The History of the Tuesday Club

The History of
the Ancient
and Honorable
Tuesday Club

BY DR. ALEXANDER HAMILTON

VOLUME I

Edited by Robert Micklus

PUBLISHED FOR THE INSTITUTE

OF EARLY AMERICAN HISTORY AND CULTURE

WILLIAMSBURG, VIRGINIA

BY THE UNIVERSITY OF NORTH CAROLINA PRESS

CHAPEL HILL AND LONDON

The Institute of Early American History and Culture is
sponsored jointly by the College of William and Mary and
the Colonial Williamsburg Foundation.

The paper in this book meets the guidelines for permanence
and durability of the Committee on Production Guidelines for
Book Longevity of the Council on Library Resources.

Library of Congress Cataloging-in-Publication Data

Hamilton, Alexander, 1712–1756.
    The history of the ancient and honorable Tuesday Club /
by Alexander Hamilton; edited by Robert Micklus.
        p.   cm.
"Published for the Institute of Early American History and Culture,
Williamsburg, Virginia."
    Includes index.
    ISBN 978-0-8078-9727-0 (pbk.: alk. paper)
    1. Annapolis (Md.)—History—Colonial period, ca. 1600–1775—
Fiction. 2. Tuesday Club (Annapolis, Md.)—History—18th century—
Fiction. 3. Maryland—History—Colonial period, ca. 1600–1775—
Fiction. I. Micklus, Robert. II. Institute of Early American
History and Culture (Williamsburg, Va.) III. Title.
PS763.H35H57   1990
813'.1—dc20   89-30768
                                                                    CIP

The publication of this work was made possible in part through a grant from the Division of Research Programs of the National Endowment for the Humanities, an independent federal agency whose mission is to award grants to support education, scholarship, media programming, libraries, and museums, in order to bring the results of cultural activities to a broad, general public.

Publication of these volumes was made possible by a grant from a fund established by DeWitt Wallace, founder of Reader's Digest.

The editor is grateful to the John Work Garrett Library of the Milton S. Eisenhower Library at the Johns Hopkins University and to the Manuscripts Division of the Maryland Historical Society Library for permission to publish this edition.

For J. A. Leo Lemay

ACKNOWLEDGMENTS

This edition is dedicated to the man who introduced me to the world of the Tuesday Club, who showed me early on that scholarship is hard and proud work, and whose sound advice and continued support have firmly established him as perpetual president of my club.

My thanks also to the honorary and longstanding members who contributed to this edition: John Hales, H:M:, who deserves a special place among the clubical worthies for having given up the better part of a summer to help me proofread my typescript against Hamilton's manuscript; Gregory Stiverson, H:M:, who provided useful comments on the biographical sketches; Georgia Brady Barnhill, H:M:, whose remarks on Hamilton's illustrations are included in this edition; Norman Fiering, L:S:M:, who guided this edition through its early stages; Daniel Williman, L:S:M:, and Saul Levin, L:S:M:, who provided transcriptions of the Latin and Greek passages and helped to track down many of the classical allusions; Gil Kelly, L:S:M:, who helped to make many a note more noteworthy; and Edward King, L:S:M:, who designed this edition.

I am particularly grateful to the oldstanding member who has helped me through every phase of this project from beginning to end, Cynthia Carter Ayres, a person whose eye for consistency and attention to detail make her an editor's editor. Together we have cared for and corrected this edition as if we were raising a child. We did the best we could; now it's time to send it a-clubbing into, I hope, a hospitable world.

Finally, I want to thank the Tuesday Club itself. Loquacious Scribble, Jonathan Grog, Quirpum Comic, Prim Timorous—you and your companions have taught me much about friendship, trifles, and laughter.

CONTENTS

Volume III

The History of the Ancient and Honorable Tuesday Club, VOLUME III

LIST OF ILLUSTRATIONS

Volume II

LIST OF MUSIC

INTRODUCTION

Although Dr. Alexander Hamilton, alias Loquacious Scribble in his comic narrative, *The History of the Tuesday Club,* once came close to losing his nose at the hands of the club's president during a furious clubical skirmish, he should not be confused with, nor was he related to the Alexander Hamilton who lost his life at the hands of Aaron Burr. To be sure, in *The History of the Tuesday Club* Hamilton relates the infamous duel that occurred in the streets of Annapolis on June 19, 1752, when Loquacious Scribble confronted that arrogant fomenter of clubical mischief, Coney Pimp Front-inbrass, during the great clubical Battle of Farce-alia; but at the approach of the formidable Frontinbrass, "mounted on a lofty Chariot . . . drawn by two fiery Steeds" and armed with "a whip of an Enormous Size . . . which he smacked as he drove along," Scribble "did not stay to make him any answer, but ran precipitately into [a] back alley and Immediatly betook himself to flight, to save his bacon" (III, 65–66). No one was shot; no one was even injured. It was just another afternoon's entertainment in the life of the Tuesday Club.

This Alexander Hamilton was born in Edinburgh on September 26, 1712, fifth son of Mary Robertson Hamilton and William Hamilton (professor of divinity and principal at the University of Edinburgh), at a time when Edinburgh was rapidly becoming one of the intellectual centers of Europe. Hamilton attended the University of Edinburgh and received his medical degree from that institution in 1737. Like other eighteenth-century Scots, he left his homeland shortly after receiving his medical degree for "the simple [reason] . . . that Scotland was a poor country in which too many competed for too few resources."[1] Following the lead of his oldest brother, John, who had established a profitable medical practice in Maryland, Hamilton emigrated to Annapolis during the winter of 1738, choosing the better prospects for professional advancement that the colonies offered.

Hamilton arrived in Maryland at the beginning of the period now commonly referred to as the golden age of Chesapeake culture (1740 to 1770), but had anyone called it that in 1738 he probably would have taken his pulse and checked his temperature. Maryland culture had indeed developed

---

1. William R. Brock, *Scotus Americanus: A Survey of the Sources for Links between Scotland and America in the Eighteenth Century* (Edinburgh, 1982), 18. Hamilton offers much the same explanation himself in the *History* (see I, 83–84).

in important ways by 1738. Under the influence of the Bordleys, Carrolls, and Dulanys, Annapolis in particular had gone through a period of rapid expansion shortly before Hamilton's arrival.[2] Yet colonial Annapolis still offered newcomers only the scant cultural menu of horse racing, dancing at the local armory, or drinking and dining at one of its many taverns—no university, no circulating library, no theater, and no literary clubs or scientific societies. Hamilton was not impressed. He was used to Edinburgh, and by comparison the majority of the people and the living conditions in Maryland were, he felt, crude. Five years after his arrival, when he referred to Maryland as a "Barbarous and desolate corner of the world,"[3] he was only half joking. Hamilton learned to cope with the crude living conditions in Maryland by laughing at them; more important, he helped to change those conditions so that by the time he died two decades later the idea of culture existing in Maryland was no longer a laughing matter.

Like many colonial physicians, Hamilton worked double time as a physician and apothecary. Good physicians were scarce throughout the colonies, and those with Hamilton's training were much in demand.[4] Most of the time he was too busy to be homesick, but during his leisure hours he keenly missed the society of his friends back home, especially his friends at the Whin-Bush Club in Edinburgh. A few months after his arrival he nostalgically invoked his brother Gavin to "be so good as Remember me to all the Members of the whin-bush Club, . . . Inform them that every friday, I fancy myself with them, drinking twopenny ale, and smoking tobacco, I Long to see those merry days again."[5] Letters from home and the compan-

2. Nancy T. Baker discusses the developments that had taken place in Annapolis before Hamilton's arrival in "Annapolis, Maryland, 1695–1730," *Maryland Historical Magazine*, LXXXI (1986), 191–209. Three particularly informative studies of the social and economic changes that Maryland as a whole had undergone are Russell R. Menard, "Population, Economy, and Society in Seventeenth-Century Maryland," *ibid.*, LXXIX (1984), 71–92; Charles Albro Barker, *The Background of the Revolution in Maryland* (New Haven, Conn., 1940), 27–43; and David Curtis Skaggs, *Roots of Maryland Democracy, 1753–1776* (Westport, Conn., 1973), 30–56.

3. AH to Robert Hamilton, Sept. 29, 1743, Hamilton Letter Book, Dulany Papers, MS. 1265, Box 3, Maryland Historical Society, Baltimore.

4. The deplorable state of the medical profession in colonial America has been well examined by Richard Harrison Shryock, *Medicine and Society in America, 1660–1860* (New York, 1960), 1–18; Brooke Hindle, *The Pursuit of Science in Revolutionary America, 1735–1789* (Chapel Hill, N.C., 1956), 36–58; Whitfield J. Bell, Jr., "Medical Practice in Colonial America," *Bulletin of the History of Medicine*, XXXI (1957), 442–453; and Bell, "A Portrait of the Colonial Physician," *ibid.*, XLIV (1970), 497–517. For further information on medicine in the colonial South, see Richard Beale Davis, *Intellectual Life in the Colonial South, 1585–1763*, 3 vols. (Knoxville, Tenn., 1978), II, 906–928.

5. AH to Gavin Hamilton, June 13, 1739, Hamilton Letter Book.

ionship of his brother John helped to alleviate Hamilton's homesickness, but what he needed most was a good club.

To help fill this void, Hamilton joined the Ugly Club of Annapolis in 1739. In *The History of the Tuesday Club* he reports that, unlike the Ugly Club made famous by the *Spectator,* membership in the Annapolis Ugly Club was not determined by any physical deformity:

> It was Sufficient for [a member] Sincerely to profess and believe that he was not handsom, till he was declared to be a monstrous ugly fellow by the Ladies in public company. . . . A man was to show his Sincerity in this opinion of himself, by assuming a certain Slovenliness and peculiarity in his dress, by never throwing away his time at a looking Glass, and diligently evading all foppish and finical airs and affectation, . . . but, if he ever observed any oddity of Gesture, affected by another man, such as a wink, a cast of the Eye, a sudden toss of the head, . . . or wry twist of the mouth, . . . these he was Strictly to Imitate, . . . as being real deformities and deviations from nature in a much higher degree than bodily distortions and blemishes (I, 117–118).

From 1739 to 1744, this club met mainly "to argue and debate upon various Subjects, and to discuss points of a knotty and abstruse nature," but some of the members eventually became so contentious that "all Sort of Clubical cordiality and friendship, began to decrease, and at last was quite extinguished, so that the Members drop'd off one by one, and from a numerous Club, it dwindled to nothing, and at last expired" (I, 126–127).

Shortly before the Ugly Club disbanded, Hamilton also entered the contentious world of Maryland politics.[6] In 1743, "at the desire and Request of many of [his] fellow Citizens," he ran for the office of common councilman of Annapolis "in opposition to a certain creature of the Court."[7] Hamilton was not politically ambitious; he was, however, a gentleman, and in his day "the quality that most nearly epitomized what was needed to make a gentleman was 'liberality,'" including "a certain disposition . . . to under-

6. The struggles between the proprietary and anti-proprietary (court and country) parties in colonial Maryland have been enlarged upon in numerous works, but see especially Ronald Hoffman, *A Spirit of Dissension: Economics, Politics, and the Revolution in Maryland* (Baltimore, 1973), 44–59; Skaggs, *Roots of Maryland Democracy,* 84–109; Aubrey C. Land, *The Dulanys of Maryland: A Biographical Study of Daniel Dulany, the Elder (1685–1753) and Daniel Dulany, the Younger (1722–1797)* (Baltimore, 1955), 62–75; and Land, *Colonial Maryland: A History* (Millwood, N.Y., 1981), 151–178.

7. AH to Gavin Hamilton, Oct. 20, 1743, Hamilton Letter Book.

take important responsibilities in the community at large."[8] Hamilton met his obligations as a gentleman, but Maryland elections were far from gentlemanly.[9] "There arose such tumults at giving of the votes in the Mayors Court," he wrote his brother Gavin, "that the majority of the Aldermen left the Bench in a passion. . . . In the afternoon the tumult was so high that the partizans went to Cudgelling and breaking of heads, . . . and they have been afraid ever since to proceed upon the Election." Eventually the election was decided in Hamilton's favor. At the time he questioned whether he would ever run for office again. "I doubt I shall stand again," he told Gavin, "for tho I be a Lover of Liberty, and abhor force or oppression of any kind, and especially when they are exercised by an Insolent Government party, yet I like better to be a peace maker, than an Instrument of disturbance in any Shape."[10] Gentleman that he was, he kept his seat as common councilman for the rest of his life.

But Hamilton's greatest concern in 1743 was not the health of the body politic; it was his own health. He was in such a "Low State, with fevers and a bloody Spitting," that by the end of September 1743 he intended to return to Great Britain. Over the next few weeks, however, he began to recuperate. "I am now Considerably better," he told Gavin, "but am followed up with an Incessant cough, which no medicine whatsoever can abate or deminish, this makes me apprehensive that the consequence will be a confirmed Consumption."[11] To improve his health, Hamilton spent the following summer away from the muggy Maryland climate touring the northern colonies. On May 30, 1744, he set out on horseback with his black slave Dromo on a four-month journey from Annapolis, Maryland, to York, Maine, and back, a trip totaling 1,624 miles. Upon his return to Annapolis, he compiled a narrative of his travels, the *Itinerarium*. First published in 1907, the *Itinerarium* has been called "the best single portrait of men and manners . . . in colonial America."[12]

8. Rhys Isaac, *The Transformation of Virginia, 1740–1790* (Chapel Hill, N.C., 1982), 131.

9. A good study of the turbulent nature of elections in colonial Maryland is Robert J. Dinkin, "Elections in Proprietary Maryland," *MHM*, LXXIII (1978), 129–136.

10. AH to Gavin Hamilton, Oct. 20, 1743, Hamilton Letter Book.

11. *Ibid.* Hamilton announced his intention to leave in a broadside advertisement dated Sept. 29, 1743.

12. J. A. Leo Lemay, *Men of Letters in Colonial Maryland* (Knoxville, Tenn., 1972), 229. For further discussion of the *Itinerarium*, see Robert Micklus, "The Delightful Instruction of Dr. Alexander Hamilton's *Itinerarium*," *American Literature*, LX (1988), 359–384. Two editions of the *Itinerarium* are available: Albert Bushnell Hart, ed., *Hamilton's Itinerarium: Being a Narrative of a Journey from Annapolis, Maryland, through Delaware, Pennsylvania, New York, New Jersey, Connecticut, Rhode Island, Massachusetts, and New Hampshire, from May to September, 1744* (St. Louis, Mo., 1907; repr. New York, 1971); and Carl Bridenbaugh, ed., *Gentleman's Progress:*

Shortly following his return to Annapolis, Hamilton helped to form the Tuesday Club, which met for the first time on May 14, 1745. Over the next eleven years almost everyone of some importance in the northern Chesapeake Bay area either joined or visited the Tuesday Club. In the beginning there were seven members besides Hamilton: John Bullen, captain of the Annapolis Independent Company and commissioner of the Paper Currency Office; William Cumming, Sr., a Scot, arrested during the Jacobite rebellion of 1715 and transported to Maryland, where he became a lawyer and a member of the Lower House; the Reverend John Gordon, a Scot, pastor of St. Anne's, Annapolis, and later of St. Michael's, Talbot County; Robert Gordon, a Scot, Annapolis merchant, judge of the Provincial Court, and commissioner of the Loan Office; John Lomas, an Annapolis merchant; Witham Marshe, secretary to the Maryland Commissioners at the treaty of Lancaster in 1744 with the Six Indian Nations and later secretary for Indian affairs; and William Rogers, chief clerk of the Prerogative Court. A varied bunch, but many of them Scots and all of them public servants in one capacity or another.[13]

As the Tuesday Club grew, its lists expanded to include many of colonial Maryland's most distinguished residents and visitors, such as the Reverend Thomas Bacon, clergyman, musician, philanthropist, compiler of the *Laws of Maryland at Large,* and one of colonial Maryland's most prolific authors; John Beale Bordley, judge, member of the Upper House, author, and member of the American Philosophical Society; the Reverend Thomas Cradock, clergyman and author; Jonas Green, public printer of Maryland, poet, and publisher of the *Maryland Gazette;* the Reverend Alexander Malcolm, clergyman, author, and musician; the Reverend James Sterling, clergyman, poet, and playwright; the sons of Daniel Dulany the Elder; and numerous other members and visitors, not the least of whom was Benjamin Franklin. All comers were welcome, and most men of any note who came to Annapolis visited the Tuesday Club.

The regular members—or the "longstanding members," as they liked to boast of themselves—were limited in number to fifteen. In *The History of the Tuesday Club* they appear under pseudonyms typifying their characters and roles in the club: John Beale Bordley (Quirpum Comic, Master of Ceremonies); Stephen Bordley (Huffman Snap); John Bullen (Bully Blunt, also Sir John Oldcastle, Club Champion); Charles Cole (Nasifer Jole, Presi-

---

The Itinerarium of Dr. Alexander Hamilton, 1744 (Chapel Hill, N.C., 1948; repr. Westport, Conn., 1973).

13. For further information on these figures and the ones mentioned in the following paragraph, see the Biographical Sketches, below.

dent); William Cumming, Sr. (Jealous Spyplot, Sr., Attorney General); William Cumming, Jr. (Jealous Spyplot, Jr.); Edward Dorsey (Drawlum Quaint, Speaker); Richard Dorsey (Tunbelly Bowzer); Walter Dulany (Slyboots Pleasant); Jonas Green (Jonathan Grog, P.P.P.P.P.—Purveyor, Punster, Punchmaker General, Printer, and Poet—and later P.L.M.C.—Poet Laureate and Master of Ceremonies); Thomas Jennings (Prim Timorous, Sergeant at Arms); John Lomas (Laconic Comas, Orator); Alexander Malcolm (Philo Dogmaticus, Chancellor); William Thornton (Solo Neverout, also Protomusicus, Chief Musician and Attorney General); and, of course, Hamilton himself (Loquacious Scribble, Secretary and Orator). Other longstanding members came and went, but these were the mainstays.

Every other Tuesday for the next eleven years, longstanding members, honorary members (those who could attend whenever in Annapolis without having to entertain the club), and visitors met, normally at the home of the high steward for the night, to share a side of bacon, some bread and cheese, a bowl of punch, but mainly each other's company and conversation. Hamilton establishes the formula for a boon club companion early in *The History of the Tuesday Club,* maintaining that "none but your merry, droll, facetious, Jocose, good humored, risible companions, punsters, comical Story tellers, and *Conundrumifiers,* ought to be members of those nocturnal assemblies, called Clubs, for the Quintessence, marrow and main fulcrum of Clubs consists in gaiety, Jollity, pleasantry and Jocosity" (I, 72). On the other hand,

> Those Solitary, moaping, morose, humdrum fellows, who evade, shun, run and fly, from all company, hate the Sight of men, as if they were Tygers, bears, Serpents, hobgoblins, Rhinoceroses and Panthers, . . . are mortal and Irreconcileable enimies to all Clubs, Jovial meetings, and humerous Conversations.
>
> When I see a fellow of this Stamp, with his Clouded brows, and Lowring countenance, *monstrum deforme Ingens,* I Imagine I behold a black cloud, rising from the dirty blustering South east, saturated with hollow murmuring Smouldering blasts, sending before it grumbling, tumbling, Jumbling thunder, and Infectious puffs of pestilential Steams, darkening the face of the fair day with polluted murky and Stiffling vapors, exhalations and damps, saturated, loaded, Impregnated and overcharged, with morbific Sulphureous atoms, bursting from the mouth of Tartarus it self (I, 69–70).

The Tuesday Club was no place for such humdrum fellows.

The combined talents of the members of the Tuesday Club provided an almost limitless fund of entertainment. Those members familiar with law—and some not so familiar—entertained the club by conducting numerous mock trials; those with a flair for speechmaking—and some flaired better than others—entertained the club with their rhetorical effusions; and those gifted with musical talents—and some not so gifted—entertained the club by reciting popular songs and performing their own compositions. But the greatest source of entertainment in the club was the wit of its two principal comedians, Hamilton and Jonas Green—Loquacious Scribble and Jonathan Grog. As club orator, Loquacious Scribble took every possible occasion to impress the club with his erudition by haranguing them with numerous bombastic speeches, especially at each of the club's anniversaries, when he annually delivered a learned and lengthy speech commemorating the grandeur of the occasion. At those times his rhetorical talents were complemented by the literary talents of Jonathan Grog, who traditionally delivered his anniversary ode following Scribble's speech. Grog further entertained the club on many other nights with his humorous verses, practical jokes, puns, and conundrums. Together they jointly shared the distinguished post of club "Conundrumificators," but Grog was the indisputable master and the more bawdy of the two. "Why is the king's prick," he asked the club one evening, "in marking down a Sheriff like an Elephant?"—to which Jealous Spyplot, Sr., rightly answered "Because it always *Stands*" (II, 116). "I shall beg leave to observe," Hamilton notes, "lest it should escape the observation of the Reader, that there seems to be an uncommon delicacy and Elegance in most of the Conundrums, composed by Jonathan Grog Esqr, as may be seen in the one Just now mentioned, Concerning *The king's prick*, which is not only a perfect Conundrum, but Contains also a delicate pun, as the word *Prick* may be Interpreted various ways" (II, 117).

Although it might be difficult to tell from a brief sampling of their elegant humor, Hamilton and Green are the best comic team in colonial literature. They further teamed up in the *Maryland Gazette*, which Green began publishing in 1745. From 1746 to 1750 Hamilton contributed various pieces to the *Gazette*, including an essay on the impertinent question "What News?" (Jan. 7, 1746); a cure for distempered authors and a mock advertisement to catch a runaway wit (Feb. 4, Mar. 18, 1746); an essay on curiosity (Jan. 27, 1747); a dream vision on the fate of the contributors to the *Gazette* (June 29, 1748); a tale for melancholic scribblers (Aug. 31, 1748); a piece on odd orthography (Apr. 12, 1749); and a parody of Masonic ceremonies (Jan. 24, 1750). These humorous pieces helped to make the *Maryland Gazette* one of colonial America's most entertaining newspapers.

While writing for the *Maryland Gazette*, serving the Tuesday Club,

recording and revising the club's minutes, and administering to his pa-
tients, Hamilton also found time, on May 29, 1747, to marry Margaret
Dulany, daughter of Daniel Dulany the Elder. His marriage to the "viva-
cious" Miss Dulany was "the social event of the season,"[14] but much lamented by Stephen Bordley, who had hoped that Hamilton would remain,
like himself, one of the Tuesday Club's few surviving bachelors:

> Yet in vain was that hope, since I am now obliged to hold out alone
> against the numerous and powerful host we . . . formerly provoked
> by our united hostilities,—for poor Hamilton is gone!—not dead,
> but married, he was the day before yesterday obliged to surrender
> discretion to throw himself up to the money of Peggy Dulany, and is
> already become what you would from your knowledge of the lady
> now suppose him to be, a very grave sober fellow.[15]

As Bordley well knew, Hamilton's marriage to Margaret Dulany could only
enhance his fortunes and lift his spirits. Hamilton was glad to be married,
and although he and his wife had no children—at least none that survived
birth—they apparently enjoyed their life together.[16]

His marriage into the Dulany family produced several changes in
Hamilton's life, the first of which was a change in religion from Presbyteri-
anism to Anglicanism. It simply made good sense socially to practice the
Anglican faith in a predominantly Anglican colony, and Hamilton was an
eminently sensible man socially and religiously. Like his Latitudinarian
friend the Reverend Thomas Bacon, Hamilton believed in a rationally ordered universe, one in which the "revealed Law of God" was consistent
with the "Law of Nature."[17] For Hamilton, as for Bacon, God was a benevolent deity who "hath been pleased to make all Men . . . dependent one
upon the other, and by a mutual Exchange of Service and Assistance, to
contribute to the Comfort and Support of each in Particular, as well as the
general Benefit of the Whole."[18] The Anglican church, which stressed a

14. Land, *Dulanys of Maryland,* 191.
15. Stephen Bordley to Witham Marshe, May 30, 1747, Bordley Letter Book, MHS.
16. Hamilton's mother wrote more than once that she had received letters from him and his wife attesting to their happiness together (see Mary Hamilton to AH, July 15, 1748, Feb. 15, 1749, and Oct. 25, 1749, Hamilton Letter Book). Margaret Dulany remarried in 1757 after Hamilton's death. She and her second husband, William Murdock, had two children, Rebecca and Margaret.
17. Bacon, *Four Sermons, upon the Great and Indispensable Duty of All Christian Masters and Mistresses to Bring Up Their Negro Slaves in the Knowledge and Fear of God* (London, 1750), 1st sermon, p. 35.
18. *Ibid.,* 2d sermon, p. 56.

similar brand of "rational piety,"[19] came close enough to Hamilton's own beliefs that, even though he considered some of the church's sacraments foolish, he was able to join in good faith. Two years later he was elected vestryman of St. Anne's, a position he held until March 30, 1752.

Hamilton's marriage also produced significant changes in his financial and political status. Despite his whiggish sentiments (voiced in the letter to his brother Gavin cited earlier), Hamilton's experience as an observer and as a participant in the tumultuous world of Maryland politics had led him to lean increasingly toward moderation and stability, and consequently toward the proprietary camp. With the aid of the Dulanys, in 1753 Hamilton represented the court party in the election for the Lower House seat of his recently deceased club companion and old proprietary faithful, Robert Gordon. Once again, the election was contested, but Hamilton was officially sworn in on October 9, 1753. He served as a member of the Lower House until the Assembly adjourned on July 25, 1754, when he resigned, probably because of poor health.

Hamilton much preferred the convivial world of clubbing, and in 1749 he and several Tuesday Club members founded a Freemason's lodge in Annapolis. So much has been written about the anxieties that Freemasonry caused the church or state and about all the nefarious rituals that Freemasons reputedly conducted behind closed doors[20] that the least sensational but perhaps most essential fact about Freemasonry has often been overlooked: in an age when clubbing was the thing to do, being a Freemason was as much a part of the normal social fabric of eighteenth-century life as being a member of any other club. In his "Discourse Delivered from the Chair, in the Lodge-Room at *Annapolis,* by the Right Worshipful the Master, to the Brethren of the Ancient and Honourable Society of *Free and Accepted* Masons," Hamilton provided the framework by which not just all Freemasons but all enlightened men sought to structure their lives.[21] The "upright man," in control of his passions and guided by the "Lights of Reason" in his pursuit of liberty, was obliged, he concluded by saying, to

19. Henry F. May, *The Enlightenment in America* (New York, 1976), 67.

20. The best scholarly analysis of the various controversies that Freemasonry provoked during the 18th century is Margaret C. Jacob, *The Radical Enlightenment: Pantheists, Freemasons, and Republicans* (London, 1981). For the relationship between Freemasonry and Hamilton's *History,* see Robert Micklus, "The Secret Fall of Freemasonry in Dr. Alexander Hamilton's *The History of the Tuesday Club,*" in *Deism, Masonry, and the Enlightenment: Essays Honoring Alfred Owen Aldridge,* ed. J. A. Leo Lemay (Newark, Del., 1987), 127–136.

21. Hamilton's speech appears at the end of the Reverend John Gordon's Masonic sermon, *Brotherly Love Explain'd and Enforc'd* (Annapolis, Md., 1750).

perform works of "*Charity, benevolence,* and *Brotherly Love.*" Freemasonry, Hamilton well understood, was not some mysterious, subversive organization but part of the eighteenth-century club of man.

A few months later, Hamilton published *A Defence of Dr. [Adam] Thomson's Discourse on the Preparation of the Body for the Small Pox, and the Manner of Receiving the Infection* (Philadelphia, 1751), a twenty-seven-page pamphlet in support of his old friend and medical school classmate. Thomson's methods, Hamilton felt, had been impugned by the "ill natured Sneers and rude Reflections" of a pack of "Physical Dunces," one of whom, he claimed, had recently reported to him a

> newly discovered Method of curing dangerous Dysenteries, by Means of a certain pneumatic Operation. He informed me of "a Patient, dangerously ill with a *Bloody Flux,* at the Point of Death, who, finding some Difficulty in Respiration, desired his Servant . . . to apply his Mouth to his, and blow with all his Force into his Lungs, which the good natured Fellow did several Times; and, to the great Surprize of every Body, the seemingly forlorn Patient recovered." Whether such a Whimsical Cure as this be natural, I leave you to judge: For I shall make no Remark upon it; only, I think, the Gentleman might easily make an Improvement on this Discovery by applying his Mouth to a certain Part, through which he might convey his Air or *Flatus* more immediately into the Place, where that Distemper has it's Seat (pp. 3, 4, 16).

It is not known whether this particular "*Guess-Doctor*" took Hamilton's advice, but his satiric attack eventually elicited an apology from Dr. John Kearsley, Thomson's principal detractor.

Hamilton was unable, however, to defend himself against the consumption that had threatened his health since his first summer in Maryland. Although he managed to visit Gen. Edward Braddock's battered army in the summer of 1755, his poor health made it increasingly difficult for him to attend the Tuesday Club with any regularity.[22] On February 11, 1756, he turned the business of recording the club's minutes over to his friend William Lux of Annapolis. But even though he was forced to abdicate his position as record keeper, Hamilton continued to work on *The History of the Tuesday Club* right up until his death. Dr. Upton Scott, a club member who

22. Elaine G. Breslaw reproduces Hamilton's lengthy letter concerning Braddock's defeat by the French and evaluates his appraisal of the disaster in "A Dismal Tragedy: Drs. Alexander and John Hamilton Comment on Braddock's Defeat," *MHM,* LXXV (1980), 118–144.

administered to Hamilton along with his brother John, wrote that Hamilton suffered from "excruciating pains" during his final months:

> His Brother directed the Treatment, & visited him occasionally, whilst it was my melancholy duty daily to watch the progress of his disease, & by my friendly attention render him all the aid & consolation which the Nature of his complaint would admit of. A liberal Use of Opiates was requisite to make life bearable, & when relieved from pain he amused himself by writing this History, indeed the love of whimsicall drollery was so predominant in his constitution, that, a few days before his death, when I called upon him, I found him just finishing a Story that he had been employed in writing, which he read to me with as much Glee & delight as he was wont to do at the Club, laughing at the same time most heartily.[23]

As Scott states in his letter, Hamilton was the "Life & Soul" of the Tuesday Club. Things were not the same without Loquacious Scribble. The club met for the last time on February 10, 1756, even though Hamilton did not die until Tuesday, May 11, 1756, which would have been the club's eleventh anniversary. In the *Maryland Gazette* for May 13, 1756, Hamilton's good friend Jonas Green lamented the passing of the man they had all come to love:

> On Tuesday last in the Morning, Died . . . ALEXANDER HAMILTON, M.D. Aged 44 Years. The Death of this valuable and worthy Gentleman is universally and justly lamented: His medical Abilities, various Knowledge, strictness of Integrity, simplicity of Manners, and extensive Benevolence, having deservedly gained him the Respect and Esteem of all Ranks of Men.—No Man, in his Sphere, has left fewer Enemies, or more Friends.

No man, too, has left behind a more unusual manuscript than *The History of the Tuesday Club*. There are many indications, particularly the numerous references to his "readers" throughout the text, that Hamilton intended to publish the *History*. But whether because of its unfinished state, or because of its reflections on several of the club's still-living members, or because the obvious person to print it, Jonas Green, had neither the time

---

23. Scott's letter (dated Aug. 28, 1809), which attests to Hamilton's "strict honour & integrity" and calls him "the most eminent Physician in Annapolis," is in the Howard Family Papers, MS. 469, MHS. An abridged version of the letter appears at the front of the "Record of the Tuesday Club," MS. 854, MHS.

nor the heart to prepare for publication Hamilton's huge manuscript once
his friend was gone, *The History of the Tuesday Club* remained in the hands
of a private few following Hamilton's death.

That is unfortunate, for one can only conjecture about the influence
that *The History of the Tuesday Club* might have had on colonial literature.
Its influence might well have been great, for it is a book that is both rooted
in its time and well ahead of its time. It is particularly rooted in its time as a
political satire of the proprietary struggles in colonial Maryland,[24] in its rich
allusiveness to contemporary political, literary, and scientific developments,
and in its humorous treatment of the outcry against luxury, probably "the
greatest single social issue" during the 1750s.[25] But above all, the *History* is a
splendid gauge of eighteenth-century wit, loaded with pseudo-learned essays and digressions, surprising metaphors and allusions, raillery and repartee, bombastic letters and speeches, doggerel verses and mock trials, brain-
teasing riddles and conundrums, delicate and often indelicate puns, even
nonsensical hieroglyphics and missing passages—and, of course, a generous
dose of scatological humor and "polite smutt."[26] Hamilton's wit runs the
gamut of eighteenth-century comedy—from satire to humor to irony to
farce—creating a comedic extravaganza matched, perhaps, but unsurpassed
in eighteenth-century literature.

But *The History of the Tuesday Club* is more than just a comic micro-
cosm of its times; it is a unique and innovative narrative. It is, to use one of
Hamilton's favorite words, a "puzzlementationfuul" book. Hamilton em-
ploys and burlesques so many literary and nonliterary forms that one hardly
knows what to call the *History*. In each of its fourteen books, he typically
treats the reader first to an opening essay on some grand or trivial subject,
then continues his narrative of the club's misadventures, introducing letters, speeches, trials, indictments, commissions, set dramatic pieces, poetry,
drawings, and music—anything he can to embellish his narrative. It is an

24. For further discussion of the political implications of the *History*, see Elaine G. Breslaw,
"Wit, Whimsy, and Politics: The Uses of Satire by the Tuesday Club of Annapolis, 1744–1756,"
William and Mary Quarterly, 3d Ser., XXXII (1975), 295–306, and Breslaw, "The Chronicle as
Satire: Dr. Hamilton's 'History of the Tuesday Club,'" *MHM*, LXX (1975), 129–148.

25. John Sekora, *Luxury: The Concept in Western Thought, Eden to Smollett* (Baltimore, 1977),
75, 66. In Hamilton's day *luxury* meant extravagance in one's domestic and political behavior;
it therefore implied not only drunkenness, gluttony, lust, avarice, ceremony, vanity, effeminacy,
and affectation, but also ambition, pride, enervation, corruption, and subjection. The first set
of vices, many feared, inevitably led to the second set. In a humorous way, that is precisely
what happens in the *History*. (For further development of this thesis, see Robert Micklus,
"'The History of the Tuesday Club': A Mock-Jeremiad of the Colonial South," *WMQ*, 3d Ser.,
XL [1983], 42–61.)

26. Bridenbaugh, ed., *Gentleman's Progress*, 177.

extraordinary attempt to merge various literary, rhetorical, and artistic modes into one narrative—but what, finally, *is* it?

Although Hamilton would have been the last to admit it, *The History of the Tuesday Club* is a comic novel. Written between the publication dates of the two great comic novels of the eighteenth century—Henry Fielding's *Tom Jones* (which Hamilton read and admired) and Laurence Sterne's *Tristram Shandy* (which was published after Hamilton's death)—*The History of the Tuesday Club* in many ways resembles both. Two of its most prominent features—the introductory essays to each of its fourteen books and the dominant voice of its witty, self-dramatizing narrator—owe much to the example Fielding set in *Joseph Andrews* and *Tom Jones*. But Hamilton's narrative is, by design, far more experimental and discursive than the "architectonic" *Tom Jones*.[27] More often than not, the *History's* loose plot—concerning the rise of the Ancient and Honorable Tuesday Club to its peak of clubific felicity, and its fall as the insidious forces of luxury, ambition, and pride infest its members—is lost behind a maze of digressions. In the end, the plot hardly matters; structurally and thematically, digression is everything. In its intrinsic structural and thematic discursiveness and in the variety of verbal high jinks Hamilton incorporates into his narrative, *The History of the Tuesday Club* anticipates *Tristram Shandy* as much as it imitates *Tom Jones*.

Like *Tristram Shandy*, *The History of the Tuesday Club* is a comic novel that borrows heavily from the "anatomy," a genre particularly popular during the eighteenth century.[28] As Northrop Frye has argued, the "anatomist"—Swift, for instance, in *Gulliver's Travels* or Voltaire in *Candide*—is primarily concerned with "intellectual themes and attitudes" and with "piling up an enormous mass of erudition about his theme or . . . overwhelming his pedantic targets with an avalanche of their own jargon." The novel

27. The symmetrical structure of *Tom Jones* is the focus of Robert Alter's chapter "The Architectonic Novel" in *Fielding and the Nature of the Novel* (Cambridge, Mass., 1968).

28. Throughout this paragraph, I use *anatomy* as Northrop Frye defines it in *Anatomy of Criticism: Four Essays* (Princeton, N.J., 1957), 308–314. In Hamilton's day, of course, it would have been used more typically to describe a treatise such as Robert Burton's *Anatomy of Melancholy* (which Hamilton parodies in bk. II, chap. 1) rather than a narrative prose work. Anticipating his critics, Hamilton also refers to the *History* as a "prolix Rhapsody" (I, v), a word that by the 18th century had come to imply a literary work of miscellaneous or disconnected pieces. At one point Loquacious Scribble mentions in a letter that the Tuesday Club has yet to appoint an "able Historiographer, to connect and form [the club's affairs] into an uniform Rhapsody" (I, 535), a notion that would have been recognized as a ludicrous contradiction in terms. Although the *History* resembles—and indeed burlesques—the rhapsody, Hamilton was clearly poking fun at those who might perceive his narrative as nothing more than that.

and the anatomy are not, however, mutually exclusive; indeed, particularly during the eighteenth century they frequently converged in the same work. "It was Sterne," Frye says, "who combined them with greatest success. *Tristram Shandy* may be . . . a novel, but the digressing narrative, the catalogues, the stylizing of character along 'humor' lines, . . . the symposium discussions, and the constant ridicule of philosophers and pedantic critics are all features that belong to the anatomy."[29] Much the same can be said of *The History of the Tuesday Club*. It is a comic novel whose narrative centers around the social behavior of a humorous cast of characters, but at the same time one whose narrator provides a comic anatomy of eighteenth-century society and ideas.

Hamilton himself, of course, did everything possible to disassociate himself from the common herd of "novel" writers. Like Fielding and other eighteenth-century novelists, he chose to call his narrative a "history" and would not have been flattered had anyone in his day called *The History of the Tuesday Club* a novel any more than Fielding would have been flattered had anyone called *The History of Tom Jones* a novel. The reason is clear from their remarks concerning novels and romances throughout their works. Lennard J. Davis argues that there was "a profound rupture, a discursive chasm between these two forms" in eighteenth-century England, and so "the romance is not usefully seen as a forebear of, a relative of, or an influence on the novel."[30] Davis's observation is at once insightful and misleading. There *was* a sharp break between the romance and what we *now perceive* as the novel as it was emerging in the works of novelists such as Fielding by midcentury. But at the time they were writing their novels, "novel" and "romance" were virtually synonymous and equally pejorative terms: both were perceived as being overly concerned with the past, with impossible situations, and with idealized characters. During an empirical age that valued factual observation and expected writers to focus their narratives on daily life, most authors consciously avoided associating their narratives with either genre.[31]

---

29. *Anatomy of Criticism*, 311, 312.

30. *Factual Fictions: The Origins of the English Novel* (New York, 1983), 25. Davis presents a strong argument for the influence of contemporary news and journalism, rather than popular romances, upon 18th-century fiction, but he overstates his case, I think, when he claims that by midcentury most English writers clearly distinguished romances from novels (pp. 103–104).

31. The best study of the movement toward historicity in narrative during the early 18th century is Michael McKeon, *The Origins of the English Novel, 1660–1740* (Baltimore, 1987). McKeon nicely summarizes the early-18th-century perception of romance and of particular romances that Hamilton mocks (see especially pp. 26–28, 52–64). A good study of Fielding's attitude toward romance is James J. Lynch, *Henry Fielding and the Heliodoran Novel: Romance, Epic, and Fielding's New Province of Writing* (Rutherford, N.J., 1986).

Writers such as Hamilton and Fielding therefore turned not toward the "novel" or "romance" in defining their narratives but toward "history," the most respected prose genre in the eighteenth century.[32] By the end of the seventeenth century the conception of history as a genre had become blurred by European writers who called their romances "histories" simply because their narratives were based on real characters. "In these enlightened times," Hamilton facetiously observes, history

> received additions and Improvements which it never before had, and was dressed up in very fine and Gaudy trappings, to the Immortal Geniuses of that age, we owe, the new and rare Invention of Romance writing, a kind of History, altogether Novel, (hence some kinds of Romances are called *Novels*) and hitherto unknown, from these great Historians, came the Prodigious Histories of *Amadis De Gaul, Amadis de Grece, Don Bellianis, Esplandian, Palmerin,* and a hundred other voluminous pieces, equally witty amusing and Instructive. These were the Heroical Histories of the times. There were also the amorous Histories of *Cassandra, Cleopatra, Clelia,* & *Almahyde,* all adapted to excite amorous and tender passions, particularly among the readers of the fair Sex (II, 26).

Hamilton's complaints about "Romantic Historians" who have "palm[ed] upon the world, a hideous collection of fables" (II, 4) are typical of the eighteenth-century attempt to restore the factuality of history and to establish factuality as the foundation of any good prose narrative.

Rather than associate himself with these romantic historians, Hamilton, like Fielding in *Joseph Andrews,* defines his narrative as a "true history."[33] By doing so he meant not only to indicate that his narrative was rooted in fact but also, like Fielding, to distinguish between "a naively empiricist and a more 'imaginative' species of belief."[34] Some historians,

32. As H. Trevor Colbourn observes, by midcentury "the testimonial on history's behalf was overwhelming" (*The Lamp of Experience: Whig History and the Intellectual Origins of the American Revolution* [Chapel Hill, N.C., 1965], 5). History was so respected that, as Jerry C. Beasley points out, the 1740s witnessed the "elevation of private experience to the status of public history," and private experience accordingly became the substance of narrative "histories" during this period (*Novels of the 1740s* [Athens, Ga., 1982], 43). Hamilton also plays upon what his contemporaries would have perceived as the double meaning of "history" and "historian": as not only a narrative of actual events but also a narrated story or *histoire* told by a *histor* who shapes and interprets events (Leopold Damrosch, Jr., argues this point well in *God's Plot and Man's Stories: Studies in the Fictional Imagination from Milton to Fielding* [Chicago, 1985], 273).

33. Hamilton's conception of "true history" and the distinctions he draws between history and romance are very similar to Fielding's remarks in *Joseph Andrews,* bk. 3, chap. 1, bk. 9, chap. 1, and *Tom Jones,* bk. 4, chap. 1.

34. McKeon, *Origins of the English Novel,* 404.

Hamilton felt, were "too strictly attached to what they call truth and demonstration," and others were "only dry drivelling narraters of Incidents and
facts" (I, 2). For Hamilton, as for Fielding, the "true historian" sought not
simply to present facts accurately but to frame those facts with "the proper
and decent seasoning of apposite remarks and observations" (I, 2); to create
characters who were combinations of "light" and "shade" rather than one-
dimensional (I, vii); and most of all to copy Nature in all its fullness (I, 4).
What both authors were attempting to define as "true histories" we now
call novels.

   In his opening chapter, "Of History and Historians," Hamilton, much
like Fielding in his "Bill of Fare to the Feast" in *Tom Jones,* invites the
judicious reader to partake of his historical feast and to keep in mind the
distinction between his learned labors and the more dubious labors of romance writers or novelists. "Histories founded upon truth, and wrote in a
plain, easie and natural Stile," he says,

> are Sirloins of beef plainly dressed, wholesome, hearty and nourish-
> ing to a robust and healthy Stomach, but those erected upon fiction,
> and stuffed with Bombast and fustian phrazes, are vapid, windy,
> unwholsom and adulterated with your damn'd sauces and pickles,
> fitted only for crazy and luxurious apetites, which require a Spur to
> excite them to a proper pitch, and are apt to breed worms, maggots
> and monstruous Crudities, in the brains and Intelects of such stu-
> dents as feed upon them. Such are Romances, novels, fairy tales,
> Love adventures, . . . and other such verbose trumpery, with which
> the french Artists have crouded our Libraries, as their Cooks have
> confounded our kitchens and loaded our tables, with Devilish Ra-
> goos, fricassies, anduilles, amulets, Solomongundies, and the like.
> The first kind of Cookery breeds as many crudities in the Intellect of
> the readers, as the other does in the Stomachs and habits of the
> eaters (I, 3–4).

"The History which I am now about to present to [the reader]," Hamilton
asserts, "is none of your vamped up Frenchified pieces of Cookery, it is a
Solid and Serious performance, plain and homely, and withal true, every
article thereof, being copied exactly from nature and the life" (I, 4).

   Hamilton's declaration of intent is in part a serious attempt to distinguish his narrative from previous narratives and in part an ironic pose
designed to fool no one. Immediately after establishing his high seriousness
he discusses the "dignity and Importance" of antiquity, first stating that of
all things men revere "Antiquity holds the foremost Rank" (I, 7), then

providing one irreverent account after another of the antiquity of ancient nations and families, and finally of the antiquity of "old rotten rags, . . . rusty nails, Jaw bones and Shank bones, perhaps honeycombed by the pox, teeth, beards, whiskers, parings of nails, Smoak tails and the like" (I, 21). Hamilton's digressive account of the dignity of antiquity undercuts the very notion that antiquity carries any particular dignity, just as his digressive narrative itself undercuts the grandiose declarations of authors who take themselves and their works too seriously. His most bombastic digressions, similes, or allusions typically end, of course, with his soberly observing that he values brevity at all costs "for fear this history should exceed the Size of a portable volume" (I, 93). But that does not prevent him from swelling his narrative to three volumes, or from creating one of the most bombastic characters in eighteenth-century literature to play his role as secretary in the *History*, Loquacious Scribble. "Such a Surprize and astonishment as possessed the old hoary and Squalid anarch Chaos," Scribble informs President Jole at the start of one of his anniversary speeches,

> when he was waked out of his eternal Slumbers, by the elucidation of the Celestial lights, when Creation first sprung, such a Surprize, I say, Honorable Sir, must at this Instant possess my Sensorium when I behold the members of this here ancient Club, Incumbent over those capacious bowls, replete with precious punch, most Splendidly elucescent, with those Glittering and Lumeniferous badges, like so many oriental and bright planets, Rising upon the watery deep, and adorning the azure Expance with their Immortal Irradiations! whilst you, Great Sir! like the Solar Center of this grand Clubicular System, dispence Inexhaustible Lustre to all, and, from your fountain undeminished, the whole emanation of light proceeds, the Splendor of our Longstanding members being nothing else, but the reflected glory of your honor, our most honorable president (II, 136).

Scribble continues in this vein, also praising the club's champion, Sir John, in this manner, when Jole interrupts him, saying "I think we have [had] enough of this Stuff" (II, 137). And if it's not Jole interrupting him, it's Sir John saying "Hoh! why so much Fiddle come farts about nothing?" (II, 304) or "Phogh! damn the fustian" (III, 212).

These are hardly the markings of a "Solid and Serious performance" written in a "plain and homely" manner. Rather, they are the markings of an author who loves nothing better than to deflate the customary grandeur of any topic or occasion by bombastically inflating it beyond recognition or digressively whittling it away to nothing. Some readers, Hamilton is aware, will deplore his trifling methods and his trifling preoccupation with club history. After circuitously haranguing his readers on the importance of not wasting time in the opening paragraph of his preface, he acknowledges that

> some people, who may find time enough to throw away in reading
> of this, will undoubtedly exclaim, Well! and what the Deuce is the
> meaning of these grave observations? . . . Many, I am satisfied, will
> either be mightily astonished, or pretend to be so, that any Mortal
> Wight, could waste, as they Call it, so much precious time, besides
> paper and ink, in compiling and Collecting, the History of, (as it
> may seem to them) a Ridiculous Club, whose chief pastime (they'll
> say) appears from the face of the History it self, and from the Gro-
> tesque Stile of its Idle Author, to have been the carrying on, a Silly,
> Stupid and unmeaning farce. Very well, my good friends, what if
> I should grant you all this, . . . the Subject of this History is a
> farce, and a very Silly one too, since you will needs have it so, . . .
> I will not Indeed so easily grant you that it is an unmeaning one,
> since it bears an exact resemblance to many other farces in human
> life, esteemed (tho they are not really so) of a more Serious nature
> (I, x–xi).

Hamilton allows, too, that he might have spent his time more profitably than by composing this silly—though not unmeaning—farce; he will not concede, however, that he has spent his time any more foolishly than the critic who would take him to task for his foolishness. "If I have laid out much time in writing of these triffles, as you call them, pray," he argues,

> have not you and many others as wise as either you or I, that is, in
> their own Conceit, laid out an equivalent of time, upon equivalent,
> if not greater triffles, only with this difference, that this triffling
> Scribble of mine, required some thought and application, and your
> triffling Occupations require no thought at all. . . . Have I not been
> poring reading studying and turning over Ancient Authors, and
> modern wits, in the composition of this History, to the great Solace
> and Improvement of my Rational, Intellectual and Gelastic faculties,
> when you, and twenty other such Loggerheads as you, who pretend
> to call me to account for it, have been exercising the keenest acumen
> of your obtuse thoughts upon a game at whist, . . . bawling at a
> boxing match or Cock pit, . . . fumbling and tumbling a whore in a
> bagnio, . . . or taking an afternoons nap, after having spent two
> hours more than what was necessary in beastly cramming. . . . Now,

I would Seriously ask you, which of us have been employed to the best purpose, you, in these triffling pastimes, . . . or I, in writing this (as you call it) Silly history (I, x–xia).

According to Hamilton, life is a comedy full of trifles—great and small, to be sure, but, regardless of the size, still trifles—and the most trifling figure of all is the critic who cannot enjoy the human comedy. "All that passes in this . . . petty scantling of time," he says, "which we have allotted us to peregrinate thro' this absurd worldly wilderness, and to rant our Comical . . . parts out upon this terrestrial Stage, is but of a triffling nature" (I, 297–298). Why, then,

> should any . . . finical coxcomb of a Clubical Critic, . . . pretend to say, that this our famous History, is more triffling than any other history, or this our ancient and honorable Club more triffling in it's constitution, . . . than any other Society whatsoever, great or small. . . . Pray does not an Emperor eat, drink and sleep as much as a [club] president; does he not stink at times as hideously as a president? . . . may he not be poxed as well as a president? may he not have the plague, . . . the Ripples, the whiffles, nay the Itch as well as a president? Nay, may he not play the fool as much as a president? what then is the difference between an Emperor and a president, . . . a triffle, believe me, a very triffle, and not worth Contending for (I, 298, 302).

"Oh how I pity you," Hamilton concludes his tirade against these "perverse anticlubarians,"

> for the want of that blessed humor, which set Democritus a Laughing, and Heraclitus a crying, . . . for, ye dry withered Stocks of human Society, . . . you can neither laugh nor Cry in earnest, . . . [but] like a flitch of Smoked bacon, . . . you go out of [the world], dry, dead, musty, Insipid and Sapless, having never in your lives enjoyed the Sweets and delights of clubical humors and recreations, without which life is not worth enjoying, but is a *tabula rasa* . . . in which nothing of Sense or Significancy can be read or discerned (I, 307, 310).

The History of the Tuesday Club is not designed for, nor can it hope to reform these "Incorrigible Anticlubarians" (I, 309); it is designed for those who, like Hamilton's favorite authority, Democritus, know how to laugh good humoredly at the "Sempiternal Comedy . . . acted from day to day on this great earthly stage" (I, 464). Who can observe "this medley of absurdity," Hamilton wonders, "without Laughing Immoderatly, either with Democritus, or any other Gelastic Philosopher; and who can blame the members of the . . . Tuesday Club, for Laughing at all the world, as well as at themselves, and furnishing a fund of Laughter to all those who have a turn for the Gelastic humor" (III, 351). *The History of the Tuesday Club* will appeal to many readers of many different interests, but most of all to those interested in exercising and improving their gelastic faculties. I want to welcome those readers to the world of the Tuesday Club. "Begin in the middle of the Book & read backwards" if you like, "then forwards & skip about; I think now & then you will find something that will set you a roaring."[35]

35. In a letter dated May 4, 1824, James Carroll addressed these remarks to a member of the Baltimore Library Company upon presenting him with his copy of the "Record of the Tuesday Club." Carroll's remarks, like the rest of his delightful letter, apply equally well to the *History*. The entire letter appears in Elaine G. Breslaw, ed., *Records of the Tuesday Club of Annapolis, 1745–56* (Urbana, Ill., 1988), xxxiv.

COMPOSITION

Four separate stages of composition went into the making of *The History of the Tuesday Club*. As the club's secretary, Hamilton first kept its minutes from 1745 to 1756; during that time, he also prepared a fair copy of the minutes, the "Record of the Tuesday Club"; he then drafted the *History*, a fictionalized account of the club's proceedings; and finally he rewrote the *History* from first page to last, replacing the names of the club's members with pseudonyms and further embellishing the narrative. The following paragraphs summarize my conjectures about the probable dates of composition of these four stages. (Locations of the manuscript holdings are provided in parentheses.)

1. Minutes of the Tuesday Club, volumes I and II (John Work Garrett Collections, The Milton S. Eisenhower Library, The Johns Hopkins University, Baltimore, Maryland; Peter Force Collection, Series 8D, Item 170, Library of Congress). These are the actual minutes of the club (written in several hands, but mainly Hamilton's), composed at or shortly after each meeting from May 14, 1745, to February 11, 1756. The first volume runs from May 14, 1745, to February 25, 1755; the second volume, from May 27, 1755, to February 11, 1756. The second volume contains only thirty-seven pages of minutes, eight of which are missing (pp. 9–16, or most of Sederunt 241).

2. "Record of the Tuesday Club" (MS. 854, Maryland Historical Society, Baltimore). This is a careful revision of the minutes, covering the period from May 14, 1745, to April 22, 1755. It includes club drawings and music. Although Hamilton indiscriminately referred to this revision and to the original minutes as "record books," I use "Record" to refer only to the volume of revised minutes. (Hamilton himself titled this volume "Record of the Tuesday Club.") It is uncertain when Hamilton began revising the minutes, but it was probably no later than 1750. Elaine G. Breslaw's edition, *Records of the Tuesday Club of Annapolis, 1745–56* (Urbana, Ill., 1988), includes the "Record" and the second volume of minutes.[1]

3. Draft of the *History*, volumes I and II. (The only extant portion of

---

1. Breslaw suggests in her edition that Hamilton possibly began revising the minutes in 1755, but that seems unlikely. By fall 1752, he had begun working on the *History* itself. Although he continued to revise the minutes beyond that date, it seems unlikely that he would have begun the formidable task of revising them at the same time that he was devoting so much energy to the *History*.

the drafted text [containing pp. 465–700 of volume I and the index to that volume] appears at the end of volume III of the manuscript of the *History*. The table of contents has been mistakenly placed at the front of the "Record"). Hamilton states in the *History* that he "began to Collect and Compile the History of the Club" in the fall of 1752 (III, 118); he probably stopped working on the draft around January 22, 1754, the date of the last event (Quirpum Comic's trial) listed in the table of contents. The table of contents is divided into twelve books but not into volumes. However, the last page of the extant portion of the draft says "End of the first volume" (Book VI, p. 700); the index, too, has "Contents of The first Volume" placed at the top, suggesting that after he finished all twelve books and the table of contents Hamilton decided to divide the draft into two volumes of equal size. He then numbered the first seven hundred pages and provided an index to volume I. That he provided page numbers for only the first six books in the table of contents suggests that he probably stopped working on the draft after indexing volume I. Rather than spend his time numbering the pages of volume II and indexing that volume, he turned to the final version of the *History*. For a transcription of the draft, see Robert Micklus, "Dr. Alexander Hamilton's *The History of the Tuesday Club*" (Ph.D. diss., University of Delaware, 1980), IV, 1475–1721.

4. *The History of the Tuesday Club*, volumes I–III (John Work Garrett Collections, The Milton S. Eisenhower Library, The Johns Hopkins University, Baltimore, Maryland; pages 503–564 of volume III are in the Dulany Papers, MS. 1265, Box 3, Maryland Historical Society, Baltimore; sections of volume III are missing [pp. 301–332, 455–502, and the final pages; I provide transcriptions from the "Record" for those portions of the narrative]; a draft of the dedication and the first two pages of a draft of the preface have been mistakenly placed at the front of the "Record"; the remaining portion of Hamilton's draft of the preface is also in the Dulany Papers). Hamilton probably began writing the final version of the *History* around September 9, 1754, the date of the dedication. The title page to volume II states that that volume was written in 1755, and the eyewitness account of Dr. Upton Scott, Hamilton's good friend and fellow Tuesday Club member, indicates that Hamilton continued writing the *History* up until his death in May 1756 (letter dated Aug. 28, 1809, Howard Family Papers, MS. 469, Maryland Historical Society). Hamilton numbered all the pages of the *History*, but he did not have time before dying to finish numbering the table of contents or the index to volume II. (I doubt that he ever completed an index to volume III.) Hamilton had simply copied the table of contents from his draft, adding only one more chapter heading to Book

XI and eight more to Book XII. As he was writing Book XII, however, he divided it into three books—making a total of fourteen in all—and added two more chapters to Book XIV not listed in the table of contents. Hamilton initially intended the final version of the *History*, like the draft, to contain only two volumes and twelve books. But to take his mind off his illness he continued writing up until his death, and the twelve books swelled to fourteen and the two volumes to three. Before dying he wrote "vol. 3d" in the text at Book XI and mistakenly placed "Volume III" alongside the heading for Book X in the table of contents. Since Hamilton did not have the chance to provide a title page to volume III or to change the book and chapter headings in the table of contents to accurately reflect the expansion of volume III, I have done both for him. I have also finished numbering his table of contents and have provided page numbers for his index to volume II.

PROVENANCE

Alexander Hamilton's widow, Margaret Dulany, gave his manuscripts (including "Man," a lost poem in blank verse) to his old friend and Tuesday Club associate Dr. Upton Scott. The sole surviving club member, Scott kept the manuscripts in his possession until 1809, when at age eighty-five he lent *The History of the Tuesday Club* to the Baltimore Library. Scott presented the library with three volumes of the *History*, two of which were already bound, and requested that they bind the third. Because he considered pages 503–564 (and whatever else there may have been) of volume III as part of an unfinished fourth volume, I suspect that Scott kept those pages in his own possession, which possibly accounts for the different locations of the manuscripts today. Judge George W. Dobbin later acquired the *History* (minus pages 503–564 of volume III), which was then purchased by the Johns Hopkins University in 1905, where it is presently housed in the John Work Garrett Collections of the Milton S. Eisenhower Library (Upton Scott to unidentified person, August 28, 1809, Howard Family Papers, MS. 469, Maryland Historical Society, Baltimore; Scott to unidentified person, August 28, 1809, "Record of the Tuesday Club," MS. 854, MHS; Sarah Elizabeth Freeman, "The Tuesday Club Medal," *Numismatist*, LVIII [1945], 1314).

BIBLIOGRAPHICAL NOTE

Only three chapters of *The History of the Tuesday Club* have previously appeared in print: a modernized version of book 10, chapter 3, concerning the "decathedration" of Nasifer Jole (printed anonymously, but probably by the editor, Dr. William Hand Browne, in the first volume of the *Maryland Historical Magazine* [1906], 59–65); Elaine G. Breslaw's transcription of book 13, chapter 4, concerning the celebration of the club's ninth anniversary (in "The Chronicle as Satire: Dr. Hamilton's 'History of the Tuesday Club,'" *MHM*, LXX [1975], 129–148); and my own transcription of book 8, chapter 1, concerning Hamilton's burlesque of the eighteenth-century conception of tragicomedy (in "Dr. Alexander Hamilton's 'Modest Proposal,'" *Early American Literature*, XVI [1981], 107–132).

Hamilton and *The History of the Tuesday Club* have been only passingly mentioned—when mentioned at all—in general studies of colonial literature and culture (but see Richard Beale Davis, *Intellectual Life in the Colonial South, 1585–1763*, 3 vols. [Knoxville, Tenn., 1978], III, 1383–1390). The most complete study of Hamilton and his works is Robert Micklus, *The Comic Genius of Dr. Alexander Hamilton* (Knoxville, Tenn., 1990). J. A. Leo Lemay provides an excellent chapter on Hamilton in *Men of Letters in Colonial Maryland* (Knoxville, Tenn., 1972), 213–256. Elaine G. Breslaw, "Dr. Alexander Hamilton and the Enlightenment in Maryland" (Ph.D. diss., University of Maryland, 1973); Breslaw, "Wit, Whimsy, and Politics: The Uses of Satire by the Tuesday Club of Annapolis, 1744 to 1756," *William and Mary Quarterly*, 3d Ser., XXXII (1975), 295–306; and Breslaw, "The Chronicle as Satire: Dr. Hamilton's 'History of the Tuesday Club,'" *MHM*, LXX (1975), 129–148, provide informative discussions of Hamilton's social and intellectual milieu and of the political satire in the *History*. The only other essays dealing with the *History*'s value as literature are Robert Micklus, "Dr. Alexander Hamilton's 'Modest Proposal,'" *Early Am. Lit.*, XVI (1981), 107–132, and Micklus, "'The History of the Tuesday Club': A Mock-Jeremiad of the Colonial South," *WMQ*, 3d Ser., XL (1983), 42–61.

Numerous books and articles provide additional insights into the Tuesday Club and its members, including (chronologically) [John G. Morris], "History of the Annapolis 'Tuesday Club,'" *American Historical Record*, II (1873), 149–155; Frank B. Mayer, "Old Maryland Manners," *Scribner's Monthly*, XVII (1878), 315–331; Elihu S. Riley, *"The Ancient City": A History of Annapolis, in Maryland, 1649–1887* (Annapolis, Md., 1887), 131–136; Lawrence C. Wroth, *A History of Printing in Colonial Maryland, 1686–1776* (Baltimore, 1922), 75–95; Walter B. Norris, *Annapolis: Its Colonial and Naval Story* (New York, 1925), 62–66; Joseph Towne Wheeler, "Reading and Other Recreations of Marylanders, 1700–1776," *MHM*, XXXVIII (1943), 37–55, 167–180; Wheeler, "Literary Culture in Eighteenth-Century Maryland, 1700–1776," *ibid.*, 273–276; Sarah Elizabeth Freeman, "The Tuesday Club Medal," *Numismatist*, LVIII (1945), 1313–1322; Anna Wells Rutledge, "Portraits in Varied Media in the Collections of the Maryland Historical Society," *MHM*, XLI (1946), 282–326; Rutledge, "A Humorous Artist in Colonial Maryland," *American Collector*, XVI (1947), 8–9, 14–15; David Hackett Fischer, "John Beale Bordley, Daniel Boorstin, and the American Enlightenment," *Journal of Southern History*, XXVIII (1962), 327–342; Robert R. Hare, "Electro Vitrifrico in Annapolis: Mr. Franklin Visits the Tuesday Club," *MHM*, LVIII (1963), 62–66; Shunsuke Kamei, "Cultural Clubs in Colonial America, 1720–1750," *Studies in English Literature* (English Literary Society of Japan), English Number (1963), 37–70; Rosamond Randall Beirne, "The Reverend Thomas Chase: Pugnacious Parson," *MHM*, LIX (1964), 1–14; Joseph C. Morton, "Stephen Bordley of Colonial Annapolis," *Winterthur Portfolio*, V (1969), 1–14; Richard Beale Davis, "The Intellectual Golden Age in the Colonial Chesapeake Bay Country," *Virginia Magazine of History and Biography*, LXXVIII (1970), 131–143; J. A. Leo Lemay, "Franklin's 'Dr. Spence': The Reverend Archibald Spencer (1698?–1760), M.D.," *MHM*, LIX (1964), 199–216; Lemay, "Hamilton's Literary History of the *Maryland Gazette*," *WMQ*, 3d Ser., XXIII (1966), 273–285; the chapters on Jonas Green, James Sterling, and Thomas Bacon in Lemay, *Men of Letters*, 187–212, 257–312, 313–342; David Curtis Skaggs, "Thomas Cradock and the Chesapeake Golden Age," *WMQ*, 3d Ser., XXX (1973), 93–116; Skaggs, *The Poetic Writings of Thomas Cradock, 1718–1770* (Newark, Del., 1983); William E. Deibert, "Thomas Bacon, Colonial Clergyman," *MHM*, LXXIII (1978), 79–86; James R. Heintze, "Alexander Malcolm: Musician, Clergyman, and Schoolmaster," *ibid.*, 226–235; Mary M. Starin, "The Reverend Doctor John Gordon, 1717–1790," *ibid.*, LXXV (1980), 167–191; Aubrey C. Land, *The Dulanys of Maryland: A Biographical Study of Daniel Dulany, the Elder (1685–1753) and Daniel Dulany, the Younger (1722–1797)* (Baltimore, 1955); Land, *Colonial Maryland: A History* (Millwood, N.Y., 1981), 179–205; Elaine G. Breslaw, "Merrymaking in Old Annapolis: The Tuesday Club," *Baltimore Sun Magazine*, Mar. 24, 1974, 22, 24, and 33; Breslaw, "A Dismal Tragedy: Drs. Alexander and John Hamilton Comment on Braddock's Defeat," *MHM*, LXXV (1980), 118–144; Breslaw, "The Tuesday Club of Annapolis,"

Maryland Heritage News, I (1983), 12–14; Robert Micklus, entries on Thomas Bacon, Jonas Green, and Alexander Hamilton in Emory Elliott, ed., *Dictionary of Literary Biography: American Colonial Writers, 1735–1781* (Detroit, Mich., 1984), XXXI, 19–22, 96–98, 101–107; and Micklus, "The Secret Fall of Freemasonry in Dr. Alexander Hamilton's *The History of the Tuesday Club,*" in *Deism, Masonry, and the Enlightenment: Essays Honoring Alfred Owen Aldridge,* ed. J. A. Leo Lemay (Newark, Del., 1987), 127–136.

Two editions of the Tuesday Club's minutes and music are available: Elaine G. Breslaw, ed., *Records of the Tuesday Club of Annapolis, 1745–56* (Urbana, Ill., 1988); and John Barry Talley, *Secular Music in Colonial Annapolis: The Tuesday Club, 1745–56* (Urbana, Ill., 1988).

EDITORIAL METHOD

For my doctoral dissertation I prepared a literal transcription of *The History of the Tuesday Club;* since then, I have become convinced that a dissertation is the only place suitable for an exact reproduction of Hamilton's manuscript, and that to publish a literal transcription of the *History* would be a disservice to him. Hamilton was a superb prose stylist, but he did not live long enough even to complete volume III of the *History,* let alone to proofread the entire manuscript. His inability to add the finishing touches to his manuscript shows in many ways: in the missing page references for the index of volume II; in the increasingly sketchy nature of the drawings toward the end of that volume; and in his misspellings, his sometimes careless capitalization, and his often peculiar lack of punctuation throughout the *History.* To be sure, like other eighteenth-century authors, Hamilton's composition habits were consistent mainly in their inconsistency. Still, he did observe certain rules of spelling, punctuation, and capitalization. To ignore those rules for the sake of presenting an exact transcription of the *History* would serve only to display an editor's, not Hamilton's, ignorance of them.

I have therefore made some changes in this edition in spelling, capitalization, and punctuation according to Hamilton's normal practice. Given the length of Hamilton's manuscript and its unfinished state, the changes that I have made are relatively few, and on the whole this edition remains as untidy as the original. One need only compare the punctuation in Hamilton's draft with that in the corresponding pages of volume I of the *History* to discover that he was not an exceptionally tidy author. With no particular consistency, he omitted or added punctuation marks in the *History* that were present or absent in the draft. (His spelling and capitalization also fluctuate inconsistently from one version to the next.) So even though it would be a simple matter to tidy up the *History,* I have made changes only in instances that I am certain are unintentionally awkward, ambiguous, or distracting. Where none of these problems arise, I have retained Hamilton's original usage, even though his normal usage might justify making a change. (He normally placed commas between all compound sentences joined by conjunctions, for instance, but to add commas in every instance where he failed to do so would be, as he would say, an act of supererogation.) In short, my intention has not been to lend the *History* a consistency that the manuscript itself does not possess, but to maintain its inconsistencies and, at the same time, to keep Hamilton's prose from appearing silly or cumbersome in ways he clearly did not intend. The specific policies I have followed in making changes are outlined below.

The length of Hamilton's manuscript has made the task of normalizing the *History* initially exasperating but ultimately rewarding. There is little guesswork involved in editing a manuscript of this size, for pattern after pattern unmistakably emerges. The initial temptation (and I fell) is to compile chart after chart of what Hamilton did 90 percent of the time in any given case, and to suppose that, after having pinned down his "normal" usage for virtually every spelling quirk, punctuation mark, or capitalized word, one then has the license to change the 10 percent that does not fit the pattern. So one changes the 10 percent that does not fit here and there until eventually one realizes that the 10 percent that does not fit is part of the pattern, too, and that the infernal itch to tinker with that 10 percent is the editor's obsession, not the author's. The ultimate advantage of editing a manuscript the size of the *History*, then, is that it naggingly reminds an editor that the inconsistencies are also normal, that there are patterns to the inconsistencies as well as to the consistencies, and that the only way to maintain an author's normal usage is to leave his text as unmolested as possible. That is what I have sought to do in this edition. To do otherwise, I think, is to have an author—particularly an eighteenth-century author such as Hamilton—speak in a language he did not use. For better or worse, the voice that emerges from the pages of this text is Hamilton's.

Additions, Cancellations, Overwritings, and Repetitions

Having written about the Tuesday Club in three previous forms, Hamilton had a good idea of what he wanted to include in the *History* by the time he sat down to write it. His cancellations and overwritings are therefore few and insignificant (anyone interested in them should consult my dissertation). I have, of course, included all his additions.

I have added words to Hamilton's text (and included them in my list of substantive changes) only when they are absolutely necessary to make sense of a given sentence. But where I suspect that Hamilton intended to omit a word, I have retained his original usage. (In one of his speeches, for example, President Jole, whose mercantile style of speaking is characterized by his frequent omission of subjects in his sentences, says, "as I know, that is not so good a musician as Poet." Jole obviously means "that he is not," but I have retained the original.) I have also silently added the first word on a new page when Hamilton supplied a catchword but neglected to repeat the word at the top of the next page.

Bracketed Material

Hamilton frequently inserted material within brackets, normally to indicate an aside or interruption during club speeches. I have also used brackets when I have supplied a word or phrase that is missing (because of a tear) or obscured in Hamilton's manuscript. Whenever possible, I have traced the word or phrase back to its most immediate source before the *History* (i.e., I have looked first in Hamilton's draft and then in the "Record"). I have therefore rarely needed to guess at missing or obscured letters, but because they are illegible in the *History* itself, I have nevertheless placed them within brackets.

Capitalization

Hamilton's capitalization habits were inconsistent. To be sure, he capitalized certain parts of speech more often than others (nouns more often than verbs, adjectives more often than adverbs, and so on) and certain types of words more often than others (e.g., he was especially fond of capitalizing a whole slew of mock-heroic adjectives such as *Glorious, Heroic, Illustrious,* and *Remarkable*). But it was not unusual for him to capitalize the same words in one sentence that he left uncapitalized in the next. Since he followed no particular system of capitalization, I have retained his original usage with only a few exceptions.

I have capitalized the first word in any sentence, paragraph, or line of poetry. For proper names and place-names, I have closely followed Hamilton's normal usage—meaning not only what he did 90 percent of the time, but also what he did in that 10 percent that might at first appear unusual. For instance, Hamilton usually capitalized both halves of place-names or proper names such as Wapping Dock and Slyboots Pleasant. But it was not unusual for him to capitalize only half of a place-name (Wapping dock, cape Breton) and only the first half of a proper name (Slyboots pleasant, Ignotus warble). I have therefore retained his capitalization in these cases, and in the handful of instances where he neglected to capitalize either half, I have capitalized only one, not both.

I have capitalized all words beginning with uppercase letters that differ in shape from their lowercase letters (*B, D, E, F, H, I, J, K, L, P, Q, R, T*). Hamilton capitalized three of these letters—*I, J,* and *T*—at least twice as frequently as the other letters in this group for the simple reason that he apparently found it easier to use *I, J*, and *T*, all of which he normally wrote with a similar single stroke, than to go back and dot his *i*'s or *j*'s and cross his *t*'s. Since it is impossible to determine which of his *I*'s, *J*'s, and *T*'s Hamilton would have changed to lowercase had he published the *History*, I have left them all capitalized.

A second group of capitalized letters in the *History* generally differ only in size from their lowercase letters (*A, C, G, M, N, O, U, V, W, X, Y, Z*). Because the size of Hamilton's script often changes radically from page to page—sometimes from sentence to sentence—I have determined whether or not a given word in this group should be capitalized first by judging whether its first letter is appreciably larger than its remaining letters, then by comparing it with similar words in the first group of letters, where Hamilton's capitalization is beyond question. Although the auxiliary verb *could* or the preposition *of*, for example, sometimes appears to be capitalized, the fact that Hamilton never capitalized *did* or *for* in similar instances suggests that what might appear to be capital letters in the former cases are more a result of haste than design. In such instances I have treated these letters as lowercase in keeping with Hamilton's normal usage. But wherever the possibility exists that he may have intended to capitalize a word in this group, I have left it alone.

The last letter—the capital *S*—poses particular problems for anyone who edits eighteenth-century manuscripts. As with other eighteenth-century authors, Hamilton's *S* looks exactly like his long *s*. The only way to determine whether or not a given word beginning with *s* should be capitalized, therefore, is to compare it to what Hamilton normally did with similar words in the first two groups. If he normally capitalized similar words, I have treated the long *s* as a capital; if he did not, I have treated it as a lowercase letter.

End-of-Line Hyphenation

Hamilton normally used a double hyphen for end-of-line hyphenation; occasionally, however, he used a single hyphen, and sometimes he carelessly omitted any hyphenation whatsoever. As a rule, he used the double hyphen to indicate that a word should be transcribed without a hyphen (e.g., *man* = *ner* becomes *manner*, and *long* = *standing* becomes *longstanding*). Where he used a single hyphen at the end of a line, I have retained the hyphen if the word is hyphenated elsewhere within a line in his manuscript, but I have treated it as a hasty double hyphen if the word is never hyphenated elsewhere within a line (e.g., *long- standing* becomes *long-standing,* but *man- ner* becomes *manner*). Where Hamilton neglected to provide any end-of-line hyphenation, I have spelled the word as it appears elsewhere within a line (e.g., *long standing* remains *long standing,* but *man ner* becomes *manner*). As the above examples suggest, a compound word such as *long-standing* can be spelled three different ways depending on Hamilton's end-of-line hyphenation.

On rare occasions Hamilton placed what appears to be a hyphen at the end of a line when the mark he used is actually simply a line (e.g., "there may be allowed, two dishes of desert, and no more, Butter - [end of line] Cheese, and all Sorts of Garden Stuff, in their proper Seasons, not being Included in the name of deserts"). Hamilton obviously meant "Butter, Cheese," in the preceding example, not "Butter-Cheese." Because the line in cases such as this might be intended to signify a pause, and not merely to take up space, I have added punctuation (in this case a comma) when appropriate.

Greek and Latin Passages

I have spelled all Greek words as they appear in the *History,* except where Hamilton occasionally used eighteenth-century ligatures that cannot be reproduced typographically. I have expanded the ligatures in those instances. Hamilton was not particularly fussy about accents and breathings: sometimes he used them accurately, sometimes inaccurately, but more often than not he did not bother to use them at all. I have therefore left the accents and breathings as they appear in his manuscript.

In Latin passages I have retained the abbreviation ʒ, which Hamilton generally used in place of *-ue* endings (as in *annoqʒ domini*), and the ⁹, which he used to indicate any abbreviated word. (Ordinarily, the ⁹ takes the place of *-us* in eighteenth-century manuscripts, whereas its variant, ʒ, takes the place of *-es, -et,* and *-m* endings, but Hamilton used them more loosely.)

Italics

Hamilton followed no particular system to signify whether a word or phrase should be italicized. Sometimes he used an italic script, sometimes he underlined, and sometimes he did both. I have italicized all underlined words; where a word or phrase appears to be both italicized and underlined, I have simply italicized it. Usually Hamilton italicized foreign words and phrases, titles of books, forms of address, proverbial phrases, and oaths; I have followed his normal practice and have italicized all such words.

Pagination

Hamilton's pagination is occasionally unreliable, moving, for instance, from page 270 to 171. In such instances, I have silently corrected his errors. When his pagination overlaps, I have added a letter (e.g., a second page 245 becomes 245a).

Punctuation

It would be a waste of time and energy to note every punctuation change I have made in this edition. In his haste to complete the *History* Hamilton often failed to provide punctuation in chapter, letter, or poem headings, and at the end of footnotes, paragraphs, or stanzas of poetry. To keep the *History* from being pointlessly distracting, I have silently added the proper punctuation in these and similar instances that do not affect the rhythms of Hamilton's poetry or prose. I have listed all punctuation changes, however, that I have made within the stanzas of his poetry or the paragraphs of his narrative.

Most of the punctuation changes I have made are additions rather than substitutions or cancellations, and a majority of these additions appear at the end of Hamilton's manuscript lines. His repeated omission of punctuation at the ends of lines suggests not only his haste to move on to the next line, but also his apparent assumption that a break at the end of a line—be it poetry or prose—marks a pause normally signified by a period, comma, or some other form of punctuation. Hamilton's failure to provide end-of-line punctuation is a perfect excuse for an editor to tinker with the rhythms of his prose and verse. But regardless of whether an omission appears at the end of a line or within it, I have added punctuation only in instances where Hamilton's original usage is awkward or ambiguous in ways that he clearly did not intend. For the same reasons I have occasionally substituted or cancelled previously existing punctuation. My policies regarding individual punctuation marks are outlined below.

APOSTROPHES

Hamilton inconsistently used apostrophes to identify possessives (*its* or *it's, president's* or *presidents*), plurals (*Cyruses* but *Solyman's, Specieses* but *Rhombus's*), contractions (*don't* or *dont*), and numerous other abbreviated words or omitted letters. I have retained his usage, adding or omitting apostrophes only to prevent an occasional misreading (when *well* should be read as *we'll* or, perhaps, *I'll* as *Ill*).

BRACKETS

Occasionally Hamilton used brackets in place of parentheses, but normally they function in the *History* to enclose stage directions or asides during club speeches ("I shall accuse no other babbler [Here Mr Crankum looked about towards his left hand, where Mr Secretary sat,]"). I have added brackets only where Hamilton omitted one or the other bracket, or where he used a parenthesis instead of a second bracket.

COLONS

Hamilton never used colons to separate independent sentences and very rarely to separate a series of parallel clauses or phrases. Rather, he normally reserved colons for abbreviations, and when an abbreviation occurs within or at the end of a sentence, the colon usually doubles for other punctuation ("Jealous Spyplot Junr: Quirpum Comic, and Prim Timorous, were . . . all unanimously admitted"). As in the preceding example, Hamilton often placed colons after abbreviated words ending with superscripts (which have been brought down to the line in this edition); just as often, however, he did not. If Hamilton provided a colon after the superscript, I have kept it; if he did not, I have added colons only to prevent misreadings (e.g., M^r appears as *Mr* and *Esqr* appears as *Esqr,* but *d^0* [*ditto*] appears as *do:* rather than *do* and *Proceed^s* [*Proceedings*] appears as *Proceeds:* rather than *Proceeds*). I have also added colons where Hamilton neglected to follow his normal practice with particular abbreviations (e.g., *Dec:* or *vizt:*).

COMMAS

Like other eighteenth-century authors, Hamilton treated the comma as the most protean of punctuation marks. Huge one-sentence paragraphs littered with comma splices appear throughout the *History,* so that commas abound in places where we normally expect to find periods, semicolons, or colons. To Hamilton, the comma obviously signified pauses of various lengths; moreover, the host of comma splices in the *History* are an integral part of his intentionally digressive writing style. Most readers sensitive to the rhythms of Hamilton's prose will quickly adjust to his all-purpose commas and recognize many of the situations in which they commonly occur, as in the following instances where Hamilton used them much as we would use semicolons: "but it was too late, the enimy had secured the Doors";

"it was not at all necessary, that a man should be hard favored . . . , it was Sufficient for him Sincerely to profess and believe that he was not handsom." These and other comma splices in the *History* may initially pose some difficulties for readers, especially when a clause or phrase is ambiguously sandwiched between two independent clauses ("it is a true observation, that men are to be wrought upon by degrees, when any new model or form of Government Religion or Clubs is proposed, they must be soothed, flattered, cajoled, cozened and hoodwinked"). But once we recognize that, in keeping with his digressive writing style, Hamilton usually added subordinate clauses or phrases onto already existing independent clauses, we have little trouble unscrambling sentences of this sort. (In the preceding example, for instance, the break occurs between "proposed" and "they," not between "degrees" and "when.") At other times, Hamilton more unpredictably scattered commas throughout his sentences, and occasionally his sentences require every ounce of the reader's ingenuity to unscramble them. But that is all part of the fun of reading the *History*, and although I have often added and sometimes omitted commas in this edition (for reasons discussed below), nowhere have I replaced Hamilton's commas with other punctuation merely to make his sentences more accessible to modern readers.

Actually, it is less difficult for modern readers to adjust to finding commas in place of other punctuation than to finding no punctuation at all in places where we normally expect to see commas. Yet in certain constructions Hamilton repeatedly omitted commas, especially in the following situations.

1. In a series of verbs, nouns, adjectives, or other parts of speech ("murdered massacred and expelled"; "cough fart, and sneeze"; "Gluttony letchery and Idleness"; "punctillios Ceremonies, and distinguishing badges of honor"; "a nauseous fowl mouthd and beastly toast"; "gay, airy volatile fellows").

2. When couplings of verbs, nouns, adjectives, or other parts of speech appear in a series ("fringe scollop, shape and proportion"; "mollify malax, soften, intreat and request"; "Simpletons fools, asses and Idiots"; "traiterous rebellious, Scandalous and Submissive letters").

3. When a prepositional phrase, preceded by a comma, splits a subject and verb ("titles and dignities, in all polite societies have a certain fixed value").

4. When an appositive, preceded by a comma, splits a subject and verb ("death, the Confounder of all human projects interrupted him").

5. Before or after transitional words or phrases ("how many for Instance, sleep one half of their time and dream the other half").

To be sure, in these instances Hamilton sometimes employed commas as we would, and occasionally I have added commas in the above situations—especially in cases such as item 3—to avoid exceptionally awkward or ambiguous constructions. But the exceptions are few. Hamilton felt no qualms about omitting commas in these situations, so generally I have maintained his usage in all such instances.

In the following instances, however, it would be equally misleading *not* to supply commas.

1. When a majority of items in a lengthy series are separated by commas and there is no apparent reason other than hastiness for Hamilton's omitting punctuation ("Ignoramus[,] blockhead, dunce, rogue, liar, knave and fool"; "nasty, blewbellied, blanket ars'd, hip-shotten, maggot eaten, round about[,] Snuff besmeard, flyblown Son of a whore").

2. When a subordinate clause follows or interrupts an independent clause ("There are two maxims . . . generally received as true ones[,] tho' for my part, I think them at best but paltry Stuff"; "Certain it is, tho I know not how it happens[,] that the mind is more sprightly and active in company").

3. When a nonrestrictive clause or phrase follows or interrupts an independent clause ("he was called upon to deliver the Copy of that Commission[,] which he did"; "even the punishment of the gelastic Law, which was inflicted on this occasion[,] was nothing to that vociferous heroe").

4. When a clause or phrase other than a prepositional phrase or appositive interrupts the subject and verb of an independent clause ("Some, insensible of either mirth or anger[,] have sunk into soft Repose").

5. When a missing comma before a conjunction joining two independent clauses makes the sentence as a whole awkward to read ("as the saying is, the proof of the pudding is in the eating[,] so, the proof of what I here write, will be elucidated by reading what I have there wrote"). Where no confusion arises, however, I have not added the comma ("Jonathan Grog was declared victor and he drank a toast to the Club").

6. When no punctuation appears between two independent clauses joined by a conjunctive adverb ("the prop of your honor's understanding is crazy, and very much needs repairing[,] therefore, I move to your honor . . .").

7. When no punctuation appears between two independent clauses and the first word of the second clause is not capitalized ("Mr Neilson was like

all other Illustrious men[,] he had blemishes blended with his excellencies").

Except in the instances noted above, and in a few other restricted cases that require no elaboration (before *vizt:,* for instance, as in "it's members were now chiefly composed of Slaves[,] vizt: the Slaves of the honorable Nasifer Jole"), I have added commas only to prevent ambiguous, sometimes silly readings of particular sentences ("Roundhead Muddy after supper[,] stood up, and addressed himself to his honor"; "A dull parson, once holding forth in his pulpit[,] the whole congregation, except this natural, fell fast asleep"). All of these additions are consistent with Hamilton's normal usage.

I have omitted commas only when the word (or words) following a comma is an obvious afterthought ("I now invest you with our Club badge, medal"; "From a nice observance of these rules, of ceremony"), and occasionally when Hamilton awkwardly separated two words for no apparent reason ("it was a piece of the most notorious, nonsense"; "under which many strange and dreadful mysteries were, couched"). But Hamilton habitually used commas in what may seem to us the most unlikely places— between any subject and verb, before any prepositional phrase or conjunction—so, aside from the exceptions just mentioned, I have not omitted any of his commas.

DASHES

Aside from using dashes as we would to mark an interruption or to emphasize a word or phrase at the end of a sentence, Hamilton frequently used dashes to separate direct or indirect quotations. Where he has failed to do this, I have added and noted the dash ("When Demetrius took Megara he asked Stylphon a Philosopher, if he had lost any thing,[—]Not I sir indeed replied he, I carry nothing about me, which you can make prey of"; "sometimes . . . it would be heres to you,—and heres to you—and thank you Sir,[—]and pledge you Sir"). Often other punctuation precedes a dash ("[they] triffle thro' a triffling life, in a promiscous multitude and medley of triffles,—But 'tis well we have these toys to . . . keep them out of mischief"); in the few instances where Hamilton carelessly added other punctuation *after* a dash, I have omitted the other punctuation and noted it in my list of punctuation changes ("As if Pone was not bread.—, if Pone be not bread, . . . what is it").

EXCLAMATION POINTS

Hamilton occasionally employed commas instead of periods in exclamation points. It may appear that he used this curious punctuation mark only to separate a string of exclamations, but no such pattern exists. Rather, it whimsically crops up from time to time, and because it is distracting and not consistent with his normal practice, I have used regular exclamation points throughout this edition.

FLOURISHES

Hamilton often placed a flourish after the salutation or at the close of club letters, but he also used commas at these times. I have used commas in place of his flourishes throughout this edition.

PARENTHESES

More often than not, Hamilton placed other punctuation before parentheses, but he adhered to no particular pattern. Sometimes he provided punctuation within parentheses: "Human wit (if I may be allowed the expression,)"; sometimes he provided punctuation before and within parentheses: "These meddling Coxcombs, (some of whom had almost been committed to the flames for Heresy,)"; and sometimes he provided no punctuation at all before or after parentheses: "every thing turned uproar and Confusion, which produced much cursing and swearing, and hence accrued fines (for they had Laws in this Club, which imposed fines upon certain trespasses) this soured the members at one another." Like colons and dashes, parentheses (and brackets) often take the place of other punctuation in the *History,* so it would be a mistake to add a period, for instance, between "trespasses" and "this" in the last example above. I have not added other punctuation before, within, or after Hamilton's parentheses, and I have added parentheses only where he carelessly omitted the first or second one.

PERIODS

It would be easy to assume from reading Hamilton's manuscript that "he did not bother with periods."[1] Sometimes he used no punctuation at all at the end of sentences (most of these instances occur at the end of his manuscript lines), and as I have noted above, often he used commas in place of periods. Yet unmistakable periods appear throughout the *History.*

1. Elaine G. Breslaw, "The Chronicle as Satire: Dr. Hamilton's 'History of the Tuesday Club,'" *Maryland Historical Magazine,* LXX (1975), 135.

Indeed, periods sometimes appear in what may seem to modern readers the most unlikely places, creating sentence fragments ("It could be called but a Compliment paid the president, and no Privilege. Which Solo Neverout Esqr, in a long frothy noisy Speech absolutely denied") or separating a series of items ("they call an Ale house, a *bouzing ken*. a beggar born and bred, a *Clapperdudgeon*. a pretended Dumb man, a *Dummerer.*"). I have retained Hamilton's usage in these instances and in all instances where a period unmistakably separates two independent sentences.

In general, I have made relatively few changes involving Hamilton's use of periods in this edition. I have replaced periods with commas (but never with semicolons or other punctuation) only when they are followed by an obvious afterthought ("Thus we find . . . Charity made use of as a pretext. a very bad precedent, and a dangerous Stroke to the liberties of the Club"), or when an uncapitalized conjunction or conjunctive adverb, preceded by a period, separates two independent sentences ("[Ceremonies] alone distinguish the high and great from the Low and Inconsiderable. for, as virtue and merit, . . . come not under the Cognizance of the grosser Senses, . . ."). I have changed commas to periods only when the majority of items in a series are separated by periods and the remaining commas create misreadings ("they call . . . Money *Lour*. Virgins *Dells*. Strumpets, *Doxies,* Beggars, *Maunders*. Hats, *Nab Cheats*. Hands, *Fambles*. Staves, *Filches*. to steal *Filsh*. Rayment, *Back cheat,* Food, *Belly Cheat.*"). I have added periods when no punctuation appears between two independent sentences and the first word of the second sentence is capitalized ("the president, assumed his Timber Countenance, which was an Infallible Sign, of his being highly displeased[.] The Secretary, to prevent the Rising Storm, . . . offered to read a paper in Club intituled a Remonstrance"). When no punctuation appears between two independent sentences and the first word of the second sentence is not capitalized, however, I have added a comma in keeping with Hamilton's normal usage ("Mr Neilson was like all other Illustrious men[,] he had blemishes blended with his excellencies"). In effect, I have added periods according to Hamilton's normal usage, but never merely to avoid a comma splice.

QUESTION MARKS

Hamilton separated a series of questions with commas, semicolons, question marks, and sometimes with all three; in all such instances, I have retained his usage. Like exclamation points, question marks occasionally have commas instead of periods; as with exclamation points, I have used regular question marks throughout this edition.

QUOTATION MARKS

Hamilton punctuated quotations inconsistently. Often he provided other punctuation before and after quotations, but sometimes he simply left extra space to indicate a pause; often he placed commas or periods before the second quotation mark, but sometimes he placed them below or after it; and often he enclosed quoted passages within single quotation marks, but frequently he enclosed them within double quotation marks and sometimes within combinations of both. In the first two cases, I have followed his normal usage, appropriately adding commas or periods before and after quotations and transposing commas or periods following the second quotation mark. But I have departed from Hamilton's normal usage in the third case because evidence suggests that he enclosed the majority of his quotations within single quotation marks in the *History* merely to save time. Throughout his draft and well into the first volume of the *History*, Hamilton used double quotation marks to enclose quoted material. But midway through volume I he began using single and double quotation marks interchangeably, and in volumes II and III he almost exclusively used single quotation marks. He apparently decided that double quotation marks were too much of a bother, not that they were improper for enclosing quotations. I have therefore used single and double quotation marks according to modern practice, and as Hamilton himself normally did in his draft and the first half of volume I.

Hamilton usually followed the eighteenth-century convention of placing quotation marks along the left-hand margin of his paragraphs, but sometimes he placed them only within his paragraphs, and sometimes he did both or combinations of both. I have placed quotation marks only at the beginning and end of direct quotations. Because Hamilton inconsistently added or omitted quotation marks around indirect quotations, I have retained only those around direct quotations to avoid confusion.

ROMAN NUMERALS, ARABIC NUMERALS, AND CAPITAL LETTERS

Hamilton sometimes placed commas, sometimes periods, and sometimes both after roman numerals, arabic numerals, and capital letters. Consequently, the periods in these cases sometimes also function as commas ("Charles I. who deserved . . ."). I have retained his usage in all such instances, supplying punctuation according to the rules established above only when he has omitted it completely.

SEMICOLONS

Wherever one might expect to find a semicolon, it is likely that Hamilton has used a comma instead. I have therefore added no semicolons in this edition. As with periods, I have occasionally changed semicolons to commas when a word or phrase following the semicolon is clearly an afterthought.

QUESTIONABLE ADDITIONS

Hamilton frequently doubled over the final loop of a letter or carried down the tail of a letter in such a way that he appeared to be adding commas without lifting his pen. These types of letters often occur in places where he normally used commas; but they appear equally often where he normally omitted commas, so unless he physically lifted his pen to add a comma, I have treated the loop or tail as part of the word, not as a punctuation mark. If further punctuation is required, I have added it and included it in my list of punctuation changes.

Spacing

Hamilton often lifted his pen while writing compound words and words with prefixes or suffixes (e.g., *common wealth, can not, over grown, there fore*). But he also lifted his pen in writing even the simplest monosyllabic words, so I have not divided a word such as *commonwealth* unless the space between the two words is clearly as great as the space between most of the other words in a given line. I have been especially reluctant to divide words that Hamilton repeatedly separated by a double end-of-line hyphen.

Spelling

Hamilton's multiple spellings of the same words or sounds are not an indication of his carelessness, but rather an indication of the indefinite nature of standard spelling rules at the time he wrote the *History*. It was not unusual, for instance, for him to use a single or double vowel, or a single or double consonant for the same word, sometimes in the same paragraph (*kept* or *keept, Intelect* or *Intellect*). As the spirit moved him, he sometimes dropped a silent *e* (*falshood, wholesom*), added or doubled a short *e* (*Proseperity, moderen; keept, streech*), dropped a short or silent *i* (*necessarly, transcript; aganst, villanous*), dropped the *h* in a word ending with *th* (*sevent*), changed a final *t* to *d* (*Sederund*), and so on. It would be foolish even to attempt to normalize Hamilton's spelling in these and similar instances. I can only promise the reader that, however odd a particular spelling may at first appear, if one is patient one will find several more just like it.

I have therefore made few spelling changes. If Hamilton spelled a particular word or sound the same way more than once, I have assumed he knew what he was doing. I have been especially wary about changing spellings that likely reflect his Scottish dialect. It hardly seems coincidental, for instance, that he used the spellings *havy* (*heavy*) and *plasantry* (*pleasantry*) only a few paragraphs apart. I have, however, changed obvious misspellings (*hononor*) and less blatant misspellings that one could probably find some justification for retaining, but that arise in ordinary words Hamilton always spelled otherwise (*istead*). I have changed a word that he spelled the same way more than once only when it could be misread to mean something else, and when the change I have made is consistent with his normal usage. It is confusing, for example, to see *they* spelled *the,* so even though Hamilton spelled it that way three times in the *History,* I have spelled it as he normally did hundreds of other times. Since all superscripts have been brought down to the line in this edition, I have also expanded the few words beginning with the thorn to avoid misreadings (*the* for *ye,* for example).

ABBREVIATIONS

Hamilton abbreviated numerous words and phrases in English and in Latin, and he particularly enjoyed mocking law Latin by almost incoherently abbreviating it. The abbreviations are part of the fun of reading the *History,* and I have retained rather than expanded them.

FALSE STARTS

In this edition I have ignored all false starts. (I included them in my dissertation.) Hamilton wrote the *History* so quickly that it would be pointless to note every false start (e.g., *lwrong*) or slip of the pen.

LIGATURES

Hamilton normally wrote *ae* as a ligature, occasionally in such a way that it might easily be mistaken for a double *e.* I have used *æ* for all those ligatures and *ae* for the few instances where he did not write *ae* as a ligature. Hamilton generally did not use the ligature *œ,* but in the few instances where he did I have reproduced it as such.

SUPERSCRIPTS

Hamilton's practice concerning superscripts was inconsistent. Sometimes he raised, sometimes he raised and underlined, and often he neither raised nor underlined the last letter or letters of abbreviated words and titles (*Secretary*, for instance, appears abbreviated as *Secret^ry*, *Secret^a*, and *Secretry*). Since he showed no particular preference in handling superscripts, I have chosen the least distracting method of bringing them all down to the line.

REMARKS ON THE DRAWINGS
Georgia Brady Barnhill

By his own admission in *The History of the Tuesday Club,* Hamilton "had a foolish Sort of a Genius for drawing" (III, 118), and among the more intriguing features of this edition are the many drawings he incorporated into his narrative. These illustrations predate any printed literary illustrations for an American text by almost fifty years. The next significant illustrations of American origin appeared when Elkanah Tisdale designed and engraved illustrations for John Trumbull's *M'Fingal* (1794).[1] Because of the uniqueness of Hamilton's drawings, some commentary on them is appropriate here.

The History of the Tuesday Club contains forty-eight completed drawings—thirty in volume I and eighteen in volume II. In addition there are vignettes of the club badge and seal, the presidential badge and cap of state, and the shield on the presidential canopy. Volume II contains an unfinished frontispiece, an unfinished pencil sketch, and two pages with ruled rectangles and titles below intended for illustrations that were never completed. Volumes II and III contain numerous blank leaves that Hamilton apparently left for illustrations he planned to include but never completed. These blank leaves support Robert Micklus's contention that the manuscript was left incomplete at Hamilton's death.[2]

The illustrations are uniform in technique. Hamilton used a combination of pen and black ink and wash applied with a brush. Each drawing is

Georgia Brady Barnhill is Andrew W. Mellon Curator of Graphic Arts at the American Antiquarian Society in Worcester, Massachusetts. She wishes to thank the Bibliographical Society of America and the American Philosophical Society for grants that supported the research for this essay, and the American Antiquarian Society for a research leave in 1986.

1. Donald C. O'Brien, "Elkanah Tisdale: Designer, Engraver, and Miniature Painter," *Connecticut Historical Society Bulletin,* XLIX (1984), 83–96.

2. The "Record of the Tuesday Club" (Maryland Historical Society, MS. 854) contains twenty-three of Hamilton's drawings. The Dulany Papers (MS. 1265) contain several additional drawings, three of which pertain to the Royalist Club and two to the Tuesday Club. A second portrait of George Neilson is in the Dulany Papers, and portraits of Beale Bordley, Richard Dorsey, and Walter Dulany are in the "Record" (these portraits are missing from the *History*). The members are given their proper names, although Latinized, in the "Record" drawings and appear wearing their club badges, which Hamilton omitted from the portraits in the *History*. Since Hamilton's technique improved over time, the illustrations in the *History* are better drawn.

contained within a rectangle ruled with a pen and iron gall ink, the same used for the writing of the text and for the inscriptions on the drawings. The single graphite sketch in volume II of the manuscript indicates that Hamilton used a pencil to delineate the basic features of the illustrations; the pencil is not dominant, however, in the completed drawings.

Ten of the drawings in volume I and three in volume II are portraits. The first, Congal de Rutherin, was, according to the inscription, copied from "an antique marble bas-relief dug up from the rubbish dumps of an old monastery near Drumlanridge." Hamilton has correctly drawn a fac-simile of a relief, as if taken from a funerary monument. Although a fictive portrait, it is realistic, not idealized as were so many funerary portraits. The other portraits in the *History*—of various members of the club—all share the format of bust-length mezzotint portraits popular in England and in the colonies during the first half of the eighteenth century: each portrait is surrounded by an oval frame set into a larger rectangle, with spandrels normally of a different tone than the immediate background of the portrait within the oval. Space below the portrait is reserved for the title and any additional inscription.

In a very economical style, Hamilton captures the salient features of the club's members, occasionally exaggerating certain characteristics. Al-though his drawings have been called caricatures, most of them correspond to his verbal sketches.[3] Hamilton's lack of drawing expertise renders his attempts awkward, but this is not tantamount to caricature. Several of the portraits do, however, contain a good deal of exaggeration, a prime exam-ple of which is the portrait of the club's president, Charles Cole (Nasifer Jole). Hamilton devotes several pages to describing Jole, noting that he was "of a fair complexion, long and Sharp visage; somewhat Inclinable to a Square countenance, his nose aqueline, his chin of a Considerable length and prominent, in short, he is what many call in their vulgar Stile somewhat hatchet faced" (I, 160). Jole's aquiline nose and pointed chin are used to good advantage in the formal portrait and distinguish him from the other members in the group scenes. Since Jole often dressed flamboyantly—red was his favorite color—we can only regret that Hamilton's portraits are not in color.

Two other interesting portraits are of Hamilton himself (Loquacious Scribble) and Jonas Green (Jonathan Grog). Unlike Jole's exaggerated por-

---

3. Anna Wells Rutledge, "A Humorous Artist in Colonial Maryland," *American Collector*, XVI (1947), 15; J. A. Leo Lemay, *Men of Letters in Colonial Maryland* (Knoxville, Tenn., 1972), 253.

trait, Hamilton's self-portrait—one of the few extant colonial self-portraits[4]—is a direct representation of himself holding a volume labeled "Record of the Tuesday Club." The portrait of Jonathan Grog, poet laureate and master of ceremonies, is curious because of its singular format, which seems derived from an antique coin, cameo, or seal. A profile of Algernon Sidney of somewhat later date is derived from a seal cut by the seventeenth-century die cutter Thomas Simon.[5] Perhaps Hamilton was inspired by a similar source. He was no doubt also familiar with images of Julius Caesar, commonly portrayed with a crown of laurel leaves. John Burdett of Williamsburg, for example, had twelve portraits of the Caesars in his collection.[6] Hamilton obviously meant to bestow a particular dose of flattery on his good friend Jonas Green by portraying him in this manner.

Six other illustrations in volume I depict incidents concerning the Tuesday Club's precursors—the Whin-Bush Club, the Royalist Club, the Red-House Club, and the Ugly Club. Among the more interesting of these is the violent performance depicted in "Mr Neilson's Battle with the Royalist Club," in which the various objects described in the text are seen flying through the air, the punch bowl is overturned, and chairs are used as battering rams. The compactness of this scene, the lack of space between any of the figures, and the omission of any background rivets attention on the action and adds to the immediacy and intensity of the scene. Whereas the introduction of too much detail diminishes the impact of some contemporary English literary illustrations, Hamilton was careful to avoid unnecessary distractions in scenes such as this. He was, however, capable of setting a scene if he considered it appropriate, as in his drawing of the Ugly Club. In this illustration he follows his text closely, including cobwebs in the corner, chalked figures on the wall, and cracked panes in the leaded glass window. When he wished to provide a detailed setting, Hamilton did so with competence.

The remaining illustrations in the *History* depict the club's proceedings or incidents discussed in the club. Four of these concern individuals delivering speeches to the club. That Hamilton was able to differentiate these

4. Ann C. Van Devanter, *American Self-Portraits, 1670–1973* (Washington, D.C., 1974) lists only three from the colonial period. No drawings from the colonial period are reproduced in Marvin Sadik and Harold Francis Pfister, comps., *American Portrait Drawings* (Washington, D.C., 1980).

5. Frank H. Sommer III, "Thomas Hollis and the Arts of Dissent," in *Prints in and of America to 1850*, ed. John D. Morse (Charlottesville, Va., 1970), 137.

6. See Joan Dolmetsch, "Prints in Colonial America: Supply and Demand in the Mid-Eighteenth Century," in *Prints in and of America*, ed. Morse, 59.

stock situations at all is a testament to his invention. Three additional drawings concern the club's anniversaries. The pattern for these occasions was set the first year when the members, regular and honorary, assembled at the home of the president and marched in procession to the meeting place under the admiring gaze of the citizens of Annapolis. Like the proceedings, these drawings resemble carefully staged theatrical scenes: the action is in the foreground and the background is sketchily represented by a few buildings with figures in the windows. "The First Grand Anniversary Procession" is the simplest of the three; the other two are more elaborate. Hamilton's drawings of the anniversary processions and other events reflect the increasing pomp and ceremony in the club's proceedings, but with a simplicity that humorously undercuts his baleful lamentations against the degenerate effects of luxury.

Although his style is distinctive, Hamilton was surely influenced by other eighteenth-century painters and illustrators, particularly William Hogarth (1697–1764). In the *History* Hamilton pays homage to "the genius of the Celebrated Hogarth" (III, 345–346) and further suggests Hogarth's influence in his verbal sketch of President Jole: "when Speeches were made that displeased [Jole]," he writes, "there followed an elongation of countenance, and a droping of the Lower Jaw, which some of the members called his timber Countenance, which would have afforded no uncommon hint to the famous Hogarth" (I, 230). For the most part, Hogarth concerned himself with series of paintings and prints rather than illustrations for books. He did, however, illustrate a number of literary works during the 1720s and 1730s. Hogarth's figures are less slender than those of his contemporaries and his lines more deeply incised on the plates, making the figures emerge from the paper. His abandonment of the pretty faces typical of eighteenth-century illustrators and the robust character of his drawings no doubt afforded an uncommon hint to Hamilton.

Although Hogarth was the most familiar English artist and illustrator, Hamilton may have been acquainted with the drawings of several of Hogarth's contemporaries. The portrait painter John Vanderbank (1694–1739) was also known for his illustrations for the second edition of *A Select Collection of Novels and Histories* (1729) and for Jacob Tonson's edition of *Don Quixote* (1738). Hamilton was perhaps influenced by Vanderbank's manner of focusing attention on the protagonists in any given episode and on their unusual physical characteristics. George Bickham, Sr. (d. 1769), and George Bickham, Jr. (d. 1749), both designed and engraved illustrations for numerous literary works and for *The Musical Entertainer* (1737–1739), which contained two hundred carefully engraved vignettes illustrating the lyrics.[7] Given Hamilton's interest in music, he was likely aware of this publication. He was probably also familiar with illustrated editions of Shakespeare's plays, particularly Jacob Tonson's edition (1709), illustrated by François Boitard (ca. 1670–ca. 1717), and he may well have been influenced by Boitard's son, Louis Philippe Boitard (d. ca. 1760), who created book illustrations and scenes of London life, and whose engravings, like Hamilton's drawings, are linear, precise, and awkward.

The most prolific and highly regarded engraver in London in the 1730s and 1740s and, according to Hanns Hammelmann, the man most responsible for bringing from France "the vogue of the elegant engraved book of the rococo [and] the notion that a book should not only be pleasant to read, but also attractive to look at and to handle" was Hubert François Burguignon Gravelot (1669–1773). Gravelot's influence extended to other book illustrators including Hogarth and Francis Hayman, with whom he used to "take his evening ale."[8] Among his works for London publishers were illustrations for *The Dramatick Works of John Dryden* (1735), *The Kit-Kat Club* (1735), *The Works of Shakespeare* (1740), and the first French edition of Fielding's *Tom Jones*—all of which Hamilton probably saw. Particularly in *Tom Jones*, Gravelot's delicate French rococo style at times seems out of place in illustrating some of the rougher and more boisterous scenes in the novel. Hamilton's inelegant style, better suited to the content of the *History*, was perhaps a reaction against the delicate style Gravelot sought to introduce in England.

Gravelot's and Hogarth's drinking companion, Francis Hayman (1708?–1776), was also a prolific illustrator as well as a painter of historical subjects, conversation pieces, narrative scenes, and theatrical portraits. He and Gravelot collaborated on the illustrations for Samuel Richardson's *Pamela* (which Hamilton read) and for Thomas Hanmer's edition of Shakespeare's plays (1743–1744). Hammelmann notes that, particularly in his illustrations for *Fables for the Female Sex* (1744), Hayman "introduced a more homely touch of local genre into the French manner, and this steadily increased in the work of later artists."[9] Hamilton was probably familiar with Hayman's illustrations for the *Fables* and his frontispieces to the second

7. Hanns A. Hammelmann, *Book Illustrators in Eighteenth-Century England* (New Haven, Conn., 1975), ed. and completed by T. S. R. Boase, 15–16; Nancy R. Davison, "Bickham's *Musical Entertainer* and Other Curiosities," in *Eighteenth-Century Prints in Colonial America: To Educate and Decorate*, ed. Joan D. Dolmetsch (Williamsburg, Va., 1979), 98–122.

8. Hammelmann, *Book Illustrators in Eighteenth-Century England*, 38, 39.

9. *Ibid.*, 5.

edition of Tobias Smollett's *The Adventures of Roderick Random* (1748); in any event, there are stylistic parallels between Hamilton's drawings and Hayman's illustrations in these works, particularly in their manner of differentiating individuals and capturing everyday details.

Of the dozen portrait painters active in colonial America during the Tuesday Club's lifetime, two were connected with the club.[10] John Hesselius (Signior Sehesslius; 1728–1778) was active in Maryland in 1750 and 1751. At Sederunt 187 (October 10, 1752), he was ordered to paint a portrait of Charles Cole. This commission was apparently never filled, and no explanation is offered in the *History* (III, 117).[11] John Wollaston (Squeak Grumbleton) visited the Tuesday Club on January 23 and May 25, 1753. During his residence in Annapolis, his paintings were publicly exhibited. Dr. Thomas Thornton, another occasional visitor to the club, in 1753 published a poem in the *Maryland Gazette* entitled "Extempore: On Seeing Mr. Wollaston's Pictures in Annapolis."[12] Other members of the Tuesday Club, including Hamilton, must certainly have seen Wollaston's paintings.

Both Hesselius and Wollaston were skillful portrait painters working within a traditional Anglo-American style. As such, their aim was to present the sitter in the most agreeable pose and to minimize any irregularities of facial structure, while using elegant settings and attributes (clothing, books, etc.) to provide a sense of affluence befitting the subject. Although Hamilton clearly was familiar with such portraiture, he did not follow its conventions himself. Instead he used the simpler format of bust-length portraiture and emphasized precisely the physical features of his sitters (long noses, pointed chins) that Hesselius or Wollaston would have minimized. In this manner Hamilton successfully and comically differentiated his subjects.

Arguing against the common perception that illustrations were mere embellishments, Dr. John Oldfield stated in 1742 that they were "capable of answering a higher purpose, by representing and illustrating many things, which cannot be so perfectly expressed by words," particularly during

10. Richard H. Saunders and Ellen G. Miles, *American Colonial Portraits, 1700–1776* (Washington, D.C., 1987), 30.

11. See Elaine G. Breslaw, ed., *Records of the Tuesday Club of Annapolis, 1745–56* (Urbana, Ill., 1988), 372. The portrait is not listed in Richard K. Doud, "John Hesselius, Maryland Limner," *Winterthur Portfolio,* V (1969), 129–153.

12. The poem appeared in the *Maryland Gazette,* Mar. 15, 1753. It is attributed to Thornton by J. A. Leo Lemay in *A Calendar of American Poetry in the Colonial Newspapers and Magazines and in the Major English Magazines through 1765* (Worcester, Mass., 1972), 159. The poem is reprinted in George C. Groce, "John Wollaston (fl. 1736–1767): A Cosmopolitan Painter in the British Colonies," *Art Quarterly,* XV (1952), 140.

scenes of great passion, where the illustrator can "supply the imperfection of the reader's imagination, and the deficiency of the description in the author."[13] At their best, Hamilton's illustrations serve precisely that purpose. The many scenes he depicts, such as the "Club Hubbub concerning the Records," serve not merely to ornament the text but to accentuate particularly lively moments therein and to enhance the reader's imaginative participation in those moments. To be sure, Hamilton's drawings are crude, awkward, at times even clumsy. The work of an untrained amateur, they nonetheless indicate a knowledge of contemporary English illustration and a good understanding of how illustrations should relate to the spirit of the text. They serve, moreover, to capture the physical aspects of an important segment of society in colonial Maryland. Most of all, they bring the comic world of the *History* to life. They are a significant contribution to the corpus of American art.

[Editor's Note: Nearly all of Hamilton's drawings (except for his drawing of the modern theater, half of which is missing) have held up well over time and can be reproduced clearly from photographic copies. Hamilton did not live, however, to complete four of the drawings in volume II. (There are no drawings in volume III for the same reason.) Of those four, two—the frontispiece and the "Deputation of the Club to His Lordship"— are very sketchy. It is quite possible that the last thing Hamilton worked on before dying was the central figure in the frontispiece to volume II. The last drawing of any substance in the *History* is the deputation drawing; Hamilton apparently stopped in the middle of that drawing and went back to provide the frontispiece. Shortly before and after the deputation drawing, two blank pages appear in Hamilton's manuscript where he planned to include drawings of the "Great Clubical Battle of the Great Seal" and of "His Lordship Recathedrized." I have omitted those pages; the two pages with sketches, however, do appear in this edition.]

13. "Advertisement concerning the Prints," in Jacob Tonson's edition of *Don Quixote* (London, 1742), xxv.

REMARKS ON THE MUSIC

The original music in *The History of the Tuesday Club* includes—in order of appearance—the anniversary ode for 1750, composed primarily by Hamilton (the overture, air and minuet for his honor [the club's president], and pastorale were composed by Thomas Bacon); the anniversary ode for 1751, which includes the "Club March against Sir Hugh Maccarty," both by Bacon; the "Grand Club Minuet *con variatione*" (1751), a "Minuet for Sir John" (1751), and a "Minuet for His Honor" (1752), all by Bacon; the anniversary ode for 1753, which includes a minuet for the chancellor, a minuet and a gavotte for his honor, and a minuet and a march for Sir John, "by several hands" (probably Alexander Malcolm, William Thornton, Charles Cole, and Hamilton, but not Bacon); a "Minuet for the Poet Laureat" (1753), perhaps by Hamilton; a "Grand Club Jig" (1753), by Thornton; an "Overture for His Honor's Entertainment" (an overture for the 1752 anniversary ode, never set to music), which concludes with a "Gavotta Burlesqua for His Honor," both by Bacon; a "Minuet for the Attorney General" (1753), by Bacon; and "The Jurors for the City Bring" (1755), by Cole. Earlier versions of Bacon's pieces in the 1750 ode, the complete 1751 ode, the 1751 "Minuet for Sir John," the 1752 "Minuet for His Honor," and the "Attorney Generals Minuet" appear in the "Tuesday Club Record Book," MS. 854, Maryland Historical Society, Baltimore.

The manuscript pages of the music are in very poor condition. Hamilton wrote the music on both sides of the paper, and over time the ink has bled badly through the pages, creating numerous lines of music that look like indiscernible masses of gray. Moreover, the pages are badly worn and torn in spots, apparently from much thumbing and passing about during the club's meetings. Some pages, particularly in the 1751 ode, contain more holes than music. Fortunately, the copy of the 1751 ode appearing in the "Record" is fairly legible, making it possible to reconstruct much of that ode in the *History*.

Rather than provide modernized transcriptions, I have sought to restore the music as nearly as possible to its original condition so that I could provide readable copies of the original scores for this edition. I began restoring the music in a rudimentary way for my dissertation, but only recently have I found a means of making the original scores legible enough to print. By darkening all the notes, scales, and words on my copy of the music, cutting out as much of the blank gray area between the scales as possible, and then making a photocopy of my copy on the lightest possible setting, I was able to eliminate most of the gray that had accumulated over time and to make the music itself more legible. I then repeated the entire process a second time. As a result, the music printed in this edition appears almost as it did when the Tuesday Club first passed it about.

Where holes appear in the manuscript pages of the music, I have supplied the missing measures whenever possible with the corresponding measures from the "Record." I have indicated in brackets the few instances where a given measure or line is illegible in either the *History* or the "Record." Only one section was beyond redemption: the "Grand Club Minuet," which appears immediately following the 1751 ode in the *History*. The Tuesday Club must have particularly enjoyed playing that piece and passing it about, for it has virtually crumbled into illegibility. Regrettably, the only copy of the "Grand Club Minuet" is the one in the *History;* had another copy been available in the "Record," I would have restored that selection as well.

For a conjectural reading of the "Grand Club Minuet"—and conjectures on the passages I have indicated as illegible—and for modernized transcriptions of all the musical pieces in the *History,* see John Barry Talley, *Secular Music in Colonial Annapolis: The Tuesday Club, 1745–56* (Urbana, Ill., 1988). Talley has done a remarkable job not only of reconstructing and evaluating the club's original music, but also of researching all the borrowed songs and catches that the members played in club. His transcriptions helped me to decipher some of the more obscure measures in the club's music. Aside from obvious differences in the appearance of our two versions—Talley uses modern equivalents of Hamilton's symbols and standardizes his many backward or upside-down notes, whereas I have reproduced the original, quirks and all—there are various substantive differences between my restorations and Talley's transcriptions. For the most part, our versions agree. But sometimes we have read notes and entire measures differently, and sometimes—as in the "Gavotta Burlesqua" and the "Grand Club Jig"—our versions differ considerably.

In an age that witnessed an "invasion of music by the amateur in search of diversion," an age when almost "every gentleman played the violin, and every lady the flute,"[1] it is likely that all of the Tuesday Club's members

---

1. Homer Ulrich, *Chamber Music* (New York, 1948), 115.

contributed to their musical performances in one capacity or another. The principal composers were Bacon and Hamilton, in that order of musical ability. Bacon's works, Talley writes, display "considerable structural skill," and Hamilton's melodies are "usually interesting, often expressive, and well formed," although corrections to the 1750 ode show that "someone [probably Bacon] attempted to make musical sense out of some of the stranger passages."[2] The principal musicians were Bacon (violin and viola da gamba), who was appointed musician *con stromenti* to the club, Malcolm (flute and violin), Hamilton (violoncello), Daniel Wolstenholme (flute), Robert Morris (violin), William Lux of Annapolis (organ and harpsichord), and Jonas Green (French horn), who also wrote the words to the odes. Everyone lent their voices, but William Thornton, Protomusicus, outsang them all. Hamilton reports in the *History* that, because of his "uncommon talent at Singing," Thornton was appointed musician *con voce* "by unanimous consent" and that whenever he voted he was required "to sing it in a musical manner, else his vote to go for nothing" (I, 283). Charles Cole, the club's president, also entertained the club with numerous songs. Cole acquired his musical talent, Hamilton says,

> merely by the force of Genius, having never been taught, and his talent this way lies in vocal execution, he having a number of old Songs by him, to the words of which, he affirms, he never is at a loss to find a tune, and Indeed, give him words at any time, and he'll Immediatly clap a tune to them, with so Sweet and small a voice, and so delicate a trill, that some people have doubted whether or not he has in his youth been Italianized, but, be that as it will, . . . he has a most exquisite pipe, and, were he not obliged sometimes to wear his Spectacles, to read the words of the Song, . . . his voice would be quite clear, and without asperity, but this nasal machine, will sometimes in the high notes, occasion a Snuffling, which a nice ear will easily excuse, seeing the cause is known to proceed from no natural defect (I, 162).

Other of the club's members no doubt emitted equally strange noises from time to time, and no doubt they were also forgiven their trespasses. The Tuesday Club's music, Talley rightly argues, demonstrates that "a high level of musical sophistication existed in the American colonies well before the formal establishment of a concert tradition."[3] But the level of sophisti-

2. Talley, *Secular Music in Colonial Annapolis*, 114, 116.
3. *Ibid.*, 121.

cation was finally less important to the members than the act of participation. For Hamilton, music was meant to "soften and humanize" mankind (III, 116), to make man more sociable to man. If that meant having to put up with a few snufflings and assorted noises, it was worth it.

REMARKS ON THE NOTES

All internal references in the notes are to Hamilton's original pagination, which appears in brackets in the margins of this edition.

Rather than insult the reader by providing superfluous notes on commonplace classical, biblical, and historical allusions, I have generally noted
only those allusions that the average reader of this edition might not immediately recognize. Similarly, despite Hamilton's sometimes whimsical
spellings, nearly all the words he used are comprehensible to modern readers or available in any good dictionary. I have noted only those words that
Hamilton coined (e.g., *scabarabused*) or that have become unfamiliar to
most readers (e.g., *lcorice*, a variant of *lickerous*, an archaic word meaning
"lecherous or greedy").

I have frequently incorporated information from the following refer-
ence works into my notes: for biographical information, I have used the
Dictionary of National Biography, the *Dictionary of American Biography*,
the *Encyclopaedia Britannica* (1910–1911 edition), the *Century Cyclopaedia of
Names*, *La Grande Encyclopédie* (1886 edition), and *Webster's Biographical
Dictionary*; for literary allusions, the *Oxford Companion to English Literature*,
the *Oxford Companion to the Theatre*, the *Oxford Companion to American
Literature*, the *Oxford Companion to French Literature*, the *Dictionnaire des
Lettres Françaises*, the *Oxford Companion to Spanish Literature*, E. Cobham
Brewer's *The Reader's Handbook of Allusions, References, Plots, and Stories*,
and, often the most useful of all, Robert Watt's *Bibliotheca Britannica*; for
words, maxims, and proverbial phrases, the *Oxford English Dictionary*, the
Century Dictionary and Cyclopedia, the *English Dialect Dictionary*, the *Scottish
National Dictionary*, Eric Partridge's *Dictionary of Slang and Unconventional
English* and *Dictionary of the Underworld*, Burton Stevenson's *Home Book of
Proverbs, Maxims, and Familiar Phrases*, *Brewer's Dictionary of Phrase and
Fable*, G. L. Apperson's *English Proverbs and Proverbial Phrases*, Morris
Palmer Tilley's *Dictionary of the Proverbs in England*, Mitford M. Mathews's
Dictionary of Americanisms, and Bartlett Jere Whiting's *Early American Prov-
erbs and Proverbial Phrases*; and for classical allusions, the *Oxford Classical
Dictionary* and *Harper's Dictionary of Classical Literature and Antiquities*. I
have also used the following more specialized reference works whenever
possible: for identifying artists, Michael Bryan's *Dictionary of Painters and
Engravers*, the *Dictionnaire des Peintres, Sculpteurs, Dessinateurs, et Graveurs*,

and the *Dictionary of Artists in America;* for musicians, the *International Cyclopedia of Music and Musicians;* for folklore, the *Standard Dictionary of Folklore* and *Brewer's Dictionary of Phrase and Fable;* for alchemists, the *Bibliotheca Chemica;* for saints, the *Oxford Dictionary of Saints;* and for an occasional event in British history, J. P. Kenyon's *Dictionary of British History.* An invaluable source of information on the songs Hamilton alludes to has been John Barry Talley, *Secular Music in Colonial Annapolis: The Tuesday Club, 1745–56* (Urbana, Ill., 1988).

I have tried to find sources for all of Hamilton's quotations or secondhand stories. Though it is impossible in many cases to pinpoint the exact edition that Hamilton may have used, for direct quotations (such as the passage from James I's *Counterblaste* on I, 45–46) I have referred to an edition printed prior to his writing the *History;* for indirect quotations, however (such as the allusion to Dryden on I, 47), I have referred to more recently edited texts, since Hamilton has only paraphrased his source anyway. Where Hamilton has referred to a "certain author" who says something profound, I have done my best to track down the author and the quotation. In some cases I have been successful; in others where I have not, I suspect that the "certain author" is sometimes Hamilton himself.

TUESDAY CLUB PSEUDONYMS

Bavius, Bard	Thomas Chase
Bluechin, Jocifer	Michael Earle
Blunt, Bully (Sir John Oldcastle)	John Bullen
Boniface, Mr.	perhaps John or Anthony Stewart
Bowzer, Tunbelly	Richard Dorsey
Bumbasto, Col.	?
Bumper, Abraham	James Calder
Butman, Comico	William Fitzhugh
Carpentiro, Giovanni	John Carpenter
Charlotto, Don John	John Charlette
Cheary, Chantum	Richard Hill, Jr.
Comas (Comus), Laconic	John Lomas
Comic, Quirpum	John Beale Bordley
Coppernose, Comely	Anthony Bacon
Courtly, Curious	Abraham Barnes
Crankum, Crinkum	William Lux (of Annapolis)
Dogmaticus, Philo	Alexander Malcolm
Fibber, Humbug	?
Fluter, Joshua	James Hollyday
Frontinbrass, Coney Pimp	Thomas Cumming
Furbisher, Capt.	John Troy
Gabble, John	John Bacon
Goggle, Dormer	Sidney George
Grog, Jonathan	Jonas Green
Grumbleton, Squeak	John Wollaston
Gundiguts, Dumpling	Mark Gibson
Hasty, Joggle	George Atkinson
Hop-a-kickie, Mr.	[?] Jennings
Jaunter, Jeronimo	Upton Scott
Jerkum, Jehoiakim	probably Alexander Hamilton
Jole, Nasifer	Charles Cole
Laconic, Prim	Edward Tilghman
Lardini, Signior	Thomas Bacon
Leidemont, Mr.	Samuel Middleton
Lisper, Mr.	perhaps Samuel Mitchelson

Maccarty, Sir Hugh (Col. Rormis)	[?] Morris
Makefun, Merry	Robert Morris
Mevius, Bard (Mevius Pumpkin)	Thomas Cradock
Motely, Prattle	Witham Marshe
Muddy, Roundhead	Andrew Lendrum
Neverout, Solo (Mr. Protomusicus)	William Thornton
Philalethes, Dr.	perhaps Dr. John Hamilton
Philo-Bavius, Mevius	probably Jonas Green
Phraze, Courtly	Edward Lloyd
Phrazeobundus, Signior	Philip Key
Pickeringtonus, Gasperus	Stephen Pickering
Pleasant, Slyboots	Walter Dulany
Polyhistor, Dr.	Dr. John Hamilton
Polypharmacus, Dr.	Alexander Hamilton
Precisio, Giovanni	Daniel Wolstenholme
Pyrgos, Dr.	[?] Towers
Quaint, Drawlum	Edward Dorsey
Ramble, Dio	Dennis Dulany
Ranter, Roughby	James Richard
Rhubarb, Dr.	Archibald Spencer
Rodomantus, Rev.	James Sterling
Round, Broadface	Rev. John Hamilton
Scribble, Loquacious	Alexander Hamilton
Scriblerus, Martinus	probably Alexander Hamilton
Sehesslius, Signior	John Hesselius
Sly, Smoothum	John Gordon
Smirker, Theophilus	James Dickinson
Snap, Huffman	Stephen Bordley
Snuffysnout (Snuffybeak), Stentor	Robert Swan
Social, Serious	Robert Gordon
Spruce, Seemly	William Rogers
Spyplot, Jealous, Sr.	William Cumming, Sr.
Spyplot, Jealous, Jr.	William Cumming, Jr.
Spyplot, Prettyman	Alexander Cumming
Surly, Huffbluff	Robert North
Swagbelly, Swillum	John Addison
Swallowbeak, Samuel	Samuel Stringar
Swashgut, Madonna	Catherine Jennings
Sylvius, Nathaniel	Samuel Wood
Thereum, Hereum	Robert Holliday

Thoughtless, Giddy   John Ellis
Timorous, Prim   Thomas Jennings
Tomlinsonus, Joannes   John Thompson
Vitrifrice, Electro   Benjamin Franklin
Volens, Nolens   Thomas Thornton
Warble, Ignotus   Samuel Hart
Whiner, Rev.   Charles Lake
Wisely, Oldham   Richard Snowden
Wouldbe, Spatterdash   William Wilkins

BIOGRAPHICAL SKETCHES

Oldstanding (Original) Members, Longstanding (Regular) Members, Honorary Members, Visitors, and Associates

In compiling the sketches of individuals who were members of the legislature and of the clergy, I have relied particularly on Edward C. Papenfuse *et al., A Biographical Dictionary of the Maryland Legislature, 1635–1789,* 2 vols. (Baltimore, 1979–1985) and on Nelson Waite Rightmyer, *Maryland's Established Church* (Baltimore, 1956). Complete bibliographic information is provided below for items cited in abbreviated form in the sketches. All unpublished Maryland records are in the Maryland State Archives, Annapolis.

BDML	Edward C. Papenfuse *et al., A Biographical Dictionary of the Maryland Legislature, 1635–1789,* 2 vols. (Baltimore, 1979–1985)
Land, *Dulanys of Maryland*	Aubrey C. Land, *The Dulanys of Maryland: A Biographical Study of Daniel Dulany, the Elder (1685–1753) and Daniel Dulany, the Younger (1722–1797)* (Baltimore, 1955)
Lemay, *Men of Letters*	J. A. Leo Lemay, *Men of Letters in Colonial Maryland* (Knoxville, Tenn., 1972)
MG	*Maryland Gazette*
MHM	*Maryland Historical Magazine*
MHS	Maryland Historical Society, Baltimore
Newman, *Anne Arundel Gentry*	Harry Wright Newman, *Anne Arundel Gentry: A Genealogical History of Some Early Families of Anne Arundel County, Maryland* (Annapolis, Md., 1970)

| Newman, *To Maryland from Overseas* | Harry Wright Newman, *To Maryland from Overseas: A Complete Digest of the Jacobite Loyalists Sold into White Slavery in Maryland, and the British and Continental Background of Approximately 1400 Maryland Settlers from 1634 to the Early Federal Period with Source Documentation* (Annapolis, Md., 1982) |

Addison, John (1713–1764). "Swillum Swagbelly." Honorary Member (admitted 1747).

Native Marylander; son of Thomas Addison (1679–1727) and Elinor Smith (1689–1761); husband of Susannah Wilkinson (d. 1774); Anglican; captain by 1747, and colonel by 1760; probably a planter; member of Lower House, Prince George's County, 1745–1757.

Atkinson, George. "Joggle Hasty." Honorary Member (admitted 1745).

Annapolis merchant; his notices in the *MG* show him frequently leaving for England, then returning to Annapolis to sell his goods (see Feb. 7, 1750, Mar. 22, 1751, Sept. 6, 1753).

Bacon, Anthony. "Comely Coppernose." Honorary Member (admitted 1749) and Agent for the Club in London.

Brother of Thomas Bacon (q.v.); received the B.A. from Trinity College, Dublin, in 1739, shortly before leaving for Maryland; began as a tobacco trader in Maryland and eventually became one of England's wealthiest tycoons (Lemay, *Men of Letters*, 188, 313; see also L. B. Namier, "Anthony Bacon, M.P., an Eighteenth-Century Merchant," *Journal of Economics and Business History*, II [1929], 20–70).

Bacon, John (d. 1756). "John Gabble." Honorary Member (admitted 1751).

Son of Thomas Bacon (q.v.); probable author of "A Recruiting Song, for the Maryland Independent Company" (*MG*, Sept. 19, 1754); on Sept. 30, 1754, Lt. John Bacon marched from Annapolis with a party of soldiers; he was later killed and scalped about five miles from Cumberland Fort (Lemay, *Men of Letters*, 300; *MG*, Oct. 3, 1754, Apr. 8, 1756).

Bacon, Thomas (1700?–1768). "Signior Lardini." Honorary Member (admitted 1745) and member of Eastern Shore Triumvirate.

Native of the Isle of Man; in Dublin, he published *A Compleat System of the Revenue of Ireland* (1737), established the *Dublin Mercury* (1741–1742), and edited the *Dublin Gazette* (1742); in 1743 he abandoned his publishing career and in 1745 was ordained and licensed for Maryland; rector of St. Peter's, Talbot County, by 1746; published *Four Sermons, upon the Great and Indispensable Duty of All Christian Masters and Mistresses to Bring Up Their Negro Slaves in the Knowledge and Fear of God* (London, 1750); active in establishing charity schools; compiled *Laws of Maryland at Large* (Annapolis, Md., 1765); accomplished musician and one of colonial Maryland's most prolific authors (Lemay, *Men of Letters,* 313–342; see also William E. Deibert, "Thomas Bacon, Colonial Clergyman," *MHM,* LXXIII [1978], 79–86).

Barnes, Abraham (d. ca. 1778). "Curious Courtly." Honorary Member (admitted 1747).

Immigrated to Virginia from England between 1740 and 1744; married Mary Elizabeth King (1715–1739), then Elizabeth Rousby (by 1743); Anglican; Gent., 1747; colonel by 1756; merchant, land speculator; member of Lower House, St. Mary's County, 1745–1754, although temporarily dismissed in 1749 for using liquor to influence the electorate; Maryland delegate to Albany Congress (1754); supporter of proprietary power.

Belt, Joseph (ca. 1680–1761). Visitor.

Native Marylander; son of Elizabeth and John Belt (d. 1698); married Hester Beale (1706), then Margery Wight (d. 1783); Anglican; Gent., 1726; colonel, 1726; merchant, planter, and modestly wealthy landowner; member of Lower House, Prince George's County, 1725–1737.

Bladen, Thomas (1698–1780). Associate.

Native Marylander; son of William Bladen (1670–1718) and Anne Van Swearingen; married Barbara Janssen (1737); Anglican; Gent., 1720, and Esq., 1744; officeholder and land speculator; governor of Maryland from August 1742 to October 1746, when he was dismissed for being "quarrelsome."

Bordley, John Beale (1726/1727–1804). "Quirpum Comic." Longstanding Member (admitted 1749) and Master of Ceremonies.

Native Marylander; son of Thomas Bordley (ca. 1683–1726) and Ariana Vanderheyden (d. 1729); married Margaret Chew (d. 1773), then Sarah Fishbourne (1776); studied law under his half brother, Stephen Bordley (q.v.); Anglican; Esq. at death; elected to American Philosophical Society (1783); judge, planter, and agronomist; member of Upper House, 1768–1774; opposed intemperance and slavery; read extensively and published many books, including *A Summary View of the Courses of Crops, in the Husbandry of England and Maryland* (Philadelphia, 1784), *Yellow Fever* ([Philadelphia, 1794?]), *On Monies, Coins, Weights, and Measures, Proposed for the United States of America* (Philadelphia, 1789), and *Essays and Notes on Husbandry and Rural Affairs* (Philadelphia, 1799) (see Elizabeth Bordley Gibson, *Biographical Sketches of the Bordley Family, of Maryland, for Their Descendants* [Philadelphia, 1865]; Olive Moore Gambrill, "John Beale Bordley and the Early Years of the Philadelphia Agricultural Society," *Pennsylvania Magazine of History and Biography*, LXVI [1942], 410–439; and David Hackett Fischer, "John Beale Bordley, Daniel Boorstin, and the American Enlightenment," *Journal of Southern History*, XXVIII [1962], 327–342).

Bordley, Stephen (ca. 1710–1764). "Huffman Snap." Longstanding Member (admitted 1749).
Native Marylander, son of Thomas Bordley and Rachel Beard (d. 1722); never married; attended school in London and was admitted to the Inner Temple in 1729; returned to Maryland in 1733 to practice law; Anglican; Hon. at death; lawyer, naval officer (Annapolis, 1755–1762), attorney general (1756–1763), commissary general (1762–1764); member of Lower House (Annapolis, 1745; Anne Arundel County, 1749–1751; Annapolis, 1754–1756), and Upper House, 1759–1763 (see Elizabeth Bordley Gibson, *Biographical Sketches of the Bordley Family, of Maryland, for Their Descendants* [Philadelphia, 1865], and Joseph C. Morton, "Stephen Bordley of Colonial Annapolis," *Winterthur Portfolio*, V [1969], 1–14).

Bullen, John (d. 1764). "Bully Blunt," "Sir John Oldcastle." Oldstanding Member (admitted 1745) and Club Champion.
Bullen was a modestly wealthy Annapolis landowner; husband of Sarah and father of John (Wills, 1761, Box B, No. 109); elected mayor of Annapolis in 1749 (*MG*, Oct. 4, 1749); his obituary reads: "Monday last [March 12], Died, of a Complication of Disorders, in an advanced Age, JOHN BULLEN, Esq; one of the Commissioners of the Paper Currency Office, an Alderman of this City, and formerly for many Years in the Commis-

sion of the Peace for this County, and Captain of the City Independent Company" (*MG,* Mar. 15, 1764).

Burman, Anne. Associate.
Various advertisements in the *MG* suggest that Hamilton's Burman was Anne Burman, an Annapolis storekeeper (see, e.g., July 28, 1747, Aug. 23, 1753).

Calder, James (ca. 1695–1755). "Abraham Bumper." Honorary Member (admitted 1745).
Immigrated to Maryland ca. 1727; husband of Katherine Murray; Protestant; lawyer and planter; member of Lower House, Kent County, 1739–1744. Calder's obituary states that he long practiced law "with great Repute" and that he was "greatly esteem'd by all who knew him" (*MG,* Apr. 17, 1755).

Carpenter, John (d. 1748). "Giovanni Carpentiro." Associate.
Husband of Elizabeth Plater (Test. Procs., Box 49, No. 27); his obituary reads: "Yesterday died here Capt. *John Carpenter,* who had long been a worthy Inhabitant of this City, and was many Years Commander of a Ship from *London* in the Tobacco-Trade; and who, by a diligent Application and honest Industry, had acquired a considerable Fortune, with a fair Character" (*MG,* Nov. 2, 1748).

Carter, Ann. Associate.
Hamilton might be referring to any number of Annapolis ladies, but Ann Carter, daughter of Robert "King" Carter and wife of Benjamin Harrison (m. 1722), seems as likely a choice as any for the directress of the Syllabub Club (Richard Beale Davis, *Intellectual Life in the Colonial South, 1585–1763,* 3 vols. [Knoxville, Tenn., 1978], III, 1258).

Charlette, John. "Don John Charlotto." Clerk of the Kitchen (appointed 1753).
Husband of Ann; owner of two houses in London (Wills, 1764, Box C, No. 27). Hamilton's humorous treatment of the constant feuding between Charlette and Charles Cole (q.v.) was apparently no joke. The following advertisement, which Cole ran in the *MG* for nearly three months, implies that Charlette had decided to abdicate his position as Clerk of the Kitchen without Cole's permission.

Whereas a Certain *John Charlett,* hath lately published in the MARY-
LAND GAZETTE, No. 176 . . . his Intention of going to *England* . . .
and hath, since that Time, absented himself from my service, to
whom he is now a Servant, under Contract, at considerable yearly
Wages; which contract he hath not performed . . . but left his said
service, without giving me the least Warning, to my very great
Prejudice and Damage. He is harboured, encouraged, and entertained, by some persons in this Town [Club members?]; to whom I
give this Public notice, that if they continue so to do, I shall take
such measures both with him and them, as the Law directs (*MG,*
Oct. 26, 1748).

Chase, Thomas (1703–1779). "Bard Bavius." Baltimore Bard.
    Immigrated to Maryland from England; son of Samuel Chase and
Henrietta Catherine Davis; brother of Richard Chase, the Maryland clergy-
man; married Matilda Walker (1740), then Ann Birch (1763); educated at St.
John's College, Cambridge, and at Sidney Sussex, where he studied medi-
cine; ordained in 1739 and inducted into Somerset Parish on the Eastern
Shore in 1740; rector of St. Paul's, Baltimore County, from February 1744/
1745 until his death (Rosamond Randall Beirne, "The Reverend Thomas
Chase: Pugnacious Parson," *MHM,* LIX [1964], 1–14).

    Cole, Charles (d. 1757). "Nasifer Jole." Longstanding Member (ad-
mitted 1745) and President.
    Regrettably little is known of Cole's life. He was appointed warden of
St. Anne's, Annapolis, in 1741 (*MHM,* VIII [1913], 355). Cole's will (dated
1753 and revoked in 1757) indicates only that he was an Annapolis merchant
(Wills, vol. 30, p. 511, Box C, No. 60). His obituary reads: "Last Tuesday
Evening [July 5], Died here in an advanced Age, Mr. CHARLES COLE, Merchant, who had resided in this City above Forty Years, and was formerly a
very considerable Trader. This Gentleman was a Batchelor, who, it is said,
Repented of nothing in his latter Years, so much as that he had not Married
while he was Young" (*MG,* July 7, 1757).

    Cradock, Thomas (1718–1770). "Mevius Pumpkin," "Bard Mevius."
Baltimore Bard and Honorary Member (admitted 1753).
    Immigrated to Maryland from England in 1744; son of Arthur Cra-
dock and Ann Marson; married Catherine Risteau (ca. 1728–1795) in 1746
(*BDML,* s.v. "Risteau, George"); ordained in 1743 and licensed for Maryland; appointed rector at St. Thomas's, Baltimore, in 1745, where he served

until his death; author of numerous sermons, a translation of the Psalms, and the "Maryland Eclogues in Imitation of Virgil's" (see David Curtis Skaggs, "Thomas Cradock and the Chesapeake Golden Age," *William and Mary Quarterly*, 3d Ser., XXX [1973], 93–116).

Cumming, Alexander (1721–1774). "Prettyman Spyplot." Honorary Member (admitted 1750).
Native Marylander and resident of Baltimore County (Wills, Box 15, No. 19); son of William Cumming (q.v.) and Elizabeth Coursey; petitioned Maryland legislature for damages suffered while quartering the king's forces in his father's house in Annapolis (1754), but was denied payment (*BDML*, 246). Cumming's name often appeared in the *MG*, but only to indicate that he had returned from abroad.

Cumming, Thomas (d. 1774). "Coney Pimp Frontinbrass." Honorary Member (admitted 1750) and Agent for the Club in America.
Native of Scotland and a printer in Cork, Ireland; a "sensible Quaker" merchant who was living in New York by 1750–1751, when he visited Philadelphia, met Benjamin Franklin, and then traveled to Maryland and Virginia, where he acquired many friends and business associates. Established in London by 1754, Cumming made a trading voyage to the east coast of Africa, securing a trade agreement from a native ruler; following his return to England, he proposed to Pitt an expedition that led to the capture of the French Fort Louis at Senegal in 1758 (*The Papers of Benjamin Franklin*, ed. Leonard W. Labaree *et al.* [New Haven, Conn., 1959–], X, 345n–346n).

Cumming, William, Sr. (ca. 1696–1752). "Jealous Spyplot, Sr." Oldstanding Member (admitted 1745) and Attorney General.
Transported to America after being arrested in England (ca. 1716) as a Jacobite rebel; sold as a servant; married Elizabeth Coursey (1719/1720), then by 1742/1743, Margaret Thomas (d. 1804); Anglican; studied law while servant to Thomas Bordley and became a practicing lawyer in Maryland; member of Lower House, Annapolis, 1732–1734.

Cumming, William, Jr. (1724–1793). "Jealous Spyplot, Jr." Longstanding Member (admitted 1749), then Honorary Member.
Native Marylander; son of William Cumming (q.v.) and Elizabeth Coursey; planter and attorney; fined £25 during the Revolution for allegedly drinking to His Majesty's health (*BDML*, 246).

Dickinson, James (ca. 1726–1787). "Theophilus Smirker." Honorary Member (admitted 1750) and member of Eastern Shore Triumvirate.

Immigrated, possibly from Cumberland County, England, and resided in Talbot County, Maryland; married Rachel Taylor (1748); Anglican; Gent., 1750, and Esq., 1754; merchant; member of Lower House, Talbot County, 1768–1770; freed six slaves (1781) and ordered in his will that his nephew John Singleton (1750–1819) free all of his remaining slaves.

Dorsey, Edward (1718–1760). "Drawlum Quaint." Longstanding Member (admitted 1745) and Speaker.

Native Marylander; son of Caleb Dorsey, Gent. (1683–1743), and Elinor Warfield (1683–1752); married Henrietta Maria Chew (ca. 1704–1736/1737), stepdaughter of Daniel Dulany, the Elder, in 1748; Anglican; Esq., 1753; lawyer; member of Lower House, Frederick County, 1757–1760.

Dorsey, Richard (1714–1760). "Tunbelly Bowzer." Longstanding Member (admitted 1750).

Brother of Edward Dorsey (q.v.); married Elizabeth Beale, widow of William Nicholson, and resided in Anne Arundel County (Admin. Bonds, Box 62, No. 40); his obituary reads: "Early on Tuesday Morning last [Sept. 2], Died at his Plantation near Town, of the Gout in his Stomach, Head and Bowels, Mr. RICHARD DORSEY, aged 47 Years, Clerk of the Paper Currency Office, and for about 20 Years past, a very worthy Magistrate of this County" (*MG,* Sept. 11, 1760).

Downie, George (d. 1750). Associate.

Husband of Mary; Annapolis "Musitioner" (Wills, 1750, vol. 27, p. 405; Test. Procs., 1750, Box 50, No. 39); possibly the same George Downey who frequently advertised as a soapmaker in the *MG* (see, e.g., May 23, 1750).

Dulany, Daniel, Jr. (1722–1797). Frequent visitor.

Native Marylander; son of Daniel Dulany (1685–1753) and Rebecca Smith (ca. 1695–1737); husband of Rebecca Tasker (1724–1822); completed Eton in 1738 and entered Middle Temple in 1742 (called to the bar in 1746, a form of recognition rarely accorded a colonist); lawyer until 1763, then a planter; member of Lower House, Frederick County, 1749–1757, and Upper House, 1757–1774; argued against Stamp Act but opposed Sons of Liberty and advocated neutrality during the Revolution (see Land, *Dulanys of Maryland*).

Dulany, Dennis (1730–1779). "Dio Ramble." Honorary Member (admitted 1750).

Native Marylander; son of Daniel Dulany and Rebecca Smith, and brother of Daniel Dulany (q.v.) and Walter Dulany (q.v.); entered the British navy in 1743 and remained in the service for several years; clerk of Kent County from 1754 to 1777; died without issue (*BDML*, 285; *Maryland Journal* (Baltimore), Dec. 21, 1779; see also Land, *Dulanys of Maryland*).

Dulany, Walter (d. 1773). "Slyboots Pleasant." Longstanding Member (admitted 1745).

Native Marylander; son of Daniel Dulany and Rebecca Smith, and brother of Daniel Dulany (q.v.) and Dennis Dulany (q.v.); married Mary Grafton ca. 1745; Anglican; Gent., 1747, and Esq., 1764; merchant, investor, naval officer, contractor, landowner, and officeholder (see Land, *Dulanys of Maryland*). His obituary states that he was "one of the Lord Proprietary's Council of State, Commissary General of this province, and one of the aldermen of this city" (*MG*, Sept. 23, 1773).

Earle, Michael (1722–1787). "Jocifer Bluechin." Honorary Member (admitted 1754).

Native Marylander; son of James Earle, Jr. (ca. 1694–1739), and Mary Tilghman (1702–ca. 1736); husband of Mary Carroll; Anglican; Gent., 1749; commander of a merchant ship, 1744, and merchant by 1753; member of Lower House, Cecil County, 1751–1763.

Ellis, John (d. 1747). "Giddy Thoughtless." Visitor.

Ellis's obituary reads: "The Ship *Montague*, Capt. *John Ellis* late Commander, is arrived in *James* River, *Virginia*, from *London*, but last from *Gibraltar*; Capt. *Ellis* died on the Passage; he often loaded in this Province, was a worthy honest Commander, and is lamented here by all that knew him" (*MG*, Sept. 1, 1747).

Fitzhugh, William (ca. 1722–1798). "Comico Butman." Honorary Member (admitted 1753).

Native Virginian, moved to Maryland ca. 1752 and resided there until his death; son of George Fitzhugh (ca. 1690–1722) and Mary Mason (ca. 1697–1728); married George Turberville's widow (née Lee), then Ann Frisby (1727–1793); Anglican; Esq. and colonel by 1752; planter, owner of a grist mill, fulling mills, and a distillery by 1783; member of Lower House, Calvert County, 1754–1761, and Upper House, 1769–1774; close friend of George

Washington and Thomas Sim Lee (1745–1819); fought in French and Indian War and became a wealthy landowner.

Forty, John (d. by 1765). Visitor.
Resident of Baltimore County; he apparently left little property and had no relations in Maryland (Wills, 1753, Box F, No. 33; Inventories, 1765, Box 17, No. 16).

Franklin, Benjamin. "Electro Vitrifrice." Visitor.
The *MG* for Jan. 17, 1754, states that Franklin had "arrived in Town, to regulate and settle the Affairs of the Post Offices"; Franklin's affiliation with Annapolis is discussed in Robert R. Hare, "Electro Vitrifrico in Annapolis: Mr. Franklin Visits the Tuesday Club," *MHM*, LVIII (1963), 62–66.

George, Sidney (d. 1774). "Dormer Goggle." Visitor.
Native Marylander; son of Joshua George (ca. 1695–1748) and Allice Docwray; Protestant; Gent., 1749; attorney; member of Lower House, Cecil County, 1751–1754.

Gibson, John (d. 1790). Associate.
Native Marylander; son of Woolman Gibson, Gent. (ca. 1695–1742), and Elizabeth Dawson; husband of Elizabeth (d. 1797); Anglican; Gent., 1777, and Esq. at death; planter; member of Lower House, Talbot County, 1777–1782.

Gibson, Mark. "Dumpling Gundiguts." Longstanding Member (admitted 1745).
Gibson's advertisement in the *MG* for Feb. 18, 1746, reads: "At the Subscriber's Brewing-Office in *Annapolis,* any Person may be supplied with the best Sorts of Malt Liquor, at reasonable Prices."

Gordon, John (1717–1790). "Smoothum Sly." Oldstanding Member (admitted 1745), Master of Ceremonies, then Honorary Member and member of Eastern Shore Triumvirate.
Born in Aberdeen, Scotland; inducted into St. Anne's, Annapolis, in 1745, where he preached against the Rebellion of 1745 (including his "On Occasion of the Suppression of the Unnatural Rebellion, in Scotland," which was advertised in the *MG,* Oct. 14, 1746); became rector of St. Michael's, Talbot County, where his whig principles permitted him to function

throughout the Revolution until his death (see Newman, *To Maryland from Overseas*, 79, and Mary M. Starin, "The Reverend John Gordon, 1717–1790," *MHM*, LXXV [1980], 167–191).

Gordon, Robert (ca. 1676–1753). "Serious Social." Oldstanding Member (admitted 1745).

Immigrated ca. 1719 (probably from Scotland) and settled in Annapolis; husband of Agnes (see *MG*, Nov. 8, 1753); Anglican; captain by 1723 and Esq. by 1724; merchant and officeholder; member of Lower House, Annapolis, 1725–1752; his obituary reads:

> On Sunday Evening last died, of the Gout in his Lungs, in the 77th Year of his Age, ROBERT GORDON, Esq; who was for many Years a very reputable Inhabitant of this City, one of the Aldermen . . . as also, one of the Judges of the Provincial Court, and one of the Commissioners of the Loan Office: He executed his public Trusts with Diligence and Integrity: In private Life he constantly maintain'd the Character of an honest Man, a quiet inoffensive Neighbour . . . and a pleasant and agreeable Companion . . . and on Tuesday last in the Evening his Remains were honourably interr'd, the Funeral Sermon being delivered by the Rev. Mr. BACON, and Persons of all Ranks accompanying his Corps to the Grave (*MG*, Sept. 13, 1753).

Green, Jonas (1712–1767). "Jonathan Grog." Longstanding Member (admitted 1748), P.P.P.P.P. (Purveyor, Punster, Punchmaker General, Printer, and Poet), then P.L.M.C. (Poet Laureate and Master of Ceremonies).

Descended from a family of printers, including his father, Timothy, public printer of Connecticut; probably moved to Maryland shortly after his marriage to Anne Catherine Hoof in Philadelphia (1738); public printer of Maryland from 1738 until his death, publisher of the *MG* from 1745 to 1767, poet, and alderman of Annapolis (Lemay, *Men of Letters*, 193–212; see also Lawrence C. Wroth, *A History of Printing in Colonial Maryland, 1686–1776* [Baltimore, 1922], 75–95). Green's obituary reads: "On Saturday Evening last died . . . Mr. JONAS GREEN, for Twenty-eight Years Printer to this Province, and Twenty-one Years Printer and Publisher of the MARYLAND GAZETTE: He was one of the Aldermen of this City. It would be the highest Indiscretion in us, to attempt giving the Character he justly deserved, only we have Reason to regret the Loss of him, in the various Stations of Husband, Parent, Master, and Companion" (*MG*, Apr. 16, 1767).

Gresham, Sarah (d. 1756). Associate.

Widow of John Gresham (d. 1752); Annapolis merchant and owner of a plantation near South River Church (*MG*, Jan. 23, 1752, Nov. 28, 1754, Oct. 28, 1756); her will, which was witnessed by Jonas Green, indicates that she was probably well-to-do, leaving her son Richard properties in Gravesend and Northfleet, England (Wills, Box G, No. 72).

Hamilton, Dr. John (1697–1768). "Dr. Polyhistor." Honorary Member (admitted 1745).

Older brother of Alexander Hamilton; married Mary Scott in 1722 (*BDML*, 390); also a physician, John preceded his brother in coming to America and establishing a medical practice; he resided in Calvert County, owned a water mill, and left everything to his grandchildren (Wills, vol. 36, pp. 461–464). His obituary reads: "He has left, few, very few Equals, and none superior to him, in the Character of a skilful, and able Physician, and of an honest, humane, benevolent Man" (*MG*, Mar. 31, 1768).

Hamilton, Rev. John (d. 1773). "Broadface Round." Honorary Member (admitted 1745) and member of Eastern Shore Triumvirate.

Immigrated from Ireland and was inducted into St. Mary Anne's, Cecil County, in 1746; married Lettice Short, then Jane Peck (1757); active in the formation of the Corporation for the Relief of Widows and Orphans (see Wills, vol. 39, pp. 373–374).

Hart, Samuel. "Ignotus Warble." Honorary Member (admitted 1745). Married Catherin Gardner (1742) and apparently resided in Anne Arundel County (St. Margaret's Parish Register, MHS).

Henderson, Captain. Visitor.

The *MG* for Dec. 4, 1751, notes that Captain Henderson of the *Nancy* supplied Daniel Wolstenholme (q.v.)—and probably other merchants associated with the Tuesday Club—with fresh goods.

Hepburn, John (1710–1775). Visitor.

Resident of Prince George's County; survived by his son Samuel Chew Hepburn and his daughter Ann Leeke (Wills, Box 12, No. 11); appointed one of the judges of assize, on the Western Shore, in place of William Rogers (q.v.) (*MG*, Aug. 9, 1749); several notices in the *MG* suggest that he was a wealthy landowner (see, e.g., May 30, 1754; see also his will). Hepburn's obituary reads: "On Monday the 14th instant, died at his house in Upper-Marlborough, in the 65th year of his age, JOHN HEPBURN, Esq; for many years one of the judges of the provincial court, which important trust, he executed with the fidelity and uprightness becoming a good magistrate—in private life, he approved himself the tender husband, the affectionate and indulgent parent, the humane master, the beneficent neighbour, the faithful friend, the polite companion, and the man of nice honour, and unshaken integrity" (*MG*, Aug. 24, 1775).

Hesselius, John (1728–1778). "Signior Sehesslius." Visitor.
Probably a native Marylander; son of Gustavus Hesselius, a native of Sweden naturalized by the Maryland General Assembly in 1721, and his wife Lydia; married Mary Woodward (1763); church warden and vestryman, St. Anne's, Annapolis, 1763–1764; portrait painter and one of the most prolific painters of the pre-Revolutionary period (see Newman, *To Maryland from Overseas*, 92; Theodore Bolton and George C. Groce, Jr., "John Hesselius: An Account of His Life and the First Catalogue of His Portraits," *Art Quarterly*, II [1939], 77–91; and Richard K. Doud, "John Hesselius, Maryland Limner," *Winterthur Portfolio*, V [1969], 129–153).

Hill, Richard, Jr. (d. 1755). "Chantum Cheary." Honorary Member (admitted 1747).
Hamilton calls him Richard Hill "of Philadelphia," probably because Hill was born and raised in Philadelphia at the home of his father, Richard Hill (1673–1729; see *Dictionary of American Biography*); Hill had established residency in Anne Arundel County by 1735; his connection with Samuel Stringar (q.v.), a fellow surgeon (Test. Procs., vol. 30, p. 27), suggests that this is the Hill to whom Hamilton is referring, and probably the same Hill whose death notice appeared in the *MG*, May 15, 1755.

Holliday, Robert (d. by 1748). "Hereum Thereum." Honorary Member (admitted 1745) and member of Eastern Shore Triumvirate.
Baltimore County physician; husband of Achsah (Wills, 1747, Box 7, No. 46; Inventories, 1748, Box 11, No. 44).

Hollyday, James (1722–1786). "Joshua Fluter." Honorary Member (admitted 1745).
Native Marylander; son of James Hollyday (1696–1747) and Sarah Covington (1683–1765); never married; Anglican; admitted to the Middle Temple in 1754 and returned to Maryland in 1758 to practice law; member of Lower House, Queen Anne's County, at various intervals from 1751 to 1770

(see George T. Hollyday, "Biographical Memoirs of James Hollyday," *Pennsylvania Magazine of History and Biography*, VII [1883], 426–447).

Jacques, Lancelot (1709–1791). Frequent visitor.

A French Huguenot who came to America as a refugee and sought to develop the country by starting iron furnaces, constructing and operating the Catoctin Furnace in Frederick County (T. J. C. Williams and Folger McKinsey, *History of Frederick County, Maryland*, 2 vols. [Frederick, Md., 1910], I, 106); numerous advertisements in the *MG* further indicate that he was a merchant "at his Store fronting the Court House" in Annapolis (June 14, 1749).

Jennings, Catherine. "Madonna Swashgut." Associate.

Annapolis storekeeper whose house was such a familiar spot that an advertiser in the *MG* directed his friends to his new dwelling "near the widow Jenning's" (Dec. 6, 1753; see also Nov. 20, 1751, Feb. 27, 1752). Jennings moved to Frederick Town, Frederick County, where her will was probated in 1765 (Wills, vol. 33, pp. 250–251).

Jennings, Thomas (d. 1759). "Prim Timorous." Longstanding Member (admitted 1749) and Sergeant at Arms.

Resident of Anne Arundel County; husband of Rebecca and father of Elizabeth and Ann (Admin. Bonds, Box 61, No. 37); he was a judge and a modestly wealthy landowner (*MG*, Jan. 3, Mar. 21, 1750). Jennings's obituary reads: "Sunday last Died here, after a tedious and lingering Indisposition, Mr. *Thomas Jennings*, Chief Clerk of the Land-Office, and for a great many Years in the Commission of the Peace for this County; by whose Death his Family has lost a tender Husband, indulgent Father, and kind Master; and the Community, a very useful, honest, and inoffensive Member" (*MG*, Aug. 30, 1759).

Johns, Kensey (d. 1763). Visitor.

Probably the son of Aquila Johns (*MG*, Mar. 13, 1751); husband of Susannah (Admin. Bonds, Box 66, No. 40); commander of the *Rumney* and the *Long* (*MG*, Apr. 13, 1748, Apr. 4, 1750, Mar. 6, 1751). Johns's obituary reads: "On Thursday last Died at his House at *West-River*, KENSEY JOHNS, Esq; High Sheriff of this County [Anne Arundel]. He was a tender Husband, affectionate Father, sincere Friend, upright Magistrate, humane Officer, kind Neighbour, and chearful Companion: His Death is sincerely lamented by all his Friends, and the Loss to his Family is truly deplorable, being snatched from them in the very Prime of Life, aged no more than 42 Years" (*MG*, June 2, 1763).

Key, Philip (1696/1697–1764). "Signior Phrazeobundus." Visitor.
Immigrated to Maryland from England ca. 1720; married Susannah Gardiner (d. 1717), then Theodosia Lawrence (d. 1772); Anglican; Gent., 1738, and Esq., 1750; merchant, planter, lawyer; member of Lower House, St. Mary's County, 1728–1731, 1734/1735–1737, and Upper House, 1763; died a wealthy landowner. Key's obituary reads: "On Monday the 20th of this Instant, Died, at his Seat in *St. Mary's* County, in the LXVIIIth Year of his Age, the Honble PHILIP KEY, Esq; one of the Council of this Province. He was a truly pious and devout Christian, an affectionate and tender Husband, an indulgent and fond Parent, a humane Master, a warm Friend, a friendly Neighbour, and a most agreeable and chearful Companion. His Death is sincerely lamented by his Family, and all his numerous Friends and Acquaintance" (*MG*, Aug. 30, 1764).

King, Thomas (d. by 1761). Associate.
Resident of Anne Arundel County; husband of Rachel (Admin. Bonds, Box 54, No. 35); King's advertisements as a shoemaker, such as the following notice, frequently appeared in the *MG*: "Notice is hereby given, That *Thomas* King, Shoemaker, who formerly kept his Shop at the Gate-House of the City of *Annapolis*, now keeps his Shop at the Old Prison" (Sept. 22, 1747).

Lake, Charles (d. 1764). "Rev. Whiner." Associate.
Rector of St. Anne's, Annapolis, from 1740 to 1743, and of St. James's, Herring Creek, from 1749 until his death; proposals for the Reverend Lake's system of divinity, the *Florilegia Sacra*, were advertised in the *MG* for Nov. 14 through Dec. 5, 1750.

Lendrum, Andrew (d. 1769). "Roundhead Muddy." Longstanding Member (admitted 1749), then Honorary Member.
Possibly A.B., Trinity College, Dublin, 1739; inducted into St. Anne's, Annapolis, in 1749 and resigned shortly thereafter to become rector of St. George's, Baltimore County, where he remained until his death; the notice of his induction into St. Anne's appeared as follows in the *MG*: "Wednesday last the Reverend Mr. ANDREW LENDRUM was Inducted into this Par-

ish, in the room of the Reverend and Ingenious Mr. JOHN GORDON, who is
Removed, to the great Grief of his Parishioners, to *St. Michael's* Parish in
Talbot County" (Apr. 5, 1749).

Lloyd, Edward (1711–1770). "Courtly Phraze." Honorary Member (admitted 1745).
   Native Marylander; son of Edward Lloyd (1670–1718/1719) and his wife
Sarah (1683–1755); married Anne Rousby (1721–1769) in 1739, then a second
wife (name unknown); Anglican; colonel by 1741; Esq., 1747; planter, merchant; member of Lower House, Talbot County, 1738, 1739–1741, and Upper
House (served several terms); died a wealthy landowner. Lloyd's obituary
reads: "Lately died at his Seat, on *Wye* River, in *Talbot* County, greatly
lamented, EDWARD LLOYD, Esq; formerly one of his Lordship's Council of
State, and Agent and Receiver General for this Province: He was a tender
and affectionate Parent . . . and a polite and agreeable Companion. As he
was possessed of great Wealth, so was he remarkable for his Hospitality to
Strangers, and Benevolence to real Objects of Compassion" (*MG,* Feb. 8,
1770).

Lomas, John (d. 1757). "Laconic Comas (Comus)." Oldstanding Member (admitted 1745) and Orator.
   Lomas lived in Annapolis with his wife Margaret (*MHM,* X [1915],
128). Various advertisements in the *MG* show that Lomas was an Annapolis
merchant and owned a plantation near South River, and that he left for
London in 1749 and returned in 1750 (the time of his absence from the
Tuesday Club) (Apr. 7, 1747, Mar. 8, 1749, Aug. 30, 1749, June 20, 1750).
Lomas moved to Glasgow by 1754 and died in Liverpool (*MHM,* IV
[1909], 196–197; *MG,* June 30, 1757).

Lux, William, of Annapolis. "Crinkum Crankum." Longstanding
Member (admitted 1753).
   Native Marylander; Annapolis merchant; advertised goods for sale in
MG (see, e.g., Sept. 4, 1751). He left his entire estate to his "dearest friend
and relation," William Lux of Baltimore (q.v.) (Wills, 1772, vol. 38, p. 824).

Lux, William, of Baltimore (1730–1778). Visitor.
   Native Marylander; son of Darby Lux (ca. 1698–1750) and Ann Sanders
(ca. 1705–1785); married Agnes Walker (1731–1783) in 1752; Anglican; Gent.,
1752, and Esq., 1778; wealthy merchant and land speculator; participated in

the Stamp Act controversy, 1765, and was one of the organizers of the Baltimore Sons of Liberty, 1766.

Lyon, William. Visitor.
Probably Queen Anne's County physician (Inventories, 1767, vol. 93, p. 59, 1770, vol. 104, p. 351); notices in the *MG* also imply that he was a druggist who sold his wares at his shop in Baltimore (Nov. 4, 1746, June 19, 1755).

McPherson, Alexander (d. 1776). Visitor.
Resident of Charles County; husband of Elizabeth and father of five children; tobacco planter and modestly wealthy landowner (Wills, 1775, vol. 40, p. 488; Inventories, 1776, vol. 122, p. 387).

Malcolm, Alexander (d. 1763). "Philo Dogmaticus." Longstanding Member (admitted 1749), Chancellor, then Honorary Member.
After meeting Hamilton in Massachusetts, Malcolm was inducted into St. Anne's, Annapolis, in 1749 when Andrew Lendrum (q.v.) resigned; he was inducted into St. Paul's, Queen Anne's County, in 1753, and in 1755 became master of the Queen Anne's County school, from which he was forced to resign. His obituary calls him "a Gentleman who has obliged the World with several learned Performances on the Mathematics, Music, and Grammar" (*MG*, June 30, 1763); his *New Treatise of Arithmetick and Bookkeeping* (Edinburgh, 1718), which had reached several editions by his death, was assessed as "the best in English and perhaps any other Language" (*New Hampshire Gazette* [Portsmouth], July 22, 1763). For further information on Malcolm's career, see James R. Heintze, "Alexander Malcolm: Musician, Clergyman, and Schoolmaster," *MHM*, LXXIII (1978), 226–235. According to Heintze, Malcolm's *A Treatise of Musick, Speculative, Practical, and Historical* (Edinburgh, 1721) established him as "the most significant music theorist to have immigrated to the colonies during the eighteenth century" (p. 226).

Marshe, Witham (d. 1765). "Prattle Motely." Oldstanding Member (admitted 1745), Secretary, then Honorary Member.
Marshe is best remembered as secretary to the Maryland Commissioners at the treaty of Lancaster in 1744 with the Six Indian Nations (and author of the "Journal of the Treaty Held with the Six Nations by the Commissioners of Maryland, and Other Provinces," Massachusetts Histori-

cal Society, *Collections*, 1st Ser., VII [1801], 171–200), and as Sir William Johnson's secretary for Indian affairs (Lemay, *Men of Letters*, 246).

Middleton, Samuel (d. 1770). "Mr. Leidemont." Host.
Husband of Anne and father of three sons and one daughter (Wills, Box M, No. 55). He owned and operated Middleton's Tavern and the ferry at Annapolis; Middleton's Tavern is still standing and still thriving.

Mitchelson, [Samuel?]. "Mr. Lisper." Visitor.
Since Mr. Mitchelson is given a dubious character in the *History*, perhaps he is the Samuel Mitchelson who was convicted for stealing, and then convicted for prison breaking (see *MG*, Dec. 25, 1751).

Morris, Robert (d. 1750). "Merry Makefun." Honorary Member (admitted 1747) and member of Eastern Shore Triumvirate.
Born in Liverpool; son of Andrew Morris, mariner, and his wife Mauldin (Newman, *To Maryland from Overseas*, 125). In the "Narrative of the Principal Incidents in the Life of Jeremiah Banning" (1793), Banning writes: "As a mercantile genius it was thought he [Morris] had not his equal in the land. As a companion and bon vivant he was incomparable. . . . He gave birth to the inspection law on tobacco and carried it through though opposed by a powerful majority. He was the first who introduced the mode of keeping accounts in money. . . . At repartee he bore down all before him. Mr. Morris was father to the present Robert Morris, . . . the most distinguished merchant of his time in America" (in William F. Boogher, *Miscellaneous Americana: A Collection of History, Biography, and Genealogy* [Washington, D.C., 1895]). Morris's obituary, relating the unusual nature of his death, appeared as follows in the *MG*.

> On Thursday last died at his House in *Oxford*, Mr. ROBERT MORRIS, Merchant, Agent and Factor of *Foster Cunliffe*, Esq; of *Liverpool*. He received his Death by a Gunshot Wound in his Right Arm, which melancholy and unfortunate Accident happened in this Manner:—The Friday before his Death, upon the Arrival of the *Liverpool Merchant*, a Ship of Mr. *Cunliffe's*, he went on board her with some Company; and, after a small Stay there, went into the Boat to come ashore; at which Time the Captain was about paying him the usual Compliment with his Guns. Mr. *Morris* . . . being under an unusual Apprehension of Mischief, desired the Guns might not be fir'd 'til he was astern of the Ship: But the Captain, not

apprehensive of any Danger . . . unfortunately gave the Signal for firing, whilst the Boat was aside of the Ship. . . . The Wadding of the first Gun pass'd near the Head of Mr. *James Dickenson,* who sat by Mr. *Morris;* and that of the third did the Mischief. The Breechings were indiscreetly left under the Guns, and the Ship had a heel to the Side next the Boat; otherwise this sad Accident could not have happened. . . .

The Bone of his Arm was broke a little above the Elbow, and a large Wound and Contusion was made in the Flesh.—The Wound began to mortify the next Day, but by the Skill and Assiduity of the Surgeons who attended him, the Mortification was stopped, and there was good Hopes of saving both his Life and Arm, until Wednesday Evening, when he was seiz'd with a violent Fever, which carried him off next Afternoon (July 18, 1750).

The rest of the obituary confirms Banning's high opinion of Morris.

North, Benjamin (d. by 1761). Visitor.
The inventory of North's personal effects, witnessed by William Rogers (q.v.) and William Lux of Annapolis (q.v.), indicates that North was a mariner who lived in Baltimore County and owned very little (Inventories, 1761, Box 15, No. 13).

North, Robert (d. by 1751). "Huffbluff Surly." Honorary Member (admitted 1745).
Resident of Baltimore County; son of Thomas and Ellen North of Whittington, Lancashire, England (Newman, *To Maryland from Overseas,* 130); father of three children; wealthy landowner (Wills, 1749, Box 8, No. 2; Accounts, 1751, vol. 30, p. 141).

Pickering, Stephen (d. by 1765). "Gasperus Pickeringtonus." Visitor.
Anne Arundel County merchant; sued by Sarah Gresham (q.v.) and bailed out by the Reverend Charles Lake (q.v.); his will, witnessed by Lake and the Reverend Archibald Spencer (q.v.), indicates that he was a gentleman with apparently little property; he had no children (Inventories, Box 72, No. 56; Wills, 1753, Box P, No. 41; Accounts, 1765, vol. 53, p. 309).

Raitt, John (d. 1758). Visitor.
Native of Scotland; husband of Ann (Admin. Bonds, Box 60, No. 7); wealthy merchant. Raitt first sold his goods "at his Store over against Mr.

[Beale] *Bordley's*, near the Stadt House in *Annapolis*," then "removed from the House over against Mr. *Bordley's* in *North East* Street, to the House where Mr. *Ashbury Sutton* lately lived, near the Dock in *Annapolis*" (*MG*, June 15, Dec. 7, 1748). He left bequests of £1,000 to each of his five children (Newman, *Anne Arundel Gentry*, 264). Raitt's obituary reads: "On Thursday last died here, after a short Indisposition, greatly Lamented by his Family and Friends, and on Friday was decently Interred, Mr. JOHN RAITT, a Merchant in this City, and late Sheriff of *Anne-Arundel* County, which Trust he Discharged to the intire Satisfaction of all with whom he had any Concerns" (*MG*, July 6, 1758).

Richard, James. "Roughby Ranter." Associate.
Sheriff of Baltimore County. Richard's defense of his reputation against what he considered the slanderous attacks of Richard Chase and others (including Thomas Chase [q.v.]) appeared in the *MG* for July 28, 1747; Richard was vindicated in court in his dispute with the Chases (see Lemay, *Men of Letters*, 200, and Rosamond Randall Beirne, "The Reverend Thomas Chase: Pugnacious Parson," *MHM*, LIX [1964], 7). Other notices in the *MG* indicate that Richard was a wealthy landowner (see, e.g., Sept. 30, 1746), and unless there were two James Richards, he was also an Annapolis merchant (*MG*, Nov. 18, 1746, May 19, 1747).

Richardson, Thomas (d. 1768). Visitor.
Probably born in Scotland; Annapolis merchant and business associate of Anthony Stewart (q.v.) in the rum trade (Wills, 1768, vol. 36, pp. 478–479; Inventories, Box 80, No. 16). Richardson's obituary reads: "On the Evening of Friday last, Mr. THOMAS RICHARDSON, late of this City, Merchant, was instantly kill'd by a Flash of Lightning, which melted his Watch, Shoe, and Knee Buckles.—He was sitting in a Room at Mr. ADAIR's, in BALTIMORE-TOWN, with another Person, at a small Distance, who was struck down, but soon recovered. . . . Mr. RICHARDSON was a young Man, in the Prime of Life, and possess'd many good Qualities, which justly entitled him to the Esteem of a numerous Acquaintance" (*MG*, June 23, 1768).

Ridout, John (1732–1797). Visitor.
Immigrated to Maryland from England in 1753; son of George Ridout (1702–1779) and Mary Hallett; husband of Mary Ogle (1746–1808); Anglican; Esq., 1753; protégé of Horatio Sharpe (1718–1790) and served as his secretary during Sharpe's term as governor; planter; member of Upper

House (served several terms); died a wealthy landowner. Ridout's obituary reads:

> On Friday the 6th instant, at his house in the city of Annapolis, after a short illness, departed this life John Ridout, Esquire, in the 66th year of his age. In the amiable character of this useful and worthy member of society were uniformly and eminently displayed soundness of judgment, evenness of temper, benevolence of heart, integrity and prudence in conduct. A kind and affectionate husband, a tender and discreet father. . . . Sensible, polite and social in his manners, obliging, beneficent and unassuming in his deportment, his loss is deeply regretted by his friends and neighbours (*MG*, Oct. 12, 1797).

Rogers, William (1699–1749). "Seemly Spruce." Oldstanding Member (admitted 1745).

Born in New England; resident in Annapolis by 1720; husband of Mary Townley (d. by 1725); chief clerk and register of the Prerogative Court, 1736–1749 (*BDML*, s.v. "Rogers, John"). Rogers's obituary reads: "Last Saturday Morning died here, very much lamented, after a long and lingering Indisposition, in the Fiftieth Year of his Age, and on Sunday Evening was decently interred, WILLIAM ROGERS, Esq; a Gentleman born and bred in *New-England*, but had long been a worthy Inhabitant of this Place; where he was greatly belov'd and esteem'd. He enjoyed many Posts of Honour and Trust, which he discharged with Judgment and Fidelity; and has left a sorrowful Widow and three Children" (*MG*, Aug. 2, 1749).

Scott, Andrew (d. 1766). Visitor.

Prince George's County physician and surgeon; husband of Mary Abington. After ending an extremely unhappy marriage, Scott left Maryland in the early 1750s and settled in New Bern, North Carolina, where he continued to practice medicine until his death (George F. Frick, James L. Reveal, C. Rose Broome, and Melvin L. Brown, "The Practice of Dr. Andrew Scott of Maryland and North Carolina," *MHM*, LXXXII [1987], 123–141).

Scott, Upton (1724–1814). "Jeronimo Jaunter." Longstanding Member (admitted 1754).

Scott came to America from Glasgow in 1753, bringing a letter of introduction from his teacher, Dr. Robert Hamilton, Alexander Hamilton's cousin (Lemay, *Men of Letters*, 244); in September 1756, he married Elizabeth Ross, the wealthy daughter of John Ross, Esq. (*MG*, Sept. 9, 1756); he died a modestly wealthy physician (Admin. Bonds, 1814, Box 112, No. 14; Wills, Box S, No. 20). Scott's glowing obituary appeared as follows.

Departed this life, on Wednesday evening the 23d ult, at the advanced age of 90 years, Dr. UPTON SCOTT, a native of Ireland, but for more than 60 years a most distinguished inhabitant of this City.

Society seldom mourns the loss of a more excellent and valuable member, than the venerable man whose decease we now record. Through the course of a life, protracted far beyond the ordinary span of human existence, his career has been one unbroken tenor of virtue, dignity, and usefulness. Pure in his principles, discerning in his judgment, unshaken in his attachments, he has been the hereditary counsellor and friend of many generations, and has enjoyed the successive confidence and affection of grandsire, son and father, who have been successively enlightened by his wisdom, and enobled by his friendship.

Bred among heroes, whom history delights to honour, and in scenes which though at present dimly seen "through the long vista of departed years," have not yet lost their interest, his soul was of that lofty cast which befitted the chosen friend of Wolfe, while the treasures of his mind, enriched by the constant accumulations of experience, and the elevated and endearing qualities of his heart, rendered him the oracular adviser of the young, the boast and ornament of the aged.

A Gracious Providence lengthened to him not merely "the frail tenure of a feverish being," but the diviner bounty of moral and intellectual pleasures; and at a period of life when most men, despoiled by time of the feelings and faculties which make life a blessing, seem but as melancholy mementos of mortality, the vigour of his understanding, and the unchilled ardour of his affections, rendered this venerable man the soul of an extensive circle of family friends and connections, in whom as in a common centre, their affections and enjoyments converged and were united (*MG*, Mar. 3, 1814).

Sedgewick, John. Visitor.
Anne Arundel County mariner; husband of Sarah Gaither (b. 1726) (Wills, 1753, vol. 30, p. 511; Newman, *Anne Arundel Gentry*, 90, 447). Sedgewick appears in the *MG* as commander of the ship *Friendship* (May 2, 9, 1750).

Snowden, Richard (1687–1763). "Oldham Wisely." Honorary Member (admitted 1745).

Resident of Anne Arundel County; husband of Elizabeth and father of three sons (Inventories, 1766, Box 73, No. 32). Snowden's obituary reads:

> Yesterday Morning Died, at his Seat on *Patuxent* River, near his Iron-Works, in the 76th Year of his Age, the venerable Mr. RICHARD SNOWDEN, a Gentleman universally and deservedly Esteem'd, who has left a sorrowful Widow, numerous Offspring . . . and Acquaintance, to lament a most tender Husband . . . and agreeable Companion. He was of a most benevolent and humane Disposition, remarkably Hospitable and Generous in his Entertainment of Strangers, as well as his intimate Acquaintance. By a diligent Application to the extensive Business which he was a long Time engag'd in, he acquired an affluent Fortune, with a fair unblemish'd Character; and led the Life of a Christian truly worthy of Imitation. . . . *Mark the perfect Man, and behold the Upright, for the End of that Man is Peace.* Psal. xxxvii. 37 (*MG*, Jan. 27, 1763).

Snowden also seems to have held some trade as a tobacco dealer (*MG*, July 31, 1751).

Spencer, Archibald (1698–1760). "Dr. Rhubarb." Visitor.

Physician, lecturer on experimental philosophy, and apparently a deist who was nevertheless ordained a minister and licensed for Virginia in 1749; rector of All Hallows Parish, Anne Arundel County (from September 1751), where he remained until his death (J. A. Leo Lemay, "Franklin's 'Dr. Spence': The Reverend Archibald Spencer [1698?–1760], M.D.," *MHM*, LIX [1964], 199–216). Spencer's obituary states that "while he seemed in good Health, . . . he declared, with great Indifference, his Expectation of a speedy Death, and afterwards met his Fate with a singular Constancy and Resignation" (*MG*, Jan. 17, 1760).

Sterling, James (1701–1763). "Rev. Rodomantus." Visitor.

Born in Ireland; matriculated at Trinity College in 1716; immigrated to America in 1737, having already established himself in Dublin and London as a poet and playwright; inducted into All Hallows Parish, Anne Arundel County, where he remained until his resignation in 1739, when he was appointed rector of St. Anne's, Annapolis; resigned from St. Anne's in 1740 to accept a more lucrative position at St. Paul's, Kent County, where he remained until his death; continued to write poetry—mostly occasional—

while living in America, and many of his pieces appeared in the *MG*. Sterling's obituary says that for his "uncommon Abilities and extensive Learning, particularly in all the Branches of polite Literature, [he stood] unrival'd in this Part of the World" (Lemay, *Men of Letters*, 257–312; *MG*, Nov. 17, 1763).

Steward, John. Visitor.
A John Stewart of London advertised in the *MG* for Sept. 26, 1750, as a merchant. This is possibly the same John Stewart who opened a store in Anne Arundel County in partnership with William Lux of Baltimore (q.v.) (*BDML*, s.v. "Lux, William").

Stewart, Mr. "Mr. Boniface." Visitor.
This could be any number of Stewarts, but it is possibly John Stewart or Anthony Stewart, business associate of Thomas Richardson (q.v.) in the rum trade (Inventories, Box 80, No. 16).

Stringar, Samuel (d. 1747). "Samuel Swallowbeak." Mentioned.
Anne Arundel County physician; husband of Lydia Warfield (Admin. Bonds, Box 47, No. 49); Stringar's obituary reads: "Last Wednesday died, much lamented, at *Elk-Ridge,* in this County, Dr. *Samuel Stringar,* formerly Mayor of this City" (*MG*, Aug. 25, 1747).

Swan, Robert (1720–1764). "Stentor Snuffysnout (Snuffybeak)." Visitor.
Affluent Annapolis merchant, of Scottish ancestry; he apparently died childless, leaving everything to his nephews (Inventories, 1765, Box 72, No. 29; Wills, 1764, Box S, No. 107). Swan also "carrie[d] on the Business of Tanning, and Currying of Leather, and Shoemaking" (*MG*, May 7, 1752). Swan's obituary reads: "Friday last Died here, in the 44th Year of his Age, Mr. ROBERT SWAN, Merchant, one of the Common-Council of this City: And on Sunday his Remains were very decently Interr'd" (*MG*, May 10, 1764).

Thompson, John. "Joannes Tomlinsonus." Visitor.
Annapolis merchant (see, e.g., *MG*, May 30, 1750, Mar. 5, 1752).

Thornton, Thomas (d. 1791). "Nolens Volens." Visitor.
Thornton was licensed for Maryland in 1754; the *MG* for Apr. 24, 1755, notes that the Reverend Mr. Thomas Thornton had lately arrived from

London (probably for the first time); he served as curate to the Reverend Thomas Bacon (q.v.) at St. Peter's, Talbot County, until he was appointed to Port Tobacco Parish in 1762; in 1779 he and his wife Mary were living in Kent County (Inventories, 1779, Box 34, No. 5); sometime prior to 1785 he moved to Virginia, where he held parishes until his death.

Thornton, William (d. 1769). "Solo Neverout," "Protomusicus." Long-standing Member (admitted 1745), Chief Musician, and Attorney General.
Merchant and shipowner (*MG,* Nov. 11, 1746, Jan. 16, 1751); Thornton owned land in Prince George's and Anne Arundel counties and apparently moved from Annapolis to Baltimore County before his death; he was the brother of Thomas Thornton (q.v.) and left most of his possessions to his son William (born to Sarah Heigh) (Wills, 1769, Box 37, No. 80). Thornton's obituary reads: "On Friday last died, at BALTIMORE-TOWN, Mr. WILLIAM THORNTON, formerly Sheriff of this County [Anne Arundel].—A Gentleman much respected by his Friends and Acquaintance" (*MG,* Feb. 9, 1769).

Tilghman, Edward (1713–1785). "Prim Laconic." Honorary Member (admitted 1747).
Native Marylander; son of Richard Tilghman (1672/1673–1738/1739) and Anna Maria Lloyd (1677–1748); married Anna Maria Turbutt ca. 1738, Elizabeth Chew (1720–1759) in 1749, and Juliana Carroll (b. 1729) in 1759; Anglican; Gent., 1737, and Esq., 1740; colonel by 1755; member of Lower House, Queen Anne's County, 1745/1746–1748; died a wealthy landowner.

Troy, John. "Capt. Furbisher." Visitor.
Notices in the *MG* show that a Capt. John Troy commanded the snow *Polly,* and that he, Lancelot Jacques (q.v.), and William Thornton (q.v.) apparently dealt in the slave trade (June 14, 21, 1753).

Wallace, Charles (1727–1812). Visitor.
Native Marylander; son of John and Anne Wallace; married Catherine (ca. 1731–1795), then Mary Bull Rankin (ca. 1747–1834); Anglican; Gent., by 1757, Esq., by 1776; staymaker, tavern keeper, land developer, and merchant.

Wilkins, William (1700–1761). "Spatterdash Wouldbe." Visitor.
Resident of Annapolis; husband of Deborah and father of five children (Wills, 1761, Box W, No. 73). Wilkins's obituary reads: "Saturday last Died here, after a long Indisposition, Aged 61 Years, and on Tuesday was decently

Interr'd, Mr. WILLIAM WILKINS, who was for a great Number of Years Prosecutor in our Mayor's Court, and a very useful Clerk to many Committees in the Lower House of Assembly" (*MG*, Mar. 5, 1761).

Wollaston, John (fl. 1736–1767). "Squeak Grumbleton." Visitor.
Portrait painter; probably the son of John Woolaston, London artist of the early eighteenth century; came to America in 1749 and remained nearly ten years, producing over three hundred portraits from New York to Virginia (including portraits of Maryland's most prominent families); influenced Gustavus Hesselius and probably his son John Hesselius (q.v.); according to George C. Groce, outside of New England Wollaston's influence on colonial painting was "greater than that of any English artist . . . prior to the Revolutionary War" ("John Wollaston [fl. 1736–1767]: A Cosmopolitan Painter in the British Colonies," *Art Quarterly*, XV [1952], 133).

Wolstenholme, Daniel (d. 1795). "Giovanni Precisio." Visitor.
Immigrated to Maryland from England; resident in Annapolis by 1750; husband of Deborah (d. 1807); Anglican; merchant, planter; member of Lower House, St. Mary's County, 1765–1766, 1768–1770; a Loyalist, Wolstenholme in 1775 refused to sign the Association of Freemen of Maryland.

Wood, Benjamin (1715–1753). Associate.
Wood's obituary reads: "Last Friday died, after a very long and lingering Illness, at the House of *Jonas Green*, where he had lived upwards of Eleven Years . . . Mr. BENJAMIN WOOD, Printer, aged *38*, born at *Tattershall* in *Lincolnshire:* He had a good Education, well understood the learned Languages, and was an ingenious and skilful Artist" (*MG*, Aug. 2, 1753).

Wood, Samuel (d. by 1759). "Nathaniel Sylvius." Visitor.
Resident of St. Mary's County; he left his few possessions to his daughter Ann and sons Samuel and Jonathan (Wills, 1758, vol. 30, p. 527; Accounts, 1759, vol. 43, p. 354).

Woodward, Mr. Associate.
This might be any number of Woodwards, but I suspect it is either Abraham Woodward of Anne Arundel County, whose will was witnessed by William Rogers (q.v.) (Wills, 1744, vol. 24, pp. 7–8), or, more probably, Henry Woodward (1733–1761). He was a native Marylander; son of Amos Woodward (d. ca. 1735) and Achsah Dorsey (ca. 1704–1741); married Mary Young in 1755; Anglican; Gent., 1756, and Esq., 1759; planter, engaged in

some mercantile business; member of Lower House, Annapolis, 1757–1758. He was associated with Stephen Bordley (q.v.) and left his land and houses—one of which may have served as the meeting place for the Tuesday Club—to his wife (Wills, 1761, vol. 31, pp. 465–467). Woodward's obituary reads: "Saturday Night last, Died, at his Plantation near Town, after a short Illness, in the 28th Year of his Age, Mr. HENRY WOODWARD, a few Years since one of the Representatives for this City. He has left an inconsolable Widow, and Four young Children, to lament an affectionate Husband and tender Father" (*MG*, Sept. 24, 1761).

Woolf, Garrett. Associate.
Born in Germany and naturalized by an act of the Maryland General Assembly in 1727 (William Hand Browne *et al.*, eds., *Archives of Maryland* [Baltimore, 1883–], XXXVIII, 406–407); as Hamilton indicates, he was a cordwainer in Annapolis (Test. Procs.).

The History of the Tuesday Club

Volume I

FRONTISPIECE.

[Hamilton's drawings are reproduced in this edition courtesy of the John Work Garrett Library of the Milton S. Eisenhower Library at the Johns Hopkins University. The location of each drawing in the manuscript is indicated in brackets following the illustration.]

The History of the Ancient and Honorable Tuesday Club

From the earliest ages down to this present year.

Volume I

Autor Noster, ita describit Heroas Clubicos, ut Incertus hæreat Lector, an eruditi magis fortesve essent, corporisque potius aut animi viribus pollerent.[1]

---

1. "Our author so describes the Clubical heroes, that the reader remains uncertain, whether they are more erudite or brave, and whether they are more powerful in strength of body or of mind."

Contents of the
History of the Ancient and honorable
Tuesday Club

Volume I

Book I

Book II

From the transmigration of the Club to America, to the first Sederunt of the ancient and honorable Tuesday Club of Annapolis in Maryland.

Book III

From the first Sederunt of the ancient and Honorable Tuesday Club, to the Cathedration of the Honorable Nasifer Jole Esqr President.

Book IV

From the Cathedration of the Honorable Nasifer Jole Esqr President, to the first grand anniversary procession.

Book V

*From the first grand Anniversary procession, to the foundation of the Eastren
Shore Triumvirate.*

Book VI

*From the foundation of the Eastren Shore triumvirate, To the Creation of the
Chancellor, and Striking of the Club Medals at London.*

Dedication

To the Most Learned, the Attorney General of the Ancient and honorable Tuesday Club,[1] and his Successors.

Learned Sir,

 As it is more than probable that the Honorable the President, and the Longstanding members of the ancient & Honorable Tuesday Club, in their profound wisdom and Sagacity, will pitch upon you, and your Learned Successors, as keepers of their Valuable archives and historical Chronicles, as well as of their *Corpus Juris* or body of Laws, so I, their humble historiographer am of opinion, that I cannot dedicate these my Labors to a fitter person than to your most erudite and Learned worship (to speak in Clubic Stile), and to your Successors in that Eminent laborious, and *Puzzlementationful* office, which you have the honor to possess in our Ancient and honorable Club, under the kindly and benign Influences, and Cherishing beams of his honor the president, whose Smiles and prolific Aspect, produces Learned Ideas, as plentifully and thick, In your Worship's Capacious Cranium, as the Sun breeds Insects on a dunghill, Pardon, dear Sir, the allusion.

 There are two maxims often made use of in Common discourse, and [ii] generally received as true ones, ‖ tho' for my part, I think them at best but paltry Stuff, & if not absolutely false, yet nighly border on falshood, vizt: 1st That the truth ought not to be spoken at all times, and 2d, that we ought to be tender of the Characters of the dead.[2] These maxims may be esteemed good rules for some Dedicators and historians (nay Indeed for most,) to

---

 1. William Thornton (see biographical sketch).
 2. According to G. L. Apperson, *English Proverbs and Proverbial Phrases* (London, 1929), the following passage appears in Sir Roger L'Estrange's translation of Seneca's *Moral Essays* (ca. 1680): "The thing was true; but all truths are not to be spoken at all times" ("On the Happy Life," chap. 7), but I have not located this passage in any of the first three editions of L'Estrange's translation (1679, 1682, 1685), or in the original "De vita beata." In any event, Hamilton is perhaps recalling John Gay's remark that "Truth should not always be reveal'd" (*Fables,* 1st Ser., no. 18 [1727; rpt. Los Angeles, Calif., 1967], line 24). The second maxim has been attributed to Chilon, one of the Seven Sages of Greece, although Plutarch gives Solon the credit for it.

observe, who, Carried away, either by the power of Flattery, or, by their pestilent Inclination to party, or pusilanimous fear of the anger and resentment of men in power, vent in their Compositions, ten falshoods for one truth, hence it is that the public is loaded with such a quantity of lies and Rodomontades, and Impudent barefaced Gasconades, that little or no Confidence can be put, either in dedicatory or historical writings, so, that it may, to our Shame be said, that the History of *Amadis de Gaul* or *Esplandian*[3] afford as much Genuine truth, as do our Modern Histories, of England, France, Spain, &ct: and one may as well go to the Devil, the father of Liars, for the Gospel of truth, as to these Dedicators for a genuine Character of a Great man, or to these Historians for a fair Impartial and true Narration of facts, our herd of Dedicators, for example, observing exactly, the above Silly and Impertinent maxims, will Impudently load their patrons in the face of the discerning world, who well know the Contrary, with Eulogiums and praises, which they never merited, tho' Ignorant as children and Idiots, they must be called learned, tho' Stupid & dull ‖ as [iii] owls, they must be lively and facetious, tho' ugly as Swine, they must be handsome & well made, tho wicked and worthless as the Devil, they must be decked and adorned with all the Moral Virtues. Again they must Surely be descended from noble and Illustrious progenitors, tho' this present generation can well Remember their Grandsires peddling and hawking, and mumping about the Streets, this Romantic Ancestry must also be virtuous, brave & honorable, tho' many an honest man knows, and will swear to it, that there never was a pack of arranter Rascals unhang'd than they.

If it be not from a superstitious regard to the above absurd maxims, suggested by party zeal, pusilanimity, and a mean turn for flattery, and productive of an utter disregard for truth, whence does it arise, that we shall find a couple of grave historians, giving opposite Characters to one and the same person? whence comes it, that what the one calls white, the other pronounces black? whence does it proceed that they are still in different Stories, like two Suborned Irish evidences, one giving it this way another that, in such a manner, that the bewildered reader, does not know, or cannot determin, which of them is the greatest liar? Is it not also, from the fear of disobliging, and drawing down upon themselves, the resentments of great men and Illustrious families, that no Historian dares honestly Compile the genuine memoirs and transactions of those very times in which we

---

3. Amadis de Gaul is the chivalric hero of *Amadís de Gaula,* a 15th-century Spanish or Portuguese romance. Esplandian, the son of Amadis de Gaul, is a valorous knight who battles the Turks and eventually marries the daughter of a Greek emperor. *Las sergas de Esplandián* (1510) was a sequel to *Amadís de Gaula.*

[iv] live, whence the Circumstances ‖ and facts are so mashed and broken, so
      mangled and obscured, by this foolish method of proceeding, that they are
      rendered utterly Incorrigible, and, Instead of being bettered, by the Histo-
      rians of the Succeeding age, who often Labor under the Disease of a bad
      memory and worse Judgement, the whole mass turns out to be a hodge
      podge, almost unintelligible, and quite Irreconcilable to Nature and Com-
      mon Sense.

         Conscious of these evils, flowing from too Strict an observation, of
      these above mentioned Impertinent and foolish maxims, I have not either
      in quality of a Dedicator or Historian, allowed myself to be guided by
      them, but have all along had a Strict regard to truth and Nature, and
      whatever the truth is, or wheresoever she is to be found, I bring her out to
      fair View, without any regard to foppish forms and Ceremonies, and I care
      not a fig who takes offence at it, nor Indeed, would I entertain so Slight a
      regard for that Amiable Goddess, (who the Ancient Mythologists tell us, is
      hid in a well)[4] as to deviate from her in the least title either for fear or favor,
      hence you'll find, if you take the trowble to read the following history, that I
      have therein given every one his due, without partiality, favor or affection,
      there, all comes out to open light, be it what it will, good or bad, and I
      hope, nay am assured, that I have been as little Partial to myself as to others,
      however, as the Saying is, the proof of the pudding is in the eating, so, the
[v]   proof of what I here write, will be elucidated ‖ by reading what I have there
      wrote, but, as I apprehend, You will not give yourself the trowble to read
      such a prolix Rhapsody, as is the following history from end to end, having,
      it is likely, things of greater Importance, or at least, things which you
      believe to be of greater Importance, whereon to bestow your precious
      moments, I shall only refer you to this here Dedication, which I now
      address to your Learned worship, which, as it is none of the Longest, I
      hope you will take the trowble to peruse, both for my Sake and your own,
      that is, to vindicate the Conduct of both to the present times and also to
      futurity in this here affair; you will find in this Epistle Dedicatory, an eikon
      or Image of the History it self in minature, and therefore I put it to your
      Conscience, as a Learned man, and Clubical Lawyer, to Judge with equity
      and declare with Candor whether I have acted herein like the Common
      herd of Dedicators, who load their patrons with so many fine Qualities,
      and so many transcendent perfections, that they can scarce see themselves
      for Sunshine, such a prodigious glare of light is thrown about them. No
      Sir, I hope I have talked to you, in a plain easie and natural manner, in the

      _____

      4. This expression has been attributed to Heraclitus and other ancients.

same honest open Candid and pure Stile as I talk of his honor the President and his Longstanding members in the Subsequent History, It is true, I might, had I thought || fit, have Ennumerated your good qualities as an [vi] attorney General, profoundly versed in the *Corpus Juris Clubicalis,* might have Extolld your gravity, Depth of Judgement, eloquence, Elocution, Erudition, probity and undaunted perseverance, in doing the duties of Your great and honorable office, to this I *dares* to say you would have had no *Animosity,* and it would have done all very well, and perhaps a Couple of pages of this Stuff, tho *Judgematically* executed, might have lulled every reader (except you and I) asleep, for, it is to be supposed, that Self love, natural to us both, as creatures of the human Species, might have Counteracted the Hypnotic quality of the Stuff; But then Good Sir let me ask you Seriously, if I should not by this means have brought myself upon a *Precipe?* for would it have been fair dealing with the world to paint out all your excellencies and good qualities, in a Clubical Capacity, without also giving an Impartial Account, and putting you in mind of a few little foibles (I mean Clubical ones) which all who know you, allow you to be possessed of, and I am Confident, you know yourself so well, that you'll allow what I say to be true. In fine, should I have mentioned your good Qualities, without || glancing by the way at a few of your foibles, I should have made of you but [vii] a very Sorry picture, all light and no Shade, and Just in the ridiculous taste of our Dedication painters, who make such Tawdry things, such be-bugled, be-spangled and be-tinseled Images of their patrons, that they serve for nothing but the public to stare gape and laugh at; it stands to reason then, that if I do you and the public Strict Justice, I ought also at the end of the list of your accomplishments & perfections, to have summed up your failings, which to be Sure, you as a reasonable man, a Philosopher, and a Lawyer, can never deny you have, unless you would make yourself a monster in nature, which a Character absolutely perfect must absolutely be— But I think it is now high time to drop, both your perfections, and Imperfections here, and (after heartily wishing that you may still be Reforming and Improving every day in your life,) to subscribe myself, Learned Sir,

From my Study   Your most Humble Servant
Septr the 9th 1754   *The Author.*

[viii] The Preface

Nothing more Common in every man's mouth than That time is precious, and therefore ought to be well husbanded, and yet, precious as this time is, we meet with but few, who are nigh so careful about saving it, as about saving their money, since we see it often squandered away, in foolish, vapid, tasteless, foppish and Impertinent conversation, and, that even among such people, as have the Assurance to call themselves men of taste, we find it also lavished, in Silly unimproving and Childish diversions and amusements.—How many for Instance, sleep one half of their time and dream the other half? how many follow Chimerical and Romantic pursuits, and gallop full Speed after a Shifting Cloud, how many plod and plod on from day to day, and do nothing but build Castles in the Air, how many are Entertained with a tooth pick, a Shuttle cock and battle door,[1] a pair of dice, a Cup and ball, a game Cock, a pair of Cudgels and foiles, a Race horse, a fiddle, a bagpipe, a french horn, a ring of bells and a pack of Cards, [ix] for much the ‖ greatest part of their time, and triffle thro' a triffling life, in a promiscous multitude and medley of triffles,—But 'tis well we have these toys to amuse the great Babies of the Age, and keep them out of mischief, to which it is the nature of children to be prone,—These serve to keep our human puppies and kittens in play, for, were it not for these curious Inventions, very properly called time killers, they would, after running alittle round and Round in pursuit of their own tails, or perhaps the tails of others, drop asleep, for want of a proper Stock of Consistent Ideas, to employ the mind, which being a very busy and active principle, cannot be a moment without some Subject to work upon, for, should it ever be in this Idle Situation, it Immediatly drops its clog the body, for a space, and retires to the Inner chambers of the brain, hence, we find, all such Animals, as have not their Intellectual Chambers well furnished, pass a very large portion of their time in Sleep, this is a Sure Criterion, by which we may know to what degree of propinquity, the Rational approaches to the brutal nature, for all Philosophers have allowed the latter but a small Stock of Ideas, and these [x] very Simple, it was therefore highly ‖ expedient, that many bawbles and

---

1. A *battledore* is the racket used in badminton.

14

chip in porridge² amusements, should be Invented and Introduced, to keep at least three fourths, of what we presume to call the rational world awake, and the Remaining fourth out of mischief.

Some people, who may find time enough to throw away in reading of this, will undoubtedly exclaim, Well! and what the Deuce is the meaning of these grave observations? I'll tell them In short what they mean; Many, I am satisfied, will either be mightily astonished, or pretend to be so, that any Mortal Wight, could waste, as they Call it, so much precious time, besides paper and ink, in compiling and Collecting, the History of, (as it may seem to them) a Ridiculous Club, whose chief pastime (they'll say) appears from the face of the History it self, and from the Grotesque Stile of its Idle Author, to have been the carrying on, a Silly, Stupid and unmeaning farce. Very well, my good friends, what if I should grant you all this, since you are pleased to assert it, the Subject of this History is a farce, and a very Silly one too, since you will needs have it so, I will not Indeed so easily grant you that it is an unmeaning one, since it bears an exact resemblance to many ‖ other farces in human life, esteemed (tho they are not really so) of a more   [xi] Serious nature, I will grant you too, that I the Compiler, am more Silly if possible in collecting the history of this arrant farce, than any of the members of that ridiculous and foolish Club, (as you esteem it,) in acting of it, and I have squandered a deal of precious time, Ink and paper, besides fire and Candle, in the Compiling of it, *Iamque opus exegi nugosum, oleumq₃ perdidi,*³ Now, when all this is granted, Let us examine how I, the Compiler, of this here farcical history, differ from other men, with regard to the Importance and utility of my painful Labors to others and myself, and, how this, as a history, differs from other Histories, with regard to its Subject and Contents.

If I have laid out much time in writing of these triffles, as you call them, pray, have not you and many others as wise as either you or I, that is, in their own Conceit, laid out an equivalent of time, upon equivalent, if not greater triffles, only with this difference, that this triffling Scribble of mine, required some thought and application, and your triffling Occupations require no thought at all, at least none worthy of a rational being, for the very pursuit of them is directly repugnant to thought and reflec- ‖ tion, and   [xa] proceeds originally from a privation of both. Have I not been poring reading studying and turning over Ancient Authors, and modern wits, in the composition of this History, to the great Solace and Improvement of my

2. A *chip in porridge* is a matter of no importance; here, trivial amusements.
3. "Now I have performed a trifling work, and wasted my oil."

Rational, Intellectual and Gelastic⁺ faculties, when you, and twenty other such Loggerheads as you, who pretend to call me to account for it, have been exercising the keenest acumen of your obtuse thoughts upon a game at whist, piquet, Cribbage, put or all fours,⁵ and stocking the *Sensorium Commune* with a rabble of black and Red Spots, called Spades, Clubs, harts and Diamonds, while you have been gazing and gaping at a Sign post, bawling at a boxing match or Cock pit, sotting in an alehouse or Tavern, over trite Sophisticated and Stupifying Conversation, and more Sophisticated and Stupifying liquor, while you have been nodding over a Silly news paper, funking abominable mundungus,⁶ scalding your guts with politic Coffee, or Listening to hawkers ballad, while you have been fumbling and tumbling a whore in a bagnio, gaping at Henlys Nonsense,⁷ or taking an afternoons nap, after having spent two hours more than what was necessary in beastly cramming, while you have been talking away the precious hours, about fiddlers, fools and farces, handing about the bumpers, drinking of [xia] bawdy ‖ toasts, and singing obscene Songs, while you have been reading of smutty books, and luscious ballads, triffling at a tea table, or playing the fool at a great man's levee, or, if you Employ any thought at all about these, your paltry amusements and pastimes, 'tis perhaps how to dress and deck out your mortal Clay, to entrap the Ladies, how to ensnare the virtue and Innocence of some Simple girl, how to erect a character upon the ruins of your neighbour's, how to live upon and get drunk at other peoples expence, how to tell a plausible lie to promote your own Interest, and how, for the same noble and generous view, to circumvent your neighbour, in a bargain, or in short any other Idle or vicious occupation, which requires a deal of low Cunning, but little thought. Now, I would Seriously ask you, which of us have been employed to the best purpose, you, in these triffling pastimes, and wicked and pernicious Schemes, which, upon a Strict examination, you'll find, Consume much the greatest part of your time, or I, in writing this (as you call it) Silly history; I believe upon a due Scrutiny I shall have the advantage of you, as my employment has been in it Self at least Indifferent and harmless, whereas yours must turn out to be prejudicial both to yourselves and others.

As to this History, it needs no apology, let it speak for it self, if it

4. *Gelastic,* meaning "risible," stems from the Greek "to laugh."

5. *Put* is a card game for two, three, or four players, resembling Nap, three cards being dealt to each player; *All Fours* is a card game for two players, and so named from the four particulars by which it is reckoned (High, Low, Jack, and Game).

6. *Funking abominable mundungus* means "smoking raunchy tobacco."

7. John Henley (1692–1756), or Orator Henley, contributed to the *Spectator* as "Dr. Quir" and published numerous works on oratory, theology, and grammar.

cannot plead its own Cause, it deserves no advocate, every trevat ought || to   [xii]
stand upon its own legs, and every tub upon its own bottom, if this History
has no bottom or legs to stand upon, e'en let it tumble down a gods name.

Histories are no farther Instructive, than as they display to us human
nature in a true picture, & as a picture is not compleat, without the Coloring and Shading, to fill up the design or outlines, so history is not compleat, without proper observations remarks and reflections, Interspersed or
Interlarded with the bare Narration of facts, which last I take to be the
Outlines or Sketch of the historical picture, and the other the Shading or
coloring, which raises and Emboldens it, and makes it more forceibly strike
the eye, the more then of these observations and remarks are disseminated
in a historical piece, the more Instructing it becomes to the understanding
of the reader, and Indeed, as to the bare narration of facts and occurrences,
there is really but a triffling difference between the histories of the smallest
Clubs, and those of the greatest Empires and kingdoms, we find in the
latter, a parcel of mortals, denominated Emperors, kings, potentates and
princes, contending and scrambling, about little parcels and portions of this
terrestrial ball, we find State politicians racking their Invention to bring
about Certain Schemes, and still, like a parcel of earth moles, Counter-
mining and undermining one another, we find generals, or rather licenced
banditti, leading forth great armies, pillaging & laying || waste vast coun-   [xiii]
tries, burning towns and cutting throats, and all to acquire for themselves
or masters, a certain perishing power, eminence and grandure, or Certain
Sonorous titles, we find grand and grave councils and Senats in deep Con-
sultation, about things that are as plain and Self evident, as that two and
two make four, and In fine we find the whole world in an uproar, about
certain matters in themselves, abstractedly of a very mean Consideration,
and of a perishing transitory Nature, can any thing worse be said of these
trivial Transactions, that are to be met with in Clubs, whose members being
men, (tho esteemed in a Lower rank in life) have the very same affections
and passions, with those mortals called the great, and go upon pursuits and
Schemes of a parallel and like Insignificant and ridiculous Nature, for the
bringing about purposes equally vain and transitory, tho under a different
Class and denomination.

If Histories of Nations and kingdoms then, are only capable to Instruct, in so far as they Justly point out the passions Incident to human
Nature, and their effects, and exhibit a general Character of Mankind, and,
in so far as they are Salted and Seasoned, with useful Remarks and observa-
tions, I hope the same may be allowed to the Histories of Clubs, || which   [xiv]
are composed of men, as well as greater Societies, I have done my utmost,

to Season the following history with such apposite observations and remarks, upon such Incidents, as were worth observing and remarking upon,
so, that I hope, my Readers, if any there be, may Gather some Instructions
from them, if so, my reward is Sufficient, but if none will be at the pains to
read these historical Collections, which may be the case for aught I know, I
am satisfied, and quite easy about the matter, they may, and will do, Just as
they please, nay, even should they apply these Labored papers, to wipe a
part wch decency forbids me to name, I shall not Care one single farthing,
and nevertheless, shall sleep as Sound as usual, Remembering that golden
Maxim of Epictetus, never to make myself, over Solicitous or uneasy, about
matters that are Intirely in the power of another, and altogether out of my
own reach or command.[8]

8. See Epictetus, *Moral Discourses,* bk. 1, chap. 1, "Of the Things Which Are, and of Those
Which Are Not, in Our Power."

The History of the Ancient and Honorable Tuesday Club

Book I

From the earliest ages, to the Transmigration of the Club
to America, and the foundation of the Red-house Club,
of Annapolis in Maryland.

Chapter I

Of History and Historians.

History has always been classed among the most useful and Instructive
writing. Hence Historians, among the numerous herd of writers, are deservedly honored and esteemed.

Various are the Subjects of History, The transactions of Empires, kingdoms, Republics and *Clubs,* yield an Inexhaustible fund of matter, not to
mention the atchievments of great men and Presidents, a Sort of History
Called Biography, in which many incidents relative to the public are Interwoven.

Yet notwithstanding this great variety of Subjects, and redundancy of [2]
matter, which the various Scenes around us afford for History, we find that
good Historians are very thinly sown; which I cannot account for in a more
plausible manner, than that the talents necessary to produce a good Historian, are so many and so great, that it is a rare thing to find one man
possessed of them all, or even a moderate portion of them. Some wanting
Judgement and Invention of their own, copy too Slavishly from others &
are not masters of a proper stile and expression, some confide too much in
common rumor, others are too strictly attached to what they call truth and
demonstration, some are only dry drivelling narraters of Incidents and facts,

and like Slovenly cooks neglect the proper and decent seasoning of apposite remarks and observations, others Indulge too great a Luxuriance of Stile, and stepping out of their rank, turn poets, some will be too Superstitious and credulous, others too Sceptical, and in fine the far greatest part, if not the whole herd, will have a wicked or rather Senseless byass to a party.

    I am not now to dwell upon Historical writings in the Stile of a panegyrist; That, as I apprehend, being not only foreign to my purpose, but a task for which I am by no means equal, tho honored at present, with [3] the office of Orator, to that ancient || and honorable Club, of which I am now to collect the history. I may perhaps be allowed, without vanity, some small talent in declaiming, in praise of Illustrious personages, as the Honorable Nasifer Jole Esqr, president of the aforesaid ancient and honorable Club, but to expatiate in praise of history, or any such extensive, and Complicated Subject, is beyond my province.

    As good eating and drinking serve to nourish the body, so good reading and study Invigorate the mind. Among the various viands, which are cooked in our Literary kitchens, where Learned authors are the Cooks, I take History to be a dish, when dressed clean and plain, of all others the most Substantial and nourishing, and can be compar'd to nothing so aptly as to a Sirloin of Good Roast beef, served up in it's own gravie, with a plain pudding, if you please, but without any addition of pickles, or adulterated and Sophisticated Sauces, which confound and spoil the natural relish of the meat, and rob it of its nutritive and Salutary Virtues, allow me here to compare the gravie and pudding to useful and Solid reflections, and the pickles and Sophisticated Sauces, to party Scurrilities, palpable falshoods, mean Subterfuges, and poetical bumbast or Impertinent fustian, relished only by vitiated palats.

    Histories founded upon truth, and wrote in a plain, easie and natural Stile, are Sirloins of beef plainly dressed, wholesome, hearty and nourishing [4] || to a robust and healthy Stomach, but those erected upon fiction, and stuffed with Bombast and fustian phrazes, are vapid, windy, unwholsom and adulterated with your damn'd sauces and pickles, fitted only for crazy and luxurious apetites, which require a Spur to excite them to a proper pitch, and are apt to breed worms, maggots and monstruous Crudities, in the brains and Intelects of such students as feed upon them. Such are Romances, novels, fairy tales, Love adventures, private, or Secret memoirs of Courts, and persons of Quality of both Sexes, and other such verbose trumpery, with which the french Artists have crouded our Libraries, as their Cooks have confounded our kitchens and loaded our tables, with Devilish

Ragoos, fricassies, anduilles, amulets, Solomongundies,[1] and the like. The first kind of Cookery breeds as many crudities in the Intellect of the readers, as the other does in the Stomachs and habits of the eaters.

The History which I am now about to present to your worships, is none of your vamped up Frenchified pieces of Cookery, it is a Solid and Serious performance, plain and homely, and withal true, every article thereof, being copied exactly from nature and the life, and yet, Simple and true as it is, I shall be bold to affirm, that it contains as great a variety, and as many Surprizing and unaccountable events, as any true history that ever yet appeared, and, the Characters of the eminent persons therein concerned, are so nicely ‖ touched, as to strike at first view, and excite in the mind of   [5] the Reader, the Idea of a well executed piece of painting, in it self so highly picturesque, as to force the attention and admiration of all that view it.

While I am penning these prologomena, to this most excellent history, my genius and parts, are not alittle furbished up, sharpened and exalted, by the delightful prospect, of procuring to myself thereby Immortal fame, and a lasting Character, to be transmitted to future ages, [a] and Indeed it gives me no small pleasure to reflect, that a thousand years hence, I shall share the same rank of honor, with Herodotus, Diodorus Siculus, and Halicarnasseus, Xenophon, Plutarch, Justin, Trogus, Polybius, Cæsar, Tacitus, Salust and Livy,[3] as also I shall stand in the same degree with Homer, Hesiod,

(a) Vide, *Life of Colley Cibber,* written by himself.[2]

1. *Andouilles* are hog's guts stuffed with other entrails, cut into small pieces, and seasoned with pepper and salt; *salmagundies* are composed of chopped meat, anchovies, eggs, onions, oil, and condiments.

2. Hamilton is probably alluding to the following remarks Cibber addresses to Alexander Pope: "You may ask me, why I give myself all this Trouble? Is it for Fame or Profit to myself, or Use or Delight to others? For all these Considerations I have neither Fondness nor Indifference" (*An Apology for the Life of Colley Cibber,* ed. B.R.S. Fone [Ann Arbor, Mich., 1968], 6–7).

3. Herodotus (ca. 480–ca. 425 B.C.) was the famous Greek historian known as the "Father of History." Diodorus Siculus was a Roman historian who flourished under Caesar and Augustus until at least 21 B.C. and wrote a world history in 40 books, from the beginnings of history to Caesar's Gallic War. Dionysius of Halicarnassus (fl. ca. 25 B.C.) was a Greek literary critic and historian who lived in Rome during Augustus's reign. Xenophon (ca. 427/428–ca. 354 B.C.) was the Greek philosopher and historian remembered as one of the most prolific writers of antiquity. Plutarch (before A.D. 50–after 120) was the Greek biographer and moral philosopher especially remembered for his *Lives* of 46 Greeks and Romans. Pompeius Trogus was the Augustan historian noted for a universal history, *Historiae philippicae,* coming down to us only in the abridgment of Marcus Junianus Justinus of the 3d century. Polybius (ca. 200–after 118 B.C.) was the Greek historian of the rise of Rome to world power. Tacitus (ca. A.D. 56–ca. 117) was the Roman historian best remembered for his *Germania,* a description of the Germanic peoples and their origins, *Agricola,* an account of the Roman conquest of Britain, and *Annals,* a review of the period from the death of Augustus to the death of Nero. Sallust (probably 86–

Pindar, Æschylus, Virgil and other ancient poets, there being in this work, abundance of poetical flowers, and noble flights, which by the bye, I must honestly own, to be Sprouts of the Luxuriant Genius of Jonathan Grog Esqr, poet Laureat to that ancient and honorable Club, of which I now Collect the History. These great, these Invaluable advantages, I shall Enjoy, as being Historiographer, to the most Honorable Mr President Jole, some degrees I hope, above those celebrated authors, who have penned the His-

[6] tories of *Tom Thumb, Jack and the Gyants* & || *the wise men of Gotham,*[4] and a hundred degrees above our moderen french Romance compilers, to read whose works, is enough to give any Christian the Spleen, such as the Authors of the *Grand Cyrus, Clelia, Almahyde, Amadis de Gaul, Amadis de Grece, Don Bellianis, Cassandra, Cleopatra*[5] and a hundred other such volu-minous writers, to whom not (to say) only the Tobacconists and spice Shops, but even the Houses of office, have been of late years so Infinitely Indebted, who, had they not been supplied from these vast piles of waste paper, would have been at a Sad loss how to wrap up their grocery and haberdashery, and besides, many honest well meaning Christians, must have run the risque of befowling their fingers, in using the tender leaves of vegetables, which are not of so tough a nature, as that same other Historical Stuff is, besides the risque they must have run, of getting that most griev-ous distemper called the piles, by means of the Corrosive down that often abounds upon the leaves of the said vegetables, which like so much low

---

35 B.C.) was the Roman senator and historian especially remembered for his history of the conspiracy of Catiline. Livy (59 B.C.–A.D. 17) was the Roman historian whose massive history of Rome ranges from the foundation of the city to the death of Drusus in 9 B.C.

4. Although Hamilton was surely aware of Henry Fielding's burlesque play, *Tom Thumb, a Tragedy* (1730), the context here suggests that he is referring to the famous nursery tale. *Jack the Giant-killer* is another famous nursery tale. By "the wise men of Gotham" Hamilton is proba-bly referring to the *Merrie Tales of the Mad Men of Gotam by A. B.* (possibly Andrew Boorde [ca. 1490–1549], a physician). This collection of tales concerns Gotham, a village in Notting-hamshire, whose inhabitants acquired a reputation for folly, perhaps as a result of an actual incident in which they feigned idiocy to prevent King John's displeasure.

5. The first three titles were written by Madeleine de Scudéry (1607–1701), prolific author of French romances. *Artamène; ou, Le grand Cyrus* (1649–1653) deals with the love of Cyrus, grandson to the king of Media, for Mandane; *Clélie* (1654–1660) concerns the Clelia who escaped the power of Porsenna by swimming the Tiber; and *Almahide* (1660) is a story of the Moors in Spain. For *Amadis de Gaula,* see p. iin, above; *Amadís de Grecia* (1530), by Feliciano da Silva (fl. 16th century), is a Spanish sequel to *Amadís de Gaula;* and *Don Bellianis* (which Hamilton later refers to as Don Bellianis of Greece) is probably a reference to *The Honour of Chivalrie* (1598), the story of Prince Don Bellianis and his love for the Princess Florisbella. *Cassandre* and *Cléopâtre* were written by Gauthier de Costes de La Calprenède (1614–1663), French author of several lengthy romances. *Cassandre* (1644–1650) concerns the daughter of Darius and wife of Alexander; *Cléopâtre* (1647–1656) involves a supposed daughter of Antony's Cleopatra.

Itch, would vellicate in a dreadful manner, the Tender plicæ of the Rectum, where it terminates in the anus; and here I shall terminate this Chapter, lest I vellicate the ears of my reader by talking too much in my own praise.

Chapter II   [7]

Of Antiquity, It's dignity and Importance.

Among other things of great value and Significancy, to which my bretheren Historians, by general Consent have given the preference, as communicating a Certain lusture and Dignity, to Nations, persons and things, to which they are accidentally annexed, that of Antiquity holds the foremost Rank.

From this position, which certainly no man in his senses will presume to deny, may be clearly prov'd, the Dignity, grandure, worth and excellency of that Club, of which I now Compile the History, since it can be made evident, by authentic Records, that it is as ancient as Time itself.

Wealth, a royal or noble birth, offices of honor, titles and dignities, in all polite Societies have a Certain fixed value, and may be called excellencies of the first Class; Honesty, truth, Candor, Charity, Humanity, Piety, and such other Scholastic terms, which your Venders of Ethics call moral virtues, are of a fluctuating nature, having sometimes a modicum of worth, at other times no worth at all Annexed to them, according as they tally or Correspond with the prevailing modes of the times in ‖ which they make [8] their appearance, these are of the Second Class, their Intrinsic worth being very hard to be ascertained by our polite moderen Connoiseurs.

But still at all times and in all Circumstances, Antiquity Carries with it a certain value, and takes place of every thing else, being an Inestimable prize, for which Historians in all ages have eagerly contended, each aledging and mantaining that his own Nation has the Justest claim to it. Among the Ancients, the Ægyptians and Scithians Contended long for the precedence in point of Antiquity, and I cannot find that the Dispute was ever determined in favor of either party; the Chief moderen disputants on this point, are the Irish, British and Spaniards of Old Castile, Aragon and Leon, but the Chinese Chronology, lately struck in, and outdid them all,[1]

---

1. Travel accounts of China were plentiful in the latter 17th and early 18th centuries, but the one that most thoroughly discusses Chinese chronology is Gabriel de Magaillans, *A New*

the first confining themselves to the narrow Compass of the Mosaic history, the last restricting themselves to no Compass at all.

Now, since it is generally agreed, that antiquity Carries with it a certain dignity and excellence, it will be worth while to enquire

I   Upon what this Dignity and excellence is founded, and

II   To consider, whether or not there be some exceptions to this general rule, that antiquity Carries honor and Dignity along with it. That is, if [9] there are not some || beings in nature both of the animate and Inanimate Class, that are rather depreciated by their antiquity, and therefore neglected scorned and undervalued.

I   As to our first enquiry, upon what the merit and Dignity of Antiquity is founded, we may say, that antiquity claims, or rather exacts respect, on account of its hoary and venerable aspect. Ancient Nations, Clubs and families are respectable, because they could not thro' so many centuries have mantained an uninterrupted Succession, from father to Son, from president to president, and from Generation to generation, unless they possessed in themselves some Glaring excellencies by which they outshone and at last eclipsed other Nations Clubs and families, or were concerned in some great and heroic actions, which spread their name abroad, and handed down their glory to Succeeding ages. But let us examine alittle of what nature these actions were, upon which this merit was founded. We find many ancient nations, supporting and aggrandizing themselves, by the bold and valorous actions of their Heroes and warlike Spirits, these Illustrious Banditti, used to range the face of this globe without controul, plundering, knocking on the head, burning, hewing to pieces and extirpating, the helpless and forlorn of their own Species, what Glory, what renown, was not acquired by our Cyruses, Alexanders, Cæsars, Pompeys, Scipios, [10] Annibals, || Tameralanes, Osman's, Solyman's[2] and a hundred others, who made it their constant practice to scour the earth, Sword in hand, to acquire

---

History of China, Containing a Description of the Most Considerable Particulars of That Vast Empire (London, 1688); see especially chap. 3, "Of the Antiquity of the Kingdom of China, and What a High Opinion the Chineses Have of It." Hamilton is perhaps recalling this account, which establishes the precedence of Chinese antiquity, but he is apparently directly referring to a more contemporary account that I have not located.

2. Cyrus the Great (ca. 600–529 B.C.) was the founder of the Persian empire. Scipio Africanus (236–184/183 B.C.) was a great Roman general who helped establish Rome's domination in Spain, Africa, and the Hellenistic East. Hannibal (247–183 B.C.) was the great Carthaginian general. Tamerlane, or Timur-Leng ("Timur the Lame"), ca. 1336–1405, the famous descendant of Genghis Khan, ruled by terror and desolation over parts of Turkestan, Siberia, Persia, and India. Osman I (1259–1326), the founder of the Ottoman Empire, conquered northwestern Asia Minor and assumed the title of emir (ca. 1299). Suleiman I, the Magnificent (1494–1566), was a Turkish ruler who reformed the administration of his country and added Belgrade, Budapest, Baghdad, Algiers, and other territories to his empire.

to themselves glory, and to found great Empires and states, on the Ruins, calamities and distresses of little petty kingdoms, which Empires and states in time, became very ancient, and therefore very honorable and venerable. We find few or none of these great states and Empires, laying the foundation of their fame and honor, upon the aforesaid stale props called the moral virtues, Some small Inconsiderable States indeed, we find setting a Value upon these, the Spartan common wealth rested for a few Centuries upon such weak Supports, bequeathed, and as it were palm'd upon them by an old doating Lawgiver called Licurgus,³ but finding that by the virtue of these wise Laws, as some called them, they could not subdue Greece and were at the same time forced to resist the temptation of amassing riches by hostile Spoils, they violated their Sanguinary Law against such as should possess gold or Silver money, and finding they could follow this Laudable practice with Impunity, the old foolish regulations were kick'd out of doors, their little political fabric fell to the ground, and having changed their ponderous and Cumbersome Iron money, for precious Gold and Silver, they at the same time bartered their temperance for excess, their Integrity and Simplicity for cunning and fraud, Their Justice for oppression and Iniquity, their plainness and humility for Luxury and pride, and by these laudable pursuits, became at last Ill- ‖ ustrious slaves to Philip of Macedon, [11] and his mad-cap Son Alexander, called the Great, and Succeeding Eminent Tyrants; The same fate had the Athenian State, the same had the Roman Republic; They all found these supports too weak, and therefore had recourse to more Certain ways, and means, such as cutting of throats, burning, plundering, slaying, masacring and extirpating whole Nations, proscribing their own Citizens, and killing them up, like Sheep in a pen, by hundreds and by thousands, whereby the Strongest was at last Sure of engrossing all the power to themselves, amassing great treasure, and from this opulence sprung their permanency, Grandure, power and honor.

As for Clubs, the honor which they derive from Antiquity, evidently arises from this; that their Constitution and oeconomy must be founded upon very Solid and Sound maxims, rules and Laws, by which only they have preserved their being thro' a long tract of time, and enjoyed an uninterrupted Succession of presidents, a glaring Instance of which, I hope, soon to make appear, in the course of this our History. As for that ancient and honorable Club, the Free and Accepted Masons,⁴ many are of opinion,

---

3. Lycurgus was the traditional founder (probably fl. 9th century B.C.) of Sparta's constitution and social and military systems, and consequently of the "good order" they created.

4. Hamilton was Grand Master of the Annapolis Freemasons, and other club members also belonged. Many of his apparent jibes at the Freemasons throughout the *History* are obviously more affectionate than malicious. For a discussion of Hamilton's use of Freemasonry in the

(who perhaps know nothing of the matter) that, the main Excellence of their Constitution, and principal Cause of their Antiquity rests on their admirable Talent at keeping a Secret.

[12]   Now, permit me a word or two relating to the honor conveyd to families by antiquity. We find the || scots, welsh, Irish and Spaniards, the most noted people for antiquity of families, and every one knows, who has read their Histories, that they were anciently divided into families and Clans, and over each Clan, there reigned an absolute petty prince, called the Chief of the Clan, poor enough in every thing but honor & Ancient pedigree, who was by trade a Butcher, and his Subjects or vassals, might properly be called his bull dogs, (I must here be understood metaphorically, for those princes had too much honor and Noble blood in them, to apply their thoughts or diligence, to any low mechanic Craft) these warlike Clans, used to pelt one another continually, and every butcher, and every bull dog, had a greater or smaller proportion of honor, according to the numbers he had worried or butchered. Those families then, that escaped total extirpation, during this general hurly-burly, stood the most ancient in the heralds list, and, as their antiquity exhibited a glaring proof of their Superior Valor, and military Skill, it must necessarily follow, that as they centered all honor, in this Sort of butchering trade, These surviving ancient families were with great reason esteemed the most honorable, hence, we find, in these our degenerate days, that the great Representatives of these ancient families,

[13]   always take the right hand, the door the wall || and the road, of our upstarts of a Later date, tho' loaded with more dignified titles, and hence, we find, that these honorable people the Spaniards, are to this day so fond of Bull fighting and assasinating, the British of Bull and bear baiting, Stage and Cock fighting, and the Irish of your great overgrown bulls. Duelling is indeed a more polite and Gentleman like manner of Butchering, Introduced by our Beaus and petti maitres of the last Century.

    II   As for exceptions to this general rule, which is the Second part of this enquiry, they shall be cleared up as I go along.

    If these above delivered, be not the true reasons why antiquity, has given precedence to Nations, Cities, tribes, families and Clubs, I must own, I can give no better to satisfy those who may question their validity; this reason only I have still in reserve, which they may accept or reject as they please, vizt: that they are of greater antiquity than others, and therefore are Justly entituled to the preference.

History, see Robert Micklus, "The Secret Fall of Freemasonry in Dr. Alexander Hamilton's *The History of the Tuesday Club,*" in *Deism, Masonry, and the Enlightenment: Essays Honoring Alfred Owen Aldridge,* ed. J. A. Leo Lemay (Newark, Del., 1987), 127–136.

The City of Jerusalem, which we may reckon the most ancient city now in being, (as Babylon is no more) unless we admit the monstrous Chronology of the Chinese, is not only venerable for its antiquity, but is to be reckoned in the foremost rank, as being a holy City, which sets it in a point of view above all others, for holy || things as well as holy men, (I mean men [14] of the holy Cloth) are always to have the preference, else whence comes it that Churches and Chapels are made Sanctuaries for knaves and Villains and assasins, but because they are Sacred Ædifices and the ground on which they stand is holy, in the same manner we find that his holiness the pope, is exalted one or two degrees above human nature, nay often equaled to Almighty God, and takes place of all Catholic princes on Earth, and even in England, a reformed Country, his grace the Archbishop of Canterbury, tho' he gives place to the king out of mere Civility, yet takes the Right hand and precedence of all the peers in England—Therefore it is, that Jerusalem, an ancient holy City, has cost such Seas of Christian and Infidel blood, for as to wealth, magnificence or extent, it is not to be named among Cities of the fifth or Sixth Class. The Epithet holy adds a Character and lustre to many things as well as to Cities; but how Cities, Stone walls, bricks, planks, or any other kind of dead matter, can with any propriety be stiled holy, is not my business to enquire, I leave that therefore to our Learned Divines.

The City of Athens, which retains it's name & pritty nigh its ancient place to this day, is now notwithstanding its great antiquity, sunk into obscurity, and is of no note or character, being Inhabited by a parcel of Servile drudges, and Ignorant peasants, Infinitely || short of the Spirit, [15] learning and valor of its ancient Inhabitants.

The City of Rome, of old, the mistress of the world, Tho it was founded by a parcel of Banditti, and Inhabited by the valiant cutthroats of all the nations round her, yet, is venerable, and honorable, on account of her antiquity, and is now also classed among the holy Cities, as being the Residence of our holy father the Pope, and many other holy prelates and priests, who enjoy great wealth in a spiritual capacity, who share the patrimony of the poor fisherman among them, who understand good living perfectly well, and how to carry on their Spiritual merchandize, and bring it to the best market, as to their knowledge and abilities in other matters, belonging to their holy function, it is none of my business here to dwell upon them, being Intirely foreign to my Subject.

Many nations have laid a great Stress upon their antiquity, and reckoned it a badge of honour, there are none of our Nations now on the European Continent Southward of Lapland and Greenland, or in the Greatest part of Asia westward of mount Taurus or Imaus, That can lay

claim to antiquity any farther back, than the Incursions of the Goths, Van-
dals, Tartars, Huns, Lombards and Sarazens into these countries, Greece
[16] and Italy are now Inhabited by a mungrell people Intirely || differing in
language and manners, from their ancient Inhabitants, heroes and worthies,
as consisting now chiefly of Slaves, peasants, Dervises, Fiddlers, rope dancers, pantomimes, Singers and Idle overgrown loitering priests, much the
same may be said of Germany, France and Spain, &ct: The Islanders to the
westward, or the Irish, Scots highlanders and Welsh, are those who have the
best claim for Antiquity among the Europeans, and they picque themselves
much on their antiquity, and the great honor and dignity they derive there-
from, and Surely it is a very honorable thing and what they have great
reason to be proud of; But the Irish excell all in their Chronology, for, it
appears from their Authors, transcribed faithfully, by that accurate and
Learned Historian, Doctor Keating, that a colony settled in that ancient
Island, long before the General Deluge, for two of Cains Daughters landed
there, of whom a certain Irish poet of great Credit and authority sings
thus.[5]

> Tri hingiona Chaid hin Chain mar aon
>   is Seth Mac Adhaimh,
> Ad chonaire Banba ar uus as
>   Meabhair liom aniom thus.

> The two fair Daughters of the Cursed Cain
> And Seth the Son of Adam first beheld
> The Isle of Banba.(*)   (*)Ireland

[17]   Some other Antidiluvian Settlers in that ancient Island, it is said, had
the luck to escape that great calamity of the General Deluge, which is most
wonderful, and can be accounted for no other way than thus; as that Island
has been called, time out of mind, the Island of Saints, probably these were
such Saints as could by their Sanctity save that Island from the general
disaster, as a few Saints, according to holy writ, could have saved the Cities
of Sodom and Gomorrah, from being consumed by fire, however, I believe
none, but the aforesaid Authors of the Ingenious Doctor Keating, and the

---

5. Geoffrey Keating (1570?–1644?) was an Irish writer and priest whose most important work
was a history of Ireland from the earliest times to the English invasion, *Foras feasa ar Eirinn*
(Foundation of knowledge on Ireland [1629]), which was written in the Irish language and
borrowed heavily from popular Irish folklore and poetry. Hamilton loosely transcribes and
translates Keating's Gaelic, which more literally means: "Three virgin daughters of Cain, /
With Seth, son of Adam, / They first saw Banbha, / I remember their adventure" (*The History
of Ireland,* ed. David Comyn [London, 1902–1914], I, 138–139).

learned Composers of that Authentic and Canonical Record, the *Psalter of Cashel,* [a] ever Imagined, that any human Creature but Noe and his small family, weathered that disaster, notwithstanding the great learning, veracity, and Consistency of these Irish Poets and Historians, I am humbly of opinion, that the Indian natives of America, and the Æthiopians of Afric, tho not quite so civilized and learned a people as the ancient Irish, nor such great Saints, bid the fairest for being the most ancient and unmixed people now in the known world, and therefore have on that Score the Justest claim to honor & precedence.

It is well known, that families at all times have picqued themselves much upon their antiquity and || on that score alone have taken precedence [18] of others, in many respects not a whit Inferior to them, the Macdonalds of Scotland, are now accounted the most ancient family there, and for that reason alone are to be honored and esteemed, by all true Scotsmen and lovers of their Country.

Having thus considered the merit which those of the human Species derive from antiquity, I think it proper now to bestow a word or two upon the brute creation, who have been much valued upon this very account, we are Informed by many Authors, and among others, the Abbe le Boe, that Horses are much more valued among the Arabians, for their being of an ancient Stock or family than for many other qualities, whether it be their being adapted for the Chace, course, battle, Saddle or draught,[7] we have an account somewhere (I forget where) of certain very ancient Mares, that were Impregnated by the westerly wind, and brought forth Colts, remarkable for their Swiftness,[8] this ancient Stock was highly valued, and, let me remark by the bye, that if our women were to be so Impregnated, that is, by

(a) An old foolish legend, on which some Irish historians lay great Stress.[6]

6. In his history of Ireland, Keating often refers to this ancient compilation of historical, genealogical, and legal subjects, traditionally ascribed to Cormac mac Cuilenan, who died at the beginning of the 10th century; the work supposedly was lost or was carried off by the Danes (see *History of Ireland,* ed. Comyn, IV, 422; *The History of Ireland,* trans. John O'Mahony [New York, 1857], lxxiv, n. 3).

7. Jean-Baptiste (Abbé) Dubos (1670–1742) was a French historian and the author of the *Histoire critique de l'établissement de la monarchie française* (Paris, 1734) and *Réflexions critiques sur la poésie et sur la peinture* (Paris, 1719–1733), which argues that poetry can be judged only by the emotions it produces, not by fixed rules and principles. For Dubos's remarks concerning Arabians and their horses, see *Critical Reflections on Poetry, Painting, and Music,* trans. Thomas Nugent (London, 1748), II, 396–399.

8. According to Homer, Achilles' horses, Xanthus and Balius, were the offspring of Zephyrus (the west wind) and Podargé (one of the Harpies); Homer also mentions other divine horses, bred by the north wind on mortal mares grazing in the meadows before Troy (*Iliad,* bks. 16 and 20).

the westerly wind, or any other wind you please, we should not only have a glorious breed, of gay, airy volatile fellows, and most accomplished beaus [19] and belles, but we should find few of the fair Sex, willing to run ‖ the risque of the thraldom of matrimony, where it is Commonly reported, the Husband Carries the Sway, and rules the roast, tho' I believe in many cases, it happens Just the reverse.

There is a relation given by a Certain Arabian writer, of a horse, that belonged to one Ibrahim, an Arab, whose genealogy was traced all the way back to the Removal of Abraham and his family to Canaan,[9] having sprung in a direct line, from a Sprightly Courser in that Caravan, but, as to the qualities of this horse, good or bad, nothing is said, therefore it will now be a hard matter to determin, whether he was the better or worse as to his morals, by reason of the great antiquity of his family, and I shall not dip into this Inquiry, since my Arabian Author is Intirely silent upon that point.

The above named Abbe le Boe, tells us of a horse of the same Illustrious family, whose lineal Genealogy was traced by authentic records, for at least 500 years back.[10]

Much might be said of the antiquity of the families of monkeys, parrots, cats, dogs, hawks, and other tameable and domestic animals, but this I shall wave, having no purpose or design to swell these my observations into a bulky Volume, but only to mention Just as much as may serve my purpose, in these matters, tho' by the bye, if any of the posterity of Tobit's Dog, [20] ‖ whose proper name has not been transmitted to us by His historiographers, or Ulysses's Dog, mentioned In the *Odyssy*,[11] could be found at this day, these two canine families would be very Ancient, and Indeed, when the honor and dignity of a family, flows from nothing else but it's antiquity, I, for my part, cannot see, why the families of Dogs, and even mites and maggots in Cheese (could records of them be handed down) might not with equal Justice claim honor on that Score, as the families of Certain rational Animals called Men.

As to Inanimate beings, it is well known, what a value they receive from their antiquity, the rust of an ancient medal, the mold of an old Stone, the powder of an old worm eaten post, are often much more valued, than

9. Ibrahim Pasha (fl. 16th century) was grand vizier of Turkey and a favorite of Suleiman the Magnificent, but I have not located an account of this allusion to his horse. It seems reasonable to assume, however, that Hamilton has not invented the story, since some of the most famous thoroughbreds have been named Ibrahim.

10. *Critical Reflections on Poetry, Painting, and Music*, II, 398.

11. A dog accompanies Tobias, the son of Tobit, and the angel Raphael on their journey to Ecbatana, narrated in the book of Tobit in the Apocrypha; Ulysses' dog, Argos, is mentioned with honor in the *Odyssey*, bk. 17.

ten thousand times their weight in diamonds and Gold dust, a Statue of Praxateles, a Scetch or design of Apelles, Zeuxis or Protogenes, a piece of engraving of Tubal Cain, a musical Composition of Jubal's,[12] will at any time bring an estate to the happy possessor, and pour in heaps of that Earthly Mammon, so much Coveted by Men in owr times, since by this, great honors, and all the favorite Luxuries and delecacies of life are procured, and not only so, but the man who has the good fortune to possess a *quantum Sufficit* of it, need never puzzle his brains to procure a character, by ap- || plying himself to the practice of any single virtue, or species of [21] Industry, for this lucky circumstance alone, without the aid of qualifications mental or corporeal, will make him seemingly esteemed, respected, and really followed, flattered, caressed, and often couzened, by multitudes of his good friends, and hangers on, who get the Scent of his golden piles; Tho a Villain, he will be Called an honest and an honorable Gentleman; tho' Graceless they'll say *please your grace,* tho a blockhead and Illiterate, he'll be made to believe he is a profound Scholar, and dub'd a patron or Mecenas to the Muses, tho' ugly he will be an Adonis, and all his faults and deformities will be patterns for Imitation; In fine tho' he may deserve the gallows, he will be as safe from that quarter, as if he had the Innocence of a Lamb, while poor rogues must hang and be Damn'd for want of that same precious metal, to salve their knavery and Crimes withal, but to evade digressions and come to the point.

  We come now to old rotten rags, worm eaten Chips and pieces of wood, rusty nails, Jaw bones and Shank bones, perhaps honeycombed by the pox, teeth, beards, whiskers, parings of nails, Smoak tails[13] and the like, which, when once they have procured the character of having once been part || of the aparrel or body of some ancient Saint or Anchorite, Im- [22] mediatly have a Superlative virtue and veneration annexed to them, have the power of working miracles, that is, of curing Incurable distempers, and even raising the dead to life, and (which is the most essential quality they possess, without which, all the rest would be good for nothing) they can

---

12. Praxiteles (fl. 4th century B.C.) was an Athenian sculptor noted for his ability to depict various types of emotion. Apelles (fl. 4th century B.C.) was a famous Greek painter whose portraits included Philip, Alexander, and their circle. Zeuxis (fl. early 5th century B.C.), the Greek painter best remembered for his portrait of Helen of Troy, was said to have died laughing at his painting of an old woman. Protogenes (fl. late 4th century B.C.) was a Greek painter and sculptor whose works are characterized by their excessive elaboration. Tubal-Cain was the son of Lamech and Zillah and the "instructor of every artificer in brass and iron" (Gen. 4:22). Jubal was the son of Lamech and Adah and the "father of all such as handle the harp and organ" (Gen. 4:19–21).

13. A *smock tail* is a woman's undergarment, shift, or chemise.

convey wealth into the treasury of Holy Church, and supply Sufficient means to mantain and support a great number of holy pamper'd priests and prelates, who take infinite pains for the Salvation of Souls, and while they Indulge in plenty, ease and Luxury (for they follow no hard labor, or any Sort of Craft or trade, by which the community might be enriched, it being expressly contrary to the wise rules of their respective orders, and Incompatible with that pious and devout life, to which they dedicate themselves, the Community being obliged to enrich them) they, out of pious fatherly love and Charity to their poor, needy, close shorn and Starving flock, put themselves in the Station of Drones in a hive, and while they devour the best honey, and the fruits of the painful labor of others, lead a lazy loitering life, for the good and Salvation of Souls, Charitably exposing themselves to [23] damnation & perdition, like the Epicure, who enjoyed all || his good things in this life, and had his portion of bad things in the next, can any thing be more brotherly and charitable than this, and all is brought about by the virtue of these antiquated rags, and lumber & other such venerable trumpery, which a man to look at, would think worthy of nothing but the dunghill, but having once heard their virtues explained, must be rapt in admiration at the wonderful power of antiquity.

Things animate and Inanimate, that derive no manner of merit from their antiquity, are Superannuated men and women, monkeys, Cats, and such like animals, who, the more ancient they grow, are looked upon with greater contempt, nay, sometimes with hatred and abhorrence, how many deplorable Instances have we in history of old cats, old women, and old men, being looked upon as Infernal witches and Wizards, and familiars of Satan, and have therefore deservedly been delivered up to temporal tormentors, and exalted on Gibbets, drowned in water, and Consumed by raging fire.

As for Inanimate things that bear the Stamp of antiquity, an old Coat, wig, cap, Shoes, provided they do not exceed the compass of a century or [24] two, or have never belonged to any pious Saint or eminent || Hero, they are so far from possessing any merit on account of their antiquity, that they are reckoned absolutely Infamous, and convey Shame and Contempt to their wearers and owners.

Why this should be, and for what reasons, will require more learning and Philosophy, than I am master of to determin, and therefore, I think it best to say nothing at all on the Subject, but leave it to abler pens.

I should now proceed to speak of the antiquity of Clubs, having, like the most Reverend, most learned, and most Ingenious Doctor Warburton, in his *Divine Legation* and other writings,[14] thro' an Infinity of windings, turnings and perplexed arguments, and a great and pompuous display of historical and critical Learning, come within Sight of my point at last, but this being a copious subject, I reserve it for another Chapter, as the above named Reverend and Learned Author, has reserved the conclusion of his great and ponderous argument, for another volume or volumes, which, pray God, may come out sometime or other, to the Confusion of all Deists and freethinkers, as bulky voluminous, and verbose as the former, else we shall be most woefully left in the lurch.

## Chapter III			[25]

Of Clubs in general, and their Antiquity.

By *Clubs* I mean those societies, which generally meet of an evening, either at some taveren or private house, to converse, or look at one another, smoke a pipe, drink a toast, be politic or dull, lively or frolicksome, to philosophize or triffle, argue or debate, talk over Religion, News, Scandal or bawdy, or spend the time in any other Sort of Clubical amusement. Out of this definition I expressly exclude, all your card matches and meetings, those properly belonging to the celebrated moderen assemblies called Routs and Drums,[1] which are many degrees Inferior to Clubs, as being less ancient.

It has been observed by some ancient philosophers, particularly one Sir Isaac Newton, that there exists a certain affection or fellow feeling, between all bodies in nature, by which they have a strong tendency, to approach, one towards another, to Join, and even to Incorporate, and that a perfect antipathy is never, a partial one seldom to be met with;[2] This has been called by

14. William Warburton (1698–1779), bishop of Gloucester, frequently engaged in theological controversy. His writings include *The Divine Legation of Moses Demonstrated* (London, 1738–1741), which argues that Moses' divine mission is implied by the very absence in Mosaic law of any reference to future life.

1. A *rout* is a fashionable gathering or assembly, evening party or reception, much in vogue in the 18th century; a *drum* is also an assembly, especially of fashionable people at a private house.

2. The analogy between the attractive power of gravitation, which governs the behavior of physical bodies, and the attractive power of love and sociability generally, which governs human conduct, was frequently drawn in the 18th century (see, e.g., George Berkeley's essay in the *Guardian*, no. 126, Aug. 5, 1713). The roots of the idea antedate Isaac Newton's discovery of

these Philosophers, the power of attraction, which we find prevails and governs very much, among men and other Animals, and occasions that great propensity in human nature, to unite and form into Clubs.

[26]   In these Clubs, formed thus, by one Individual attracting another, we find that the several members are apt to ‖ communicate to each other, their own faculties and dispositions, their own sentiments and particular turn of thought, whether this is done by the perpetual flying off of thin Surfaces from one member to another, as the old philosophers used to account for vision,[3] before the discovery of optics, or, by the communication of some Imperceptible Sympathetic qualities, to speak in the clear Style of the Schools, I cannot take upon me to resolve, this being a more Intricate and difficult enquiry than perhaps most men may Imagine; I am only certain that the fact is so, that there is a particular Sympathetic Social quality in Mankind, that makes them fond of Clubbing, whether they be adapted for conversation or not; this may be undeniably proved, from the example of many moderen Clubs, which have consisted of members, who had little or no turn or talent for that Sort of conversation, that is carried on by Language or speech, or, at least, if they used Speech, it was to no better purpose, than one that says *Bo to a goose,* their whole dialogue consisting in, you've baulk'd your glass—you drink kelty[4]—put about the bowl—fill tother pipe—here's to you—pledge you—and such like short Sentences.

Is it not probable then, that the whole and Sole pleasure of such humdrum Clubs, consists in barely looking at one another, in successively kissing the Glass or bowl, or benevolently Intermixing the Smoke of one

the laws of universal gravitation, but certainly Newtonianism underlay much of the 18th-century commentary on the subject. If Hamilton is indeed making a specific reference to Newton, he could be recalling the passage that concludes Newton's *Principia* (1687), where Newton remarks that there is "a certain most subtle spirit which pervades . . . all gross bodies; by the force and action of which spirit the particles of bodies attract one another . . . and cohere" (*Sir Isaac Newton's Mathematical Principles,* trans. Florian Cajori [Berkeley, Calif., 1946], 547).

3. The "old philosophers" are Democritus and all the Atomists. The prevailing Scholastic view before the 18th century had been that visual perception occurred as a result of the transmission of minute bodies from the object to the eye. Aside from theories of idealism, like the Platonic, this was the only kind of explanation of sense knowledge before the understanding arose that the reflection of light was the necessary medium of vision. A good discussion of this topic is Gordon Keith Chalmers, "Effluvia, the History of a Metaphor," Modern Language Association, *Publications,* LII (1937), 1031–1050. According to Chalmers, by the 17th century the Atomists' notion of effluvia had become useful not only as an explanation of sense perception but also, as Hamilton humorously applies it in the following paragraph, "as an explanation of any action without apparent corporeal contact" (p. 1034).

4. *Bo to a goose* is a proverbial saying meaning "opening one's mouth," or, in this context, "babbling"; *kelty* is a term denoting the complete draining of a glass of liquor.

pipe, with that of another, to account for this Strange, tho' true Circumstance, let us suppose, that there is some very Subtile Effluvium, or Aura, that goes from one member to another, and Communicates a titulation or pleasure to the nerves, by || setting the animal Spirits in a sort of undulatory [27] motion, which has puzzled our Physiologists so much to account for; If any body should object to this my hypothesis, let them consider, that here I follow the example of the learned and Ingenious Doctor Cheyne, in his Elaborate treatise of health and long life,[5]—it is to be hoped tho' that the late Ingenious experiments on electricity, will give some light into this dark phênomenon, and confirm this my new hypothesis.[6]

To this Invisible aura, perhaps it may be owing, that the Quakers, and those that are gifted with the Inward Spirit, feel the most violent emotions of that Spirit, when congregated in their silent meetings, especially, when the Sisters are assembled with them, for, I have by repeated observation found, that the effluvium is more pervading and active, when males and females are together, than when one or other of the Sexes, meet in separate Clubs.

I have heard a Story of a Quaker, named Aminadab Stiffrump, who was asked by a high Churchman (of consequence no friend to his Sect) how it came to pass, that the Spirit seldom or never operated so vigorously, as to set the friends to preaching and vociferating, but when they were assembled in their meetings? To which Aminadab answered and said, Verily Friend thou knowest, that one fire coal by itself will never make a fire, but put two or three together and they will burn briskly. Just so it is with the friends when separate and Congregated.

Now since I talk of the Spirit, it will be worth while to say a word or two concerning it.

It may be divided into two sorts, the Subtile and the gross, the Subtile [28] Spirit is that exalted aura, that moves and agitates the Saints in their congregations, of this Sort, the Zealous and pious Mr George Whitefield[7] has

5. George Cheyne (1671–1743) was a Scottish physician and mathematician whose works include *An Essay of Health and Long Life* (London, 1724; 9th ed. 1745) and *The English Malady; or, A Treatise of Nervous Diseases of All Kinds* (London, 1733).

6. A good contemporary account of the experiments of Jean Antoine Nollet, Benjamin Franklin, and others appears in *Histoire de l'Académie Royale des Sciences* (Paris, 1753), 6–39. Hamilton may also be referring to the medical applications of electricity proposed by Ebenezer Kinnersley, a club visitor (see J. A. Leo Lemay, *Ebenezer Kinnersley: Franklin's Friend* [Philadelphia, 1964], 72).

7. Whitefield (1714–1770) was an English evangelist whose dynamic oratorical style and religious zeal made him the leader of the Methodists in England and a great reviver of religious sentiment in America during the Great Awakening.

such a large Share, that he often throws his female hearers into fits, by the copious emissions thereof, which flow from him when he preaches.

The grosser Sort consists of the Spirit of wine and brandy, of Rum, Whisky and such liquors, which very often gives a philip to the former, and asists the Saints very much in their Devotions, this is what is always used in those assemblies called Clubs, and when it first rises to the Alembic of the head, it Surprizingly produces good humour, makes the dumb to talk, the morose good natured and merry, the mistuned musical, the enimy a friend, hence we find frequently after Cracking of the Second bottle in Clubs, abundance of friendship professed, a profusion of cordiality, hearty em- braces, and Shakings by the hand, musical vociferations and Singing of catches, with loud peals of laughter, but when the gross fumes begin to rise, by augmenting the fire, that is, when the empty bottles are piled up by dozens, then they gradually go into Disputes, brawls, Scuffles, quarrells, 'tis *bella, horrida bella,*[8] and thence ensue broken heads, bruised bones & horrid bloody noses.

Of these Societies called Clubs, there are numberless kinds, which I [29] shall not pretend to treat of par- ‖ ticularly, other Authors having done that before me, to much better purpose, than I, with all my Clubical learning can pretend to, and therefore, I shall directly proceed to say alittle, concern- ing the great antiquity of these Societies.

I have heard of a certain author, who took abundance of pains to prove the antiquity of music, and very learnedly traced it from Jubal,[9] its reputed Inventor, who, according to the Mosaic chronology, must have been born some centuries after the creation. Of consequence, for that space of time, vizt: between the Creation and the birth of Jubal at least, every thing in nature must have been mistuned, the birds could not warble or modulate, till the same Jubal taught them, or set them proper lessons, there was no melody or regular cadence in the human voice, till Jubal formed and Insti- tuted it, even the divine Plato's harmony of the Spheres was nothing but discord till Jubal regulated their Chorus, how then will you say could Jubal discover this art of music, or from what hint, if it is affirmed that it was from the well timed Strokes and Chimings of Tubal Cain's hammers upon

8. "Wars, frightening wars" (Vergil, *Aeneid* 6.86).

9. Hamilton is referring to his friend Alexander Malcolm's *A Treatise of Musick, Speculative, Practical, and Historical* (Edinburgh, 1721). In chap. 14, "Of the Ancient Musick," Malcolm claims that "of all human Arts *Musick* has justest Pretences to the Honour of *Antiquity*." Malcolm traces instrumental music back to Jubal, but, he writes, "we have sufficient Reason to believe that *Musick* was an Art long before [Jubal's] Time; since it is rational to think that *vocal Musick* was known long before *Instrumental*" (pp. 463–464). Hamilton is being intentionally difficult in interpreting his friend's argument.

his anvil, there follows a *reductio ad absurdum,* as the Logicians term it, for how in the name of wonder could Tubal's hammers become musical before Jubal taught them, but to cut short this Ingenious Enquiry, in order to establish this learned authors assertion for an undenyable truth, it will be necessary to suppose, that neither men, birds nor beasts, had throats, or vocal organs before Jubal's time, nor had they the power of framing Sounds, either articulate or Inarticulate, emitted up- || wards thro' the [30] throat, or downwards thro' the anus, since some nice ears have discovered a kind of music even in the fundamental eructations, as may be seen in a learned treatise concerning the practice and theory of farting, by that Ingenious Philosopher, Don Fartinhando puffendorst.[10] Consequently, that curious Supposition, that the Language of Adam and Eve in paradise was hebrew, must fall to the ground, for, granting this Author's assertion to be true, they must have conversed only by signs, it is also necessary to suppose, that bodies before Jubals time, were not Sonorous, therefore, when struck against one another, they yielded no Sound, or at least, that Sound was not varied, so that it was the same thing to strike a bell or a drum, as if you had thumped a cushion, the emission of Sound from both, was one and the same, till Jubal gave each of them their particular and proper tone.

Were I to trace the origin of these Societies called Clubs, in the same manner, as this Ingenious Author, has done that of music, I should bring myself under the same dilemma, for example, should I affirm, that Cain, by building a City in the land of Nod, was the first erector of Clubs, because, it is in towns and Cities, that those Societies are commonly held, I might in the opinion of many Superficial Critics, talk very plausibly, but to cut the matter short, and clear away all Rubs, Stumbling blocks and cavils, I will venture to say that Clubs and Clubbing, began as soon as the first men were || created, and therefore are certainly as ancient as mankind & very nigh as [31] ancient as the Globe it self, therefore, I think, that Clubs may cope with any thing in nature for antiquity, and, were I disposed to be tedious and Impertinent to my readers, I could prove the uninterrupted Succession of Clubs, from the very beginning, down to the ancient and honorable Tuesday Club of Annapolis in Maryland, now the Club of Clubs, and the only true ancient Club upon Earth, as plainly and perspicuously, as some Roman Catholics and Nonjuring Clerks of the Church of England, have proved the uninterrupted Succession of Bishops, from the time of the Apostles, down to the hierarchy of both these Churches, which, as they both affirm, are the only true christian catholic Churches in the world.

10. *The Benefit of Farting* . . . *Explained by Don Fartinando Puff-indorst* (London, 1722) is attributed to Jonathan Swift.

And thus having settled this great and Important point, I proceed to the next Chapter.

Chapter IV

Some Scraps of Ancient History relating to Clubs.

The Cruelty of time is such, that nothing can move his pity, nothing excite his compassion, he is an universal glutton, a gormandizer of all things, he is an Anthropo-phagite or cannibal, feeding as freely upon human flesh as any thing, he is a Camelion, for he lives on the fleeting air, a Salamander, for he consumes even fire it self, that universal consumer, [32] which he ‖ does by short snaps, as may be proved by many new experiments of electricity; nay he is an Ostridge, for he devours Iron, he is in short,— what not? and among the numberless things of which he makes garbage and waste, Empires, kingdoms, Cities, Republics, noble families, and, *O lamentabile dictu,*[1] even Clubs themselves are not exempt from his Iron teeth, for, many of these have flourished for a time and made a great Show, 'till he thought fit to gulp them up into his horrid Maw, and then were they no more heard of or mentioned, that Club, which has eluded his rage at all Seasons, is not now in being, tho' the ancient and honorable Fraternity of the Free and accepted Masons, which is a kind of ubiquitarian Club, affirm, that they have found means, from the very beginning of things, to elude his traps; but whether it really be so, is their business to prove, and none of mine to deny; my task being to rake out from the ruinous Remains of hoary antiquity, the first origin of the ancient and honorable Tuesday Club of Annapolis in Maryland, of which I have, (I hope not rashly) undertaken to pen the history.

In the earliest ages of the world, it is supposed, that Clubs consisted as they do now, of Certain Select knots of men (hence the name Club, as these knock-down weapons are most commonly made of the most knotty part of [33] the tree) ‖ that met together, either in the field, or under covert of a tent or house. It may be conjectured with some Show of probability, that the first societies of this sort, assembled in some Cave or grotto, or in some thicket or grove, hence we may derive the origin of the ancient Rural or Sylvan Deities, of Pan, the Satyrs, Bacchus, Silenus, and their followers, who were

1. "O sad to say."

probably Jolly drunken Club Companions, but this was before the Cultiva-
tion of arts and Sciences, when men were barbarous and unpolished, and,
by these Clubs, it is thought, they were first Civilized, and taught the use of
arts and Arms, Love, dress and the bottle, hence the members of these early
Clubs were deified, and those Satyrs, were nothing but the first beaus, that
appeared in wigs, with long rolld Cues, wearing also full bottomd manes,
Smart Cock'd hats with feathers, high heeld Shoes &ct: &ct:—hence, the
Ignorance of the age, and the wild fancy of Succeeding poets painted them
like Devils, with long hair, monstrous ears, tails and Cloven feet.

   We cannot possibly ascertain the time when it became customary to
elect presidents in Clubs, but probably it was very early, since we find
Apollo, a Celebrated ancient beau, distinguished by the Ladies for his excellent voice, in Singing of love Songs and opera airs, and also for his playing
on the fiddle and flute, he had a Smattering too in Physic, having read
Colepeppers *Midwifery*[2] Six times over, which art he also taught his Sister
Lucina,[3] remarkable for his dexterity in handling the curling tongs, powder
puff and perfume box, of an exquisite taste in ‖ the choice of fans, necklaces,   [34]
tweezer cases, and other ornaments of dress, in many of which accomplishments, the present honorable president of the ancient and honorable Tuesday Club, has remarkably distinguished himself, we find, I say, this same
Apollo, presiding over a female Club of Nine Muses, who met on the top
of a Mountain Called Parnassus, of which Apollo, Homer and Hesiod,
poets that lived nigh two thousand years agoe, talk as familiarly, as if they
had been his Intimate acquaintance, tho we have reason to believe, that the
said Apollo, flourished many Centuries before their time.

   But, in all probability, Clubs in ancient times, when they found the
Conversation become disorderly, noisy, or quarellsome, or when they observed some ambitious Spirits, grasping at power and precedence, and Inclinable to oppress and distress the members, saw it fit to chuse from
among their members, some wise, discreet, venerable and awful person, to
moderate in the Club, and to keep them in order, this person was distinguished by the title of *APXON, Præses, Dux,* President, and appellations of
the like Signification according to the difference of Languages and Idioms.
Whether these presidents from the beginning were *Jure Divino,* or by Civil
Institution or appointment, has been the Subject of much dispute, the
advocates for the first, have urged the divine Authority or Command ‖ of   [35]

---

2. Nicholas Culpeper (1616–1654) was the English author of numerous works on astrology
and medicine, including *A Directory for Midwives* (London, [1651]).
3. The Roman goddess who presided over childbirth.

the above mentioned Apollo, who was none of your *Diiminorum gentium,*[4] but one of the privy Councellors of Jupiter *optimus maximus,* others laugh'd at this Assertion, and mantain that the said Apollo never trowbled his head about it, having other guess[5] fish to fry, much Learning has been display'd in this controversy, and the parties are not yet agreed, nor never will while the world stands, as it is none of my business to dip into disputes, I shall leave every man at liberty to think of it as he pleases, nor, shall I declare my own opinion in the affair, least I should, by the opposite party be thought a very Silly fellow, and this my history be thrown aside by them, as wretched Stuff and not worth reading.

It appears that these presidents were Invested with great power and authority, and some, from ambitious views of extending that power, have tyraniz'd it in a most astonishing manner, so as to excite grumblings, discontents, Seditions, rebellions, and Infinite mischiefs in their respective Clubs, it is Inconceivable to think what havoc has been made, and what hub-bubs have been occasioned among the members of many Clubs, by the Tyrrannical and arbitrary proceedings of presidents in all ages, if any one gives himself the trowble to turn over ancient Clubical History, he will be Surprized to find the number of broken heads, bruised noses, black Eyes, dislocated Jaw bones, and bloody teeth, of many valiant members of Clubs, who have gloriously stood up, and shed their precious blood In defence of

[36]   Clubical Liberty, against the Tyranny of arbitrary ‖ presidents, he will stand amazed at the number of broken Glasses, bottles, decanters, candlesticks, mugs, Juggs, platters, tobacco pipes, bowls, Sticks, cudgels, truncheons and Clubs, that have been exhibited on these melancholly occasions, not to mention the tearing of numberless coats, Jackets, Shirts and the burning of wigs.

Thus, we find, tho civil power and authority was first established for good and wise purposes, in Clubs, yet there have not been wanting wicked presidents who have abused that power, by grasping at more than what was their due, while they and their adherents, have had the Assurance to affirm, that being above Clubical Law, they were accountable to none, but were at liberty to perpetrate all manner of vilanies, and to commit all Sorts of Crimes unpunished, and all upon the Strength of their *Jure Divinoship,* derived, as they assert from the aforesaid Apollo, by which they absurdly conclude, that the Constitution of all Clubs, is theocratical, and all Presidents gods, and privy Councellors to Jupiter *optimus maximus,* because Apollo's parnassean Club was a Theocracy, and he himself a privy councel-

4. "Lesser gods."
5. Here and throughout the *History,* Hamilton uses *guess* in the same sense as "kind of."

lor in the Court of the said Jupiter, but it is the opinion of many Learned men (for I here as I hinted above wave giving my own opinion) that most of these wicked presidents, may more properly be stiled representatives of, and privy councellors to the Devil, and their Government truely Diabolical, but this by the way of digression, let us thence draw this reflexion, || O [37] thrice happy, ancient and honorable Tuesday Club of Annapolis! for thou flourishest under the benign Sway of the Gentle, the pacific, the mild, the merciful and the Honorable Nasifer Jole Esqr, thy Illustrious president, whom heaven preserve for ever-more, *Amen.*

We have no certain accounts of any particular Clubs before the general Deluge, tho' doubtless there were such Societies among the Antidiluvians, we meet with a dark hint of the sons of God cohabiting with the daughters of men, from whence sprung a Club or Association of Gyants, the same as is supposed, who, according to the poets attempted to dethrone Jupiter, but this account being very obscure, I leave it Just where I found it. Some Ingenious Historians have alledged, with some Show of probability, that there was an Antidiluvian Tradesman's Club, of which Tubal Cain was president, who is said to have first formed a regular Lodge of Free masons, that there was also a Club of Musicians, of which Jubal was Chief, and a Club of Bowmen and hunters over which Lamech presided.[6]

Immediatly after the Deluge, we find Noe given to Clubbing, for he plants a vinyard and drinks the Juice of the grape with his bon-companions, and gets fuddled, and this, for aught we can find from Scraps and fragments of ancient History, was the first origin of our Fuddling Clubs, and it is said, that some members drank so hard, at the first Institution of these fuddlecap Societies, that their countenances || turned first florid, then purple, and at [38] last they plied it so hard, that many became black in the face with mere force of Drinking, and this, I think, more naturally accounts for the origin of the Moors and Negroes, than any other fine spun reasons that have been delivered to the Accademie Royal de Sciences,[7] or any other learned Society on Earth, who have proffered very great Rewards to the literati, to account reasonably for this strange phænomenon; and, as I look upon myself, to be the Author of this very useful Discovery, I hope the Republic of letters will allot me a handsome reward, suitable to my merit, at least I expect a medal

6. For a good discussion of the longstanding confusion between Jubal and Tubal-Cain and the respective clubs they founded (with passing references to Lamech as well), see volume 2 of Paul E. Beichner, *The Medieval Representative of Music, Jubal or Tubalcain?* (Notre Dame, Ind., 1954).

7. I have searched in vain for any reference to the origins of Moors and Negroes in the *Histoire de l'Académie Royale des Sciences.* However, Pierre Barrere (d. 1755), a French physician, did publish *Dissertation sur la cause physique de la couleur des Nègres* (Paris, 1741).

from the Royal Society, and to be entered a member of that learned body, as
the smallest recompense for my Study and application in making this Important discovery; I may meet with some, perhaps, who may treat me, as
his contemporary Physicians treated Doctor Harvey, when he first discovered the Circulation of the blood,[8] who mantained that Hippocrates, Galen, and many others, were the first discoverers of it, They may attribute
this my discovery to Pythagoras, Aristotle, or some other ancient Philosopher, but they must quote a better authority for it than that of το σωμα
κυκλος εστι,[9] for, I will undertake to make it plain, either by fair disputa-
tion *viva voce*, or in writing, that none ever thought of this before me; The
Short and the Long of it is no more than this, Some of Noe's Jolly family,
[39] probably Ham, drank 'till he became || black in the face, goggle eyed, flat
nosed and blubber liped, and thus his posterity have remained ever since,
hence we may conclude, that it was of some deep coloured wine they
Drank, such as the Alicant and Benecarlo, that are made In old Spain, and
what confirms this, is that the Spaniards, by even the moderate use of this
wine, (for they are reputed a very Sober and temperate people) are generally of a dusky Swarthy complexion, tho' some have erroniously attributed
that color in the Spaniard, to a mixture of the Moorish blood, which
cannot be, for these abominable Infidels were murdered massacred and
expelld by them, in the very same manner as the Indians of South America
were, to promote the good christian cause of Holy catholic Church, some
Centuries agoe, which, as it originally took root from the blood of the
Saints, so it needs to water and nourish it plenty of worthless Infidel blood,
and besides, had this been the case, that tawny cast must have been now
wore out, from among our moderen Spaniards, also, if this is to be attributed to the Moorish blood, why are not the Spanish ladies, noted for their
fair complexion, of the same hue with the men; the reason is plain, the
women there are kept so Strictly to rules, that they are not suffered, by their
austere lords and masters, to Indulge in the Rites of either Bacchus or
Venus.

Soon after the flood, we find Nimrod at the head of a Club of warriors
and hunters, and also we read of a Great Club, or assembly of bold adventurers (as that learned Cosmographer Heylen calls them,)[10] that assembled

8. William Harvey (1578–1657) was the famous English physician who in 1616 proposed his
theory on the circulation of the blood.

9. Literally, "the body is a wheel."

10. Peter Heylyn (1600–1662) was the English author of works on ecclesiastical history and
of *Microcosmus, or a Little Description of the Great World* (Oxford, 1621; enlarged and reissued as
Cosmographie in 1652). Heylyn relates the story of Babel and refers to its founders as "the first
Adventurers" in his introduction to the *Cosmographie* (see pp. 7–9 of the 1658 edition).

in the plain of Sinaar, and erected a most Stupenduous tower, ‖ which they   [40]
probably Intended for a Club house, and with which they thought to
overtop the Clouds, but their conversation becoming confused and Irregular, they could not understand one another, and so were obliged to disperse,
and form themselves into various Clubs, this has been the fate of many
Clubs since, and even at this day, where it frequently happens, that while
the members are vainly building Castles in the air, they either do not, or
will not understand each other, and thus, a misunderstanding, as it is called,
arising among them, they separate, and become members of other Clubs,
for that of Clubbing, is so natural to mankind, that every man must necessarily be in some Club or other, a remarkable Instance of this, happened
lately in the Synod of the Seceding bretheren among the Clergy in Scotland, who not understanding one another in point of Doctrine, or Rather
in point of ambition for popularity, separated Into many Clubs or Synods,
and very Solemnly declared each other heretics, pronouncing the dreadful
Sentence of excommunication, against each other, then the Reverend Mr
Ralph Erskin, excommunicated the Reverend Mr Fisher and his Synod, the
Reverend Mr Fisher excommunicated the Reverend Mr Wilson and his
Synod, and the Anathemas flew about as thick as hops.[11]

I might, since I have dip'd so far into the Subject of ancient clubs, trace
the origin of the ancient and honorable Tuesday Club of Annapolis In
Maryland, from the uninterrupted Succession of Clubs thro the first ages,
after the General Deluge, down to the present times, still finding, as ‖ I   [41]
went along, some Club or other, that met on Tuesday, and this I might do
with the same propriety, as the ancient & honorable fraternity of Free and
accepted Masons, do, by their printed constitutions (of which many fair
Editions are now extant and may be had for money of the booksellers) trace
their Society from Noe, Tubal Cain, king Solomon, king Hiram of Tyre,[12]

11. Ralph Erskine (1685–1752) was a Scottish seceding divine and religious poet whose
preaching was remarkable for its pathos, and the author of *Faith No Fancy* (Edinburgh, 1745), a
repudiation of the image of Christ as man. James Fisher (1697–1775) was one of the founders of
the Scottish secession church and primary author of *The Assembly's Shorter Catechism Explained
by Way of Question and Answer*, 2 parts (Glasgow, 1753–1760), long regarded as the standard
manual for catechismal instruction in the secession church. William Wilson (1690–1741) was a
Scottish seceding divine who sided with Erskine and Fisher and published *A Defence of the
Reformation Principles of the Church of Scotland* (Edinburgh, 1739) and several other collections
of sermons. These three men seem to have been opposed more to the general assembly of
Scotland than divided among themselves. They were all in agreement, at least, about the
fundamental issue behind their secession: each regarded the congregational right of appointing clergy as sacred and opposed the general assembly's act allowing that right only to the
heritors and elders of the church.

12. Hiram, king of Tyre (970–936 B.C.), befriended Solomon and David and helped erect
Solomon's temple and David's palace.

Pythagoras &ct: down to those famous moderen Architects, Inigo Jones, and Sir Christopher Wren,[13] so, I say, might I follow the tract of Clubs, from those famous presidents Apollo, Bacchus, Silenus, Alexander the Great, &ct: down to the Honorable Nasifer Jole Esqr, the prime and paragon of moderen Presidents, but I leave that to the Reverend Doctor Warburton, and others more versed in antiquities and Critical learning, and also, for another weighty reason I ommit it, that is, least I should make this work too voluminous and bulky.

I shall therefore hasten towards the main point of my Subject, and omitting the Clubs of ancient greek Philosophers, who used to assemble in the porticos (the same to them as our Coffee-houses are to us at this Day) as also the private assemblies, of those that were Concerned in the Mysteries, which were properly the Ancient Lodges of Masons, and the meetings of the Bacchinals, which were mad Clubs, like our late moderen Mohooks, and the Celebrated Hellfire Society;[14] The mysteries of the Bona Dea,[15] [42] which were ‖ female Clubs, resembling much our moderen Gossopings, after a lying in, and a thousand others of the like nature; in the following Chapter, I design to proceed to the more Immediate Spring and origin of the Ancient and honorable Tuesday Club of Annapolis in Maryland.

Chapter V

The more Immediate origin and rise of the Ancient and honorable Tuesday Club, of Annapolis in Maryland.

It has been the misfortune of most Historians, while they grope, fumble and blunder in the dark, among the Rubbish of Antiquity, and vainly

13. Jones (1573–1652) was the English architect who designed settings for court masques by Ben Jonson and others. Wren (1632–1723) was the famous English architect best remembered for designing the Pembroke College chapel and Saint Paul's Cathedral in London.

14. The Mohock Club was one of the more frolicsome, blasphemous, and rakish clubs that thrived in England around 1712 (see Robert J. Allen, *The Clubs of Augustan London* [Cambridge, Mass., 1933], 105–119). Hamilton may have heard of Boston's Hellfire Club, a group of wits who contributed to James Franklin's *New-England Courant* in the 1720s (see Shunsuke Kamei, "Cultural Clubs in Colonial America, 1720–1750," *Studies in English Literature* [English Literary Society of Japan], English Number [1963], 40). However, given the context, Hamilton is probably referring to the rakish Hell-Fire Clubs (there were actually three) that flourished in England in the 1720s (see Allen, 119–124).

15. The Bona Dea was a Roman goddess of unknown name, probably an earth spirit protective of women. Rites in her honor were celebrated annually in December and were attended only by women.

try to tack together fragments, and broken hints of history, to produce a Chimêra, or monstruous birth, which seems to every Judicious Reader, altogether Inconsistent in it self, ridiculous, and Indeed Incredible, hence we have, what are called the fabulous accounts of the Poets, the Stages and periods of the Golden, Silver, Brazen & Iron ages, which, in themselves, duely perpended & considered, contain as much of the Legend, as the famous books of knight Errantry, or the accounts of the Miracles, done by the Saints of holy Catholic Church.

That I may evade splitting upon this dangerous rock, I shall lay aside [43] all disquisitions and Dissertations, concerning ancient times, enveloped In obscurity, and at once making a skip, shall trace in a direct line, our ancient and honorable Tuesday Club of Annapolis, from a Celebrated Club, called the ancient and venerable Tuesday (or whin bush) Club of Laneric,¹ in the ancient kingdom of Scotland, which was in its highest Glory, about two centuries before the usurpation of Oliver Cromwel, In the Presidentship of the venerable Congallus de Rutheren, consequently, about the middle of the Reign of Henry VI of England, It is found, by the ancient Records of that Club, now remaining, for all before that time were lost, by means of the national feuds subsisting in that unhappy kingdom, that there were then 350 Living members in the Club, Some few Traditional Stories, are yet

1. While probably exaggerated, most of what Hamilton says about the Whin-Bush Club is based upon fact. His reference to the club's association with Clydesdale, for instance (see p. 48), is verified by Allan Ramsay (see p. 59n, below). In "A Petition to the Whinbush Club" Ramsay offers himself to the club as a

> Native of *Clydsdale's* upper Ward
> Bred Fifteen Summers there,
> Tho, to my Loss I'm no a Laird
> By Birth, my Title's fair
>> To bend wi' ye and spend wi' ye
>> An Evening, and gaffaw,
>> If Merit and Spirit
>> Be found without a Flaw.

In an explanatory note to the poem, Ramsay further observes: "This Club consists of *Clyds-dale*-Shire Gentlemen, who frequently meet at a diverting Hour, and keep up a good Under-standing amongst themselves over a friendly Botle. And from a charitable Principle, easily collect into their Treasurer's Box a small Fond, which has many a Time relieved the Distresses on indigent Persons of that Shire" (*The Works of Allan Ramsay*, ed. Burns Martin and John W. Oliver [Edinburgh, (1951)–1974], I, 210–211). For verification of Hamilton's membership in the Whin-Bush Club, see his letter to his brother Gavin, where Hamilton implores him to "be so good as Remember me to all the Members of the whin-bush Club, especially to the Right honourable, the Lord Provost, and other magistrates and officers of that ancient and honour-able society, inform them that every friday, I fancy myself with them, drinking twopenny ale, and smoking tobacco" (June 13, 1739, Dulany Papers, MS. 1265, Maryland Historical Society, Baltimore).

CONGAL æ DE RUTHERIN

marmor antiquum Baſſo Relievo, ex rudens vetens Canobii prope Drumlanridge exfoſſus.

[An antique marble bas-relief dug up from the rubbish dumps of an old monastery near Drumlanridge.]

[facing page 43]

told at Christenmass meetings, of this ancient and venerable Club, long before this period, as that the venerable Aidan was president, at the time of the coming of Fergus I from Ireland, when Coyl was king of the Britons, he was famous for playing on the bagpipes, and added the Drone pipe to that Instrument, which before Consisted of one single treble pipe only, The venerable Ferithar was president in the time of Fergus II king of Scotland, and was only remarkable for his being a very great ‖ devourer of Brose, a   [44] dish, made of the fat Skimmings of Salt beef broth and oatmeal; The venerable Fethelmach was a noble Pict, and was Killed by king Kenneth II and his Clan at the extirpation of that Nation, he is famed for having Invented the high Relished Dish of Cock-a-leekie, and the Comfortable Soup called Dads and Blads.[2]

What Sort of Liquor that ancient Club drank in these early times is not mentioned in their Records, but, since the latter part of the Reign of Eliza-beth of England of Glorious, and the beginning of the Reign of James the Sixth of Scotland of Shitten memory, in the Presidentship of the venerable Sir Walter Wadle, we are pretty certain, that they drank twopenny ale and smoked tobacco, for punch was not as yet received among them till after the restauration, when the manufacture of the Sugar Islands began to prosper and Increase; whether this same punch, which has been much extoll'd, by many of our moderen Bowzers, as a most beatific liquor, and exactly like the Nectar of the Gods, furbished up and Improved the wit and humor of this venerable Club, does not appear by the Records of the same, they rather seem to me, to have flagged in their conversation, since the use of this compound guzzle, for, before this time, when Simple twopenny ale was their drink, some lively Sparks of wit and humor passed amongst them, at every Se- ‖ derunt, but since the use of tobacco and punch, we find nothing   [45] in these records, but "James such a one, fined one penny for coming *Sero*, or late to Club, Robert such a one fined four pence for absence, without being able to render a satisfactory reason, and Andrew such a one, fined Sixpence for Swearing." But the advocates for punch will not allow, that

2. The club presidents, Congallus de Rutheren, Ferithar, and Fethelmach, appear to be Hamilton's inventions. The British kings, however, are real. Aidan (d. 606) was the king of the Scottish kingdom of Dalriada, but after announcing his intention to govern it as an indepen-dent kingdom, he was defeated by Ethelfrith, the king of Northumbria. Fergus I was the legendary king of Scotland who came from Ireland ca. 330 B.C. to assist the Scots against the Picts and Britons. Fergus II (d. 501) was the first Dalriad king in Scotland. Kenneth II (d. 995) was a Scottish-Pictish king who tried to consolidate the warring territories of Scotland. By "Coyl" Hamilton is perhaps recalling Coilus, British king of the first century A.D., referred to in Geoffrey of Monmouth's *History of the Kings of Britain*. For other information on the Whin-Bush Club members, see p. 60n, below.

this hebetude of humour, in that venerable Club, was at all produced by the fumes of that glorious Liquor, but rather by the thick and gross steams of Tobacco, and, to support this argument, they quote a book of great authority, composed by a royal author, entituled the *Counterblast*,[3] which being bound up in a large, learned and ponderous volume of his other works in Folio, which is now scarce to be seen, for the benefit of my readers, I shall here quote these passages.

"Shall we, I say, that have been so long civil and wealthy in peace, famous and Invincible in war, fortunate in both,—shall we, I say, without blushing, abase ourselves so far, as to Imitate those beastly Indians, Slaves to the Spaniards, refuse to the world, and as yet Aliens to the holy covenant of God; It seems a miracle to me, how a custom, springing from so vile a ground, and brought in by a Father[(a)] so generally hated, should be welcomed upon so slender a warrant, it was neither brought in by king great [46] conqueror,[(b)] or learned Doctor of Physic,— || and that the suffumigation thereof cannot have a drying quality, it needs no further probation than that it is a Smoke, all Smoke and vapor being of it self humid as drawing near to the nature of the air, easie to be resolved again into water, whereof there needs no further proof but the Meteors, which being bred of nothing else but the vapours and exhalations, sucked up by the Sun, out of the Earth the sea and waters, yet are the same Smoaky vapours, transformed into rains, dews, Snows, hoar frosts, and such like watery meteors, as by the contrary, the rainy clouds, are transformed and evaporated into blustering winds— This Stinking Smoke then, being sucked up by the nose, and Imprisoned in the cold and moist brains, is by their Cold and wet faculty, cast forth again, in watery distillations, and so are you made free and purged of nothing, but that wherewith you willfully burdened yourselves—a Custom loathsome to the eye, hateful to the nose, harmful to the brain, dangerous to the Lungs, and, in the black Stinking fumes thereof, nearest resembling the Stygian Smoke, of the pit that is bottomless."

(a) Sir Walter Rauleigh, who was a father of learning and a brave Soldier, and therefore hated by Gondemar,[+] the Spanish Ambassador, and his creature king James, which was the same as to be universally hated, at least in that corrupt and Sycophantish court.

(b) Here his majesty tells a gross lie.

3. Hamilton is referring to James I's *A Counterblaste to Tobacco* (London, 1604), a serious, carefully reasoned treatise against smoking. For the most part, Hamilton accurately transcribes King James's text, although in the original text "it was neither brought in by king great conqueror, or learned Doctor of Physic" precedes "It seems a miracle to me. . . ." Hamilton's derogatory notes and his patching together of snippets of King James's prose make the argument against tobacco seem a good deal sillier than the original.

4. The count of Gondomar, Diego Sarmiento de Acuña (1567–1626), as Spanish ambassador to England (1613–1618, 1619–1622), successfully prevented James from aiding Spain's enemies.

The advocates for punch, from these learned passages prove, that this venerable Club, was stupified by the fumes of Tobacco, for, say they, this Learned and Royal Author Clearly demonstrates, that these Stinking fumes, moisten the brain, and Create Clouds there, so as to obscure the understanding or Sensorium; for, according to Dryden, a Celebrated poet, || great wits are nighly related to madmen, and according to Sir Richard [47] Blackmore, a noted Poet, a Learned Physician, and withal a knight Baronet, the brains of all madmen are very dry and parched,⁵ therefore the brains of great wits are in a degree of temperature, between those of madmen and heavy dull fellows, that is, they are temperatly dry, but, as the fumes of tobacco moisten the brains, they must necessarily render men heavy and dull. *Q:E:D:*

This venerable Club was under a total eclipse, during the Cromwellian usurpation, in the presidentship of the venerable Zachary Auchmoutie the great, and part of the time of the Venerable Jeremiah Majoribanks, for Oliver Imagining that they were a Cabal a plotting against the common wealth, seized their Records, and dispers'd them, but, upon these being examined, by a learned Committee of the *Rump,* there appeared nothing of politics or State matters in them, but only Simple facts, relating to fines and forfeitures, and drinking of toasts in bumpers &ct:

But, in the Presidentship of the venerable Rowland Macpherson, on the happy restoration of the Steuart family, who, to be sure, had an Indefeasible hereditary right to the British crown, derived in a curve line, direct, Indirect and collateral, from William the Bastard of Normandy, who, acquired it partly by conquest, Sword in hand, and partly by an Authentic last will and testament of Edward the Confessor, those valuable records were again restored, to this venerable club, when most || of the other national [48] records were lost, a lucky Incident, and what at this day will give us great Insight into the history of the ancient and honorable Tuesday Club of Annapolis.

These circumstances I deliver as authentic, having the honor to be myself, a standing member of that venerable Club of the whin bush of Lanneric, and have a hundred and a hundred times over seen and perused their Records, during the Secretaryship of the learned and Ingenious Mr

---

5. Hamilton is alluding to the following lines from *Absalom and Achitophel:* "Great Wits are sure to Madness near ally'd; / And thin Partitions do their Bounds divide" (*The Works of John Dryden,* ed. Edward Niles Hooker et al. [Berkeley, Calif., 1956–], II, 10, lines 163–164). Blackmore (d. 1729) was physician to Queen Anne and author of several lengthy poems and essays, including *Creation: A Philosophical Poem Demonstrating the Existence and Providence of God* (1712).

John Duncan, who was then, and is now, for aught I know, Secretary of that ancient and venerable Club, who was so kind as to communicate to me, some anecdotes, relating to the government and policy of that ancient and venerable Club, which I shall give to my readers in the thread of this History, in proper places, where they will naturally occurr.

In order to be admitted a member of this venerable Club, it was necessary, among other notable qualifications, for a man to be of the Shire of Clydsdale, either by his own birth, or that of his father or Grandfather, and some, upon proving that their great grandfather was of that Shire, or that their cousin germans or Cousins once removed, were natives of that Shire, were Indulged so far as to be admitted, provided, that they were men of a truly Clubical Genius or Disposition, that is, could drink a bumper, smoke a pipe, crack a Joke, or tell a waggish Story, nay, I remember one Instance of a Gentleman's being admitted who was a native of the Town of Sanquhar in [49] the north, ‖ whose ancestors, time out of mind, had been born there, upon a Supposition, that his grandfather had once travelled thro' Clydsdale, in his way to Galloway, and had a new heel Clapped to his boot, by a Clydsdale Cobler, but in fact, the Chief merit on which he was admitted, was, his having married a Daughter of the Late Sir John Norris,[6] admiral of England, with whom he had a world of money, and Indeed, we find, that thro' petticoat Interest, many men have had very honorable promotions, and have been entrusted with Employments of the greatest profit and emolument, not from any personal qualifications of their own, but, by the transmitted excellencies of their wives, Sisters and daughters, who, from their extreme handsomness, or some other equivalent property, become the prime favorites of great men, and I must here observe, that it is no extraordinary thing to see men admitted members of venerable and honorable Clubs upon female merit alone, since by that ladder, some have Climbed to the highest Titular honors, and procured to themselves, Principalities, Dukedoms, Lordships, Papacy, Cardinal-hats and Bisho-pricks, not to mention numberless places of an Inferior rank, procured Solely, by the Influence of certain commodities, in the possession only of the fair Sex; I myself know a certain man, who, for certain reasons, shall be nameless, who now lives in a certain City, whose wife at a Certain time, found out a method to please a certain Lord, which procured for her husband, a certain handsom [50] yearly Income, who, had it ‖ not been for that (he having no certain good

6. Norris (1547?–1597) was an English military commander who fought under Essex against the Irish (1573) and, with Sir Francis Drake, commanded the fleet that ravaged the coasts of Spain and Portugal in 1589.

qualities to recommend him) would certainly all his life time have been a beggar.[7]

As for Signior Pasquelino de Marzis, now master of Ceremonies to this venerable Club, tho' a native of Italy, yet he being grandson to Mathew Paisly (which name was Italianized into Pasquelino) who was Censor in the Presidentship of the venerable Sir Walter Wadle, and the Venerable Tobias Hodge, he had a good title to be admitted a member.

I must observe here, after what I have mentioned above, that it is a mighty great advantage for a man to be born in some particular places, how happy for instance, were those born in Clydsdale, upon this single privilege, of being qualified to be Members, of this ancient and venerable Club, happy were they also, whose fathers and grandfathers were born in that Shire before them, happy, for a simular reason, are all those who are true born Englishmen, being by that circumstance alone, bless'd with liberty, the quiet enjoyment of property, and absolute exemption from popery, Slavery, pagan Idolatry, Mahometan Superstition, bribery and corruption. O Glorious Nation! whose natives surpass all mankind besides in Courage comeliness and vigor! who wallow in the delights of good eating and drinking! who know not what it is to live upon scraps, dry crusts, and Soup meagres, like the Raw bon'd French and Spaniard! but abound all the days of your lives in lusty beef, Glorious pudding, and Invigorating ale!

Chapter VI   [51]

A Succinct account of the Ancient and Venerable Tuesday (or whin bush) Club of Lanneric, in the kingdom of Scotland.

The ancient and venerable Tuesday (or whin bush) Club of Lanneric, was time out of mind governed by a president, who, once he had attained the Chair, continued *durante vita,* or *quam diu bene se Gesserit,*[1] for we have an Instance of one being deposed, vizt: the Venerable Luke Tomlinson, who was degraded in 1502 for heresy, and eating roast beef on Good fridays. This place was neither elective nor hereditary, but was possessed by se-

7. Hamilton is apparently referring to one of the more dubious affairs in the life of the profligate Frederick Calvert (1731–1771), sixth Lord Baltimore and proprietor of Maryland from 1751 until his death.
1. "During his lifetime," or "so long as he behaves himself well."

niority, the oldest member of the Club, always holding it, but in case there was a parity of age, that person who was the member of the longest Standing, took that place of honor, from whence we derive the title of *Longstanding member*, in the ancient and honorable Tuesday Club of Annapolis, the members of that Club, taking to themselves that title, from a certain noble emulation and ambition, sometime or other to ascend the chair, each in his turn, and not from any Waggish Entendre, as some Imagine was Intended by Jealous Spyplot Esqr, when he Revived that Significant term, in the ancient and honorable Tuesday Club. In case two or three members, were of equal age, and of equal *Long standing* (I desire none may misinterpret my words in the manner that some evil minded females, have done the myster-

[52] ies of the Free Masons) then, and then only, the Chair was elective ‖ and the Club determined the affair by a majority of voices. Under this president were several officers, vizt: a Senior and Junior Baylie, a censor, a Treasurer, a master of Ceremonies, a poet Laureat, and a Secretary, who, all, but the Master of Ceremonies, Poet and Secretary, were appointed and Commissioned by the president, the last three being chosen by the Club, the first were called State officers, the other officers of the commons, The Senior and Junior Baylies, sat at the Right and left hand of the Chair, The Censor was an officer of Great authority, and it was his business to remark and bring to a trial, all trespasses and misdemeanors committed in Club, before the worshipful the Baylies, as also, to take into custody all offending members, and them to keep without bail or Redemption, till the Issue of the Cause was tried, I do not find by the Records that they ever had any Champion, or military discipline in this Club, their Constitution was so pacific, that they had no occasion for one, neither had they a chancellor or great Seal, the Presidents own privy seal, serving all Clubical Commissions and Instruments of writing, it was the Secretaries business to enter the proceedings in the book of Records, (and nothing was entered there, without the Presidents consent,) to draw up Indictments Impeachments, declarations, and Informations against offenders, The treasurer kept the Club

[53] box, and the fund was ‖ collected, by every present member's clubbing one penny at each Sederunt, and by fines; the master of Ceremonies Introduced Strangers, Installed new members, and performed the honors of the Club, to the venerable the President, The poet Laureat, on particular occasions, exercised his genius in praise of the venerable the president and Club, and Repeated certain ancient Clubical verses at the admission of new members.

As to the Laws of this venerable Club, they were few and Simple, one Law was, that the Club should meet once a week upon Tuesday Evening, at the Hour of Six, Summer and winter, and not to exceed eleven o clock at night, and, by the very old records we find, that this venerable Club, went by the name of the Tuesday Club of Lanneric, but, in the Presidentship of the venerable Mr President Majoribanks, the day of meeting of this Club was changed into Friday, for what Reasons is not known, unless it was upon account of the Turbulent times of persecution, which broke out sometime after the happy restoration, when so much countenance and favor was shown to papists and high Church Caviliers, that Sober discrete moderate whigs could not sleep in a Sound Skin. It is thought, that then, the members of this venerable Club, being all true blue whigs, and many of them concerned in the battle of Bothwell Bridge,[2] in Clydsdale, they were obliged to abscond and skulk, and || met under the shelter of the whin or [54] furz bushes (like Mr Cameron's congregation,[3] which met under the Canopy of the heavens) that they might not be discovered and routed by the blood thirsty Caveliers, who were on the Scent after them, so, being constrained to assume the Sham name of true Catholics, for their own Safety, they absconded on fridays, pretending to be fasting and praying, while all the time they were soaking their noses in twopenny ale, smoking tobacco, and devouring bread & cheese, this food they were particularly fond of, and one of their Baylies, vizt: Anthony Dottle, choaked, while he was voraciously swallowing a great mouthful of Cheese in Club, in the year 1650; This custom they continued for some time, lurking in the fields among the furz and broom, 'till the times began to relax in their Severity, then they betook themselves to a taveren, which hung out for a Sign a whin bush, (hence their moderen name of whin bush Club) in honor of this club; their day of meeting still continued to be friday, and their meetings were very private (this was in the presidentship of the venerable Praise-god Maccartie) 'till the happy revolution, at the coming over of King William of Glorious memory, and, in the presidentship of the venerable Theophilus Petticrue, then they sung whig Songs with all the Jollity and freedom Imaginable, mounting a large table, clapping each his wig under his right foot, holding a pipe of tobacco in one hand and a || bumper of punch in the [55] other. From that time the Club has continued to meet on fridays, and, as the different Sects and parties in politics and religion, at that time, were fond of taking new names, and laying aside the old, as the Cameronians,

2. In the battle fought on June 22, 1679, the rebel Covenanters of southwest Scotland were defeated by 10,000 men under the duke of Monmouth. Of about 4,000 rebels perhaps 200 to 400 were killed and 1,200 captured.

3. Richard Cameron (d. 1680) was a Scottish Covenanter and field preacher who formally renounced allegiance to Charles II and whose followers, the Cameronians, later constituted a sect of Reformed Presbyterians in Scotland.

covenanters, anticovenanters, whigs, tories, Revolutioners, Jacobites, so, this venerable Club, from their late place of meeting, took the name of the whin bush, changing for it the ancient name of the Tuesday Club of Lanneric, which ancient name is now kept up and preserved, only by the Ancient and honorable Tuesday Club of Annapolis, which proceeds in a direct line, from the Ancient and Venerable Tuesday (or whin bush) Club of Lanneric, and is indeed the Self same Club, as shall presently be made appear, by the most authentic historical proofs.

Having but Just now mentioned bread & cheese, It will be proper to take notice in this place, that this ancient and venerable Club, had a Standing law, that nothing was to be admitted of eatables but this, which was only to give a relish to their Liquor, formal Suppers taking up too much time, and occasioning too much Ceremony and Confusion in the Club, this Law, the ancient and Honorable Tuesday Club of Annapolis at first adopted, in Laudable Imitation of their patrons of the whin bush, but Luxury by degrees crept in among them, and they now Indulge themselves

[56] In sumptuous Suppers, which some have ‖ attributed to the custom established by that Club, of Celebrating their anniversary, at which time, the honorable Mr President Jole, out of the overflowings of his generosity and respect to the club, always provides them in a most elegant entertainment, and the longstanding members, (as it is natural for the Inferior class of mankind to ape those above them) in Imitation of his honor, try who shall outdo one another, in pomp and elegance of Club Suppers, and this is not alittle promoted, by the ambition and Emulation of the females, related to the Club, to shine & be remarkable in this particular.

This circumstance will admitt of a few grave reflexions; all allow, that Luxury is a destructive thing, and sooner or later fatal to every society or Community that once admits of it; as having a tendency to Introduce abject Slavery, by means of its being a promoter of bribery and Corruption, yet, we have Instances of the wisest Societies, that have, sometime or other fallen into her traps; Did not the Greeks, a wise and warlike Nation, after having for several ages, mantained their honor and dignity, in arts and arms, and Integrity of Morals, sink by degrees into Softness and effeminacy, by which, the persians overcame them, after they had subdued the persians by their arms and warlike prowess; and what are they now? how degenerated from their ancient honor and bravery, are they any better than a parcell

[57] of Quacking, pedling, rope dancing Juggling ‖ knaves, and withal, abandoned Slaves to the Law and government of Mahomet; what now are the Romans? once a wise honorable and warlike people, who ruled the world, and grasped the Globe at a handful, are they any wise like the Ancient

Romans, or do they Resemble them in the least feature? No. They are a
parcel of Singers, dancers, fidlers, pipers, effeminate catamites, Silly eu-
nuchs and Idle Sauntering priests. Where now are their Scipios, Cæsars,
Pompeys, Luculluses, Catos, Ciceros, Virgils, Horaces and Lucretias?[4] are
they not sunk into these pigmy mortals, called by the soft and languishing
names of Signior Corelli, Vivaldi, Tessarini, Torelli, Martini, Geminiani,
Alberti, Valentini, Lampugnani, Senesino, Farinello, Bonancini, Beneditto,
and Seniora or Madona Auretti, Violante, Berberini &ct:[5] we may thence
see & beware of the danger of admitting luxury into any Society, and, tho
wise Societies and nations, have embraced this Cockatrice, yet that does not
at all prove, that there is any good to be had of her, and tho' the ancient and
honorable Tuesday Club, of Annapolis, be one of the wisest Clubs that ever
yet appeared, yet she may see the time, when her constitution will feel the
Smart of admitting Luxury to gain ground among her longstanding members, when she may receive such a Shake, as she may never be able to
recover, and, tho she may not thereby be quite extinguished, yet may she
sink from her || present grandure excellence and conspicuity, to the obscure   [58]
degree of an Infamous ale-house Club, like those that are held in your
Chop-houses at the back of Change alley, where poor poets, and poorer
military officers, the first mantained on Short commons by the muses, the

4. Lucullus (probably fl. ca. 75 B.C.) was a Roman soldier, administrator, and patron of the
arts. Lucretia, the wife of Tarquinius Collatinus, was raped by Sextus, son of Tarquinius
Superbus, then took her own life.
   5. Arcangelo Corelli (1653–1713) was an Italian violinist and composer of sonatas especially
distinguished for his dance movements. Antonio Vivaldi (1675?–1741), Italian violinist and
composer of operas and sonatas, greatly influenced the development of violin concertos. Carlo
Tessarini (1690–1765) was an Italian violinist who established the form of the violin sonata with
three movements. Giuseppe Torelli (1658–1709) was an Italian violinist and composer who
established the concerto form as used by George Frederick Handel, Corelli, and others. Giovanni Battista Martini (1706–1784) was an Italian monk, composer, and music theorist who
wrote the *Storia della musica*, 3 vols. (Bologna, 1757–1781). Francesco Geminiani (1687–1762)
was an Italian violinist and composer noted for his concertos and sonatas. Domenico Alberti
(ca. 1700–1740) was an Italian musician and composer of sonatas remembered for the device
now known as the Alberti Bass. Valentini could be either Pier Francesco Valentini (d. 1654), an
Italian composer of madrigals and of a canon with more than 2,000 musical combinations,
Giuseppe Valentini (b. 1681), composer of violin and bass solos, or Giovanni Valentini (fl. 17th
century), composer of madrigals, masses, and sonatas. Giovanni Battista Lampugnani (b. ca.
1706), an Italian conductor and composer of operas, was in London in 1743. Francesco Ber-
nardi Senesino (ca. 1680–ca. 1750) was an Italian male mezzo-soprano who performed in many
of Handel's operas from 1720 to 1733. Carlo Farinelli (1705–1782) was an Italian male soprano
who performed operas in London in 1734 and was famous throughout Europe for his extraordinary range. Bonancini is probably Giovanni Battista Bononcini (1670–ca. 1750), an Italian
composer and an associate of Handel's in England. Beneditto is probably Benedetti, an Italian
singer who appeared in London around 1720. The three women were probably also Italian
singers who appeared in London in the 18th century.

latter allowing all for the back, and little or nothing for the belly, devour their poor threepenny meals, amidst poorer conversation, and leave Devil a Scrap for their fellow Dogs to feed upon—But to return to our history—

As all Societies, have certain mysterious Ceremonies, at the admission of members, so this venerable whin bush Club, have proper rites which they use on this occasion, and, which I shall here mention, that we may afterwards compare them with the ceremonies used by the ancient and honorable Tuesday Club of Annapolis, on the like occasion, and see how nighly they agree.

When I was admitted a member of that venerable Club, which was in the year 1737, In the Presidentship of the present venerable Mr Neal Gilpin, I was conducted into a private Room, by Mr Secretary Duncan, and two other Standing members of that venerable Club, They first asked me my age, to which having answered, they asked me where I was born, and receiving a proper reply, they demanded next where my Father and Grand-

[59] fathers were born, and these last being born In Clydsdale, they Clap'd ‖ a hat upon my head, stuck a bunch of furz into my button hole, (here I cannot but remark the great Simplicity of the badge of this venerable Club) made me subscribe the book of Rules, pay a fee to the Secretary, and conducting me with great State into the Club room, delivered me over to Signior Pasquelino De Marzis, master of Ceremonies, who first presented me to the venerable Mr Neal Gilpin, the President, and in a Set form of words, proclaimed me a Standing member, of the ancient and venerable whin bush Club of Lanneric. The venerable President took me most graciously by the hand, to whom I made a Complimentary Speech, and drank a bumper, or Quaff full of twopenny ale, and had a Clean pipe and tobacco presented to me, then these verses were Solemnly pronounced, by Mr Allan Ramsay, Poet Laureat.[6]

> As this furz is ever green,
> And this pipe streight white & clean,
> May your virtue still remain,
> Unchang'd, chast, pure, without a Stain,
> Which, if it does, then you we dub,
> A Standing member of this Club.

---

6. Ramsay (1686–1758) was a Scottish poet and bookseller noted for his elegies and satires, his collections of old Scottish and English songs (*Tea-table Miscellany* [1724–1732] and *The Ever Green* [1724]), which helped revive vernacular Scottish poetry, and his principal work, *The Gentle Shepherd* (1725), a pastoral drama. I have not found these verses in Ramsay's works.

The Whin Bush Club, admitting a member.

[facing page 58]

Tho these verses at first hearing, seemed to me alittle upon the hobbling order, yet in my opinion they Contain an excellent Sentiment, and a most beautiful metaphor and Similie.

[60]   Having thus delivered some anecdotes relating to the constitution of this venerable Club, which I think Sufficient to show, that it was the ancient and venerable Tuesday Club, and, that the Ancient and Honorable Tuesday Club of Annapolis in Maryland, is no other than the same Club transmigrated to America, In order to preserve the thread of this history Intire, I shall here give you, the Lineal Succession of the Presidents and respective officers of this venerable Club, from the year 1440 (for the Records go no further back, all before that period being lost) in a kind of Chronological table, with which I shall close the first book of this History.

A

Chronological
Table

of the

Ancient and Honorable Tuesday
Club
of Annapolis in Maryland

from the year 1440
Down to this present time[7]

---

7. In the following chronology, Hamilton apparently has invented a good many of the Whin-Bush Club names (e.g., Donough deagh Deagha and Jervais Fuckater are obvious inventions), or he is having fun with the family names of his contemporaries and friends (e.g., Craigie, Dalgleish, Abercrombie, Strachan, Murdoch, and even Majoribanks are all Scottish surnames, though none of those I have located has the given name Hamilton provides). Indeed, I would suspect the entire table of being a fabrication except that at least four of the characters named—three of them poets laureate—did exist. For Allan Ramsay, see p. 59n, above. David Lindsey was possibly Sir David Lindsay (1490–1555; Hamilton shortens his life seven years), a popular poet of great influence in his day, noted for satirizing the vices of the clergy and exposing the disorders of church and state. Zachary Boyd was probably the Reverend Zachary Boyd (1585–1653; Hamilton grants him another seven years), rector of Glasgow University (1634–1635, 1645), who wrote *The Last Battell of the Soule in Death* (Edinburgh, 1629), "Zion's Flowers" (MS at Glasgow University Library), and many other devotional works in verse. Harbottle Grimston (1603–1685; Hamilton adds seven years—he apparently did not think anyone would be silly enough to check these dates), was a member of Parliament, and I suspect that Hamilton may be toying with the names of other members of Parliament as well.

[62] A:C:	Presidents	Baylies	Censors
1440	The venerable *Congallus de Rutherin* uncertain when he tooke the Chair, the records being lost before this year, pres: after this 16 years	*Godofredus Gallatly* *Gustavus De Bruce* obiit 1449 Succeeded by *Gawen Macclewraith*	*Jordanus Crie* obiit 1452 Succeeded by *Ebenezer McLeash*
1457	The venerable *Donough deagh Deagha* lineally descended of the monarchs of Ireland Presid: 12 years	*Godofridus Gallatly* ob: 1460 Succeed: by *Duncan Davis* *Gawen Macclewraith*	*Ebenezer Mcleash*
1470	The venerable *Dongallus Auchtermughty* Præs: 15 years	*Duncan Davis* *Gawen Macclewraith* ob: 1482 Succ: by *Oneal Norton*	*Ebenezer McLeash* obiit 1477 Succed: by *Jacob Craigie*
1486	The venerable *Duncan Fairlie* præs: 9 years	*Duncan Davis* ob: 1489 Succ: by *Job Drumlanridge* *Oneal Norton*	*Jacob Craigie*
1496	The venerable *Luke Tomlinsonus* præs: 6 years, and was deposed for being a Lollard, eating roast beef on Good friday and other heretical practises	*Job Drumlanridge* ob: 1498 Succ: by *Jervis Dennison* *Oneal Norton*	*Jacob Craigie*
1502	The venerable *Alexander Pujolas* pres: 32 years aged 96	*Jervis Dennison* ob: 1518 Succ: by *Darby Yare* *Oneal Norton* ob: 1508 Succ: by *Andrew Jolly*	*Jacob Craigie* ob: 1503 Succ: by *Fulk Dallas* ob: 1529 Succ: by *Doctor Pengueasel*

A:C:	Treasurers	Masters of Ceremonies	Poets Laureat	Secretaries	[63]
1440	Gundy Galbreath	Alexr: Maccarty obiit 1443 Succeeded by Jodocus Gundy	Godfrey Connor an Irish bard	Gustavus Coulter obiit 1448 Succeeded by Joannes Duns Scotus, Grandson to the Philosophus Subtilis	
1457	Gundy Galbreath ob: 1463 Succ: by Jervais Dalgleish	Jodocus Gundy	Godfrey Connor ob: 1465 Succ: by Sylvester Fulk	Joan: Duns Scotus ob:1467 Succ: by Archibaldus Petrie	
1470	Jervis Dalgleish deposed for profane Swearing anno 1487 Succed: by Jonas Bogle	Jodocus Gundy obiit 1483 aged 95 Succ: by Andrew Logie	Sylvester Fulk ob: 1484 Succ: by Luke Fodry	Archibald: Petrie obiit 1485 Succ: by Robertus Kirk	
1486	Jonas Bogle	Andrew Logie	Luke Fodry	Robertus Kirk	
1496	Jonas Bogle ob: 1501 Succ: by Mungo Mcafferty	Andrew Logie	Luke Fodry	Robertus Kirk	
1502	Mungo Macafferty ob: 1512 Succ: by Michael Dougharty ob: 1526 Succ: by David Killigrew	Andrew Logie ob: 1506 Succ: by Geofry Tough expelld for drunkenness 1534 Succ: by Laughlan Mclean	Luke Fodry ob: 1510 Succ: by Laughlan McIntosh ob: 1526 Succ: by David Lindsey	Robertus Kirk ob: 1519 Succ: by Constantine Forbes	

A:C:	Presidents	Baylies	Censors
1535	The venerable *Gustavus Ockletree* The great præs: 11 years	*Darby Yare* ob: 1537 Succ: by *Andrew Dalziel* *Andrew Jolly* ob: 1539 Succ: by *Thomas Pintleridge*	*Doctor Pengueasel* ob: 1536 Succ: by *Donald McLaurie*
[64] 1547	The venerable *Alexander Kilspindie* Præs: 18 years	*Andrew Dalziel* ob: 1563 Succ: by *John Short* *Thomas Pintleridge*	*Donald Mclaurie* ob: 1551 Succ: by *Thomas Troop*
1566	The venerable *Mathew Pendragon* the Great of the Race of Arthur king of Britain præs: 7 years	*John Short* *Thomas Pintleridge* ob: 1567 Succ: by *Robert Cameron*	*Thomas Troop* ob: 1571 Succ: by *Jervais Bogie*
1574	The venerable *Arthur Kilbuckie* præs: 21 years	*Robert Cameron* *John Short*, expelled the club for blasphemously saying, he knew many priests that were damnd rogues 1567 Succ: by *Robert Drumore*	*Jervais Bogie* ob: 1595 Succ: by *Ringan Dobson*
1596	The venerable *Giles Punton* præs: 13 years	*Rob: Drumore* *Rob: Cameron* ob: 1603 Succ: by *Giles Breckendridge*	*Ringan Dobson* ob: 1608 Succ: by *Ezekiel Orum*
1610	The venerable *Sir Walter Wadle* Pres: 8 years	*Robert Drumore* ob: 1611 Succ: by *Constantine Abercrombie* *Giles Breckendridge*	*Ezekiel Orum* ob: 1612 Succ: by *Dermot McLeod*

A:C:	Treasurers	Masters of Ceremonies	Poets Laureat	Secretaries	
1535	David Killigrew ob: 1539 Succ: by Geo: Montgomery	Laughlan Mclean	David Lindsey	Constant: Forbes ob: 1539 Succ: by John Trotter	
1547	George Montgomery ob: 1553 Succ: by Giles Borlin	Laughlan Mclean deposed for whoring 1552 Succ: by Jervais Fuckater	David Lindsey ob: 1548 Succ: by Obadiah Mowat	John Trotter	[65]
1566	Giles Borlin ob: 1569 Succe: by Daniel Hog	Jervais Fuckater killd by an Irishman for excessive farting and belching in Company, 1572 Succ: by Duncan Tweedie	Obadiah Mowat ob: 1569 Succ: by Adam Thacker	John Trotter ob: 1567 Succ: by Willm: Mclatchy A:M:	
1574	Daniel Hog, expelld the Club, for perpetual Sleeping and loud Snoring 1677 Succ: by Mungo Strachan	Duncan Tweedie ob: 1594 Succ: by Adam Bell	Adam Thacker ob: 1593 Succ: by Jasper Bamph	Wm Mclatchy A:M: ob: 1585 Succ: by Obadiah Primrose	
1596	Mungo Strachan ob: 1598 Succeed: by Neal Craig	Adam Bell	Jasper Bamph ob: 1599 Succ: by Tobias Mowbray	Obadiah Primrose ob: 1603 Succ: by Malcolm Purdie	
1610	Neal Craig ob: 1610 Succ: by Mathew Paisly	Adam Bell ob: 1612 Succ: by John Auchtermoughty	Tobias Mowbray ob: 1613 Succ: by Thomas Jolly	Malcolm Purdie	

A:C:	Presidents	Baylies	Censors
1619	The venerable *Tobias Hodge* præs: 10 years	*Const: Abercrombie* *Giles Breckendrige* ob: 1620 Succ: by *Anthony Dottle*	*Dermot Mcleod* ob: 1623 Succ: by *Robert Restlerig*
1630	The venerable *Zachary Auchmoutie* Præs: 18 years	*Const: Abercrombie* ob: 1631 Succ: by *Jasper Tough* *Anthony Dottle*	*Robert Restlerig* ob: 1633 Succ: by *Donald McNash*
[66] 1649	The venerable *Jeremiah Majoribanks* præs: 9 years	*Jasper Tough* *Anthony Dottle* ob: 1650 being choaked with Cheese in Club Suc: by *Simon Spindle*	*Daniel McIntosh* went beyond Sea 1651 Succ: by *James Gorie*
1659	The venerable *Praisegod Maccarty* Præs: 15 years	*Jasper Tough* ob: 1660 Succ: by *Thomas Tubbs* *Simon Spindle*	*James Gorie*
1675	The venerable *Theophilus Petticrue* præs: 20 years	*Thomas Tubs* ob: 1681 Succ: by *Joseph Affleck* *Simon Spindle*	*James Gorie* obiit 1676 Succ: by *Ambrose Peezle*
1696	The venerable *Rowland Mcpherson* Præs: 16 years	*Simon Spindle* ob: 1699 aged 90 Succ: by *Gavin Prue* *Joseph Affleck*	*Ambrose Peezle* ob: 1698 Succ: by *Diego Trelawny*

A:C:	Treasurers	Masters of Ceremonies	Poets Laureat	Secretaries	
1619	Mathew Paisly went beyond Sea 1620 Succ: by Josh Murhead	John Auchtermoughtie	Thomas Jolly	Malcolm Purdie ob: 1621 Succ: by Joseph Aikenhead	
1630	Josh Murhead ob: 1639 Succ: by Donald Duncaster	Jno Auchtermoughtie ob: 1632 Succ: by Duff Murdock	Thomas Jolly, deposed for composing doggrell Rhimes, 1631 Succ: by Simon Mavis	Joseph Aikenhead hang'd for atheism, 1640 Succ: by David Crighton	
1649	John Muirhead ob: 1650 Succ: by Duncan Strang	John Murdoch ob: 1652 Succ: by Ringan Fairy	Simon Mavis ob: 1650 Succ: by Zachary Boyd who translated the Bible into elegant verse	David Crighton ob: 1650 Succ: by Neal Mclaster	[67]
1659	Duncan Strang ob: 1672 Succ: by Harbottle Grimston	Ringan Fairy ob: 1663 Succ: by Godfrey Purdie	Zachary Boyd ob: 1660, and left a legacy to the college of Glasgow, to print his Sacred pindarics Succ: by Simon Goldie	Neal Mclaster ob: 1669 Succ: by Joseph Irwin	
1675	Harbottle Grimston ob: 1692 Succ: by Daniel Waigle	Godfrey Purdie ob: 1694 Succ: by Moses Mcguire	Simon Goldie ob: 1676 Succ: by Duncan Mcgregor owtlawd	Joseph Irwin	
1696	Daniel Waigle Died drunk 1705 Succ: by Gilbert Farqhar	Moses Mcguire	Duncan Mcgregor owtlawd & killd in a duel 1697 Succ: by Joseph Dallas	Jos: Irwin ob: 1697 Succ: by James Mccaupie	

A:C:	Presidents	Baylies	Censors
1713	The venerable *Sir John Kirkaldie* sirnamed *Cruikshanks* præs: 14 years	*Joseph Affleck* ob: 1715 Succ: by *Dugal Patullo* *Gavin Prue*	*Diego Trelawny* ob: 1718 Succ: by *Thomas Waughop*
1728	The venerable *Mas: James Gillespie* præs: 7 years, in his time, 1732, this club settled a Colony in America	*Gavin Prue* ob: 1729 Suc: by *Duncan Gordon* *Dougal Patullo* ob: 1736 Succ: by *Andrew Gutterie*	*Thomas Waughop* In 1728 *George Neilson* a member of this club founded the Red house Club in Annapolis in Maryland
1736	The venerable *Mr Neal Gilpin* now in the Chair	*Duncan Gordon* *Andrew Gutterie* now baylies	*Thomas Waughop* ob: 1739 Succ: by *Sawny Mccawl* now Censor

[68] anno

1728	Erection of the Red house Club of Annapolis in Maryland, by Mr George Neilson, a Standing member of the ancient and venerable Tuesday (or whin bush) Club of Lanneric, this Club was Governed by a Rotation of Presidents, first President Mr George Neilson.
1732	Translation of the Seat of Government in the Red house Club.
1736	Death of Mr Geo: Neilson & dissolution of the Red-house Club.
1739	Foundation of the Ugly Club, by a residue of the members, of the Red house Club, this Club Governed by a rotation of Presidents, Mr Spruce Limberloins Secretary, Mr Vocifer Leatherlungs Orator.[8]
1744	Dissolution of the Ugly Club.
1745	The Revival or Settlement of the ancient and honorable Tuesday Club in America, by a residue of the members of the Ugly Club, this at first Governed by a rotation of Stewards, till the Election of the Honorable Nasifer Jole Esqr perpetual president, in November the same year, whom God preserve long in the Chair.

A:C:	Treasurers	Masters of Ceremonies	Poets Laureat	Secretaries
1713	Gilbert Farqhar in 1716, George Neilson a member of this Club was transported to America for his Loyalty to the pretender	Moses Mcguire ob: 1714 Succ: by Donald Braidie	Joseph Dallas ob: 1715 Suc: by Tory Rory killd the same year in the battle of Shereifmoor and Succ: by	James Mccaupie ob: 1714 Succ: by Laughlan McIntosh M:D:
1728	Gilbert Farqhar ob: 1730 Succ: by Archb: Halyburton	Donald Brade ob: 1735 Suc: by Signr: Pasquelino de Marzis who plays the violoncello, and	Peter Birnie ob: 1728 Succ: by Allan Ramsay who wrote his elegy and is now poet Laureat of	Laughlan Mcintosh M:D: ob: 1733 Succ: by the Learned and Ingenious Mr John Duncan
1736	Arch: Halyburton ob: 1737 Succ: by Daniel Bradie now Treasurer	is now master of Ceremonies	this Club	now Secretary

8. I have not been able positively to identify many of the names and pseudonyms of the Red-House Club and Ugly Club members. The only extant portion of Hamilton's draft of volume I (in which he provides actual surnames rather than the pseudonyms in the *History*) does not concern these precursors of the Tuesday Club, though occasionally I have managed to identify a pseudonym by comparing the index for the draft with that for volume I. Regrettably, then, Mr. Pedantius, Surly Sourface, Captain Swarthy, Andrew Vapor, and Major Vaunter remain a mystery. However, Hamilton does identify Mungo Macfun as Samuel Minskie (p. 106); the administration bond for Minskie reveals that he lived in Anne Arundel County with his wife Catherine and that he died in 1739 (Box 42, No. 1, Maryland State Archives, Annapolis). This bond was signed by Joshua Hopkinson (Joshua Swash in the *History*; Hamilton sketches his character on pp. 125–126), confirming that he and Minskie were indeed close friends. Moreover, either Spruce Limberloins or Vocifer Leatherlungs is the John Euens in the index to the draft, possibly John Evans (d. ca. 1766), a planter who lived in Prince George's County with his wife Eleanor (Wills, Md. State Arch.). Thomas Long was perhaps Thomas Long of Frederick County; the inventory of Long's possessions (Box 11, No. 34, Md. State Arch.) indicates that he died by 1781, that his wife's name was Jane, and that he was a friend of John Gibson's (see p. 86n, below). George Neilson (d. 1736) was the founder of the Red-House Club. A native of Scotland who joined the Jacobite rebellion in 1715 and was taken prisoner at Sheriffmuir, Neilson arrived in Virginia in 1716 as a Jacobite prisoner and was purchased by Charles Digges of Calvert County, Maryland. After serving his time, Neilson moved to Annapolis, where he began to brew and sell beer and then became a tavern keeper; his inn was used at least once as a meeting place for the Provincial Council in 1727 and for various business meetings (J. Thomas Scharf, *History of Maryland from the Earliest Period to the Present Day*, 3 vols. [Baltimore, 1897], I, 355, 388; William Hand Browne *et al.*, eds., *Archives of Maryland* [Baltimore, 1883–   ], XXV, 487, 501). Neilson was, indeed, a disputatious and tenacious fellow. In 1722 he initiated a grievance against William Digges and Charles Carroll over a large quantity of malt that they had agreed to provide him; he continued the grievance until 1733, when it was finally settled in their favor (No. 5, Chancery Court I.R.2, pp. 487–503, 631, Md. State Arch.).

History of the Ancient and Honorable Tuesday Club

Book II

From the transmigration of the Club to America, To the first Sederunt of the Ancient and honorable Tuesday Club of Annapolis in Maryland.

Chapter I

A learned Dissertation, in the Stile and manner of the Ingenious Mr Robert Burton.[1]

Those Solitary, moaping, morose, humdrum fellows, who evade, shun, run and fly, from all company, hate the Sight of men, as if they were Tygers, bears, Serpents, hobgoblins, Rhinoceroses and Panthers, and of the fair Sex, as if they were no better than Basilisks, cocatrices, harpies and Crocadiles, *Lemures Nocturni, mentulæque tersores,*[2] are mortal and Irreconcileable enimies to all Clubs, Jovial meetings, and humerous Conversations.

When I see a fellow of this Stamp, with his Clouded brows, and Lowring countenance, *monstrum deforme Ingens,*[3] I Imagine I behold a black

---

1. Burton (1577–1640) was vicar of Saint Thomas's in Oxford, rector of the parish of Seagrave, Leicestershire, and author of *The Anatomy of Melancholy* (Oxford, 1621). The influence of Burton's *Anatomy* appears throughout the *History,* not just in this chapter. Hamilton frequently parodies Burton's inflated rhetoric and pilfers passages from the *Anatomy,* and he dubiously honors Burton by signing his own translations of Latin doggerel "Robertus Burtonus." Hamilton clearly intended to set forth an anatomy of humor at Burton's expense, and nowhere does he parody Burton more effectively than in this chapter (pp. 74–75, for instance, are lifted almost verbatim from Burton's preface, "Democritus Junior to the Reader").

2. "Night demons and penis purgers" (similar to Horace, *Epistulae* 2.2.109).

3. "Unnatural, deformed monster" (similar to Vergil's description of Polyphemus, *Aeneid* 3.658).

69

[70]   cloud, rising from the dirty blustering South east, saturated with ‖ hollow murmuring Smouldering blasts, sending before it grumbling, tumbling, Jumbling thunder, and Infectious puffs of pestilential Steams, darkening the face of the fair day with polluted murky and Stiffling vapors, exhalations and damps, saturated, loaded, Impregnated and overcharged, with morbific Sulphureous atoms, bursting from the mouth of Tartarus it self.

——*Corpus onustum*
Histernis vitiis, animum quæque pergravat una. Horat:[4]

This disposition, according to Lemmius, *Institut, ad vitam optimam* Cap: 26, causes dryness of the brain, frenzy, dotage, and makes the body Dry, lean, hard and ugly to behold, the humors become a dust, the Eyes sunk in the head, the nose turns Sharp, the Jaws fall, Choler is Increased, and the whole body inflamm'd.[5]

These fellows ought never to be concerned in Clubs, compotations, merry meetings, Jovial frolicks, delectable Sports, or Juvenile Entertainments, for, they mar, spoil, disturb, destroy, contaminate, confuse and Interrupt all mirth and good humor.

Your Insipid, havy dull drivelling moralizers, Criticisers and Censors on the times, I do veryly think, also, are not at all fitted to be members of free, frolicksome, gay and Gamesome Clubs, those who will draw a moral
[71]   Conclusion, out of a decayd turnip, or rotten Cheese, and gravely ‖ infer from thence, that all flesh is grass; make a bad omen of two Straws accross, a Salt Seller overset, a Jacket buttoned awry, or a Coffin, as they call it, in the candle, or a Stocking wrong side out, or the glowing of ones face, or the Itching of ones elbow, or the noise of the worm Called the Death watch, are as little fit to make Companions of, and therefore, I would have all such fellows banished from our Clubical, as Plato banished Poets and musicians from his Philosophical Commonwealth, for they are fit for nothing but to be shut up in Solitary desolate caves or celles, and there to

4. "A body loaded with yesterday's vices, any one of which crushes the soul" (Horace, *Sermones* 2.2.77).

5. Levinus Lemnius (1505–1568) was a Dutch physician and author of *The Touchstone of Complexions* (London, 1565), *An Herbal for the Bible* (London, 1587), and *The Sanctuarie of Salvation, Helmet of Health, and Mirrour of Modestie and Good Maners* (London, 1592). Hamilton is referring to Lemnius's "How to Lead a Life That Shall Be Most Excellent," the supplement to his popular *The Secret Miracles of Nature* (London, 1658). In chap. 26, "Moderation in Sleeping and Waking," Lemnius writes: "Immoderate watching is hurtful for all ages, but most hurtfull for old age, as is also fasting, for both those dry the brain, and besides that they make men frantick and doting, they dry the whole body, and make it lean and starved" (p. 341). Hamilton embellishes the passage and yanks it out of context, which has nothing to do with misanthropy.

become mouldy, musty and worm eaten, with a pack of Lazy, loitering Idle monks, Hermits and Anchorites, and, to pass thro' the world silently, without leaving any the least trace or tract or path behind them, as a Ship in the wide ocean, or a bird in the air.

There is also a Set of fellows, of a Grum, Sullen, boisterous, Surly, Growling, captious disposition, who cannot bear a Jest, quirp, pun, conundrum or witty repartee, but Immediatly upon such being vented put on a threatning, passionate, furious countenance and are for nothing but Swords, daggers, pistols, blood, fire and destruction, *Sevit atrox Volscens,*[6] these are not fit to be on the face of the Earth, and therefore *a priori,* not qualified or adapted to be in Clubs (since all Clubs are earthly) where good humor and plasantry, should rule the roast, and appear in every countenance.

Having excluded these, and many others, whom it is needless to en- [72] large upon, such as your eternal wranglers, disputers, contradictors, falsifiers, Sceptical Doubters &ct: from our Clubical Commonwealth, I will now assert and mantain, that none but your merry, droll, facetious, Jocose, good humored, risible companions, punsters, comical Story tellers, and *Conundrumifiers,* ought to be members of those nocturnal assemblies, called Clubs, for the Quintessence, marrow and main fulcrum of Clubs consists in gayiety, Jollity, pleasantry and Jocosity.

What shall I then say, to every true Clubical genius but this.

Utere conviviis, non tristibus utere Amicis,
Quos Nuga et risus et Joca salsa Juvant,[7]

and, as Marselius Ficinus, winds up his epistle, to Bernard Canisianus,[8] so will I conclude this learned Chapter, with an advice to all free, honest, open Club Companions, and lastly, bestow a mild word or two on the Criticks.

Live merry my friends, void of care, perplexity, anguish, grief, live merrily, *letitia Cælum vos creavit,*[9] again, and again I request you to be merry, if any thing trowbles your head, or frets your guts, neglect it, let it pass, and this I enjoin you, not only as a Philosopher, but as a Physician, for, without this mirth, which is a Clearer of the head, (for laughing is

---

6. "Savage Volscen rages" (Vergil, *Aeneid* 9.420).

7. "Indulge in banquets, cultivate friends who are not sad, / Who are delighted by trifles, laughter, and spicy jokes."

8. Marsilio Ficino (1433–1499) was a learned Italian philosopher who revived Platonic philosophy and is best remembered for his translations of Plato and Plotinus. Hamilton is referring to Ficino's *Epistolarium familiarum* (1495), but he has faithfully lifted Ficino's advice—and the Tiresias story immediately following it—from Burton's chapter "Mirth and Merry Company" in the *Anatomy of Melancholy.*

9. "Heaven made you for joy."

preferable to Sneezing) and enlivener of the fancy, there is no Science, no
[73] wisdom, mirth is the life and Quintessence of Physic; medicine and || what-
ever is applied to prolong the life of man, without this, is dull and dead,
and of no force, *dum fata sinunt vivite læti*, says Seneca the Philosopher, ὀ
βιοσ βϱαχους, says Hippocrates the Physician,[10] and I say, be merry, be
merry.

> Would you shun Charon the ferryman,
> Consult Doctor Diet, Doctor Quiet and Doctor Merriman.

It was Tiresias the prophets councel to Menippus, that travelled all the
world over, even down to hell itself to seek content, and his last farewell to
him to be merry, Contemn the world, (sayth he) and count it and its
vanities and toys, Trash, lumber, trumpery and Rubbish, this only covet all
your life long, be not curious in other men's affairs, or ever Solicitous in
any thing, place not your happiness in what is Intirely in the power of
another, but with a well composed and contented estate, enjoy yourself
within yourself, and above all things, and by all means be merry, and keep a
constant Sunshine and Clear weather, within the precincts of your pericranium, thus will you enjoy peace and Quiet and pleasure to yourself, and
communicate Satisfaction, and delight to your neighbour.[11]

And now, ye Learned Dons of the Critical tribe, ye Myrmidons of
Billingsgate, ye Sons of Erynnis[12] and Spawn of Medusa, ye empoisoned
Snakes that lurk in the flowery herbage of literature, It is evident, I have
excluded you together with the aforesaid Humdrum fellows from our
Clubical Commonwealth, I know well what Sentence you will pronounce
upon me, but snarl, revile, cavil, carp and oppose what you will.

[74]   *Allatres licet usque, nos et usque,*
        Et gannitibus Improbis lacessas.[13]

I know what you'll say, *aperto ore*,[14] you'll blame my Doric Dialect, unpolished Stile, tautology, apish Imitation, a Rhapsody of rags raked together
from dunghills, excrements of authors, fopperies, toys, tumbled and Jum-
bled and Crumbled higglede-pigglede, without Invention, art, Judgement,

___

10. "While the fates permit, live happily"; "life is short."
11. Tiresias was the legendary blind Theban seer. Menippus (fl. 3d century B.C.) was the
originator of the seriocomic style in literature.
12. *Erinyes* was the Greek name for the Furies (the avenging deities, Alecto, Megaera, and
Tisiphone).
13. "However much you will rail at us / And provoke us with your constant snarling"
(Martial, *Epigrams* 5.60.2).
14. "Openmouthed," i.e., with a big mouth.

wit, learning. Raw, rude, crude, harsh, fantastical, absurd, Insolent, Indis-
creet, vain, Scurrile, Indigested, idle, Silly, dull and dry—and what care I?
all this I confess, and freely own that I affect it, and all of you together
cannot say worse of me, than I do of myself, unless you prove this to be a
History of lies, which I defy you to do. Like other Authors, I pilfer out of
old books, stuff up new comments, scrape Ennius's dunghills, and drink
from Democritus's well,[15] I contribute my Quota, to stuff our Libraries full
of putrid papers, and also to furnish every close stool and Jakes, *Scribo
carmina quæ legunt cacantes,*[16] they'll serve also to put under Christenmass
pies, wrap up Spice and tobacco, and keep roast meat from burning; and
tho' the perusal of them may keep some fools Idle, yet it will keep them out
of mischief; I grant you, these Lucubrations are not worth reading, therefore lose no time, I pray you, in perusing this vain Subject, as I have in
writing on it, all the Apology I shall make is that I have precedents for it, an
apology which Sure may serve me, a Simple Scribbler, since it has hereto-
fore served The wisdom of the British Nations In Parliament assembled, ||
and the profound wisdom of our grave Judges and Lawyers; who have [75]
taken precedents for their Rule, in matters every whit as exceptionable, by
the Standard of right reason, *Uno absurdo dato mille sequuntur, perfugium
iis qui peccant,* others as absurd, vain, Idle, Illiterate, *non nulli alii Idem
fecerunt,* so that of me or you, it cannot be said as a certain old Author said
of a very great man, *Oinom, Duonorum, pleorumei virom Illom optimom esse
Consentiunt,* perhaps you yourselves have acted as absurdly as I, *novimus et
qui te &ct:* we have all of us our faults and blind Sides, *scimus et hanc veniam
&ct:* Thou Censurest me, so have I done others, and may do thee, *nam
dubito multos lectores hic fore stultos, cedimus inque vicem &ct:* is *lex talionis*
and *quid pro Quo,* go on now censure, criticise, scoff, rail.[17]

15. Ennius (239–169 B.C.), one of the founders of Latin literature, was famous for his influence on subsequent Roman writers, all of whom borrowed from him. Vergil in particular
admitted that "he gathered gold from Ennius's dung heap." The Democritus referred to here is
again Robert Burton, who signed himself Democritus Junior and who borrowed lavishly from
earlier authors. Burton himself reflected on plagiarism, comparing authors to apothecaries,
who make new mixtures by pouring from one vessel into another.

16. "I write poems that they read while shitting" (Martial, *Epigrams* 12.61.10).

17. "Given one absurdity, a thousand follow: a refuge for those who go wrong"; "certain
others have done the same"; "of the good men, a great many agree that he was the best man";
"we who know you"; "we know, and pardon this"; "for we concede that many readers here will
doubtless be fools, and vice versa"; "this is the law of retaliation and quid pro quo." The
"certain old Author" could refer to almost anyone, but it is most likely Isocrates. The Greek
version of the passage appears in Engelbert Drerup, *Isocratis opera omnia . . .* (Leipzig, 1906–),
I, 143.

Nasutus sis quisque licet, sis denique Nasus,
Non potes in nugas dicere plura meis,
Ipse ego quam dixi.[18]

And thus, having Called whore first, I go off with flying colors.

Chapter II

The History and Character of Mr George Neilson, and the Cause of his
coming to America.

It is the Indispensable duty of all Historiographers, and Biographers, to collect and compile, in the most Impartial, Candid, and unprejudiced manner, the Glorious actions atchieved by great men, and faithfully to transmitt them to posterity.

[76]   The lives of great princes, Generals, poets, Philosophers, orators, and founders of Clubs, hold the first Rank in Biography, and shine like the Stars of the first magnitude among those of Physicians, Logicians, magitians, arithmeticians, musicians, Lawyers, Divines, mechanics and Almanac makers, which may be Compared to the fainter constellations.

Micat Inter Ignes
Luna minores. Horat:[1]

The Illustrious person, of whose life I am now going to give some account, as being the founder of a Club, Immediatly derived from, and established upon the constitution, and police of the Ancient and venerable Tuesday (or whin bush) Club of Lanneric, stands therefore in the foremost rank of such worthies as have decorated Biography.

As the public is generally curious, to know the Stature, dimension, features, dress and air of Great and Illustrious men, I shall here present my readers with the portraiture of our Hero, and finish it off as well as I can.

Master George Neilson then, was a man of a small Stature, about four feet eight Inches high, of which he Cared not to lose one quarter of an Inch, for he strutted in his walk, and stood bolt upright like a pike, he was of a slender make, long visage, nose Inclinable to the aqueline, his chin

18. "You can turn up your nose if you please, and turn into one finally; / You can't say more against my nonsense / Than I have said myself" (Martial, *Epigrams* 13.2.1).
1. "The moon shines out among the lesser fires" (Horace, *Carmina* 1.12.46).

Mr George Neilson

[facing page 76]

alittle peacked, his eyes lively and full of motion, he was neither bandy
legg'd nor battle Ham'd, nor Spla footed, as it is said most Scotsmen are,
but he had, I know not what Sort of peculiarity about his legs, which I
[77]   cannot otherwise describe, but that it did not resemble ‖ that of any other
person, but, we often find, that great and Illustrious men, have had Certain
peculiarities in their make, Thus, Alexander the great had a wry neck,
Ptolomy Physcon, king of Ægypt was pot Bellied, Julius Cæsar was bald,
Cicero had an excressence like a vetch on his Eyebrow, Hannibal was cock
eyed, Monsieur Scarron was made like the letter Z, Monsieur St Evermond
had a bottle nose, and a large bump on his forehead, The Duke of Luxem-
burg was Hump backed, and Alexander Pope Esqr, had a crump Shoulder.[2]

Having given this short description of his person, I shall next delineat
his dress, he wore one of your large Revolution hats, tho in principle, he
was an Antirevolutioner, under that, a very voluminous tye wig, which
covered two thirds of his face, and hung down before half way to his pocket
holes, and the bob behind depended to within two Inches of his loins;
Round his neck, he usually wore a large twisted neck cloth, which was
drawn thro' the fourth or fifth button hole of his upper coat, which was
commonly very much daubed with Snuff, that he took, from out of a large
Mull, that he Carried with him as his constant fellow traveller, his loins
were girt with a leatheren belt, at which hung a small Sword, of the length
and Size of a Spanish Spado, with which he used to defend himself on all
occasions against Insults. As to his other aparrel, there was nothing re- ‖
[78]   markable, that differed from that of other men, only, when he went a
horseback he was commonly armed with pistols.

I shall now give a detail of his political principles, and learning, and
wind up the whole with a catalogue of his virtues and vices.

Mr Neilson was in principle a Jacobite, having Imbibed in his tender
years, before the maturity of his Judgement, (as indeed most Jacobites do)
the heroic tenets and maxims of that Illustrious party. He firmly believed
that kings were *Jure Divino,* and God's vicegerents upon Earth, and therefore, their actions of what nature soever were not to be enquired into or

2. Ptolemy VII (184?–116 B.C., nicknamed Physcon, or "fat paunch") was a friend of culture
but extremely vicious and dissolute. Paul Scarron (1610–1660) was a French burlesque drama-
tist and novelist who was deformed and paralyzed in his lower limbs. Charles de Saint-Denis,
sieur de Saint-Évremond (1613–1703), was a French exile who spent most of his later years in
England, associating with the wits and courtiers of the day and writing essays on a variety of
literary and philosophical topics. François Henri de Montmorency-Bouteville, duc de Luxem-
bourg (1628–1695), was a French soldier who served in wars against Spain and Holland and was
created marshal of France in 1675.

Canvassed; That they had an Indefeasible hereditary right to their Dominions, provided they were true kings, and not usurpers, and Creatures of popular formation; That they were accountable to no earthly power; That the Steuart family had the only Indefeasible and Indisputable title and Right to the Crown of Great Brittain France and Ireland, and were the only True Defenders of the faith; and that all and every person or persons, who secluded them from that Claim and right, were *Ipso facto*, Usurpers, traitors and Rebels, If any one contradicted him in these tenets, by alledging that the hereditary right of the line of British kings was Interrupted by three Illustrious bastards, viz: William of Normandy, Called the Conqueror, the Son of a base mechanic; The Issue of John of Gaunt, Duke of Lancaster, by his concubine Catharine Swynford, from whom sprung Henry VII, in a direct line; and Robert Steuart, ‖ the first of that name, had a bastard by [79] Elizabeth More, who succeeded, by a Scotch act of parliament, his lawful Issue by his queen being excluded; he would either answer them by drawing his Sword, and bidding them encounter cold Iron, or presenting his pistols, and daring them to smell powder, but when he had a mind to be more moderate, he would convince them by this Silencing argument, by which he proved beyond dispute, the uninterrupted legitimacy, of the royal line of those princes, vizt: that they possessed the miraculous power of curing the king's evil by the touch, a power, which neither the House of Orange, nor that of Hanover, could ever pretend to.

    As to Mr Neilsons Religion, I can say but very little, he having never been very communicative on this point, Some however, have Imagined he was a nonjuror, others, a high flown Episcopalian, others a Roman Catholic, and there have not been wanting some, who have maliciously asserted that he was a Presbyterian, an Anabaptist, Seventh Day man, Quaker, and even a muggletonian,[3] nay some have suspected him for a Jew, and of the Seed of Abraham, because forsooth he did not love pork, and was thought to be circumcised, but, as for the first, it is a food, which many Scots men detest, and yet are no Jews, and as for the other, we all know, that their are some Circumstances, a man may be under, that may oblige him to part with a Slice of his foreskin, and when that is the case, there is so small a difference between the Scar, made by the priests knife and the Surgeons, that they cannot easily ‖ be distinguished, but, as this affair is at best uncertain, I [80] shall leave it where I found it.

3. A member of a sect founded in 1651 by Lodowicke Muggleton (1609–1698) and John Reeve (1608–1658), who claimed to be the "two witnesses" of Rev. 11:3–6; Muggleton, a journeyman tailor, was imprisoned and fined for blasphemy.

His Learning was of a mixed kind, having a Spice of every thing, it is said he understood the languages, being thought a critic in Erse, Low dutch and Law french, the first he acquired in the highlands of Scotland, being led to converse much there, by reason of his political principles, the Second he learned among the Dutch Regiments quartered in Scotland, and the last by his diligent application to the common law, which last, (a Strange unaccountable taste) he studied more for pleasure than profit, as to latin and greek, he was always shy of showing his knowledge in either, and therefore it cannot be ascertained how deep a Clerk he was in these languages; True Indeed, it is said of him, that being asked the English of *Sancta Maria,* he made answer, he did not know, but he might possibly say so on purpose, to discourage the opinion that prevailed, of his being a Roman Catholic, we cannot certainly affirm, that he was versed in any of the Oriental tongues, such as the persic, turcic, Arabic, Syriac or Coptic, tho' some alledged that he spoke all these fluently, but I am rather apt to think, that it was a very broad Scots dialect, which he spoke with great volubility, especially when in a passion.

Having thus dispatched the Languages, we next remark on his Skill in the liberal Arts and Sciences, he was a bold musician, and could play in a [81] very extraordinary || manner upon several Instruments, such as the violin, Bass viol, flute, Hautboy and Bassoon, and some say that he handled the Jews Harp with great dexterity; but the Bassoon excelled all his other performances, for by means of this Solemn Instrument, he used to draw many of the Rustics about his door, who flocked to the Sound, as the Stones and trees did of old to the Sound of Orpheus's Harp,[4] with this difference, that, as the harp of the latter used to animate Inanimate beings, so *vice versa,* the Bassoon of the first, used to Inanimate animated beings, or Convert human Shapes into Stocks and Stones.

In other things also, he was Profoundly versed, such as Physiognomy, palmistry, Judicial astrology, Cookery, Pastry, Chemistry, Pharmacy, and many other accomplishments, which we cannot here Ennumerate, In fine, he was such an extraordinary Genius, in his way, that a Certain Poet wrote an Epitaph on him,[5] which for its Justness and Singularity I shall here transcribe.

Poor Neilson's gone, a warlike Scot,
What was he, and what was he not?

4. The most popular version of this myth appears in Ovid, *Metamorphoses* 6.86–109; see also Vergil, *Georgics* 4.494.
5. If Hamilton himself was not responsible for this doggerel, the author was probably the club poet laureate, Jonas Green, who would have taken this occasion to exercise his genius.

He liv'd, 'till this his dissolution,
In Sanguine hopes of revolution,
He liv'd in hopes of better days,
But Grew Impatient with delays,
And still he would have liv'd, no doubt,
Poor man, but that his Rum was out,
And all he left behind they tell you,
Was an old plaid Nightgown & his Nelly.[a]

Now, as to Mr Neilson's moral Character, he was reckoned one of those people whom the world Calls good natured men, being apt to let his Substance go out faster ‖ than it came in, of a free liberal and open disposition, for which many wise men esteemed him a fool, and those who profited by his lavishness, never once gave him thanks for his favors, but after the manner of the world, used to receive as fast as he gave, and then laugh in their Sleeves, he was esteemed a man of great veracity, except only in two points, and these were, when he talked either of his family or travels, on both which topics many Imagined that he shot flying,[6] for, on the first, he would fall into Rhapsodies, of great Princes, dukes and Earls of the Name of Neilson, the Progenitors and Chiefs of his family, on the latter he dealt much in the marvelous, as many Great travellers do, among the other prodigies he had seen in his travels, he would talk of Churches twenty miles Long, of Spiders as large as a Sheep, of men 15 or 20 feet high, of Scots Lairds worth 20000 ~~lib~~ Sterling a year, and among his own exploits, he used to relate, how he once spited[7] 24 woodcocks on the wing, at one Shot upon the ramrod of his Gun, and strung them all exactly thro' the Eyes, and such like Stories, he was of such a noble and elevated Spirit, that he would never stoop to ask favors of any body, tho' he sometimes stood in need of the asistance of others, and some say, that his virtue in this particular, carried him so far, that he died in very great want and extreme necessity, yet his Inate Spark of heroism, made him desirous that the world should believe, he was in very opulent Circumstances.

Mr Neilson was a man of very warm passions and stood much upon points of honor, very apt to be highly provoked at Slight affronts, and upon all occasions of this Sort, out flew the Spado, or pistol, & his common expressions ‖ on these occasions, were to desire his adversary, to smell [83]

[82]

(a) Mr Neilsons housekeeper.

6. As J. A. Leo Lemay suggests, *shooting flying*, or *shooting a bird on the wing*, had become synonymous by Hamilton's time with telling a tall tale ("The Tall Tales of a Colonial Frontiersman," *Western Pennsylvania Historical Magazine*, LXIV [1981], 46n).

7. *To spit* is to string together (needles) by passing a wire through the eyes.

powder, or kiss cold Iron. These excursions or flights passed upon many simple people, and they submitted to the prowess of his Invincible Arm, but Mr Neilson sometimes met with undaunted heroes, who were not to be Intimidated by these methods, and once in particular, a Gygantic Champion, clapped him in a hamper, with his tie wig, Sword, and other warlike Accoutrements about him, and throwing him headlong into the river, he narrowly escaped a drowning, and after he was draggd out of the water, he Remained as mute as a fish, and made no more words of the matter.

It will be expected here, that I should give an account of our heroe's parentage and place of birth, but as both are uncertain, I shall only say, that he was born in the Lowlands of Scotland, either in the City of Edinburgh, or that of Air, which is only conjectured from his dialect or Speech, and so leaving these two ancient Cities, to contend for the Honor of this great man's birth, as Seven Grecian Cities did for the birth of Homer,[8] I shall Conclude this Chapter, with an account of the reason of his coming to America.

The general reason that is given for the Scots leaving their own country, is, that it is a place where they have but very cold comfort; The Climate, tho healthy, being unkindly and uncomfortable, the country poor, Gener-[84] ally barren, and badly stocked in provisions, and that the || natives, being of a bustling, pushing disposition, cannot rest at home, where nothing is to be got, but range about to all parts of the world, Improve their fortunes, hence it is, that in all quarters of the Earth, many Scots men are to be found. This I grant may be the case with many of that nation, but it was by no means the case with our heroe, whose departure from his native country, we have reason to believe was Involuntary.

The Case then with Mr Neilson was this, being a Loyal and hearty espouser of the cause of the Steward family, in the year —15, he took the field, with many other valiant and hardy Champions, who then made a bold attempt, to set James VIII, as they called him, upon the British Throne, and after many Skirmishes, and one decisive battle at Sherrifmuir,[9] where much blood was spilt, and many bones broke to no purpose, our heroe fled, among the rest of the vanquished Rout, and being unluckily taken, luckily escaped a hanging, and was sent over Seas to America, to plot out the

8. Hamilton is probably drawing his information from the discussion of Homer's life in Pope's preface to his edition of the *Iliad,* where he states that Salamis, Ithaca, Colophon, Io, Colony, Smyrna, and Chios all claimed to be Homer's birthplace (see *The Poems of Alexander Pope,* ed. Maynard Mack [New Haven, Conn., 1951–1969], VII, 43–45).

9. An engagement during the Fifteen rebellion (Nov. 13, 1715), between 10,000 Jacobite rebels under the earl of Mar and 3,300 loyalist Scots under the duke of Argyll. After an indecisive confrontation, Mar retreated and his rising collapsed.

remainder of his life, with others of that Loyal party, to retale rum & punch
& to found Clubs.

Chapter III

*Of the turn and genius of the Annapolitans to Clubbing, at, and after
the arival of Mr George Neilson in America.*

At the time when this great personage arrived in America, with many
of his countrymen, equally concerned with him, in the same loyal and
honorable undertaking, the Annapolitans were very ‖ much addicted to   [85]
Clubbing, so that I shall speak within Compass, If I say, that there were
then at least 40 clubs in that City.[1] Since then, I must own, that the Clubbing humor is much abated among them, there being now at this day, not
above four or five Clubs, and, to make up this number, we must reckon the
Free masons and Routs, which by many connoiseurs, are not in a strict
sense reckoned Clubs, the first, dealing in mysteries, which they keep Intirely to themselves, and submitting to a great number of Rulers, such as
Grand masters, Deputy Grand masters, masters and pass masters, the latter
are governed and managed Intirely by the Ladies, being mixed assemblies
of male and female, and among these last, the disputes for Precedency, are
not as yet, nor ever can be adjusted, the first of these Societies, for want of
proper presidents, cannot be called Clubical, the latter, on account of their
moderen Institution, deserve not the name of Clubs.

The Clubs that prevailed at this time In Annapolis, were all bouzing or
toaping Clubs, there were wine Clubs, punch Clubs, Rumbo Clubs (for
Grog was not yet invented) Flup Clubs,[2] Lambs wool Clubs, Bishop Clubs,

1. Hamilton may be exaggerating a bit, but there certainly were a good many clubs in
colonial Maryland. Another Marylander, Henry Darnall, observed that in Maryland "there are
settled Clubs in every County, where they talk over Affairs" (*A Just and Impartial Account of the
Transactions of the Merchants in London, for the Advancement of the Price of Tobacco* [Annapolis,
Md. (1729)], 12). Given the relish with which Marylanders apparently approached clubbing,
perhaps some of the clubs Hamilton mentions in the *History* actually existed (e.g., the College
Club, the Red-House Club, the Ugly Club, the Eastern Shore Triumvirate, the Hiccory Hill
Club, the Saturday Club, and the club at Charles Town in Cecil County). However, the
standard works on colonial culture, including Richard Beale Davis, *Intellectual Life in the
Colonial South, 1585–1763*, 3 vols. (Knoxville, Tenn., 1978), do not include any information on the
clubs, nor does the *Maryland Gazette* or the indexes of the *Maryland Historical Magazine* and
the *Virginia Magazine of History and Biography*.

2. Here and in the next paragraph, Hamilton uses *flup* for *flip*, a mixture of beer and liquor
sweetened with sugar and heated with a hot iron.

negus Clubs, Syder Clubs, Rum Clubs, Bub Clubs, and Syllabub Clubs, The last of which were all female Clubs, tho' some Sorts of beaus and pritty fellows were admitted to them, who, in their mein and address approached nighly to the Feminine Gender.

To describe every one of these in Particular, would take up too much time, and consume a world || of paper and Ink, I shall therefore only say, that the main Intent and purpose of the meeting of these Clubs, was to drink and be merry, and among them all, it was hail fellow, well met, there being little or no distinction, tho the wine Clubs punch Clubs and bub Clubs were reckoned in the first rank, as also the Syllabub Clubs, and the Secret negus and Bishop Clubs, which were composed of Ladies, The Rumbo Clubs, Lambs wool and Flup Clubs were reckoned the Second degree, and the Cyder and Rum Clubs of the Lowest Class.

The favorite liquor in the female Clubs, as I have said, was Syllabub, which they drank avowedly and publicly, they had, tis true, other liquors, which they used in their privy councils, of a more diuretic nature, such as Bishop and Negus, which they were unwilling should be used at any time, but when shut up in the Conclave, least it should be thought by the men, (O horrid!) that they were adicted to strong liquors, which all fine Ladies must Surely abominate, or seem to abominate, by keeping these shut up in their Closets, only to look at, or smell at when vaporish, and Indeed they Chose not to let any of the Males see them tipple these liquors except Mr J—n G—bs—n,[3] who was their Secretary and privy Councellor, on all occasions, and is said, used to get so far Into their councils and Confidence, as to be permitted to hold the ——, while some of them —— but this being a piece of Secret History, my readers must excuse me, if I do not speak plain, therefore, as to the above breaks and dashes, I leave all my wise politic and discerning readers || to fill them up with what words they please. The Reverend and Pious Mris A—— C——,[4] who had more of the Coquette than the prude in her Character, was Leader and directress of these female Clubs, sometimes Indeed, this wise Lady would Graciously condescend to permit them to drink this Negus and Bishop in a more open manner, but always with this proviso, that, upon the approach of any of the Male Sex, except the aforesaid Mr J—n G—bs—n, who was by some thought to be of the doubtful Gender, they should Clap the bowl or tankard under their petticoats, so soon as the adversarry came in Sight, and keep them snug in the same manner as the dutch frows do their Stoves.

Such of these Clubs as were Composed of Male members, were Gov-

[86]

[87]

3. John Gibson (see biographical sketch).
4. Perhaps Ann Carter (see biographical sketch).

erned by kings, and were called the Royalist Clubs, they were therefore, so
many distinct monarchies, as Ireland was, before the English conquest, but
then, the Reigns of these monarchs were Commonly very short, for, they
might perhaps hold up an hour or two, and then be fairly knocked under
the table, they acquired their Royalty by conquest, he who could drink off a
large bowl of punch at a draught, being Immediatly Crowned king of the
Club, and he held his place, till another drank off a larger, so that, in one
night, you might see all the members of one of these Clubs, crowned king,
each in his turn, and each in his turn fall flat under the Table, This method
of Conquest was easier, than that enjoined by Pope Adrian IV, who, thinking that he had ample authority, to dispose of all the kingdoms in the
world, very || generously gave unto Sancho, Brother to the king of Arragon, [88]
the Land of Ægypt, then in the possession of the Sarazens, and he should
have it, if he would take the pains to conquer it, and accordingly proclaimed him king of Ægypt, Sancho Informed of this, would not be behind
hand with his holiness in curtesies, and so, he gravely proclaimed the pope
Caliph of Bandas, which he might conquer and possess if he pleased;5 I say,
these Club Conquests of the Bowl, were much easier accomplished, than
the Conquests proposed by this pope, for to effect these last, men, money, a
wise head and good conduct were requisite, whereas the first might be
affected with a wide Swallow, Long breath, and no further conduct was
necessary, than to conduct the bowl to the head, which, in this case, proved
so much the better, the less brains or wisdom it contained, as there was
thereby a Greater vacuum in the Skull to receive the Intoxicating fumes.

In these Clubs, the king had an absolute power to command any of his
Subjects, to drink as often and as much as he pleased, but then he was
obliged to pledge him in a Cup of an equal Capacity.

When they went to war in these Clubs, (and their wars were generally
civil or Intestine) it was only with offensive arms, and generally did not
break out, till it grew very Late, and several monarchs, one after another,
had mounted the throne, and one after another fallen prostrate or Supine
under the table, these offensive weapons were bottles, de- || canters, candle- [89]
sticks, glasses, and sometimes, when they used great ordenance or heavy
artillery, Chairs and Stools, till at last, O tragic Scene! the floor was strowed
with the Slain, and much good christian liquor was shed, and flowed about,
blended with the frothy Spewings of the knocked down Combatants.

5. Adrian IV, or Nicholas Breakspear (1100?–1159), the only Englishman ever to become pope
(1154–1159), was especially famous for giving Ireland to Henry II. Sancho VI (d. 1194) was king
of Navarre (1150–1194) whose war with Aragon and Castile (1173–1180) was terminated by an
alliance with Aragon.

The Royalist Club.

[facing page 87]

The only Club among these, that was distinguished by a particular name, I find to be that called the College Club; but for what reason this Club was so called I cannot conjecture, unless it was this, that one of their members was a parson, and had had a College education. This parson had the honor to be crowned king of the Club, much oftner than any other member, he having a very Strong (I dare not say an empty or a hard) head, like most of his cloth, so that it was not a small quantity of Liquor that would knock him down; This Club was soon dissolved, and Mr Neilson gave a very Learned and Ingenious reason for it, which was this, that they Indiscreetly Intrusted the Clergy, with too much power, and suffered the priesthood to meddle too much in State affairs, which conduct, will at last Surely prove the ruin of every kingdom, State, commonwealth and Club, since the Gentlemen of the crape, once they are exalted to power, always prove the most Cruel and oppressive Tyrants, and, he gave a glaring example to support this learned argument, which was, the calamities and hardships the Christian princes labored under, for several centuries, by rashly clapping no less than three crowns at once, upon the head of a certain old doating parson at Rome, ‖ who at last grasped so much power, that he made many wise men teach, and fools believe the doctrine, that he had a full and unlimited power to depose kings, and kill them at his pleasure, an Instance of the Truth of this gentleman's observations, we may have occasion to exhibit, in the History of the Ancient and Honorable Tuesday Club. [90]

How Mr Neilson disliked the Regal government in Clubs, and how he, with much pains, labor and perswasion, established the presidential Government in it's place, and Erected a Club near upon the plan of the Ancient and Venerable Tuesday (or whin bush) Club of Lanneric, by virtue of a Special commission, from the venerable Mr Neal Gilpin, we shall show in the Sequel.

Chapter IV

The first Institution and foundation of the Red-house Club of Annapolis, by Mr George Neilson and other Illustrious personages.

Mr George Neilson, after his arrival in Annapolis, Took some time to look about him, and having maturely considered, the wretched and Confused condition, that the Clubical constitutions were under in that City, he set himself Strenuously about working a Reformation in these Clubs, and,

having an ample Commission in his pocket, under the Privy Seal of the
[91] Venerable Mr Neal Gilpin, Impowering him to erect Clubs || in any of his
majestie's plantations in America, he made the best use of the power conveyd to him by that commission.

His first business was, like all other wise and long headed politicians,
to hear all and say nothing, for which Reason, he, in the beginning, attended these Clubs like a Pythagorean Philosopher, resolving with himself
to keep a Strict Silence, till such time as he should discover the bent and
Genius of these Clubs and the humours of the members, at the same time,
he constantly had his Scouts out, to make observation, and bring him due
Intelligence, these were some Ingenious persons, his own countrymen, who
perhaps may make, some of them, a conspicuous figure in this history; they
frequented these Clubs themselves, drank with them, roard with them,
laughd with them, fought and squabbled with them, and were Crowned
kings with them; but they carried their policy farther in making cunning
enquiries into the particular private Characters of the members, by frequently visiting the matrons and old women of the City, where Certain
Gossoping Clubs of females, Informed themselves carefully of every private
occurrence in families, and as carefully divulged them again, sometimes
by way of Secret, and sometimes with openness and frankness free of all
reserve.

Upon account of this silent, reserved, and politic behavior, Mr Neilson
passed among these people, for either a bashful Sheepish fellow, or a mo-
[92] rose Sullen com- || panion, and some Imagined he was melancholly mad,
others, that he was in love, and, if he had not constantly drank his bumper
in his turn, and tossed off the Bowl, and suffered himself to be crowned
king by the Club, without saying a word, they would have expelld him from
their Clubs as an useless member.

Mr Neilson, by this behaviour, put a very great constraint upon himself, for he was naturally of an airy and volatile disposition, much adicted to
talking and fond of displaying his Learning and parts, besides, being of a
hasty and passionate temper, it Cost him many a hard Struggle to contain
himself, when any of these Club wits passed their Jokes upon him, and
made him the but of the company, which they were very apt to do, upon
the account of the oddity of his appearance, vizt: his oblong Sharp visage,
his peaked Chin, his Snuff besmeard countenance, his large wig and his
long Sword, Sometimes his passion would so ferment and fret within his
breast, that his color, would come and go in his face, now turning pale as
chalk, and then as red as a turkey Cock, and, it is said, he was once screwd
up to such a pitch, by their running their rig, and making their game and

Mr Neilsons anger restrained by Philosophy

[facing page 92]

fun of him, that he was seen to lay his hand on the hilt of his Sword, but, his Philosophy, overcoming his passion, he quickly retracted it again, and composed his countenance.

I might on this occasion, to decorate this history have Introduced the Goddess Philosophy, in a beautiful Similitude, pulling Mr Neilson, by one [93] of the ties of his wig ‖ to restrain his heroic fury, as Homer has Introduced Minerva, pulling the yellow Locks of Achilles, upon a paralell occasion,[1] but I purposely evade these Similies and allusions, for fear this history should exceed the Size of a portable volume.

Mr Neilson and his Scouts, having at last discovered by Indefatigable application and Industry, the Disposition and bent of these Club members, and finding that like other men they were mightily Inclined to party, upon this ground they laid their plan of Reformation, and set upon erecting a new Club on a different model, by strictly observing, that known Machiavelian maxim *Divide et Impera*,[2] Imitating therein, the glorious example, of their Illustrious and Royal Countryman King James VI of Scotland & I of England, who first set on foot, the two famous and Irreconcileable parties of whig and Tory, which names they adopted, about the time of the Infamous and Scandalous revolution, which has sapped the foundation of true Church, established Presbytery and Phanaticism, Introduced the toleration act, and brought the Nation most damnably in debt, these two prevailing parties, have shone with great Glory in their particular Spheres, ever since the time of that learned wise and Cunning Monarch, and their Contentions have Cost one of that monarch's Sons his head, and his Grandson his Crown, and perhaps these parties and disputes, may last as long as the English can say they are a free people, and when that ceases, probably all parties will be swallowed up in one.

[94]   The two parties that contended in these Clubs I shall Call The royalists and the Levellers; the royalists were those that stood up for the kingly government, in the Shape in which it now existed, these were your Stout toapers, who made no bones of tossing off a gallon bowl at a draught, and procure for themselves the regal crown at any time, The levellers were those, whose Swallows were not so wide, nor Stomachs so capacious, or, whose heads were not so Strong, those argued, that it was unjust to measure a man's merit by such a criterion, that, as they were not themselves the

1. See Homer, *Iliad* 1.261–268.
2. This maxim—"divide and conquer"—has been attributed to Machiavelli, although he actually argues against the sense of it in his *Discourses* (see bk. 2, no. 25, "To Attack a Divided City in the Hope That Its Divisions Will Facilitate the Conquest of It Is Bad Policy").

makers of their throats, Stomachs and heads, they could by no means either Increase or deminish their capacity, width or Strength, They therefore thought it would be expedient, and for the Interest of the whole Club, to lay aside that barbarous way of electing kings, and to allow each member to take it by turns, each having a certain time allotted him to reign, as king over his fellows, and, that every member might be suffered to drink as much or as little as he pleased. The other party argued, that custom was a Second nature, that it was extremely dangerous to the State, to alter old established customs, and, that a man by a Steady perseverance, might bring himself to any thing, and to confirm this, they very learnedly quoted ancient authors, and historians, whose authority they held to be as Sacred and Valid, as many of our divines do that of the fathers, such as Polybius Livy Herodotus ‖ and Xenophon, who says the persians eat once a week, and [95] stoold once a month,³ they also gave Instances of men, who, by force of custom, lived Intirely upon cable ropes and candles ends, and eat flint Stones, without Receiving any hurt, as old Saturn once devoured a Stone, and for aught we know, digested it well enough, and Mithridates, king of Pontus made poison his common diet, and numberless moderen examples they give of Jugglers eating fire, pitch, tar, knives, Swords, hatchets, halberts, pikes, poakers and the like indigestable materials, and yet were as healthy as other men, nay, they Instanced several frenchmen, that would eat Carrion, and one in particular called Monsieur Esteron, who flourished in the beginning of this present Century, who could make a Comfortable male of a Sir reverence,⁴ provided it was of such a Solid consistence, as to admit of Chawing.

These disputes and Cavils, gave Mr Neilson and his Scouts an opportunity to carry on their laudable Schemes, with all the Success they could wish, their business was to blow the coals, and spread the flames of party, so that in a little time, the Disputants from Serious, grave and Learned arguments, came to abuse, as is very usual in political, as well as religious controversy, particularly the latter. Ignoramus, blockhead, dunce, rogue, liar, knave and fool, were Common ‖ appellations, among them, and some [96]

---

3. Since the Persians were notorious for their heavy eating, it is doubtful that Xenophon made this claim about them.

4. Even though the name "Esteron" is apparently not an invention (the French doctor Pierre d'Estiron flourished in the 14th century and other Frenchmen surely had the same name), it is doubtful that one existed at the beginning of the 18th century who could dine comfortably on human excrement. Rather, it seems likely that here and throughout this paragraph Hamilton is simply poking fun at the 18th-century preoccupation with scatology, in this case at the expense of the French.

were branded with the usual names of Atheist, Infidel, Reprobate, and such like; the Advocates for the Bowl, who were reckoned the High-Club party in this dispute, alledging that the opposite party or Low-Club Gentlemen, denied the authority of Revelation, because in Scripture it is said that Noe planted a vinyard, and drank liberally of the Juice thereof, that wine chears the heart of man, and oil maketh his face to shine, and finaly somewhere we find the following passage, *drink wine for thy Stomach's Sake,*[5] and some learned comentators think that the most authentic manuscripts have it, *Drink punch,* and that the word οινω, *wine,* has been Surreptitiously put into the text, by some Ignorant ammanuensis, instead of πυνσιω, either thro' design or Ignorance, for if they suppose the π or Initial letter to have been erased in a copy, and the υ made pritty nigh to meet at the top, so as to resemble an ο, and also the σ obliterated, it would stand thus, υνιω, which by an easy transposition of the ι before the ν, makes οινω, and thus this error might have crept in, but others more probably conjecture that this corruption of the text was made by the priests, who wanted an authority from Scripture, for drinking all the wine themselves, & giving the laity, nothing but a dry wafer, or Crust.

[97]   Mr Neilson and his emissaries, espoused the party of the levellers upon this occasion, as the fittest persons to bring about their purpose, as Cromwell and his Independants, espoused the party of the Presbyterians to bring about their Designs upon the Royalists, but this conduct was expressly contrary to his own political maxims, for in other State controversies, he and his followers showed themselves always to be Strenuous Royalists and Cavaliers, arguing loudly and boisterously for the *Jure divinoship* of kings, and hereditary indefeasable right, and non resistance, and passive obedience in the Subject, and such like favorite topics, and damning to the Infernal pit, all Revolutioners, whigs, presbyterians, Hanoverians, and sneaking low churchmen, but this is no novelty, for we shall find the wisest men sometimes shifting sides, and taking that party which suits their Interest best, according to the doctrine of our Moderen polite philosophers, who think that right and wrong, truth and falshood, do not really exist in the nature of things, but are only Specious terms to be made use of by politicians and Statesmen, hence we see, the now Earl of Bath, heretofore Mr Poultney, a wise Statesman and politician, who, has of late from a Clamorous patriot, in the house of Commons, become a very complaisant, moderate, and I may say, silent peer in the house of Lords.[6]

5. 1 Tim. 5:23.
6. William Pulteney (1684–1764) was a Whig political leader and member of Parliament who served as secretary at war (1714–1717) before contributing to the downfall of Robert Walpole's

It is Inconceivable what hardships, abuses, and Scurrilous usage, this [98] great personage suffered and went thro' to bring about this laudable Scheme, for clubical liberty. They would call him a hundred abusive names in half an hour, such as lousy scabby scot, poor rascally pedlar, Itchified Son of a bitch, Scoundrel, knave, fool, ass, Goose, blockhead, ugly beetle browd, squint eyed, Lenteren Jaw'd, Jacobitish, Skip kennel Scrub, nasty, blewbellied, blanket ars'd, hip-shotten, maggot eaten, round about, Snuff besmeard, flyblown Son of a whore, and conclude all, with the epithet of bloodthirsty traitor and Rebel and No-nation Spawn of Vexation. This, for some time, Mr Neilson bore with christian like patience, notwithstanding the natural heat and Impetuosity of his temper, but at last, an Accident happened, which brought about the great end, that he and his asociates had been for a long time plotting, and it was thus.

One Evening, Mr Neilson being at one of these Royalist Clubs, upon a dispute arising concerning Clubical Government, The king called him a Gallows fac'd Rebel; Mr Neilson, who was alittle warmed with liquor, and not brooking this harsh apellation, hastily drew upon his majesty, and in a trice overset him and his throne, Immediatly all was in an uproar, decanters, Glasses, and Tobacco pipes flew about like hail, his majesties guards at last seized upon Mr Neilson, tore his tye wig and neckcloth, stuffed his mouth full of tallow and Candle wick, wrung his nose, || broke his Sword, and [99] tossed his whole box or mull of Snuff in his Eyes, and taking him by the legs and arms, carried him out of doors, and threw him headlong into a puddle, so that he was the most woefull Spectacle ever was beheld by the eyes of any Christian, and leaving him there, in a most miserable nasty pickle, his Scouts soon had Intelligence of it, and, coming to his asistance, they beset, begirt and besieged the Club house; but it was too late, the enimy had secured the Doors, and fortified the place, so strongly, that they found the fort Impregnable, and resolved to turn the Siege into a blockade; but being much annoyed with Stink-pots from the besieged, they were obliged to raise the Siege and march off.

Immediatly after this tumult, the Club Royalists, who found that several of their members had a warm Side towards Mr Neilson, and his party, in order to put a stop to this Scism and division, raised a hot persecution against the Neilsonists, the most cruel punishments were Invented, for those, whose consciences would not allow them, to toss off the bowl to be made king, the whole quantum of punch was poured upon their heads, which made them look like drowned rats, they were condemned to be pica-

---

government; requested to form his own government, Pulteney refused and became a comparatively silent member of the House of Lords.

Mr Neilson's battle with the royalist Club

[facing page 98]

fousted, and Scabarabused,[7] and had the most unmerciful thumps on the back, and blows on the breech bestowed upon them, and withall, had their Crowns most miserably Clapperclaw'd, so that when they came abroad they ‖ seemed most pitiful Spectacles, being all over bumps, bruises and [100] Scratches. This Inhuman persecution, naturally raised pity and Compassion, in the breasts of many, and being daily Joined by fresh numbers, they unanimously pitched upon Mr Neilson for their leader, upon this, an Intire Separation was made from the Royalists, and Mr Neilson Conveen'd his adherents in a house in Market Street, which was painted red, where having harangued them in a very Learned manner, he proposed, that they should Erect themselves into a Club, under different regulations from the Royalist Clubs, which Regulations he should propose to them, then pulling some papers from his pocket, among which was his Commission under the Venerable Mr Neal Gilpin's hand and privy Seal, and a Scheme or plan of a Club, he read both with a Clear and audible voice, and they unanimously agreed to form themselves into a Society, under the name of the *Red house Club,* the constitution and Government of which, we shall give a Succinct account of, in the following Chapter.

Chapter V

Description of the Red-house Club, it's Customs, Oeconomy and Government.

Our hero having thus drawn his party together, they began daily to Increase, and the other, vizt: that of the Royalist Clubs, to decline, so that in the space of one ‖ or two years there was not the least trace of the latter [101] left, this Great Revolution happened In the beginning of March, in the year 1728.

The Red house Club being once established and set on foot, Mr Neilson applied himself Intirely to the forming of it's constitution and Government, for which Reason he Chose to himself a privy Council, from among the members. The Chief of these Councellors, were such Gentlemen, his countrymen, who had bore a Share, and gone Snacks with him in both his

7. *Pica-fousted* seems to be Hamilton's invention, deriving from the Spanish *picar* ("to pierce") and the obsolete *foutch* ("sword"); *scabarabused,* another invention, obviously means "abused by striking with a scabbard," or "scabbarded."

adverse and prosperous fortune. The names of the principal of them were as follows, Mr Jealous Spyplot, Attorney at Law, Mr Andrew Vapor, Mr Surly Sourface, Capt: Serious Social and Mr Mungo Macfun.

The names of the Chief of the others, who had made a Secession from the Royalist Clubs, were Capt: Seemly Spruce, Major Vaunter, and Mr Prim Timorous. These were of Mr Neilsons privy council.

At the first meeting of this Clubical Council, on the first of April (commonly called fools day) in the year 1729, Mr Neilson proposed Erecting a government by presidents, which was agreed to, but being a man of Great foresight, wisdom and penetration, he Judged that it would not be proper, In the Infancy of this Club, to propose appointing any person perpetual president, by Seniority or personal merit, according to the excel- [102] lent ancient constitution of the whin bush Club of Lan- ‖ neric, revived, or rather continued since, in the ancient and honorable Tuesday Club of Annapolis; least it should be thought, that he Intended to seize the tyranny into his own hands, and make himself absolute, especially, as he knew it was suspected, that his Jacobitish principles, made him a favorer of Arbitrary power, it was therefore agreed, that this Club should be Governed by a rotation of presidents, and each should have the Chair in his turn.

This Club had it's first Regular meeting upon the 14th Day of May, in the year 1729, and Mr Neilson being Reckoned the person of Greatest ability, and the Chief founder of the Club, was, by unanimous voice appointed first Archon or president, to continue in place for the Space of two months, which was reckoned a Sufficient time, to model and form aright, the constitution of the Club.

They were appointed to meet once a week, at the Red house in Market Street, at Six o'clock in the evening, their laws and Regulations were few and Simple, and tended Chiefly to exclude luxury and excess in eatables and drinkables, to prevent wranglings and disputes and all disorders of that Sort, an example worthy the Imitation of all Clubs, which, if duely observed, would settle them upon a firm and lasting foundation.

As to eatables in this Club, they at first seldom went higher than Bread and Cheese, Smoked gammon, or roasted oysters, punch was their Chief [103] liquor, and sometimes in cold ‖ nights used warm flip. Some of the Club members smoked tobacco, and some not, Mr Neilson himself only using tobacco in the form of Snuff, of which he sucked up a vast quantity, he would Indeed handle a clean pipe, twisting it about, and turning it first one way, and then another, and often putting it to his mouth, as if he was a smoking, this he did in Complaisance to the other members, that smoked, that he might seem at least to accompany them, and appear Sociable, an excellent piece of policy, which all rulers ought to observe, for nothing gains the hearts of a people more, than their Rulers Imitating them, tho' in triffles, Mr Neilson has been closely Imitated in this very thing by the Honorable Nasifer Jole Esqr, who, it must be owned, has copied from this eminent personage, many of his amiable qualities.

Taking of Snuff also, prevailed very much in this Club, according to the example of their founder, tho few or none of the members took it before, which shows how apt Inferiors are to Imitate their Superiors, in every thing they do, and this ought to be an Incitement to great men, governors and presidents, to give those beneath them good example, which would contribute more to reform mankind, than the preaching of a hundred thousand parsons, Indeed, some have thought that the taking of Snuff in this Club, grew to a vice, tho Mr Neilson took it for a good purpose, to wit, to help contemplation, and Philosophical Cogitation, || to which he [104] was much addicted, as also to promote the consumption of the Staple Tobacco, yet others took it only In Imitation of him, and went to that excess, that you might have swept at least a large boxfull of Snuff, from the breasts and lappets of the members coats on a Club night, and they stuffed their nostrills with it to such a degree, that many of them Snuffled, which made some Ill natured people out of doors, reflect upon the members, and wickedly assert, that most of them were far gone in a distemper, which, for modesty and decencie's Sake, I shall not here mention or name.

The Conversation of this Club, was of a mixed kind, Sometimes they would dip into politics, and examin with great candour and moderation, the merits of the Cause upon both Sides of the Question, but they were very Cautious how they argued against the *Jure Divinoship* of kings, Indefeasible hereditary right, and the Independancy of the Church upon the State, the last of which, the Reverend and Learned Doctor Warburton, has in an elaborate and voluminous tract, proved as clearly as it ever can or will be proved;[1] knowing that these were Sacred points, which Mr Neilson would not suffer them to profane or Jest with, and therefore, when they entered upon these Solemn topics, they seldom durst go any farther than Significant nods winks and Shrugs.

Sometimes they would talk of Religion, and were || permitted to de- [105] clare their opinion freely, in the great points of predestination, free will, the lawfulness and unlawfulness of eating black pudding, the Sacred and divine Institution of tythes, passive obedience, non resistance, reprobation, abso-

---

1. Hamilton is probably referring to Warburton's tract *The Alliance between Church and State; or, The Necessity and Equity of an Established Religion and a Test-Law Demonstrated* (London, 1736).

Mr Neilson taking Snuff with the Red house Club

[facing page 102]

lute decrees, propitiatory Sacrifices, lay baptism, and such like profound and Ingenious topics, but, in points of this Sort, they agreed perfectly well, understanding little more than the bare words; there being a toleration in this Club, for all Sorts of Religions, which was a very wise and politic provision, and contributed much to its growth and Interest, preventing Infinite wrangles and disputes.

Bawdy they did not often touch upon, and when they did it was very cleanly wrapt, so that it scarce would have tickled the ears of a vestal, and, that was Generally, when it grew late, and they had drank so liberally, that Bacchus began to Introduce Venus by toasting the Ladies all round, which was an established custom of the Club, the worst discourse of that Sort, that passed among them, was such a Lady, and such a Gentleman mounted upon her, the B:C:J:C:[2] the mother of all Saints, the universal Chymist, and sometimes, when merrier than ordinary, they would say here's ——t's health, and such like, which are favorite toasts to this very day among our politest and best bred people.

When they drank the Ladies after Supper, they ‖ would often use [106] epithets, answerable to the Initial letters of the Ladies name that was toasted; thus, suppose the Initial letters to be B:R: It might be beautiful and rich Miss B:R: or Buxom and Rompish Miss B:R: or Bold and Rattling Miss B:R: &ct: which display'd in a very elegant manner, the wit, learning and humor of the members; But, if any member used a word, which his fellow had used before him, he was condemned to drink kelty in a bumper, and, that was the greatest excess, that ever this Club came to in drinking, they often also told comical and delectable Stories, by which the whole Club would be set in a roar of Laughter, their Greatest Genius at this, was the Celebrated Mr Samuel Minskie, alias Mungo Macfun, by birth a high German.

Sometimes they would converse upon the price of tobacco, the fineness or badness of the weather, the Scarcity of news, the dearness of goods, of this much and that much percent advance and deduction, and sometimes for half a night together, it would be heres to you,—and heres to you—and thank you Sir,—and pledge you Sir, but this only happened when conversation run low, which generally was when the liquor was not good, and this was always determined by the opinion of an Ingenious Gentleman, vizt: Doctor Samuel Swallowbeak, who was taster to the Club, and Indeed to all the Clubs in this place, by which office he enjoyed the benefit of drinking at

2. This abbreviation means the "bad character" (the mark formerly set on a soldier guilty of misconduct) of someone or something whose initials were J. C.

[107] || free cost, which he liked very well, for he loved good liquor dearly, but loved his money Infinitely better, if this Gentleman said it was Sad Stuff, they then drank but sparingly, and he got a larger share for himself, but, if he smacked his lips and declared that it was good, and only wanted alittle more powder, then it went down their throats with force Sufficient to drive a mill.

They were very cautious about Swearing in Club, tho' some modest oaths upon particular occasions, they would not scruple to use, which oaths were pronounced with great Solemnity and composure of countenance, When the truth of any thing was to be urged, admiration expressed, or abhorrence declared. These were Commonly, *as God shall Judge me—as I am a living Soul—god save the king, the Lord proprietary, and all the rest of the Royal family,—I wish I may die on this Spot alive,* and the like modest oaths and exclamations, which were particularly used by Mr Prim Timorous, a worthy member of this Club, and afterwards a Longstanding member of the ancient and honorable Tuesday Club of Annapolis, which shall be shown in its proper place.

These were the Chief customs of this worthy Club, which was ruled in a mild and gentle manner by Mr Neilson, as often as he had the presidential power in his hands, and, as all the other members followed his example, they were Continually blessed, with a mild and Easy goverment, there being no such thing as one tyrant to be found, among their presidents, from their first Institution, to their dissolution.

[108]   ## Chapter VI

The translation of the Seat of Government in the Red house Club, the Cause of its dissolution, and the place of meeting converted to a Nunnery.

This Club was for some considerable time governed by a Rotation of presidents, and, we do not find, that there were any Subaltern officers in the Club, excepting only the taster, it does not appear that they had even a Secretary or kept Records, or, if there were any Records they are lost, for, what is here delivered, is collected only from oral tradition, for the Greatest part of which we have been obliged to Mr Prim Timorous, a member of that Club, and since Serjeant at Arms to the honorable Nasifer Jole Esqr, president of the ancient and honorable Tuesday Club.

But, as there is a Constant fluctuation among Sublunary things, and

nothing, not even Clubs, tho well Constituted, are exempt from this muta-
bility, the Seat of Government, or place of meeting in this club was
Changed in the year 1732, which happened thus.

The house where they met was struck with Lightning, and was thereby
shattered in such a woeful manner, that it became unhabitable, all that
were In it at that time were stunned or knocked down, excepting one old
woman, who happened to be in the Cellar making candles, who was not
hurt, which lucky escape, has since been ascribed by many, to the tallow
with which she was besmeared all over, from head to foot, and tallow, wax,
rozin and such like, being non electrics, ‖ the elementary fire only Glanced   [109]
upon the Surface of the old womans Skin and Cloaths, but did not penetrate her body, by which means she escaped, if this should be true, it would
be prudent for those who are afraid of Lightning, to have a Slush bucket
always at hand, to besmear themselves with, which I think would be an
easier preservative against it, and less expensive, than fixing iron rods and
wires upon houses, for, this Method will preserve people from it out of
doors, as well as within, and, perhaps this may be the reason, why the
native Indians of America, (a quarter of the world very subject to violent
thunder gusts) smear their bodies all over with bears grease.

Some people skilled in omens and prodigies, affirmed, that this
prodigy foretold an utter dissolution of the Club, others more truely pro-
phetical, said, that it did not portend a dissolution, but only a translation of
the Club, from one place of meeting to another, which they affirmed they
discovered, by the circumstance of the old Woman, and they explain it thus,
Age say they is a State which is approximated to that translation called
Death, which, tho' it shifts the place, or rather habitation of the Soul, yet
does not destroy it's entity or existence, therefore, the Circumstance of the
old woman, showed that the Club was to shift its place, but not to lose Its
entity or existence, but these Gentlemen have two difficulties to get over,
e'er they establish their argument, first they must prove, that Spirit ‖ can be   [110]
said to possess or shift a place as matter does, and Secondly, they must
answer all the learned arguments, that our moderen Smarts have urged
against the Immortality of the Soul, and a future State, else their argument
falls to the Ground, *with these objections, or Reasons under it* as Mr Drawlum
Quaint used to say, in his Speeches to the ancient and honorable Tuesday
Club, when honored with the office of Speaker there. However, this prediction was reckoned by some, a very cunning and wise one, but some critics
who pretended to see farther, alledged that it was a very easy and natural
prediction, and, that those who were no prophets, might make a hundred
such in half an hour, for, what could be more plain, than that the Club must

shift its place of meeting, seeing the house by this accident became ruinous, and unfit alike for Clubs as tennents.

It was reported that some great prodigies were seen alittle before this happened, such as meteors like blazing Stars with long tails, which appeared and vanished again in a Second of time, and also, Strange noises were heard, of Screech owls, crickets, dismall howlings of dogs, and crowing of cocks at midnight, these unusual appearances, it was said, portended this event, others affirmed that these were prodigious forerunners of Mr
[111] Neilson's Death, which happened about ‖ four years after, and quoted examples from History of various Phênomena of the like nature, before the death of great men, many believed this, and marvelled much thereat, tho' there were not wanting some prophane atheistical persons, who laughed at all this, and affirmed that there was nothing in it, these being only natural appearances, that the Shooting Stars, (as they are Called) happened always either in Clear hot weather, or in Clear, frosty nights, and that owls hooted and screamed, dogs howled and barked, and Crickets chirrup'd at all times, and even Cocks, before and after the Great and Solemn feast of Christenmass, were observed to crow Incessantly all night long, and would still continue to do so, even tho' there was no such Club as the Red-house Club, or no such man as Mr Neilson,—but these foolish arguments we reckon only *Gratis dictu.*

This Club then, changed its place of meeting to a large house near Bloomsbery Square, where were many Spacious apartments, but one of these they pitched upon, in particular, for the Club to sit in, where, for a considerable time, in great peace and tranquillity, they smoked their pipes, took their Snuff, drank their punch, eat their gammon and bread and Cheese, and carried on a Clubical conversation, concerning various Subjects.

In this happy State were they, when the death of Mr George Neilson,
[112] put an end to all their Glory by ‖ putting an end to their peace and quiet, which is a lesson to men in prosperity and easy circumstances not to be too vain or secure, for adversity and distress may suddenly come upon them, e're they are aware; In short, after the Death of their founder and leader, they split into factions and parties, every one aspiring to the management of affairs, and showing a desire to rule the roast, but none being of capacity or wisdom equal, or even nigh to their Illustrious founder, they bilged upon this Sandbank, and like a mouldering wreck, gradually separated one from another, till at last from a numerous Club, they became nothing, and from their ruins Immediatly after, there sprung up another Club, which we shall describe in it's proper place.

As it is usual for historians to make some Sage reflexions, on the persons of great men after their Death, It will be proper here to bestow a word or two on our Club heroe.

Mr Neilson was like all other Illustrious men, he had blemishes blended with his excellencies, Imperfections Interwoven with his perfections, but the quantum of the first bore so small a proportion to that of the latter, that he may Justly be Classed among the most perfect Clubical worthies, that have decorated Clubical History, we shall weigh and examine his perfections and defects, both of body and mind.

If Mr Neilson was of a hasty passionate temper, he was at the same time placable, and his passion like a flash ‖ broke out and disappeared in an Instant, if he was opinionative dogmatic and positive, in any thing he asserted, he had at the same time such a clear Judgement and understanding, that he was seldom or never in the wrong box; if he was profuse and extravagant, he was also of a genteel and polite taste, and withal, Generous to an excess; If he was refractory and ungovernable in Company, he was also a Loyal Subject, to such as he thought had an Indefeasible hereditary right to reign over him; if he had some little Irregularities in his life, and was too much given to women, we must remember, that he was quite orthodox in his religious principles, having copied these from the perfect pattern of the Celebrated University of Oxford, tho he was not educated there, if he was at times given to prophane Swearing, he was at other times much addicted to fervent devotion and prayer. [113]

Again, if his visage was long, his forehead was high, If his nose was crooked, his eyes were lively, if his chin was peaked, his complexion was good, if his body was slender, it was at the same time streight and well proportioned, if his legs were Comically made, his feet were small and neat, If his walk was hobbling, yet he danced to the admiration of all that beheld him, and if he was of a small Stature he was well built, and thus, having exactly balanced his perfections and Imperfections, I here leave this Illustrious Clubical heroe, to sleep in peace with his fathers.

After the breaking up of this Club, the house was converted to a nunnery, several females fixing their habitation in it, who afterwards were dignified with the name ‖ of nuns; It will perhaps seem strange to some how this should have happened, but Instances of the like nature may be produced from history both ancient and moderen; That famous ancient Rotunda, the Panthæon at Rome, which was originally appropriated for the habitation of the heathen Deities, is now converted to a christian chapel, under the name of the Church of all Saints, and is Inhabited by a great number of holy Saints, who have now as much adoration paid them, as [114] these old Deities ever had, and a preferable adoration, since this is offered by Christian, whereas that was paid by pagan devotees; Indeed, as for the Materials, of which these christian Deities are made, the difference is little, they being the Self same Stones and blocks of wood, of which the pagan Divinities were Confabricated; We have it from Scripture history, that the Temple of Solomon, which was a consecrated Ædifice, set apart for divine worship, at last became a den of thieves; The ancient City of Babylon, Inhabited by magnificent monarchs, and a polite people, was turned into dens for Lyons, tygers, panthers, and all manner of wild beasts, The Nunneries and Monasteries in England, In the Reign of Henry VIII, were found to be Surprizingly metamorphosed, from the habitations of holy men and women, professing Celebacy and Chastity, into brothwells, bawdy houses and bagnios, The City of Rome, once the habitation of men of the Sword, is now a dwelling for holy and peaceable men of the Gown, and, it is [115] scarce yet out of the memory of our Grand- || fathers, that the Royal palace of Whitehall, was in the time of the Rump and roundheads, converted into Stables and apartments for Grooms, of which event, there was an old prophesy, concerning an ass, whose master [a] was hanged Drawn and quartered, in the wise Reign of James I, for this ass, it seems brayd in a treasonable manner, against that Second Solomon and his Courtiers, the Prophesy runs thus.

> Some seven years since, Christ rid to court,
>   And there he left his ass.
> The Courtiers kick'd him out of doors,
>   Because they had no grass. [*]   [*]Grace
>
> The ass went mourning up and down,
>   And thus I heard him bray,
> If that they could not give me grass,
>   They might have given me hay.

(a) Mr Williams, a councellor of the temple, and a Roman Catholic, who was executed at Tyburn for publishing a Satyrical book against the King and ministry entituled *Balaam's Ass*. Howels *Familiar Letters*.[1]

1. The story of Balaam's ass seems to have aroused considerable theological controversy and satirical retort during the 17th century. The verses Hamilton transcribes appeared in James Howell's (popular author and friend of Ben Jonson) *Epistolae Ho-Elianae: Familiar Letters*, 2d ed. (London, 1650; see vol. III, letter XXII, "To Dr. W. Turner," 35–36). In his note to the poem, Howell says that *Balaam's Ass* was "compos'd [more than 20 years ago] by one Mr Williams a Counsellor of the Temple, but a Roman Catholic, who was hang'd drawn and quarter'd at Charing Cross for it" (p. 35).

> But Sixteen hundred, forty three,
>   Who'eer shall see that day,
> Will nothing find within that court,
>   But only grass and hay.

These nuns It is said, resembled the Roman vestals in one thing, that they fed and kept up a perpetual fire, and were ‖ visited every night, by [116] many of the priests and votaries of Venus, who seldom went away from them, without carrying some of that same Sacred fire, or rather *Ignis fatuus*,[2] concealed in their Breeches, these priests payd divine honors to these Nuns or vestals, and worshiped them with great devotion, for, they seldom or never went In their presence, but they fell down upon their knees, and seemed moved and agitated with great extasies, fetching deep Sighs, and earnest groans, but we shall leave these nuns and priests, to carry on their pious frauds, and proceed with our Clubical History.

Chapter VII

The Rise of the Ugly Club, from the Ruins of the Red house Club.

As Empires, kingdoms and States may be compared to the Hydra, new ones springing up continually from the Downfal of the old, so it is the same with Clubs, for no sooner is one of these nocturnal assemblies dissolved, or dissipated, but Immediatly another Rises up in its place, as is plainly exemplified here in our History, for scarce was the Red-house Club, a branch of the ancient and venerable Tuesday (or whin bush) Club of Lanneric, at a period, but Immediatly sprung up from it's remains, like the Phoenix from its own ashes, a Club Called the *Ugly Club,* a description of which we are now to give.

A residue of the members of the Red house Club, vizt: Major Vaunter, [117] Mr Prim Timorous, and some others, after their dissolution, laying their heads together, laid out the first plan for forming of this club, which they agreed should be called the Ugly Club.

My Readers are not here to Imagin, that they assumed that appellation, upon account of ugliness of feature, or deformity of body in the

---

2. As Hamilton was no doubt aware, *ignis fatuus* literally means "foolish fire" (a flamelike phosphorescence produced over marshes by the spontaneous combustion of decayed vegetable matter, which eludes those who attempt to follow it).

members, like another Club of that name described by the *Spectator*,[1] it was
not at all necessary, that a man should be hard favored, crooked, or hunch
backed, to qualify him to be a member of this Club, it was Sufficient for
him Sincerely to profess and believe that he was not handsom, till he was
declared to be a monstrous ugly fellow by the Ladies in public company, for
then, as that Sex are perfect Judges of beauty, propriety of feature and
proportion of body in the other, and, as it is their constant custom, when
on this Subject, to express themselves Contrary to what they think, all those
declared ugly by them were Reckoned unqualified to be members of this
Club, and all declared handsom, by the same fair Judges, perfectly qualified
to be admitted to it. A man was to show his Sincerity in this opinion of
himself, by assuming a certain Slovenliness and peculiarity in his dress, by
never throwing away his time at a looking Glass, and diligently evading all
[118] foppish and finical airs and || affectation either in his gesture of body,
Speaking or gait in walking, but, if he ever observed any oddity of Gesture,
affected by another man, such as a wink, a cast of the Eye, a sudden toss of
the head, to one Side or other, or wry twist of the mouth, or knitting of the
brows, a sudden turning round upon the heel, while he is spoke to by
another, these he was Strictly to Imitate, and perfect himself in, as being
real deformities and deviations from nature in a much higher degree than ·
bodily distortions and blemishes, which the members of this Club, did not
think Carried in them so much deformity, as to entitle their possessors to a
Seat in their Society, this kind of affectation Mr Spruce Limberloins, a
distinguished member, being Secretary to this club, was perfect in, having
set for his pattern and example, a certain eminent Squire, under whose
direction and precepts, he had been brought up, Some will object here, I
suppose, to our excluding the beaus and pritty Gentlemen, who are as
much given to affectation, and deviate from nature as widely as any Set of
men whatsoever, but, let it be remembered, that the fopperies and affectation of these gentlemen, are original, and not Imitated, besides, they are
much ridiculed (that is praised) by the Ladies, who being perfect Judges of
what is handsom and pritty, the antics of these fops, beaus and pritty Gentlemen, cannot be Classed with such things as are termed ugly.

[119]		Nevertheless, there were some particular bodily blemi- || shes and de-
fects, which a man might possess, that no ways disqualified him from being
a member of this Club, such as a remarkable Scar on the face, freckles,

1. The Ugly Club is mentioned in nos. 17, 48, 52, 78, 87, and 553 of the *Spectator*, but the most
extended account of the club—and the one to which Hamilton is probably referring—appears
in no. 32.

[facing page 118]

Squint eyes, deep pock fretting or a nose set awry, or a good many of those pimples called by some courage bumps, these were not objected to when any person proposed himself as a member; Some peculiarities in dress also, qualified people to be members of this Club, such as a Stocking slackly gartered, or put on all of one Side, full of derns or holes; Greasy leather breeches, Codpiece unbuttoned, with Shirt hanging out, a Shoe down at heel and buttoned the reverse way, ragged ruffles, Slouch hat, wig uncombed and uncurld, dirty hands & face, long beard and the like; a certain Slovenly Stile in discourse too was reckoned a qualification, such as Coarse homespun Similies, gross metaphors and allusions, pronounced with a harsh tone of voice and a horse laugh.

But what Chiefly gave this Society the name of the Ugly Club, was the Squalidness of the Room where they sat, and held their meetings, it being a large Ghastly apartment, of an old Building, made use of for a School Room, the plaister of the walls and Ceiling was much decayed, and cracked, moldy, dirty, and in several places fallen off, around the walls were many names engraved and done with Ink Chalk and marking Stone, and some human faces and figures of a Strange wild fancy, with monstrous noses, unconscionable mouths, and horrid Staring eyes, the Cieling was Smoked [120] In several places with a Candle, ‖ and very much garnished with cobwebs, and the Clay Nests of worms and wasps, many panes of Glass in the windows were broke and Cracked, the window Sills and Shelves covered with dust, which had been collecting there for half a century. The floor was Squalid, full of Spots, and plaistered in many places with dawbs of dirt, collected from Chaws of tobacco, and such like plastic Substances, which having been trod upon, adhered, and in a manner Grew to the plank, the furniture of the Room, consisted of a parcell of old forms and desks, which served the members of the Club to sit and loll upon, there was only one antiquated elbow Chair, which was set apart for the president of the Club.[2]

Thus was it Solely upon account of the Slovenliness of the members (who looked when met like a parcel of ragged philosophers) their affectation of odd gestures, and the dirtiness and unseemliness of the Club room, that this Society had the name of the Ugly Club; and not from any bodily deformity in the members themselves, for, in that respect, some of them were proper enough men, and tollerably well made.

Their Chief members were Major Vaunter, Joshua Swash Esqr, John

2. According to Charlotte Fletcher, the Ugly Club met in the King William's schoolroom ("An Endowed King William's School Plans to Become a College," *Maryland Historical Magazine*, LXXX [1985], 160–161).

Cork, Thomas Long, Mr Prattle Motely, Mr Pedantius, Mr Spruce Limberloins, Captain Swarthy, Mr Vocifer Leatherlungs, and Mr Loquacious Scribble.

I shall now proceed to give an account of their Constitution and government, and the Cause of their Dissolution.

Chapter VIII [121]

An account of the Constitution and Government of the Ugly Club, Its dissolution, and the first Scheme for erecting the Ancient & Honorable Tuesday Club of Annapolis in Maryland.

Tho Mr Neilson, when he first founded the Red house Club, did not model that Society exactly after the plan, of the ancient and venerable Tuesday (or whin bush) Club of Lanneric, yet he Intended to have done it by degrees, and was proceeding very Successfully in that Laudable Scheme, when death, the Confounder of all human projects Interrupted him; It may be asked by some short sighted persons, unacquainted with human nature, and therefore Ignorant of the humor, and disposition of Clubs, why did he not do it at once? to which we need only answer, that such sudden Innovations, are dangerous and destructive to Schemes, let them be never so laudable, that great man did more, than half a dozen others could have effected, by lessening the Character of the Royalist Clubs, setting up a presidential government, and establishing a Society on an opposite footing. Had he at first, slap dash, adventured, to Introduce Baylies, Censors, Masters of Cerimonies, and such like State officers, into Clubs, his project in all probability had failed, and his party entirely deserted him, for, it is a true observation, that men are to be wrought upon by degrees, when any new model or form of Government Religion or Clubs is proposed, they must be soothed, flattered, Cajoled, cozened and hoodwinked, as being most obstreperous animals, that may Slyly be led, but never forcibly drove.

The founders of the Ugly Club, being some of the most Judicious and [122] politic members of the Red house Club, and having been of Mr Neilson's privy council, were hearty favorers of his Schemes, & therefore, set off with a full purpose, to model this new Constitution, according to the plan of that great Club politician, they therefore made the best use of their commission from him, and appointed in this Club several officers, vizt: a Treasurer, Orator and Secretary; The treasurers was a Circulating office, he continuing only for a stated time, and the Club was also Governed by a Rotation of Presidents, a new Chairman being elected at the end of every two months, the Honorable Major Vaunter was first president, the offices of orator and Secretary were permanent, and the persons best qualified were put into these places. Vocifer Leatherlungs Esqr was Orator, a man of Good action and Gesticulation, of easie fluent and Copious Speech, and a loud Clear delivery; he used some very elegant expressions in his Orations, which were afterwards adopted by Succeeding Orators, in the ancient and honorable Tuesday Club, These were *This here Club, That there argument, These here laws,* and so forth.

The Secretary was Mr Spruce Limberloins, a person of great abilities and uncommon understanding, being very well versed in the common Law, he very Carefully entered the proceedings of the Club into a folio book, which record would have been exceeding valuable, and of Great use In Compiling this History, but It was unfortunately burnt, with many other useful papers and books belonging to that Learned Gentleman; the Secretary did not always ‖ Strictly confine himself to his office, but sometimes would make excursions and encroach upon the Orators province, which laid the first foundation for the Dissolution of this Club, for, these two great men becoming Jealous of one another (as great men often do) Strenuously contending for the palm of victory in the oratorial way, it grew at last to hot and violent disputes, and wrangling, and Ended in hatred and aversion to one another, as we shall show presently, this is no uncommon thing in human Society, there being often two or more men of an aspiring Genius in a Club or Neighbourhood, who get together by the ears, and like a couple of prize fighters or wrestlers, striving who shall be uppermost, each draws his faction after him, there arises a division of parties, the fabric of the constitution receives such violent Shokes, that at last, it tumbles about our ears, and lies in ruinous heaps, never again to be repaired.

I shall mention three more extraordinary Geniuses, Members of this Club, who made no Contemptible figure in it, either as notable Slovens or queer fellows, vizt: Mr Pedantius, Mr Prattle Motely, and Joshua Swash Esqr.

The first was a man of Letters, having for some time exercised the office of Schoolmaster In the City of Annapolis, and exerted himself to admiration, in that conspicuous Station, he was remarkable for wearing dirty Linnen nightcaps in Summer, and Greasy worsted Ditto in winter, and for having long nails, and he used to wash his face and hands duely

[123]

twice a year, vizt: at Christenmass and Lammas, which ‖ gave him a Just   [124]
claim to be a member of this Club, he understood *Qui Genus,* and *propria*
Quæ maribus perfectly well, and could repeat *As in presenti,*[1] from begining
to end, without Stammering or hesitating, with a delectable and musical
tone of voice, in the Right Recitativo taste, he was an Hybernian by birth,
and was pritty well stocked in that Sort of modest assurance, which is
reckoned peculiar to that Nation. He had a particular turn to Mechanics,
and made such great Strides towards the discovery of the *perpetuam mobile*
and the Longitude, that it is thought, by many competent Judges, had his
Means or purse been Sufficient, he would have effected them both. Like
others of his profession he was positive dogmatic and Imperious, treating
all persons, as if they were his pupils or Schoolboys, much given to dispute,
and always Sure he was in the Right, and Commonly used to get the better
of the Argument, by quoting greek and latin Authors, which few or none of
the Club understood.

    Prattle Motely Esqr, had studied the Law in his younger days, which
had given him a habit of perpetual dictating, wrangling and Disputing, he
had pritty much of the Misanthrop in him, and was too apt to entertain a
bad opinion of mankind In General, believing and asserting, that most men
were either fools or knaves, when he conversed in Club, he seldom or never
kept to one Subject a minute together, but would Ramble up and down
from topic to topic, abuse people in Superior Stations, with the names of
Pimps ‖ and Bunters,[2] and conclude all with a hearty pinch of snuff, and   [125]
half a Dozen round Oaths. He affirmed often, that he was much skilled in
Secret History, and in the Heraldry and Genealogy of families, and often
would assure the Company, that he could tell such Stories, of such and such
persons, as would make their blood boil, and their hair stand on end, and
when he had thus raised their Curiosity to a great pitch, with such Rodo-
montade expressions, he'd either leave them on the rack, or allow them to
guess, if they could, what these pieces of Secret History were, or, if they got
it out of him, it proved either some stale Story they had heard before, or
some piece of buffonery, which excited laughter more than admiration,
horror, or resentment; nevertheless, he was a very good Club member, and
Contributed much, by his facetious Conversation, to promote the Mirth
and good humor of the Company, for his Sarcasms, and nicknames, were

---

    1. "What genus," or "what kind"; "belongings which by sea"; "as at present" (legal ter-
minology).
    2. *Bunter* is a cant word for a woman who picks up rags from the street, which is used, by
way of contempt, for any low, vulgar woman.

only Reckoned as words of Course; he Indeed had an unlucky ambition to rule the roast in all Companies, and his chief talent lay in Exercising the office of a Sir Clement Cotterell.[3]

Joshua Swash Esqr, was by profession a Lawyer, and had the honor to possess the place of Prosecutor for the County, he was a man of very few words, and loved much the circulation of the Bowl, so that it was thought he was for the most part muddled and often fuddled; The most that he said was *here's to ye again,* or *Herefordshire kindness,*[+] he had the best title of any of the members to be of this Club, by reason of his ragged appearance and his settled Philosophical Countenance; once when it was his turn to sit in the Chair as President, he wore a great Jockey || coat, and standing up with profound gravity and awful Solemnity to give some orders, or directions to the members, this Surtout fell open, and discovered the tattered State of those garments which it covered, which put me somewhat in mind of robes of state. He had little or no regard or passion for the fair Sex, tho' he was no woman hater, therefore the Ladies declared him a very handsom fellow, and often toasted him, which procured his admission into this Club.

[126]

I was myself a member of this worthy Club, some time before it's dissolution, but, as I had no office in it, but that of an ordinary member, I shall not here Characterize myself, but defer that, till the time, when I shall appear in this History, a degree above the Rank of Common members, In the ancient and honorable Tuesday Club, In the Quality of their Orator and Secretary.

Their Chief employment in this Club, was to argue and debate upon various Subjects, and to discuss points of a knotty and abstruse nature, they often also, exercised themselves in law pleadings, and argued cases and pled causes, with great elegance, distinctness and perspicuity, in this Sort of Declamation, Messrs: Limberloins, and Leatherlungs exercised themselves much, and had almost all the talk to themselves, by this means each Improved his talent to admiration, for they Learned how to wrest a meaning, to Quibble and play upon words, prevaricate, and make the best of a bad Cause, and both turned out afterwards, very Eminent Lawyers, tho the first soon gave up his practise for a County Clerkship, which he Thought was a more Conscientious Calling.

3. By Hamilton's day the name Sir Clement Cotterell was virtually synonymous with the master of ceremonies. The original Sir Clement Cotterell of Wylsford, Lincolnshire, was groom-porter to James I and muster-master of Buckinghamshire by 1616. Like his ancestor, the Sir Clement Cotterell who flourished in the early 18th century was master of ceremonies and a noted antiquarian besides.

4. Roughly, "and here's to you"; the people of Herefordshire were renowned for toasting those who toasted them.

However, the wrangles, debates and disputes of these two Gentlemen, [127] and the turbulent Disposition of Prattle Motely Esqr, led this Club into parties, and then every thing turned uproar and Confusion, which produced much cursing and Swearing, and hence accrued fines (for they had Laws in this Club, which Imposed fines upon certain trespasses) this soured the members at one another, and all Sort of Clubical cordiality and friendship, began to decrease, and at last was quite extinguished, so that the Members drop'd off one by one, and from a numerous Club, it dwindled to nothing, and at last expired.

After the Decease of this Club, which Indeed could not be of long Continuance, having no such able Genius as Mr Neilson's to support it, out of its remains sprung a Club, which since has made the most Shining figure of any that have yet appeared in America, vizt: the ancient and Honorable Tuesday Club of Annapolis, in the frame and Constitution of which, In process of time, arose the real likeness and Image, of the Ancient and Venerable Tuesday (or whin bush) Club of Lanneric, being nothing but that very Club It Self, translated to America, the effecting of this, was what the Great Mr Neilson aimed at, with all his might, but the Inexorable Destinies, cut the thread of his life, before he had half accomplished his Laudable design, however, he had the honor to lay the foundation of this great Superstructure, tho he enjoyed not the pleasure of seeing it perfected.

This happy lot fell upon persons much less conspicuous than he, viz: Prattle Motely Esqr, and Loquacious Scribble M:D: who were the only two members of the Late Ugly Club that stuck together and Strenuously operated to keep alive || the taste for Clubbing in Annapolis, for which purpose [128] they called to their asistance two very able politicians, vizt: Jealous Spyplot Esqr, Serjeant at Law, and the Revd Mr Smoothum Sly parson of the parish, the first had been a companion of the Great Mr Neilson in his trowbles, came to America with him, and was also of his privy council in the Red house Club, he was a Gentleman of great discernment, and could see into men's breasts and fortell Events at a distance, as well as any Conjurer of the Age. The latter was a Gentleman very well adapted for Clubs, being of a free airy disposition, full of compliment and panegyric to all, and of a Jocose turn, much given to quaint Repartee, dowble Entendre, & withal a hearty & loud laugher, these four gentlemen having procured four more to be of their party, whom we shall afterwards mention, laid the first foundation of that famous Club, whose History I now write, but, I would not have my readers here to misunderstand me, they were not so much the founders of the Ancient and honorable Tuesday Club, as the Settlers and revivers of that Club in America, for the time of their foundation is uncertain, They being as ancient as the ancient and Venerable Tuesday, (or whin-bush) Club of Lanneric, of which we have given a short history in the preceeding Sheets, and now proceed to Scenes of greater action and Importance in the following Books.

End of the Second Book.

Members of the Ancient & honorable Tuesday Club,
at its first Sederunt.

Loquacious Scribble M:D:	Capt: Serious Social
The Revd Mr Smoothum Sly	Capt: Bully Blunt
Prattle Motely Esqr:	Capt: Seemly Spruce
Jealous Spyplot Esqr	Mr Laconic Comas

The History of the Ancient and honorable Tuesday Club

Book III

From the first Sederunt of the Ancient and honorable Tuesday Club, to the Cathedration of the Honorable Nasifer Jole Esqr President.

Chapter I

Of Great and Illustrious personages, whose names only have been transmitted to posterity.

It has so happened, to the great hurt and Dammage of Posterity, that several Eminent Clubical heroes, and Illustrious personages, have very unjustly, and undeservedly been deprived of that Reward, which is for ever due to Clubical merit and virtue, by an entire ommission, of all their famous actions, which have perished in oblivion, by means of the woeful and Lamentable neglect of Club Historiographers, and Secretaries, and we know no more of them, but their bare names, their lives, in all other respects being one entire blank or Chasm.

Several of these worthies I shall here mention, ‖ of whom it is uncertain who they were, tho' we may probably conjecture that they were members of some Certain Clubs, that have been long obselete, and the last of my roll, shall be a very famous and Illustrious moderen Clubical Worthy, who was President of a great Club, but what seems most strange, it is a matter of mighty doubt, among the Learned in Club History, whether this hero or his Club had ever any real existence. [130]

The two first which shall appear upon my list are famous persons, who always go together, by the Name of John-a-Nokes and John-a-Stiles;[1] these we often hear mentioned in bargains, conveyances, deeds, testaments, bonds, declarations &ct: and very often we find them going to Law together, a mischievous practice, used for many ages, both among friends and foes; It is so uncertain at what time these Illustrious personages lived, that several people have doubted, whether there were such men ever alive, tho' others alledge they came in with William the Conqueror, and were properly called, de Nokes and de Stiles; and Consequently their Descendents, if any remain, are of as ancient a family as any in England. I make no doubt of their having once flourished, and that they were very eminent men, but, as to their Country, parentage and birth, these must for ever remain in the Dark, unless some Casual medal or Tombstone not yet ploughed or dug up, or some ancient manuscript, not yet found should agreeably Instruct us. There seems to be something Inconsistent and contradictory, in the traditions handed down concerning them, for, sometimes, we find John a Nokes, conveying great Estates to John a Stiles, and sometimes John a Stiles is exercising the same Generosity to John a Nokes, sometimes Nokes

[131] is prosecuting Stiles in the most violent manner, || and at other times Stiles becomes plaintiff and Nokes defendant, Nokes often makes his will in favor of Stiles, and bequeaths him Immense estates and possessions, again Stiles bestows very great legacies upon Nokes; Stiles often beats Nokes and abuses him with very Scurrilous and oprobrious language, and again Nokes uses Stiles in the same rude and Rascally manner. But for these Inconsistencies in the transactions of these great men, we must Intirely blame the carelessness of historians. The only certain thing that is known of them, is, that they were good friends to the Gentlemen of the Law or long robe, helping them out at a dead lift upon all occasions, and filling up many blanks and deficiencies in their pleadings, for, as these gentlemen, never transact business, or plead without a fee or reward, being professed Enimies to all Causes *in forma pauperis*,[2] and, as we find these two worthies oftner named in their briefs, than any other Clients, we Judge from that, that they must have feed their Lawyers handsomly.

The two whom I shall next name, are John Doe and Richard Roe,[3] who Surely were, and are now, for aught I know, men of great credit and Character, for, in all our Courts of Justice, we shall find them named, as pledges and Surities for the appearance of plaintiff and defendant, which

---

1. Names formerly given to fictitious persons in an action at law.

2. Literally, "in pauper's form"; referring to cases in which the court allows an indigent petitioner to plead without paying court costs.

3. Names signifying any plaintiff and defendant in an action of ejectment.

makes me conclude, that not only their Credit must be very great, but they must be Gentlemen of distinguished humanity, generosity and good nature, seeing they run so many risques, for persons to whom they are utter Strangers, and yet, there is one very Surprizing circumstance in the traditions concerning them, that is, tho those gentlemen never ask any Questions, concerning the circumstances of those people, for whom they ‖ become [132] engaged, yet I never yet could find that they lost one farthing by their becoming Surities or pledges, but, at the same time, with regard to their Pledgees, the balance between them is exactly even, for, if they never lost a penny, they never gained any thing by it, nay, I am told, not so much as thanks, for people were in time so habituated to those pledgors that it is thought as absurd to thank them for their favors, as to thank a chair for supporting one's bum, a razor for shaving one, or a pair of Gloves for keeping ones fingers from the Cold; for certain it is, where no distinction is made in bestowing of favors, they lose the name of favors, tho' some profane people have a very loose and Improper way of Speaking, such as, I a'nt Cold, thank these Gloves, and this Great Coat, I am Clean Shaved, thank this razor; I sit easie, thank this elbow Chair &ct: these expressions are every whit as extravagant, as if one at Law should say, I have good Pledges, thank John Doe and Richard Roe.

Another Eminent person whom I shall mention is Jeck with the Lanthorn or Will with the wisp as some Call him, by the Ancients called Mr Ignis Fatuus.+ This Gentleman was supposed to be of a melancholy turn, and therefore a constant night walker, having never once been known to make his appearance in the day, which is a Strong proof that he is a frequenter of some humdrum Clubs, and is seen a nights either going to, or coming from some such Club or Clubs, he loves a rural retirement, and is very famous among the Country people, having never once been seen in great Cities, he affects walking thro marshes and bogs, and by this means has misled many who have attempted to follow him, and made them run into Ditches and ‖ quagmires, to the great danger of their lives and dam- [133] mage of their Cloaths; it is said, he sometimes will make so free with Travellers on horseback, as to vault upon the horses mane & ride merrily before them; but he seldom keeps his Seat long, Jumping and skipping about like any Harlequin,⁵ as to his Religion, he is Inclinable to that of the

4. Jack-o'-lantern and will-o'-the-wisp were two of the many names for ignis fatuus (see p. 116n, above).

5. In Italian commedia dell'arte, Harlequin is one of several stock characters along with Columbine, Pierrot, Pantaloon, and others. In English pantomime, which was derived from the Italian commedia and to which Hamilton is probably referring, Harlequin is a mute

new light, and treats his followers in the same manner, as the Reverd: and pious Mr George Whitefield A:B: used to do his disciples, giving them first a Glimmering of the road or path, and then leaving them as much in the dark as ever. He will sometimes go on board Ships among Sailors; (*In Navigiorum Summitatibus ascendit,* saith Eusebius)[6] and wantonly climb to the mast head, but these cattle love his company, and always make him welcome, because, loving to keep out of danger, he always comes at the end of a Storm.

The next remarkable worthy, is he who goes under the Name of Robin Goodfellow,[7] he has always been esteemed a very courteous civil and obliging Gentleman, he would at any time condescend, for a mess of milk, to grind Corn, cut wood, scour peuter, empty piss pots, or do any other kind of drudgery work in a family, Thelosanus lib: 7 Cap: 14, calls this ancient worthy by the name of Trullus and Getulus, and says that in his time he travelled to France, and learned the fashions, and has appeared heretofore in the highlands of Scotland in the form of a hairy man, and used to take great delight in drawing water dressing meat, and sweeping the hearths Clean.[8]

[134]   Another obscure Gentleman of renown, is he whom the Italians Call Foliot, the English Hob Goblin, known in our Nurseries by the name of Raw head and bloody bones,[9] He generally loves to frequent old forlorn houses, and ruinous castles; he will make Strange noises in the night, howl sometimes pitifully, and then laugh again, cause great flames and sudden lights, fling Stones, rattle Chains, shave men, open doors, flap them to again with great Clapping & Jarring of rusty hinges, fling about plates, Stools, Chests, bedsteads and tables, and look out at windows, grinning

---

character who is supposed to be invisible to the clown and to Pantaloon and who rivals the clown for the affections of Columbine.

6. Eusebius (ca. 260–340) was a historian and theologian whose thought was inspired by the transformation of the Roman Empire into a Christian kingdom under Constantine and who tried to demonstrate the superiority of the Bible over pagan philosophy. This passage, in which Eusebius is criticizing pagan superstition, means "he climbed in the tops of ships" (*Contra philosophos,* chap. 48).

7. A merry domestic fairy, famous for his mischievous pranks and practical jokes; also known as Puck.

8. Tholosan was the pseudonym of René Milleran (b. 1665), a French grammarian known during the 18th century for his compilation of imaginary words and names, *Lettres familieres et galantes, et autres sur toutes sortes de sujets,* 6th ed. (La Haye, 1705).

9. A hobgoblin was an impish, ugly sprite (a variant of Rob-Goblin, or the goblin Robin). In the *Anatomy of Melancholy* Burton refers to a kind of hobgoblin that "frequent[s] forlorn houses, which the Italians call *foliots*" (I, II, i, 2) and uses Cardan as his authority (see following note). Rawhead and Bloody-Bones were famous bogies who were the terror of children.

with a Strange uncouth Countenance, as if he had the dry belly ake, this account Cardan gives of him Libro 16. *De rerum varietate,*[10] he appears to be one of these Sorts of people that are *occupati nihil agendo,* and that make a mighty pother *de lana Caprina,*[11] as the Learned express it.

I shall but Just mention that famous ancient Gentleman Called Tantar-abobus,[12] of whom nothing is said, but *that he lived till he Died,* wherefore he has become a worthy pattern, to those Sort of Philosophers among the Vulgar, who never think of any thing but the present time, their concise Philosophy prompting them to use this worthys name in a proverb, viz: "I care not, let the world wag, for I shall live as long as Tantarabobus, and he lived till he Died," happy would it have been, for multitudes of poor wretches in this world, had Alexander the Great, Julius Cæsar, Hannibal, and Kouli Can,[13] mighty men at arms, and Saint Athanasius, St Ambrose, Saint Cyryl,[14] and other Zealous Christian Saints, followed the example of this Indolent worthy Tantarabobus, who as he never was the au- || thor of [135] any good during his long life, so none can lay any bloodshed or mischief at his door.

I come now to speak of some Saints, priests and popes, of whom we know little more than their bare names, the Seven Champions of Christen-dom[15] are all Saints of this Class, one of the principal of them is Saint George, the English Champion, we know little more of him, than that he killd a monstrous dragon, it is true, Spencer has given him a whole Legend in his poem of the fairy Queen, but, as that is Intirely allegory and fiction, the Incidents are as applicable to George a Green[16] as to St George; and by

10. Cardan, or Geronimo Cardano (1501–1576), was an Italian mathematician, physician, and astrologer whose writings include *De subtilitate rerum* (1551) and numerous works on astronomy, astrology, rhetoric, and medicine. Hamilton's allusion is to book 16 of Cardan's *De rerum varietate* (1557), "On the different kinds of liver."

11. "Busy doing nothing"; "over goat's wool," or "over trifles" (Horace, *Epistulae* 1.18.15).

12. Perhaps Hamilton's invention, a combination of *tantara* (fanfare, or trumpet flourish) and *bobus,* or *bogus,* meaning "a counterfeit sound," or in this case, "a counterfeit name."

13. Kublai Khan (1216–1294) was the founder of the Mongol dynasty in China.

14. Saint Athanasius (ca. 295–373), the theologian who played an influential part at the Council of Nicea, was the leader in the fight against Arianism. Saint Ambrose (ca. 339–397), the bishop of Milan whose teachings influenced Augustine, also opposed Arianism and supported strict orthodoxy in general. Saint Cyril (376–444), the Alexandrian archbishop, defended orthodoxy and persecuted the Novations, the Jews, and the Nestorians.

15. The patron saints of England, Scotland, Wales, Ireland, France, Spain, and Italy (Saint George, Saint Andrew, Saint David, Saint Patrick, Saint Denis, Saint James, and Saint Anthony).

16. The poundmaster of Wakefield, Yorkshire, who single-handedly resisted the attempted trespass of Robin Hood and his men; to be "as good as George a Green" is therefore to be resolute and dutiful.

the bye, this George a Green, tho we have no documents of his ever having been Canonized, yet he must have been a person of excellent qualifications, for ever since his time, his name has been used in a proverbial Comparison, vizt: *were you as good as George a Green;* but what this worthy was really good for, cannot now be known from any records extant.

Saint Patrick, the Irish Saint is another, of whom we have but very Imperfect accounts, but the most remarkable thing related of him, is his swiming a river, after his head was struck off, with that very Identical head in his teeth, a genuine Irish miracle.

Were I to mention all the Saints named in the Calendar, of whom nothing but their bare names is known, I should compose a whole volume or Index of names, and therefore, I shall take notice of only a few more, The most remarkable of these obscure Saints is Saint Viar, mentioned with

[136] honor, by Doctor Conyers Middleton in ‖ his *Letter from Rome,*[17] who has not left behind him one single circumstance to make him famous, it is said indeed that he was *PræfectuS. VIARum* under some of the twelve Cæsars, and that is Indeed all we know of him, besides the Circumstance of his being a Saint.

There is also Saint Amphibolus, who lived in the time of Saint Alban,[18] the british martyr, the only circumstance we know of him, is, that he was the Cloak of the said St Alban, and was Sainted, because he suffered martyrdom in company with him, Tho some have gone so far, as to assert, that this holy Cloak was Bishop of the Isle of Man, and consequently, was very moderate in his principles, doing neither good nor harm.

Several other Saints there are likewise, of whom we have nothing but their names, of whom Saint Januarius is the most Eminent, and besides there are Saint Ocularis, Saint Auricularis, Saint Mammillaris, Saint Mentu-

17. Middleton (1683–1750) was educated at Trinity College, Cambridge; his chief works include the *Life of Cicero* (London, 1741) and the latitudinarian *Free Inquiry into Miracles* (London, 1748), which aroused much controversy by concluding that postapostolic miracles were unreal. Hamilton is purposefully misconstruing Middleton's *Letter from Rome,* 2d ed. (London, 1729), in which the story of Saint Viar is used to point out the ridiculous nature of idolatry. In the *Letter,* Viar is a Spaniard whose sainthood is demonstrated when his people produce a sacred stone with *S. Viar* on it; antiquaries, however, prove the stone to be only a fragment of an old Roman inscription in memory of a Praefectus Viarum, or overseer of the highways.

18. Amphibalus was the cleric who supposedly converted Saint Alban and whose name was invented by Geoffrey of Monmouth from the cleric's cloak (*amphibalus*) used by Saint Alban to conceal his identity. Saint Alban (d. ca. 304), the first British martyr, was put to death during the Diocletian persecution. A layman, he sacrificed his life to save the life of a priest by disguising himself in the priest's cloak.

laris, Saint Vulvaris,[19] and so forth. These Saints have done Infinite dammage to Physicians and Apothecaries, and conveyd thousands of pounds out of their pockets into those of the priests, by means of a certain latent virtue they have of Curing distempers in all parts of the body, such as headakes, toothakes, Pleurisies, Colics, and even the venereal Distemper, which has been of such vast Emolument, for this Century past, to certain obscure doctors of Physic.

There is a person, whether a Saint or a hermit, or both, I cannot be certain, nor Indeed is he known by any other name but that of the Wandering Jew,[20] this person is said to have been strolling from place to place, like a Scotsh pedlar, for upwards of Seventeen hundred years, Several persons of great ‖ credulity and moderate credit, have affirmed that they have seen   [137] him, and, it is believed by many, that he will persevere in this Strolling way, to the end of the world, or at least, to the long, and longer yet to be wished for Millennium.

As for the Seven Sleepers[21] and their dog, who sleeped in a Cave for 500 years, we need not wonder that nothing is known of them but this Sleeping bout, since Sleep is a State of torpor or Inactivity, in which the only thing we can be Employed about is dreaming, an employment, which several people exercise, to as great perfection when broad awake, as others do when fast asleep.

Prester John[22] is another obscure worthy, whose place of Residence and proper office is not yet fixed, many believe him to be an Emperor, a king, a great prince; but all agree in this, that he is a priest, but if so, he is a priest of whom we know as little as of the Ancient Melhisedec,[23] who is mentioned only by Name in Sacred History, and all that we know of him, is that Abraham paid him the tythes of the Spoils taken in battle, which

19. These are all invented names (for different parts of the body) except Saint Januarius, the bishop of Beneventum who was beheaded during the Diocletian persecution in 305.

20. A widespread medieval legend concerned a Jew who refused Christ comfort while Christ was bearing his cross to Calvary and who was therefore condemned to wander over the face of the earth until the end of the world.

21. The seven noble Christian youths of Ephesus who fled the persecution of Decius (250) and concealed themselves in a mountain cave, which Decius ordered to be walled up; they slept for around 200 years, and after awakening and telling their story, they died.

22. Legendary Christian priest and king who is alleged to have reigned both in Asia and in Africa in the 12th century.

23. Melchizedec was the high priest of Salem "who met Abraham returning from the slaughter of the kings" and received a "tenth of the spoils" (Heb. 7:1–4). The proximity of this allusion to the Selden allusion below suggests that Hamilton is recalling the story of Melchizedek and Abraham related in the first chapter of Selden's *History of Tythes* (see p. 137n, below).

Circumstance alone, I think, is Sufficient to convince all prophane cavillers at the divine right of tythes, but, as this age has come to such a gross degree of Infidelity, as to give little or no credit to quotations from Scripture, and the pious and Learned labors of the Revd Mr Commissary Henderson, on that Subject,[24] for even our nobles of the English Nation, (witness the late learned Henry Saintjohn Lord Bolingbroke, in his letters against the Authenticity of Sacred History)[25] have run much into that Strain, we shall to reclaim them (tho we have reason to think it will be as much in vain, as foreign to our present purpose) relate a miracle, which is quoted by the Learned Selden, in his book upon tythes.[26]

[138]   "It happened on a time, that Saint Austin, the famous Archbishop of Canterbury, in the time of the Saxons, had a dispute with some Lord concerning the tythes, he refusing to pay them, upon this, the Archbishop, on a Solemn day, at Church, pronounced a curse upon all those who refused to pay the tythes, forbidding them to come within the rail of the altar; he had no sooner pronounced this Interdict, than the Corps of a man, that lay enterred within that rail, miraculously rose from the grave, and very gravely walked out of the Church; the Archbishop calling him back, asked him who he was, and what was the reason of his rising out of his grave; he replied that he had Layn buried there 170 years, and, that he was in his life time Lord of the Mannor, and had refused to pay the tythes, upon which the priest of the parish excommunicated him, and, upon the Archbishops pronouncing the Curse, he was obliged to rise from his grave, and quit that holy ground, where he lay enterred, the Archbishop asked him if he knew who, or where that priest was, he answered that he lay buried in the same

24. Jacob Henderson (d. 1751) was born in Ireland, ordained in 1710 and licensed to Virginia, appointed commissary for the Western Shore of Maryland in 1715, and then reappointed commissary for the whole colony in 1729. Henderson was embroiled in a dispute over ministers' salaries, and Hamilton is probably alluding especially to Henderson's *The Case of the Clergy of Maryland* ([London, 1729]); see J. A. Leo Lemay, *Men of Letters in Colonial Maryland* (Knoxville, Tenn., 1972), 120–121.

25. Henry Saint John, Viscount Bolingbroke (1678–1751) was an English statesman who supported Robert Harley and the Tory party, managed the peace negotiations at Utrecht (1713), acted as James the Pretender's secretary of state and drew up his declaration for invasion, and after returning to England, retired and wrote numerous political tracts. Hamilton is referring to Bolingbroke's *Letters on the Study and Use of History* (London, 1752), in which Bolingbroke argues against the credibility of miracles.

26. John Selden (1584–1654) was an eminent lawyer of the Inner Temple whose *Historie of Tithes* ([London], 1618) offended the clergy and was suppressed; he was noted also for his treatise *De diis Syris* (London, 1617), which established his reputation as an Orientalist. The passage on Augustine appears in the *Historie of Tithes* (see the tale of Augustine and the lord of Cometon, chap. 10, pp. 272–274), but Hamilton has loosely paraphrased the story and added the derogatory remarks. (Selden does not say, for instance, that the priest refused to stay on earth because he had "no personal Interest in the thing.")

Church, at a small distance from the altar, upon this the Archbishop, Solemnly called him by his name to appear, and lo, the priest rose from his grave also; The Archbishop urged him to absolve the lord, which he did, and this Lord quietly retired to his rest again, within the rail of the Altar. The Archbishop would fain have persuaded the priest to stay on earth, to make Converts, with regard to paying of the tythes, but he also retired to his grave, positively refusing to grant the good Archbishop this boon, as having no personal Interest in the thing, however, upon this miracle, the Lord, with whom the Archbishop had the dispute, quietly payd the tythes ever after"—let our prophane denyers of the divine right of tythes read this Story and tremble, be convinced and converted.

There is but one pope, whom I shall mention among these nominal [139] worthies, and it is Pope Joan,[27] who is said to have been a female pope, and put an arch trick upon the wise Cardinals of the Conclave, there is nothing more known of this pope or popess, but this piece of waggery, this Story is denied by all true and Stanch catholics, who say, it is only a Scandalous lie, Invented by the Heretics, to throw a Slur upon holy Church, but, I would ask them, for what reason the Cardinals now use a Groping Chair at the Installment of the popes? is it not to be certain of the virility of the Candidate, and, that they may never again have such another trick playd them.

Tom Folio[28] is another worthy of this class, who is often mentioned, in conversation, it is uncertain when and where he lived, but we have reason to believe, that he was a profound Critic in title pages, and had treasured up in his head a voluminous catalogue of books, since it is a common appellation, bestowed upon all such (since his time) as talk much of books which they have never read, dipt into or understood, such people being properly stiled Tom Folios.

Many others besides these I have mentioned might be Introduced among the nominal worthies, such as messiurs Jack-a-napes, Jack-a-Dandy, Joannes ad oppositum, The man in the moon, Archæus Faber, and Tom Fool,[29] but let those I have already exhibited serve as a Specimen of the great worth and dignity of these obscure heroes.

27. The mythical female pope who supposedly succeeded Leo IV (855); she disguised herself as a monk so that she could gain admission to her lover, the monk Folda. After being elected pope, she was discovered when she gave birth during her enthronement.

28. Thomas Rawlinson (1681–1725), an English book collector, was satirized by Joseph Addison in the *Tatler* (no. 158) as "Tom Folio," but Hamilton may be referring to a more mythical figure.

29. A Jackanapes is a pert, apish little fellow (originally, the name probably signified a tame monkey [*Jack*] from Naples). A Jack-a-dandy is a smart, bright little fellow. For variations of the man in the moon myth, see *Brewer's Dictionary of Phrase and Fable*. Jan Baptista van Helmont (1577–1644) in chap. 5 of his *Oriatrike, or Physick Refined* (1662) defines the Archaeus

Since we cannot certainly tell what Sort of people those worthies abovementioned were, I think, to fix the matter, and In some measure to satisfy posterity, we may take upon us to pronounce, with great verisimili-
[140] tude, that ‖ they were all once on a time, members of certain Clubs, and by that means, their names have been handed down, in winter Evening Stories, Legends, Law papers, proverbs and the like, tho' their actions have been most of them buried in oblivion, thro' the Neglect of Clubical Historians and Secretaries.

I shall mention but one other worthy before I conclude this Chapter, by Name, Sir Hugh Mccarty Esqr, an Illustrious person, whose name has spread far and near within these two or three years, being the Honorable the President, of the Ancient and Right honorable Monday Club of New York,[30] as it has been called; but still one Strange peculiarity attends this great man and his Club, that tho' both be of very moderen date, yet not one Soul, far or near, can be found, that can upon oath or honor declare, that they ever saw that Illustrious personage, or ever were once in his Club, or heard any thing at all of it in the City of New York, where it was said to meet, tho he, and his Club were both very famous in several places at a distance, from that City, like the new Island lately Discovered by Admiral Anson's Crew,[31] known every where, but in the very place where it lies, and for this reason, I have Introduced him and his Club, in the Catalogue of these worthies merely nominal, and as I shall have occasion to say a great deal of this noble personage, in the Sequel of this history, I shall drop him here, together with his club, and, flattering myself, that my labor and pains, will preserve the worthies, of the ancient and honorable Tuesday Club, (of which I may Justly say, I am the faithful Secretary,) from that misfortune, of having little else but their bare names known to posterity, I with pleasure pursue the thread of my history.

Faber as the "chief Workman, containing the fruitfulness of generations and Seeds, as it were the internal efficient cause," and suggests that in the "*Archeusses* of the bowels . . . the planetary Spirits do most shine forth, even as also, in the whole influous *Archeus*" (*Van Helmont's Works* [London, 1664], 35–36). A Tom Fool is a clumsy fool, fond of practical jokes.

30. Sir Hugh (or Colonel Morris, as Hamilton calls him in the "Record") and his Monday Club remain a mystery. Carl Bridenbaugh alludes to the Monday Club in *Cities in Revolt: Urban Life in America, 1743–1776* (New York, 1955), 163, but he has borrowed his information from Hamilton.

31. George Anson, Lord Anson (1697–1762) was an English admiral who commanded a squadron in the Pacific, inflicted damage upon the Spanish, and circumnavigated the world (1740–1744).

Chapter II   [141]

The first Sederunt of the Ancient and honorable Tuesday Club, and the wise Laws then framed.

Such of my readers, as have perused the last chapter of the preceeding book, if their memory be not very short, will Remember, that Messiurs Prattle Motely and Loquacious Scribble M:D: the residue of the Ugly Club, called to their asistance Jealous Spyplot Esqr, Serjeant at Law, and the Reverend Mr Smoothum Sly, parson of the parish, in order to form a new Club, and fix it upon a better and more lasting foundation, than any of the Clubs hitherto erected, They presently got four more to Join them, vizt: Captn: Seemly Spruce, a Jolly boon companion, and no early Starter, being one who usually wore his Sitting breeches at a nights compotation, Captn: Serious Social, of the same kidney, and noted for Singing of old Club Catches, Mr Laconic Comus, a Jolly old cock, of Surly aspect and few words, but gifted with an excellent musical voice, and a Sincere lover of the Bowl and tobacco pipe, these had formerly been members of the Red house Club; and Captn: Bully Blunt, a person of a very happy turn to the Burlesque, which made him an exceeding good Clubs man.

These Gentlemen then, meeting upon Tuesday the 14th day of May, in the Year 1745, the same month and day on which the Red house Club met under Mr George Neilson Sixteen years before, formed and erected themselves into a club, which they called by the name of the *Tuesday Club;* they met first at the Lodging of ‖ Doctor Loquacious Scribble, who first exer- [142] cised the office of Steward, and Chairman to the Club; and the Candles being lit, the punch made, and the pipes fairly set a going, after two or three rounds of the punch bowl, they applied themselves to make and pass some wholesome Laws, for the good government and regulation of the Society, In which, they did not trust so much to their own Judgement, and Invention, as some vain people are apt to do, but took for a pattern, the regulations and laws of other Clubs, particularly those of the ancient and venerable Tuesday, (or whin bush) Club of Lanneric, of which, they reckoned themselves a direct continuation, on the same line, and, upon this position they assumed the name of the *Ancient and honorable Tuesday Club, of Annapolis in Maryland,* and thus having fixed their ancient and honorable title, they, at their first Sederunt established the following Laws.

[facing page 142]

Law I. That the meeting of the Club be weekly, at the members houses, by turns, thro' out the year, upon Tuesday evening.

Law II. The Steward for the time being, shall provide a gammon of bacon, or any other one dish of dressed vittles and no more.

Law III. No Liquor shall be made, prepared or produced after eleven o clock at night, and every Member shall be at liberty to retire at pleasure.

Law IV. No members shall be admitted without the concurring con- [143] sent, of the whole Club, and after such admission, the member shall serve as Steward next meeting.

Having passed these laws with great wisdom and Sagacity, they betook themselves again to their punch and pipes, and then, the Gammon, according to Rule, appeared on a Side-board, with some plates in a heap, and knives and forks, there not being so much as the formality of a Cloth laid, and every member at pleasure arose from his Seat and helped himself, without taking up time in Saying of Grace, setting Chairs, passing compliments, about taking place at table, or trowbling themselves about shifting of dishes, handing of plates Spoons, cruets mustard pots &ct: and Servants running over one another, which not only wastes much time, but creates more noise than is needful.

Happy, O happy had it been for this ancient and honorable Club, had they always kept to this golden mean of frugality and temperance, but the mode soon changed, and Luxury crept in by degrees, as we shall find in the Sequel.

This first Sederunt was finished in a gay and Jovial manner, by the Singing of several ancient Catches, at which Capt: Serious Social was a good hand, and sung the following, holding up a large punch bowl well Replenished, which I think worthy of a place in this history, because it became afterwards a Constant Club Catch.

Club Catch sung by Capt: Serious Social

Merry meet, and merry part,
Here's to thee with all my heart.
One bowl in hand, and another in store, [144]
Enough's enough, and we'll have one more.

Nothing more, worth remarking passed at this first Sederunt.

At Sederunt Second, May 21, which was held by Jealous Spyplot Esqr, the Evening passed in putting round the bowl and Smoking; but, on the 28 of may, when the Club was held by Capt: Serious Social, the order of honorary members was established, and Mr Abraham Bumper was made an honorary member of this ancient and honorable Club; These honorary members, of whom we shall find many admitted in the course of our History, had a right to attend the Club meetings as often as they were in the place, and were not obliged to serve the Club at any time as Stewards, an excellent policy in the Club, to Increase and add to their Strength and Importance, and to spread their fame abroad, without much expence or trowble, from these honorary members, arose, in process of time, a considerable Society, Called the *Eastren Shore Triumvirate,* depending upon this ancient and Honorable Club, as shall be related in its proper place.

Before this Sederunt broke up, the Steward, Capt: Serious Social, being in a very gay and pleasant humor, took up the punch bowl, and with a musical voice, sung the following Catch, which went round the members.

Club Catch sung by Capt: Serious Social

There was a man of very great fame,
Signior Domingo was his name.
He was a man not given to quarrel,
But now and then, with a Sma' beer barrel,
And, when he died, he was so kind,
As to leave this very bowl for us behind.

[145]

The next meeting or Sederunt of the Club, was at Capt: Bully Blunt's, which was on the 4th of June, when the Club passed another Law, vizt:

Law V. That Immediatly after supper, the Ladies shall be toasted, before any other healths go round.

This Law stood in force for a great while, but at last gave place to the King and the Club, and even that submitted to the high Steward's health, as he was stiled.

This Law shows the great regard, that this ancient and Honorable Club had for the Ladies, and, there will appear in the Sequel of this History, more marks of honor and respect, which this Club conferrd upon this amiable Sex, tho' it must be owned, that there were in the Club at that time, two longstanding members, that were remarkable for their disregard to, (I will not say, utter Indifference for) the Sex, for, one of these gentlemen, loved a piece of old hat very well (as the Saying is) but his humor led him to partake of it in a hugger mugger way, as for the other, he was a Sort of apathy, had not the least Inclination for that Sort of amusement, and Indeed, never much affected being In the company of the Ladies, If my readers have a Curiosity to know, who these members were by name, I must beg to be excused, not thinking it proper, to mention names in this history,

when any thing that looks like Satyr ‖ or accrimination is laid at the door of [146]
a member, for tho' a regard to truth, obliges me as an historian to mention
every circumstance, yet, a regard to my own quiet, and the good will of
others, constrains me to forbear naming of names upon all occasions, and
therefore, I shall leave my Judicious Readers to guess, who I mean in this
particular, and in many other particulars of the like nature, which may occur
in the course of this History.

    And, now, since I am upon the Subject of the Club's regard for the fair
Sex, I must not omitt an order that passed at this Sederunt, which, some-
how or other, by the fault of the Clerk or Secretary, was not entered in the
book of records; and that was the Introduction of certain utensils into the
Club, these were Sand boxes to spit in, as most of the members smoked,
and some Chawed, this contrivance was fallen upon to prevent abusing and
soiling the floors of the rooms where the Club sat, and these conveniencies
were carried about with great pomp and Solemnity, from one Stewards
house to another, every time the Club met, but cleanly and useful as they
were, and contrived for the ease of Servants and neat house wives, whose
chief ambition and Care of life, is to make their plank floors shine like glass,
yet, were they soon dismissed, because, it was thought, that the married men of the Club, were afraid of falling under the Ridicule of the
Batchellors, by showing in this, a more than Common care and Sollicitude,
about Incurring the displeasure of their wives.

Chapter III

*The Introduction of the Batchellor's Cheese into the Club, the passing
The Gelastic law, and other matters of Importance.*

    We shall meet with some Histories, where there is nothing ‖ but a dry [147]
relation of facts, without any useful reflections, or observations interspersed, which are Indeed the Salt of History, and afford it a Savor which
makes it agreeable to the palat of every Judicious reader, without this, it
would look like the York-shire Squire's Story of himself and his friend,
which consisted chiefly of—and so quoth he, and so quoth I, and so we
agreed on this, and so we differed on that, and so I went there, and so he
came here, and so—and so—and so &ct:

    Whoever reads this history, must not expect to find any such trumpery
in it's structure and composition; I never Intended it for the entertainment

of nurses children and Shallow wits by a winters fire, but have adapted it to
the taste of the learned & Ingenious, by Interlarding the narration of facts
In several places, with proper and apposite observations and remarks, and
these, my readers are to expect to meet with, wherever the nature of the
Subject will permit, and, if any Slender wits happen to be among my
readers, I advise them, for their own ease, to pass over these learned Remarks, as being above their capacity and understanding, but, I hope all my
learned Readers will esteem them the very marrow and Cream of this history, and therefore read them over with attention and Carefully store them
up in their Intellectual warehouses and magazines, which, as the learned
Descartes says, is in the middle Ventricle of the brain, near the pineal
Gland, where memory keeps her court.[1]

This virtuous and frugal Club, Imagining that they were still too lavish
in allowing a Gammon of bacon, or one dish of dress'd vittles for Supper,
passed at Sederunt 5th June 11, the following Law, viz:

Law VI. That such as are batchelor members of the Club may have a
Cheese upon one Side board, instead of dress'd vittles.

[148]   This not only exhibited, a Singular Instance of frugality and moderation, but also, a high degree of Indulgence to those batchelor members,
who, not always having cooks at home, and for the most part, little or
nothing for Cooks to lick their fingers upon, must be at abundance more
trowble in providing, than such of the members as were matirmonized,
they likewise showed in this an Instance of heroic temperance and moderation, much like that of a certain Roman General; who, when foreign ambassadors came to have audience of him, was busied in boiling a turnip for
his own Dinner.

(*)Happy then was it with the members of this ancient and honorable
Club, for, without Interruption, let or molestation, they could sit with their
legs across, loll upon the table or an Elbow chair, smoke their pipes, kiss the
Glass or bowl, in their turns, converse upon Clubical matters, either grave
or facetious, drink toasts either loyal or amorous, crack Jokes, frame puns
or conundrums, and, should their Stomachs call for a whet, without Ceremony or trowble to themselves or fellow members, they might rise up, go
to the Side board, and after having taken their Slice of cheese or Sliver
of Gammon standing, return again to their compotation, Jocosity, and
Clubical conversation, how charming, how regular, and how much like the

(*) Vide anniversary Speech in 1754, almost verbatim the same with this paragraph.

1. Hamilton is probably recalling Descartes's 1664 *Essay on Man* (*Traité de l'homme*), in which
Descartes explains that memory is located in the pineal gland (see *Oeuvres de Descartes,* ed.
Charles Adam and Paul Tannery [Paris, 1897–1910], XI, 177–178).

Simple frugality of the Golden age was this, and how different from that luxury and profuseness that prevails in most of our moderen Clubs, where, the whole apparatus of a formal table is Introduced, the Club room is pestered with the passing and repassing of Servants, the hobnails of whose Shoes, make a miserable Clamping over the planks, and, when this is over ‖ it proves only a prologue to the confusion and Superfluous Ceremony that [149] succeeds, for, as soon as the Steward gives the Signal that Supper waits, there is hawling of Chairs, crossing over, Casting off, figuring in, right and left, like so many people at a Country dance, There is—pray Gentlemen take your places—as the Steward's prologue,—there is grace to be said, of which not one word can be heard, for talking and laughing, then follow Sharp reproofs from the Chaplain, and grumblings from the offending members; next it is—pray take a Seat—Pray Sir sit here—here's room enough—excuse me Sir, I eat no Suppers—I seldom sup a nights Sir—for my part, I never sup Sir. Then comes the table conversation—Here boy, some bread—Pray shift that Dish this way—who carves best?—what do you chuse Sir?—pray gi' me leave to help you—Shall I help you to this pray good Sir?—Shall I help you to that—Sir, your most humble—pray Sir help yourself,—hold good Sir—here's enough—dont you chuse Sauce—please to hand me that mustard,—pray shove the vinegar cruet this way—a clean plate there—This is fine veal, that's delicious mutton—these apples are well baked, these cheese cakes are not done,—of all things commend me to pudding—do you love Cold pudding Sir—no good Sir, my love is set-tled,—pray Sir eat 'tother Custard,—boy, some Small beer—a glass of wine you—Sir, my humble Service—Sir your health—yours Sir,—and yours Sir,—and yours Sir—your most obedient humble Servant—pledge you Sir—fill me a glass of Claret there ho—avast you Son of a bitch, none of your bumpers damn you!—well, come away, let's have at this turkey and oys-ters,—my Stars and garters what a twist of the under Jaw you have got,—I play a good knife ‖ and fork, thanks be praised—here take away,—and so [150] they get up one by one, and fall to picking their teeth, sauntering about the Room, or standing with their bums to the fire; I would ask what pleasure there can be in all this, except only that of eating and drinking, which, as it is a pleasure we enjoy in Common with the brute, and often employ to baser purposes, the destruction of health and constitution, we ought to glory but little in, as the pious Mr Dods, the Reverend Mr Dolittle, and several other learned Divines tell us,[2] as for the table conversation on these

2. Probably John Dod (1549?–1645), Puritan divine known as "Decalogue Dod" for his exposition of the Ten Commandments (1604). Thomas Doolittle (1632?–1707) was a Noncon-formist tutor and preacher who published several volumes of religious writings, including *A*

occasions, have I not given a Specimen of it, is it any thing but mere balderdash, so confused, and so noisy, that I defy the wisest head in Christendom to methodize it, and, after all Impediments are removed, and the Club forms itself again round the great table, how dull, how sleepy are the members, when their Stomachs are overcharged, how flat, how low the Conversation, what yawning, what gaping, what Streching of limbs, what Nodding, what Sleeping, what Snoring, or rather driving of hogs! Oh! Oh! Tis Lamentable to behold, how much better is it to spend the time, in witty conversation, such as punning, framing quaint Conundrums, cracking Sly Jokes, telling comical Stories, singing old catches, or composing extempore Rhimes, but alas! all this is only preaching to the wind, and beating the air in vain, for one may preach to eternity, and never reform the manners of Clubs, nay more, the manners of mankind in General, till the example of great men and presidents shows them the way.

I come now to relate a transaction, which shows in a very conspicuous Light, the wisdom of this ancient and honorable Club; It is a truth not to be disputed, that the greatest pest of Clubs, and the most common disturber of the peace of those ‖ Societies, is that violent propensity in human nature to dispute, every one thinking himself the wisest and most learned person in company, and therefore not obliged to yield one ace to the opinion or Judgement of another. This has been the cause of the dissolution of many Clubs, and, where disputes have arisen about such Important matters, as what is the right, and what the wrong end of a black pudding, at what end one shall break an egg, with most ease and conveniency to eat it, which is the most amicable, or familiar way of Saluting a friend, to shake him by the hand, or clap him on the Shoulder, what is to be reckoned among men of nice honor, the greatest affront, a twitch o' the nose, or a kick o' the breech, the consequences of these learned disputes, have been fatal to those Clubs, where they have been fomented or encouraged, have entirely broke them up, and rendered those who were before, good Club Companions and friends, bitter enimies to one another, to the great hurt and Dammage, of that Social Clubical disposition, which nature has been so careful to Implant in mankind.

[151]

Complete Body of Practical Divinity (London, 1723). Like most divines, Dod and Doolittle frequently admonish their readers against the dangers of excessive eating and drinking, but I suspect that Hamilton is especially recalling their treatises on the Lord's Supper. In *A Briefe Dialogue, concerning Preparation for the Worthy Receiving of the Lords Supper* (London, 1627), Dod discusses the dangers of excessive eating and drinking in his section on the sins against the Fourth Commandment; in *A Treatise concerning the Lords Supper* (London, 1667), Doolittle writes: "It is an hainous sin that those that are reeling in the street, . . . rather than degrading themselves below the rank of men" and "reducing them[selves] to the Primitive Institution, . . . should be seen kneeling at the Sacrament" (p. 3).

This sage Club therefore, considering how dreadfully fatal the consequences might be, if such Subtile disputes were suffered to take place in their Society, thought of a method to prevent this mischief, and fell upon the most effectual remedy, which shows their deep Judgement and Sagacity; they pitched upon ridicule, as the most effectual way to Cure it, and Indeed, we find it to be true, that men are much sooner laughed out of their follies and faults, than cured of them by grave admonition and advice, they therefore at Sederunt 6th, June 18, passed the following law.

Law VII. That if any Subject of what nature soever, be discussed, that levels at party matters, or the administration of the Government of this Province, or be disagreeable to the Club, no answer shall be given thereto, but after such discourse is ended, the Society shall laugh at the member offending, in order to divert the discourse.

This Law was called the *gelastic Law,* and, in its Substance and Structure, shows the wisdom and Sagacity of the Longstanding members, of this ancient and honorable Club, as much as any Law framed by them, either before or since, and, we shall find in the Sequel, this Law put in execution, against several offending members, sometimes with effect, and sometimes with none at all, which shows us, how difficult a task it is, for even the utmost Strech of human wisdom, to frame a Law or Laws, that cannot be evaded, at the same Sederunt there passed another rule, vizt: [152]

Law VIII. That Mr Prattle Motely, shall be Secretary of the Club during pleasure.

At the next Sederunt, (Mr Laconic Comas being Steward) two Gentlemen were proposed by the Reverend Mr Smoothum Sly, to be admitted members of the Club, vizt: Mr Nasifer Jole, of whom we shall have a great deal to say in the next chapter, and Mr Dumpling Gundiguts, of whom we shall say all in this place that can be said of him, that is, that he was only noted for his being a very fat unwieldy man, and a vociferous Singer in Club, making more noise than music, at this Sederunt the Gelastic Law, was the first time put in execution, against Mr Secretary Motely, who entered into a prolix harangue concerning the Consciences of Lawyers.

Chapter IV

The private Character of Nasifer Jole Esqr, and other prodigious matters.

I am now entering upon a chapter in this History, in which I shall have occasion for the asistance of all the muses, which Inhabit Parnassus, from

[153] its top to its bottom, from the highest of the ‖ Sublime, to the lowest of the bathos; from Virgil to Bavius, from Milton to Pryn and Wythers, from Cervantes and his follower Henry Fielding Esqr, to the Reverend Mr Gazeteer Eachard & the Celebrated Mr John Bunyian.[1]

Upon the celebrated 2d of July, O:S: in the year 1745, a day ever to be remembered by the ancient and honorable Tuesday Club, at Sederunt 8, Mr Secretary Motely being Steward, were admitted to the Club several members, vizt: Messieurs Nasifer Jole, Dumpling Gundiguts, Drawlum Quaint, Slyboots Pleasant, and Joggle Hasty; The first of these Gentlemen is the Subject of this dignified and distinguished Chapter, and Indeed, will be the Chief heroe of our Succeeding History, as for the others, we shall mention them only occasionally as we go along, according to the Station they hold, and figure they make in the Club.

Mr Nasifer Jole, otherwise Carlo Nasifer Jole, was a native of old England, and the County of Kent claims the honor of his birth, he often Justly values himself on his being born an Englishman, and is not alittle fond of letting it be known, that he is a man of Kent, sprung of a race of ancient heroes and true british blood, not a kentish man,[2] who is only the mungerell Issue of the Roman, Saxon, Norman, Dane, Scot, pict, and a hundred other mixed foreign Nations, that gained footing in England but of late.

He was educated in the mercantile way, and made such progress in the Science of traffic and trucking, that he could tell at his fingers ends, all the noble Ingredients that Compound the Character of a reputable merchant, or storekeeper, & could distinguish such from a Scots pedlar at a miles distance without the help of a perspective glass, his chief Characteristic of a
[154] merchant, was one that bought very Cheap, and ‖ sold at a living price, as he called it, which golden rule he followed himself, as much as in him lay, and his distinguishing mark of a pedlar, was a fellow, that presumed to vend his wares at a low, or what some call a reasonable rate, (whatever price he

---

1. Bavius (fl. 1st century B.C.), a Roman poetaster, was rescued from oblivion only by Vergil's contempt. William Prynne (1600–1669), a Puritan pamphleteer, wrote against Arminianism and endeavored to reform the manners of the age, for which he was confined to the Tower of London. George Wither (1588–1667), an English author, was noted for his satires (*Abuses Stript and Whipt* [London, 1613]), his pastorals, including *The Shepherds Hunting* (London, 1615), and his *Hymnes and Songs of the Church* (London, 1623), written after he became a devout Puritan. John Eachard (ca. 1636–1697) was an English divine and satirical writer whose works include *The Grounds and Occasions of the Contempt of the Clergy and Religion Enquired Into* (London, 1670) and two dialogues ridiculing Hobbes's philosophy (1672, 1673).

2. A man of Kent is one born east of the Medway; these men went out with green boughs to meet William the Conqueror and consequently obtained a confirmation of their ancient privileges from the new king. A Kentish man is a resident of the western part of the county.

The Honorable Carlo Nasifer Jole Esq.ᵣ President of the Ancient & Honorable Tuesday Club.

Prandum flos, alta infidens icce Cathedra,
Consortii nostri et decus, et gloria.
Dedito, a Hugo, tu Cognominate Macuarti,
Vedmum nam caput nostra tiara timnit.

purchased them at) to the prejudice of the Reputable merchant, he would prove very clearly, by unanswerable arguments, that 300 per cent, tended more to the public good, (vizt: the good of the merchants or Storekeepers, who were of public Service) than 50 per cent, because, said he, 300 per cent, is a living price, and enables the merchant to carry on trade and commerce, with vigor and life, whereas, any thing under that is a pitiful peddling price, and occasions trade, (vizt: Storekeeping) to languish and decay, that high prizes for goods in the retale way, was what Chiefly made the nation (vizt: the Storekeepers and merchants) flourish, but low prizes were the ruin and bane of Society, i:e: The Society of Storekeepers or merchants. He would often endeavor to Inculcate this doctrine to Ignorant people, who could not comprehend how this could be, and endeavored to perswade them, that it was much more for their advantage and Interest to give a reputable merchant half a crown a yard, for any kind of Stuff, than to buy the same Stuff of a Scots pedlar for one & Sixpence, the wares of the first being good, those of the latter trash, but, I never heard that he made any pros-elytes to this way of thinking, not only because this doctrine was *gratis dictum*,[3] as the Logicians term it, but because the Sordid Love of money is so generally prevalent, that people would still buy where they could at the Cheapest rate, which made Mr Jole very much admire at their Stupidity and Ignorance in thus preferring Scots pedlars, to merchants of repute & Character.

[155]   Mr Jole had a great part of his education on board a man of war, where he had learned many useful arts, particularly that of Cookery, and he was such a proficient in that noble Science, that he understood as well as any notable husiff, how to stew a frecassée, or ragout, mix, compound, boil or bake a pudding, or raise a pasty, and he knew his own Skill in these Impor-tant operations so well, that with reason he picqued himself upon it, and people approved of, and acquiesced in his Judgement herein so far, that they often eat of his dishes with high relish and pleasure, Indeed, his fond-ness for these niceities, and desire of applause on that Score, might Justly be called his weak side; for, tho' he was a person pritty tenacious of his prop-erty, yet, he would spare no expence in making a Show with such delicacies, and dainties, and any hungry fellow or abandon'd Epicure, might get a good meal out of him, as often as he pleased, by only praising his Cookery, and saying that it put one in mind of *Old England;* for he was so passionatly fond of Old England, as we have said, and every thing belonging to it, that nothing in the world was to be compared to the manners, customs, eating,

3. "Freely asserted."

Clothing, drinking, air, Soil, Language and Commodities of Old England, in short, with him old England was all in all, but if this was an Infirmity in Mr Jole, it is an Infirmity generally Incident to human nature, in which, there is Ingrafted, such a Luxuriant Slip of vanity, that the wisest man that ever stept on two legs, may be cajoled or managed in this manner, if any artful Sycophant or flatterer, is lucky enough to hit upon, and humor his natural foibles, in fine, among all men, let their professions be what you will, it is the same now a days, as it was in the days of Tully, when ‖ in his [156] epistle to Atticus he says, *Nemo unquam poeta aut Orator, qui quenquam se meliorem arbitraretur,*[4] some may apply this to the present case, by using the words *Coquus* and *Culinarius,* instead of *poeta* and *Orator.*

Carlo Jole had a very elegant taste, in most things relative to houshold affairs, which he acquired by long and painful experience and application, during the many years that he spent in a Single life; he understood perfectly well how to set out a mantle piece or bofett, with plate, Glass and China, in the neatest and most Showy order; how, and in what places to dispose of flowers in the season, how to paper candlesticks and adorn glass Sconces, how to hang pictures, filigrams and pettipoints, and such like ornaments in a room, how to cut papers for decoying the flies from the hangings and Valence of beds, and how in the most charming and elegant taste to dress up a nosegay, for which he always kept a choice Collection of flowers in his Garden, that looked like a pleasant thicket or grove, shaded over with trees, bearing variety of fruits, such as apples, peaches, cherries, and Covered below, with all Sorts of kitchen Stuff, vizt: Cabbage, coleworts, Spinage, beets, carrots &ct: and Indeed, this curious gentleman showd the elegance of his taste, as much in the disposition and order of his Garden, as in any other knick-knack that he had about him, and, as to nosegays, which we but Just now mentioned, it was his practice in Spring, Summer and fall, never to go to bed, without at least half a dozen of these about him, vizt: one at his head, one stuck in his mouth, one in each hand and one on his breast, and at all times, when he went to Church, he wore one in his buttonhole, so beautifully decked, that it attracted the eyes of all the Congregation, ‖ particularly those of the Ladies, while he kept twirling a [157] Charming pink Iris, Jonquille, or Ænemonie betwixt his finger and thumb, and often applying it to his nose, which was of no moderate Size, some suspected, as Mr Jole was a Batchellor, that he Intended thus to lay traps, or attract the Regards of the fair Sex; for this purpose, it is thought also, he

---

4. "There was never a poet or orator who considered anybody better than himself" (Cicero, *Epistulae ad Atticum* 14.20.3.8).

often used perfumes, such as musk, ambergrise, Civet, Bergamot, and the like, tho others affirm, that his design in that (and those were such as thought he was little attracted by the vanities of the fair Sex) was to conceal or Improve a perfume of a Ranker nature, which he contracted by keeping a number of favorite brutes about him, called by the greeks γαλαι,⁵ of which we shall speak by and bye, and, if he used these perfumes for this purpose, he Surely is as Justifiable, as was Demosthenes the Athenian Orator, who held in his mouth at all times when he declaimed in public, a parcell of small pebble Stones to correct the natural uncouthness of his Speech & pronounciation.

He had a curious and elegant taste in cutting out patterns of work for Sempstresses, and would save a deal of trowble to these gentle Nymphs by cutting out all his own Shirts, and nightcaps, and Instructing them how to work them up, and some of his patterns I have seen, so beautifully Scolloped, and Jagged round the edges, that it was even delectable and wonderful to behold, and excited grand Ideas of the Sublimity of his Imagination, and fertility of his Invention, nay more, sometimes this Ingenious gentleman, would use the needle himself, and dern and patch to the admiration of all that saw his work.

[158]   In setting out a table for an Entertainment, it was ‖ delightful to behold in what elegant order and Symmetry the table furniture was disposed, how charmingly the cloth was plaited, and pinched with regular figures in many places, how the plates, knives, forks, dishes, Salts, boats, cruets, casters &ct: were ranged in beautiful order, and how curiously the napkins were folded, and how delightfully perfumed.

Mr Jole in short, showed a delicacy of taste in every thing he had about him, both as to cleanliness and order, even in the disposition and arangement of the toys in his Shop, in which he dealt, to the great emolument of the Children of the place where he lived, who purchased of him at a good living price; those toys were piled up in pyramids, prisms, cylenders and Cones, and other Geometrical figures on the Shelves (which showed his Skill in the Mathematics) so as to attract the eyes of all passengers, particularly the longing and admiring eyes of Children and Schoolboys; they shining with as great Resplendency and Lustre, as does the throne of the great Mogol, Thick sown with diamonds, pearls, rubies, emeralds, Sapphires, topazes, and other precious Stones, in this manner shone the Shop

5. Mr. Jole keeps a bevy of cats about him, for which he is sometimes chided by other club members; it is probably no coincidence, then, that Hamilton has used the Greek word for *weasles* in referring to Jole's cats.

of Nasifer Jole Esqr, with little looking Glasses, bugles, Spangles, Isinglass and tinsel.

Some Cynical Mortals, may probably object here to these particulars in the character of this great man, and with a Sneer say, Well, what then? is this your Club hero? what is all this but triffling, and a Silly fancy or taste for bawbles and toys? but, in answer to those morose remarkers, I shall only produce some instances from history, of certain great men, who amused themselves with things rather more trivial and Insignificant, and shall give one recent example of the moderen taste this way.

Dioclesian the Emperor, gave up his Sceptre and turned Gardiner; Constantine wrote 40 books of husbandry; the austere Cato was an excellent cook, and wrote a Great book on the art of Cookery, Lysander, when ambassadors came to him talked ‖ of nothing but his orchard; what shall I   [159] say of Cincinatus, Tully and many others, who delighted in pruning, planting and Grafting, nay Domitian the Emperor was mightily pleased with fly catching. Augustus was entertained playing with nuts among little Children, and a Certain Right Reverend and Learned french Bishop, whose name I have forgot, used to shut himself up in his chamber, and spin tops, and ride Hobby horses with a favorite child, his pupil, or probably his nephew, Sir Hans Sloan, that noted Physician and Philosopher, with many learned members of the Royal Society, took great pleasure in handling and tumbling over, little pieces of metal, with the pictures and heads of a great many Rogues of Antiquity, stamp'd upon them, and also, used often to divert themselves, with placing in regular order, Shells, feathers, flies, Cobwebs, and such like toys, and exercise their great and profound learning, in making florid lectures on them.[6]

6. Diocletian (A.D. 245–316), Roman emperor who ruled during a period of extreme difficulty, resigned the emperorship in 305 and turned to tending his cabbages. Constantine (ca. A.D. 285–337) was the Roman emperor who restored the empire to its former strength and converted to Christianity (Hamilton is perhaps recalling Constantine's *Liber de agricultura*). Cato (95–46 B.C.) was the famous Roman praetor noted for his Stoicism and adherence to old Roman principles (Cato concludes his *De agricultura* with some recipes, especially for preserving, but he did not produce a book solely on cooking). Lysander (d. 395 B.C.), Spartan general and statesman who destroyed the Athenian navy at Aegospotami, was noted for his impolite reception of his guests (see the section on him in Plutarch's *Lives*). Cincinnatus was a model of integrity and frugality who, according to Roman tradition, was called from the plow in 458 B.C. and appointed dictator to free Minucius from the Aequians, then returned to his farm beyond the Tiber. Domitian (A.D. 51–96), Roman emperor noted for his strict enforcement of public morality and his attempt to impose Greek refinement on the Romans, was also known for his extreme cruelty and is said to have spent hours each day in strictest privacy, catching flies and piercing them with a sharp instrument. Augustus (63 B.C.–14 A.D.), the great Roman emperor, often amused himself by playing at dice, marbles, or nuts with little boys (see

Even in his Dress Nasifer showed a peculiar elegance of taste, he always went clean, and neat, tho never tawdry, he wore a large full flaxen wig,
sometimes too a laced hat, his favorite color was red, for he often wore a
Scarlet Coat, edged round with gold galloon, and ornamented with gold
buttons and button holes, but this was properly his military dress, he being
Leutenant General of the Independent foot Company of Annapolis, and
had formerly been ensign thereof, but was promoted, in reward of his brave
behaviour in the Dangerous expedition of that warlike Corps, against the
Nanticock Indians, whom they took prisoners to the number of about 30,
out of a boat at Wapping dock at Annapolis, and Conducted them safe to
the City prison, without stricking one blow, or sheding one drop of Christian blood.[7]

Carlo Nasifer Jole was exactly, and to a title, as genteel in his undress,
as in his high military dress, he wore a red or green velvet cap, a large blue
[160] wrapper, Girt about with a red || military sash, a blue Silk Jacket with Silver
mounting, and a genteel clouded cane; which last, vanity did not prompt
him to Carry, but necessity obliged, being at times much afflicted with the
gout, for the violent pains of which, his most effectual cure was Immerging
his legs in Cold water.

Our heroes person, which in general was genteel and well made, sett
off his dress, rather more than his dress his person, he is of a fair complexion, long and Sharp visage; somewhat Inclinable to a Square countenance,
his nose aqueline, his chin of a Considerable length and prominent, in
short, he is what many call in their vulgar Stile somewhat hatchet faced; his
body is thick and well built, of a middle Stature and every way proportional
except a little (tho' not disagreeable) *prominentia chínium,* resembling somewhat the description of Rob Morris in the old Scots Song,[8] who is described in the following distich thus.

Suetonius, *The Twelve Caesars,* sec. 83 of "Augustus"). Sloane (1660–1753), president of the
Royal Society (1727–1741) and president of the College of Physicians (1719–1735), was a noted
naturalist with a penchant for collecting the kinds of curiosities Hamilton pokes fun at.

7. In 1742 the Nanticokes briefly participated in a revolt against the English settlers on the
Eastern Shore of Maryland. While the Nanticokes and other tribes on the Eastern Shore were
engaged in a war dance, a Choptank Indian exposed the plot and the revolt came to an abrupt
end. The Nanticokes were severely reprimanded by the Maryland Assembly for their part in
the uprising, and by 1744 the Nanticokes removed themselves from the province to live among
the Six Nations. For a good discussion of this and other disputes concerning the Nanticokes,
see Frank W. Porter III, "A Century of Accommodation: The Nanticoke Indians in Colonial
Maryland," *Maryland Historical Magazine,* LXXIV (1979), 175–192.

8. "Auld Rob Morris" appears in Ramsay's *Tea-table Miscellany* (I, 59–60) and in *Calliope, or
English Harmony,* 2 vols. (London, 1739, 1746). The comparison between Jole and Rob Morris
is none too flattering. In the song, a girl's parents try to coerce her into marrying Morris, and
she swears she would rather die than marry such a poor excuse for a man.

Auld Rob Morris, I ken him fou well,
His arse it sticks out like ony peet creel.[9]

His presence is grand and majestic, especially when he ascends the Club
Chair, and sits erect in it, his walk is stately and upright, tho' alittle on the
hobble, which is not natural but from a gouty weakness in his feet, but he
has contracted a habit of Seesawing often when he sits, especially if he be
telling of a Story, at which he has a particular genius or knack, and tho' he
be somewhat circumstantial or prolix, yet, he seldom fails to fix the attention of his hearers, and affords them abundance of Instruction and agreeable amusement.

As to his religion, he values himself much upon being of the Church of
England, as by Law established, which he declares he thinks is the only true
Church in the world, he has a profound regard for all Creeds received by
that Church, particularly the Athanasian Creed, which he esteems a most
excellent composition, || and to be believed by every true and Sincere chris-   [161]
tian, on pain of eternal Damnation, as that admirable and excellent *Sym-
bolum,* expressly bears in it self; he is Intirely wedded to the Strict observation of the fasts, feasts and hollidays of the Church; and accounts all those
to be heretical Presbyterians (for whom he has a very high Contempt, not
only as foolish fanatics, but most of them lousy Scotsmen) who neglect
them, especially the Martyrdom of that most pious martyr Charles I, of
Savory memory, whom those hellish presbyterians (as some say) butchered
in a most Inhuman manner; he carries his observation of feasts so far, as
even to regulate his diet by them, Pancakes for example he looks upon to be
profane and Insipid food, at any other time of the year but Shrovetide, tho
never so well relished with wine and Sugar, and he also esteems it highly
absurd, to eat plumb porridge or minced pies, except at christenmass and
the hollidays.

The chief of Mr Joles Learning, besides that of cookery pastry, and
other parts of housewifery, consists in divinity and music, his knowledge in
the first he picked up, from a Curious collection of old books of Sermons,
bound In parchment and many of them printed in a black character, with
learned marginal notes, which Sermons were chiefly preached, by Learned
Divines, in the Halcyon days of K: James I. when punning and quaint
Sayings were very much in vogue, and diligently practised, encouraged and
rewarded, by that wise monarch and his Sententious courtiers, when it was
usual for men of bright Geniuses to pun themselves into bishopricks and
places at court, a noble example this, and what all great princes & crowned

9. Peat basket.

heads ought to observe, vizt: to encourage and promote all Ingenious and Learned men. For this reason Chiefly Mr Jole admires these Quaint Ser-
[162] mons, affirming that there ‖ were no such sermons to be met with now a days, which every one will frankly own to be true, yet, fond as he is of this Sort of learning, and quaint Sententious writing, there is nothing he detests more than awkward Imitations of it, as appears in his displeasure with, and opposition to the Club Conundrums, and the dislike he expressed to that pestilent and assuming humor of punning in Jonathan Grog Esqr, a Long-standing member and poet Laureat of the Club.

His knowledge in music, he has merely by the force of Genius, having never been taught, and his talent this way lies in vocal execution, he having a number of old Songs by him, to the words of which, he affirms, he never is at a loss to find a tune, and Indeed, give him words at any time, and he'll Immediatly clap a tune to them, with so Sweet and small a voice, and so delicate a trill, that some people have doubted whether or not he has in his youth been Italianized, but, be that as it will, (tho it may be said of him, as it was of *Aurelius Philippus Paracelsus Theophrastus Bombastus de Hohenheim, Testimonium virilitatis prebet rigida barba*)[10] he has a most exquisite pipe, and, were he not obliged sometimes to wear his Spectacles, to read the words of the Song, when he sings by book, his voice would be quite clear, and without asperity, but this nasal machine, will sometimes in the high notes, occasion a Snuffling, which a nice ear will easily excuse, seeing the cause is known to proceed from no natural defect, among many other favorite Songs, which shall afterwards be mentioned, Mr Jole had one of the amorous kind, entituled, *Whilst I gaze on Cloe trembling*,[11] which Song in the printed editions, wants about twelve or 15 Stanzas, which Mr Jole
[163] used to sing to the tune,[12] ‖ this Induced some to believe, tho' Mr Jole never showed it, or seemed to be vain of it, that he had a poetical Genius, and had added several verses to that ancient Song with his own accurate

10. Full name of Paracelsus (1493–1541), a famous Swiss physician, alchemist, and astrologer. The quotation about him—the source of which is uncertain—means "A stiff beard bears witness of virility." Not surprisingly, Jole is never depicted wearing a beard.

11. "Whilst I gaze on Chloe trembling" appears in Ramsay's *Tea-table Miscellany* (II, 5) in only 4 stanzas. That Jole, a man who has no passion for the ladies, would invent another 12 or 15 stanzas about the raging passion of a frustrated lover is humorous indeed. This song also appears in *Calliope, or English Harmony*, in Charles Coffey's ballad opera *The Devil to Pay* (1731), which was performed in Annapolis in 1752, and as "The Lukewarm Lover" in John Watts's *The Musical Miscellany*, 6 vols. (London, 1729–1731), II, 76.

12. Hamilton's sentence breaks off here without telling us what Mr. Jole was singing to the tune of (although it hardly matters, since Jole was probably warbling off-key anyhow). *To the tune* perhaps simply means "accordingly" or "appropriately."

hand, Some of these verses are in themselves very Sublime and poetical, one of which, for its beauty and Singularity, I cannot ommit here quoting.

Here there lies Interr'd a Squire
Underneath this marble Stone,
Who for Loving did expire,
And he never Lov'd but one.

This verse in particular Mr Jole would sing with so lamentable a voice, as to draw tears from the eyes of the most flinty hearted, tho many affirmed that these tears flowed not from Commiseration, but from a certain gelastic conquassation.[13]

This Illustrious gentleman has a very pritty taste for antiquities, of which he keeps a curious collection by him, now to show, to all Con- noiseurs who are desirous of seeing them, these are petticoats, Scarfs and Caps that belonged to his grandmother, hats, nightcaps and ruffs of his great grandfather, the little Spoon, with which his grandfather was fed when a child, his own baby Cloths, in which his mother dressed him, with the Stains of the Slabber carefully preserved on the bibs to this very day, and several other Curiosities and Nicknacks, on which the old Gentleman can exhibit a whole afternoon's lecture, in a very pleasant and Delectable manner, and elegantly expatiate upon the Superexcellency of all ancient things, and how vastly they exceed every thing of a moderen date, for, he is an enthusiastic admirer of antiquity, posi- ‖ tively asserting that all old [164] things are best, tho' it is doubted whether he will have the assent of the fair sex, for the truth of this general proposition, however, Mr Jole's taste in this is not Singular, for we find several Learned universities, fond of keeping antique remains in their musæums, such as, the pen of Duns Scotus, with which he wrote his Subtile Philosophy, the bonnet or cap of Aristotle, the Inkhorn and Candlestick of John Knox, the Skull of Buchanan &ct:[14] which shews that there is a real value in these ancient reliques.

As I talked but Just now of the fair Sex, it will be proper here to enquire, how far Mr Jole was ever engaged with them, he has lived always

13. Severe shaking caused by laughter.
14. John Duns Scotus (1265?–1308?), known as Doctor Subtilis, was one of the great medi- eval Scholastic theologians. Knox (1505–1572), generally considered the leader of the Protestant Reformation in Scotland, was the author of the *Treatise on Predestination* (1560) and the *History of the Reformation of Religion within the Realme of Scotland* (1587). George Buchanan (1506–1582), a Scottish historian, scholar, and poet, published *Detectio Mariae Reginae* (1571), a violent attack on Mary, Queen of Scots, *Rerum scoticarum historia* (1582), long regarded as a standard source of Scottish history, the tragedies *Baptistes, Medea, Jephthes,* and *Alcestis,* and some good elegiac and occasional poetry.

Single, having been, as it is thought, ever averse to the Clog of a wife, and a man of too much prudence and Solidity ever to keep a concubine, for this reason the world is not likely to be much entertained with his amours, and the transactions of his life would therefore afford very unfit materials for a novel; It being a question whether he ever permitted a woman to come nigher to him than arms Length, or a modest and decent distance, so as to hold Indifferent discourse, for, tho' he never showed any affection to the Sex, yet, he would deign to converse with them as rational Creatures, which showed, that he was too much of a christian to believe with some Philosophers, that women had no Souls,[15] but then he would behave himself with the same Indifferent coldness, as one man does to another, or as one maid would accost another.

Yet, as man is a Sociable animal, and the most Savage and retired have at times their Darling companions, so, this celebrated Gentleman, Judging his own Species, unworthy to make constant companions and Intimates of, chose a Society of Cats for his friends, fellows and playmates, both at bed [165] and board, and so far did his extra- ‖ ordinary charity and benevolence extend to those Cats, that he would deign to converse with them in the most familiar manner, giving some of them a christian like education, for he had some that he taught to sit erect, and clap their fore feet or paws together in a praying or begging like posture, he would stroke down their soft Skins, apply their mouths to his, give the females, Silk and velvet beds, in which to lie in, or deposit their kittins, and when, for fear of their multiplying too much, he would order some kittens to be drowned or buried alive, he was so tender hearted, that he would not see the execution, but shut himself up, and grieve for some time, as a tender mother does for her babes; nay, it is said, that he once buried a favorite Cat, with great form and ceremony, like a christian, he gave her a band box for a Coffin, and had an epitaph wrote upon her tombstone, it would delight your eyes to see the great benevolence of this good Gentleman to these domestic brutes, for you could never step into the house, but you would find all these his favorites great and little, about their kind benefactor, some upon his Shoulders, others on his head and neck, some on his knees and others crawling up

15. Hamilton is alluding to the traditional Turkish belief that had become commonplace in 18th-century England. In the famous opening lines of his *Epistle to a Lady*, for example, Pope writes: "Nothing so true as what you once let fall, / 'Most Women have no Characters at all'" (*The Twickenham Edition of the Poems of Alexander Pope*, vol. III, pt. ii, ed. F. W. Bateson [London, 1951]); see also Samuel Butler's "Women": "The Soules of women are so small / That Some believe th' have none at all" (*Satires and Miscellaneous Poetry and Prose*, ed. René Lamar [Cambridge, 1928], 220).

upon his back and belly, while he stroked one, patted another, tickled a third, and tossed another gently away from him, tho' they, like Saucy favorites, would sometimes make too familiar with their patron and protector, and oblige him at times to use a small Switch, with which hed gently scourge them out of the room, in fine the Great Nasifer, in the midst of his cats, looked like the Grand Signior in the midst of his Seraglio, and by means of his good discipline and advice, they were all so modest and well bred that when he entertained Company of the human Species, not one of those brutes would dare so much ‖ as to appear, or even to peep, but all   [166] retired to their proper Chambers, and appartments allotted for them.

Some may think it very Strange, that Mr Jole, a Gentleman born and bred in a christian land, should pay so much deference and respect, to these brute creatures, Indeed, had he been a Turk, they'll say, whose religion enjoins a respect to dogs and cats, and such like brute animals, and whose enthusiasm prompts them to build hospitals for them: had he professed himself a Pythagorean philosopher, or an Indian Santon, who believe that the Souls of their grandfathers are lodged in these brutes, and transmigrate from Animal to Animal: had he been an ancient Ægyptian, who made divinities of these creatures and paid them divine honors: In fine, had he been a persian Dervis, who understood thorro-ly the Language of brutes, there might be some plausible reason for his amusing himself in this manner; but as he is an old Englishman, and a protestant, and Christian of the Church of England, as by Law established, there is no other way they'll say, for accounting for this odd humor, but by ascribing it to mere whim and fancy, but, granting it was no other but this last, have we not the example of many ancient great worthies, who were delighted with the same Sort of amusements, does not Homer tell us, that Hector was very familiar with and held several Grave Conversations and conferences with his horses; are we not told that Toby had a dog that followed him when he went forth, does not Spartian Inform us that Adrian the Emperor, was so Enamoured with dogs and horses, that he bestowed Sumptuous monuments and tombs on them, and buried them decently ‖ in graves;¹⁶ dont we find that Caligula   [167] had such an opinion of his horse's abilities, that he created him Consul of Rome, and dressed him in purple like a wise Senator, Lampridius affirms, that the Emperor Severus kept tame Pheasants, ducks, partridges, peacocks,

16. Hector exhorts his horses in the *Iliad*, bk. 8, 224–239. Tobias's dog is noted above (see p. 20n). Aelius Spartianus (fl. 3d century A.D.) was one of the principal authors of the *Historia Augusta* (for the story of the Roman emperor Hadrian's affection for his dogs and horses, see *The Lives of the Later Caesars* [London, 1967], 80).

and about twenty thousand ring doves and pigeons in cages, Alexander Severus was often pleased to play with whelps and young pigs, The famous Montaigne, speaks feelingly of his favorite puss,[17] and, the great Ladies in the great Turks Seraglio, at this very day, keep a great many cats, to pass away the time, not to mention our best and politest Ladies of quality in England, who converse much with monkies, Lapdogs, parrots and Squirrells, where then is the Great wounder, that our Clubical heroe should keep about him some 40 or 50 Cats, for his amusement and recreation.

Carlo Nasifer Jole, tho' he had no great communication with mankind, was thought to be a friend to human nature and a well wisher to Society, for, he always expressed a great aversion and hatred to thieves, rogues and villains, in such a manner, that, whenever he heard of any wretches accused of theft, robbery or murder, he was for tucking them up, without the ceremony of a trial, Some Indeed said, that this proceeded from a rigid temper and cruel disposition, and therefore pronounced him a Mysanthrope, but I must beg leave to be of a contrary opinion.

In fine, Mr Jole was of a very Suspicious temper, cared not to trust any body, and was exceeding fond of power and authority, of which we shall see many Instances, in the Sequel of this History.

[168]   Having said thus much of our heroe, in order to prepare our readers, for encountering him in his Clubical Character, thro' the following history, I now proceed to the thread of my narration.

After the admission of the abovenamed Gentlemen, into this ancient and honorable Club, it was agreed at Sederunt 8th

Law IX. That members shall be admitted for the future, by way of balloting, as also the passing or making of any new rule or Law.

At Sederunt 9th July the 9th 1745, Dumpling Gundiguts Esqr, being Steward, 26 ballots, marked N & Y. were produced in Club, by Mr Secretary Motely, according to the Law for that Intent, made and provided, and at Sederunt 11th (the 10th I purposely omitt here) July 23, Nasifer Jole Esqr, being Steward, the following law passed.

---

17. Aelius Lampridius (fl. early 4th century A.D.) was a Roman historian and one of the collaborators in the *Historia Augusta* (Aelius Spartianus, however, wrote the chapter on the Roman emperor Severus [A.D. 145/146–211], which does not mention his affection for birds, nor do any of the other allusions to Severus in the *Historia*. Severus Alexander (A.D. 208/209–235) was adopted by Heliogabalus and made emperor at age 13 when the latter was murdered. Montaigne writes particularly of his fondness for animals in the two essays "Of Cruelty" and the "Apology for Raimond Sebond." Hamilton is probably referring to a passage in "Of Cruelty," where Montaigne remarks: "When I play with my cat, who knows but that she regards me more as a play thing than I do her? (We amuse each other with our respective monkey-tricks; if I have my moments for beginning and refusing, so she has hers)" (*The Essays of Montaigne*, trans. E. J. Trechmann [New York, 1946], 444).

Law X. That the book of Rules belonging to the Society, and likewise the Ballot boxes, be Lodged with the Steward, and by him be delivered to his Successor in that office.

At the same Sederunt, Doctor Polyhistor, was made an honorary member, and the *Great bell of Lincoln* was sung for the first time by Nasifer Jole Esqr, a large bowl of Rack punch, being carried in procession Round the great table, typically representing the great bell, while the members followed it in Regular order, shouldering tobacco pipes, this was the first appearance of pomp and pegeantry, in this ancient and honorable Club. The Catch called the *Great Bell,* as it is often mentioned in this history, I shall give a Copy of as follows.

The Great Bell of Lincoln, sung by Nasifer Jole Esqr   [169]

The great Bell of Lincoln
It rings once a year,
But we're not for Lincoln
While this Bell rings here. (a)

Chorus There are five men to raise her (b)
And at whitsontide rings,
Then turn the bell over
And see how she rings. (c)

Now the bell is turnd over
And has lost her old Strings,
And she must be mended
Before she will ring.

New frame, new wheel,
New Clapper, new Strings,
Then turn the bell over
And see how she rings.

Chorus Drink right, or else your wrong,
Poor Tom is dead and gone.
To—m, To—m

At this Sederunt there passed abundance of Learned discourse, between Capt: Seemly Spruce, and Mr Joggle hasty, two long Standing members,

(a) Here they sound upon the bowl with a tobacco pipe.
(b) Here 5 take hold of the bowl, and raise it up high in the air.
(c) Here they drink.

The Tobacco-pipe procession.

which arose upon this || Question, vizt: whether or not a man, born and   [170]
bred a taylor and understanding no other craft, either of head or hand,
might be qualified to take holy orders, and become a parson of a parish?
The first asserted that the transition was natural, for, as his first employ was
to make up breeches, to cover his customer's bums, so his second occupation, would be to make up breaches among his flock; but the other took
this In Snuff, and would not assent to the argument, so this great point of
the breeches and breaches, still remains undetermined, this was the first
time that punning took place in this ancient and honorable Club, which
Ingenious art, received great Improvements afterwards, from the facetious
Jonathan Grog Esqr, poet Laureat of the Club.

Chapter V

*The expulsion of the Batchellor's Cheese, and the Signal Loyalty of the
Longstanding members, with an Instance of their amorous disposition.*

We have now discussed the primitive, Simple times of this ancient and
honorable Club, and must bid farewell in a little Space, to that virtuous
and heroic frugality, which prevailed in it at it's first Institution, for now
Luxury[a] began to peep from behind the Scene, and prepare for her pompous entry upon this Clubical Stage, and, Indeed, to carry on our metaphor,
this bold actress took one great Stride at her first advance, and proceeded
afterwards, with a *grand pas,* to expell Simplicity and plainness from the
Club, and to Introduce, pomp show and || extravagance, her constant pages   [171]
and attendants, while another, her companion and coactor, with the like
buskined pride, plaid the part of a momus or mimic, this was no less a
person than Ceremony, as much a beau, as the other is a belle, whom we
shall soon see also, showing his pragmatical front, upon the most conspicuous part of the Scene, and Introducing certain fantastical punctillios, forms
and modes, by which he so disguised and poisoned the manners and behavior of the longstanding members, of this here ancient and honorable Club
(as indeed he does those of all mankind, especially such as are in higher life,
for he is never seen among beggars & Clowns,) that they did in no manner
seem to be the same persons they were at their first Institution.

It was at Sederunt 10th July 18, Drawlum Quaint Esqr, being Steward,

(a) Vide 9th anniversary Speech, almost verbatim the same wt the following.

that the batchellor's Cheese was Expelled the Club, by an express Law, in which it was declared

Law XI. That Cheese shall no more be deemed a dish of vittles, and therefore the use of it as such in the Club is forbid.

The Chief moover for this Law, was Nasifer Jole Esqr, whom we shall find afterwards by gradual Steps Introducing high relished dishes and dainties into the Club, he began first with rack punch, here madam Luxury first pop'd her head from behind the curtain, with her far fetched commodities, presently after this, come the bowl and tobacco pipe procession, then her adjutant Ceremony followed her beck; then an Iced cake makes it's appearance, as we shall relate in its place, and thence Mr Jole proceeded gradually in his Schemes, and slap dash, there followed a whole troop of frecassees, ||

[172] ragous, hashes, soups, pasties, pies, puddings, dumplings, tarts, Gellies and Syllabubs, and it is thought, that it was by these artful Steps, that this politic gentleman raised himself to the presidential Chair, and advanced one Step, or Six inches above the other Longstanding members.

The Chief argument that was brought against the Cheese Law, was, the absurdity of it, when compared with a preceeding law, which allows a gammon of bacon, or any other one Dish of Dressd Vittles, now this law of the Cheese said they annulls of course the law of the Gammon, or dressed Vittles, for, it never once was Imagined, by any man in his right Senses, that cheese is a dish of dress'd vittles, but rather a relisher or desert, therefore they asserted *a priori,* that this law of the Cheese was in itself void, as being absurd and nonsensical, and also directly repugnant to Clubical liberty, for which reason the Cheese was expelled as a nauseous, Stinking and Clownish mess, but it is not the first time, that good Laws, ordained for the establishment of frugality and temperance, have been annulled upon the like Specious pretences, and Luxury and Epicurism, have met with Strenuous advocats to support their Cause, and vindicate the practice of these effeminate Vices, whoever doubts of this, needs only read, the Learned and Ingenious Doctor Mandeville, his *Fable of the bees,* where I think, it is seemingly made out, beyond all question, if you will take the Doctor's own word for it, that private vice is public emolument.[1]

On the same Sederunt, the Club having news of the taking of Cape Breton, from the french, by the Sea and land forces under Warren and

---

1. Bernard Mandeville's (1670–1733) *The Fable of the Bees* (London, 1714), designed to illustrate the essential vileness of human nature, was at the heart of the controversy over luxury that Hamilton satirizes in the *History.* Mandeville argued that the taste for luxury in a populace stimulates the economy in general, providing benefits to all; virtuous frugality, on the other hand, is the ruin of active commerce.

Pepperell,[2] || drank several loyal toasts, such as Success to his majestie's arms [173]
by sea and land. Generall Pepperel. Commodore Warren. The several Land
and Sea officers. The brave Soldiers and Sailors. the perpetual possession of
cape Breton to the English. Prosperity to all his Majesties Plantations.
Governor Shirly.[3] The Colony of new England, and the like. By these loyal
and well affected toasts, this ancient and honorable Club, showed their firm
and Steady attachment, to the present happy Establishment, and, there
being no opposition in Club, to any of these toasts, we may pritty surely
conclude from thence, that all the Longstanding members were Stanch
whigs, and averse to all Jacobitish principles and maxims, a happy Circumstance, and what has contributed much, among other Concurring causes, to
the prosperity and Stability of this ancient and honorable Club, we have all
of us reason to pray, that this noble Spirit of Liberty, may grow and Continue among us, and, that no bribery, corruption and Luxury, may gain
footing so far, as to extinguish so noble, heroic and generous a disposition.

While these matters were transacting in Club, the members had a visit
from the Hon: Coll: Courtly Phraze, who made his appearance so suddenly, that none present could certainly tell, in what manner he came into
the Room, tho' many affirmed, that he seemed to them to enter back
foremost; and turning his face to the Company, made a most profound
bow, passed some polite compliments, and sitting down gravely, told the
members that he had Just now left the Company of the Ladies, those dear
angelical creatures! for the Colonell, was always a person || noted for his [174]
courtly polite behaviour and address to the fair Sex, the Collonels discourse
concerning the Ladies, put the members of the Club into an amorous vein,
and there was not one there excepting Mr Jole, but resolved to have his Girl
that very night; Drawlum Quaint Esqr, the Steward seemed to be more
agitated by this amorous enthusiasm, than any of the other members, for,
he went out of Club, attended by Loquacious Scribble M:D: and was

2. Sir Peter Warren (1703–1752), a British naval officer, helped capture the French fortress of
Louisburg on Cape Breton Island (1745) and helped defeat the French off Cape Finisterre
(1747). Sir William Pepperell (1696–1759), an American general, assisted the British in capturing Louisburg, was created baronet (the first American so honored, 1746), served in the
French and Indian War, and was promoted to lieutenant general in 1759.

3. William Shirley (1694–1771), colonial governor of Massachusetts (1741–1749, 1753–1756),
planned the expedition against the French at Louisburg, served on a commission in Paris to
determine the boundary between New England and French North America (while visiting
England, 1749–1753), and was appointed major general (1755) at the outbreak of the French and
Indian War. On the great joy and sense of achievement with which the conquest of Louisburg
was received in the American colonies, see Nathan O. Hatch, "The Origins of Civil Millennial-
ism in America: New England Clergymen, War with France, and the Revolution," *William and
Mary Quarterly,* 3d Ser., XXXI (1974), especially 417–422.

resolved not to return, till he had blunted the edge of his desires, with some Gentle and kind Nymph, but, his resolution did not carry him thro' thick and thin, for, he was so terrified, at the Sight of a Superannuated female, who, upon his knocking opened her door to him, that all his tender Ideas vanished like Smoke, and taking to his heels, as if the Devil had been after him, he run faster back than he went forth, and took his Seat again in Club, quite out of breath.

It was not so with Laconic Comas Esqr, and Mr Secretary Motely, two Stanch Longstanding members, the first a widower, the other a batchellor, who, after the dismissing of the Club, went in pursuit of some fair Nymphs, who that night were assembled at a dance, and carried the Steward with them, but what their adventures and exploits were, we shall not relate here, as having nothing to do with the History of the Club, which is of too grave and Solid a nature, to admit of the detail and relation of amours, these triffles, properly belonging to Romances and Novels, and therefore cannot be any credit to True histories such as this.

At this Sederunt, the Hon: Col: Courtly Phraze was admitted an honorary member of the Club.

[175]   Chapter VI

Some of the Members seized with a furor poeticus, and some account of the Baltimore Bards.

Much about this time, appeared an epidemical distemper in the Club, which broke out, no body can tell how, it was what Physicians might properly call a κακο-ηθεια or μανιας ποιητικης,[1] *malignitas poetica*, or *Furor poeticus*, several of the members having been taken in an unaccountable manner, with fits of Rhiming, and writing of Rhimes, those that seemed to be most affected with it were Messiurs Sly, Motely, Blunt, Quaint and Scribble, tho' none were writers but the two last, however, the whole Club was in some measure touched with this malignity, so that they could scarce speak to one another, but in Rhime and Jingle, and even Mr Solo Neverout, sometime after, admitted a Member of the Club, who had never before shown the least genius or turn to Rhiming or versification, nay even made a Jest of it in his laughing way, and ridiculed all poets and poetasters,

1. "Poetical wickedness or madness."

was so Infected as to break all at once into blank verse, and with great violence and vociferation, exclaimed to the Surprize of all present,

With dowble Lustre, Beckie's beauties shine.

And when he was desired to proceed farther, and make a Couplet of it, he bawld out in a furious manner,

Rise Jupiter, and snuff the moon!—

Upon which the company thinking he was crazed left him ‖ to himself, and   [176] urged no more questions, since which his muse has been altogether silent, having overshot herself at her first setting out, except one faint Essay in Rhime which she made, but we shall relate that in its proper place.

We have reason to believe, that this poetical Contagion took its rise first in the north, and therefore was of the frigid Sort, for, in the county of Baltimore, there appeared two Celebrated Bards, vizt: Bard Bavius, and Bard Mevius,[2] who, having broke out into most violent fits of Rhiming and versifying, Infected many people around them with the same distemper, the first essay, which the conjoint Muses of these two Northeren Bards pro-duced, was an original piece called the *Baltimore Belles,* of which perfor-mance we shall say something in its proper place, intending first, to discuss other matters, in which these bards were concerned, more particularly relat-ing to the Club.

The first bold Stroke that appeared of this kind was from the cele-brated Bard Mevius, who, one day being In church, hearing the Reverend and pious Mr George Whitefield hold forth, was diverted in his attention to the Sweet words of that Inspired Saint, by some Ladies, who sat in a pew Just before him, with the whiteness and beautiful Length of whose Necks, or perhaps both, he was so miraculously Charmed, that, Intirely forgetting where he was, he fell directly to Composing of verses on this delightful Subject, and hammered out a very pritty epigram of eight lines, the Stile and turn of which was so peculiar, that it is yet unequalled by any bard that has since appeared, and is really an original, ‖ having never been paralelled   [177] in former ages, by any of the Bards of Antiquity.

Immediatly, upon the appearance of this amorous epigram, which was Industriously handed about in manuscript both by the friends and foes of the Bard, the first to praise and extoll his lofty genius, the latter to ridicule his pertness and vanity, each acting according to the opinion they had

2. On Bavius, see p. 153n. Mevius was another poetaster who incurred Horace's and Vergil's wrath. Here, the names synonymous with bad poetry are pseudonyms for Thomas Chase and Thomas Cradock (see biographical sketches).

preconceived of our Bard; the critics were in an uproar against it, they took this poor Bards performance all to pieces, as is the custom with Critics in these our degenerate days, and discried more blunders and Inaccuracies in it than there were words, Some of the Longstanding members of the Ancient and honorable Tuesday Club were among these Critics, particularly Messieurs Blunt, Sly, Quaint and Scribble, who exercised the acuteness of wit and Genius pritty Smartly upon this unfortunate Bard, and were Joined by others, both bards and Critics in Baltimore and Elsewhere, from Criticising in prose, they went to Satyrizing and Lampooning in Rhime, So the Baltimore Bards & the Critics of the Tuesday Club strenuously contended who should outrhime, and who should outcriticise each other, there was nothing but paquets, papers and Scrowls handed about, stuffed with abundance of repartee and railery, as is usual in these cases, and some who thought them wiser than themselves admired much their wit, while others who had no opinion of their wisdom laughed at their folly and assurance, and condemned them much, as Idle and mischievous, in trowbling people that thought no harm with such poetical Jargon, which set many tongues a [178] wagging in a Scandalous manner, and prompted many peaceable ‖ christians to quarrel and fall out one with another who before lived in perfect amity, not to mention the Idle habit some contracted by it, in squandering their time in Composing of Silly rhimes, vainly Imagining that they had a poetical turn, tho they found themselves at last miserably mistaken, and were obliged to bear the Laugh of the public with patience, seeing they had drawn it upon themselves, by their own folly and vanity.

It came at last to that pitch, that even the weekly Journal of Mr Jonathan Grog, entituled the *Maryland Gazette,* was stuffed with comments, Reflections and Satyrs on this unfortunate Bard and his performances,[3] so, that it is thought he must Infallibly have sunk under the pressure, of this formidable hostile power of Critics, had not an Invulnerable Champion, stood up in his defence, vizt: the tremendous Bard Bavius, who was reckoned by many the compleatest bard of the two, and Indeed, the most extraordinary bard, that was to be found, far or near, and not to be daunted, or put out of countenance, by the conjoint forces of all the Critics put together.

This Illustrious Bard, was of a stern, Severe countenance, whose Severity and Sterness, was of great use to the other, naturally mild, modest

---

3. Although Hamilton says the *Maryland Gazette* was "stuffed" with remarks concerning this battle between the Baltimore Bards and the members of the Tuesday Club, I have not located any comments other than those he specifically mentions later in this chapter.

and timorous, since he was much asisted thereby, in bearing the violence
and fury of the Attacks made upon him, by his professd foes, the Critics and
Bards of the Tuesday Club.

This Gygantic auxiliary Bard, mustering up all his force and straining
the Sublime of his genius to the utmost, advised the other, to show the
dignity of his muse, by outsoaring all those pitiful bards and Critics, that set
up against him, and, that he should have his asistance, in whatever Subject
he undertook, it was then resolved, by these two eminent Baltimore Bards,
over a bowl of punch and a pipe of tobacco, to pen a Sublime panegyric on
|| the celebrated toasts and beauties of their county, under the title of *The*   [179]
Baltimore Belles. This piece was then Immediatly set about, and the Muses
Invoked, and being finished by these rapid Geniuses in a few hours, was
carefully revised, corrected, and wrote out fair, It was read by Bard Bavius,
in a Sonorous and theatrical tone of voice, much approved of by both
bards, and after a Second third and fourth reading, was left lying on the
table for further perusal and consideration, or, rather to be exposed to the
ey, of the public, that it might meet with the applause it so Justly deserved;
being such a specimen of the Sublime, as exceeded the execution of all
Bards whatsoever, either ancient or moderen, since the days of Pindar.

This piece then, Lieing on the table in a taveren, soon had readers
enough of all capacities, from the Scholar to the dunce, from the Gentleman to the Clown, and various were the opinions that were given of it,
Some shook their heads at it and pronounced it to be damn'd Stuff, others
attempted to read it, but stammered and blundered so, that they threw it
down with seeming Indignation and disdain, before they had mumbled out
three lines, some said that the Rhime was Good, and the verse smooth
enough, but the Sense past their Comprehension, these were the Sentiments of the Baltimore Connoiseurs concerning it, and the bards all this
time Lay perdue, expecting to have their opinion asked thereupon, which
hapened to their wish, and accordingly, they pronounced it an excellent
piece, and declared, that if Pope had been alive and In America, they should
have Judged it to be of his composition, a remarkable Instance this, of the
fondness and tender Indulgence of Bards towards their own performances,
who, like fond parents, always Imagine, that their own brats, are the hand-
somest, best, Sweetest, comliest of any in the world, but, their soun- || ding   [180]
the praises of this composition so extravagantly, soon made the Critics smell
a rat; for, they being a sagacious discerning Sort of people, Immediatly
took the Scent, and discovered the piece to be a production of these very
bards who extolld it so much, & they clenched the discovery in this cunning
manner, they heartily Joined with them in praising the piece, and, by this

decoy, Bard Mevius, was prevailed upon to own that he had a great hand in it, but nevertheless he confessed, he was much obliged to his friend Bard Bavius, who shared the most considerable part of it, for the whole Excellent plan, Invention and Machinery was his; and as for his own part, he had only asisted in some degree in the versification and Rhime, so soon as the critics were Informed of this, they set up a furious cry against these Illustrious Bards, and, like a pack of blood hounds, hunted them in such a manner, as to allow them no Sort of repose or rest. Bard Bavius stood out, with great Intrepidity against them, bawling, railing, scolding, reviling and cursing in as loud a key as they, but Bard Mevius, was obliged, from his natural Timidity, to look out for lurking holes, and skulk from the violence and rage of these furious critics.

The news of this soon reached the Clubical Bards and Critics at Annapolis, together with a copy of the composition it Self, who set about it, tooth and nail, and gave it no quarter. One, under the name of Doctor Philalethes, published in the *Gazette* No 34 an Infallible receipt to cure the Epidemical and afflicting distempers of Love and the poetical Itch.[4] Soon after, another Learned Physician, who stiles himself Doctor Polypharma- ||

[181] cus, in *Gazette* No 41 publishes another recipe,[5] and seems to be diffident of the efficacy of the former, according to the humor of great Physicians, who commonly prefer their own Nostrums, to those of all the faculty besides, this Learned Gentleman, describes Bard Bavius, under a violent delirium or *furor poeticus,* excited by a *febris Amatoria,*[6] which he cautions us not to mistake for the Chlorosis or green Sickness, in his fits of raving he repeats severall passages of the celebrated piece of the *Baltimore Belles,* on the Doctor's first feeling his pulse, he exclaims thus.

> A well turn'd praise requires the nicest Skill,
> And he who writes ill natur'd must write ill.

And again, upon being asked how he did, he bawls out

> Then let the Muse her tuneful numbers raise
> And praise the beauties for the Sake of praise.

Soon after he accosts the Doctor thus.

> In every charm, some glorious goddess place,
> And let the Charm the glorious Goddess grace,

---

4. Hamilton is referring to a notice that appeared in the *Md. Gaz.,* no. 34 (Dec. 17, 1745), 3–4 (see Appendix 1).
5. This notice appeared in the *Md. Gaz.,* no. 41 (Feb. 4, 1746), 4 (see Appendix 2).
6. "Amorous fever."

> Let Venus hail her for the wife of Jove,
> And Juno take her for the queen of Love,
> Let Pallas frowning &ct:

Upon this the Doctor applies cupping Glasses, as he says, to his head, and gives him a large dose of hellebore, which procures a copious and fætid Stool, after which the Bard exclaims

> Maria sings, now bid the Muses hear
> Or Call Apollo from the Crystal Sphere.

Polypharmacus on this, suspects a calenture, plies him with cooling Glysters [182] to Relieve the encephalon, and Claps Sinapisms to his feet, and soon after, he breaks out thus.

> See, Lovely Risteau![7] happy, hapless Maid!—
> Happy the man whom this fair Maiden loves,
> O happiest he, whom this fair maid approves,
> Great is her worth, yet useless and unknown,
> Or useful to her charming Self alone.

This last, the Physician observes, is a most remarkable Instance of the Bathos, and by this, he percieved that the Violence of the Distemper abated, and gives him his famous remedy, which he calls his *Neutrum quid,*[8] the Composition of which may be seen in the said *Gazette* No 41, if now to be found.

Soon after this Bard Bavius wrote his celebrated Letter to the City of Annapolis, which he Intends as a kind of prose Dunciad, Introducing all his critics and opponent Bards in some Ridiculous Character or other, here he learnedly criticises on the term *Neutrum Quid,* and, assuming the Character of a Physician himself, he proposes a Remedy, or *Methodus Medendi,*[9] so very much out of the common road, that never any thing like it was seen either before or since, nor, I believe, ever will be, in this transient world, the piece it self being Inimitable, and extraneously extravagant, in short, to cure those frantic poets, as he calls them, Mr Jonathan Grog, (to whose name we shall have occasion soon, to clap with propriety the title of *'Squire*) was to put them into his press or typographical machine, and, an operator with a Spatula || was to extract excrementitious matter from their fundament, [183] while Parson Sly was to sing a Psalm, to Comfort them under the operation; in this prophylactic dissertation our Bard displays his profound skill

7. Catherine Risteau was the wife of Thomas Cradock (see biographical sketch for Cradock).
8. "Something that is neither of the two."
9. "Method of healing."

The Phrensy of a Ballimore Bard

and knowledge in Chemistry, by absolutely pronouncing Doctor Polypharmacus a dunce, for using the term *Neutrum quid*, which he says is in it Self
Stark nonsense, as Intending something that is only chip in porridge, or
neither Chalk nor Cheese, then he slides into a Learned Enquiry into the
nature of Ordure and excrement, to which he elegantly compars the works
and compositions of his Antagonist Bards.

This Learned Epistle made some noise for a time among the wits and
critics, particularly of Annapolis, and produced several learned criticisms,
dissertations and essays; and certain critical and Explanatory Notes were
wrote upon it in the names of Martinus Scriblerus & Hurlothrumbo,[10] the
first in a grave, the other in a Burlesque Stile, all which learned papers,
paraphrazes and Commentaries, are they not to be seen laid up in the
Musæum, of the Curious and Ingenious Mr Jonathan Grog, even at this
Day.

Bard Bavius, the only person now aimed at (since his associate Mevius,
had altogether retired and absconded,) was also attacked by another wit,
who appeared in the *Maryland Gazette* No 47, under the Character of an
advertiser;[11] This wit assumes to himself, the name of Jehoiakim Jerkum,
and is thought to have been personated, by one or more of the Longstanding members, of the ancient and honorable Tuesday Club, takeing upon
them the Character of a Master advertising his run away Servant; Bard
Bavius is mentioned ‖ in this advertisement, under the names of Bard & [184]
Bavius, he is described as a fellow disordered in his Senses, wearing a String
of Bells about his neck, carrying with him several Stollen materials from the
works of Pope & Prior, together with abundance of Trash of his own. A
nasty Fellow, whose discourse turns chiefly on excrementitious Subjects, of
uncertain parentage, and therefore, in himself an original, praising for the
Sake of praise, and Censuring for the Sake of censure, apt to bewray himself
in company, thro' a relaxation of the *Sphincter ani*, and then lay the blame
on others, an Enimy to the Presbyterians, tho' himself a Muggletonian, the
profit of his poems for one hundred years to come, is offered to those who
go on the *Chace* after him, and apprehend him, as it appears to be a difficult
thing so to do, besides what the Law allows in such cases.

This Burlesque advertisement, utterly silenced Bard Bavius, and consequently, the other Baltimore Bard, whose Champion he was, and effectually

10. Martinus Scriblerus was a pseudonym sometimes used by Pope (the *Memoirs of Martinus
Scriblerus*, a prose satire against false learning, was published in the second edition of Pope's
works [1741]). *Hurlothrumbo* was the title of a popular burlesque (1729) by Samuel Johnson, a
Manchester dancing master.
11. Hamilton is referring to a notice in the *Md. Gaz.*, no. 47 (Mar. 18, 1746), 4 (see Appendix
3).

cured that pestiferous *furor poeticus,* which had for some time raged in Baltimore, and set many people a quarrelling, and as many a Laughing, and, the members of the ancient and honorable Tuesday Club, that were concerned in this conflict and victory, valued themselves much upon it, as having largely Contributed to the peace and quiet of the public, nothing being more destructive to the good order of Society and private families, than the Scribble of the *Poetæ Minorum Gentium,*[12] whether Panegyrical or Satyrical, handed about either in Manuscript, or from the press.

---

[185]   ## Chapter VII

The drinking of Lamb's wool at Batchellor's hall, and the Danger of the Clubs being converted into a State Club.

Those who have read the beginning of the preceeding Chapter of this history, will remember, that it was there said, that Bard Mevius Composed an elegant epigram upon some Ladies in Church, while the Reverend Mr Whitefield was holding forth from the pulpit, a true Copy of that masterly piece here follows.

> *On The two Miss ******'* as they sat before me,*
> *hearing of Mr Whitefield—An Extempore Epigram.*
>
> Plac'd as I was, such charms within my view,
> Say, Whitefield, what could all thy Rhet'ric do?
> In vain the nonsense trickl'd from thy tongue,
> In vain with canting harmony you sung;
> Their blooming beauties more perswasive prov'd,
> My heart with greater energy they mov'd,
> Their Swan-like necks my ravish'd eyes did bliss,
> Courted the touch, and tempted me to kiss.
>
> *Mevius*

This epigram was first handed about, in the Author's own hand writing, without any Annotations critical or explanatory, but it was not long before a certain Critic, thought to be a member of the Ancient and honorable Tuesday Club, and afterwards Secretary and orator to the said Club,

---

12. "Lower-class poets."

annexed to it some Critical remarks, annotations and Queries, to the following purpose.

Quere. Where were the Author, the Ladies, and Mr Whitefield at the [186]
time of composing these verses? probably in Church.

Quere. Whether nonsense be any part of Rhetoric?

Quere. Whether Canting harmony be a proper term in music? unless
the author, or somebody else, bore a part of the Chorus or Song with Mr
Whitefield, harmony being a term only applicable to two or more voices or
Instruments, singing or playing in concert?

Quere. Whether the Ladie's necks resembled those of Swans by their
extraordinary Length, whiteness, or both?

Quere. Whether or not the bard kissed the Ladies, and if so, where?
Probably in church.

This Clubical Critic or observator, at the end of these queries takes
notice, that the author of this epigram is not to be forgiven for that
thought, tho altogether new, of placing the most powerful Charms of the
fair Sex behind, or *a posteriori*, by which great Injustice is done to their
Sunny eyes, ruby lips, rosy cheeks, Ivory forehead, and pearly teeth, as also
to their Snowy breasts and alabaster arms as our moderen bards stile them.

This notable Composition, with these annotations anexed, having
come into the hands of some of the members of the Ancient and honorable
Tuesday Club, vizt: Messrs Blunt, Sly, Motely and Scribble, they with some
others, had a Set meeting, at a place called Batchellor's hall, and having
called a few more bright geniuses to their asistance, there took the matter
into their Serious consideration, over a large Tankard of Lamb's wool, a
reviving Liquor, the pierian Spring of the moderen muses, compounded of
white wine, Sugar and roasted apples, and, when the generous liquor had
furbished up their wit, they began to make learned observations on the
backward beauties of the fair Sex, which they committed to writing, and
among other productions || their conjoint muses hammered out the follow- [187]
ing piece.

Verses on the Baltimore Bard

A Parson in Church, with some Swan necks before him ⎫
To kiss and to touch, he hardly forbore'um,   ⎬
Being Check'd by the awe of the *Sanctum Sanctorum*,   ⎭
Had they and the poet been but in the Dark,
He'd have thrown off the parson, and put on the Spark,
And now, Mr Parson, If we may advise,
Pray pick up your swans under other disguise,

The drinking of Lambs wool at Batchellors Hall

[facing page 188]

For if thus with your verses you play fast and loose,
Instead of a Swan, we shall think you a goose,
And thus, you at last will be left in the Lurch
And bring a disgrace on the Cloth & the Church.

After these Clubical poets had thus Indulged and let loose their genius, against this devoted Baltimore Bard, they Commissioned one of their number, to Inclose the original Epigram with the Queries and annotations annexed, and the above answer to it, to Mr Roughby Ranter of Baltimore county, whom they pitched upon as their Mecenas, being a great encourager of such Sort of Gelastic, and Jocular Learning, the letter wrote to this Gentleman, was to the following purpose.

Sir,

One of your Baltimore Bards, (for we hear you have many) has pritty much diverted our Town Connoiseurs, by Comparing the necks of some of our Annapolitan Ladies to those of Swans, in an Epigram Composed by him in Church, ‖ seated behind those Ladies, to hear the as yet unheard of [188] doctrines of the famous Mr Whitefield, our Illustrious american apostle, an able Critic has subjoined his remarks, and one of our Bards (for with us also, the Spurious Sons of Apollo abound) has wrote a reply to it. You have the whole Inclosed, and we leave it to your Judgement to determin, whether the Streams of Helicon run purer in Baltimore than with us in Annapolis, we cannot at all forgive your bard for that thought, (tho altogether new) of seeing the most powerful Charms of the Ladies behind, and therefore, from this argument *a posteriori,* we Conclude, that, as the Gentleman has the honor to be of the Clergy, he ought to beware, how he broaches such novel Doctrines, Least thereby the Interest and power of the Clergy should be Impaired, which would necessarily be attended with some fatal Consequences to the Church. We are Sir,

To Mr Roughby ⎱   Your most obsequious Servants
Ranter, *These* ⎰   *Mevius Philo-Bavius*
                                      Martinus Scriblerus.

The Contents of this letter were exposed to the view of Bard Bavius, and maturely considered, and pondered by him, and, soon after, appeared, in the hands of many, a copy of finished and elegant verses, by him Composed, which were sent under Cover to a Gentleman of Rank and Eminence in the City of Annapolis,[1] they are as follows.

1. Probably Jonas Green, editor of the *Md. Gaz.,* who never published these verses.

[189]   *Verses to the Bard on the Ladies backward beauties*
          By a Baltimore Bard

          veniam petimus, dabimusque vicissem. Hor: de art: poet:[2]

          The lovely Sex, my friend, are charms all o'er,
          And strike behind as powerful as before.
          In H—n—s—n's Shape is seen as fine a grace,
          As that which shines in H—mm—nd's Smiling face,
          Bright as the Sun, they shine from every part,
          Charm every Eye, and ravish every heart,
          If thy cold heart no beauty can delight,
          Tis not for want of Charms, but want of Sight,
          Then friend be wise, your ill plac'd Jeers give oer,
          Who sees no Charms behind, sees none before.

Thus melodiously did Bard Bavius sing, nor did his melliflous muse desist, 'till the reiterated provocations of the Junto of Bards and Critics at
Batchellors hall, had put him into a violent rage, in the midst of which
Frenzy he wrote his dirty Epistle to the City of Annapolis, much about the
time that the Learned Doctor Polypharmacus had him in the powdering
tub, and there flagrantly acted, contrary to his own maxim, vizt: He that
writes Ill natur'd must write ill. At last Jehoiakim Jerkum silenced him for
ever—and thus the Baltimorian muses gave up the Ghost. But the Bards
and Critics of Annapolis did not here desist but Emploied their Genius in
Satyr. Mongst These Drawlum Quaint Esqr, a Longstanding member, and
afterwards Speaker of the ancient and honorable Tuesday Club, made a
most considerable figure, having Composed two Satyrs, one Entituled the
Reverend Scout, and another the *Spiritual Rake,* both now in the Custody of
the Revernd Mr Smoothum Sly, among these Satyrists appeared the Ingenious Capt: Giddy Thoughtless, who, one evening over a bowl of punch,
composed a Satyr on Bard Bavius, of which we have only a fragment left,
which we give here as a Specimen of what the rest must have been, and pity
it is that so excellent an original should be lost.

          *** me ***** Lord.
          ******* one single Turd
          **** for ***** flat
          ******** a nine taild cat.

          2. "We seek pardon, and give it in our turn" (paraphrased from Horace's *Ars poetica,* chap.
11).

A Ladie's neck no more is like a Swan,
Than you ye monster's like an apish man.

The above fragment was snatched out of the hands of an Ignorant Clown, [190]
who was Lighting his pipe with the only remaining copy of this excellent
piece, and the words wrote down, are what remained unburnt; I shall here
give one entire Song, of the Satyrical kind, wrote by the Junto upon these
bards, which has been accidentally preserved from the rage of time.

Song on the Baltimore Bards, by the Junto at Batchelor's hall

I
Ye Baltimore Bards, while your fame we reherse,
   The muses we cannot Invoke,
Since we ne'er should expect they would dictate our verse
   While singing so arrant a Joke.

2
This too would resemble some Clerks of our day,
   Who act as absurdly as think,
In the morning on Sundays they preach & they pray,
   In the evening they sing and they drink.

3
Say wonderful bards, how your muse is Inspird?
   By what magic power does she sing,
By the Demon of Moorfields,[3] or punch is she fir'd,
   For she drinks not the Helicon Spring.

4
Say, does she not soar to a wonderful height
   In Clubs of our Raking gallants,
When o'er punch and Tobacco on Sundays at night
   The Cuckold and Cuckoo she Chants.

5
To the Tune of the Cuckold, pray Chant it no more,
   For on this I will venture my oath,
Your Slut of a muse will turn out Common whore
   And shortly will Cuckold you both.

6
As Cuckolds are hooted and scoff'd in the Streets
   For their horns, so may you for your wit.

---

3. Bethlem Royal Hospital, popularly known as Bedlam, was at one time located in Moorfields, an outlying section of London.

Rank fools you appear by your billingsgate Sheets,
And your Poems, shall soon be b—s—t.

Soon after, the Junto of Bards and Critics at Batchellor's hall, having nothing left to exercise their wit upon, broke up, but yet the Spirit of poetry still
remained among the members of the ancient and honorable Tuesday Club,
and we shall see it often breaking out, with vigorous coruscations in the
Sequel of this History, till at last the whole force of it, like a collected *Ignis*
[191] *fatuus,* which before was diffuse || and erratic, centered in the most Sublime
Genius of Mr Jonathan Grog, now poet Laureat to the ancient and honorable Tuesday Club.

I come now to a remarkable part of our History, but before I enter
upon it, I shall discuss some matters of Lesser consequence; as I Intend to
ommit nothing, which relates to the Laws and Rules of this Club, and the
execution of them, nor Indeed, the least title relative to their Sports, pastimes and Recreations, as I look upon this here Club, to be a pattern for all
other Clubs, that are now, or shall be in after ages.

At Sederunt 12th July the 30th 1745, Joggle Hasty Esqr, being Steward,
Mr Secretary Motely having taken his departure for England, Loquacious
Scribble M:D: was appointed Secretary to the Club, and had the book of
Records delivered to him, and that Gentleman, will in the course of this
history, make a considerable appearance, not only as Secretary and Record
keeper, but as Orator of this here Ancient and honorable Club, in both
which offices, he has distinguished himself in a very remarkable manner,
sometimes highly pleasing, and at other times much disgusting his honor
the president, and the Long standing members of the Club, and, it must be
owned Indeed, that his Clubical Character, was always dark and Mysterious, and never could be thorro'ly understood by most of the Members,
which made his honor the President extremely Jealous of him, and these
Jealousies were much Increased, by the Suggestions of some Longstanding
[192] Members, particularly Capt: Blunt, || afterwards Sir John Oldcastle, tho'
some alledge, that this was only a political fetch in Sir John, to render his
honor uneasy in his Chair, to which Seat of honor, he, the said Sir John,
ambitiously aspired, for many reckoned the Secretary a main pillar of the
Club, and the Ingenious artist, by whom the whole Clubical machinery was
set and kept in motion, tho' it must be owned, that he was of a positive
fractious and fiery temper, and often excited Commotions and disputes in
Club, by making absurd and Phantastical motions, under pretence of check-
ing the grouth of Luxury, and arbitrary power in the Club, for he was
always a Strenuous Stickler for the one dish law, and an opposer of the box,
which first gave his honor the president cause to take offence at his con-

duct; he had a considerable Share of vanity, for he lov'd on all Occasions when haranguing the Club as orator, to tire out their patience with long quotations from obselete Authors, that wrote in the dead Languages.

Tho' there passed abundance of dispute at this Sederunt, concerning law 4th, which many were for altering or rescinding, yet, the members were in a very merry vein, and Mr Smoothum Sly, sung the following Scots Song.

Club Song, sung by Mr Smoothum Sly[4]

Down in yon meadow a Couple did ta-ry,
The wife she'd drink nathing but Sack or Canary,
The Husband Complaind to her friends very early,
O If my wife would Drink hooly and fairly.[5]
Chorus Hooly and fairly, hooly and fairly,   [193]
    Oh! if my wife would drink hooly & fairly.

A logg with her cummers[6] I would her allow,
But when she has mair, shes apt to get fou,
And when she's fou, she's unco Gamstary,[7]
Oh! if my wife would drink hooly & fairly.
Chorus Hooly &ct:

She drank her Stockings, she drank her Shoon,
And next, she drank her bran new Gown,
And eke the Smoke that Civer'd her early,
Oh! if my wife would drink hooly & fairly.
Chorus Hooly &ct:

First she drank Crummie & then she drank Glairie,[8]
Next she drank my bonny gray Marie
That Carried me ay thro' the dubs & the Lairie,[9]
Oh! gin my wife would drink hooly and fairly.
Chorus Hooly &ct:

4. The earliest known version of this song, including several additional verses, appeared as "The Drunken Wife of Gallowa" in *Yair's Charmer* (Edinburgh, 1751). It is included with an introduction in James Johnson, ed., *The Scots Musical Museum*, 6 vols. (Hatboro, Pa., 1962; orig. publ. Edinburgh, 1787–1803), II, 180–182.
5. "Gently and cautiously."
6. "A pint with her female friends."
7. "Very unruly."
8. "She drank the cow and then the whites of the eggs."
9. "Muddy pools and the swamp."

When she comes hame, she lays at the Lads,
And Ca's the lasses baith bitches and Jades,
And me my sell, an auld Cockold cairlie,[10]
Oh! If my wife would drink hooly and fairly.
Chorus Hooly and fairly, hooly and fairly,
    Oh! If my wife would drink hooly and fairly.

At this Sederunt it was moved by Drawlum Quaint Esqr, That Mr Solo
Neverout, should be admitted a member of this here Club, which motion
raised a very warm and obstinate dispute, Jealous Spyplot Esqr alled- || ging
that the said Neverout had too much of the States man, and politician in
him to make an agreeable member, and tho it was evident, by the laws and
constitution of this here Club, that politics and State matters were all-
together excluded as being triffling Subjects below its dignity & Importance, yet, he found, some Longstanding members,[(a)] who had assurance
enough to attempt making a breach in so excellent and wise a constitution,
by proposing the said Neverout as a member, therefore, since the said
Neverout, was known to converse daily with States men, and politicians,
and, assuming the character and air of a politician and States man himself,
to enter into the Cabinet councils of great men, mimicking their Stiff for-
malities, feignd friendship, horse Laughs, and empty promises and protes-
tations, it was a very dangerous and rash proceeding to admit the said
Neverout, as a member of this here Club, as by that means probably, the
Longstanding members, would not only be in danger of contracting some
of these absurd and fantastical habits, but, these great men and politicians,
the said Neverout's associates, would foist themselves into the Club, by his
Interest, and thereby this here Club, would become a State Club, which
Metamorphosis, would assuredly work its ruin and downfall.

    As Mr Spyplot was looked upon, to be a long standing member of a
deep and Solid understanding, this objection had great weight with many
of the members, and some had no regard at all to it, who thought that || Mr
Spyplot was no wiser than his neighbours, tho' one of the privy council of
the celebrated Mr George Neilson, yet, it had like to have obstructed Intirely, the gentleman's election into the Club, but, after a great deal of
dispute, and abundance of altercation, Mr Solo Neverout was unanimously
admitted a member by the Ballot, and we shall see in the Sequel of this
history, that this gentleman, was so far from Introducing state members,

[194]

[195]

(a) This was the first time the term *Longstanding members* was Introduced Into the club.

10. "Cuckolded pipsqueak."

that he was one of the greatest opposers to the creating of such in the Club, when exorbitant power, and boundless ambition had gained the ascendant there, 'till he was created an officer of State himself, by the honorable the president, and then, like other politicians, who have compassed their ends, by having their mouths stop'd, he became utterly silent on that point, tho abundantly clamorous and noisy on others.

At Sederunt 13th August 6th, Mr Slyboots Pleasant being Steward, it was resolved

Law XII. That no member for the future shall be admitted into this Society, without his personal appearance antecedent to his admission.

This, and Law 16th was occasioned by some gentlemen applying to be admitted into the Club, and afterwards retracting.

At Sederunt 14th August 12th, Mr Secretary Scribble being Steward, the Club purchased a leaden tobacco box, painted and gilt, of Nasifer Jole Esqr, price eighteen Shillings, and Solo Neverout Esqr, an Eminent Long Standing member took his Seat in Club, at this same Sederunt, In Consequence of his election at Sederunt 12th.

At Sederunt 15th, August 20th, Mr Secretary || Scribble being deputy [196] Steward, for Jealous Spyplot Esqr, The following Laws were made.

Law XIII. That if any member be absent four nights successively, from the Club, and gives no reason for his absence, or offers no plausible excuse, he is *ipso facto* excluded from the Society.

Law XIV. That the full number of Regular members of the Club be fifteen, but the number of the honorary members Indefinite.

Law XV. That at the admission of every new Member, the Catch called the *Great Bell of Lincoln,* shall be sung by Nasifer Jole Esqr.

At this Sederunt Mr Jole sung the abovementioned Catch so well, that it was the cause of passing the above Law, the members being willing to make as many occasions as possible, to have the opportunity of hearing the fine well tuned voice of that gentleman, Capt: Serious Social too, at this Sederunt, exercised his musical talent, in singing the following song, which became ever since a favorite Club air.

Club air, sung by Cap: Serious Social

Jog hooly good man, or the bed'il fa,
Jog hooly good man or the bed'ill fa,
The bed is made of rotten timmer,
And if it fas it'l smoor our good Mither,
And she'll Cry out and shame us a'.

Jog hooly good man or the bed'ill fa',
The bed, it's tied at head and feet
With Simmer won hay and thats right Sweet,
And In comes the Crummie Cow she eats it a,
Jog hooly Good man or the bed'ill fa'.

[197]   At Sederunt 17th 10th September 1745, Capt: Bully Blunt being Steward, Mr Joshua Fluter was admitted an honorary member, and Mr Joggle hasty forfeited his Seat in Club, by transgressing of Law 13th.

At Sederunt 18th Septr: 17th, Capt: Seemly Spruce being Steward, it was ordained

Law XVI. That no mention shall be made, by any member of the Society, of any person whatever, desirous to be admitted, before such person appears himself in the Society, and desires the same.

Law XVII. That the Secretary Ingross the rules and Laws of the Club, at the end of the book of Records, in the same order as they are passed.

Upon Sederunt 20th October 1st, Mr Laconic Comas being Steward, Mr Oldham wisely, was admitted an honorary member of the Club.

And upon the following Sederunt October 15th, Drawlum Quaint Esqr, being Steward, Capt: Huffbluff Surly, and Mr Ignotus Warble, were created honorary members.

At Sederunt 23 Novr 12th, Nasifer Jole Esqr, being Steward, the following Law was passed.

Law XVIII. That the meeting of this Society shall be once a fortnight, any Law to the contrary notwithstanding, and that as usual, on tuesday evening.

Thus we find already the effects of Luxury and unnecessary expence in this Club, that Society, which before, met amicably once a week, and enjoyed themselves over a bowl, pipe and Gammon or cheese, now find, that by reason of the unnecessary expence of Set Suppers, introduced of late into the Club, it was Inconvenient to all, or most of the members, to have such frequent meetings, we shall likewise find more of it's pernicious effects pre-
[198]   ‖ sently taking place, and that is, settling an arbitrary and despotic power in the Club, for, Nasifer Jole Esqr, at this Sederunt, so far outdid all the other members at entertaining, having now Introduced an Iced Cake, which was dealt about in large lunceons to the members, we find an entry at this Sederunt upon the Book of Records to this purpose.

"The whole Society this night express their Satisfaction at being entertained in a very agreeable manner, by the Steward, elegance and mirth being promoted effectually, without transgressing the rules of the Society.

It is therefore the opinion of this Club, that some Signal mark of honor, or distinction, be conferr'd upon the Steward, in reward of the honor he has done the Society, as soon as may be."

I shall beg leave to make a Reflexion or two upon this transaction and these entries.

Some people may rashly conclude, upon reading the above entry, that the Longstanding members of this here Club, were Epicurean Philosophers, but soft and fair, let us before we draw rash conclusions, beware of swerving from truth and Justice, in matters of this weight and consequence, let us neither allow too much merit to these Longstanding members, nor detract too much from the Character of that worthy ancient Philosopher Epicurus; In the first place, I deny that the members of this here Club were in the least degree Philosophers in this particular circumstance, or lovers of Science, but, were more properly Philogasters, or Lovers of their Belly, For I never yet heard that Luscious eating and drinking, was any one of the Seven liberal arts and Sciences, but rather one of the many beastly appetites or lusts, that men are subject to, *ergo,* in whatever case these Longstanding members were Philosophers, ‖ they were none in this. As to Epicurus, some [199] fools have entertained a notion of him, that he affected tippling and Gormandizing, loved to lie in down beds, to cloth in Silk, to keep his concubines, and take his afternoon's nap, but I believe nothing at all of the matter, being persuaded that he was a Sedate, temperate, and Sober Sage, who thought that the greatest happiness consisted in an absence of bodily pain, and the Enjoyment of mental pleasure, by the practice of virtue and Temperance; but, how Idle it is to think, that Luscious eating and drinking, soft lying, Laziness, and an excessive Indulgence of venereal pleasures, could be Ingredients in this Philosophers System of happiness must appear, when we reflect, that he knew as well as we do, that these excesses constantly bring with them, gouts, Rheumatisms, Sciaticas, gravels, Scurvies, poxes, toothakes, colics, boils, blotches, Scabs, and all the plagues of Pandora's box, which are accompanied with pain, rack and torment Inexpressible.

We may see by this transaction, with what cunning and gaining methods, men of an ambitious turn will attempt, to raise themselves, we may also see, how liable to corruption human nature is, and, how men will be Induced to barter liberty, and every other valuable possession, for a little good belly timber, or what we call Eatables and drinkables, and if many do not exchange their liberty directly for that consideration, yet they truck it for money, which is the *Alma Regina,* and procures all these Gimcracks.

Magister artium, Ingeniique largitor venter.[11]

Smooth Language and cunning coaxing too go a great way in driving this Scurvey bargain. Therefore, it was a wise provision in the Athenians, of old, who were under ‖ a democratical government, like that of this here Club at it's first establishment, to take off their great men, so soon as they became popular, nothing conducing more to Introduce an absolute Tyranny, than the popularity of one man, we see the Sad effects of this corruption and venality, at our Elections for burgesses and Representatives; the man who treats best & gives most Cyder and punch, and makes the most Coaxing, wheedling and pallabering Speeches, being always returned by the Giddy constituents, tho' perhaps less qualified for the trust than another, who either could not, or would not be so lavish of his money and words.

I shall here observe also, how prone all men are to flatter and cajole those, from whom they have already received and yet expect to receive favors; it is presumtously said in the above entry "That elegance and mirth were promoted, without transgressing the Rules of the Club," but I may with Confidence aver, that the fact was not so, for, the one dish or gammon Law, was most audaciously violated, and trampled under foot, there having been, that very night, a formal laid out table, garnished with boiled and roast, pies, tarts and Custards, besides, the needless apparatus of a table Cloth, napkins, knives, forks, and two or three removes of plates, all in decent order, hence we see, that when people go about flattering of Great men, they will not stick to put even the most palpable untruths upon Record, *O tempora, O mores!*[12] and thus I conclude this Long Chapter.

Chapter VIII

The Election and Cathedration, of the Honorable Nasifer Jole Esqr, President.

We are now come to that period, where we must bid adieu to Clubical Liberty, for, as the end of the Roman Li- ‖ berty, was at the time of their admitting a perpetual Dictator, so, the period of the Liberty of the ancient and honorable tuesday Club, was, at their election of a perpetual President.

[200]

[201]

11. "Generous queen"; "it is the teacher of arts and the fertile womb of genius" (Persius, *Satires,* prologomena, 11).

12. "Oh the times, oh the customs!" (Cicero, *In Catilinam,* speech 1, sec. 1).

*It may be well observed here, how artful men will gain upon the opinion and affections of a people, when they observe a mild, easie deportment and behavior towards them, and when they heap benefits and favors upon them unasked. This was the very case with Nasifer Jole Esqr, and the long standing members of the ancient and honorable Tuesday Club; This gentleman wore a complacent and mild countenance, always adorned with a Smile, and like Cæsar of old, flattered the people, that by gaining the ascendant over their affections, he might the more easily seize the Tyranny into his own hands, and govern their persons as he thought fit, neither did he spare any bounty in the way of entertaining, for, at the very first time of his being Steward, he Introduced into the Club that expensive Liquor called rack, (so bewitching to our Refined palats, because it is so far fetched) as has been Related above, and had a large table in the next Room, elegantly spread, the cloth and napkins nicely pinched, and perfumed Sweetly with Lavander and roses, and several elegant dishes of meat, were curiously Ranged on this Table, the passage, between the Club room and Supper room beautifully Illuminated, with Sconces nicely disposed, in the figures of diamonds, triangles, Stars and circles, at the second time of his serving Steward, which was Sederunt 23d, he added an Iced cake to the entertainment, which was dealt about in Luncheons || to the members, curiously [202] wrap'd up in clean white paper, this Cake, this fatal Cake, Compleated the Catastrophe of the Clubs liberty, and, as Esau sold his birthright to Jacob, for fair words and a mess of porridge, so this unhappy Club, bartered their Liberty to Nasifer Jole Esqr, for an old Song, Rack punch, plumb pudding, four pound of Candles, and an Iced Cake!

But tho I condemn the conduct of the Club in this affair, yet, that I may do Strict Justice to that great and Illustrious personage, Nasifer Jole Esqr, I am Sincerely of opinion that the Club could not have pitched upon a milder or more Complacent governor than he, for, at all times, he has shown himself benign, gentle and easie to be entreated, and, excepting only in that nice point of giving up the least article or particle, of his valuable prerogative and privileges, of which he is Justly tenacious, he has spared no pains to humor the Club, in every thing they desired, as will be plainly seen in the Sequel of this History. But what tho' the Club be in a great measure happy and easie, under the government of this polite and accomplished *Archon,* yet, it cannot with any Certainty be expected, that it will always remain so under that of his Successors, who, not minding his example, may turn out to be bloody and Cruel Tyrants.

(*) Vide anniversary oration 9th, almost verbatim the same with this and the following paragraph.

It happened then, upon the memorable 26th of November, 1745 O:S: at Sederunt 24th, Mr Secretary Scribble being Steward, that the Club resolved to Chuse a perpetual president or Chairman, and The Illustrious Nasifer Jole Esqr, was proposed || by Mr Smoothum Sly, as a proper person for the presidential Chair, But, Capt: Bully Blunt stood up, and opposed it, telling the Club That he did not know that Nasifer Jole Esqr, or any esquire whatsoever, had any Juster claim to the Chair, than any other member or Esquire, That, he humbly conceived, without the least grain of Vanity, that, he himself being also an Esquire, deserved as much that eminent place and office, as any Longstanding member in this here Club, and therefore hoped that this here Club, would do him the Justice to elect him president, and so put in his claim, To this a member made reply—That if corpulency and enormous Size of body was a qualification for the Chair, Captain Blunt in that respect only was Sufficiently qualified; but really if this here Club, was to Chuse a president, for that qualification alone, they might as well pitch upon Mr Spyplots great Dog Mars, and place him in that honorable Seat. It was also observed by the same member, after alittle pause, That Captain Blunt, was not at all in a proper dress, for such a Solemn ceremony, as that of being elected a president, for, granting that he was every other way worthy of the place, yet, the Dirty night cap, the long beard, and the greasy banyian, was by no means a propper apparel, in which to ascend a presidential Chair. Upon this, Captain Blunt Retired, and, in a few minutes after, to the Great Surprize of all the members, appeared, dressed out in his regimentals, as fine as || if he had Just been taken out of a band box; with a fair Ramilee wig, a clean Shaved beard, a clean Ruffled Shirt, a Laced wastcoat and Sword, but all this fracas prov'd in vain; for, on putting about the vote, the members gave their voices for Nasifer Jole Esqr, and Captn Blunt had no other vote but his own, and Nasifer's, who modestly gave him his. Upon this Nasifer Jole Esqr, with great modesty declared to the Club, his Insufficiency for this high and dignified office, and Solemnly protested that it was a thing he by no means desired, and wished it had pleased the members to bestow it upon a person more Qualified for and worthy of the place. But this was only like Cæsar's putting aside the Crown faintly, when offered him by Mark Anthony, and Indeed, these professions with most of the members passed for words of course, and bare formal and complimentary Speeches, as is usual with great men on such occasions, when they are promoted or advanced, who, to save appearances at least, and keep up a state or form, pretend Insufficiency and want of merit, tho' neither themselves nor hearers believe these expressions and terms of humiliation to be true in fact, but this Illustrious president had a good Precedent, for this

[203]

[204]

procedure, it being Customary, for the honorable, the Speaker or Chairman of the House of Commons, to profess himself insufficient at his election, and humbly desire, that a man of Greater Abilities may be put in the Chair, as soon as this election was over, it was entered in the book of Records

"That Nasifer Jole Esqr, upon account of the Elegant entertainments given by him to the Club, and his known abilities, was voted perpetual president, or Chairman of the Club, and had Immediatly the following privileges granted him."

Law XIX. 1mo   That the President shall have the Sole power to nominate his own Deputy, in case of necessary absence.

Here it must be observed, that the Club Inconsideratly gave up all   [205] power inherent in them, to appoint deputy presidents, and they soon felt the bad consequences of this, for at several times, the president refused absolutely to name or Commission his deputy, and therefore, by a following law, they took to themselves, a power of chusing a *deputatus Electus,* but the president never would give up this valuable privilege, and says that this here other Law, is no Law at all, till they revoke the first, which they never can do; for, as he is a perpetual president, the Law, which gives him his privileges, must necessarily be a perpetual Law, This ought to be a Seasonable warning to all free Clubs, how they part with their power of election, to any president whatsoever, because, they put it in the power of that president to throw the constitution into Disorder, whenever he pleases, by depriving it of a proper head or ruler.

2do   That upon every Club night, the Steward for the time being, shall acquaint the president of the time and place of meeting, that he may know the appointed Deputy, In case the President cannot attend, and to acquaint the Club when met, of the person named to take the Chair.

This I observe was giving the Steward a deal of trowble to very little purpose, and is only a needless piece of State or form, which absolutely supposes great men or grandees to have shorter memories than other people. Why could not the president, as well as any other member, know and remember the stated times of meeting every fortnight, and send his orders to the Secretary, concerning his Deputy, whose propper office it was, (and not the Steward's) to deliver it to the Club.

3tio   That the President shall have the privilege of taking out one single nay, if at any time such shall happen in balloting, the other being all the Contrary part, or yeas, and in Cases where a majority carries in Club, he shall have the Casting vote where there happens a parity.

The last part of this privilege, I think is not to be objected to, because   [206] it is the undoubted right of all presidents and Chair men to have the casting vote, but the first part of it entirely annulls the wise law of unanimous consent, in electing members and making new Laws, some Sederunts before this so warmly Disputed, and Grants a greater privilege than any president ever yet had, by striking at the root of a fundamental and constitutional Law.

4to   That the president shall alone have the power of Judging, when the Gelastic Law ought to be put in Execution by making some Signal for executing the same.

This is another unwarrantable privilege, and seems quite preposterous, and contrary to the Law of nature, nay even to the Law of nations and Clubs, that any President shall take upon him to direct me, when, or how to laugh, or cry, or Grin, whensoever he pleases; I believe I may safely affirm that Laughing, or crying or grinning, must come naturally, and cannot be forced, and I should laugh at any man Indeed be he a president or not, that would take upon him to Command the muscles of my face, whensoever he thought fit; In fine, this seems to be a villanous privilege, because it makes of the members a parcel of momuses, histrios or Commedians, or rather poppets, subject to the caprice and will of the president.

5to   That if any motion is made in Club, the president is to be first addressed by the moving member, giving him his proper title.

This, I grant, is a very Just privilege, and what all presidents as moderators of Clubs ought to have, tho' the Club afterwards pretended to rescind it, and order the address to be directed to the Speaker, on account of the Presidents Strange in attention in such cases.

[207]   6to   That at the common expence of the Club there ‖ shall be procured a chair for the president, raised one Step above the other Seats or chairs in the Room.

This privilege several of the members grumbled at, particularly Jealous Spyplot esqr, who always thought that every member there ought to be on a Level.

Then it was Resolved, that in case other privileges should be thought proper, to be conferrd upon his honor the President, they should be considered and argued, at some of the Subsequent Sederunts of the Club.

Mr President seemed, with great reluctance and modesty, to accept of these valuable privileges, but afterwards, like all men in power, proved very tenacious, not only of them, but of some others that were since given him.

Then was he led by two members, vizt: Mr Smoothum Sly, and Mr Secretary Scribble, to a Semicircular Smoking Chair, which happened to be in the Room, and set down in it with his back to the door, which Capt: Blunt perceiving, Invidiously thrust open the door, and, his honor getting

The unlucky adventure at the Cathedration
of the Honorable Carlo Nauger Sole Esqr

[facing page 207]

hastily up, the Chair was overset, and, to the Surprize of every body, there Tumbled out a Close Stool pan, which as good luck would have it, had none of its proper contents in it, thereupon, Capt: Blunt, observed with a Sneer, That the President had made a Shitten entry into his office, and he hoped he would make the like exit.

Thus, was this great man exalted to the office of perpetual president of this ancient and honorable Club, and to this day, has kept his Seat Steadily in that Chair, and we shall now see him make a considerable figure thro' the Course of this History, sometimes ruling in peace and quietness, sometimes in the midst of disturbance and hurly burly, sometimes exalted, sometimes depress'd, by his Inconstant and unruly Longstanding members. The Club ordered Jealous Spyplot Esqr, to prepare a proper chair, for the president, against the next meeting of the Club.

[208]   At this Sederunt, Signior Lardini was made an honorary member; This gentleman, we shall find, making a considerable figure as musician *Con stromenti*, and musical Composer to the Club, as also, Chief Triumvir of the worshipful Eastren Shore Triumvirate.

Thus, this ancient and honorable Club, by creating a perpetual president, came nigher to the model of the ancient and venerable Tuesday, (or whin bush) Club of Lanneric, but deviated from that excellent ancient constitution, in this Important circumstance, that they gave a much greater power and more privileges to the Honorable Nasifer Jole Esqr, than any Venerable president, of that ancient and venerable Club ever had, in the memory of man.

End of the third book.

List of the members Regular and honorary, of the Ancient and
Honorable Tuesday Club, that were in the Club, between the 14th of
May & the 26th of November 1745.

Regular members	Honorary members
Loquacious Scribble M:D: Secr:	Mr Abraham Bumper
Prattle Motely Esqr Secr:	Doctor Polyhistor
Revd: Smoothum Sly	Mr Oldham Wisely
Jealous Spyplot Esqr	Mr Joshua Fluter
Capt: Bully Blunt	Capt: Huffbluff Surly
Capt: Seemly Spruce	Mr Ignotus warble
Mr Laconic Comas	Signior Lardini
Capt: Serious Social	Coll: Courtly Phraze
The Hon: Nasifer Jole Esqr pres:	
Mr Dumpling Gundiguts	
Drawlum Quaint Esqr	
Mr Slyboots pleasant	
Mr Joggle Hasty	
Mr Solo neverout	

The History of the Ancient and Honorable Tuesday Club

Book IV

From the Cathedration of the honorable Nasifer Jole Esqr, president, to the first grand Anniversary procession.

Chapter I

Of Club stile, and Clubical terms, necessary for the understanding of this history, as also of Great Club-offices and officers, their nature, dignity and privileges.

For some Centuries past, at least, since the Æra of the Gothic Ignorance, when Learning Arts Clubs, and every thing that had a tendency to humanize and civilize mankind, were almost totally extinguished, and nothing prevailed but a Savage ferocity and rude use of arms, it has been the Custom among our moderen Literati, and Cultivators of arts and Sciences, to clog and Encumber these arts and Sciences, with certain uncouth and Cramp terms, called Technical terms, borrowed and compiled, from either dead or outlandish Languages, such as the Greek, latin, old French and Arabic, to the no small hindrance and discouragement, of the painful, laborious, poring and brain beating Student, who, before he can understand aright, || The Substance or marrow of any art or Science, must spend half [210] his life in exploring the meaning of these terms used in that art or Science, this necessarily forces him to the drudgery of learning many other Languages besides his mother tongue, and he must spend much of his precious time, in the dry and tedious toil of turning over many of these (too often) Impertinent and voluminous compositions called Dictionaries, whereas, had these terms been expressed, in the vernacular or vulgate tongues, either by words of the same Signification, or a Circumlocutory description, when such words cannot be found, how much easier, how much shorter would his task have been.

Whether an enthusiastic reverence for the Superior abilities of the ancients, who surely were the first Inventors, or a Supine Indulgence and remissness in the moderens, was the cause of these latter, not taking the trowble to alter those terms of art, and adapt them to the particular languages of the Countries where they were received, is not my business here to enquire, but, I shall be bold to make a few observations on this General Corruption, that in these latter centuries has overspread Europe, and prevailed so far, as to gain footing even in Clubs.

This Idle piece of foppery, has extended it Self so far, as to Infect not only the professors of Science and literature, but has taken place even among mechanics and tradesmen, who too have their particular terms of art, and uncouth names and designations, which extend even to their tools, and the materials upon which they work. Nay, Divinity, or Theology, as [211] some are pleased to call it, because they would have both a greek ‖ and latin term, which in plain english, is nothing but a discourse or doctrine Concerning God, his nature and attributes, in which, all mankind, for the Sake of their own happiness and good are so nearly concerned, has been hampered Cramped, obscured, and rendered mysterious, I may say unintelligible, by a parcell of Lucrative, covetous and designing Schoolmen and priests, who, Instead of the practice of piety and morality, the main purpose and design of Religion and revelation, have crammed up the heads of the Ignorant and Superstitious mob (for I account all those gentlemen mob, who take things Implicitly and depend upon the say so of others, without exercising their own reason and Judgement) with Idle Stuff, concerning orthodoxy and hetrodoxy, heresy and heritics, Ceremonies, rites, Songs, riddles, rebuses and fiddlesticks, and perswaded them, that they may go to heaven by Legerdemain, or Slight of hand as it were, climbing up on piles and mountains of Mitres, Copes, Surplices, Chalices, crosiers, hoods, Cowls, cassocks, bagpipes, fiddles, Crucifixes, pictures, tinckling bells, pixes,[1] Consecrated wafers, triple Crowns, bunches of keys, altars, hour glasses, folio books, bells, bell ropes and cats o' nine tails, which last, are for alittle good Christian-like Jerking & Scourging, with a penny or two by the bye for the poor priests, to Indulge in Gluttony letchery and Idleness, and also to enable the chast nuns, to pray for the Souls of the Dead, who never once thanked them for it, to deliver Sinners out of purgatory, and commit Iniquity in their Cloysters.

1. A *pyx* is the vessel containing the Host, or consecrated bread of the Sacrament.

This profitable trade and cunning Science, under the Specious title of [212] Christianity and religion, as bad wares are commonly vended, by having fine outlandish names given them, has, in all ages gained much ground among frail Sinful men, because it points out to them, as they foolishly believe, a streight, wide and direct road, whereby they may go speedily to heaven, and yet fornicate, adulterize, Gormandize, tipple, rob, steal, swear, forswear, and Cut throats all the way as they go along, and fare never the worse for it, be never an ace the less christians, and Surely hit the mark at last, remembering to pay the priests and holy church their perquisites, else all this pegeantry turns out good for nothing, and the same, as if you should rub your arse with a brick bat.

What a lamentable thing is it, that thus a plain and easie matter is rendered difficult and Intricate by such far fetched technical terms and confounded Trumpery, what occasion have they, but for the greed of filthy Lucre, to perplex with difficulties, and involve in terms, such as *transubstantiation, Consubstantiation, reprobation, Sanctification, regeneration, predestination, Supererogation, free grace, adoption &ct:* a matter, which consists only in, *fear God, love your neighbour, and honour the king,*—and above all, *do as you would be done by*—this, I suppose, every man may understand at first hearing, or reading of a certain book Called the new testament (condemned from the perusal of the vulgar, by certain cunning priests, as containing ‖ dangerous doctrine,) without being at the trowble to rummage the Fathers, [213] or Commentators for a nice explication of it, for this would be like descending into deep and dark Caverens, to explore the light of the Glorious sun, or rather, as the famous Sir Rowland that mad peer of France did, like sending their wits and Senses a gadding to the moon,[2] that they might know where to look for them, should they ever have occasion to use them.

The learned gentlemen of the Law and Physic have been guilty of this absurdity to a very Scandalous degree, and to undertake the Study of either has now become a labor, almost Insurmountable, *Hoc opus hic labor est,* as the poet tells us;[3] we shall hear a Gentleman, of the first of these learned professions, talk of *Prochain amy, en son tort, apportionment, Essoin, oyer* and *terminer, fieri facias, scire facias, Warrantum, murderium, rautum, riotum, nolo presequi, ne exeat Regnum, billa vera, Ignoramus,* and a thousand other such cramp terms, by which no well meaning Christian could once Imagin,

2. Roland was the famous paladin who was defeated by the Spanish at Roncesvalles (778) and later became a legendary hero in French literature. Hamilton is referring, however, to the humorous account of Roland's efforts to recover his senses in Lodovico Ariosto's *Orlando furioso,* 34.66–71.

3. "This is the task, this is the work" (Vergil, *Aeneid* 6.129).

that he meant and Intended, *one's nighest relation, in ones own wrong, Division, Barring all delays & excuses, to hear and determin, you shall Cause to be done, you shall Cause to be known, a warrant, a murder, a raut, a riot, I forbid prosecution, he shall not leave the province or kingdom, a true bill,* and *we know nothing at all of the matter.*

In Physic again, we shall often hear, a Learned Gentleman in a full bottom wig, black coat, with a Snuff box in his hand, and a cane dangling [214] at his wrist, ‖ enveloped in a large Scarlet Rockela,[4] outward marks, ensigns and Symbols of learning and Philosophy, holding forth, concerning *Symptoms, prophylaxis, Idiosyncrasy, Gruma, coagulum, Phlebotomy, venesection, cathartics, eccoprotics, emetics, Juleps, pills, troches, ecclegmas, decoctions, apozems, incision, unguents, liniments, Embrocation &ct:* which an Intelligent man at first hearing would Imagin to be words framed on purpose to conjure up the Devil, and the Devil himself, were he conjured up, unless he understood latin greek and arabic, would never discover that this Learned don, meant by these Phrases, only *Signs of a distemper, method of cure, disposition or tendency, curd like matter, Blood letting, a purge, a vomit, a mixture of Sugar and distilled waters, little round balls to swallow, small flat things in various Shapes, or Tablets, thick mixtures of honey, Sugar and oil, broths made of herbs, cutting the flesh, ointments,* and *greasing the Skin with them.*

This fantastical Custom, has not only prevailed among the Learned, but also among the Ignorant, vulgar, and that even the lowest, tho' I dare not say the most vicious or wicked class of mankind, vizt: Gypsies, Theives, pickpockets and vagrant beggars, who have Invented terms of art, and framed a Language of their own, which Indeed excells the learned Jargon in this particular circumstance, that they are not Indebted to other Languages for their terms of art, but Invent them whenever they have occasion.

[215]   Thus, they call an Ale house, a *bouzing ken.* a beggar born and bred, a *Clapperdudgeon.* a pretended Dumb man, a *Dummerer.* a Shuffling Impostor, a *Crank;* Strong liquor, *Hum.* Money *Lour.* Virgins *Dells.* Strumpets, *Doxies.* Beggars, *Maunders.* Hats, *Nab Cheats.* Hands, *Fambles.* Staves, *Filches.* to steal *Filsh.* Rayment, *Back cheat.* Food, *Belly Cheat.* Good words *Ben whids.* Stand on your Guard, *Fumbumbus.* a man *Cove.* Beaten, *Lumb'd.* a pot of ale, *Gag of ben bouse.* Rogues *Claws.* Hedges, *Ruffmans.* To lie with a maid, *Twang a Dell.* Pigs, *Grunting Cheats.* Chickens, *cackling Cheats.* Hens *margery praters.* to steal a buck of Cloaths, *mill a Lag of duds.* And several of these cant words as they are called, have in our days been adopted, by persons of quality, rank and politeness, to the great decoration

4. A *roquelaure* is a knee-length cloak.

and Improvement of our Language, for, from whence, if not from this pure fountain, came these elegant words, now much in use at court, vizt: *Bully, cully, bite, bamboozle, bumbaisd, humbug, fun, queer, Bunter*,[5] and many such like elegant terms and epithets. It is commonly urged, by the learned professors of law and physic, that the great and cheif design of their terms of art, is to conceal the mysteries of their particular crafts from the vulgar, and to humor a Sort of foolish people, of whom there are a considerable number, in all places, who think there is nothing extraordinary in plain language and common phrazes, and I know not but our Theologues and Gypsies, may have the same use for their particular terms of art.

Is it then to be wondered at, that Clubs, and particularly the ancient [216] and honorable Tuesday Club, should have a stile and terms of art peculiar to themselves, since all Societies, learned and unlearned, have had their technical terms and favorite stile.

Let none of our Readers then, stare gape and be astonished, when they meet in the course of this club History, with such as these following terms and Phrazes, vizt: *Sederunt, Cathedration, puzzlementation, this here Club, that there Club, long standing members, old standing members, Presidential, Clubical, Clubific, Clubified, conundrum*, and its derivatives, *conundrumify, conundrumification, Conundrumatic, conundrumatical, conundrumish, conundrumation, capation, arguefication, anticlubarian, Grogorian*, and some others of less note, but let them be assured that they are all very proper, Significant and elegant Club phrazes, and proper Club stile, coined and Introduced, by certain of the members of greatest note and Eminence.

But to recapitulate, they'll say, why *this here Club*, and *that there Club*, might not *this Club* and *that Club* do as well; I grant it might, with regard to speaking of this Club, and that Club in General, but then it does not so clearly express this club at present sitting, or that Club at present sitting, for, the particles *here* and *there*, point out emphatically, something *here* present, or *there* existing, whereas, the other way of Speaking, does not at all define the Club *Congregatim*, or existing as a Club, This I think is Sufficient to Justify the expression, not to mention the Example of people of rank and quality, who use this expletive much even in their Common discourse, the Phrazes *this here* and *that there*, being favorites at St James's ‖ and in the army, the two British accademies of politeness and propriety of [217] Stile, there is besides to be considered the weight authority and example of many of our great orators and barristers, for by them, *this here* and *that there*

5. A *bully* is the protector of a prostitute; a *cully* is a dupe; a *bite* is a sharper or swindler; to *bumbaze* is to perplex or bamboozle; to *fun* is to cheat or hoax; a *bunter* is a low, vulgar woman.

are often used, as beautiful expletives of discourse, and serve much better to fill up a gap, than coughing, Spitting, wiping ones face or mouth with a fine Cambric handkerchef, rubbing ones forehead, shifting ones wig and screwing ones mouth into a political grin, taking a pinch of Snuff, or a quid of tobacco, which are all practised to perfection by orators, when they are at a loss what to say next; now, *this here Club Sir*, and *that there Club Sir*, pronounced in a slow deliberate and drawling manner, as they are only words of Course, that require no attention, flowing out as it were mechanically, may give the orator an opportunity, to rake out from among the rubbish and Lumber of his fancy, what he is next to say.

As to *Longstanding members*, I have said enough of that in the last Chapter of the first book, where I have clearly show'd the Significancy of the term, and its origin; *Old Standing members* are those who were of the Club at its first Institution, and I think it a very proper term, cavil at it who will.

But they'll say, why *Presidential*; I shall only answer why Substantial, circumstantial, and many other derivatives of the like nature.

Again, who ever before heard of *Cathedration*, very true, 'tis a new Coind clubical term, and pray is it not as good as Castration, damnation, consideration &ct:

As for *Sederunt*, it is a latin word, and signifies they sat, being used much in the Journals of the Scots parliaments, and the number annexed expresses the number of Sittings, the Club has sat, vizt: Sederunt 20th or Sed: 24: this arose from the whin bush club.

[218]   As to the rest, take them in the lump, I think that *Clubical* is as proper as comical; *Clubific*, as pacific; *Clubified*, as horrified; *capation*, as coronation; *puzzlementation*, as fermentation; *arguefication*, as qualification; *Anticlubarian*, as antitrinitarian; *Grogorian*, as historian; but as for *Conundrum* and it's derivatives, I must beg leave to enlarge alittle upon it.

It is uncertain whence the word *conundrum* it self is derived,[6] it seems to be a word of an odd Sound, and conveys a Sort of Burlesque Idea; (if I may so speak) being much of the same nature with the french *Turlupinade*, tho' that by the Bye signifies a pun; but as puns and Conundrums are cousin germans, or brother and Sister's Children, we may look upon the two words, as pritty much alike; Turlupin[7] was a famous Droll, who flour-

6. The origin of *conundrum* is, as Hamilton suggests, uncertain; it is referred to as an Oxonian term, having possibly originated in an Oxford joke.

7. Turlupin was the stage name of Henri Legrand (d. 1637), one of a trio of French actors who performed at the Hôtel de Bourgogne in Paris in the early 17th century (not the 15th, as Hamilton suggests) and delighted the public with their coarse popular farces.

ished in the 15th Century, and Invented, or rather Improved very much the Science of dowble Entendre; (a Science much cultivated since his time by the Jesuits) and used in a droll and waggish Sense, some words of an ambigous meaning, or simular Sound, and therefore, punning, since his time has been Called by the French *Turlupinader;* but to find the true Etymology of *Conundrum,* will be no such easy matter, however, to satisfy the Curious, I shall here deliver what I know Concerning it, tho' to me, the derivation seems to be somewhat strained and far fetched.

Every one, who understands the french Language, knows what is meant by the word *Con,* which, for fear of offence to modest ears, I shall not translate into English, it is derived then, says my author, from this french ‖ word *con,* and two english words added to it, vizt: the words *under* and *him,* [219] but the two last words for the ease of our polite pronouncers and writers have been contracted thus, *und'r'um,* and the whole Joined together make *Conund'r'um,* which without the break and apostrophæs, make the plain word *Conundrum;* why the word should be analysed in this awkward manner, I cannot tell, unless the Imagination and wit is as much exercised by a new broached conundrum, as the limbs and members are, at the broaching of a new maidenhead, but least I offend the modest, I shall have done.

As for the derivatives of this celebrated word used in our Club stile, I shall now knock them off, as fast as peas, *Conundrumify,* I assert, is as proper as Shipify, *Conundrumification,* as recapitulation; *Conundrumatic,* as problematic, *Conundrumatical,* as fanatical; *Conundrumish,* as funnish, punnish (which last too, is a Club phraze) rummish or rammish, *conundrumation,* as modulation, or 'Nation, which some people use for Damnation, and thus have I explained, and accounted for these words, Introduced into the Club, by members of note, and Called Club Stile.

And now, since I talk of members of note, it will be proper, before I conclude this Chapter, to say something of high Club offices and dignified officers.

Offices and officers, are alike necessary in Civil Government, as in Clubs, the last being a Consequence of the first, for an officer cannot exist without an office, no more than an office without an officer, ‖ But which of [220] them had the prior existence, or if they existed at first Synchronously, I shall not here determin, leaving that nice enquiry to your Subtle metaphysicians; Thus, in a kingdom or monarchy, there must be a King, or Supreme magistrate to govern in Chief, and under him, must be his ministers, and Subordinate magistrates, to support the head and first mover of the great political Machine, these are great officers, and under them are smaller fry, such as Constables, bum bayliffs, Catchpoles, Jailors and Hangmen, equally necessary to the public, tho' of a baser metal. Now, as to the necessity of these offices and officers, I believe none will question it, but, as to the offices being well executed, and the officers properly qualified to execute their functions, it is to be supposed all will grant, that is not so absolutely necessary, and that especially in the very highest offices and first rank of officers, else why should we often find, a Savage and Inhuman brute, in human Shape, a bitter Enimy to every other Creature in human Shape, a murderer ravisher, plunderer, and oppressor sitting at the helm, and yet the Ship of the Common wealth, steering a smooth course, why do we so often observe, fools, boys and Changelings, sitting in Councils of State, and yet matters pritty well managed, blockheads fill Judicial Chairs, and yet the affairs of Justice go Swimingly on; Cowards lead Armies, and yet victory pop into our mouths, Covetous and rapacious men entrusted with the public treasure, and yet the fund very carefully managed, and fair accounts rendered of it; But in most cases, the Lower Class of officers, must of necessity be men well qualified, that is, they must be Sly cunning, Strong

[221] fisted ‖ rugged fellows, else they never could cleverly catch their fellow rogues or keep them when cought, or even whip or hang them with any decency or good grace, hence, I doubt not, some will conclude, that your catchpoles, Bum-bayliffs, Jaylors and hangmen, are the most worthy and meritorious persons in office, in a kingdom or state, being always persons of great qualifications and abilities for the Important offices they hold and are entrusted with, whereas, your high and dignified officers, are often children, fools, Ignoramuses, pimps, knaves, cowards, covetous and Cruel fellows, which qualities render them, not quite so fit for their exalted offices, as their bretheren of the Lower class are for theirs, to whom many of these very qualities are of Singular Service.

Indeed, where certain qualities, called by many, necessary qualities, are wanting in Superior officers, these are very well supplied, by Certain badges of State, which have a mighty power and virtue to Influence and awe the herd of mankind; such as Seats called thrones, and chairs of State, canopies, maces, mitres, Crowns, triple Crowns, caps of State, full bottomd wigs, white Staves, ribbons, Stars, garters, truncheons, Swords and the like,[a] which being exposed to the view of the populace, or carried in procession, (tho' really in the nature of things no better than a fools cap and bells, with a bladder full of peas on a pole) Inspire a mighty awe and reverence for the proprietors & possessors of them.

As it is in Civil governments, so is it in Clubs, which are civil govern-

---

(a) Vide the frontispiece.

ments in minature, there is a necessity for a president or head, who, in order to qualify him- || self better than nature has done for his high office, [222] must have certain marks and Symbols of State and dignity, such as a chair of State, a cap of State, a badge of state, a canopy of State; these are all absolutely necessary to equip a President of a Club, in order to Inspire a proper and decent awe into the Subordinate members; His officers of State, and Superior officers, such as chancellor, champion, Mr of Ceremonies, must likewise have their ensigns of honor, as a Seal, a Sword, a fan, or some such flurting⁸ Instrument, and their particular privileges. As for his Inferior officers, such as his musician, orator, Secretary and Serjeant at arms, it is only requisite the first two be endued with a clear voice, the next have a quick and Stiff pen, and the last should be a Strong fisted resolute fellow, to qualify each of them for their respective offices, and to keep the Longstanding members in that awe and Subjection, which their duty requires of them, all these great qualifications, we shall find in the respective officers of the Ancient and honorable Tuesday Club, and thus, having briefly discussed this Important Subject, I now proceed with our History.

Chapter II

Of a great Club Ball, and matters of Gallantry, with the Clubical Character, of Nasifer Jole Esqr.

I have heard it said of a certain orator and Rhetorician, who used in his time to mount the rostrum with a *bon grace,* and hold forth with a *grand eclat,* that what puzzled him more than any thing else, in his oratorial and Rhetorical compositions, and exercises, || was how to make a good conclu- [223] sion, or ending, for, as to the exordium, or beginning of an oration, it was as easy as to whistle, and he could flourish it away in that part after a very Sublime manner, but how to end or conclude, or indeed where properly to stop, without making many an Impertinent circumbendibus, was the diffi- culty, *hic labor, hoc opus;*¹ that is, it required the art of hocus pocus.

The Honorable Nasifer Jole Esqr, now president of the ancient and honorable Tuesday Club, was just in the same Situation as this orator and

8. Derived from *flurtƶd* (flowered, figured) or *fleuret,* an ornament shaped like a small flower.

1. Hamilton has purposely botched the passage from Vergil noted above (p. 213).

Rhetorician; he had begun, alas, with too great Success, to Introduce excess and Luxury in matters of eating and drinking into this here Club, and it would have been well, had he stopped there. Had he gone no farther, than rack punch, iced cake, plumb pudding, custard, Sillabub, apple pie, partridge pye, Ragoos, fricassees, hashes and venison pasties, things might have gone tollerably well. But, at Sederunt 25th Decr: 10th 1745, The Club being held at the house of Jealous Spyplot Esqr, Steward, The Chair of State being prepared as ordered at last Sederunt, and set forth, at the head of the Club Table, the Honorable Nasifer Jole Esqr made his appearance, in a flamming Suit of Scarlet, a magnificent hat, bound round with massy Scolloped Silver lace, a fine large and full fair wig, white kid Gloves, with a gold headed cane, and I cannot be certain whether or not he had a Silver hilted Sword, with a beautiful Sword knot of Ribbons, white Silk Stockings rolld, large Shining Silver Shoe buckles, his coat and vest edged round with [224] gold twist, the buttons gold & gilt Spangles, ‖ the button holes trimmed with gold and several brilliant rings upon his fingers, his Shoes shining like a looking glass, his beard close shaved, and his nails close pared, in this luxury of dress did he ascend the chair of state, and looked like a flaming comet in his perihelion, the laced hat resembling the resplendent body of the Star, the flaxen wig the tail, and the other sparkling parts of his dress, the Shining constellations surrounding it, so that had Hermes, Zoroaster, or Ptolomy,[2] or any of the ancient Astronomers have seen him, when it was usual to translate Heroes to the Skies, and make constellations of them, they probably would have alloted this Clubical hero, a place in the heavens, and he would have decked the Celestial Sphere, under the name of *Præses Jolæus,* and might have sat there in State in the *Cathedra Cassiopæa,* as he sits now in State in the Grand Cathedra of the ancient and honorable Tuesday Club.

Thus did this great man, Inconsideratly Introduce the Luxury of dress, into this here ancient and honorable Club, and we shall soon find some of the Longstanding Members Imitating him in this, and, such as never knew before, any other than a Simple plain dress, members wont to come to club *sans ceremonie,* with night caps not over clean, Slouch hats, ragged round

2. Hermes Trismegistus, the name given to the Egyptian god "Thoth the very great," was the reputed author of philosophical-religious treatises and various works on astrology, magic, and alchemy. Zoroaster, the Greek name for Zarathustra (a figure of Aryan legend known to the Greeks as early as the 5th century B.C.), was credited with an immense number of works dealing with theology, astrology, and magic. Ptolemy (fl. A.D. 127–148) was a celebrated mathematician, geographer, and astronomer whose major work, the *Almagest,* is a complete textbook of astronomy as the Greeks understood it.

The Hon. nae: Jole.Esq: first mounts the Presidential Chair of State

[facing page 223]

the brim, long beards, banyans and greasy wrappers, in laudable Imitation, of their worthy predecessors of the Ugly Club, now we shall find, turning beaus, and Indulging themselves in all the extravagance of dress and finery, appearing in regimental Suits, long flowing black gowns, bands, and full bottomd wigs.

[225]   The extravagance of the members went so far at this Sederunt, being extremely elevated at seeing their honorable president exalted for the first time in his Chair of State, as that the following order was made, vizt:

"That on Tuesday, the 31 of December instant, there shall be a ball held at the Stadt house, for the entertainment of the Ladies, at the common expence of the Club, and the president is pleased to appoint the Secretary, to prepare the same against the time appointed."

O Luxury! O excess! whether wilt thou arive at last, wilt thou not, now thou hast begun, go on in an unwearied round, 'till thou hast utterly ruined and anihilated this ancient and honorable Club?

At this Sederunt the Reverend Mr Broadface Round, and Doctor Hereum Thereum, were made honorary members of the Club.

Against the approaching time of the Ball, the Secretary applied all his diligence to make proper preparations, and, as there was to be a cake provided for the Ladies, and having little or no Judgement in the Structure of a cake himself, he went pensively along one morning, βη δε ακεε παρα θινα,³ to consult his honor the president concerning this cake, as a person thorro'ly skilled in that nice part of pastry; and found him sitting in his Saloon in a dishabille, with some of the Club papers before him, which showed the care that this great man took, about every thing relating to the Club, he made his obeisance, which the president was graciously pleased to return, and being permitted to sit down, he opened to his honor, the

[226] business, about which he came, vizt: the Ball ‖ cake, concerning the confabrication of which, he humbly desired his honor, would be pleased to give him his advice.

His honor seemed to wave the Subject, by saying he did not chuse to be concerned in the affair, at which the Secretary seemed to be not alittle astonished, as he discovered by this behaviour a secret, before unknown to him, and this was that his honor was not pleased with the order of the Ball, which Indeed, after some pause, his honor frankly owned to this officer, thus confirming his suspicion, and said, at the same time that out of complaisance to the club, he did not care to Interpose his authority in that affair, but allowed them to proceed in it unmolested, as he found they were

3. "He went silently along the shore of the loud-roaring sea" (*Iliad* 1.34).

bent upon the thing, but had they taken his advice, which they ought to have done, considering his station and dignity, he would have advised them to a much more gentile and polite way of treating the Ladies, than that common and thread bare method of giving a ball. The Secretary Intreated his honor to declare how that was to have been done. After some Sort of reluctancy his honor told him "That it was thus, in the manner of the Christenmass gifts of old times, for, in my notion of things (said he) the old methods, are much the Gentilest and prettiest, and, had it been ordered thus, I should have condescended to make the cake with my own hands, but now, as it is, I shall not concern myself with it, but thus it is," and so he proceeded see-sawing, and rolling up his handcerchef on his knee, for this great man was very apt to do so while he was discoursing or telling of a Story, "in my Grandmothers time, who was a very notable woman, and understood ceremonies as well as any, it was customary to send a Slice of cake, and half a pint of canary or sack, at christenmass, upon a neat Silver ‖ Salver, to every lady in the neighbourhood, and this method I would have [227] had the Club to take to treat the Ladies, instead of that foolish way of giving a ball." The Secretary listened to this with great attention, and breaking Silence, owned that the method was very pritty and Genteel,—but then, honorable Sir, said he, we should have occasion for at least twenty or thirty half pint decanters, or Cruets, for so many Ladies are there in the place, who ought, and will expect to be treated,—That difficulty is soon Removed, Replied the president, for, I could have furnished the Club with twice as many decanters or cruets, if wanted, from my store, at half a crown a piece—upon this the conversation ended, and the Secretary made his leg and took his leave, being Sufficiently convinced, as I believe every one else, who reads this, will be of the reasons his honor had, for dissapproving the ball, and advising the other way of entertaining.

The ball then was held at the time appointed, which happened to be an extreme cold night, and therefore the better for dancing, there were a great many Ladies and Gentlemen, and most of the members of the Club attended, the Cake was froze, but the wine and punch retained their Liquidity, the Longstanding members that chose to dance, danced; and those that chose not, looked on, and drank a bumper now and then to expand the Animal Spirits, by the frigid air drove to the Centre, there were danced many minuets, country dances & Jiggs, and, there was as much bowing, cringing, complimenting, Curtsying, oggling, flurting and Smart repartees, as is usual on such occasions, and the Reverend Mr Sly, tho the gravity of his Cloth, would not permit him to dance, yet he made by much the Smartest figure, in Squiring the Ladies, comparing them, as they stood in a row, to the milky way, and telling them, that he hoped, most of the young Ladies in the Ring, were travelling fast, towards that same Galaxy or milky way, ||

[228] and abundance of other droll witty and facetious repartees, puns, dowble entendres, and gallant Sarcasms passed, 'till that Gentleman, being called upon, by a lady to dance; he pretended to step aside alittle for his hat and gloves, but took care to abscond, and not make his appearance again that night upon the dancing Stage. In fine, every thing was conducted with great elegance, and mirth prevailed in the company, nothing being wanting to compleat all, but the presence of his honor the president, who, by his absenting that night, showed that he was not altogether pleased, with this piece of Gallantry.

As we have given in a preceeding part of this history, the private Character of his honor the president, we shall here give a small Sketch, of what we may call, his clubical Character.

The President, tho' he possessed many good qualities, yet, like other mortal men, on this Side the grave, he had his particular foibles, which I, as his historian, am obliged faithfully to recount, out of the great Regard I have for truth, and I shall promise, to be as little sparing to the other Longstanding members, and even to myself, in that way, as to his honor.

His chief foible was ambition and love of power, a fault peculiar to great men and heroes, this appeared by his extreme desire to grasp as much of that, as he possibly could, by his endeavoring to have all matters transacted in the Club, Solely by his own authority and Influence; by his enforcing and procuring Laws, to lodge the whole governing and managing authority in his own hands; by his extreme tenaciousness of the privileges already granted him, and vehement desire to have more added to them; by his Jealousy of the other members who had any privileges which he was ||

[229] apt groundlessly to Imagine, Jarred or Interfered with his own, this will appear in his future conduct, with regard to the Chancellor, a high officer of the Club, who he thought was a grandee of too great power and Influence, and therefore, he used all means and methods to render him, his office and great Seal, of no effect or Significancy.

He was also very positive, and not to be convinced, by the clearest arguments, where he had the least Suspicion, that these arguments had a tendency to subtract from his Clubical authority, and the dignity of his office.

He was at times very sharp and satirical, while in the Chair, against those who offended him, by any thing they said or did in Club, and the Secretary in particular, felt the poignancy of his Satyr upon many occasions, which made him often scratch, where he did not itch, make wry faces, and sit uneasy in Club.

He was extremely Inattentive, or affected so to be, for the most part, when any member was speaking, or delivering his opinion in Club, particularly, if that Speech or opinion, was not altogether according to his own notions, and, by the bye, his notions and conceptions of things, almost always differed from those of the Club, this Strange inattention he showed, by holding a conversation in whisper, with those who sat next him, while a member was delivering himself to the Chair, nay often, when a member or Stranger drank to him, he would not advert or take any notice, tho' they bawld 'till their throats were sore, and hunchd him 'till their elbows aked, many thought this was only an air of grandure and State, it being peculiar to some Great men to be Inattentive, while address'd by their Inferiors.

He was very fond of punctillios Ceremonies, and distinguishing badges [230] of honor, thinking they contained in themselves something very edifying, expressive and Significant, and the long Standing members soon finding out this weakness, in a Course of a few years, loaded him with ceremonies, and ornamented him with a superfluity of pompous accoutrements, till at last they effectually cured him of this malady, for he smelt a rat, and grew sick and tired of these farces as will appear in the Sequel.

He was precise to the utmost nicety in all his proceedings relating to the Club, both in and out of the Chair, and would be uneasy if a pin was stuck in a wrong place, or any thing out of rank and file in the Club room, or upon the Club table.

Vanity was none of the least of his foibles, and it was thought he had some opinion of the Elegance of his form and features, for, he generally chose, when in the Chair, to sit opposite to a large looking Glass, and to turn and wriggle his body into different attitudes, in order to show himself to himself to the best advantage, to stroke down his face and beard, adjust the foretop of his wig, and to affect a complacent Smile and Smirk of the countenance, tho' at times, when Speeches were made that displeased him, or Snappish replies or retorsions were given him by the Chancellor, there followed an elongation of countenance, and a droping of the Lower Jaw, which some of the members called his timber Countenance, which would have afforded no uncommon hint to the famous Hogarth.

Even when he was in his highest Zenith of power in the Club, and ordered, and did Just as he pleased, he still expressed a Sort of uneasiness and dissatisfaction, that || his power and authority was not greater, which [231] made him often exclaim in conversation, that the members of the Club, had only amused him with a false show, in setting him in a chair of state, and bestowing certain Sham titles and privileges upon him; for that still, notwithstanding all this pomp and ceremony, he looked upon himself as a president and no president, seeing the members would not be ruled entirely by his will, but still acted by their own, tho sometimes his honor would forget this ungrateful Subject, and would in a pleasant humor, compare himself to the King, his State officers to the Nobles or peers, and the other members to the commons, whom he regarded as people of little or no account or Signification, then indeed, would his honor, with a Sweet Smile in his countenance, talk very pleasantly, of our Chancellor, our knight and Champion, our Protomusicus, our attorney General, our Master of Ceremonies, our poet Laureat, our Secretary &ct: for both in his conversation and writing, he assumed the royal Stile of we us and our.

But this worthy and honorable Gentleman, if like other mortal men, he had his little foibles, he was at the same time endued with very great qualities, of which, his forgiveness, long Suffering, and Surprizing patience were none of the least; often has he been Insulted, and affronted even in the Chair, by petulent and Saucy long standing members, and as often has he bore it with heroic resolution, and Surprizing composure of mind; once was he dragged out of it, pulled about the room, tossed and hursled from corner to corner, his ruffles tore, his ensigns of State threatned to be burnt, [232] he himself called a traitor, a tyrant, nay even an old || fool, yet after all this, could this great man forget and forgive; Often has he showd an extreme Solicitude to humor and please the Club, and to provide every thing handsom and Genteel for them, while he has had little thanks for the same, some maliciously alledging, that he did this more out of a vain desire of making a Show, than any other motive. Many a week has he spent, in preparations for Anniversary solemnities, and even ordinary times of serving, he has traversed the whole town twice or thrice in a day, after the Butchers, Tallow Chandlers, and Tobacco pipe merchants, appearing often, notwithstanding the dignity of his office, with troops of these Sort of cattle about him, and would often deign, to carry himself thro' the street, bundles of tobacco pipes, and other such provision for the Club, many a day, and many a night, has he spent and watched in his kitchen, amidst Steam grease and Slush, sweating over the fire, cutting, sliceing, kneading, seasoning, boiling, roasting, stewing, baking and preparing delicacies for the entertainment of the Club, often, while he was racked with the excruciating pains of the gout, has he walked, trotted and run about in great anguish to serve the club, often has he Immerged his feet in cold water, to the great peril of his life, merely to overcome the attacks of the gout, that he might be able to do the

Services of the Club, often has he neglected his own affairs, for the affairs of the Club, and has lost many a night's rest, and wore out his Spectacles in perusing and examining Letters, commissions, petitions, remonstrances, Songs, poems, odes, Summons, epigrams, accrostics, Club conundrums, and other Clubical papers of great ‖ Importance and Significancy, to the [233] danger of his eyesight health and understanding, often has he with great modesty declined being flattered and cajoled by the longstanding members, and Sincerely professed, that, as to power he desired no more of it, than what was Just necessary for the good and wellfare of the Club, and this, he has often declared from the Chair, with the same Sincerity as some of our princes of the Steward family declared from the throne to their obstreporous parliaments. Often has he, with great Complacency and good nature, sung and warbled Sweetly from the Chair, (for he had an excellent small musical pipe,) love ditties and witty Songs, for the entertainment of the long Standing members, tho some were Ill natured enough to say, that he did this out of emulation to Excell Solo Neverout Esqr, Chief musician, in short, his good qualities were so many, that he was the admiration of all members, and all Clubs, and were we to lose, this great and worthy president, heaven only knows when or where we could procure such another.

Chapter III

Of the Introduction of the Club box, and other Important matters.

"Ye Gods! what havoc does ambition make among your works!"—says the Celebrated Mr Addison in the first Scene of his Tragedy of Cato,[1] and, I Introduce this pathetic exclamation, at the beginning of this Chapter very ‖ much *a propos*, as it will be a seasonable preparative to my readers, and [234] prevent their being overmuch Surprized at the dreadful Havoc made by ambition, in this here ancient and honorable Club.

We have seen how Luxury has been Introduced into this here club, and gained now a Strong footing in it, but Luxury is not to be supported without means, there must be wherewithal to supply the Idle and Imaginary wants which it creates, neither can power be supported without friends, and these faithful friends being Slaves to Luxury, must have wherewithal to supply their many wants both real and Imaginary, put into their

---

1. Quoted accurately from Portius's opening speech in Addison's *Cato* (1713).

hands, of consequence, their friendship can neither be gained nor preserved without political greasing as it is called, or in plain terms tipping the Bribe, but whence are the funds to be procured to carry on this game, the answer is natural, we find that ministers of State, and those at the head of affairs, commonly have recourse to taxes upon the poor people, to supply themselves with moneys to be laid out in Secret Services, as they are called, it is Just the same in Clubs, where exorbitant power gains footing, those who have raised themselves to that power, will naturally study and practise ways and means to support and augment it, for it is a true maxim Confirmed by the experience of many ages, that no determined quantum of either power or riches, creates a Satiety, and Indeed it never was known, that either a great Emperor, or a very rich man, declared positively, that they had [235] enough of either, or wanted no more; and we shall soon || see those very practices take place in this here Club, and certain great officers created to support the authority and power of the Chair, and promote its dignity and grandure, but this was done by degrees, and Inch by Inch as it were, and, the members were first of all taxed, under a pretence of raising a fund for Charity, while the manager of that fund, thought of nothing less, in consequence of this, a treasurer was to be created in the Club, who would be an officer useful to the Chair, and a firm friend to the presidential prerogative, and Interest; and, it could not happen otherwise, since the President himself Grasped at, and actually obtained that office of trust, and, in spite of the Sophistry and Subtilety of logicians and metaphysicians; none sure could be a firmer friend to himself, than his very Identical Self, and, the Notion of the Clubs treasury or property, being Intirely in his honor's possession, and at his honor's disposal, when or how he pleased, raised among the members, first Jealousies and fears, then Grumblings, mumblings and discontents, and, last of all dreadful dissentions and bickerings, which had like to have ended in the utter ruin and final dissolution of the Club, but I shall open this Scene by degrees, and display the whole proceedings of the Chair, with regard to the treasury and the creation of great officers, as they follow one another in the order and course of our History.

It was at Sederunt 26th Janry 14th 1745–6, Capt: Serious Social being Steward, that a motion was made in Club by a member (Influenced and prompted, as is supposed, by his honor the president, who always showed an extreme desire to have the purport of this motion established into a Law) that there should be a Club box set on foot, for charity, and other [236] Laudable purposes, this carried || by unanimity, every one at last consenting to it, tho' Jealous Spyplot esqr, an old standing member showed some reluctance, and did not come easily into the thing, fortelling that it would be the cause of wrangling and Discord in the Club, and here indeed he proved a true prophet, as he was also in some other cases. Then was passed the following Law.

Law XX. That in order to raise a fund for Charity, or such other good uses as the Club shall see proper, Sixpence every club night, shall be contributed by every regular member, the payment to be made quarterly, and also, to promote this fund, every honorary member shall contribute five Shillings, at his first admission, and the same Sum yearly afterwards, so long as he continues in the Club, this fund to be disposed of, as the majority of the Club shall determin.

Thus we find by this law, a tax of Sixpence each Sederunt Laid upon the members, and Charity made use of as a pretext, a very bad precedent, and a dangerous Stroke to the liberties of the Club. We shall see in the Sequel how far this fund was applied towards charity, I cannot but observe here, that this here Club took alittle too much upon them, in taxing the honorary members without their own consent; but, I suppose it was thought that they were bound to pay something, for the honor of being called honorary members of this ancient and honorable Club.

Law XXI. That every quarter day, or day of payment, the Contents of the box shall be made known to the members of the Club, and every member shall have a note of the Sum then contained in it delivered to him by the Secretary.

Law XXII. That there shall be two locks and keys to the box, the one [237] to be kept by the president, the other by the Secretary, and the Secretary is to keep the accounts and present the State of them quarterly to the Club.

Law XXIII. That the president shall have a power of calling together the members, at any time when necessity requires, in order to dispose of the charity, and that the fund is to be paid into the Secretary's hands and lodged with the president.

This is an exact transcript from the records of the Laws made on account of the box, we shall find in the Sequel, how strictly they were put in execution, and what all this fracas about charity ended in, after having occasioned a mighty hurly burly and hubbub in the Club, between his honor the president and the long standing members.

By the last recited Law, a new privilege is added to the Chair, vizt: that of calling the members together at pleasure, to dispose of the charity, we shall find this privilege soon extended farther, and a power given to his honor to call the members together by Summons, when, and as often as he pleased, which Indeed, they never had reason to take amiss, for even on the occasions of private Committees, his honor always treated very handsomly as well as at Set Clubs, at this same Sederunt also, the two following Laws were passed.

Law XXIV. That the book of minutes shall always be Lodged in the hands of the Secretary, any law to the contrary notwithstanding, who is to produce it to the Club as often as it is called for.

[238]   *Law XXV.* That whoever stays with the Steward after the hour of eleven, the penalty of one Shilling current money shall be paid by each and every member so transgressing, into the box, at the ensuing meeting of the Club.

This is the first penal law passed in the Club, and it is plainly Intended to promote the Scheme of the box, but we shall soon find what regard was paid to it and every other Law of this Club.

At the following Sederunt on January 28, Solo Neverout Esqr, being Steward, Jealous Spyplot Esqr, presented to the Club, a curious box of black walnut, for which he had the thanks of the Club, formally delivered to him by the Secretary, and his honor the president took Immediate possession of this box, generously putting ten Shillings into it, to show a good example to the Long-standing members, his honor kept one of the keys of this box, and the Secretary the other.

Chapter IV

The Introduction of set Speeches into the Club, and the members that made the Greatest figure that way.

So Inherent is vanity in human nature, that it seems to be Inextricably Incorporated and Ingrained with it, so as that it cannot be separated or Extracted, by the most Subtile Chemistry, wash'd away by the strongest Suds or purged off by the purifying fire of purgatory itself.

This Inherent principle of vanity appears in nothing more, than the
[239] great desire most men have to Speech || making, and engrossing to themselves a great share of the talk in all places of rendezvous, such as Coffee houses, Taverens, Teatables, but more particularly in Clubs; as for those who hold forth in public assemblies, such as the members of both houses of parliament, the Gentlemen of the long Robe and of the Crape; The Theatrical Emperors, kings, Princes, heros and heroins, the Celebrated quacks of the Age; and the Tyburn Heroes and worthies, there may be other motives besides that of vanity to tempt those licenced holders forth, such as the

desire of pecuniary Rewards, offices of honor, places of profit, titles, and what we call a comfortable livelihood or a Glorious exit, Some of these orators, tho they seem to perorate powerfully for hire, yet they use the words of other men, to whom nature has been more liberal in the gifts of wit and Invention, than to the orators themselves, many of our pulpit orators for Instance, only Deliver the words of one Doctor Tillotson, one Doctor Smallridge, one Dr Clerk, one Dr Barrow and one Dr South,[1] with very few additions or Interpolations of their own, which makes it differ from the form, in which it was delivered from the mouths of the original authors, only as a hash, or Second hand dish does from the whole meat of which it is Compounded, being cut and slash'd and mash'd, and divided in a very curious manner, with the addition of a Sophisticated Sauce to disguise the true relish of the meat, our Theatrical declaimers Indeed are Intirely Indebted for their matter, to a Certain Shakespear, a certain Row,[2] a certain Congreve & others; || our orators at Westminster hall, whether [240] parliamentary or bar Declaimers, have Inexhaustible funds of discourse, from the printed proceedings and debates of parliament, and from the huge and ponderous volumes of Reports Entries, and Law Cases and precedents from time Immemorial. Our Stage Itinerants are Indebted much to the Ingenious composers of Quack bills,[3] of which numberless Specimens may be collected from the news papers, to suit all cases, and also to the facetious Elocution of that famous and Ingenious Gentleman ycleped Merry Andrew, Jack pudding, or Pickle herring,[4] and the worthies of Tyburn, to the learned Geniuses of Grubstreet, who often pen for their use last Speeches and dying words, which Speeches or words they never once

---

1. John Tillotson (1630–1694) was a Cambridge Latitudinarian who became archbishop of Canterbury. George Smalridge (1663–1719) was bishop of Bristol whose character Addison praised and whose sermons Samuel Johnson placed in the first class of those preached by English divines. Samuel Clarke (1675–1729), an English divine generally regarded as the first of English metaphysicians after Locke's death in 1704, published numerous sermons and treatises. Isaac Barrow (1630–1677), professor of Greek, geometry, and mathematics at Cambridge, was the author of *Exposition of the Creed, Decalogue, and Sacraments* (London, 1669), *Euclidis Elementa* (London, 1655), and *A Treatise of the Pope's Supremacy* (London, 1680). Robert South (1634–1716), a great court preacher favored by Charles II, was known for his humorous, pithy sermons.

2. Nicholas Rowe (1674–1718), a popular playwright, was the author of *Tamerlane* (1702), *The Fair Penitent* (1703), and numerous other plays, including *Lady Jane Grey* (1715).

3. Hamilton's burlesque of quack advertisements appeared in the *Md. Gaz.,* Apr. 12, 1749.

4. Merry Andrew, a buffoon or attendant on a quack doctor, was said to derive from Andrew Boorde (ca. 1490–1549), physician to Henry VIII noted for his eccentricity. Jack Pudding was a clown or mountebank who may have performed tricks such as swallowing large quantities of black pudding. Pickle-herring, the German term for a clown or buffoon, derived from a humorous character of that name in an early-17th-century play.

thought of or delivered, and which penitential orations are often Cryd about by the hawkers in their own hearing, before the cart has left them pendulous between heaven and earth, or the Inexorable hempen noose with cruel gripe has stop'd the volley of oaths and curses proceeding from their Inebriated throats.

But these orators that hold forth in Clubs are prompted and spur'd on Solely by vanity, and they can Surely have no other motive but this, seeing it is out of a desire to Instruct and Inform their fellow members (which supposes a Superiority of understanding in the said Club orators) that they take upon themselves the character and office of declaimers.

[241]   The desire to show a graceful action in the delivery of an Oration, may be an Incentive to many to become Speech makers; especially if we consider, that many orators have such barren fancies, that they cannot find matter enough, to frame a discourse of any Length, and would make but a very Silly figure, without some graceful action or gesture of body. And indeed, we often find stark nonsense, go much better off, with a proper and violent gesticulation, than the most finished good sense with none at all, this is so true a proposition, that Demosthenes, the famous Athenian Orator, being asked, what was the principal qualification of a declaimer? answered, Action.—what the Second?—replied action.—what the third?—still action, and so on to Infinity,⁵ and thus, we find clearly exemplified in these our days, in our Itinerant preachers, and holders forth, The Reverend Mr Whitefield, the New light men and Methodists, and also in many of our Quaker (particularly female) preachers, who, tho' there is nothing at all in any thing they say, yet never fail to surprize and move their hearers, by the strength of their action, and bodily gesture alone.

It is more than probable, that the members of this ancient and honorable Club, were, at this time actuated by this Vanity only, which made them feel an Invincible propensity to speech making, for, it could not be from any prospect of gain or reward, that they were prompted to become orators, since they were so far from receiving or even expecting any reward or præmium or perquisite for it that I do not understand, that any one member, who set up for a Club declaimer, earn'd so much as thanks for his trowble.

[242]   The first long standing member that was seized with this pestilent itch of speech making, was the Secretary, who was one, not the least stocked with vanity, in this here Club, as I promised before, to give the Character of this Club officer, I think it will come well in this place.

5. This story appears in Cicero, *De oratore* 3.213.

[From the archives of our club, look upon the Scribe
Who plows out your words, O Jole! with eternal pen,
And also recites your deeds in elegant style,
Whom you consider able to defeat Nestor at talking.]

[facing page 241]

The Secretary executed the Laborious part of his office tollerably well, by entering all the proceedings of the Club in the book of records, but then, his natural vanity, or opinion of his own self Sufficiency appeared glaringly even in this the execution of his office, for he often would, without the advice of his honor the president, or the Club, enter matters, in what manner and form he pleased, which was often the Cause of great disgust and heart burnings betwixt his honor & the Longstanding members, since the president often urged and mantained, that the Secretary had no business to enter any thing there, but by his order and direction, and, that nothing relating to what the members did or said, had any title to a place in these Records, but his Actions and his Sayings alone should be entered, while on the other hand, the members thought, that their proceedings, debates and determinations, had as good a title to a place in the records, as the acts and Sayings of his honor the president; Thus the Club and the President differed among themselves, and both with the Secretary, who, notwithstanding the many grave and Sharp rebukes, which he had from the honorable Chair, and checks and threatnings from the Club, went on in his usual way and would still enter matters as he pleased, an Instance of perverse obstinacy as well as of vanity and Self conceit, and Indeed, a positive [243] and wayward humor, was none of the least failings || which this club officer could be charged with, by which he often Introduced confusion into the Government of this here Club, thereby drawing the Indignation of his honor the president upon himself and the members; This Secretary was also of a Scheming, plotting, Restless disposition, and his plots and Schemes, tho generally carried on, under pretence of doing honor to the President, and for the advantage of the Club, yet, for the most part, terminated in mischievous purposes and attempts, either to make tools of the Longstanding members, or to derogate from the honor and prerogative of the honorable Chair, at least, this Gentleman was much belied by his honor and the Longstanding members, if he was not a Sly, cunning, Insinuating, deceitful, mischief making member, the continual Author and promoter of Brawls, wrangles, Jealousies, Grumblings, heartburnings, hubbubs and hurly burlys in this here ancient and honorable Club, and it will appear in the Sequel, when we give an account of the *Cap of State,* and the *Box No 1,* that these allegations against the Secretary were not grounded on Suspicion only; Some indeed affirmed that the Secretary was a deep politician, but his honor the president was always angry when this was mentioned and spoke of him as a person only skilled in what is called *Low Craft,* however, this may be said in his commendation, that he was a very constant and punctual attendant on the Club, and spared no pains to do every thing for its interest and advantage, where it did not Interfere or clash with his own, or stand in the way of his ambitious Schemes, to advance his own Influence in the Club, and make himself a person of weight and Importance, and in this indeed he resembled many other Secretaries and politicians, who, In Indifferent matters can give very good advice, but whenever Self is to be served, that must of necessity be done, tho every body else should go to the devil.

At Sederunt 29th febr: 25th 1745/6,[6] Capt: Seemly Spruce being first deputy in the Chair, and Capt: Bully Blunt Steward, ‖ the Secretary stood [244] up and Informed the Club that he had a discourse or Speech to deliver, and craved permission to deliver it; this Speech we must observe, had been prepared of his own head, without orders from the Club, to which he was in all probability prompted by his vanity, having surely this opinion of himself, that he had an excellent knack at Speech making, and that the Club could not otherwise than be mightily entertained and Instructed, with this Sort of Exercise, he had leave given him to deliver this discourse, tho' not without some grumblings from Capt: Blunt the Steward; who said he was for no Innovations of this Sort, Damn the Speeches says he, we meet together in this here Club to smoke, Chat, and put about the bowl, and not to hear and make Speeches, however, being permitted to deliver this Speech, he put himself into a proper attitude for it, and Imagining that he had Cond it by heart, did not use his papers, but began to repeat it with a tollerable good grace; his Subject was the advantages reaped from Society, and some encomiums on Clubs, a thread bare and trite Subject, but put together in a tollerable Stile, The Secretary had gone thro' one half of this oration, smoothly enough, without hesitating, and the Longstanding members had given a close attention to it, when an odd Circumstance happened, which made the orator stop short all of a Sudden, and obliged him to fumble in his pockets for his papers, which, having pulled out, he read very distinctly the remaining part of it, the occurrence was this, Drawlum Quaint Esqr, a Longstanding member, was more attentive than any one else to this harangue, and the better to swallow what was delivered by the Secretary sat ‖ with his neck streeched out, his mouth wide open, motion- [245] less, every limb of his body remaining as still, as if he had been a piece of Sculpture, and, in his right hand he grasped his tobacco pipe, the extremity of the Stem about two Inches from his mouth, in the very same altitude as it was, when he pulled it from his lips, this figure struck the Secretary, (happening to turn his eyes that way) in such a manner, that it obliterated at once, from his memory, all that he had been saying, and all that he had yet

6. Hamilton apparently was well aware that he had reversed Sederunts 28 and 29.

Mr Secretary Scribble delivering a Speech in Club —

[facing page 243]

to say on the Subject, so finding himself at a Stand, and that he could by no means recover himself, he stoped short for some time, and had recourse to his papers.

The Club seemed to approve of this Speech, at least they did not condemn it, and they so well liked of this custom Introduced by the Secretary, that they ordered Mr Drawlum Quaint, to prepare a Speech to entertain the Club at next Sederunt, and to chuse his Subject, and we shall soon find some other members excelling this way, vizt: Mr Solo Neverout, Capt: Serious Social, Mr Jealous spyplot & Mr Smoothum Sly, and even his honor the president himself in a remarkable manner, display'd his Rhetorical and oratorial learning, in an elegant Speech that he delivered to the Club, which we shall relate in it's proper place.

At Sederunt 28th Febr: II, 1745–6, Slyboots Pleasant Esqr being Steward, a hot dispute arose in Club concerning the Club Box, and the honorary members, vizt: whether the money in the box, should be disposed of, at the discretion of his honor the president, by the direction of the Club or by both conjointly, and, whether the Club had any power to tax the honorary members, and oblige them to ‖ contribute to this box, many violent and [246] warm Speeches were made on both Sides of the argument, for five Sederunts successively, there was abundance of bawling, Sharp railing, invective, repartee, alittle Swearing, and much taking of Snuff, both in a literal, and metaphorical Sense, at last, it was determined at Sederunt 32d April 15th 1746, Dumpling Gundiguts Esqr being Steward

Law XXVI. That the Box shall continue, according to it's primitive Institution (vid: Law 20, 21, 22, 23.)

Thus we see in part, the prophesy of Jealous Spyplot Esqr come to pass, with regard to this box, heats and dissentions already arising in Club about it, tho' as yet, there was not above 40 Shillings in the treasury, a strong Instance of that propensity in human nature, to wrangle and differ, about the veriest triffles where Interest is concerned, a Specimen also, of the ambition of presidents, who struggle and Contend, still for an addition to their power and Influence, they, never being satisfied, with the quantum of power allotted them, let it be ever so great.

At Sederunt 30th March 11th 1745–6, the Revd Mr Smoothum Sly being deputy in the Chair, and Capt: Seemly Spruce Steward; Drawlum Quaint Esqr, Delivered a long Speech to the Club, the Subject of which was honesty, this Speech was delivered without notes, but was very sarcastical and Severe, the Gentleman took almost all professions, offices and callings to task, allowing a very small portion of honesty to any Station in life, particularly to Sheriffs and other public officers, tho he seemed to be very

Franklin Quaint Esq; delivering a Speech in Club

[facing page 247]

partial with regard to the Gentlemen of the Law (the orator being himself a
|| Lawyer) this longstanding member had a peculiar action when he spoke,   [247]
which attracted the Eyes of the audience, and fixed their attention as much
as the Subject on which he harangued, he kept his body still and motion-
less, his head and Shoulders stooping forwards, extending his neck to a
considerable length, his right arm streched out, with alittle bend of the
elbow, the forefinger of his right hand in a pointing posture, wch he moved
gently up and down, his chin, when he made a pause, dropping down on
his breast, his left hand under the waste band of his breeches, and, when he
had occasion to stop in his discourse, (which was pritty often) to consider
of what he was next to say, he would like many orators spit or hawk, or
Cough, or yawn, and, for these excellent qualities in oratorial action, as well
as for his elegant Stile and phraze of *this here* and *that there,* he was soon
after promoted, to the honorable place of Speaker to the Club, as we shall
relate in the Sequel, the Satyr of this Discourse was chiefly pointed at Mr
Neverout, then Sheriff of the County, who, at a preceeding Sederunt, undertook to prove that Mr Quaint was Dead, which argument he managed
so artfully and Sophistically, that he seemed to Convince the Club that he
really was a dead member, and they actually voted him such, Mr Neverout,
the same night Elevated with his Skill in argumentation, tho' Indeed, he
had borrowed most of his reasoning from the Celebrated Isaac Bickerstaff
Esqr, in his famous controversy with Mr Patridge,[7] Student in Physic and
astrology, thought he could || go farther in displaying his great abilities, and   [248]
exhibit a Specimen of his poetical Genius, the occasion was this, Mr Quaint
had wrote a Satyr on him and some others, which he entituled the *Reverend
Scout,* In which was a relation of an adventure of Solo Neverout Esqr, Mr
Secretary Scribble, and Mr Slyboots pleasant, who had one night a Set
meeting with some Celebrated Nymphs of the town, at one of these polite
assemblies, called twopenny hops, which was held at the house of Mr
George Downie Musicioner, these Gallants and their Nymphs were observed from a low window in the Street, by two Scouts or spies, who,
having Informed Councellor Quaint therewith, he wrote the aforesaid Satyr, In which he distinguishes Mr Neverout, by the name of *Littlebreeches;*
Neverout still resenting this, was resolved to answer it in the same Satyrical

7. Hamilton is alluding to Jonathan Swift's "A Vindication of Isaac Bickerstaff Esq; Against
What Is Objected to Him by Mr. Partridge, in His Almanack for the Present Year 1709,"
especially the passage beginning: "Without entering into Criticisms of *Chronology* about the
Hour of his Death; I shall only prove, that Mr. Partrige is not alive" (*The Prose Works of
Jonathan Swift,* ed. Herbert Davis [Oxford, 1939–1968], II, 162).

and poetical Strain, but never compleated any more than one Couplet, which he made in Club, and was as follows.

> Whilst at the window, stood two prying pimps,
> Scratching and wishing, for the Buxom Nymphs.

This, we may say, was the last effort, made by the muse of this Ingenious Gentleman, the first we have given an account of in the preceeding book, we shall Indeed find in this History two other poetical performances, which he pretended to pass off for his own, but one is plainly borrowed from the Celebrated Rabelais, the other, excepting five or Six lines, was Composed by some other members of the Club.

These two great geniuses for sometime contended together with weapons of wit, and, we must own, that Councellor Quaint at last got the better, for, he gave the first provocation and had the last word to himself, this noted oration of his intirely silencing his antagonist.

[249]   At Sederunt 31, April 1, 1746, Slyboots Pleasant Esqr, being deputy in the Chair, and the Revd Mr Smoothum Sly Steward, Mr Solo Neverout, according to an order of last Sederunt, delivered a discourse of Love and Lovers, he used Notes, and had such a graceful action and delivery, and withal handled the Subject in so elegant and polite a manner, not making one single Slip, (unless you reckon his pronouncing the word *Phystologists*,[8] *Phigiogolists*, according to the modish accent and pronounciation, was a *lapsus Lingua* as the learned term it) that the Club was Intirely satisfied with his performance, requesting him to deliver it over again, which he did very Complacently, and with a Singular good grace; There was not one single touch at Satyr in the whole piece, tho many Imagined that he would have taken this opportunity, to pay off Scores with Mr Councellor Quaint.

The Reverend Mr Smoothum Sly, and Mr Ignotus Warble, an honorary member, were ordered to prepare discourses to be delivered in Club, the Subjects *ad libitum*.

At Sederunt 32, April 15th 1746, Dumpling Gundiguts Esqr being Steward, the following Law was made.

Law XXVII. That all Cases, excepting that of the admission of members, and the disposal of the money in the Club-box, shall be determined by a majority of voices.

Mr Smoothum Sly, at this Sederunt, delivered his discourse, which was upon civil government, and had the approbation of the Club in general, excepting his honor the president, who alledged he spoke too much in favor of popular liberty, to the hurt of prerogative and power in rulers, this

8. Perhaps *phytologist*, a botanist.

raising some small dispute in Club, between his honor and the Longstand-
ing mem- || bers, Mr Councellor Quaint, growing warm in the argument, [250]
told his honor, That all power rested in the Club, for, as they had placed
his honor in *that there* Chair, so they could displace him again, whenever
they pleased, a wicked whiggish maxim, absurdly mantained by such as are
enimies to the Sacred and Indelible Character of presidents; His honor
took great offence at this, and threatned to resign the Chair, getting out of
it with great precipitation, but, at the entreaty of some of the members, was
prevailed upon to resume that honorable Seat, tho' many thought that
these entreaties were needless, as his honor, upon Second thoughts, would
have done the same without them.

It was ordered that the Revd Mr Broadface Round, and Mr Abraham
Bumper, honorary members, should each of them prepare a discourse to be
delivered in Club, and also, that Mr Secretary Scribble, should prepare a
Speech to be delivered at next Sederunt, the Subjects of these discourses,
being left to their own Choice.

At next Sederunt, which was the 33d on the 29th of April, the same
year, Drawlum Quaint Esqr, being Steward, the Revd Mr Broadface Round,
delivered a discourse upon Charity, which had very great approbation from
the honorable Chair, upon this account chiefly, as it seemed to favor and
promote the Scheme of the box, of which his honor was passionatly fond,
for certain political Reasons above mentioned, and his honor never failed to
extoll every thing, that squared with the Interest of the Chair.

Mr Ignotus warble, an honorary member, delivered also a discourse
upon cheerfullness, in which he Introduced, a very pritty Comparison || or [251]
parallel, between Mr Neverout and Socrates, This Comparison was striking, being entirely new, and what none else would have thought of, it was
built upon Mr Neverout's being a batchellor, and of an amorous complexion, both which circumstances were Socrates's case, before this, the Club
never found out any such Similitude, between this moderen batchellor and
that Ancient philosopher, and were conscious of no other, than that asperity
of countenance, or hardness of favor, as some call it, peculiar to them both,
the Secretary excused himself at this Sederunt, as not yet being prepared to
deliver his discourse, and requested longer time, which was easily Granted
him.

Thus did these Club orators, shine, each in his particular sphere, in
declaiming or speech making, but Drawlum Quaint Esqr outshone them
all, still excepting his honor the President who would not (Indeed should
not) yield to any in Clubical Qualifications, and, whom we shall soon see
acting the Orator in Club, in a most Surprizing manner.

At this Sederunt, a Committee was appointed to prepare matters for Solemnizing the Club anniversary now at hand, this Committee was ordained to meet upon tuesday the 13th of May, the day Immediatly preceeding wednesday the 14th, and the honorable the president was privileged to serve always on this Anniversary day, the Club dispensing not only on this, but on all other occasions of his honor's serving, with the Law of one dish, which was only a matter of form, since he did not wait for such dispensation, but broke thro' that law long before he mounted the Chair, these two privileges more were now added to the Chair, by which the Longstanding members flattered his honor's vanity, and encouraged and countenanced his turn for Luxury.

[252]   ## Chapter V

The Celebration of the Club Anniversary, for the first time,
The Institution of the Club badges, and other significant matters.

The custom of Celebrating Anniversaries, has been practised and kept up in all ages, by all civilized nations and people, whether Jews, christians, pagans, or Mahometans, but to go no farther than the christian countries, who have Indeed been the fondest of any, in observing this ancient and universal Custom, we find so many anniversaries of Saints, anniversary fasts, and anniversary feasts, that in some Countrys, particularly Spain, whose Inhabitants are the best catholics in Christendom, above two thirds of the year is taken up by these Anniversaries, by some called holidays, these holidays are days of liberty, or rather Licentiousness, like the ancient Saturnalia at Rome, and every one is at full freedom, to bestow his time as he pleases, (excepting only, that they are debard working at their lawful Calling or trade) either in devotion drunkenness or debauchery, and tho' there be but few who chuse the first, and most of these few hipocrites and bigots, yet all pretend, that it is a religious regard to those anniversary holidays, feasts, and fasts, that makes them observe and keep them so strictly, and, as religion is a Subject, about which men have differed more widely and split into more numerous factions and Sects, than any thing else, so the disputes, wrangles and brawls have been carried to an excessive height among Christians, about these anniversaries. What differences have [253] there not been about christenmass ‖ the grand anniversary of christendom; have not some been for the celebration and observation of it and some not, have not some called it a holy-day and some with great propriety a folly-day; have not some said it was of Christian, and apostolic Institution, and some of pagan original, which they prove from the old Scots name *Yule,* or *Jule,* derived, as they say from Julius Cæsar, a pagan Roman Emperor, whose birth day they confidently affirm it was, dont even the most Zealous observers of it, spend it in a fantastical medley of devotion and mirth; do they not one day attend divine Service, Sacraments and Sermons, and another frolicks tricks, and what they call Christenmass gambols, and dont some fanaticks (as they are called) celebrate it in ridicule, by a Sort of mock feast, in which the principal dish is a goose pye; Is it not a time of Idleness, drunkeness and debauchery among most of the Common people, and of frolic and foolish pleasantry among many of the better Sort, In fine, the enimies of this Sacred Institution, do not stick to say, that the wicked priests of the Second or third century of the Christian æra, Instituted it as an Indulgence to their poor Slaves the people, allowing them a certain time in which to be as Idle and Intemperate as they pleased, to appease or Check the Clamours raised against their Sacred brotherhood, who had assumed to themselves the liberty of Indulging in Idleness and Luxury all the year round, thereby Imitating the example and policy of Mahomet their brother Cheat and Imposture, who to appease certain clamours against his own Incontinency, allowed his disciples the privilege of having four wives at once & as many concubines as they could mantain; There is also the anniversary of Easter, which is not fixed to this day, nor is it determined by Christendom in general, upon what day it shall be kept, being one of those Sorts of comical feasts of the Church called moveable feasts, and thus, different churches keep it on || different days, what fury, what rage, what [254] bloodshed, massacre & murder has not been exhibited in the Christian world, about fixing of this very anniversary, But to descend to particulars & come nigher home to our own country and Religion, with what Solemn mourning and humiliation, doth the Church of England now, celebrate the Anniversary of the Martyrdom of that most pious Saint and Martyr king Charles I. who Surely deserved to be Canonized as much as the Holy Archbishop Thomas Becket, since he was as great a champion, for that Idol of his family *Arbitrary power,* in civil matters, as the latter was for that Idol of the Roman See, absolute and uncontrouled Sway, both in Civil and Ecclesiastical affairs; How, upon this Solemn occasion does the nation then mourn for the Sins and trespasses of the nation, what grief, what contrition is not expressed, what holy Lessons and prayers are not read on the occasion, and, what volleys of christian like Curses and terms of abuse, are not thrown upon the wicked presbyterians, by the Zealous preachers at this time, but let us see how the high flowen presbyterians celebrate this anniversary, do they not demean themselves with the same Christian Spirit wisdom and Sagacity with their bretheren of the other Side, when out of a pious Spite and resentment, they, as it were openly, take the guilt of the Death of this Royal Martyr, (as he is called) upon themselves, by Ironically and Impudently, dressing, preparing and eating, a *calves head,* on that very day.

Other Anniversaries there are of less note, that is, where particular Cities, corporations, Societies or Clubs are only Concerned; Such are the anniversaries of the Birth or Coronation of princes, which are celebrated
[255] commonly by ‖ firing of great guns, by exhibiting of Squibs, crackers, fireworks, Skyrockets, Illuminations, bonfires, compotations and balls; The Anniversary of the gunpowder treason is yet, and I hope ever will be kept, in Brittain, Ireland and British America, In commemoration of that Singular delivery from a horrid and bloody popish plot, tho' the Roman Catholics, according to their wonted assurance, deny that there ever was such a plot; There is also the Grand Anniversary of the Lord Mayor of London, on which the worshipful aldermen observe the Ancient Custom of eating a great quantity of Custard, and the moderen mode of devouring mighty loads of Turtle, for which luscious dish we are Indebted to the west Indies, and also swallow down floods of Burgundy Champain, Claret and other outlandish liquors (instead of the Stout beer of old England,) with which it is said they often before the evening of that Joyful day get as drunk as Emperors and Lords.

Clubs also have their Anniversaries, which they Celebrate by solemn processions and feasts, the Anniversary of Saint John Baptist, is a great and Jolly day, with the ancient and honorable Club of free and accepted Masons, who used to strut in grand procession, with all their ornaments, Jewels, badges and ensigns on that day, Till the Burlesque fraternity of Scald Miserables,[1] Instituted a comic procession, in Imitation of them; ornamented with riders on asses Arsy-versy, dungcarts, mops, broomsticks, dishclouts, and Soot-bags, much in the Nature and humor of a Skimmington procession,[2] which Gelastic pomp and pegeantry, put a stop to the

---

1. The Scald Miserables were early-18th-century mock Freemasons, who rode on donkeys through the streets of London escorting a hearse, in which a tattered ragamuffin represented the Grand Master, followed by a bawling troop carrying columns and waving Masonic symbols.
2. An old custom in rural parts of England and Scotland, whereby nagging wives and unfaithful husbands were publicly ridiculed in effigy by a procession of their neighbors; the origin of the name is uncertain.

other, and ever since, that Right worshipful fraternity ‖ have left the street [256] clear, for their mock bretheren the Scald miserables, and make their processions in a more private manner, Round the Great hall, where they hold their general Communications.

The Ancient and honorable Tuesday Club, In Imitation of this ancient and universal Custom of Celebrating anniversaries, Thought fit, at Sederunt 34th May 14th, 1746, The Honorable Mr President Jole being Steward, to Celebrate the anniversary of the Club's Institution, by holding a great feast, and wearing badges, the feast was prepared and given by the honorable the president, and was managed in a very polite and elegant manner; at this first anniversary Indeed, there was no procession, only two of the Long-standing members, vizt: Capt: Blunt, and Solo Neverout Esqr, marched forth, with their badge ribbons, to meet his honor the president, as he came from his own house to that of Capt: Seemly Spruce, where the Anniversary was celebrated.

These badges, by order of the committee, which met at the Secretaries house, and of which Solo Neverout Esqr was Chairman, and the Reverend Mr Smoothum Sly, and Drawlum Quaint Esqr, longstanding members, and the Reverend Mr Broadface Round, and Mr Ignotus Warble, honorary members, were the Committee appointed, and Mr Secretary Scribble Clerk Comttee: The Committee Issued an order, which was Solemnly presented to his honor the president, in full Club, by Solo Neverout Esqr, Chairman, with which the Club Concurred and passed into a Law, vizt:

Law XXVIII. Ordered by the Committee, that to morrow, being wednesday, the 14th Instant May, the anniversary of the Institution of this here Club, each ‖ member shall wear a badge, fastened to a belt of yellow Rib- [257] ban, which badge, shall be a piece of card, cut into a round form, in the Center of which, shall be writ in large characters THE TUESDAY CLUB, and underneath *Libertas et natale Solum,*[3] 1746, and upon a label round the edge of the Card, the proper motto of the Club, *Concordia res parvæ crescunt,*[4] and that this badge shall be wore, by every regular, and every honorary member, that shall attend the Club meetings on the Anniversary, from this time forth, so long as the Club is in being.

This badge, we find at first was very simple, and here the Club Imitated the great example, of the Ancient and Venerable Tuesday (or whin bush) Club of Lanneric; whose badge as we observed before is only a Sprig of furz, but they differed from them in this, that they adopted a few Scrapes

3. "Liberty and native soil."
4. "Small endeavors flourish through unity" (Sallust, *Jurguitha* 10.6).

of latin, trite or common enough for their motto and Inscription, and such
was the plainness and Simplicity of the whin bush Club, that they had none
in any language whatsoever, tho their badge might have born such a motto,
as the Scots Thistle, vizt: *Nemo me Impune lacesset,*[5] seeing furz is rather
more beset with prickles than the thistle, but the Reason why this ancient
and venerable Society, rejected any such pompuous motto, was, as I conjecture, this, they were Jealous, that some acute wits, would clap to it some
foolish or Impertinent Interpretation, or Comment, as they did to the
other, that is *None shall scratch me without paying dear for their familiarity, or
Catching the itch,* which is a distemper, to which it is said the Scots Nation,
are extremly liable, and for that reason, have become the Just ridicule of
some Smarts, who perfectly know when ridicule is Justly and appositely
placed; and from this rare Joke only has proceeded an Infinite flow of
delicate wit and Satir.

[258]   It will be proper here, to give a
figure of this Simple badge, as it
appeared, at its first Invention and
Institution, for some time after it had
several additions and alterations made
upon it, the Simple Card being converted to a resplendent medal of Silver
dowble Gilt, and some other Ingenious devices added to it, an
exact description of which we
shall exhibit, in its proper
place.

This Badge Committee issued their Summons for Mr Ignotus warble,
an honorary member, to appear before the Club, at next Sederunt, to answer what should then and there be laid to his Charge, which he refused to
obey, they also humbly addressed his honor the president, that he would be
pleased to deliver a Speech from the Chair, upon Tuesday the 27th of this
Instant May, His honour so far complied, as to promise to deliver a discourse from the chair, which he did on the 8th of July following, as we shall
relate in the Sequel.

The Secretary at this anniversary delivered a discourse to the members
upon Clubs, in which he gave a succinct General History of these Illustrious Societies, their antiquity, Importance, frame, constitution and government, which speech met with approbation, but not being entered in the

5. "Nobody provokes me with impunity."

Club records, it is now Irrecoverably lost, whether there was something flat or unentertaining in this Speech, or something unintelligible, as that Club orator affected a learned Stile, peculiar to himself, or some fault in the manner of delivering it, he having used notes, we ‖ cannot now positively   [259] determin, but, it was observed, that some Gentlemen, Invited that night to the Club, fell fast asleep, while the Secretary held forth, and with some difficulty were roused by pinching and hunching, one passage in it bordered alittle on the Gelastic, for one of the members, vizt: Mr Dumpling Gundiguts, a Gentleman of a Clumpish Genius, and not at all of a risible disposition, was observed to laugh.

We have in the foregoing part of our History, observed upon the use and Significancy of Badges, and we shall observe here, that this ancient and honorable Club, showed their wisdom and Sagacity, in Inventing and using a badge, for the members of their Society, to distinguish themselves from those of other societies.

Badges have been used by great Empires and nations, and by armies in warlike expeditions, the badge of the Roman Empire was a spread Eagle, and as this is a royal bird, it was a proper type of the grandure and dignity of that vast empire, and its being spread, was a proper figure of its extent; The Turkish Empire uses a crescent, to signify, that it is still upon the growing hand, and this ensign also, shows the great Regard the Mahomedans, pay to their feasts of the new moon, The Crusards, when they went out to extirpate the Infidels, wore a red cross, to signify that they were christian Soldiers, and that they delighted in the blood of those that were enimies to the Cross.

Several Illustrious orders of knighthood, wear badges proper to their order, The Stars and Garters of England, are now, and have been for many years noble ensigns of honor and family, we all know the origin of the ‖ most noble order of the knights of the garter, and the rise of their badge   [260] and motto; the first being no other than the garter of a Lady of Quality, which she dropt, in dancing with that brave and heroic prince Edward III, at a ball, and she, suspecting some waggish Intention in that monarch, when she felt his hands fumbling about the Skirts of her petticoats, as he stooped to pick it up, took offence, after the manner of women, at this seeming Insult upon her modesty, on which that Gallant prince exclaimed *Hon'y soit qui mal y pense,* which Sentence of old french, signifies no more than, Shame be to him who evil thinks, and these words have ever since become the Motto of this Noble and Illustrious order, with which many of our European princes have been Invested. I cannot help here taking notice, (as America is the Scene of our History) of an order of Virginian knights that were founded about 30 or 40 years agoe, and I know not but may still subsist; His majesties ancient colony of Virginia is stocked with Inhabitants, which Consist of two Classes, the Grandees and the Common people, the first Class are fond of pomp Show and extravagance, and make a Shift to cast a fine dash in dress and equipage, without any certain estates to support it, as for the plebs, we only observe that they are very poor and very miserable, and therefore highly dispised by the Grandees, these Grandees being fond of some particular badge of distinction, Instituted, as I have said, some years agoe, an order of knighthood among themselves, of which, since I have not learnt the true name, I shall venture to call them by that of [261] the Tra- ‖ montane knights, or the knights of the horse Shoe,[6] their badge being a bit of Gold in the form of a horse Shoe, with this Inscription, *Juvat transcendere montes,*[7] for these Cavalier adventurers had exhibited a Specimen of heroism and true Courage, by travelling over the mountains, and having viewed a large tract of a wild uncultivated country, returned home again, all Safe and Sound from this dangerous expedition.

The herald's office shows how fond even families are of badges and marks of distinction, all great families, and even almost all little families, and late upstarts, having some badge or Symbol, which they call their *Coat of arms,* and which they wear upon their furniture coaches and equipage, with which they adorn their houses by way of picture, and which they engrave upon their plate, tho' this custom is originally gothic, and took its rise first in the days of Chivalry, when every Soldier in the field of battle, wore a Mark to distinguish him, least, his vizor being down, he should be mistaken by a friend for a foe, and afterwards this depicted Shield, like Horaces lyre, was hung up for a badge of honor, so that *mutatis mutandis*[8] it might be said by these Gothic heroes,

6. Hamilton is referring to the surveying expedition Gov. Alexander Spotswood of Virginia led to the Blue Ridge Mountains in 1716. The nickname Knights of the Golden Horseshoe stems from Spotswood's having given each man in the company a small golden horseshoe as a souvenir. See Edward P. Alexander, "An Indian Vocabulary from Fort Christanna, 1716," *VMHB*, LXXIX (1971), 303–313, and his edition of *The Journal of John Fontaine: An Irish Huguenot Son in Spain and Virginia, 1710–1719* (Williamsburg, Va., 1972), 13–19, 101–109. In both works, Alexander states that the romanticization of the Spotswood expedition began in 1845 with William Alexander Caruthers's *The Knights of the Horseshoe: A Traditionary Tale of the Cocked Hat Gentry in the Old Dominion,* but Hamilton's remarks show that a romantic tradition surrounding the Tramontane Knights had already developed, if only in a minor way, more than a century before Caruthers's novel. Before Hamilton, too, the Reverend George Seagood had printed the English translation of Arthur Blackamore's *Expeditio ultramontana* in the *Maryland Gazette,* June 17 and 24, 1729 (reprinted by Earl G. Swem, Richmond, Va., 1960).

7. "It is pleasant to cross mountains."

8. "Given the necessary changes."

Nunc arma Defunctumque bella,
Clypeum hæc paries habebit,[9]

and was an expressive history, in hierogliphic, of the warlike exploits of the family to which this ancient and battered Shield belonged, Yet now a days, very few of these ancient gothic heroical badges remain, the old families ‖ being almost all Cut off, by the natural ferocity, and barbarousness of these [262] violent times of heroism; The heralds office, however, discovering that this would turn out to be a profitable trade, as all trades are which flatter human pride and vanity, have fallen upon a way, by the force of fancy and Invention, to bestow promiscously for a fee or reward, these honorable ensigns, whether the persons deserve them or not, hence we find that many taylors, Shoemakers and weavers, who never used any other warlike or missile tools, but a needle, an awl and a Shuttle, (the first of which heroes by his mortal Steel, has destroyed many a backbiter and bloodsucker, and the Second has boldly peirced many a tough hide) have by means of a few pence, procured for their Illustrious families, the ensigns and Shields of bravery and heroism.

Now, the use of these badges is evident, they being absolutely necessary, to distinguish and render conspicous, certain families and persons, who have no other quality in nature, (except sometimes the pretended, and rarely the real merit of their ancestry) to distinguish or render them conspicuous; the above said merit, by some philosophers, being reckoned of no real value, as being not so easily transferable, as money lands and mannors, and therefore in it self only chimerical, and also, it is well known, that very few families or heads of families, are furnished with these eminent Substantial, and distinguishing badges of honor, which are called by the said Philosophers, magnanimity, Justice, Charity, gratitude, temperance, honesty, Integrity ‖ and many other such like obselete qualities, which qualities with [263] our *people of Quality,* have now become only dictionary words, of no certain Signification, but serve only to enable knaves to gull fools more easily, that is to say, such fools as believe that there is any signification at all in these words, and indeed, if these words were ever in use among persons of the first rank and fashion, they served for nothing more than Sound and expletives of discourse, as Insignificant and unmeaning as oaths among persons of Quality, or fal lal de ral in the Chorus of a Song, but now they seem to be Intirely obselete, and not of any Emolument or advantage to our families of note, tho' a Set of Idle fellows called authors, in their Epistles Dedicatory to Noble patrons, will make use of these very words, and terms of art, or

9. "Now that he is discharged from arms and war, / This wall will bear his shield" (after Horace, *Carmina* 3.26.4).

rather artful terms, for want of something else to say; Again, as nature now a days, does not distinguish our nobility and Gentry, from the common Rascallion herd of men, by any remarkable perfection of mind body or limbs, they being now Generally an Ignorant, degenerate, puny, pigmy race, it is absolutely necessary, that these Illustrious pigmies, Skeletons and dwarfs, should have their arms and badges of honor, painted upon their coaches and equipage, that they may be known for what they really are, according to their noble titles, vizt: such a Duke, such a Lord, such a Bishop, such an Earl, such a marquis, such a Baron, such a Baronet, such a [264] Squire, such a Squiret, and such a Squirt, and not || be mistaken for pages, powder monkies, Ghosts or Inhabitants of the Realms of Pluto, or stewd wretches Just come from a fluxing in an hospital.

These badges of distinction are also very Significant and useful in Religious orders, and Communities, as well as in Civil Societies, a Mitre, a crosier, a pair of Lawn Sleeves, a red hat, a broad brimd beaver or Castor with a large twist of black Ribbon called with great propriety a rose, a starched band, a black gown, a white Surplice, a rope, a Cowl, a Cassock, are certain marks and emblems of Sanctity, as they are appropriated to the holy ministers of the Church, and Successors of the apostles thro' out christendom, who seldom possess any thing more than these Symbols, properly apertaining to their holy function and character, to distinguish them from the prophane and profligate Lares,[10] and it is known to all, how much Indebted our grave and deeply learned Judges are, to that particular antic, or rather Comical Dress, which they wear on the bench in Westminster hall, which exhibits a badge or Symbol of their profound knowledge in the Law, one of the most perplexed and Intricate Sciences, that ever yet was hatched, Thanks to the great plenty of Rogues, in all professions we are blest with, by such outward Signatures too a regular Physician, or Learned fellow of the Colledge, may be distinguished from a Quack, the former always appearing in a grave Sable dress, and the latter in a gaudy Suit of [265] Scarlet, or some other || lively and stricking colour, daubed over with lace.

The Ancient and honorable Tuesday Club, in Imitation of these honorable, pious, wise, learned and politic bodies or Societies, thought fit, as we have related, to distinguish themselves from others, by a badge, peculiar to the members of that Club, and to none else.

At Sederunt 35th May 27, 1746, Mr Secretary Scribble being Steward, The following laws were passed.

10. In Roman mythology, the Lares were spirits who guarded the dwellings they once inhabited.

Law XXIX. That the proceedings of the former Sederunt shall be read at every Subsequent meeting.

Law XXX. That the Steward for the time being shall wear the Badge of the Club.

At this Sederunt also, Jealous spyplot Esqr, delivered a discourse upon trade and traffic, which was approved of.

At Sederunt 37th June 23d 1746, Solo Neverout Esqr being Steward, Capt: Serious Social, delivered an Elegant discourse to the Club upon prudence, in which he gave a fine description of the irascible and Concupiscible passions, incident to human nature, which was the more applauded, in so far, as it was known to every one, that this gentleman never was much addicted to speech making.

Chapter VI

The Creation of Sir John Oldcastle knight of the Club, and the privileges thereunto annexed, & the appointment of the master of Ceremonies.

It has been observed by wise and Cunning politicians ‖ that orators [266] and speech makers are a very dangerous Sort of people in a commonwealth, since being great masters of the pathos, they can work upon the passions of the Mobile, and set them into violent Commotions; the truth of this observation is very much confirmed by a Story of Demosthenes, a Celebrated Athenian Orator, who being told that a certain man, one of his hearers, at a public oration which he delivered, being asked what he thought of the orator, protested on his conscience, that he thought him a most dangerous pestilent fellow, to the Athenian State, and as such, ought to be banished the Republic. To which the Sagacious orator replied, without the least chagrin; that he was very glad to find one man at least in Athens at that time o' day, who had a true and Just notion, of the ancient Athenian Liberty.

If then it be allowed, that these orators and Speech makers, are a dangerous crew in a common wealth or State, it must follow of consequence, that they are alike dangerous in Clubs, seeing they have the same opportunity of practising upon the passions of the members, and setting the whole Society in an uproar. We have seen several of the Longstanding members of this ancient and honorable Club, exercising the office of orators and Speech makers, but indeed, hitherto, the mischief flowing from these declamators, has not broke out with any violence in the Club, except a small Spark, excited on occasion of that political Speech made by the Reverend Mr Sly, which was Blown up alittle by the Breath of Mr Councellor [267] Quaint, ‖ but the breath of Mr Quaint, not being vigorous enough to kindle it into a blaze, it soon went out, being smothered by the Submission and complaisance of the long-standing members. The true reason of the Inoffensiveness of this custome of Speech making, at it's first Introduction Into this ancient and honorable Club, is, it's being destributed into the hands of so many members, for almost the whole Club became orators and declaimers, at that time, and each of them pulling different ways, (as every member Intended to advance himself in particular) there arose a sort of Renitency in the body politic, which preserved the constitution from falling to pieces, and from receiving any violent Shocks, as the Springs weights and balances do in a piece of Clock work, hence I observe, with what propriety and fitness, some learned writers have compared forms of civil government to pieces of clock work, there being always in these, even when most despotic and arbitrary, some kind of renitency and Counterpulling, between the Governing and the governed; but after this general humor of Speech making droped or ceased in this ancient and honorable Club, which it soon did, the practice became more confined, and therefore more dangerous to the Clubical constitution, an officer being appointed, first, under the name of Speaker, who quickly rendered himself a person of Influence and Importance in the Club, and after that, a politic, Sly, designing, ambitious, and mischief making member of the Club, was promoted to that office, and was called Orator, who proved the exciter of much wrangling, noise, disturbance, hubbub and hurly burly in this here Club, as shall be shown in the [268] Sequel. ‖ If then it is clear, that speech making and declaiming is a dangerous thing in Clubs, when exercised by one, two or more of the members of common rank or degree, in these Clubs, how much more dangerous must it be, when practised by an officer, or officers of rank power and Influence, and what pen can describe, or tongue express, the mighty mischiefs it is capable of effecting, when exercised by the chief officer, or president himself.

Yet notwithstanding that the Longstanding members of this ancient and honorable Club, were wise enough to know and forsee, the mischiefs necessarily arising from Introducing these oratorial perorations in the Club, and had Indeed once found the Smart of it, yet O unaccountable Infatuation, or rather Stupidity! they Inconsideratly addressed the honorable the president himself, requesting him to assume the office of an Orator, by which they rashly put it in the power of the honorable Nasifer Jole Esqr, a person of great Qualifications that way, to enslave them more and more; for, as he had formerly, by his natural Civility, Complaisance and Innate politeness, Introduced Luxury in eating, drinking and dress into the Club, so now by his Silver tongued eloquence, he lulled the members into such an Insensibility, that like as if they had been all asleep, they permitted him, without the least resistance, to create two great and powerful officers in one night, vizt: a knight or Champion of the Club, and a Master of Ceremonies, by the first promotion, the Club had a Standing army established upon them, and besides, lost a powerful || advocate for their liberty and a [269] strong rival to the Chair, by the other, the Chair procured an assiduous flatterer, who not only vindicated, but even praised and extolled every act and proceeding, flowing from that fountain of power, tho never so arbitrary and oppressive, and thus was the balance of power almost unhinged, in this here ancient and honorable Club by means of a fine fustian Speech from the Chair, tho' it is suspected by some, that the force of Eloquence was not Solely Concerned in this Infatuation, but that certain Corrupt practices were used to silence some clamorous members, which were charged to the treasury in an article of Secret Services, and that hush money had been set to work at this time is almost Certain, for upon rendering an account of the treasury to the Club, the Sum in the box, fell short one Shilling and Sixpence; and his honor as box keeper, thought fit to throw the blame on Dumpling Gundiguts Esqr, with whom the box had been left for some days, tho' the Club thought, and with some reason, that the said Gundiguts was the person bribed by his honor, as he was the person of the most corrupt principles in the Club.

It has been already mentioned, how at Sederunt 34 The anniversary Committee, addressed his honor the president, that he would Graciously be pleased to deliver a discourse from the Chair, upon what Subject his honor pleased, and with this request, his honor wisely forseeing what advantages would thence accrue to the Chair, wisely complied.

And accordingly, at Sederunt 38, July the 8, 1746, Jealous Spyplot Esqr being Steward, his honor in a high presidential dress, ascended the Chair, and it being very || warm weather, he first of all pulled off a voluminous fair [270] wig, which covered two thirds of his face, and laying it Carefully, together with his hat and gloves under the Seat of the Chair, he drew from his pocket, a fair, clean, white Linnen night cap, which with profound gravity, he drew over his pericranium and ears, then pulling out a large Roll of paper in folio, and a pair of temple Spectacles, he wiped the latter with a fair Cambric handkerchef, first breathing on the Glasses to clean them, and then he saddled his nose with that catoptrical machine, and turning over the papers he put them in order, and looking round him for a little while, he fixed himself in a proper posture in the Chair of State, and, while two of the long standing members, vizt: the Secretary and Mr Neverout, held a candle to him on his right and left, behind the great chair, he, with great Solemnity, and a Clear distinct voice, without much action excepting only alittle nodding of the head, pronounced an elegant oration, of about half an hour in Length, the Subject of which was wisdom; the Stile of this oration was much like that of a Sermon, and some censorious people did not stick to say, that the very marrow and Substance of it, was taken from a Sermon composed by one Doctor South,[1] but this much might be urged in vindication of his honor the president, whom I would be loath to accuse of plagiarism, without better grounds, that it is a very common thing, for Great and Sublime Geniuses to agree in Sentiments, so far, as even to use the same

[271] words, when writing or speaking on the same || Subject, and therefore, from this very reasonable Supposition we may conclude, that his honor, and the aforesaid Doctor South, expressed themselves in the same manner on the same Subject, without the least Intercourse, or Communication one with the other, but what gave a Colour for this malicious Insinuation, were some seeming Slips his honor made, in pronouncing of some words used by the said Doctor South, such as *Chous* for *Chaos,* which made some rashly conclude, that his honor the president, did not understand the meaning of these words, but how Silly and groundless is this Insinuation, seeing it has always been customary, for great Geniuses to alter not only the Common Orthography, but also the Common pronounciation of words, Just as they please, which being Imitated by persons of small Genius, has for ever been the principal cause of the Instability and fluctuation of our Language, and pray, where is the great occasion to make a pother about *Chous* for *Chaos,* when it is known, that our politest people, and persons of the first fashion and Quality and taste, use, Instead of *Anatomy, Otomy,* for *Encyclopædia, In sickly pay day,* for *positive pos,* for *paltry paw,* for *Reputation Rep',* for *Incognito Incog',* for *plenipotentiary plenipo,* for *taste Vertu* (hence vertuoso for a man of taste) and many other Instances might be given of the caprice of great and distinguished wits, in the new modeling of old words, that are

[272] too hard to be pron- || ounced, by most of the present lisping and toothless Generation.

It was remarked, that his honor the president, in this Celebrated Speech, was remarkably Severe and Satirical upon one of the old Standing

---

1. Hamilton is alluding to "For the Wisdom of This World, Is Foolishness with God" (1 Cor. 3:19), sermon 9 in Robert South's *Twelve Sermons Preached upon Several Occasions* (London, 1692).

The hon.ble mr President delivering a Speech in Club.

members, viz: the Rev: Mr Smoothum Sly, whom he described as a person born far North, very much skilled in the art of palaber, smooth coaxing and flattering Speeches, but this Severity of his honor, was so far from Injuring that member, that it rather, in his honor's opinion, recommend'd him to a dignified office in the Club, which was accordingly Conferr'd upon him at that very Sederunt, hence we may observe, that when great men condescend so far as to take notice of little men, or to make them the Subject of their discourse, whatever Stile these great men use, pangyrical or Satyrical, it bodes good fortune to the little man, and is a Sure forerunner of their promotion, hence some have affirmed, that these great men are swayd by fear, others by Caprice.

After the delivery of this speech, the Secretary, in the best terms he could, by order of the Club, returned thanks to his honor the president, for his Gracious Speech from the Chair, and his honor, willing to preserve all forms of state, pulling his papers from under the Chair again, where he had deposited them, made a reply to the Club in form, thanking them for their civilities.

The first Symptoms of Joy, that broke out among the members, upon this gracious condecention of his honor, appeared in their Extraordinary liberalities to the box, which looked like the Largesses of a British parliament to the Crown, after a most gracious Speech from the throne, among [273] others, Slyboots pleasant Esqr, contributed one pistole, the ‖ secretary four Shillings and Sixpence, and the Sum now in the box, amounted to five pounds, three Shillings and Sixpence, an Immense Sum, to be collected in so short a space as half a year.

The next thing the Club went upon, was the making of short congratulatory Speeches to one another, in which Drawlum Quaint Esqr, outshone every one else; he, in the most Sublime manner, and with all his natural grace of action, at the command of his honor the President, thanking Slyboots Pleasant Esqr, for his liberality to the Club Box, and Mr Secretary Scribble for his constant attendance on the Club, he having not been absent one Sederunt, since it's first Institution.

At these proceedings Capt: Blunt, seemed to grumble and be uneasy; being, as he said, Justly alarmed, at the growing power of the Chair, on which, his honor the president, having some reason to be afraid of the Influence of this Old Standing member, Saluted him, by the title of knight, and Champion of the Club, under the name of The worshipful *Sir John Oldcastle,* knight of the Ancient and honorable Tuesday Club, and ordained, as a principal privilege of his noble office, that he should sit at the right hand of the Chair; Sir John, could not help showing, thro' the wonted

Sir John Oldcastle, Knight, Champion of the Tuesd. Club

[facing page 265]

gloom of his warlike countenance, some Satisfaction and Joy, at this un-
looked for promotion, but pretended at the same time not to be satisfied,
and refused to take his place, unless ushered in a proper manner, upon this,
his honor Immediatly nominated and Created the Reverd: Mr Smoothum
Sly, Master of Ceremonies, or Sir Clement Cotterell, to the ancient and
[274] honorable Tuesday Club, who Instantly rose from his Seat, ‖ took the
Worshipful Sir John Oldcastle by the right hand, and placed him upon the
right of the presidential Chair, The worshipful the knight, was stiled a state
officer, and had afterwards, at Sederunt 39th July 22d 1746, Capt: Serious
Social being Steward, the privilege of dispensing with the Law of one dish,
as well as his honor the president, this was Indeed a mere farcical privilege,
for this law was long agoe become a mock law, and disregarded by all the
members; The Master of Ceremonies was stiled chief officer of the commons, and made the honors of the Club to strangers, ornamented his honor
the president with his proper badges of State, and confirmed new members; Thus did this Club, Inconsideratly permit the raising of great officers
among themselves, and putting them above law, and hereby were Instrumental in establishing an Intollerable Tyranny over the long standing members, by strengthning the already overgrown power of the Chair, which
occasioned a deal of trowble and perplexity, to this here ancient and honorable Club, as was wisely forseen and foretold by Jealous Spyplot Esqr, a
Sagacious Oldstanding member, who always opposed these mad proceedings, and seldom Judged wrong in these cases.

His honor's Speech from the Chair, so far excelled all others, that, at
the same Sederunt, a resolve of the Club was made, that there should be no
more Set Speeches delivered in Club, unless upon the nights of quarterly
payment into the box, and upon the Anniversary of the Club's Institution,
and, the first article of this order was punctually observed, for, as there were
no more quarterly payments into the box, which soon after this Intirely ‖
[275] dropt, so, were there no more set speeches made by the members, unless,
upon the anniversary days of the Club, which were pronounced generally
by the Speaker or Secretary, and latterly by the officer stiled the Orator.

Drawlum Quaint Esqr, however was appointed to deliver a Speech on
the 14th day of October next, being the day of Quarterly payments into the
box, we shall soon see how punctually this payment was made, and that
Speech delivered, before this Sederunt broke up, the Joy of the Club appeared to rise to an excess, by their dancing in a ring round the Club table,
like a parcell of Ancient Bacchinalians, Captn Serious Social, leading up the
dance to an old Scots Song.

At Sederunt 39th July 22d Drawlum Quaint Esqr, appointed Chairman of a committee held at the Secretarie's house, upon monday the 21st Instant, read the proceedings of the said Committee to his honor the president & Club, which were declared void, because the committee was not appointed by his honor the president.

What was the business before this Committee cannot now certainly be known, because their proceedings were cancelled, but it is conjectured, that there was therein a plan or method, proposed to the Club, for Celebrating rejoicings, on account of some news lately arived, of the pretender's being defeated and taken, and the rebel army routed, by the king's troops, concerning which very matter, his honor the president, tho' a loyal and true blue whig, differed outragiously with the Secretary, in which Scuffle, the Secretary (as his honor alledged) robbed his honor of some political Club letters, and papers, snatching them away by force. In this dispute his honor opposed with all his might ‖ the design of the Club's rejoicing on that [276] occasion, which gave the Club so violent a Shoke, as had like to have ended in it's dissolution, from this transaction we may observe to what an enormous height the presidential power had already grown in this here Club; since the members, who before had a full power of forming themselves Into Committees, now saw themselves utterly divested of that power, and rendered Incapable to proceed in that manner, without his honor's express consent and appointment.

There was a meeting appointed to be held at the Steward's (Capt: Social) house, upon Saturday the 26th Instant, but the Squabble between his honor and the Secretary prevented it. Nothing material happened after this, till Sederunt 45th, except a neglect of the then members of paying their quarterly dues into the box, but these transactions are reserved for the following Chapter.

Chapter VII

The Creation of the Speaker of the Club, & his privileges, and also of the Chief musician and his privileges.

No more blue Stone good Doctor, is an old proverb, of which, I was never able to learn the first broacher, but waving such enquiries, my design in Introducing it here, is only for the Sake of the application, when any proceeding or piece of conduct, has been found hurtful to those who have practised it, or to those upon whom it has been practised, there follows an

[277] uneasy Sensation in the Suffering persons, much like that occa- || sioned by
the application of causticks in Surgery, and therefore they have the same
reason to call out, no more of this, we feel the Smart of it too much already;
One would think, that the ancient and honorable Tuesday Club, had already Sufficiently smarted, by the late proceedings of the chair, in creating
two great officers, and had very good reason to exclaim, No more officers,
good Mr President; but not a word of complaint on the matter, they were
too much benumned and stupified, to feel the twinge that was given them,
and Instead of exerting themselves to put a Stop to these proceedings, they
allowed another state officer, and another officer of the Commons to be
palmed upon them, so that it was likely that in a short time, the whole club
would become State officers, and officers of the commons, and so all the
Crew, being Quarterdeck men, as the Saying is, there would be no hands
left to heave out the long boat, and therefore, the Ship of this Clubical
common wealth, must of Consequence soon founder, or become a wreck,
none exclaimed so much against these proceedings in Club, as Mr Serjeant
Spyplot, who foresaw all the mischiefs and Inconveniencies that threatned
the Club, from this wrong headed policy, but his wise councels and wholesome advice, were not regarded, till it was too late.

At Sederunt 45th October 14th 1746, The honorable the President
being Steward, the payment into the box was again put off till next meeting, as it had been at the preceeding Sederunt, in the Stewardship of Drawlum Quaint Esqr, under pretence of there not being a full meeting of the
[278] members, but the truth was, || that the members were tired of this tax, when
they found that his honor the president held fast whatever he got, and
never would suffer a farthing of this fund to be applied, but for such uses,
as he only, in his presidential wisdom thought proper, and, accordingly, we
find, for six Sederunts following, this payment was still shifted off, when, at
Sederunt 52d febry 10th 1746/7, Capt: Spruce being Steward, we find on the
book of records this remarkable Entry, vizt:

"Some warm disputes arose in Club, concerning the box, which ended
in this general Result of the members of the Club, (except his honor the
president, who refused his assent) that the payment into the box, ought to
be voluntary, and at the pleasure of each member, and not by Constraint, or
at appointed times, and also, that no more disputes concerning the box,
should be brought upon the Carpet."

This bold Stroke of the long standing members, gave the first mortal
blow to the box, and we shall soon find this bone of contention, Intirely abolished and swallowed up, in the voracious maw of a philadelphian
Lottery.

Drawlum Quaint Esqr, having been appointed to deliver a discourse to the Club, upon Sederunt 45 octor: 14th 1746, desired to be excused from the same, upon account of multiplicity of business, and after a formal apology, he was accordingly excused, till another opportunity.

Upon which, the Secretary, in the place of Mr Quaint, delivered an extempore speech, which chiefly consisted in Encomiums upon Mr Quaint as a Speaker, of which Speech the Club approved, and he had the thanks of the same delivered from the mouth of Mr Quaint.

Hereupon, Drawlum Quaint Esqr, In consideration of his uncommon [279] Talent at Speech making, was unanimously constituted and appointed, honorable Speaker of the Club, by his honor the president; this piece of mischief, the Secretary was principally concerned in, and we shall always find this petty officer, in the sequel of this history busying himself in mischief, and contriving schemes and projects, to set his honor the president and his Longstanding members together by the ears. He was a cunning, Sly and conceal'd operator, for advancing the Authority of the Chair, and, tho the honorable the president, always took him for an enimy to, and an underminer of his prerogative and privileges, yet, it will appear in the course of this history, that all his actions, designs and plots (under a mistaken policy to advance himself) had a tendency to establish a tyrannical power in the Club.

At Sederunt 46, octor 28, 1746, Mr Secretary Scribble, being Steward, the following Laws were passed.

Law XXXI. That no disputes relating to the business of the Club, shall be entered upon when strangers are Present.

Law XXXII. That the honorable Speaker of the Club shall be addressed, when any Speech is made in Club, and that it shall be a part of his office, to sum up the argument, to the honorable Chair, when the member has done speaking.

By this last law we see, how considerable a person the Speaker is made in Club, and it may seem to some, that this privilege granted him, of being addressed by ‖ the speaking member, Jars, or Interferes with the privilege [280] 5to of his honor the president, where, it is expressly said, that when any motion is made, "the president is to be first addressed by the moving member, giving him his proper title," and this very thing, occasioned some dispute, in the trial of Mr Serjeant Spyplot, which shall be related in it's place, but there is really no such privilege given to the Speaker, great as it seems to be, for the Law does not say, that he shall be first addressed, but only addressed, which supposes still that his honor the president is first addressed by the Speaking member, who, after that necessary ceremony, directs the rest of his discourse and argument to the Speaker.

Some warm disputes happened at this Sederunt, but, upon what Sub-

ject the records do not mention or explain, however, the result was, that the
Speaker and Secretary both resigned their places, and refused to officiate,
the Speaker's reason for resigning, is thought to have been some opposition from the Chair, to his being addressed by the speaking member, the
Secretarie's reason stands upon record, vizt: that he was accused of some
artful practises against the dignity of the Chair, and tho' this accusation
might have been grounded upon plausible circumstances, considering the
Character of that Sly officer, yet he took it so much in Snuff, that he
contemptously threw down his office, and delivered up the book of Records to the Club, but was so far dissappointed in this his rash procedure,
that the honorable the Chair took no manner of notice, nor seemed to be in
the least moved about the matter.

[281]   At the following Sederunt however, which was ‖ the 47, on the 11th of
November, 1746, Solo Neverout Esqr being Steward, both these officers
got into so good a humor, that they again resumed their proper offices, this
Strange Change in two such resolute officers, could be attributed to no
better cause, than this, that his honor and the Club took no manner of
notice of their being out of humor.

At Sederunt 48 Novr: 25th, 1746, Slyboots Pleasant Esqr, being Steward, Mr Ignotus Warble, an honorary member appeared in the Club, who
having been Summoned by the last anniversary committee, to appear, to
answer to some charges, that were to be urged against him, had refused to
obey that Summons, therefore was liable to a Severe censure, but his trial
was put off, on account of the absence of Mr Speaker Quaint, and it happened luckily for that Delinquent, that it never afterwards came on, by
which means, he escaped a condign punishment, which probably might
have been Inflicted upon him.

At the same Sederunt, Solo Neverout Esqr, being gifted with an excellent musical voice, entertained the Club with a Song, which, as it became
the Subject of frequent contests and trials of Skill, between his honor the
president and him, which should sing it most musically, and apply the best
air to the words, we shall here give a transcript of it.

Club Song, sung by Mr Neverout[1]

    When Cloe we ply,
    We swear we shall die,

---

1. "When Chloe we ply" appears in Ramsay's *Tea-table Miscellany* (II, 63–64) almost exactly
as Hamilton has it. It also appears in *Calliope, or English Harmony* and in Watts, *Musical
Miscellany*, III, 81.

Her Eyes do our hearts so enthrall.
  But 'tis for her pelf,   [282]
  And not for herself,
'Tis artifice, artifice all, all, all,
'Tis artifice, artifice all.

  The maidens are coy,
  They'll pish, and they'll fie
And swear if you're rude they will bawl,
  But they whisper so low,
  By which you may know
'Tis artifice, artifice all, all, all,
'Tis artifice, artifice all.

  The wives they will cry
  My dear, if you die,
To marry again, I ne'er shall,
  But less than a year
  Will make it appear,
'Tis artifice, artifice all, all, all,
'Tis artifice, artifice all.

  In matters of State
  And party debate
For Church and for Justice they'll bawl,
  But if you'll attend,
  You'll find in the end
'Tis artifice, artifice all, all, all,
Tis artifice, artifice all.

This song Mr Neverout performed, so much to the satisfaction of the Club, [283] that they determined according to the following entry, which appears upon record.

"Solo Neverout Esqr: on account of his uncommon talent at Singing, is, by unanimous consent, appointed Chief Musician *con voce* of the Club, and, that, as often as he votes, he is to sing it in a musical manner, else his vote to go for nothing.

N:B: That as Mr Neverout's qualifications in Instrumental music are unknown, to the Club, he is not to perform upon any instrument, but his modulation and melody is to be confined to the voice only, and also, that this entry is not a state Entry, any objections to be brought against it by members now absent, to the contrary notwithstanding, and, finally, that

Solo Neverout Esqr, musician, & attorney Genl of ye Gnes: Club

[facing page 283]

the Secretary had no hand in proposing this entry, and therefore clears himself of all allegations of political designs, which may hereafter be brought
against him, by any wrangling or dangling members whatsoever."

The reason of putting in this *Nota bene* in the record was this, that
the Secretary intended thereby to clear himself of all blame that might be
thrown upon him by posterity, relating to this matter in particular, of creating another Great officer in the Club, as he had, at a former Sederunt been
severely taken to task, by Mr Serjeant Spyplot, for attempting to make a
state Club of this ancient and honorable Society, by promoting and encour-
aging the creation of the Speaker, who ‖ at Sederunt 49th Decemb: 9th   [284]
1746, Jealous Spyplot Esqr, being steward, was exalted to the dignity of a
state officer, and took the left hand of the Chair, the Champion and he,
being henceforth stiled, his honor the president's council of state. But, at
this Sederunt, the Secretary was absent, for the first time since the Institution of the Club, Therefore, whatever reasons Mr Serjeant Spyplot had for
blaming the Secretary, for procuring the creation of this Club officer, he
could have not the least color to accuse him of causing that gentleman to be
made an officer of state, Mr Neverout, had the title of *Protomusicus,* or
Musico-con voce given him, and at Sederunt 60 June 23d 1747, Slyboots
Pleasant Esqr, being high Steward, (for then that pompous title was Introduced) had this privilege granted him, which is the only one he ever had, or
is ever likely to have as Musician, of ordering any other member of the
Club, to sing, after he had sung himself.

At Sederunt 49th Decemb: 9th 1746, Jealous Spyplot Esqr, being
Steward, the following remarkable entry is found upon the Club book,
made by Mr Smoothum Sly deputy Secretary.

"Upon reading the entry of last meeting, appointing Mr Neverout to
sing his vote, Mr Speaker Quaint moved, that the said Mr Neverout, chief
musician, should not only sing his Votes, but likewise every motion he
should make in the Society, which was rejected, as the Chief musician
declined it."

This was a more politic motion, than perhaps the Club apprehended at
the time of making it, since it ‖ had a tendency, if the order had taken place,   [285]
to restrain the Chief musician from making many speeches and motions, for
the support of the Liberty and privileges of the Club, for which this Gentleman had always been a strong friend and stickler, till he was taken off, by
being made attorney general, and, of consequence, a state officer, this motion came naturally enough from the honorable Speaker, as he was now
become a mere creature of the Chair.

At Sederunt 50th January 13th 1746/7, Capt: Serious Social being Steward, the honorable the speaker appeared in the Club very late (having been detained by some matters of Gallantry) with his badges of office, for the first time, (and Indeed for the last time, for he never once wore them afterwards,) vizt: a long flowing black Gown and a band, but we do not find, that these right reverend ensigns, or Signatures of gravity and Learning, in the least brightened up the Genius of this Club orator, for he made no speeches at this Sederunt, tho' they added somewhat to the awfulness and Solemnity of his person and presence.

It was agreed in Club, at this same Sederunt, that his honor the president should have the privilege of drinking the first toast after supper, and it was observed, that the happy fair one, whom his honor chose for his toast, (for he constantly keept to one) had the good luck soon after, to be provided in a husband, which made his honor so famous among the Girls, that they petitioned him for the precedence, as we shall relate in it's proper place, in the course of this history.

[286]   ## Chapter VIII

The laudable custom of epistolary writing Introduced into the Club, the title of high Steward, and the first grand Anniversary procession.

Human wit (if I may be allowed the expression,) is an active and restless principle, it can never be kept quiet or still, but will always be nibbling, if any of my readers object to this proposition and these terms of art, in stiling wit a principle, I shall only tell them, that they must even take the proposition and terms as they stand; I never having had leisure enough to study Logic or Metaphysics; but as I endeavor, never to use reflections foreign to my purpose, so, I think I have brought in this short apothegm, much *a propos*, in this particular part of the history, for we now find the epidemical distemper of Speech making and declaiming, thrust out of doors by the members, and the whole Quantum left of that *Cacoethes*[1] lodged in the honorable the speaker, who at times was very sparing of it, and dealt it out in small parcells to the members as occasion served. What then must take place of this declaiming humor, now ceased among the members of this ancient and honorable Club? for, it cannot be supposed, that their wit can lie fallow or Idle, no, it must have something to nibble at, or a crust to

1. Evil habit.

chew, and accordingly we find the humor of Epistolary writing take place among the members of the Club, it is || uncertain who first began this [287] epistolary correspondence, the dispute lies between his honor the president, and the worshipful Sir John Oldcastle, some giving the merit of the Invention to the first, and some to the Latter, it is certain that Sir John wrote a letter of excuse to the Club, for his not attending it at Sederunt 44th, Septr 30, 1746, Mr Speaker Quaint being Steward, and another, in answer to one of Mr Secretary Scribble, at Sederunt 46th octor: 28, the said Secretary being Steward, on which Mr Speaker Quaint made some remarks, but, as neither these letters, nor the remarks are recorded in the Club-book, and his honor's letters, wrote soon after, are all fairly registered, we cannot help giving his honor the preference to Sir John Oldcastle, as to this Ingenious Invention.

The first essay of this kind from his honor, was at Sederunt 53 February 24th 1746/7, Dumpling Gundiguts Esqr, being deputy president, and Smoothum Sly Esqr high Steward, (the first who bore that title) when a letter directed to the Secretary, from his honor, and another to Mr Sly giving him the title of high Steward, were produced and read in Club.

To Loquacious Scribble Esqr,
Secretary to the Tuesday Club, These,

To be opened, and read to the Gentlemen when they are all met.

Gentlemen,

As I cannot be at the Club this night, have appointed Mr Spyplot to take my place in the Chair, || not doubting but my choice will be agreeable [288] to you all, and as I understand some of the members, will not be able to come, it's probable you'll postpone the resolves of the last Club to our next meeting, and if the Reverend Signr: Lardini, one of our worthy honorary members, be with you, as have heard he will, Mr Speaker being absent, must desire the favour of Mr Secretary to make my compliments of congratulation on his appearance in Club, after so long an absence—I wish you very merry, and hope you'll meet with nothing to obstruct it, I respectfully Salute you, and am Gentlemen,

Your most humble Servant
Nasifer Jole.

P:S: I understand that Mr Spyplot is not in town, so, if he does not come in time, have appointed Mr Gundiguts to take the Chair in his room.

The Letter to the High Steward was as follows.

To the Revd: Mr Smoothum Sly,
high Steward of The Tuesday Club, These.

Sir,   Febr: 24th 1746/7
    I Just now received your message, per the Negro Man, and, in answer
to it's contents, as I cannot be at the Club this night, have wrote to Mr
Secretary Scribble, To signify the same to you and the other Gentlemen at
meeting of the Club, and am, Sir,

Your humble Servant
Nasifer Jole.

[289]   After reading these Club letters, the Secretary, according to his honor's
desire, made a congratulatory Speech to the Revd: Signior Lardini, on his
appearance in Club, Mr Speaker Quaint being absent.

    The Stile of these letters is so peculiarly neat and elegant, that we
cannot ommit transcribing in this history all letters from his honor, that are
now upon record relating to the Club, since the ommission of this would
be an Irreparable loss to posterity, who must certainly profit, by this pat-
teren of stile and politeness. The terms in these letters—*have appointed,* for
I have appointed,—*as have heard,* for, as I have heard—*per the negro man,*
for by the negroe man, show plainly that Mr Jole had studied the mercantile Stile, and made himself perfect in that elegant and ornate manner of
writing.

    We find now how his honor established the title of high Steward in
this ancient and honorable Club, a title which remained ever afterwards,
and Surely, his honor, as president and Sovereign of the Club, had, located
in himself, a power to create as many new titles as he pleased, and bestow
them on his Subjects the longstanding members, for the same Reason as
king James I. that politic prince so deeply versed in King-craft, had an
inherent power of creating knights Baronets, an Inferior Class of nobility,
or rather a rank, which makes a cement, or fills up a gap, between the
lowest of the nobility and highest of the Gentry, tho' his honor had a
[290] different motive for acting thus, than that || prince, his honor's motive
being a generous ambition for Clubical power and grandure; whereas that
Shitten Monarch's motive was sordid avarice, and a desire to fill his coffers,
and support his extravagance, by means of the fees, which certain Rich
fools gave him for these caps and feathers, and, as his honor the president's
motive was more noble and heroic, so the thing answered the same good
purpose, as the other device did, the title of high Steward, being as it were a
cement between the State officers, or the nobility, and the officers of the
commons, or gentry of this ancient & honorable Club.

The custom of Epistolary writing Introduced by his honor, soon began to spread and take among the long-standing members, and Mr Speaker Quaint as a State officer, was the first Longstanding member, after his honor, that put it in practice, the Club receiving a polite letter of apology from that State officer for nonattendance, at Sederunt 54th March 10th 1746/7, Dumpling Gundiguts Esqr, being high Steward, which letter to the great dammage of posterity is irrecoverably lost.

At Sederunt 55th March 24th, 1746/7, Mr Secretary Scribble being high steward, Mr Laconic Comas, a worthy Longstanding member, who had been absent from the Club several months, upon a voyage to England, appeared in Club, and was Joyfully received and Saluted by all the Longstanding members, and, the honorable the Speaker being absent, the Secretary was ordered to congratulate him upon this occasion, which he did with approbation, he also congratulated, the Reverend Mr || Broadface Round, [291] an honorary member, upon his appearance in Club, after a long absence, but notwithstanding the said Speeches of congratulation, the Club saved to themselves a Speech from the honorable Mr Speaker Quaint upon this occasion, which Speech by the bye was never yet delivered.

At the following Sederunt, which was April 7th 1747, Jealous Spyplot Esqr, being deputy president and the honorable Mr Speaker Quaint high Steward, Mr Chantum Cheary of Philadelphia, and Mr Merry Makefun of Oxford were made honorary members, the latter of which Gentlemen, makes no small figure in this history, at the same Sederunt, a letter from his honor the president to the high Steward, was read in Club as follows.

To Drawlum Quaint Esqr,
High Steward and Speaker of the Tuesday Club, These.

Sir,   April the 7th 1747
I am very ill in bed with the gout [which [a]] prevents my being at the Club this night, for which am very sorry, so name Mr Spyplot to take my Seat in the Chair, and on his absence or refusal, then to chuse any other Gentleman by majority of voices, pray, my Service to all the Gentlemen, and am Sir,

Your Humble Servant
Nasifer Jole.

P:S: I would have been more particular in writing had I not been very ill.
N:J:

(a) This word [which] not in the original letter, but subjoined by the Secretary to compleat the Sense.

[292]   At the following Sederunt, april 21, 1747, Capt: Serious Social being deputy president, and Laconic Comas Esqr high Steward, the Club received the following epistle from his honor to the high Steward.

To Laconic Comas Esqr,
high Steward to the Tuesday Club—These.

Mr Comas,   April 21, 1747
     I Just received yours, and some days ago, on a considerable appearance of ammendment, I flattered my self with hopes of being at your Club this evening, but my obstinate gout has returned again, and I now, in as great pain as ever; That I am sorry to acquaint you and the other members of the Society, that I cannot Join with you in company this night, so appoint Capt: Social to take the Chair, in my room, or in his absence, to make choice of any other member, by majority of voices. I should always be very glad to see you, and am sorry for your Indisposition, which you say has prevented it, please communicate the above Contents to the Club, to whom I give my Service, in which you'll oblige Sir,

                                        Your Humble Servant
                                        Nasifer Jole.

     As the Anniversary of the Clubs Institution, happened upon thursday the 14th day of may next ensuing, the Club adjourn'd it self to that Day, no
[293] an- ‖ niversary committee being appointed, but, the honorable the president, whose privilege and turn it was to serve on that day, thought fit to adjourn farther 'till Tuesday the 26th of may, when his honor said, probably Green peas and Gooseberries would be in Season, which would be a great addition to the Anniversary Supper; It was accordingly celebrated on that day, being Sederunt 58th, with abundance of pomp and Solemnity, the Regular members, and four of the Honorary members, vizt: the Revd Messrs Broadface Round, and Lardini, Mr Merry Makefun and Capt: Huffbluff Surly, waited upon his honor the president, at his own house, ornamented with their badges and Ribbans, and went with his honor in Solemn procession, marching two and two, his honor and Sir John Oldcastle leading up the Van, and Mr Protomusicus Neverout, and Secretary Scribble, closing the rear, to the house of the honorable Mr Speaker Quaint, where the Anniversary feast was kept, his honor and his longstanding members, thus marching along, Received a very Low bow from the Great Collonel Bumbasto, then accidentally passing by, which they returned in good order, keeping their Ranks, they were Sufficiently stared at, as they passed, by persons of all Ranks and degrees, who seemed to be as

The first grand anniversary Procession.

[facing page 293]

much astonished, as the mob is at a coronation procession, or any such Idle pageantry, This was called the first grand anniversary procession, and the only one, ever honord, with the presidents presence.

[294]   Having come into the great hall, where they were to sit, his honor ordered Sir John Oldcastle to take the Chair while he looked after the Supper and Entertainment, in this his honor showed his great humility and earnest desire and willingness to oblige and serve the Club.

The honorable the Speaker, was desired by the Secretary, in the name of his honor the president and Club, to open this grand Anniversary meeting with a Speech proper upon the occasion, but Mr Speaker, not being in the humor of Speech making, like many other grandees, who are either above doing the duty of their office, or utterly unqualified for it, desired to be excused, and requested the Secretary to officiate for him, which the Secretary did, directing his discourse to Sir John Oldcastle in the Chair, and to the other members of the Club, and then in particular, to the Speaker and Chief musician, congratulating the Club, on it's entry on the third year of it's Institution; to this Speech, the honorable the Speaker returned a short answer of thanks. By these opportunities, of exercising his elocution, the Secretary found means of making himself a considerable person in the Club, and at last, acquired such a knack at making speeches, that in spite of opposition, he worked himself into the office of orator to the Club, and became thereby the author and Instigator of much mischief and discord in the Club, as will be made appear in the course of our History.

[295]   The members at this anniversary, were all in high dress, Sir John Oldcastle being dizened up in a fine Spencer wig, and a wastcoat with massy gold lace, and Mr Protomusicus Neverout, having a Jacket dawbed over with Silver lace, an Instance of the Luxury of the times.

After Supper, which was very elegant, and all served up in China, his honor the president resummed his place in the Chair, and Sir John Oldcastle, descended to his proper place at the right hand, putting on a very grim look.

The honorable Mr Speaker made a handsom Encomium on the elegance of the Club Supper and entertainment, and there was performed after Supper a Cantata of music, by a violin, violoncello, and two voices, which met with great approbation, the performers on the Instruments were Merry Makefun, Violino, Signior Lardini Violoncello, and protomusicus and another voice accompanied the Instruments. Thus did this grand Anniversary finish, in mirth & Jolity among the members, and thus I finish this fourth book of our history.

End of the fourth Book.

A list of the members Regular and Honorary, of the ancient and [296] honorable Tuesday Club, from the 26th of November 1745 to the 26th of May 1747.

Regular members	Honorary members
The Hon: Nasifer Jole Esqr præs:	Mr Abraham Bumper
Sir John Oldcastle knight	Dr Polyhistor
Drawlum Quaint Esqr Speaker	Mr Oldham wisely
Solo Neverout Esqr, Protomusicus	Mr Joshua Fluter
Loquacious Scribble Esqr Secretry	Capt: Huffbluff Surly
Revd Mr Smoothum Sly Mr of Cerem:	Mr Ignotus warble
Jealous Spyplot Esqr	Signr: Lardini
Capt: Seemly Spruce	Revd Mr Broadface Round
Laconic Comas Esqr	Mr Merry Makefun
Capt: Serious Social	Mr Chantum Cheary
Dumpling Gundiguts Esqr	Coll: Courtly Phraze
Slyboots pleasant Esqr	

The History of the Ancient and honorable Tuesday Club

Book V

From the first grand Anniversary procession, to the foundation of the Eastren Shore Triumvirate.

Chapter I

A Chapter of triffles, and concerning Clubical Critics and Anticlubarians.

Were it not for triffles, says a certain philosopher, (which I know only by hearsay) the world would be but very scurvily entertained, and life would hang on us like a heavy Clog, and our time be a burden, whoever doubts of this doctrine, let him read the works of Solomon, that Royal preacher, whom I look upon to be a philosopher of no mean degree, that knew well the nature of triffles and vanities, among which he Classes all Sublunary enjoyments, after having himself had a taste of all.

Triffles and vanities are but Synonomous terms, and therefore, all that passes in this transitory life, this petty ‖ scantling of time, which we have [298] allotted us to peregrinate thro' this absurd worldly wilderness, and to rant our Comical, or (as some are pleased to call it) tragical parts out upon this terrestrial Stage, is but of a triffling nature, why should any saucy, pert, demure, pricise, finical coxcomb of a Clubical Critic, to say no worse of him, nay, any Chuckleheaded, unexperienced, raw, Saucy Jackanapes pretend to say, that this our famous History, is more triffling than any other history, or this our ancient and honorable Club more triffling in it's constitution, government, model, form and Conversation, than any other Society whatsoever, great or small, be it Empire kingdom, Commonwealth corporation or Club.

But, to particularize alittle, what did Cæsar Conquer for? a Triffle; What did Brutus kill him for? a triffle; a Shadow, as he owns himself, what was the Grandure of the Roman Empire? a triffle a vapor, an evanescent Smoke; what was Cato's virtue? a morose triffle, what was Lucretias Chastity? a Squeamish triffle; what was Messilene's Lewdness, an Impudent triffle, what Cleopatra's pride and Luxury? a haughty puffd up triffle, I ask you, was not Socrates, tho a poor hard favored fellow, of more weight and Significancy, than all these triffles put in a bundle together; again, I ask you what is the learning and wisdom of philosophers? a triffle; what is the Splendor, equipage and pomp of great princes? a triffle; what are Crowns, triple Crowns, Coronets, mitres, Scepters, pikes, maces, truncheons, Stars [299] and Garters? all transitory, vain, perishing ‖ triffles, bawbles, toys, in which the great babies of this world delight; What is a great man, attended by his Levee of pimps, liars, flatterers, Sycophants, parasites and hungry dependants? a damnd Superlative, unequalled unparalelled triffle, a paragon of triffles, the Sum Substance, essence and cause efficient of all the other evanescent triffles about him, since he contains them all, and they him, since they think by him, act by him, live by him, move by him, breath by him, and by him they have their being, not as rational men, which god made them, before they mangled god's work—but as fools, prigs and Coxcombs, which their foolish patron molded them into, for him they adore, and him they worship, more than they do God, their Creator. What are all human Enquiries, learned discourses, Dissertations, explications, comments, paraphrases and Annotations? Triffles! Triffles! the mockery of Learning, and the very Image of Ignorance. What are all the Charms of the fair Sex, all their allurements, all their Smiles, all their blandishments, all the pleasures in the lump, which they are able to afford? perfect, paultry perishing, good for nothing triffles. To sum up all, what is this Globe and all its Contents, compared to the General System of nature? an atom, a triffle, a thing of nothing; what the General System of Nature compared to endless space? a Spec, a triffle, a grain of dust; and what are all these to the Supreme Essence? more than a triffle, and less than nothing if possible.

Say then, ye wise men of Gotham, ye round heads of this world, with [300] what face of Impudence can you ‖ assert, that this here History of ours, is a triffling History and this here Club a triffling Club, comparatively speaking, since there is not an ace difference between what you call Serious, Solid and rational, and all the triffles that you can ransac and cull out, in this our history, and in the Characters of these the heroes of our Club, which In fact are not more arrant triffles, than these other triffles that are to be met with in the histories of great Empires kingdoms, commonwealths, and in the

Memoirs of the Characters and lives of mighty Emperors, kings, Generals and Commanders of armies.

Will you have the Impudence to say, that Julius Cæsar was a greater man than Nasifer Jole Esqr, because the first was Emperor over great territories, and the latter only President of a little paltry Club; Surely no, consider the Inscription, which Cyrus the great ordered to be put upon his tomb, and you'll find no difference between great Emperors and presidents of Clubs, The Inscription runs thus, *"O Man, whosoever thou art, and from whence soever thou comest, for I know thou wilt come, I am Cyrus, the founder of the great persian Empire, do not envy me this little portion of earth that covers my body,"* and pray does not an emperor take as small a portion of the Earth to lye in, as a president of a Club, notwithstanding, his Spacious palaces.

> *Tu Secanda marmora*
> *Locas sub ipsum funus; et Sepulchri*
> *Immemor Struis domos. Horat:*[1]

Our famous dramatic poet also observes of Alexander the Great, "that he died, was buried, returned to dust, dust is earth, of earth is made Lome, with lome we stop a beer barrell." Pray can any president be reduced lower than this mighty Alexander; and then that Inimitable bard subjoins [301]

> Imperial Cæsar, dead and turn'd to clay,
> Might stop a hole to keep the wind away,
> Oh! that that earth, which kept the world in awe,
> Should patch a wall, t'expell the winter's flaw![2]

Again, will you pretend to assert with a grave composed countenance, (that is, in Sober earnest, without laughing) that the Roman, or the Russian, or the Turkish or the Persian or the Chinese Empires, are greater than this here Club, because they are Empires, & this here Club only a Club? Surely no,— and why pray? Why thus,—Is there any difference but in Size or Magnitude? are not the parts of a mite, as perfect as those of an Elephant, tho smaller? has not a mite its Sinews, nerves, arteries, veins, muscles, brain, heart, Lungs, Stomach, Intestines, genitals, legs, feet, toes, hair, Skin &ct: as well as an Elephant, and wherein do they differ but in magnitude of body? Has not the Tuesday club, it's president, State officers, officers of the Commons, Longstanding members, honorary members, and an Empire or kingdom, it's Emperor or king, prime || ministers, rulers, nobles, commons [302] &ct: and wherein I pray do they differ but in bulk.

1. "You gather the marble for cutting / Right at the edge of your grave, and, / Mindless of the tomb, build a palace" (Horace, *Carmina* 2.18.18).

2. *Hamlet,* act 5, sc. 1, lines 208–212, 213–216.

But take me along with you, ye conceited Sophisters, ye paultry rea-
soners of this world, Pray does not an Emperor eat, drink and sleep as
much as a president; does he not stink at times as hideously as a president?
does he not prevaricate, swear, cheat and lie as grossly as a president? does
he not tyrannize, oppress, fornicate, whore, kill and massacre as much, nay
more than any president? and finally, does he not die and rot after and often
rot before he dies as well as a president? Is he not subject to weaknesses,
passions, foibles and distempers as much as a president? Is he not a Sinfull
man as well as a president? may he not be poxed as well as a president? may
he not have the plague, the hyppo, the palsey, the Rheumatism, the gout,
the fistula in Ano, the Ripples, the whiffles, nay the Itch as well as a
president?[3] Nay, may he not play the fool as much as a president? what then
is the difference between an Emperor and a president, and in what does it
consist, a triffle, believe me, a very triffle, and not worth Contending for.

Again, is not an Empire bounded as well as a Club? has it not a
beginning as well as a Club, has it not a rise decay and end as well as a club?
are there not wicked men, fools, knaves, pimps, flatterers and Idiots in it as
[303]   well as in clubs? is it not subject to the vices of Luxury ‖ effeminacy and
corruption as well as clubs? what then is the great difference between Empires and Clubs? a triffle, a pitiful triffle, nothing at all, but as a drop to the
bucket, or a dust to the balance good friend Sophister.

I question not, but I shall be asked, why I should fall into this odd
Rhapsody, this rant, which they'll say looks as if it had been hatched in
Bedlam? but let me tell you my grave, Serious friends, (whom I shall take
the liberty to call by no worse name than Anticlubarians,) that your ridicu-
lous, Silly, and Idle remarks, uttered with a grave tho unmeaning face, and
an Empty head, against the Lawful recreations of Innocent mirth, and
Inoffensive drollery, has been the occasion of all this rant, so, if I have
Committed any mortal Sin, at your doors I lay it, ye Impertinent, precise,
Stiff, Starch'd up, Cynical Logerheads.

I know you'll say, ye good for nothing wiseacres, ye mock critics, and
bungling molders of modes and manners, that such Clubical pastime is
beneath the dignity of rational creatures, and wise men; but tell me, ye
pragmatical dunces, If you call yourselves rational creatures, (which grand
epithet by the bye, many foolish puppies such as you, irrationally assume to
themselves) are you never Employed about amusements less becoming a
rational nature, than these droll, facetious, gelastic and harmless Clubical

---

3. *Hyppo* is an obsolete abbreviation for *hypochondria; ripples* refers to a weakness in the back
accompanied with shooting pains; *whiffles* refers to an attack either of bragging or of farting,
probably the latter.

recreations? do you never whore? do you never game? do you never swear? do you never lie? do you never flatter? do you never Idle your time away in insipid flat, childish and unprofitable Conversation? || among fops like [304] yourselves? If so, you are rational creatures Indeed, if otherwise, you are as far to seek in point of Rationality, as the rankest Clubist that ever breathed. Wise men indeed! pray who made you wise men? on what ground do you claim that title to yourselves? is it on account of your knowledge? is it on account of your Learning? your knowledge is nothing, when compared to your vanity and Self conceit, and your Learning is Collected from broken Scraps of plays, Romances, Lewd authors,+ title pages and hearsay, do you pretend to know more than Socrates, who, tho' the wisest of the Athenians,—of the greeks, and consequently of the whole world in his time, yet declared that *he knew nothing,* yet was pronounced a wise man by the Oracle, it will be a lying Oracle Surely that declares you any other than Self conceited fools, since you differ so much from the said Socrates in conceiving a great opinion of your own knowledge, and condemning all Sorts of Clubical and Gelastic pastimes, of which that philosopher was often very fond. You wise men I say again! are you wiser than Pythagoras the Samian Sage, who thinking that the term wise men, or Sages, was a title too assuming for the Connoiseurs and virtuosi of his age, took another in it's place, by which he made it known, that he thought it not altogether so proper to arrogate to himself the actual possession of wisdom, being only an humble Enquirer after it, and therefore, he took to himself the appellation of || philosopher, or lover of Science, or wisdom, a name ever since given, to [305] those that make natural Science and morality their Study. But if you persist still, and say these Low clubical humors are Inconsistent with philosophy, pray what do you take Philosophy to be? do you think it is consistent with Philosophy, to be demure, finical, pragmatical, chagrin, foppish, fantastical and Coxcombish? Such philosophy, I believe, may suit the humor of certain Starched up fellows, such as you; I tell you ye dunces, that there is nothing more gay, more frolicksome and (if I may so speak) more Jocose than Philosophy, and I think, Mr Jonathan Grog's Anonymous poet, gives a Just description of true Philosophy under the name of virtue in the following Lines.⁵

> True virtue seldom haunts the Cynic Cell,
> Morosely wise, she wears eternal Smiles,
> The face of Innocence, is social still,

4. Unlettered, or untaught, authors.

5. These lines, part of the lengthy poem "To the Ladies" (signed by "Eumolpus"), appeared in the *Md. Gaz.,* Dec. 24, 1745.

Benevolent and free: Hypocrisy,
She scorns, and Starch Screwd up formality,
The boast of fools, and haters of mankind.

The true mark of wisdom, is a lively and Constant Chearfulness, it is *Baracco* and *Baralypton*,[6] and such like pestilent Stuff of the Schools, 'tis an affected primness preciseness and Ceremony, the darlings of triffling fops, which renders some pretended philosophers, (not Philosophy) so base and [306] Contemptible. Those that place true || philosophy then in such triffles, know no more concerning her, than what they know by hearsay, her Sole end, is to render a man more happy, in making him more wise, and what can make a man more wise than the knowledge of himself and his own species? what can conduce more to that than his going abroad in the world, and frequenting of Clubs; *Ergo*, Clubs, as they Conduce to make a man more wise, will Surely make him more happy. *Q:E:D:*

It is said of Demetrius the Grammarian,[7] that one day, popping into the Temple of Delphos, he spied there a Club of philosophers in a very merry vein, Chating, Laughing and cracking of Jokes. Gentlemen said he (putting on a precise look) I am either very much deceived, or finding you in such a giggling disposition, you seem to converse on nothing but triffles, unbecoming wise men and profound Sages, To whom Heracleus the Megarian[8] made answer, It is the business of those, (you meddling fool) who employ their whole time in enquiring, whether the future of the Verb βαλλω be wrote with a dowble λ and whence the Comparatives χειρον and βελτιον[9] are derived, to those I say, it belongs to be dull finical and stupid in Conversation, but philosophers in their Discourse, are accustomed rather to be merry and Sprightly, than precise and formal, this Demetrius [307] was Surely in his time, a thick skulld || morose clubical critic and anticlubarian, and these wise philosophers were Stanch and true Clubists.

But once more, ye perverse anticlubarians, pray who set you up for modelers of manners, and for absolute regulators of Societies? have you any right to Censure or Callumniate any thing but what is in itself really Immoral and wicked? by what authority do you set yourselves up for men of taste and wisdom above all others? what malignant Spirit moves you to call

6. These words, nonsense in themselves, are a Scholastic mnemonic for teaching the patterns of syllogisms.

7. Probably Demetrius Ixion (fl. 2d century B.C.), who disputed Aristarchan textual principles and compiled an Atticist lexicon.

8. The Megarians, members of a philosophical school founded by Euclid, or Eucleides (450–380 B.C.), were noted for their vehement disputations. Surely the irony of the "merry and Sprightly" pose of this particular Megarian did not escape Hamilton.

9. The verb *to throw*; the comparatives *worse* and *better*.

certain ceremonies forms and proceedings, nonsensical Stupid, Silly and *Clubical* indeed (which elegant term by the bye you Improperly use as an expression of contempt) while you are too dull, and too Stupidly Solem to understand, compass or comprehend, any thing at all of the true Spirit and Significancy of these gelastic mysteries, are ye not a parcel of pragmatical, foppish, strait laced Coxcombs, who Imagining you have all the Learning and Philosophy yourselves, condem every body else, who do not Imitate and follow your formal Band-box humors and precise decisions, as Simple-tons fools, asses and Idiots.

What does your humor consist in, is it any thing in the world but a dull form and precise Starchness, which you contract by an uniform stupid habit, like the Idiot, who continued to tell the Clock by force of custom, even when the Clock was no more, are you any thing else but the ecchoes or repeating watches of the leading fops and finicals of the times? do you || employ your time in any thing, but the dull, tiresome and Impertinent [308] circle of ceremony and Grimace, do you know any thing more than to make a jantee bow, a Scrape with the leg and foot, to pull off your hats to your betters, and strut by your equals without taking notice, to make formal and Starched Speeches, to fringe scollop, shape and proportion your words and actions, like a Taylor, or a pastry Cook at work, who have patterns for every mode and fashion that their Cloth and paste are to be cut and molded into, to learn to come into a room by Geometry, to drink by hydraulics, cough fart, and sneeze by pneumatics, and to pay compliments and make speeches by Gunter's scale,[10] to put on demure faces for a Show of wisdom, while your Sculls are as empty as dried Gourds, and, for all the world, like Retorts set in Snow where they may remain till the Greek Kalends,[11] before any volatile Spirit will Sublime, or produce any thing that one may smell to. Does not your conversation, consist chiefly of trite thread bare observa-tions, or cut & dry compliments coned by heart from your bretheren Cox-combs, or in censuring of triffles that are not worth censuring, or praising greater triffles that never deserved any praise; does the Sublimest pitch of your mirth, go beyond an affected horse laugh, the tribute which you pay to the stupid Sayings of some great person of Quality or fashion; does your Conversation || ever run higher for the most part than the ace of Spades, [309] and the knave of Clubs, can you talk of any thing to the purpose, but the

10. A flat rule, two feet long, marked on one side with scales of equal parts and on the other side with scales of the logarithms of those parts; it was named after its inventor, Edmund Gunter (1581–1626), the distinguished English mathematician.

11. The "Greek Kalends" is Hamilton's humorous expression for "never," since the Greeks used no calends in reckoning time.

Rubbers, the lurch, Size Cinque, Seven's the main, mattadores, the Vol, Codille,[12] Race horses, hounds, Spaniels, pointers, laced Jackets, powdered wigs, of Signior Lampuni, Madam Albinoni,[13] opera airs, farces, pantomimes, Routs, Drums, masquerades, Ridottos, Vauxhall and Ranelaw, Garric and his play mates, a few paltry Authors of the same foppish turn with yourselves, and all this by rote? Phogh! ye blind puppies, you are fit for nothing else but to be carried to the kennell and drowned! but no; we will preserve you for this use at least,—to afford matter of fun and Gelastic mirth, for our wise and facetious Clubs.

But I shall leave you here, ye Incorrigible Anticlubarians, ye cutters out and fashioners, of what you are pleased to call decency and decorum; ye danglers after a Sort of fools whom you call people of fashion, ye critics upon letters, words, points, Commas, colons & crotchets,[14] ye Shapers of fantastical plans and patterns for greater fools than yourselves to walk by, ye Eternal trifflers, I shall bid you an eternal Adieu in this very place, and henceforth take no more notice of you than if you were not in being, or [310] never had been hatched, which, had things really turned out so, || would not have been a farthing's matter, either of profit or Loss to the world, and we should never have had occasion to sing the old Song,

Wail a day! and wo be our lot!
For oh! for oh! the hobby horse is forgot.

Let me only conclude with this condolatory exclamation; Oh how I pity you, for your want of the true taste of life; for the want of that blessed humor, which set Democritus a Laughing, and Heraclitus a crying, That quickning Spirit, that divine Automoton, that rational principle, that prompts wise men, to Democritise and Heraclitize, for, ye dry withered Stocks of human Society, Ye Statues and poppets in human form, you can neither laugh nor Cry in earnest, nature has absolutely denied you the power of both, and like a parcel of upstart mushroms, ye come into the

12. *Rubbers* is the deciding match (of three) in a card game; *lurch* was originally a 16th-century game resembling backgammon, but here it probably refers to that stage in a card game where one player is enormously ahead of another; *size cinque* is a variant of *sice cinque* ("to set at cinque and sice" is to take great risks; here, to be reckless at playing cards); the *main* is the number called (from five to nine) in a card game by the caster before the dice are thrown (here, seven's the main); *mattadores* is a name applied to certain principal cards in games such as quadrille or ombre; *vol* is presumably a variant of *vole*, "a deal at cards that wins all the tricks"; *codille* is a term used in ombre or quadrille when the game is lost by the challenger.

13. On Lampuni (probably Lampugnani), see p. 57n, above. Tommaso Albinoni (1674–1745) was an Italian violinist and composer from whom Bach borrowed; perhaps Madam Albinoni was a relation of his.

14. A *crotchet* is the symbol for a note half the value of a minim.

world, and like a flitch of Smoked bacon, whose Salt is soaked out, you go out of it, dry, dead, musty, Insipid and Sapless, having never in your lives enjoyed the Sweets and delights of clubical humors and recreations, without which life is not worth enjoying, but is a *tabula rasa,* or a *Cart Blanch,* or rather a blotted Scroll or Scutcheon, in which nothing of Sense or Significancy can be read or discerned, like that great lubberly book sent by Micromegas the Siryan Philosopher to || the Accademie des Sçiences,[15] out [311] of which, the aged, purblind and Learned Secretary could not read one single Sillable or Letter, and so, in a christian like manner, I bid you for ever farewell.

Chapter II

The accusation of the Speaker and Chief musician, several Congratulatory Speeches, the Master of Ceremonies confirmed, and some other triffling occurrences.

Socrates the Athenian philosopher, (of whom perhaps, some of my readers may only have heard the bare name, which is enough for their purpose and mine too, since it ranks him in the Class of Clubical worthies) being one day standing, or walking, or Lying or sitting, (it matters not how, or where,) under a plane tree, with the beautiful Phædrus,[1] in a Sultry Summer's day, when the Sun shone bright, and the plains and the mountains and the fountains smoked again, while the Cattle stood under the Shady trees, and hung down their heads and ears, and switched their Sides with their tails to keep off the flies, and the Grasshopers Chirruped and sung, he took that opportunity to tell him a tale, how Grasshopers were once musicians, orators and poets, before the muses were born, and lived without meat and drink (as god knows many poor poets do now at this very day) and for that cause were turned by Jupiter into Grasshoppers, || which [312] is a creature, that like the Camelion, is said to live upon pure air.

It is very probable, that the honorable Mr President Jole, and the Longstanding members of the ancient and honorable Tuesday Club, re-

15. A philosopher from the star Sirius is the central character of Voltaire's *Micromégas* (1752), a Gulliverian tale about the relativity of all dimensions and the insignificance of mankind. At the close of the tale Micromégas leaves his teachings, a ponderous volume full of blank pages, to the Académie des Sciences.
1. Plato's friend and the central figure of his famous dialogue *The Phaedrus.*

membering this tale of Socrates or some other such antiquated tale, thought, that their Orator, vizt: the honorable Mr Speaker Quaint, and their musician, the good Mr Proto-musicus Neverout, were like these ancient musicians and Orators, whom Jupiter turned into grasshoppers, that is, that the diet fittest for them was air, and that they had no occasion for meat and drink, for as they vended nothing but air to the Club, in their vociferations, when the one sung and the other declaimed, so they had nothing but air in return for their Labor, that is Sound, of which air is the medium, excited either by loud laughing, or clapping of hands, by way of applause. As for other rewards, they had not so much as the value of one single farthing, to help, as the Saying is to keep life and Soul together, this cold Comfort surely, together with the notion of their being very great Club officers, and above doing their duty, made them negligent and remiss in their respective offices, so that it was now a very rare thing, to hear either a Speech from the honorable the Speaker, or a Song from the tuneful Mr Proto-musicus; which attracted the hawks eyes of that cunning and politic officer the Secretary, and gave ground for an accusation brought against these two eminent Club officers by him at two several Sederunts for negligence and remissness in their respective offices, but these accusations were

[313] little ‖ regarded by the Club, and in a manner slured over, the reason of which probably was, that his honor the president was Suspicious, (as he constantly professed to be) of the Secretaries designs, Imagining, and perhaps with some reason, that this Cunning menial Club officer, wanted one or other of these great Club officers to be degraded, that he might step into his place, as this is the common practice of great Statesmen and officers, who generally envy one another, and the understrappers among them are always on the Gape, for the places of those above them, wishing and praying daily with great fervency, that they may either be displaced, die, or go to the Devil, the Secretary probably might have some such designs in his Noddle, but then, it must have been the honorable the Speaker's place he aimed at, for, he was by nature so unfit for the other, that he knew as little how to sing, as a bull-frog or a goose, and far less than a Swan, Cricket or Grasshopper.

At Sederunt 59th June 9th 1747, Solo Neverout Esqr, being high Steward, several Congratulatory Speeches, were made in Club to the Secretary, on occasion of his late Marriage, The Reverend Mr Sly, in particular, complimented him upon that occasion, and, when he was done speaking, the honorable Mr Speaker Quaint, rising up, with that gravity, Solemnity and action, which was his peculiar talent on all such occasions, discoursed but

[314] little upon that Subject, delivering chiefly an ‖ encomium upon Mr Sly's

congratulatory Speech, in a nervous and elegant Stile, which was at all times quite natural to that Gentleman.

Thus did these polite longstanding members mutually compliment and congratulate each other, after the ceremonious manner of ambassadors, plenipo's and great councellors of State, who, when they assemble, which is but very seldom, pass off the greatest part of the time in compliment and Ceremony, but, notwithstanding, when the precedence comes to be disputed for, are loth to yeild it one to another.

At Sederunt 60, June 23d, 1747, Slyboots Pleasant Esqr, being high Steward, the Secretary vented his Spleen against the Chief musician, by accusing him of negligence in his office, as he had done the Speaker on the preceeding Sederunt, but the Club acquitted him, on account of his good performances, at other times, and as an acknowledgement of the favor, he entertained the Club, with two excellent new Songs, the one Solo, the other In company with another voice, the Songs were as follows.

New Song, sung by Mr Protomusicus Neverout[2]

When Orpheus went down to the regions below,
    Which men are forbidden to see,
He tun'd up his lyre, as old histories show,
    To set his Euridice free—To set &ct:

All hell was Surpriz'd, that a person so wise   [315]
    Should rashly endanger his life;
But, O ye good gods! how vast their Surprize,
    When they knew that he came for his wife.

To find out a punishment fit for his fault,
    Old Pluto had puzzl'd his brain,
But hell had not Torments Sufficient he thought,
    So he gave him his wife back again.

But pity succeeding, soon vanquish'd his heart,
    Being pleas'd with his playing so well,
He took her again, in reward of his art,
    Such power had music in hell.

It would seem by the above song, sung on such an occasion, that Mr Protomusicus Intended, not only to cox and sooth his honor the president,

2. "Orpheus and Euridice" appears in *Calliope, or English Harmony* and in *Universal Harmony; or, The Gentleman and Ladie's Social Companion* (London, 1745), 34.

by as it were comparing him to the great Pluto, king of hell, but likewise made an excellent elogium on himself as a musician, by likening himself to Orpheus, the other Song was to this purpose.

Club Song, sung by Mr Protomusicus[3]

Save women and wine, there is nothing in life
   Can bribe honest Souls to endure it,
When the heart is tormented with care & with Strife,
     Dear women and wine,
     Sweet women and wine,
     Dear women and wine only cure it.

[316]   Come on my brave boys, we'll have women and wine,
   And wisely to purpose employ them,
He's a fool that refuses such blessings divine
     As women and wine,
     Sweet women and wine,
     Who has vigor and health to enjoy them.

Our wine shall be old, and so my dear Jack
   To heighten our amorous fire,
Our Girls plump and Sound, they will kiss with a Smack,
     Our bottles will Crack,
     Our Lasses will smack,
     And gratify every desire.

     The Club was so well pleased with these Songs, and Mr Protomusicus's performance, that they granted him the privilege of asking any member of the Club to sing, after having first sung himself, not even excepting his honor the President, who, notwithstanding in this case, as indeed in all others questioned the power which the Club assumed to themselves, in giving any Longstanding member an Authority over him, for it always was, and is now his fixed opinion, that as president, he is above all Club law, and is at no time obliged to give reasons for his conduct, to the Club. At this Sederunt, Mr Curious Courtly, Mr Swillum Swagbelly, and Mr Prim Laconic, were made honorary members.

[317]   At Sederunt 61, July 7th 1747, Jealous Spyplot Esqr being high Steward, the Master of ceremonies was Confirmed in his office by his honor the president, but, by what particular ceremony, is not left on record, tho' it is

---

3. "The Pleasures of Life," or "Save Women and Wine," appears in *Calliope, or English Harmony*, I, 147.

thought that it was by Salutation, and Manuquassation,+ and after long dispute, the following Law was passed.

Law XXXIII. That every member of the Club, who is, or shall be honored with an office in it, provided he be in town, shall attend the Club at meetings punctually, or send his excuse in writing, to the high Steward for the time being, on the Club day, by twelve o Clock at noon, or to forfeit half a crown currency, to be paid into the hands of the honorable the president as chief treasurer, which money, is to be laid out upon rack, or other Liquors, to be agreed upon by the Society at their meeting, pre-ceeding the Anniversary of the Club, to be used on that occasion.

The cause of passing this law, it was said, was the remissness of several of the Longstanding members, in their attendance on the Club meetings, particularly Mr Protomusicus, who very often absented, and would either give no reason for his doing so, or very triffling ones, but this seems only to be a pretence, to cover a worse design, In short, it was a Scheme to enrich the box, his honor the president's darling, to do which all methods, direct or Indirect were taken in Club, || and now we find, that by the express tenor [318] of the above law, the fund in this box, is partly allotted to support the Luxury of the Club, in purchasing rack, and other expensive Liquors, and the original purpose of Charity is no more talked of, but we shall find by and bye, that those Schemes did not take, for, tho' the said protomusicus and other Club officers, often transgressed this Law, yet it is no where to be found upon record, that they ever paid the penalty into the box, tho often desired by his honor the president.

However, against this Law, the worshipful Sir John Oldcastle entered his protest; Because he said it was partially penal, making only the officers liable to the fine, and omitting the longstanding members of the Commoners.

After some warm dispute in Club at this Sederunt, concerning State officers, and officers of the Commons, it was Resolved, that the master of ceremonies, Musician and Secretary, are not State officers, but officers of the Commons, and that Sir John Oldcastle, and the honorable the Speaker, are State officers, and of his honor's honorable privy council of State.

'Tis strange to see, how soon pride, vanity, ambition and love of power, took place in this here ancient and honorable Club, in spite of all the opposition of that wise and foreseeing Longstanding member, Jealous Spy-plot Esqr.

At Sederunt 62d July 27, 1747, Capt: Serious || Social being high Stew- [319]

---

4. *Manuquassation* is Hamilton's invention for *handshake* (a quassation is a shaking).

ard, the Secretary reported to his honor and the Club, that the old record book was almost filled, and proposed to the Society, that his honor the president, or Sir John Oldcastle should Contribute for a new book, for the use of the Club, and, it being put to the vote, it was carried, that his honor the president should present the Society with a new record book, to which Resolve his honor tacitly dissented, and Indeed, this was a foolish proceeding, in the Club, being a presumption, that the taxed, had a power to tax, their tax master, who had the club treasury in his power, and therefore would be no such fool, as to part with his own private property, so long as he had the public funds in his hands.

It was moved in Club, at this same Sederunt, that Mr Protomusicus Neverout, on account of his non attendance, should be deprived of his office, and Mr Laconic Comas put in his place, but, upon it's being put to the vote, it was determined, that he should first have a hearing, and that, in case of his absence at next meeting, the Club should proceed Judicially against him.

We shall find thro' the whole course of this Club History, this Longstanding member, and officer of the Commons, the most Irregular of any of the others in his attendance on the Club, The most Inconsistent in his proceedings and Speeches in club, the most Clamorous and noisy at times [320] against the preroga- ‖ tive of the chair, and at other times the most busy in arguing for it, the most Incessant Laugher and vociferator, and yet by a peculiar good luck, that attends many people, which is not of their own Seeking, this Longstanding member escaped at all times that Just censure and punishment, which ought to have been Inflicted upon him, by his honor and the Club, many wondered how this could be, but, in short, we can only account for it thus, that he audaciously laughed in their faces, and carried off even the most Serious matters, fairly with a Joke.

Chapter III

Sir John Oldcastle's Letter censured, Club's letter to Mr Makefun, an honorary Member, other Clubical letters of no great Importance.

Tho' the Learned generally pitch upon Great and Illustrious men, that is, men of high birth and titles for their patrons, supposing them to be perfect and unerring Judges, in all Sorts of Learning whatsoever, and Intirely acquiesce in their Judgement and opinion, yet we find, that those great, Lordly and unerring Judges, notwithstanding their lofty titles, high birth and ponderous purses, which last enables them to give many a poor poet, and many a starving author a dinner, are not altogether exempt, from the || attacks and sneers of the critics, when these carping and fault finding [321] gentry, have a mind to fall foul of their works.

A glaring instance of this appeared in the reception, that a letter wrote by no less a person than the Worshipful Sir John Oldcastle, principle State officer of this ancient and honorable Club, and of his honors most honorable privy council, met with when presented and read in Club, which I shall relate, as the matter stands in the book of Records.

At Sederunt 63d August 4th 1747, The worshipful Sir John Oldcastle being high Steward, his honor the president produced to the Club a Letter, sent him by the worshipful, the high Steward, which being, in his honor's opinion (for great men are apt to compliment one another mightily, even on very Slight and triffling occasions) a *very respectful letter*, he desired the same might be read, and recorded in the book as follows.

To the Honorable The President of the Tuesday Club.

Sir,

I am to acquaint you, I have the pleasure of the worthy Club at my house, where I hope to have the honor of your good company, mean time am with due respect

August 3d   Your most humble Servant
                                              Oldcastle.

This Letter was in a very warm manner objected to by Mr Protomusi- [322] cus Neverout, as being wanting in due respect, but as his objections were Inconsistent with the respect due to his honor the president, the worshipful the high Steward, and the Club, he was gently reprimanded for the present, by the honorable the president from the Chair, but it was hoped, that this rude behavior of his, would be Sufficiently chastised by Mr Speaker Quaint, at next meeting.

At the following Sederunt, which was the 18th of August, Capt: Seemly Spruce being high Steward, there was a Law passed in Club, vizt:

Law XXXIV. That every entry, relating to particular members, or censures passed upon particular members, by this Club, as also the form and tenor of Laws, be read by the Secretary to the Club, before they are entered at Large into the book of records, that they may undergo such corrections, additions or Improvements, as the Club shall think proper, and that, notwithstanding this first reading, they shall be read as usual, at the opening of the following Club after registration.

By this Law, we may perceive, the Jealousy that had now grown in the Club, of the Secretaries makeing false entries, tho' some are of opinion that this Law was procured by the vociferation and Clamor of Mr Protomusi- [323] cus, who Imagined himself Ill used in ‖ the entry of last Sederunt, concern- ing his censuring of Sir John Oldcastle's letter, but this entry in fact was made by the Revd Mr Sly, then deputy Secretary, the Chief Secretary being absent, and concerning this very affair, some hot disputes happened in Club at this Sederunt, between the Revd Mr Sly, master of Ceremonies and Mr Protomusicus Neverout, which begun with noise and ended in nothing as many disputes do, and they were left undetermined, till Mr Speaker Quaint appears in Club, to determin and put a finishing Stroke to these Controver- sies, being Informed in nothing relating to the said Controversies, this seems to be putting a very great Confidence in the Speaker's Judgement and penetration, supposing him to be able to determin a controversy of which he knew not the least circumstance, an Instance of that Implicit trust, which understrappers, are apt to put in the Judgement and decision of great men, which proceeds from a false association of Ideas, too prevalent among the vulgar, in Joining greatness of capacity & Judgement with greatness and dignity of office.

At the next Sederunt, which was September 1st, The Revd Smoothum Sly Esqr, being high Steward, the president produced In Club a Letter from the High Steward, vizt:

To Nasifer Jole Esqr,
president of the Tuesday Club.

Sir,

[324]   As high steward of the Tuesday Club, which meets ‖ this night, in pursuance of last appointment, I think it my duty to give you this Notice, and to desire the honor of your company to preside at the said meeting to be held at the house of Slyboots Pleasant Esqr, I am with regard, Honor- able Sir,

Septr 1, 1747   Your most humble Servant and
                                       very dutiful high Steward
                                       Smoothum Sly.

[*Here endeth the first book of the Club records.*]

At Sederunt 66th Septr 15th 1747, Laconic Comus Esqr, being high steward, a letter was produced from the Secretary to his honor the presi- dent, Intimating that the book of Records of the Club was filled up, and requesting his honor the president and club to consider of ways and means to procure a new one, in order to Carry on regularly, the minutes of this Club. This was a very laudable care in the Secretary, and tended to preserve these valuable Records for the use of posterity, which, as there was not a full meeting of the members, it was postponed to another Sederunt.

Mr Merry Makefun, an honorary member, having sent a present of English beer to the Club, and entrusted a parcel of it with Mr Protomusicus Neverout, the Secretary was ordered by his honor the president and Club, to draw up a letter of thanks, to the said Mr Makefun, to be laid before the Club at next sederunt, to receive proper corrections and ammendments.

An Information was brought at this Sederunt against Mr Protomusi- [325] cus Neverout, for not acquainting the Club with an order he had from Mr Merry Makefun, to present the Club with some English beer, for which he is ordered to be Indicted next meeting by Mr Speaker Quaint.

This is the first Instance of an order for a Criminal trial, to be carried on in this ancient and honorable Club, and the Chief Musician is the first delinquent, or Culprit, we shall have occasion to relate several others in the course of this history, and this very gentleman, we shall find more than once, under the vindictive Claws of Clubical Justice.

At Sederunt 67, Octor 13, 1747, after a long adjournment, on account of birth days and horse races, the Club met at the house of Dumpling Gundiguts Esqr, high Steward, and after mature consideration, with regard to the book of Records, it was ordered, That ten Shillings Currency be paid by his honor the president, out of the box, to the Secretary, who for this Sum undertakes to provide a record book for the use of the Club; this is the first disbursment from the treasury that we find upon record, in this ancient and honorable Club, and, I believe the only one, that ever was made, from the foundation, to the final evacuation of the box, which shows how far the charitable Intentions of the box were put in practice; but, his honor the president, being Sole Judge in this affair, we need not be Surprized that none of the Clubs money had as yet been laid out on Charitable purposes, his honor being very ‖ nice and hard to please, with regard to such as were [326] proper objects of charity, not chusing, like many, who would be thought very good christians, to bestow charity, or have any the least compassion upon such as he thought unworthy objects.

The Secretary produced at this Sederunt a copy of a Letter of thanks to Mr Merry Makefun, drawn up by him, according to an order of the pre-ceeding Sederunt, of which a transcript follows.

To Mr Merry Makefun, Merchant at Oxford.

Sir,

I am enjoined and ordered by the honorable Mr President Jole, and the longstanding members of the Ancient and honorable Tuesday Club, in his and their names, to return you their thanks, and grateful acknowledgements, for the favor you lately did us, in making a present to the Club of a Sortment of English beer, by the hands of Mr Stentor Snuffybeak, in which we have more than once drank your health, and paid you that deference due to a worthy honorary member, whom we esteem an ornament to our Society.

I therefore in their name, and by their authority make due acknowledgement of the favor, being Sensible that your generosity is prompted by a [327] Sincere esteem for our Society, so wishing you all || health and happiness, we profess ourselves to be

Octor 13th 1747   Your Sincere friends and fellow members,
                                         Signed pr: Order
                                         Loquacious Scribble Secrtry

At this Sederunt Capt: Serious Social, a worthy long Standing member, voluntarily left the Club, not thro' any disgust, for he was a person of a thorro' clubical disposition, and had a true taste for the bowl, pipe and chat, but thro' age, and bodily Infirmity, he was unable now to attend these nocturnal meetings, an entry of this occurrence is found on the book to this purpose.

"Capt: Serious Social, having been 4 nights absent from the Club, without giving any reasons, is hereby excluded the Club, according to the tenor of Law 13th."

At the following Sederunt, Octor 27th, Mr Speaker Quaint being high Steward, the said high Steward represented to the Club, that in pursuance of an order, from Mr Merry Makefun of Oxford, to Mr Protomusicus Neverout, to deliver nine bottles of English beer to the ancient and honorable Tuesday Club, of Annapolis, he had sent to him, the said Neverout, for some of the said beer, for the use of the Club, and he, the said Neverout, returned for answer that he had no beer for the said Club. The Society taking offence at this rude answer, passed an order, that Mr Speaker Quaint, draw up an Indictment, against the said Solo Neverout Esqr, for [328] this, and other misdemeanors || charged upon him at some of the preceeding Sederunts, particularly, his censuring of Sir John Oldcastles letter to his honor the president, dated the 3d of august last, unjustly, as also, his being absent from the Club at this Sederunt, tho' in town, and not sending a letter of Excuse to the high Steward, according to the tenor of Law 33d, it was ordered also that Mr Stentor Snuffybeak, be Summoned by the Secretary to attend the Club at next Sederunt, to give in his evidence against Solo Neverout Esqr.

His honor the president presented in Club, a letter from the Secretary, which was read as follows.

To Nasifer Jole Esqr,
president of the Tuesday Club, These.

Honorable Sir,
   Being prevented by Indisposition, I shall not have the pleasure of attending the Club this night, at Mr Quaint's. This therefore is to Inform your honor and the Club, that I have, according to your order of the 10th Instant, dispatched the Societie's letter of thanks to Mr Merry Makefun, writ and devised in the same form and tenor, as was then read to the Club, and as is now entered in our book of minutes,—I have farther to Inform your honor and the Club, that I have, according to your Instructions, provided a new register book, for the use of the Society, which I Intended to have produced at this night's meeting, but shall be obliged to defer that ceremony to the Subsequent meeting of the Club, upon ‖ the 10th of [329] november next, when your honor serves as high Steward, and I hope then to be able to wait upon you with that duty and decency requisite upon such a Solemn occasion. In the mean time, I heartily desire to be remembered to all our worthy members, and hope, they will be most elegantly and pompously entertained by Mr Speaker Quaint, high Steward for this night, and in this, I Surely cannot be mistaken, if Mr Speaker's *Outward apparatus,* and *Decoration,* at feasts of this nature, be as *Elegant* and *Harmonic,* as his *Inward Rhetoric* and *Eloquence,* at the Club and bar, is uncommon, I am, Honorable Sir,

Octor the 27th 1747   Your most humble Servant and
                                       Trusty Secretary
                                       Loquacious Scribble.

   This is the first letter upon record of the Secretarie's proper inditing, where it may be remarked the Stile is tollerably plain and easie, having little or nothing of that Clubical Bombast and pallaber, abundance of which will be found in the Subsequent letters wrote by that officer, who, by his pernicious example, also led the way to the other Longstanding members, to Imitate the same ridiculous Stile, which disgusted his honor the president so much, that at last he would not suffer one Clubical letter directed to him to be entered upon record.

    The parallell at the conclusion of this letter of the Secretarie's, is an [330] Imitation of the elegant Phraseology || of the honorable Speaker himself, in a speech he made to a young Lady, who refused, upon her being desired to sing, which was to this purpose, "Surely Miss, you cannot but sing well, if your *Inward voice* is as harmonious, as the beauty of your *Outward form* is uncommon."

Chapter IV

Trial of the Chief musician, disputes concerning a punch Ladle, accusation and Condemnation of Mr Proto-musicus, more disputes of little Significancy.

    Delirant Reges, plectuntur Achivi, says a Certain celebrated poet,[1] whom perhaps you may be more thoroly acquainted with than I, and if not, 'tis not a farthing's matter, for our present purpose; as I only use this Adage, to apply it to the circumstances of the ancient and honorable Tuesday Club, at this Juncture, by the preposterous conduct of Mr Protomusicus Neverout, the meaning of the Saying is, "That when kings or great men lose their wits, or play the fool, the people must smart for it," but how is this applicable, you'll say, to Mr Protomusicus or the Club? why thus, Mr Protomusicus as a great man, or Club officer, tho' not a State officer, must be looked upon as a ruler in the Club, the next query will be, how this Club officer came to play the fool? and how by his playing the fool, the Club became [331] Sufferers? The State of the case is shortly thus, || the long standing members had an opportunity, of soaking their noses for one night at least in good Strong English beer, presented them by Merry Makefun Esqr, honorary member, which would have been a good and comfortable thing for them, but they were unjustly baulked of this refined pleasure, by means of Mr Neverout's secreting and keeping back that beer, in which conduct, that officer may Justly be said to have plaid the fool, for he drew upon himself thereby, the Indignation of his honor the president, the wrath of the Club, and had a Standing Joke fixed upon him, which has been kept up to this very day, and it is thought that he will never hear the last of it.

---

1. "When kings go crazy, the Achaeans are punished" (Horace, *Epistulae,* 1.2.14).

Whereupon, at Sederunt 69th Novr 10th 1747, The honorable the President being high Steward, he was, in the face of the Club, Indicted by Mr Speaker Quaint as follows.

"Solo Neverout Esqr, musician of the Tuesday Club, stands Indicted by the said Club, that he, the said Solo Neverout Esqr, being unworthily dignified with the title of musician, did, on the third day of august last, unjustly, willfully, maliciously, and with a bad Intention, censure a most elegant letter, wrote by Sir John Oldcastle to his honor the president, and that he the said Solo Neverout Esqr, on the 27th day of october last, did willfully and Insolently absent himself, from a Club, held at the house of Mr Speaker Quaint, without sending a line of ‖ excuse before noon to the said [332] Mr Quaint, the high Steward, contrary to an act of this here Club, in that case made and provided, and, that he, the said Solo Neverout Esqr being Intrusted, with nine bottles of English beer, presented by Mr Merry Makefun, an honorary member, to this Society, did, unjustly willfully and pitifully, deprive the said Society thereof, and convert the same to his own use, contrary to right Justice and Inconsistent with the honor of this honorable Society, and the dignity conferred upon him, the said Solo Neverout Esqr, by the said Society."

To all which three charges, Jointly and Severally, Mr Protomusicus Neverout, pleaded not guilty, in manner and form as aforesaid, and had allowed him for council, Mr Secretary Scribble, by whose eloquence and acuteness, the die turned up in his favor, as to the two first articles of accusation, tho the evidence was pritty Strong against him.

Upon the third Article, Mr Stentor Snuffysnout, who attended the Club at this Sederunt, was called upon to deliver his evidence, which he did in a distinct and peremptory manner, declaring in a Strong pithy voice, uttered in a loud key as high as *G Sol re in alt*, and with a particular Emphasis, That Mr Merry Makefun, had sent to Mr Neverout, and to him, (the evidence,) a large parcell of English beer, and that he had ordered one dozen and a half bottles of the same, to be de- ‖ livered for the use of this [333] here ancient and honorable Club, the moiety of which, vizt: nine bottles, had been delivered into the hands of Mr Neverout, and the other moiety he, the evidence had already delivered himself to this ancient and honorable Club.

This peremptory evidence gravelled Mr Protomusicus's Learned council, for, it was so plain against the Culprit, that he knew not how to quibble him out of this premunire or puzzlementation, as he called it, which put Mr Neverout in a Sort of huff-gruff humor, and made his council faulter in his discourse; on which, his honor the president notwithstanding his great gravity, and the solemnity of the occasion, could not forbear letting his face first expand it self, into a gelastic grin, and then burst out a laughing, most Immoderatly in the Chair, at last It came to high words and loud Swearing, between the evidence and the criminal, but the Speaker behaved with that profound gravity and decency which became his office.

However, at last, the Club Inclining to favor him, determined that he was not guilty of converting the beer to his own use, but guilty of retaining it in his hands for his own service night, for which he was reprimanded in a very Solemn and Serious manner by his honor the president from the Chair.

This Criminal trial was the first that occurred in this ancient and honorable Club, since its Institution, and was carried on with great decency and [334] Solemnity, except now and then a horse laugh, and a loud ex- || clamation from the Criminal, with two or three full mouthed Oaths from Mr Stentor Snuffysnout the evidence, who rapt out several *God Dammes* with great vehemence, and as they said swore thro' a plough Share.

Many people, deeply versed in physical causes, asserted, that the club acted wrong, in making such an uproar about this beer, for, said they, it is notorious, that the compotation of beer, very much deadens and flattens the animal Spirits, and, being a Sleepy Phlematic Guzzle, it brings on a hebetude and dullness, or a Stupidity peculiar to those hum-drum Clubs, in the neighbourhood of Moorfields, who, Immerged in beer and tobacco, sit whole nights and days together in a State of torpor or perfect Inactivity, and cannot communicate their Ideas, either by Speech or action, being only remarkable for their Swagbellies, broad faces, carbuncle noses and muddy eyes, till at last, these beer Sots losing all the little wit and Senses they had, the Devil finds an empty tenement, in their earthly tabernacles, a fit dwelling for him, and entering upon the premises, as he did of old into the herd of Swine, they become possessed, and by an easie transition, go into the neighbouring hospital of Bethelem, where ten to one they spend the remainder of their Days.

It was therefore asserted by these Ingenious naturalists, that Mr Protomusicus Neverout, consulted the Interest of the Club in what he did, and really, if we take the word of learned men for it, this assertion of theirs [335] seems to be grounded upon very good reasons; for || Henricus Ayrerus, a famous Physician, in advising an hypochondriac patient, condemns the use of beer, as also does Crato, saying *Crassum generat Sanguinem,*[2] and to confirm this, there is the old latin Sentence.

2. Perhaps a reference to Georg Heinrich Ayrer's (1702–1774) *De limitum praescriptione* (Göttingen, [1746]). Crato is probably Crito, physician at Trajan's court (ca. 100), fragments

———*Nil spissius illa,*
Dum bibitur, nil clarius est dum mingitur, unde,
Constat quod multas fæces in corpore linquat.

That is to say—

Nothing goes in so thick,
Nothing comes out so thin,
It must needs follow then,
The Dregs are left within.[3]

Robertus Burton a Club bard

And therefore, allowing the arguments of these philosophers, Mr Proto-musicus was not so much to blame in this affair as some may Imagin, but we shall see by and bye, whether this chief musician, really intended good to the Club, in an Instance of his conduct, with regard to the use to which he applied this very beer.

At Sederunt 70th Novr 24th 1747, Mr Secretary Scribble being high Steward, the following law was passed, at the Motion of the Master of Ceremonies.

Law XXXV. That henceforth from this day there shall be no disputes whatsoever, or Judicial trials carried on, or negotiated upon that night, in which the honorable the president is high Steward, or upon the anniversary of this club.

This law was procured at the Instance and ‖ desire of his honor the [336] president, whose good humor and Complaisance was such, that he chose not to have the Quiet and pleasure of the Club Interrupted or marr'd upon that night on which he entertained, a very great Indulgence this, that his honor would rather suffer the Guilty to escape (a thing that he was by no means at other times fond of) or delay their punishment, than Interrupt the pleasure the Club had in enjoying his most elegant entertainments, where the choicest dainties were always produced according to ancient custom. Yet some thought that his honors true motive for procuring this Law, was because these trials and disputes, confined him too much to the Chair, so that he had not full Liberty of trotting to and from the kitchen, to see how the Club Cookery went foreward.

---

of whose teachings appear in Galen's works (which probably contain this passage meaning "coarse food generates blood").

3. More literally, "Nothing is thicker than it / When it is drunk, nothing clearer when pissed; hence / It is plain that it leaves many dregs behind in the body." The more refined translation by "Robertus Burton" is probably Hamilton's.

At the following Sederunt, Slyboots Pleasant Esqr being high Steward, his honor the president paid to the Secretary out of the box, the Sum of ten Shillings in consideration of his having furnished the Club, with a new book of Records.

And at this same Sederunt, Mr Laconic Comus, made a motion in Club, to the Surprize of many, for he was a man of very few words, vizt: That a voluntary Contribution should be raised to purchase a handsom Silver punch Ladle, for the use of the Club—This motion came naturally enough from Mr Comus, of whom it might well be said, *mens in patinis,*[4] for the greatest part of his Cogitation ran upon punch and its appurte-
[337] nances, such as bowls, || ladles and strainers; this motion however, excited a very warm dispute, the Secretary and some others opposing the motion with all their might, alledging That there was no necessity for taxing the Club for any such thing, as there was money enough in the box, wherewith to procure any thing of that Sort, which was wanted, for the use of the Club. This objection did not at all please his honor the president, who said That it would be contradictory to the original design of the box, which was allotted for charity, to lay out that fund upon punch Ladles, or any such triffles. The Secretary upon this boldly replied That he saw no occasion for the Longstanding members being taxed to purchase triffles—at which words his honor the president frowned tremendous from the Chair, but that tremendous frown availed nothing, The Secretary harangued still and spoke very loud, and the whole Club fell into a general uproar, while Mr Comus laying down his pipe with great Indignation, rubd his forehead nose and Chin with the palm of his right hand, and often threw in the pithy Interjections, of *by God* & *God damn it—damn the box—send it to hell!* and such like, Some of the members Indeed contributed towards purchasing of this triffle, and that very Largely, and among others his honor the president himself, in order to keep the box shut, opened his purse strings, others kept their pockets shut, and were Inexorable on that Score, among whom was the Secretary, at this proceeding Mr Comus was much chagrined, To find his first, and Indeed his last motion in Club (for he never after this made another) thus Crushed and quashed, his honor the president was also much
[338] Incensed, || not for being dissappointed of this Club ladle, for he declared afterwards, that he looked upon it as a bawble, but because an open atack had been made upon the box, the pillaging of which he could not bear to hear of, as it would be as he said, Intirely frustrating the Charitable end for

4. "His mind is on the dishes."

which it was established, but great men, as well as little men ought always to Remember to be consistent with themselves at all times in arguments of this nature, for had his honor reflected on this rule, he would not have gravely proposed, a few Sederunts after this, to buy with the box money a Club table Cloth and Club Napkins, of some very fine diaper, which he had in his own Store for Sale; I would only ask, what Sort of Charity this was, after this dispute, the Club broke up in a bad humor.

At the next Sederunt, Mr Protomusicus Neverout being high Steward, this gentleman was again accused by the Speaker, for a breach of Law 30, for not wearing the Club badge, and after some arguments pro and con, he was condemn'd to drink off a bumper, which he complied with, and drank to the long continuance of the Club, and to the good agreement of the upper and lower houses of Assembly now sitting, and then, Investing himself with the Club badge, he began to ply his honor the president with bumpers of Strong beer, and dealt it so liberally about among the Longstanding members, that the whole remainder of the nine bottles, left in his hands, was soon sucked up, this shows, that he had but little regard to the health of the Longstanding members, as has been hinted above, tho' this gentleman's friends do not stick to ‖ say, that he did this to punish the Club [339] for their scurvy usage of him, and allowed them to swallow so much Strong liquor on purpose, that, feeling the bad effects of it, they might never again, make such another racket about Strong beer on a like occasion, should it ever happen, his honor the president however, by this profuseness of the high Steward at other people's expence, got so bungy,⁵ as the phraze is, that after having outsung Mr Protomusicus, and beat him at his own weapons, in the Celebrated Club Song of *When Cloe we ply,* he sung a favorite Song of his own to the Club, with great humor and Glee, together with many others, which he had in a book that he usually Carried about with him in his pocket.

*A favorite Club Song, sung by his honor the President*⁶

Where are you going my pritty maid?
I'm going a milking, Sir, she said,
Shall I go with you, my pritty maid?
You're kindly welcome Sir, she said.

5. *Bungy* means "puffed out" or "protuberant"; here, "bloated from too much drinking."
6. I have not located a contemporary copy of this tune, though apparently it was a popular tune indeed, since another version of it later appears as "Young Donald, of Edinborough Town" in *The Universal Songster; or, Museum of Mirth* (London, 1828), III, 102.

What if I Lay you down, my pritty maid?
Why then you must cover me, Sir she said,
I thank you kindly my pritty maid,
Your Kindly welcome, Sir she said.

But should I get you with Child my pritty maid?
Why then you must father it, Sir she said,
[340]   I thank you kindly, my pritty maid,
Your kindly welcome Sir, she said.

But I will not marry you, my pritty maid,
I never desird you, Sir she said,
I thank you kindly my pritty maid,
Your kindly welcome Sir she said.

The Justness of the measure, the uniformity of the Rhime and the unity or Sameness of the Sentiment or thought, (for Indeed there is but one thought runs thro the whole, tho not a very modest one,) show not only the excellence of this Song, but the great propriety of his honor's taste in chusing it to entertain the Longstanding members.

At the following Sederunt, which was the 73d, on the 5th of January, 1747/8, Jealous Spyplot Esqr being high Steward, a dispute arose in Club concerning a Claim the Secretary put in, of being deputy treasurer, under the honorable the president, as being entrusted with one key of the box; The honorable the president Claiming himself the title of sole treasurer, after many arguments pro and con, the high Steward, and the Master of Ceremonies standing up, on the part of his honor the president, and Sir John Oldcastle, and Mr Protomusicus, on the part of the Secretary, In which dispute, Mr Musician Neverout, in the opinion of the majority of the Club, made several bold and Strenous Speeches in the defence of Clubical Liberty, and in the opinion of his honor the president, and the gentlemen [341] on the other Side of the argument, arogant and assuming ‖ speeches, the affair was left undetermined, till Mr Speaker Quaint should be present in Club, to regulate and settle the dispute, this gentleman having now gained such a great character in the Club, for pleading and arguing, that they Implicitly submitted all to his decisions, but, he being a state officer, it was no difficult matter to guess, on which Side he would declare whenever the honorable Chair was concerned in the dispute, a common way with thorro' paced Courtiers, who have no opinion or private Judgement of their own, but act by a kind of public Judgement, founded upon the will and pleasure, or rather the caprice of their patrons, lords and masters, hence it is, we often find those gentlemen, gravely and confidently asserting that black is white, day is night, two and two make five, while they, and all the world besides, are Conscious of the falsity of these propositions, and political maxims.

On the same Sederunt, a debate arose in Club about who should serve upon the Anniversary of the Club next ensuing, vizt: the 14 of may 1748, whether the member in Course, or the honorable Mr President Jole, Several of the members, particularly, Jealous Spyplot Esqr, high Steward, and Sir John Oldcastle, set up in Competition for the honor, and Mr Secretary, to whose turn it fell of Course, by a Just Calculation, pleading his right, his honor generously determined the dispute, by taking it upon himself, which, as it conduced most to the honor of the Society, and the Importance of the occasion, so it was unanimously Consented to by the whole Club.

Chapter V

Election and admission of Jonathan Grog Esqr, into the Club, more Club letters, Institution of the presidential Star and badge, Speech of Jonathan Grog Esqr, to the Chair.

Magninus says, that a merry Companion is better than a Song, and, as the old proverb goes, *Comes Jucundus* || *in via pro vehiculo,* a Jocular fellow [342] to a man in the moaps is as a waggon to a Jaded foot travellar,[1] for mirth may be said to be the Nepenthe of Homer, Hellen's bowl and Venuse's girdle or Cestis, nor is mirth In my opinion at all repugnant to true philosophy, seeing the gravest and most philosophical dons, have been at times extravagantly merry, The wise Socrates would be merry by fits, would sing, dance and drink his glass, or Theodoret Damnably belies him, so would Cato, and even Tully by his own confession, in his familiar Epistles book 7th Xenophon describes Socrates as a very droll old fellow, taking on himself the Character of an Actor or comedian, and Valerius Maximus Cap: 8, lib: 8 says of him, *Interposita Arundine cruribus, suis cum filiis ludens, ab Alcibiade risus est;* he would ride hobby horses with his children, and was laugh'd at for this by Alcibiades, who was not by half so wise a man as he,[2]

1. Jean-Chrysostome Magnen (fl. 17th century), a French physician and philosopher, was the author of *Democritus reviviscens* (1646), to which Hamilton is referring. The passage literally means "an agreeable companion is like a cart on the road."

2. Theodoret (ca. 393–466), a monk, was bishop of Cyrrhus, Syria (from 423), and author of the *Church History* (spanning the period from Constantine to 428), the *Religious History,* and the *Graecarum affectionum curatio* (to which Hamilton is probably referring), which painstak-

so, many a grinning Lubber may presume, if they please to laugh at our
Clubical Sages, tho' not half so wise as they; and Horace says of Scipio and
Lælius,

Qui, ubi se a vulgo et Scena in Secreta remorant,
Virtus Scipiades, et mitis Sapientia Læli,
Nugari cum Illo, et discincti ludere donec
De coqueretur olus, soliti—

Which passage I find thus translated by an old Clubical bard.

Valorous Scipio, and Gentle Lælius,
Removed from the Scene, and rout so Clamorous,
Were wont to recreate themselves, their robes laid by,
Whilst Supper by the cook was getting ready.[3]

Robertus Burton,
Oxon: poeta Clubicus

[343] And this was often the very case with the grave, the wise the ancient and
honorable Tuesday Club, and particularly the honorable the president, who
used to lay bye his robes like Scipio and Lælius, and Bestirr himself vigorously, backwards and forewards, in a blue Silk Jacket, whilst Supper was
getting ready in the kitchen. The old greeks had their *Lubentiam Deam,*
their Goddess of mirth, and the Spartans, Instructed by their Lawgiver
Lycurgus, did *Deo Risui sacrificare,* sacrifise to the God of Laughter, after
their wars especially, and in times of peace, which was practised in Thessaly,
as appears by Appuleius Book 2d of the *Golden Ass,*[4] who was himself made
the Instrument of their laughter, why therefore might not the ancient and
honorable Tuesday Club, after their hot disputes, and In their Calmer Intervals, by the Instruction of the honorable Nasifer Jole Esqr, their wise president and Lawgiver, make themselves merry, be Jocose, and execute their
great gelastic Law, one upon another? And this we shall find they often
effectually did, making use for an Instrument on these occasions, of Jona-

---

ingly contrasts paganism and Christianity. Valerius Maximus (fl. 1st century A.D.) was a sententious and sometimes bombastic Roman historian; the passage that Hamilton attributes to him,
which literally means "Placing a hobby-horse on his shin, playing with his children, he was
mocked by Alcibiades," does appear in bk. 8, chap. 8, ext. 1 of Valerius Maximus's works.

3. Scipio is identified above (see p. 10n); his close friend Gaius Laelius shared in Scipio's
African campaign (204–202 B.C.) and became proconsul in Gaul (189 B.C.). More literally, the
passage translated by "Robertus Burton" (probably Hamilton) reads: "In the secret places
where they removed themselves from the crowd and the stage, / Courageous Scipio and mildly
wise Laelius / Were wont to joke with him [Lucilius], and to play unbelted / While supper was
cooking" (Horace, *Satirae* 2.1.71).

4. Apuleius (born ca. 123) was a poet, philosopher, and rhetorician whose *Metamorphoses*
(better known as *The Golden Ass*) is the only complete Latin novel extant.

than Grog Esqr, as the Thessalonians did of Appuleius, and, of the admission of this facetious Gentleman, we are now going to give an account.

On Sederunt 74th February 2d 1747/8, the Club assembled at the house of the worshipful Sir John Oldcastle high Steward, who, Invested with the Clubs badge in a Courteous, civil and Champion like manner, || complimented the honorable president, by meeting and Saluting him ten paces from the door; this was a piece of complaisance in Sir John, which it was feared would Introduce a bad custom, among the members, and occasion an additional trowble to the high Stewards, but, great as the personage was, who set the first example, it never was since Imitated by any of the Succeeding high Stewards. [344]

The dispute carried on in Club at last Sederunt concerning the Secretaries claim, to the title and office of deputy treasurer, which was then left undetermined, now came again upon the tapis, and was at this Sederunt, determined, settled, and Concluded, by the eloquence and Arguments of Mr Speaker Quaint, who confuted all the Strenous arguments brought against him by Sir John Oldcastle, and Mr Protomusicus, and thereupon, it was ordained, by a majority of voices, that the honorable the president should be Sole Treasurer, and that the Secretary should only have the title of key keeper; a great baulk to that ambitious and aspiring Secretary, who had been still aiming at advancement, and a multiplicity of offices in the Club, but was not able as yet, to compass his ends, tho' we shall find that he had better Success in the Sequel.

Upon a motion made by the Master of ceremonies, to Elect Mr Jonathan Grog of Annapolis, a member of the Club, he having made application, for the same to several of the members, the ballots, or Yeas and Nays were put Round by the Secretary, pursuant to the tenor of Law 9th, and being found all Yeas, the Secretary was ordered to acquaint the said Mr Jonathan Grog of this, by writing, desiring his attendance || at next Sederunt. As this gentleman, will in the Succeeding part of our History, make a very considerable appearance, as a longstanding member of this ancient and honorable Club, holding no less than five offices at one and the same time, vizt: those of purveyor, punster, punchmaker General, Printer and poet, which were signified, for brevity's Sake, by five capital P's thus, Jonathan Grog Esqr, P.P.P.P.P. it will not be amiss here, to give an Iconographical description of his person, and a Scetch of his Character. [345]

This Gentleman is of a middle Stature, Inclinable to fat, round faced, small lively eyes, from which, as from two oriental portals, Incessantly dart the dawning rays of wit and humor, with a considerable mixture of the amorous leer, in his countenance he wears a constant Smile, having never

[Hamilton's translation on back of drawing]

Behold of Clubic Bards the prime
Who sings thee, Cole, in pleasant Rhime,
And whilst his rhime is read, thy fame,
Shall live, so shall our poets name.

[facing page 343]

been once seen to frown; his body is thick and well set, and for one of his make and Stature he has a good Sizeable belly, into which he loves much to convey the best vittles and drink, being a good clean knife and forks man, tho' no Glutton, and his favorite Dish is Roast turkey with oisters, and his darling liquor of late is Grog, he professing himself to be of the moderen Sect of the Grogorians, and as some think the patron and founder of that Sect in Annapolis, which we shall have occasion to describe somewhere in this history, he is a very great admirer, Improver and encourager of wit, humor and drollery, and is fond of that Sort of poetry which is called Doggrell, in which he is himself a very great proficient, and Confines his genius chiefly to it, tho sometimes he cannot help emitting some flashes of the true Sublime, in his Club Compositions; puns, Conundrums || merry [346] tales and Jests, are the favorite Subjects, on which he Chuses to exercise his wit and talents, and we shall find him affording abundance of mirth to the Club, in his compositions of this Sort, in fine, to sum up all he is really a good humored, smooth tempered, merry, Jocose, and Innofensive compan-ion, a man of the most happy Clubical Genius that ever was known, and a Great promoter Improver and encourager of Clubific felicity, for were there 50 Clubs in the place, he'd be a member of every one of them; he is a passionate admirer of natural Curiosities, and certain little knick knacks, produced by the whimsical Inventions of art, of which he has a valuable Collection by him, some of which we may have occasion to mention in this history.

At the following Sederunt, which was held on the 16th of february, Smoothum Sly Esqr, being high Steward, and Laconic Comus Esqr, deputy in the Chair, Mr Jonathan Grog made his first appearance in the Club, and being Civily Saluted and welcomed, by all the longstanding members, he took his Seat in Club, as a Longstanding member. A Letter from his honor the president to the high Steward, was produced in Club, and read as follows.

To the Revd: Smoothum Sly,
high Steward of the Tuesday Club, These.

Sir,

As I shall not be at the Club this night, be pleased to acquaint the Gentlemen, that I have appointed Mr Comus to take the Chair in my room, and, as I || hope the most *Importand* affairs have been debated, your present [347] meeting will be attended with good harmony and agreement, I am, Sir,

Feb: 16th 1747   Your most humble Servant
                                   Nasifer Jole.

Then the following Law was passed, vizt:

Law XXXVI. Whereas several contests and disputes have happened in Club, concerning a Clause in Law 27th appointing the money in the Club's box to be disposed of only by unanimous consent, to prevent therefore such disputes for the future; Be it ordained & passed into a Law, by the president and Club now met, this 16th Day of february 1747/8, and by the authority of the same, that all resolves whatsoever, and all points which come under the consideration of the Club, shall be settled and determined by a majority of voices, excepting only the election of members, any law, rule or order of this here Club, to the contrary notwithstanding.

In this Law we find the Club, first adopting the enacting Stile, and looking upon themselves as a Solemn Legislative power, which we shall find, sometime after this they carried still farther, for their Stile and diction became at last quite parliamentary; The Club found themselves under a necessity to make such a Law as this, in order to extract the money out of the box, for such purposes as they saw proper, since no arguments, perswasions or methods of any Sort, could bring his honor the president to part [348] with one single farthing of it, except for such || purposes as were pleasing or agreeable to himself, but this law was of little or no Significancy or use, for his honor the president afterwards objected to it, as being passed in his absence, hence we see, what a fine kettle of fish this here Club had Cooked for themselves, in granting so much power to the Chair, and 'tis Lamentable to think to what a state of Slavery their rash concessions had already reduced them, but we shall soon see a flame burst out in the Club, concerning this box, which had well nigh consumed the Club it self, and compleated its dissolution, but, by the prudence and good management of the Speaker, tho' a Stanch courtier, the mischief was prevented and the affair ended in the destruction of this pestilent box, and here we may observe, that tho' the breath of the honorable Speaker, was not hot enough to kindle an unextinguishable flame in the Club, upon another occasion, yet on this exigency, the frigidity of the said flatus was such that it quickly extinguished the fire.

At Sederunt 76th March 1, 1747/8, The Club was held for the first time by Jonathan Grog Esqr, as high Steward, Mr Secretary Scribble, being by his honor's appointment deputy in the Chair, and the Revd Smoothum Sly Esqr, Deputy Secretary.

There happened at this Sederund, a kind of civil Commotion in the Club, a furious brawl having arisen between Mr Protomusicus, and the Deputy President, about the Presidential Chair, his honor the president having sent orders to the high Steward, that which ever of those two Gentlemen, should appear first in Club || should take the Chair, as deputy. The [349] Secretary appearing first, took that honorable Seat, but Mr Protomusicus entering the Club room soon after, attempted in a violent manner to pull the Secretary out of the Chair, and would have mastered him by superior Strength, but was prevented by the Interposition of the Longstanding Members.

A very Complaisant Letter, sent by the high Steward to his honor the president, was produced in Club, and being read by the Revd Mr Sly, deputy Secretary, was ordered to be entered upon record as follows.

To Nasifer Jole Esqr,
President of the Tuesday Club,
at his dwelling house in North east Street Annapolis.

Honorable Sir,   St Davids day A:M: 1747/8
    Your absence from the Club at their last meeting, on Tuesday night, the 16th of february, prevented my having an opportunity then, of returning my thanks to you, for my admittance, into that worthy and honorable Society, over which you so deservedly preside, however Sir, I hope, you will now be pleased to accept of my hearty and Grateful acknowledgements of the favor, I have heard with great regret, some few days agoe, that you were Indisposed with the Gout, but, I flatter myself, that you are now || better, [350] and hope you will dignify the Club this evening with your presence at the house of, Honorable Sir,

                              Your much obliged
                              Greatly Devoted
                              Very humble Servant
                              Jonathan Grog, high Steward.

    Before the Club broke up, a hot dispute happened between the deputy Secretary, and Mr Laconic Comus, concerning the Presbyterians, to which sect, the last mentioned Gentleman had a rooted aversion, and on this occasion Mr Comus was observed to talk more copiously & fluently, than he had ever done at any time before in Club, or ever since, which some naturalists would attribute to the power and virtue of the High Steward's Rumbo, the fumes of which, had ascended so copiously into Mr Comus's cranium, that the deputy president, and deputy Secretary, found great difficulty that night, to carry him home safe, this was a glaring instance of the truth of that maxim, that men are most apt to slide into Religious controversy, when flustered with Strong liquor.

    At the following Sederunt, on the 15th of March, Capt: Seemly spruce being high Steward, the regulation of the next Anniversary procession was agreed in Club to be referred to the consideration of a more full meeting, and the Catch of the *Great bell of Lincoln* was sung by his honor the president, in honor of the Admission of Jonathan Grog Esqr.

[351]   At Sederunt 78 March 29th 1748, Laconic Comus Esqr being high Steward, the following Law was passed.

Law XXXVII. That the president shall appear every Club Night with his badge, with the following additional Inscription upon a Square Card, to distinguish his, from the badges of the high Steward & other Members, vizt: NASIFER JOLE *armiger, Societatis Annapolitanæ, Diei martis* (THE ANNAPOLIS TUESDAY CLUB) *uti vocatur Præfectus.*[5]

Accordingly, Jonathan Grog Esqr, was ordered to prepare and produce this Card to the Club at next Sederunt, pursuant to which order, at the following Sederunt, Mr Speaker Quaint, being high Steward, the Card was produced in Club, which, upon examination, was committed to the hands of Jonathan Grog Esqr, to receive some additional alterations and Improvements.

Thus we see, that this ancient and honorable Club, not satisfied with the honors and dignities, which they had already Conferred upon his honor the president, proceeded still to heap more of these upon him, we shall find that they did not stop here, and shall also see what thanks and grateful returns they had from his honor, for taking all this pains, which I hope, will be a lesson to all Clubs, to be cautious how they go too far, in bestowing marks of honor and dignity upon their presidents.

[352]   At this Sederunt, Jonathan Grog Esqr, delivered a ‖ congratulatory speech to his honor the President, upon the occasion of his admission, and rising from his Seat he first bowed to the Chair, and then to the Club, and with a pleasant Smile on his countenance, spoke as follows.

"Mr President, Sir,

I here stand up, in quality of a Longstanding member, of this here ancient and honorable Club, to make my grateful acknowledgements of the obligations I lie under to your honor, and the Longstanding members of this here Club, in doing me the honor, to admit me a longstanding member of their honorable Society; an honor I set a great value upon, and shall always endeavor to behave myself in such a manner, as that your honor and these here longstanding members, shall never have reason to repent your having conferrd this honor upon me, I have the best reasons in the world to be satisfied with this here good Society, as I find every thing in it that is

5. "Nasifer Jole, arms-bearer of the Annapolis Tuesday Club, where he is called Prefect."

Sociable and agreeable, and besides I find that we eat and drink well in this here Club, hence must flow good humor, and as a consequence of that we must sleep well—and this here Society seems to be settled upon so firm a basis, that nothing but Death can separate the members of it one from another."

Having delivered this Speech, Jonathan Grog Esqr, bowed low to the honorable the Chair, and then to the members all round, and sat down, wearing on his face an open and pleasant Smile, while he renewd again ‖ his chaw of tobacco, which he had deposited when he rose up to speak; [353] we shall observe here, that this is the first Set Speech to the Chair, that stands upon Record, and, In its Structure and Composition, some Scattering Sparks of the authors Ingenuity and vivacity of Imagination break forth, the lively corruscations of which, we shall find abounding in all his Club Compositions.

The Speaker being desired to deliver the thanks of the Club to Mr Grog for his speech, requested the Secretary to do that office for him, which he did, and the Secretary having finished this Speech to Mr Grog, addressed Mr Speaker Quaint in a congratulatory manner, upon the occasion of his late marriage, for which he had the thanks of Mr Speaker, delivered in a very ornate and polite Stile.

Chapter VI

Clubical Letters, Celebration of the Third Anniversary, Improvement made on the Club badges; the title of Oldcastle resigned by Sir John, the Success of the Box petition.

When Roscius[1] the Actor florished at Rome, which was much about the time of the Augustine age, all Sorts of Learning and arts, were in their full perfection, the Imperial Court was crouded with polite Authors of all Sorts, Poets, Historians, Philosophers, orators and Letter writers, Such were Virgil, Horace, Livy, Tully; Just so was it at this very period, in the ancient and ‖ honorable Tuesday Club, when Jonathan Grog Esqr, that [354] Celebrated Comic poet, began to florish there, the wit and genius of several of the Longstanding members shone out with a Conspicuous Lustre, and

1. Gallus Roscius (fl. 1st century B.C.) was a famous Roman actor whose name became synonymous with the consummate artist.

continued still to Increase, ever since that happy Epocha, as will appear in the Sequel.

The first thing they Improved in, was their Epistolary writing, for, at Sederunt 80, April 26th 1748, Mr Secretary Scribble being high Steward, we find two Sublime letters wrote to his honor the president, and the worshipful Sir John Oldcastle, by the Secretary, and, as this Gentleman was the first Introducer of Set Speeches in the Club, so he was the first Improver of Epistolary writing, the Letters stand upon Record as follows.

To the Honorable Nasifer Jole Esqr,
president of The Tuesday Club, These.

Most Honorable Sir,

It being my good fortune to serve as high Steward to your honor and the worthy Club this night, your presence, to grace the Chair, and enliven the Society, would considerably add, to the pleasure I enjoy, in being honored with that Sublime office, the return of every opportunity of this kind, to serve your honor, and the worthy Club, gives me no small Satisfaction, to serve the Club to be Sure is a pleasure, whether your honor be absent or present, but I think your presence, reflects a particular dignity upon the high Steward, which as it is not ‖ in the power of even the magnanimous Sir John Oldcastle himself, to communicate in such an eminent degree as your honor, so, far less, can there be any such Innate dignity, in a deputy president, or Inferior officer,—I hope then, your honor, will be so benign & benevolent, as to do me that honor, upon which I deservedly set so high a value.

I have sent the presidential Badge, adorned and finished in such a manner, as I hope will please your honor, it is fixed upon my own badge Ribbon, to show the way, in which it is to be adapted, I could wish your honor would wear it this night, according to the Law of Sederunt 78, to decorate our Club, but that I must leave to your honor's determination, whether you will wear it this night, or deferr your appearance in it to the Grand Anniversary parade; please send back my badge Ribban, as I shall have occasion to use it this night.

I have wrote to the worshipful Sir John Oldcastle in a Sublime and exalted Stile, adapted to his dignity and office, and, I believe, he will Considerably add to the Splendor and Dignity of our Society, by his attendance, I have therefore prepared for him a magnificent Chair of State, at your honor's right hand, & am, with all due respect,—most honorable Sir,

[355]

Die martis   Your faithful high Steward and
April 26th 1748   trusty Secretary
                                                  Loquacious Scribble.

The tenor of the Letter to Sir John Oldcastle was, as follows.   [356]

To the Right Worshipful, Sir John Oldcastle knight of the Tuesday Club.

Superlatively Worshipful & dignified Sir John,

I being most extatically elevated with the propinquity of the occasion, when I shall be dignified with the ministerial dignity of high Steward, to our most Stupendous and august Society, cannot forbear, in the midst of my accumulated Raptures, writing to the honorable the president, and your Equestrian dignity, the honor of his presence, I question not, but I shall participate, but the Splendor of the grand Consistory will be Incompleat, unless your worship deigns to confer your presence, and then Indeed, O then! we shall shine with Irresistable Splendor, and magnificence, and dispell every cloud that may threaten to hang over our Significant heads, excepting only that of tobacco, the dear Specific condensator of political and Sage conceptions.

I have sent to the honorable the president his badge of office, a most Splendid Glittering ornament, made in the form of a periphery, so begilt and bespangled, as that it looks like the planetary System in minature, elucesscent in full Glory, a Just type of the Nitor^2 and harmony of our homogene Society, of which his honor the president himself, may be said to be the Solar Center, your worship that kindly planet the moon, ‖ who   [357] reflects the light she receives from the former, less constant and vigorous indeed, but milder and more benign, the rest of our officers, according to their talents may be accounted the Smaller planets, and our Commoners are Second rate Stars or Satellites, that move round the Greater or more Splendid orbs, pray excuse this poetical excursion, and if possible, let us have the honor of your worship's worshipful company, this will not only oblige the whole Junto, but, in a particular manner, Most worshipful and dignified Sir John,

Die martis   The humblest of your
April 26th 1748   humble Servants
                                         Loquacious Scribble H: Std:

At this same Sederunt it was agreed, that there should be no procession at the Subsequent Anniversary, but the members were appointed to meet at the honorable the presidents and there Invest themselves with their badges.

The above letters of Mr Secretary Scribble's show the turn which that

2. Brightness, brilliance.

Gentleman had for the Bumbast. In this Strain of writing he held for some considerable time, and Infected with it some of the Longstanding members that after this came into the Club, nay even the wise grave and Sagacious Jealous Spyplot Esqr, and the plain spoken Mr Laconic Comus did not escape this Contagion; till at Last he mixed the Sublime with the bathos, in [358] a very burlesque manner, by || affecting to blend this puffed up Stile, with some Strokes of Jonathan Grog Esqr's punnish and Conundrumish expletives and tropes.

The honorable the President mounted the Chair this night with his new badge card, which made a very resplendent Show, and was cut or fashioned in the Shape of a Star curiously Gilt painted and Spangled, of which a figure or representation is here exhibited in the margin.

As the Anniversary of the Clubs Institution was now fast approaching, matters were to be put all in Decent order, for the Celebration of that most grand and Solemn festival, and his honour the president had been constantly Employed night and day, watching, working and running about, for at least the Space of three weeks, that every thing might be put in decent rank and file, or (as the Saying is) *in gynger bread order* for this Grand feast.

[359]   The Club badges now almost wore out were renewed, and had an Improvement made upon them (which was curiously drawn by Mr Benjamin Wood) this was the figure of two hands Joined over a heart, very expressive of that cordiality, that reigns, or ought to reign among the members of the same Club; and Indeed among the members of any Society, great or small, that desires to last and prosper. The figure of this new badge card is represented in the annexed draught.

Upon the 81t Sederunt, being Tuesday the 17th Day of May, 1748, was Celebrated the third Anniversary of the Club, when all the Longstanding members, and four of the Honorary members, vizt: Collonel Courtly Phraze, Mr Oldham Wisely, Mr Abraham Bumper and Mr Joshua Fluter,

assembled In the Great Saloon in the house of the Honorable Mr President
Jole, then high Steward, and Invested themselves in their badges, and the
honorable the Speaker, and several of the members made congratulatory
Speeches to his Honor the President upon this Solemn occasion, several
loyal healths were drank after Supper, || and the entertainment as usual was
very Sumptous and elegant.   [360]

Some little contests arose at this time among the long standing members, concerning the publication of an article of news in the weekly Journal
of Jonathan Grog Esqr, relative to the Club's Anniversary,[3] which in some
measure broke and Interrupted the mirth and Jollity of the night, the Secretary and Master of Ceremonies looked much askew at one another, Sir John
Oldcastle put on first his Spectacles, and then his blusterous countenance to
examine the devoted paragraph Intended for the press, and deeply Grumbling with Indignation, took pen and Ink, and blotted out Interlined and
refined as he thought proper, Laconic Comus Esqr, mumbled and Grumbled, and was heard to swear *by God,* and *God damn it* several times, between his teeth as it were, chawing the Stem of his pipe, the Roman Catholics and Jacobites were mightily run down, and abused by some in the Club,
and by others defended, in short, there had like to have happened a lamentable brawl, but this variance was in a great measure mitigated, by an humorous Speech, delivered after Supper by the Secretary, which, not having been
recorded, is now Irrecoverably lost, and at last, they were thorro'ly recovered from their doleful dumps, by the vivacity and musical voice of Mr
Protomusicus, who Concluded the Solemnity with the following trumpet
Song.

Trumpet Air, sung by Mr Protomusicus[+]

The kings health, the kings health,
   Let the trumpet sound,
   And the glass go round,   [361]
   Huzza! Huzza! Huzza!

To the downfall of usurpation,
   And I Long to see the day,
   Confusion to him

3. Having caused such a lamentable hubbub, this article announcing the club's anniversary
was never published in the *Md. Gaz.*

4. A variation of this toast appears in Thomas D'Urfey's *Wit and Mirth; or, Pills to Purge
Melancholy,* 6 vols. (London, 1719–1720), II, 83–85.

Who would set it up again,
Huzza! Huzza! Huzza!

Some Longstanding members, who were either too strait laced in their whiggish principles, or were at bottom, no true friends to our happy constitution, alledged that this was a Jacobite Song, but the Club and Mr Protomusicus laughed at their Ignorance and presumption.

Mr Dumpling Gundiguts, having been absent from the Club, ever since the 16th of february last, and having offered no excuse, was, by the tenor of Law 13th, excluded the Club, and, as he was a longstanding member of very little Significancy, or Importance, serving only, like a Chair in a country dance, to fill up a void Space, neither his honor the president, nor the Club, were sorry for it.

At Sederunt 83d June 18th, Jealous Spyplot Esqr being high Steward, the title of Oldcastle, was taken from Sir John, at his own earnest request; because (said he) he was Informed, that one, of the title of Sir John Oldcastle was hanged, in the reign of Henry V, for being a Lollard, and he would bear no titles, on which the least mark of Infamy had been laid, whatever the Crime was, treason, heresy or felony, and besides it was his [362] opinion, that these borrowed names and ‖ titles, were beneath the dignity of the knight and Champion of this here ancient and honorable Club, who, if he had any title at all, it was very fit that he should have one peculiar to himself and none other.

At Sederunt 84, June 28, 1748, a contribution was raised among the Longstanding members for Mr Benjamin Wood, who had wrote out the New Club badges, and the money delivered to Jonathan Grog Esqr, to be paid to the said Wood, it is Surprizing to see the Stupidity and Infatuation of the members of this here Club, in this here very instance, to suffer themselves to be taxed in this here manner, when there was now upwards of Six pounds cash in the Club box, in the hands of his honor the president, but this had hitherto been a Sort of Mortmain, or bottomless gulph, into which, whatever was thrown, could never be brought out again.

On the following Sederunt, a letter from Sir John to the president, was produced and read in Club as follows.

To Nasifer Jole Esqr,
President of the Tuesday Club.

Sir,

Notwithstanding I am *fare,* from being well, that the Club may not *waite* any longer on me, I *entend* to entertain them this evening, in the best manner I can, tho' not so well as I could wish, were I in a better State of

health, but, as it so hap- ‖ pening, I flatter myself, that you, and the rest [363]
of the *worthey* members, have goodness enough to overlook what may be
amiss.

However, Sir, I hope to have the pleasure of your good Compe: which
will outshine any thing that could *possably* be in my power to do, even in the
best of times, I am, Sir, with *grate* respect

19th July 1748   Your Most humble Servant
                                            Sir John.

In this letter, Sir John follows the example of many great men, who
eminently distinguish themselves from vulgar writers, by deviating from the
Common Orthography, in many of their words.

On the following Sederunt August 2d, Captain Seemly Spruce being
high Steward, a petition signed by all the longstanding members, was presented and read in Club as follows.

To the honorable the President of the Tuesday Club, the humble Remonstrance, and petition of the Longstanding members of the said Club.

May it please the president,

Whereas, at a Sederunt of this here Club, held at the house of Capt:
Serious Social, late a worthy longstanding member of this Society, upon the
14th of ‖ January 1745, there was established and set on foot, a money box, [364]
to be applied to such uses as the Club should see proper, according to the
Laws made for that purpose, vizt: the Laws 20, 21, 22, 23, and particularly
by Law 36, passed february the 16th 1747/8 at a Sederunt held at the house of
Mr Speaker Quaint, where the money in this box, is ordained to be disposed of by a majority of voices. *Furthermore,* at the above said Sederunt, in
January 14th 1745, The Club appointed your honor, treasurer, giving you
the privilege of keeping the box, and one key thereof, while the Secretary
had the trust of the other key, and lastly at a Sederunt, held at the house of
Sir John Oldcastle (as then stiled) the Second day of febry 1747/8, your
honor was confirmed in the title of Sole Treasurer, the Secretary being only
stiled key keeper, The members here underwritten, unanimously acknowledge, that it was from the opinion they conceived of your honor's merit,
and great Integrity that they bestowed upon you, this trust, and honor, and
hope they shall have no cause to alter their mind, or change that good
opinion which they have so Justly conceived of their Honorable Chairman,
an opinion so necessary to support and Continue your honor, in the said
trust.

The members underwritten therefore upon the two following posi-

tions ground the reasonableness of their present Remonstrance, and peti-
[365] tion || to your honor, vizt: that this here box, is the Indisputable property of
this here Club, being established and set on foot, by the consent and approbation of the members, and therefore, Secondly, it ought to be disposed of
according to the pleasure of the Club, or the majority of the same, as
appointed by Law 36th, & according to the meaning and Intent of the
words of Law 20th, vizt: for Charity, or such other good purposes, as the
majority of the Club shall see proper.

As your honor then, has been entrusted with the abovesaid box and
money, it is to be hoped, that you will not refuse the Request of all the
members under written, who earnestly require and sollicit, that the money
now Remaining in the box, may be aplied to purchase tickets in the Philadelphia Lottery now on foot, by which means a public benifit or good will
be promoted, one of the noblest, one of the best and greatest works of
charity, as it regards not a few Individuals, but the whole community and is
by no means confind to private benefits, and like wise, our Stock probably
may be Increased, at least, at the worst, we can be no great losers, there
being at present, according to the Secretaries account, only five pounds
Seventeen Shillings and Sixpence Currency in the box, after deducting your
honors Share, which your honor may Chuse to dispose of as you please, a
Sum so Inconsiderable, that it cannot be applied to any use of consequence,
[366] and scarce || deserves the name of a treasury, and therefor cannot confer the
dignified title of treasurer to its keeper, this, we earnestly desire your honor
maturely to consider, and must Insist on being satisfied in our demands,
and your Orators shall ever pray &ct:

> *Signed. Sir John*
> Drawlum Quaint Spkr: Jealous Spyplot
> Smoothum Sly Mr of Cer: Cap: Seemly Spruce
> Solo Neverout Protomus: Laconic Comas
> Loquacious Scribble Secret: Jonathan Grog
> Sly Boots Pleasant

This petition was presented by Mr Protomusicus and recommended to
his honor's consideration, by that Gentleman, in a very pathetic harangue,
which done he put it into the Secretarie's hands, who read it in Club, his
honor the president, absolutely refused, to grant the request therein contained, which occasioned for some time in Club, very loud vociferation and
noisy dispute, in which, Mr Protomusicus was heard above all the other
members, sometimes bawling Insufferably loud, at other times answering
the arguments of his honor, with a great horse laugh, as was often this

gentlemans custom, & Indeed, whatever melody there was in his voice, there was none at all in this laugh of his, for the tintimarre of it struck thro one's head like a dart, as his honor the president was pleased often to say, In this dispute, Slyboots Pleasant Esqr, a Longstanding member, of a very mild and pacific disposition, and very little given to making of Speeches or talking in Club, || (making the gelastic Law his main Study, tho he never [367] laughed in such a noisy manner as Mr Protomusicus) was so provoked, at the obstinacy and unreasonableness of his honor the president, that he showed some Signs of anger and resentment, a thing extremely rare and uncommon with him, for he was a man of a very mild temper.

The Club, by preferring this petition, it is thought, did not so much want the money, to purchase Lottery tickets, tho' that was used as a pretence, they wanted in short, to knock up the box, altogether, and remove out of the way, that pestilent bone of contention, that had now been, for upwards of two years, a breaker of the peace and harmony of the Club, and Sir John, owned so much to his honor's face, as he sat in the Chair, telling him "that, that there Damn'd box, was the cause of more noise and racket than it was worth, and I wish to God, (says he) that it was at the Devil, or in hell, or some such place." At wch his honor bridled up, and looked with great displeasure on Sir John, but said nothing, for that undaunted Champion, had his honor been but in the least Snappish with him, would have knocked the Chair to pieces and sent his honor a packing, nor Indeed did this valiant knight, and his bold 'Squire Mr Protomusicus, desist 'till they had quite compassed their ends, in demolishing this terrible monster the box.

Upon the honorable the presidents denyal of the request in the petition, the members in generall protested against this arbitrary proceeding, and a great revolt from the Club was threatned, several of the Stanch old Standing members professing that they would Immediatly leave the Club; they voted however, that the money, now in the box, (excepting the Quota Contributed by his honor himself,) should be drawn out for the use above mentioned, vizt: to purchase Lottery tickets, upon which the || Secretary, by [368] order from the Club desired his honor the president to see the box forth coming, upon Tuesday the 16th of this Instant august, at next Sederunt of the Club, this Order met with no other reply from his honor, but a Stern frown; this was the boldest Stroke for Clubical liberty that ever was struck by the longstanding members of this here ancient and honorable Club, and it is thought, that the authority of the Chair, met with such a Shake upon this occasion, that it was a long time before it recovered again its wonted vigor.

At Sederunt 87, August 16th 1748, Smoothum Sly Esqr, being high Steward, the Club met in the school room, the ancient place of meeting of the ugly Club, of which we have given a particular description in the Second book of this history, and Mr Speaker Quaint, in a very elegant Speech opened to the president, the affair of the Box, entered upon at last meeting, and his honor seeing the Impending ruin that threatned the Club, if he should persist in obstinately refusing their demands, was graciously pleased to consent, that the money in the box should be disposed of, in the following manner, the Conditions being drawn up by Mr Speaker Quaint, that is to say,

"Ordered that the money now in the box, be delivered next Club Night, to the Reverend Mr Sly, by him to be disposed of as follows, that his honor the president first, and every other member of the Club afterwards, may give orders under their hands, for the disposal of their proportional parts, into the hands of such person or persons, as each member for himself shall think fit, being a resident in town & not otherwise."

As to the entry of last Sederunt, concerning the order for delivering up the Club box, it being made after Club hour, and Mr Protomusicus Neverout, not singing his motion, as he ought || to have done, it was protested against and cancelled by his honor the president and the Longstanding members.

[369]

Thus his honor the president at last yielded up his darling, thinking that he had done it on tollerable terms, since he believed, he had by the above Condition, effectually prevented the money's being laid out, in Lottery tickets (for he professed himself an enimy to all Sorts of gaming) but we shall see in the Sequel, how this money was dissipated.

Chapter VII

Solemn Surrendry of the Club box, and disposal of the Treasury, Club letters, the honorable the Speaker leaves the Club, disputes about who should succeed him, misbehavior of Sir John.

Hercules's Labors, tho' painful and difficult, were by constancy, courage, and Indefatigable perseverance, accomplished at last, and the Heroe crowned with victory and Success, in the same manner, by constancy and perseverance, was this monster of the Club-box, the cause of so much discord and dissention, hubbub and hurly burly, in this here ancient and honorable Club, totally, and finally overcome, and mortally knocked on the head, by the heroic Longstanding members; The Invincible Sir John, the Hercules and leader of the Club, being the head and Champion of this bold Clubical Enterprize.

At Sederunt 88 August 30, Jonathan Grog Esqr being high Steward, the Club box, as pestilent a box as that of Pandora, in which was five Pounds ‖ fifteen Shillings and Sixpence, was Solemnly delivered by his [370] honor the president, to the Reverend Mr Smoothum Sly master of Ceremonies, to be disposed of by him according as his honor and the longstanding members should direct, which money was afterwards laid out on lottery tickets, contrary to his honor's Intention.

Solo Neverout Esqr, chief musician, protested against a resolve of the Club; "That the Speech he made at Sederunt 86th concerning the box petition, was void, and of no effect in Clubical Law, because he did not sing it," as he alledged, that he was not obliged by any law of the Club, to sing his motions and speeches, as may be seen by an Entry of Sederunt 49th Decemb: 9th 1746, beginning "Solo Neverout Esqr upon account of &ct:" but the Club still agreed to support the president and Club's protest, against the proceeding of Sederunt 86th, and Mr Protomusicus's Speech, to support the same, as the said Speech, whether sung or said, is now thought by the Club, to have been at that time unseasonable, assuming and unpolite, wherefore he, the said Solo neverout Esqr, had the Gelastic Law put in execution against him, the whole company Joining in a most vociferous and roaring Laugh, in which protomusicus himself Joined, with most prodigious force of Lungs.

A letter was produced in Club, by his honor the President, sent to him by the high Steward as follows.

To Nasifer Jole Esqr,
President of the Tuesday Club,
at his dwelling in North east Street, Annapolis.

Mr President,

This Evening, being the 30th of the month, I am to ‖ have the honor [371] of Entertaining the *August Tuesday Club*, and, as that, as well as every thing else, looks odd and Imperfect, without a head, I hope Sir, you who have so long, and so worthily been the head of that Club, will then Be pleased to grace it with your presence, which is an honor I am anxious to be dignified with, as it has never yet been conferred on me, when I have had the honor of serving as high Steward, I am, Mr President, with profound respect, and all due deference,

From my dwelling house in	Your most obedient
Charles Street	Greatly Devoted
August the 30th 1748	Very humble Servant
	Jonathan Grog H:S:

In this letter, we may perceive, the great genius of Jonathan Grog Esqr, shining forth in a well formed pun, in the very beginning of it, and that gentleman's great Abilities in that excellent Clubical Art, will appear in many Instances thro the course of our History.

At Sederunt 92d, November 8, 1748, Mr Secretary Scribble being high Steward, the following letter from him to the President was produced in Club.

To the Honorable Nasifer Jole Esqr,
President of the Tuesday Club, These.

Honorable Sir,

As there is no body whatsoever, either natural or politic, that is good [372] for any thing, without ‖ the head, that eminent regulator and Instructor of the members, so, the members of any Society (and those of our Club among others) must, of consequence, be very torpid and paralytic, if not altogether dead and useless, when deprived of this necessary and dignified Superintendent.

It is for this Important Reason, Honorable Sir, that I would request your honor's gracious presence, this evening, at my house, where the members of our Tuesday Club, are to meet and discuss some affairs of Importance, which I am afraid they will want power and Spirits to do, unless Invigorated and Inspired, by your honor's awful countenance and presence, which too, will very much oblige and honor, Honorable Sir,

Novr 8th 1748	Your honor's diligent and faithfull
	Secretary & high Steward
	Loquacious Scribble.

In the very beginning of this letter, the Secretary plainly acts the plagiary, having borrowed or rather stole, that fine metaphor of the head, from a letter of the Ingenious Jonathan Grog Esqr, wrote to his honor the president upon a paralell occasion, which the reader may see, if he has not perceived it already, by only turning back to the preceeding page.

At this same Sederunt, an entry was made by the Secretary, which, as it

was done without Consulting his honor and the Club, was cancelled, ‖ for,   [373]
the honorable the Speaker, that useful, and eminent officer, having left
the Club, for reasons best known to himself, but not out of any disgust,
occasioned great uneasiness and Concern to his honor and the long Standing members, they being Sensible, that the Club would suffer greatly, by the
want of that State officer; The Secretary took upon him, by an ill devised
entry in the book of Records, to put the Master of Ceremonies Into that
honorable place, to officiate as Speaker *pro tempore,* till another Speaker
should be chosen by the Club, which Chagrined his honor the president
much, and the entry was cancelled, or struck out, the Secretary in doing this
had a design against the Chair, The power of which, he thought had now
grown to too great a head, and Imagined, that by putting in Mr Smoothum
Sly, a longstanding member of an officious disposition and uncommon turn
to flattery and adulation, he might, by degrees, so poison the principles of
his honor the president (the common effect that flattering arts have upon
great men) that he would be guilty of some arbitrary procedure, which
would necessaryly give a finishing stroke to that exorbitant power, the chair
was now possessed of; but this finnesse of the Secretaries would not answer
his purpose, his machinations, one after another being discovered by the
Sagacity and penetration of his honor, who looked still with Jealous and
hawks eyes, upon this designing officer. After the cancelling of this false
entry a hot ‖ dispute arose, concerning who should succeed as Speaker to   [374]
the Club, it being thought a difficult matter to cull out from among the
longstanding members, a person of that Staid gravity Solemnity, prudence
and elocution, equal to the gentleman who but lately possessed that honorable office, and indeed it is my opinion, that his equal was not to be found
in the Club. Several of the Longstanding members, and particularly the
Secretary showd a great desire to be advanced to that eminent place, but his
honor was so Chagrined at the Secretarie's Imprudent conduct, that he
absolutely refused putting any of the longstanding members into that office, and so it remained a great while vacant; In the midst of these disputes
and wranglings, Sir John, to put the Club in a good humor (being happily
in good humor himself, which was but seldom) sung the celebrated old
Song of the *Hundreds of Drury,*[1] with a very comic air, Chawing the Troll-
loll Chorus of that ditty in such an antic manner, as set the members of the
Club into a hearty laugh.

   1. This tune was originally called "The Bowman Priggs' Farewell." Harold Gene Moss includes a copy of the tune dated 1750 in "Ballad Opera Songs: A Record of Ideas Set to Music,
1728–1733" (Ph.D. diss., University of Michigan, 1970), IV, 72–73.

At Sederunt 95th Janry 3d 1748, Jealous Spyplot Esqr being high Steward, Smoothum Sly Esqr, having ascended the Chair as deputy president, by virtue of a verbal Commission, from his honor Mr President Jole, unable thro Indisposition to attend himself, Sir John objected to that proceeding, and some others of the long Standing Members, refusing him the honors due to that place, forbid the Secretary to read the proceedings of the former Sederunt, till the dispute was determined and this very Important affair settled, which was to be done, by waiting the Return of a Special messenger [375] ‖ sent by the Club, to the honorable the Chief president, accordingly, upon the return of this messenger, he was Solemnly asked by the Secretary in the hearing of the Club, *Who the honorable the President had appointed for his deputy?* and, upon answering, that he had appointed Smoothum Sly Esqr, the said Gentleman ascended the presidential Chair, accordingly, and the proceedings of last Sederunt were read according to the usual form, by this it appears, how little Confidence the Club had in the word of Mr Sly, who having of late exercised himself so much in the art of flattery, would often deviate from truth, the temper of Sir John also appears in this transaction, who was like the Dog in the manger, for he would neither take the Chair in quality of deputy himself, nor could he bear to see any other longstanding member, possessed of that honor.

Some proposals having been made at this Sederunt with regard to the Election of a Speaker, Mr deputy President declined proceeding in that affair because of the absence of Mr President Jole, and so, tho' the votes were taken, and the Election passed in favor of Jealous Spyplot Esqr, against Mr Protomusicus Neverout, the Election was Looked upon as Irregular, and the affair dropt till another meeting, thus, we find the Longstanding members, as it were, Spontaneously, without the least force or constraint, giving up the Sole power of electing and appointing of Club officers, into the hands of the honorable the president, a privilege, which he was not originally possessed of, but, once he had got it in his hands, by [376] the carelessness and overcomplaisance of the Longstanding ‖ members, he grasped it so hard, that it could never be wrested from him again, nay, he even prevailed so far upon the Club, as to make them pass two Strict Laws, to secure this valuable privilege, to him and his Successors in the Chair for ever.

It was resolved at this Sederunt, that the honorable Mr President Jole, should be addressed, to bring in the Copies of several letters, wrote to him by the High Stewards of the Club, not already given in, in order that they might be duely registred in the Club book; by this we see that his honor was now riding post haste towards Arbitrary power, and had Secreted several of the most authentic Clubical papers, and prevented the recording of them, that he might the more easily gull the longstanding members of this here Club, out of that little Scantling of liberty they had still left, it was a very politic Step in his honor also, not to appoint another State officer, by suffering the Creation of a new Speaker, the Conduct of that State officer, with regard to the Club box, being still fresh in his mind, he now found, that one officer of State and privy councellor, vizt: The worshipful Sir John, knight of the Club, was enough for him to manage, and afforded him always his handsful, as that great man, was of a restless, bustling, unsteady and ambitious temper, and a great check, to the arbitrary proceedings of the Chair.

At Sederunt 96th January 17th 1748/9, The worshipful Sir John being high Steward, and Solo Neverout Esqr Deputy President, for which he had a letter of attestation, directed and writ to him by the worshipful || the high steward, in a pithy, concise and heroic Stile, worthy the Champion of a club, as follows. [377]

To Solo Neverout Esqr, This.

Grate Sir,
   Mr President Jole
desired me to acquaint you, he expects you, Sir, to do him the honor of representing him, the said President, in the *said* presidential Chair, this night, at my Castle.

And so, I hereby acquaint you *grate* Sir, accordingly, under my hand this 17th of January 1748/9.

> Sir John,
> Of the said Tuesday Club, and always on
> the right hand of the said Chair, *and that's
> what I say.*

We may observe a peculiar elegance of Stile, manner of expression and uncommon Orthography, in all the Clubical letters of this great Champion, and in none more than in that Just now transcribed.

Sir John moved to the Club, that a Gentleman of Annapolis, was desirous to be made a member of this here Club,[2] upon which the Secretary was ordered to prepare the ballots, or *Yeas* and *Nays,* and, upon their being put round and examined, it was carried in the negative, there being two nays and four yeas.

2. See biographical sketch for John Raitt.

[378]   After Supper, Sir John, taking the precedence of ‖ the chair, took upon himself to stand up with a Settled Countenance, and drink the first toast, expressly contrary to the Rules of the Club; and not only so, but proposed a nauseous fowl mouthd and beastly toast, repugnant to modesty and good manners, drinking in plain English words, while he held a replenishd bowl of punch in his right hand, *To the pious memory of Sally Salisbury's* ——.³ Against this toast the Revd Mr Sly, master of ceremonies protested, and the Sense of it, Jonathan Grog Esqr, most devilishly wrested, asserting that the letters S.S.C. on the South Sea Shillings, did not stand for the words mentioned in Sir John's toast, but meant neither more nor less than *South Sea company,* during this whole Smutty transaction Mr Protomusicus the Deputy sat fast asleep in the Chair, and was thought not to have heard a single word that passed, thus executing his office of deputy president in such a careless manner, as if it had not been worth a pinch of Snuff, since it would have cost him no more to have kept himself awake.

Chapter VIII

A Letter of Condolance wrote to his honor the President, Election of four Longstanding members, Disputes in Club, Speech of Oldham Wisely Esqr, Honorary member, and other trivial matters.

          It was with this ancient and honorable Club, as it is with humorsome Children, to whom they say have your Cake and eat your Cake, or some ‖
[379] fractious people, to whom is applied the Scotch proverb, *you'll neither dance, nor hold the candle;* so, this Club seemed never to know when they were well, either with, or without the honorable the president, for, when he was present, it was nothing but contention, wrangling, Jangling and brangling, about prerogative and privilege, presidential authority, and Clubical Liberty, and when he was absent it was nothing but pining, whining and declining. It was now the Season of the year for his honor to be laid up with the gout, which Calamity occasioned his absence from Club at Sederunt 96th, therefore, the Club, before breaking up, ordered the Secretary, to write a condolatory epistle to his honor, upon that occasion, in the name of

---

3. Sally Salisbury (or Sally of Salisbury) is the alias of Mrs. Sarah Priddon, a fictional whore and the central character of Capt. Charles Walker's *Authentick Memoirs of the Life, Intrigues, and Adventures of the Celebrated Sally Salisbury* (London, 1723). Hamilton's draft, which reads "To the pious memory of Sally Salisbury's C—t," is a bit more explicit.

The misbehaviour of Sir John.

[facing page 378]

the Club, this was done in prose, as the poetical Genius of the Club, had not as yet broke out in its full Glory, but, on all the following occasions of the like nature, this Condolatory address was penned in verse, this Epistle Run as follows.

By order of the Deputy President and Club, January 17th 1748/9.

To the Honorable Nasifer Jole Esqr,
President of the Tuesday Club.

Honorable Sir,
It is with regret that we address your honor upon this lamentable
[380] occasion, an Occasion which ‖ affords more pain than pleasure, as the Subject is disagreeable.

That gratitude and respect, which is due from us to your honor, as our most worthy president, obliges us to express some marks of concern, for your honor's Indisposition, and therefore we have ordered our Secretary to write you this our Epistle of our proper Inditing and framing, by which, we mean to Intimate our good wishes for your honor's speedy recovery, and our Sincere concern, since that, by reason of Sickness, we reap not the advantage, of your Gracious and precious presence & direction.

Our Club is now, as it were in a State of Anarchy, the rudder wants a skillful pilot to steer this our Clubical vessel in a right course, the deputy president falls fast asleep in the Chair, Sir John, the Champion looks like a *Mope in the Moonshine,* the Ladies are but faintly toasted; music and Song are quite mute, mirth and laughter are no more, our eye-sight turns dim in the glimmering of the candles, so, that we may say, with a certain great and wise preacher, *those that look out at the windows are darkened, and all the daughters of Music are brought low.*[1]

We have only one thing left to Comfort us, which is, that the Indisposition your honor Labors under is not of so malignant and mortal a nature as to extinguish our hopes of again partaking and enjoying your honorable
[381] presence, and benign Influence, ‖ which, that it may speedily happen, is the earnest desire, and ardent prayer of, Honorable Sir,

From the Club Room,	Your most affectionate and dutiful
Jan: 17th 1748/9	members of your ancient and dignified
	Tuesday Club
	Signed p: order of,
	and in the name of the Club,
	Loquacious Scribble Secrtry

1. Hamilton has patched together two lines from Eccles. 12:3, 4; the persona of Ecclesiastes is repeatedly referred to as "the preacher."

The Secretary was ordered to copy this letter fair, and present it to his honor upon the morrow, being Wednesday the 18th Instant.

The following Sederunt, being the 97th Janry 31, 1748/9, Capt: Seemly Spruce being high Steward, and Jonathan Grog Esqr, by special Commission, deputy president, was one of the most Remarkable that ever happened in this here Club, for election of members, Ceremony and pomp.

His honor the president, having already perceived in Jonathan Grog Esqr, that extraordinary acumen and vivacity of Genius, with which nature had liberally endued that Gentleman, sent him a Special Commission, *Sub Sigillo et Syngrapho*,[2] appointing him deputy president, at this memorable Sederunt, as Judging him most qualified, of all the other Long-standing members, to perform the ceremonies and honors of the Club, upon this remarkable occasion, and, we must observe here, that this Ingenious person, was the first Longstanding member who || was honored with a special [382] commission, under his honor the president's hand and Seal, the Commission run as follows.

COMMISSION

To Jonathan Grog Esquire.

Not doubting of your prudence and abilities, for the office of deputy president, and, that you deserve to fill my Chair in my absence, I have appointed you Jonathan Grog Esqr, to be deputy president of the Club, this 31 of January 1748/9, for which this is your authority, and, I hope you will behave yourself, with due decorum and decency in your office, not admitting any Irregularities or Indecencies, to be committed in the Club, nor suffering any affront to be passed, upon the Chair, nor any of my Laws to be openly and audaciously violated, that I may have no complaint, or cause of complaint, or Criminal prosecutions, and this behavior, you shall carefully observe, as you shall be answerable therefore.

[Seal]³   Subscribed *Nasifer Jole.*

We may observe, that this Commission runs in the humble Stile, his honor expressing himself in the Singular number, using the pronouns || *I* [383] and *My*, which in the following Commissions we shall find changed for the

2. "Under seal and sign."
3. Here and throughout the *History,* Hamilton did not insert the actual seals that were originally used in club documents. He simply wrote *seal, privy seal,* or *great seal* within a fancy circle to indicate that those seals appeared in the original papers. Here and in the following pages I have placed the words he used within brackets to indicate the same thing.

plurals of the same; *We* & *Our,* being made use of, as more adapted to the presidential dignity.

Jonathan Grog Esqr, by virtue of the above Commission, having ascended the Chair, the Reverend Mr Sly, Master of Ceremonies, moved the Club, that the following Gentlemen, vizt: Mr Huffman Snap, Jealous Spyplot Junior, & Mr Quirpum Comic, should be admitted longstanding members of this here ancient and honorable Club, They having themselves made proper application, upon which motion, Mr Deputy President presented the Secretary with a Special Commission from the honorable Mr President Jole, to authorise and Enable him, to proceed and act, with full power in this election, which the Secretary read to the Club, in manner and form as follows.

North east Street, Annapolis Ss:

We hereby Authorize and Command you, our deputy Chairman for the Tuesday Club, met at the house of Capt: Seemly Spruce, our high Steward for the time being; this 31 day of January, 1748/9, In the fourth year of our presidential Government, In case Messieurs Huffman Snap, Jealous Spyplot Junior, and Quirpum Comic, should apply, to be made longstand-

[384] ing members of our Society, ‖ to admit of their request, and of the request of none others, at this Sederunt, so far, as to proceed to election by balloting, according to the Rules and Constitution of our Club, and to proceed in that election, with the same power, authority and efficacy, as if we ourself were present, and sitting in the Chair, and let our Clerk be ordered to remitt us an account, of the Issue of the Election, and, for so doing, this shall be your authority and warrant.

To Jonathan Grog Esqr,   Given under our hand and Seal, this 31
Deputy president of our   day of January, 1748/9, in the fourth year
Tuesday Club.   of our presidential Government.
                               Nasifer Jole. [Seal]

We may observe, in the form of this commission, that his honor alters his Stile, adopting now the plural Number, and Instead of the pronouns *I* and *My,* using their plurals *We* and *Our,* a Stile much more adapted to his Station and dignity as a president, and what is daily used by all princes and great men; but we must also here remark, that the president seems to assume to himself a privilege, which we find no where granted to him by the Club, and that is, a power of Granting a *Congé d'elire.*[4] It is true, he had granted him a privilege of appointing his own deputy, and this deputy was

4. "Permission to elect."

always supposed to have Conveyd to him by that appointment, the whole powers and authority of the Chief president, during the time ‖ that he held [385] his office, so that there was no necessity to grant any further particular Commissions, to Impower him to act, in the election of Longstanding members, or any other Clubical proceeding; the Club however, at this time, did not dispute the Legality of this proceeding of the president's, for fear it should have obstructed this election, but acquiesced in it, tho' sometime after this they called this power of his in question, and acted directly Contrary to it in the Election of Mr Crinkum Crankum, and Doctor Jeronimo Jaunter, now longstanding members of the Club, at the present time of my writing this history, but his honor did then, and does still assert and mantain his right to give a *Congé d'elire,* in every Case, where he is not himself present, which evinces the danger of allowing such bad precedents to be Introduced into any constitution, potentates and Presidents being always Inclined to hold fast, every privilege they have granted or conceded to them, however much the Subject may suffer, by such an exorbitant Streech of power.

The above Commission being read, the deputy president ordered the Ballots to be prepared, by the Secretary, which being done, they were elected in the following order, vizt: Mr Huffman Snap, Jealous Spyplot Junr, and Mr Quirpum Comic, and the elections were unanimous, the above Gentlemen being congratulated by all the longstanding members, and their healths respectively drank ‖ about, they took their Seats in Club [386] accordingly.

Then Mr Huffman Snap, moved the Club, that if the honorable the president's Commission had not been confined to the above Gentlemen, he would humbly propose to the Club, another Gentleman, viz: Mr Prim Timorous, who was desirous of being admitted a member at this Sederunt, upon which, the Club not presuming to proceed farther (a dangerous piece of Complaisance) without the consent of the honorable Mr President Jole, dispatched to him two Special messengers, vizt: the Reverend Mr Sly Master of Ceremonies, and Mr Secretary Scribble, with a written request from the Deputy president and Club, to Indulge them so far as to suffer them to proceed in his election, which, the honorable Mr President Jole, Readily Granted, with this further message, to be delivered to the deputy president of the Club, to drink the healths of all the new Elected members, singly, in these particular words, vizt: *That each one might be a longstanding member of the Club,* and betwixt each health, Mr Protomusicus was ordered to sing a new Song, exerting upon the occasion, his musical faculties to the utmost.

Pursuant to this Embassy and these orders, the two Gentlemen mes-

sengers, having brought along with them, Mr Prim Timorous, Solemnly delivered to the Deputy president and Club, after Supper, his honor's or-
[387] ders, and Mr Prim Timorous, being unanimously || elected by the Ballot, took his Seat accordingly, the further orders were punctually performed by Mr Protomusicus, after some trivial and Insignificant arguments upon the matter, and this was no sooner done, by this musical Gentleman, than he fell fast asleep in Club, as was his usual custom, with his pipe in his mouth, which at last he dropt and broke to pieces.

Capt: Seemly Spruce, the high Steward, it was thought, Considered Jonathan Grog Esqr, by reason of his grand commission from his honor, in the light of a Lord Mayor of London at a City feast, for he solicited and pressed him very much to eat one Custard after another at Supper, 'till he made him swallow about half a dozen pritty large ones, after having eat pritty heartily of other things, which he washed down with a proper Quantum of good punch.

The Catch of the *Old bell of Lincoln,* usually sung upon the Admission of new members, by the honorable the president, as also the confirmation of these new elected members, of which the Secretary was appointed to draw up a new form, were deferred, till his honor the president should be present in Club.

The Secretary reported to the Club, that according to an order of Last Sederunt, he had wrote out a fair Copy of a letter, ordered to be sent to his honor the President, & sent it to him accordingly upon Wednesday the 18th of this Instant January, and his honor was pleased to return for Answer, *That he was obliged to the Club, thanked them for their Compliment, and that he was something better.*

[388] As Mr Prim Timorous, now admitted a long Standing || member of this ancient and honorable Club, was heretofore a member of the red house Club of Annapolis, under the Celebrated Mr George Neilson, of whom, and of this Club of his erecting, we have given a particular account, in the Second book of our history, and, as the same Gentleman will be seen, holding a Considerable office, in this here ancient and honorable Club, vizt: that of Serjeant at arms, to the Right Honorable the Lord President Jole, (as he was at that time stiled) it will be proper in this place, to give a short Scetch of his Character.

Mr Prim Timorous was a person of a middle Stature, Inclinable to a slender make, of a mild Complacent Countenance, much given to smile, tho for the most part he carried in his look, a Sedate and Stayd gravity. He was by no means of a Loquacious disposition, for he loved better to hear others speak, than to hold discourse himself, he was always fond of Jocular and merry company, tho' he never attempted to be Jocular and witty him-self, yet, he had this Singular good quality, that he could bear a Joke passed upon himself with great good nature, and was by no means one of that morose Set, who, because they cannot be witty or arch upon others them-selves, will not bear a Jest from others, but are perpetually taking offence, looking grim, and Surly, upon the least Smart repartee or bob, which they think is pointed at themselves, Mr Timorous could bear very well to be plaid upon, and would Join heartily in the Laugh, when the Jest hit him full in the teeth, and his Laugh had something peculiar in it, his ha, ha, has, measuring such equal time ‖ as he breath'd them forth, as do the clicks of a [389] short pendulum Clock, being at equal Intervals one from another, and while he laughed in this manner, he would Clap his hands & stamp with his feet, regularly at every ha, ha, like one beating time to music, which afforded much pleasure and mirth to the company; he was very tender mouthed, when he adventured at any time to talk Smutty, and seemed to mince his words in such a manner, as if he was afraid to utter them, for which reason, he never could find in his heart, to pronounce Certain naughty english words, and paultry monosyllabs, that are used as toasts by our moderen rakes, and that in the politest companies, and are commonly wrote on the walls of houses in large Characters with Chalk Stone by our English School boys; but would always express his meaning in a Circum-locutory way, tho' no man loved better than he to hear bawdy discourse, and at all times, when such discourse happened to be Introduced, he would listen to it with all his ears, and laugh at it in his Solemn way, he was so grave and Sedate in his carriage & behavior, that many of his companions called him by the name of parson Timorous, downright swearing he was averse to, and would never venture farther than some small minced Oaths, such as *figs, ods bobs, by George,—as God shall Judge me! God!—Bless the king, the Lord proprietary and all the rest of the Royal family, may I die upon this Spot alive!*—and the like, and even these forms of Swearing, he never would use, unless taken at unawares, and, as it were Surprized into them, he was timorous both by name and nature, and much ‖ addicted to superstition, [390] having great faith in the doctrine of Witches, Ghosts, apparitions, fairies, and Devils Incarnate, now kick'd out of doors and laugh'd at, by our moderen wise men and philosophers; Mr Timorous, was, to sum up all, a good naturd peaceable Companion, neither giving offence to any body, nor taking offence at any thing, and none better qualified than he, to take him in a lump, for a good Club's man.

At Sederunt 98, February 14th 1748/9, Jonathan Grog Esqr, being high Steward, and Slyboots Pleasant Esqr deputy president, by Special Commis-

sion, the deputys Commission was read in Club, which, as it differs from
that of the preceeding Sederunt, both in Stile and form, and is exactly
according to the Stile and form of all the Subsequent Commissions, for the
Deputies of the Chair, I shall here, once for all give the form of it.

COMMISSION

To our Trusty and well beloved Slyboots Pleasant Esqr.

Not doubting of your prudence and abilities for the office of Deputy
President, and that you deserve to fill our Chair in our absence, we have
appointed you, Slyboots Pleasant Esqr, deputy president of our Tuesday
Club, this 14th day of February, 1748/9, for which this is your authority, and,
we hope, you will behave yourself, with due decorum and decency in your
[391] office, not admitting any Irregularities, or indecencies ‖ to be committed in
Club, nor suffering any affront to be passed upon our Chair, nor any of our
Laws to be openly and audaciously violated, that we have no Complaint,
nor cause of complaint, nor criminal prosecution, and this behavior, you
shall Carefully observe, as you shall be answerable therefore, and so we bid
you heartily farewell.

[Seal]   Given under our hand and Seal, at our
                                     dwelling in North east Street, this 14th
                                     day of february, in the fourth year of our
                                     Presidential Government *annoque domini*,
                                     1748/9.
                                     Nasifer Jole.

Slyboots Pleasant Esqr, by virtue of the above Commission, having
taken the Chair, a Letter was produced In Club by the Secretary, wrote by
Jonathan Grog Esqr high Steward, to his honor the President, which was
read in Club, the tenor of which follows.

To Nasifer Jole Esqr,
President of the Tuesday Club,
at his dwelling house in Northeast Street, Annapolis.

Honorable Sir,

My having been one of the late Grand Jurors, and, since that, having
had a pritty deal of business, of one kind or other, has, till now, prevented
my returning you the Commission, which you was pleased to honor me
[392] with at the last assembling of the Club, at the house of ‖ Seemly Spruce
Esqr, then high steward thereof, when your Indisposition prevented us

from the pleasure of seeing you there yourself to grace the club in the presidential Chair, but I now Sir, return it you, with a multitude of thanks, for the Singular favor then done me, the most unworthy of all the members for such a dignified Station, as that of deputy president, however Sir, as it was your will and pleasure, I did every thing as far as my ability permitted, according to the directions therein to me given, and can with pleasure acquaint you, (tho this I suppose, our worthy Secretary has already done) that no affront, or any thing like it, was offered the Chair, nor any Irregularity or Misdemeanor Committed except, that one of the extraordinary members (by whom I mean an officer) happened to *Nod*, and let his *pipe fall*, which, had yourself been there, I know you would have had Clemency enough to *Wink at*, and pass over, especially, as it was Involuntary, and the same Gentleman afterwards, *Raised his pipes* and performed with the approbation and applause not only of myself, but other Good Judges. In pursuance of your Instructions to me, Messrs: Huffman Snap, Jealous Spyplot Junr: Quirpum Comic, and Prim Timorous, were, (agreeable to the law for that purpose made and provided,) all unanimously admitted, as members of the Tuesday Club, each and every of whom, I, as deputy President, in the name and behalf of the President in Chief, took by the right hand, and bid welcome ‖ in the club, as did afterwards the other old standing & long- [393] standing members, but the grand point of Confirmation, which cannot be performed by any so well as yourself, is postponed, 'till your health, which I earnestly wish for, will admitt of your attendance, and which, I flatter myself, as it is fine weather, will be this evening, when, to serve in quality of high Steward to your honor's ancient and honorable Tuesday Club, falls to the pleasing lot of, Honorable Sir,

Charles Street	Your much obliged
Valentine's day	Greatly devoted
1748,9	Very humble Servant
	Jonathan Grog.

After Reading the Commission directed to Slyboots Pleasant Esqr, as deputy president, it was found, that the said Commission was subscribed *Nasifer Jole*, without any designation, or title, to the presidents Name, but after the said Commission was delivered by the Deputy President, to be minuted, or entered in the Club book, there appeared the term *Præs:* annexed to the president's name, which false addition, or Interpolation, was ordered to be the Subject of enquiry at a following Club, but, upon this very matter, arose a hot dispute in Club, for, it was moved, that the Secretary, or his deputy Mr Quirpum Comic, should be Indicted for this Inter-

Oldham Wisely Esqr. Delivering a Speech in Club.

[facing page 394]

polation, or high misdemeanor, and after a great many arguments and warm Speeches ‖ upon the Subject Mr Oldham Wisely, a worthy honorary [394] member, stood up after Supper in his place, and gravely pulling his pipe from his mouth, and streching out his left hand towards the Company, objected in the following terms against preferring an Indictment against the Secretary.

"Mr President, Sir,

It is with Concern what I am going to say, that I think it is not altogether equitable, to prefer an Indictment against the Chief Secretary for this trespass, as there was no such term as *Præs:* mentioned by the said Secretary, when he read the commission, to this here Club, but only *Simple Nasifer Jole*, without any additional term or designation whatsoever, therefore, I would humbly advise the Club, against such an Iniquitous proceeding."

Mr Wisely upon this sat down, and Collecting himself in his Seat, with great composure and gravity resumed his pipe, and began again to emitt Clouds of Smoke from his mouth, while the Club took his objection under their Serious consideration, and after some fine spun reasoning on the point, It was rejected.

After some Quibbling arguments used by the Secretary and his deputy, in their defence, the said Mr Wisely being asked, by the Club, what opinion he had now of the said Secretary and his deputy, as to their Innocence of the matter they were charged with, he pulld his pipe from his mouth, emitted the Smoke, spit, and made answer, that he thought worse and worse of the said Secretaries.

Chapter IX

[395]

Sublime Club Letters, Ceremonies of Confirmation, The tryal and acquittal of Sir John, the Gelastic Law executed on the Secretary.

Musical Instruments, we are told, may be tuned up to a certain pitch, to which being kept, they have a pleasant and agreeable effect, but beyond this they occasion a discordant Jarring, and become highly offensive and grating to the ear, and the Strings at last start and fly. So in Clubs, the Constitution is capable of being exalted to a certain pitch, and no farther, without being unable to support it's own weight, and at last tumbling to pieces. When the presidential power is kept within Certain bounds, and he

Contents himself with few, and those moderate titles of honor, when the State officers do their duty, and exceed not their Commission, when the officers of the commons stand up Strenously for Clubical liberty, when Club Law is duely executed, and Justice done Strictly on offenders, and matters of expence do not run too high, then all goes smoothly and Swimmingly on, and the Society flourishes, but, when the Chair aims at great power, and assumes great and Sonorous titles, such as *My Lord, Lord president, Lord presidential, your Honor, Honorable,* and *right Honorable,* titles, which Venerable presidents of Clubs || have no more business with than our Reverend Bishops and Cardinals, now a days, who Call themselves the Successors of a parcel of poor and needy fishermen, have with *your Eminence, your Grace* and *your Lordship,*—when the State officers prove loose, dissolute and obscene in their conversation, and set themselves above punishment and the Laws, when the Longstanding members quietly submitt to oppression, and unwarrantable power, when enormous crimes and trespasses are slur'd over, and all Sort of Luxury and extravagance encouraged and countenanced, when pimps in office, are flatterd and Cajoled, by worse pimps out of office, then *Actum est,*[1] the Clubical State may for a little time make a great noise and Show, but suddenly, like a fair blossoming tree upon the Coming of a blast or frost, all its pride and Glory tumbles to the Ground.

This we shall soon find to be pritty much the case with this here ancient and honorable Club, which, now in its highest glory, strained to be higher, and thus, breaking the strings, Sinews or nerves of the Constitution, every thing ran precipitatly to decay, and, tho' a dissolution did not Immediatly Happen, yet, was the beauty, order and Strength of it much Impaired, by means of Superflous ceremonies Introduced, high sounding titles, badges of honor, Seals, medals, Caps of State, Canopies of State, and the like useless trumpery, which, like the Gewgaws used in the Ceremonials of Religious worship, that divert the attention of the populace, or great mobile, from the Substance to the Shadow, || so these farcical, clubical conceits, divert the minds of the members from more rational pursuits, and set them on the hunt after pitiful bawbles. The first Remarkable appearance of this Clubical madness, broke out, in the Stile of some letters to his honor the president, wrote in so extraordinary a Sublime (such I am Sure, as Longinus never delivered any rules for)[2] that they quite turned the presi-

[396]

[397]

---

1. "That does it!" (a phrase typical of Seneca).

2. Longinus (ca. 213–273) was a rhetorician and philosopher who taught at Athens. He was generally considered to have been the author of the literary treatise *On the Sublime* until 19th-century scholars more accurately traced its authorship to the 1st century A.D.

dents head, so, that he began now, not to know, which end of him was uppermost, for, at Sederunt 99th, Huffman Snap Esqr, being high Steward, the following letters to his honor were read in Club.

To the Honorable Nasifer Jole Esqr,
President of the Tuesday Club.

Honorable Sir,   March(a) 28, 1748
     I Return your honor, the Commission your honor was pleased to favor me with, and permit me to Express to your honor, the grateful Sense I have, of that Signal Instance of your honor's favor, in promoting me to the Great and Important trust of Representing your Honor, in a Station of such eminent and exalted dignity, the good opinion your honor is pleased to express of my prudence and abilities, and, in consequence of that opinion, your honor's advancing me to an office, in its nature so elevated, and in it's execution so arduous and difficile, could not fail to excite in my breast, the most lively emotions of ‖ Joy and gratitude, but, I have the great [398] mortification to acquaint your honor, that, notwithstanding the utmost efforts of my prudence and abilities, to mantain the honor and dignity of your honor's Chair, in as great perfection as if your honor's Self had been present, a most enormous and detestable crime was perpetrated by some member, or members dissaffected to your honor's government, a crime, of so Insolent and audacious a nature, as Calls upon your honor, for the most vigorous exercise of your honor's authority, as this affair is very fully to be seen, in the records of last Club, I shall not presume to trowble your honor, with a particular recital of it here, nor shall I Insinuate to your honor, the person I suspect of this high Misdemeanor, any further, than by saying that I wish the Secretary may give your honor some better proofs of his Innocence, than barefac'd denyal, but this, I doubt all his dexterity at quibbling and Sophistry, will not enable him to do, upon as Strict an enquiry into the matter, as the Importance of it requires, I make no doubt but Sir John will be found to be at the bottom of it, notwithstanding his absence, which I must confess, is a very artful Contrivance, to prevent your honor's Suspicion of his Guilt, and, when your honor comes to reflect, upon the captious, and fractious, and Snarling disposition of the said knight, ever since the memorable dissappointment of his ill fated ambition, I dare say, your honor, will Join with me, in saying, that it is at least highly probable, that the person, who committed the above mentioned enormity, was nothing more than an humble Instrument, in the hands of this aspiring knight; give

     (a) A mistake of the month, which ought to have been february.

[399] ‖ me leave with all possible veneration, to subscribe myself, May it please your honor,

> Your honor's most obedient and
> Devoted Servant
> *Slyboots Pleasant.*

The Stile of this letter, is rather too far screwd up to the tip top Strain of Complaisance, and seems to abound with too many Superflous repetitions of *your honor,* & *your honor,* The whole of it Contains only some Sheer compliments in the form of puff paste, and an accusation of Sir John and the Secretary, and, I must own, I can by no means account for the virulence of this epistle, from either the Ambition, or ill nature of the Author, for that Gentleman seemed all along, to be the least ambitious, and was bles'd with the mildest and most complacent temper of any of the members of the Club, in short, the only account I can give of this conduct in this Long-standing member, so much out of Character, is that he had a mind to promote a Squabble, between his honor, Sir John, and the Secretary merely for fun.

The Letter from the high Steward to his honor the President, was to this effect.

To the Honorable Nasifer Jole Esqr
President of the Tuesday Club.

Most Honorable Sir,

Unpractised in that polite art and Demeanor, so natural to the mem-
[400] bers of your honor's Tuesday Club, ‖ and utterly unlettered and untaught in the ornate diction and peculiar Nitidity of Stile, conspicous, in the Episto-lary and congratulatory compositions, addressed to your honor upon occasions like this which is the motive of my now writing, It may seem to your honor somewhat bold and assuming in me, to presume addressing your honor, upon this occasion, and in this manner, especially before having passed thro' your honor's Solemn Ceremony of Confirmation, and conse-cration (if I may with propriety use that Sacred word) and also, by a dili-gent application and Study in writings of the like nature, plentifully scat-tered about in your honor's erudite book of Records, Sufficiently Instruct-ed myself, so as to be capable to write, what is worthy your honor's perusal, the hearing and approbation of your ancient and honorable Club, and the dignified degree of a spare Corner, in your honor's learned, Elaborate and ancient archives, but, seeing I am as yet a novice, and an unconfirmed member, I hope, if I make any blunder, in Stile, or propriety of address,

your honor and the Club, will humanly overlook, and not attribute my trips
to design, rudeness, or Ill manners.

I design this evening, to do myself the honor and pleasure, of attending your honor's commands, at your honor's house, to serve as your honors
willing and Chearful, tho unworthy and unqualified high Steward, where,
when that Solemn minute approaches, when I shall stand with my other
fellow novices, before your honors august Chair, to be, as it were Inaugurated, confirmed and consecrated, an effectual and true Standing member
of your || honor's ancient and honorable Tuesday Club, I earnestly beg your   [401]
honor, to give Command to your honor's Master of Ceremonies, to Instruct me particularly in every Circumstance, relating to the deportment
and carriage to be observed, when in this Solemn and awful Situation, that
I may not, to the dissatisfaction and disgust of your honorable and ancient
Club, and my own Shame and Confusion, be guilty of faults or blunders, or
any Sort of misbehavior, thro' Ignorance or Simplicity, and, by this gracious
Condecention, a permanent, and never to be forgotten obligation, will be
conferrd upon, Honorable Sir,

Anap: 28 febr: 1748   Your honors most humble
                                             Most obedient, and
                                             Most dutiful Servant & H:S:
                                             Huffman Snap.

After Reading of this very polite and high strained letter to his honor
the president, another to the worshipful Sir John, from the same hand was
produced and read.

To the Most Redoutable Sir John,
knight of the Tuesday Club.

Most puisant and Invincible Sir John,
Dreadful and horrendous have been the feats and atchievements, performed by the magnanimous knights of old, who, by their unparallelled
Chivalry, shook mountains, burst rocks in twain, knocked down Dragons
and Griffins, and made mere popets of Gyants, and all for the Sake of some
fine fair Lady, whom perhaps they never saw— || those atchievements were   [402]
most heroic, marvellous and epouvantable, as any one must know, who but
peeps into our Gotheric Romances.—But oh! ye Sempiternal astripotents!
what a more Sublime field and excellent foundation, has a knight of such a
Society as our tuesday Club to work upon, what an Infinite number of
heroic actions and Glorious Exploits, must spring from such a groundwork,
such an excellent foundation, when operated upon by a magnanimous ge-

nius like yours, for what knight I say, what emblazon'd Champion, either ancient or moderen, had ever such Subjects to exercise his valor upon and act in defence of, as the honorable the president, and longstanding members of the ancient and honorable Tuesday Club! for, such an honorable president and such longstanding members, I believe, never were heard of, seen or known, either to antiquity or these baser and Latter times, neither do I believe, shall Expecting posterity, ever be so happy as to behold such a president, such members, and above all, such a magnanimous, epouvantable and Invincible knight.

After this well adapted prelimination, I am next to sollicit you, most Invincible and heroic Sir John, to do me the honor and dignity of your knightly presence this evening, at the house of our honorable President, where I am to have the Glory of officiating for the first time as high Steward, and I doubt not but your magnanimous presence, will Inspire into me that courage and undaunted Spirit, which will be necessary, when I
[403] stand before the honorable presi- ‖ dents august chair, to be Inaugurated and confirmed a perpetual Standing member, of our Ancient Tuesday Club, I am the more bold in demanding this of you, as I know you glory, in being the valiant champion of our Tuesday Club, and the protector, of not only the whole bod thereof under the honorable the president, to whom good manners and duty require me to give the first place, but also of every particular member, and especially of persons timerous and untaught like myself, and, as I hope your magnanimity will Indulge me so far, I am, Most Invincible and Tremendous Sir John,

Annap: 28 febr: 1748   Your worship's most humble
                                        Servant and dutiful Squire
                                        Huffman Snap.

This Letter is upon the right Clubical Bombast Stile, and savors pritty much of many Dedications wrote by certain finical puppies of authors, to patrons of very little merit and Significancy, at least, patrons of far less worth and Importance, than the worshipful Sir John knight and Champion of the Ancient and honorable Tuesday Club.

After Reading these letters, and Committing them Into the Secretarie's hands to be registered in the book, the Reverend Mr Sly, Master of Ceremonies, called upon the late admitted members, to stand round the presidential Chair in order for their confirmation, and they accordingly stood
[404] up, Jealous Spyplot Senr Esqr, standing ‖ proxy for his Son Jealous Spyplot Junr Esqr necessarily absent.

Then the Secretary read aloud the form of Confirmation as follows.

North East Street Ss:

Whereas it has been reported to us, by the Reverend Mr Smoothum Sly, our Master of Ceremonies, and Loquacious Scribble Esqr our Clerk, Commissioners deputed by the Tuesday Club, in the Name, and by the authority of said Club, met at the house of Capt: Seemly Spruce our then high Steward upon Tuesday the 31 *ultimo,* Jonathan Grog Esqr being our deputy president, that the said President and Club, then and there, Solemnly met, by a Special Commission, under our hand and privy Seal at Arms, did proceed to the election of the following Gentlemen, vizt: Messrs Huffman Snap, Jealous Spyplot Junior, Quirpum Comic and Prim Timorous, by balloting, according to a rule of said Club, for that Intent made and provided, and that the said election was carried unanimously, for the said several Gentlemen abovenamed; *Be it therefore known,* by these presents, to all herein Concerned, that *we*[a] Confirm, strengthen, stabilitate, Corroborate, make valid and perpetuate, by our authority the above election, in such manner, as it shall be for ever good ‖ firm and uncontrovert- [405] able, Sufficient, valid and effectual, whatever objections may be brought to the contrary notwithstanding, and accordingly, *by these presents,* which we hereby command our clerk to enter in our book of records, *in perpetuam Rei memoriam,*[3] the above named Gentlemen, viz: Messrs Huffman Snap, Jealous Spyplot Junior, Quirpum Comic and Prim Timorous, are declared, avowed, pronounced, appointed, affirmed and Confirmed to be rightful, Lawful, effectual, firm, regular, and duely elected Standing members of the Commoners of our 'foresaid Tuesday Club, from this day forth and for ever.

To Loquacious Scribble Esqr,   Given under our hand and Seal,
Clerk of our Tuesday Club   this 28 day of february, in the 4th
                                      year of our presidential
                                      Government.
                                      Nasifer Jole. [Seal]

As the Secretary named the Gentlemen at the Conclusion of the above form, the master of Ceremonies confirmed them, one after another, by Investing them with the Club's badge, and Solemnly presenting them to the honorable the president, who Graciously took each of them by the right hand, giving them a Gentle Clubical Squeeze.

(a) Here Sir John observed, that the particle or pronoun *We,* was Improperly applied, because when this form was drawn, he was neither present, concerned, nor Consulted.

3. "In perpetual memory of the thing."

Follows the form of the master of Ceremonies his Speech, to each of the new members, when he Invested him with the Club badge, and presented him to his honor the president.

"Sir,

[406]   I as master of ceremonies of our tuesday Club, with all the Ceremony I am master of, which mastery in ceremonies, I acknowledge to be conveyd to me by the authority of our honorable president, do Inaugurate, constitute and confirm you,

$$\left.\begin{array}{l}\text{Huffman Snap}\\ \text{Jealous Spyplot Junrs proxy}\\ \text{Quirpum Comic}\\ \text{Prim Timorous}\end{array}\right\} \text{Esqr}$$

a good firm Longstanding member, of the Commoners in this our Tuesday Club, in token of which, I Invest you with this the Club's badge, and here Solemnly present you, to the honorable the president, recommending it to you, to make your acknowledgements to the honorable the president and Club, in the handsomest and best Speech you can devise."

Upon which the gentlemen tacitly assented to do so, and after the Ceremony each new member and the proxy made a low bow to the Chair, and his honor took each of them by the hand, giving them a Clubical manuquassation.

Then the honorable the president addressing himself to the new Confirmed members spoke to the following purpose.

"Gentlemen,

I had the misfortune to be under great pain, being Indisposed with the [407] gout that night in which ‖ you were admitted, or elected into the Club, and nothing gave me greater concern, than my being thus prevented from giving attendance to your admission, in which I do assure you, I should have had not alittle pleasure, but, however, tho I had not the Satisfaction to be present at your admission, the news of your Election, contributed much to my health and recovery, and I veryly believe, you will prove very worthy members of this our Club, and therefore I heartily congratulate you, upon your admission, and am very Glad we have got such agreeable members, wishing you all the Satisfaction in the thing that you can desire."

This polite Speech ended, the gentlemen made another low bow to the honorable Chair, and resumed their Seats accordingly, Invested with the proper badges of the Club.

We must observe, in the course of these ceremonies, and transactions that the longstanding members, without the least foresight or reflection, put a power into his honor the presidents hands, which he neither expected nor applied for, vizt: no less than the Sole power of electing members into the Club, it is true, they did not annex this power to the Chair, by any express law or rule, but his honor, tenacious of all powers and prerogatives given him, would never a- || gain give up this power, alledging, that none [408] could be a longstanding member of the Club, without going thro' this ceremony of confirmation, which occasioned abundance of disputes and wranglings between his honor the president and the Longstanding members, in a famous case, which will appear in it's proper place in this history.

After these Ceremonies were over, the Secretary was accused by some of the members, of the Interpolation mentioned at last Sederunt, and was called upon to answer for that misdemeanor, which he flatly denied, alledging, that the addition of *præs:* to his honor's name, was not in his hand writing, but this accusation and proceeding was discountenanced by his honor the president, who expressed his displeasure at the forwardness and petulancy of some members, in finding fault, with his manner of Signing, alledging that it was a thing entirely at his own choise, to sign all Commissions and all Clubical Instruments and papers whatsoever, Just in what manner and form he pleased, without taking Instructions or directions from the Club.

The Secretary then, delivered to his honor and the Club, two Indictments against Sir John, knight of the Club, which he was ordered to read aloud, upon which Sir John, stood up, and with a bold and Intrepid countenance said that he was ready || and prepared, to give a categorical answer [409] to all Indictments, and Libels whatsoever, which Mr Secretary or the Club should bring against him. Then the Secretary proceeded to read the first Indictment in Law latin.

Indictamentum Imum

Tuesday Club Ss:
Socii Societat, Annapolit, diei martis, anglice *The Annapolis Tuesday Club* super honorem suam present, quod dom, Joannes, eques Societat, alias, domd, Joannes Oldcastellius eques Societat, anglice dict *Sir John knight of the Club, otherwise Sir John Oldcastle knight of the Club,* nuper de Civitat, Annapol, in Comitat, predict, homo pernicios, et Seditios, pravæ mentis, et turbulent, disposition, machinans et Intendens contra honor, et dignitat, domin, presidis, Socios hujus Societat ad odium et vituperation anglice *Dislike,* person, dict, dom, presid, et gubernation, Stabilat, in fra dict, dom, presid, perturbare et incitare, et movere Sedition, et

rebellion, contra dict, dom, presidem, Decimo Septimo die Janrii, annoq3 domination, dom, nost, presid, quarto, in aulo Baccalaur,
[410] anglice *Batchelor's hall* in civitat et comitat predict, || coram ipso dom, pres, solenniter sedent, et dormient, in Cathedr, presidential, et in presentia diversor, nostror Socior, adtunc et Ibid, present, et existent, vi et armis, rautose et riotose, assaultation, fecit exicrabilem, in Cathed, et honor, dict, dom, presid, Craterum Certam, anglice *A Punch Bowl* pretii quatuor Solidar, in manu tenens Impudenter audacter, et Insolenter, crater, dict, ori suo admovens, primam post ceniam Compotavit tostam contra Leges hujus Societat, quæ Confirmant dom, nost, presid, hanc privilegiam compotand, prim, post Ceniam tostam, et hanc contumeliam perpetravit, et assaultation, fecit predict, dom, Joannes eques Oldcastellius, anglice *Sir John Knight otherwise Oldcastle* vi et armis, rautose et riotose, Insolenter Impudenter et audacter, contra Ligeantiam debitam, in malu⁹ et pernicosu⁹ Exemplu⁹ omniu⁹ alioru⁹ in tali casu delinquand⁹, et contra pacem dict⁹ dom⁹ presid⁹ cathedr⁹ et dignitat⁹.

After Reading this Indictment, Sir John said, "Hum, Hum, a fine Rigmeroll indeed! who the devil understands one word of all this Stuff"— Then the Secretary read the English Indictment as follows.

Indictment I

Sir John, You stand Indicted by the name of Sir John, otherwise Called Sir John Oldcastle, in the parish of St Anne in the County of Annarundel, knight of the Tuesday Club, for that you, as a false traitor, against the most
[411] Illustrious and Serene Nasifer, President of the said Tuesday || Club, due reverence to the said Illustrious and Serene Nasifer In your heart not having, nor weighing your duty towards his august Chair, but being moved and seduced by your own wicked Instigation, and due obedience to the said Illustrious and Serene Nasifer, utterly withdrawing, and endeavoring and Intending with all your might, the peace and Common tranquillity of this our Tuesday Club to disturb, and the Laws of the same established to overthrow, and to pull down and bring into Contempt, our said Serene president and his Chair, and the said honorable Chair, wickedly, maliciously and devillishly to usurp, you, the said Sir John, otherwise Called Sir John Oldcastle, knight of the Tuesday Club, and late a State officer of the said Club, on the 17th day of January, in the fourth year of the Dominion of our said Illustrious and Serene Nasifer, in the parish of St Annes aforesaid, in

the County aforesaid, at a place called Batchellors hall, before the said
President, in the person of his deputy, Solemnly sitting and sleeping in the
presidential Chair, and in the presence of several of the Liege members of
the said Club, with force and arms, wickedly made an open assault, upon
the Chair honor and person of the said president, in open Contempt of the
Laws of this here Club, then and there, taking into your hands a Certain
punch bowl, of the value of four Shillings, and most Impudently, audaciously and Insolently, the said punch bowl, charged with a certain liquor
called punch, to your mouth uplifting, drank the first toast after Supper,
against an express Law of this here Club, which has given that privilege, of
drinking the first toast after Supper || to the honorable the president alone,   [412]
and this contempt and open assault, you, the said Sir John, otherwise called
Sir John Oldcastle, knight of the tuesday Club, with force and arms,
rautously and riotously, Impudently, audaciously and Insolently, hast perpe-
trated, against the aleigeance, due to the honorable the President, and
setting a bad example to your fellow members, to commit the same Inso-
lence, and against the peace of his said honor the president, his Chair and
dignity. What say you Sir John, are you guilty of the matter wherewith you
stand Charged or not Guilty.

Sir John would not plead, but looked very Sour and Surly first at the
Secretary, then at his honor the president and then at all the Longstanding
members round him, every one of whom remained mute, as it is thought
thro fear.

The Champion however was not altogether silent during the reading
of the Indictment, for, at the words, *Late a State officer of the said Club,* he
Interrupted the Secretary and without rising from his Seat spoke to the
following purpose.

"*Late a State officer!*—pray Sir, why *Late a State officer?*—Mr President
Sir,—I have the honor to sit here at your right hand—I say Sir at your right
hand in quality of a State officer, of this here Club, and, I beg leave to
affirm Sir, that I was not only late a State officer, but also actually *Now a
State officer,* and permit me also to take notice Sir, that it is altogether
Irregular, nay Illegal Sir, to proceed against the nobles by way of Indictment, but, had I been guilty of any crime Sir, I ought to have been Im-
peached, and here I boldly appear Sir, and || claim the privilege of my   [413]
peerage, being, I assure you, not alittle Surprized, that you should countenance such Illegal and audacious proceedings, against a person who has the
honor to be Champion of this here Club [here Sir John laid his hand upon
the hilt of his broad Sword] and prop of the Chair, and must beg leave to

say further, Sir, that you need not be Surprized if the Chair should suffer a violent Shake, since you permit the underminers and Sappers to approach so nigh your own foundations, by digging under my props."—Then Sir John frowened & was silent.

The Indictment being read, and Sir John refusing to plead, Mr Attorney Spyplot, council for Sir John, stood up and spoke as follows.

"Mr President Sir, (here he took a pinch of Snuff)

I should be sorry—humph—That Mr Secretary should be allowed to prefer Indictments, in this here Club, Just when and how he pleases, and desire to know Sir by whose authority, and by whose advice and Instigation, this here Indictment, or rather libel Sir, has been trumpd up; for Sir, If we do not enquire into this, it is my opinion Sir—ah hey ho, [here Mr Attorney youned] it will be a dangerous affair, and I humbly Conceive, Mr President Sir, It concerns us a—a haunch—a—a haunch—a—a haunch [here he sneezd thrice] all Sir, for Sir, if Sir John, a Noble and State officer of this here Club, is laid open to these attacks libels and Insults, none of us, [414] Longstanding members of the commoners, can reckon ourselves safe, ‖ and gi' me leave to say, Mr President, Sir that your honor's Chair may be in danger, for which Mr President Sir I should be very sorry"—here Mr Attorney Spyplot sat down.

Then Sir John deigned to arise from his seat, shifted his Chaw, and declared, that he was Surprized that any one could be so audacious, as to draw up such scandalous libels against the Champion and protector of the Club.

Upon enquiry made, the Club found, that the Secretary had no authority to draw up this first Indictment, and therefore it was quashed.

Mr Secretary against this proceeding Solemnly protested, because he affirmed That he had express orders from the Club of the 17th of January last to draw up the said Indictment, to prove which he called upon Jonathan Grog Esqr, who was present and asisting at that Club, to which Jonathan Grog Esqr, made reply, that he very well remembered such orders, then his honor the president asked the Secretary if he had orders from the deputy of the Chair for that night, To which the Secretary answered That he had not, and how could he, since Solo Neverout Esqr, then deputy president, was at the time fast asleep in the Chair, to which his honor replied, that this argument was little to the purpose.

The Secretary then read the Latin Copy of the Second Indictment as follows.

[Greatest in eloquence, behold! powerful in the flow of his speech
Who has the eloquence of learned Cicero;
For what was the readiness of his well trained mouth we knew
When he bore the Clubical arms on the occasion of alarming events.]

[facing page 409]

Indictamentum IIdum

Tuesday Club Ss⁹

Socii societat⁹, diei mart⁹ Annapolitan⁹ anglice *The Annapolis Tuesday Club,* super honor⁹ suam present⁹ quod dom⁹ Joannes eques Societat⁹ alias dom⁹ Joannes Oldcastellius, eques Societat⁹, [415] anglice *Sir John knight of the* || *Club, otherwise called Sir John Oldcastle knight of the Club,* nuper de civitat⁹ Annapol⁹ in Comitat⁹ Annarund⁹ homo pernicios⁹ et Seditios⁹ prave⁹ ment⁹ et turbulent⁹ disposition⁹, timorem dom⁹ nostri presid⁹ in ment⁹ non habens vi et armis, rautose et riotose, Decimo, Septimo die mensis Januarii anno domination⁹ dom⁹ nostri presid⁹ quarto apud aul⁹ Baccalaur⁹ anglice *Batchellor's Hall,* in civitat et comitat prædict, coram ipso dom⁹ presid, Solenniter sedent⁹ et dormient⁹ in Cathedr⁹ presidential⁹ et in present⁹ diversor⁹ nostror⁹ Socicior⁹ adtunc et Ibid⁹ present⁹, et existent⁹ Certam Crater⁹ anglice *A punch Bowl,* pretii quatuor Solidor⁹ replet⁹ certo liquore, anglice *Punch,* manu tenens, Toastam Sequentem exicrabilem, abominabilem, detestabilem, horribolem, horrisonam, Immodestam, contumeliosam et damnabilem, Societati proposuit, hisce scil⁹ verbis anglican⁹ *To the pious memory of Sally Salisbury's* —— Contra Ligeantiam debitam, in malu⁹ et perniciosu⁹ exemplu⁹ omniu⁹ alioru⁹ in tali casu delinquend⁹ et contra pacem dict⁹ dom⁹ presid, cathedr⁹ et dignitat⁹.

To which Indictment Sir John said "Pish and phogh! prithee ha' done, there's too much of this Stuff, this is worse than the other, by Jupiter."

The Secretary then read the English Indictment as follows.

Indictment II

[416]	Sir John, you stand Indicted by the name of Sir John, || otherwise called, Sir John Oldcastle, of the parish of St Annes in the County of Annarundel, knight of the Tuesday Club, for that you, as a pernicious, Seditious, depraved and turbulent knight, not in your heart having the reverence due, to our most Illustrious and Serene Nasifer, president of the said Club, but, led by your own wicked and devlish Inclination, in utter contempt of the Laws of the said Club, and the authority of the said Serene President, you, the said Sir John, otherwise called Sir John Oldcastle, knight of the said Tuesday Club, upon the 17th day of January, in the 4th year of the dominion, of our said honorable president, in the parish and County aforesaid, at a place called Batchellors hall; before the said honor-

able the president, or his deputy, Solemnly sitting and sleeping in the presidential Chair, and in the presence and hearing of several of your fellow members, then and there met, with force and arms, rautously and riotously, did take into your hands, a certain punch bowl, of the value of 4 Shillings, charged with a certain Liquor called punch, and drank the following execrable, abominable, detestable, horrible, dreadful, Immodest, contumelious and damnable [here Sir John with great violence exclaimed *ha! ha!*] toast, which you, the said Sir John, otherwise Called Sir John Oldcastle knight of the Tuesday Club, expressed in the following English words, viz: *To the pious memory of Sally Salisbury's* —— against your aleidgeance due to our Lord the president, and setting a bad and pernicious example to your fellow members to be guilty of the same, and against the peace of our said Lord the president his Chair and dignity. What say you Sir John, are you Guilty &ct:

After reading this Indictment, and Sir John not pleading, the case was [417] argued for sometime and very learnedly handled by Mr Attorney Spyplot, but Sir John, having procured, by certain political devices, a very Strong party in the Club, this Indictment, to the Surprize of many, was also quashed, and Copies of both were Solemnly delivered to the Honorable Mr President Jole, to be reposited in his Store of Clubical archives, after some argumentation in the Club, whether or not they should be burnt or destroyed.

Sir John then addressed himself to the President and said "as to this last Indictment Sir, 'tis a parcell of damnd Stuff,—but as to the first, I protest, that had I not promoted drinking toasts In the Club, the whole members, as well as the deputy president, would have fell fast asleep."

It is plain from the management of these trials, that Sir John bullied and Intimidated both his honor the president and the Club; and that they were much struck with a pannic fear at the bellicose Countenance of this Club heroe, which probably would not have happened, had there been a Speaker in the Club, to manage the cause against Sir John, of equal Genius with Drawlum Quaint Esqr, the want of which able officer, the Club now felt in a particular manner, and to verify this observation, I must not ommit this circumstance, that Sir John after quashing the second Indictment, filled a bumper, and In the face of his honor and the Club, drank again, *viva voce,* the same filthy toast, for which he had been but Just Indicted, he also had his broadsword in Club this night.

It will be worth while to observe here, that in these Indictments || his [418] honor the president has the title of *Lord* given him for the first time in the

Club, and tho' the members blamed Coney pimp Frontinbrass Esqr, long after this for foisting this title upon them, yet, this makes it clear, that the Secretary first Introduced it.

The Secretary again protested against the proceedings of the Club, in their quashing the Second Indictment, and being taken up short, by his honor, and some of the Longstanding members, was attempting to speak farther in his own defense, when the Gelastic Law was put in execution against him in an Illegal tumultuous and Clamorous manner, without any Signal given by the honorable the president, this conduct the Secretary begged leave to enter as a riot or trespass and humbly craved that Indictments might be drawn up against the particular offenders, which he beg'd his honor the president to Issue his orders for, from henceforth resolving and protesting, that for his part, as Secretary of the Club, he never would draw up any more Indictments, without particular orders and authority from the honorable the president, as also, declaring, that it was his opinion, that the worshipful Sir John, knight of this Club, is less, (if at all) dissaffected to the Chair, than some pretended loyal long Standing members.

Some members, at this Sederunt, being conscious, that they had been guilty of certain trespasses, and fearing that Indictments might be ordered against them, applied to his honor for an act of Grace, forgiving all past offences, but the honorable the president declined granting it, observe here the Servile disposition of the Club.

Chapter X

Grand proposals in Club by the Secretary, Creation of a poet Laureat, Canopy of State added to the Chair, Speech of Sir John on that occasion, The master of ceremonies leaves the Club, election of a new master of Ceremonies, election of a Club Orator.

An honest Emulation for precedency in learning or virtue, is always [419] commendable (I say an honest ‖ emulation, because I would make a distinction between learning and virtue, and what are frequently mistaken for them, Pedantry and Hypocrisy, by which many rogues have Imposed upon the world,) and an ambition to excell in such excellent things, as are worth excelling in, is a glory to him that possesses it, 'tis *Ingeniorum Cos,* the whetstone of wit, and has been the cause of the rise and grouth of many a heroic action, as well as Club, on this noble and virtuous emulation (tho at first but mere banditti and Ruffians) the ancient Romans, laid the foundation of their great empire, which rose at last to such a height, as to outbrave every enimy but Luxury avarice and ambition, under the Insatiable Tyranny of which last, it fell and never rose again.

When the Ancient and honorable Tuesday Club, kept within decent bounds, as to expence, pageantry, Show, and presidential power, when they exercised their learning and bright parts in making of Speeches, penning of Letters, and striving, who should excell in this Laudable exercise, evading flattery and bombast in their Compositions of this Sort, they flourished, prospered, and grew up to that pitch of Grandure, in which they appeared at this very period, but when the power of the Chair was streched to an extraordinary extent, and the longstanding members strove one among another, who should have most favor and Influence with the honorable Chair, || then the glory power and Character of the Club began to decline. But the [420] prime cause of this declension of the grandure of the Club, was the emulation and contention among the State officers, and the officers of the Commons about precedency, which, like the Contentions between the Patricians and Tribunes of the people at Rome, laid the first foundation for Tyranny and Arbitrary power, and, the Secretary, an ambitious and turbulent officer of the Commons, was one of the Chief fomenters and promoters of this mischief, for, when he found that he could not advance himself in the Club, or gain the favor of the honorable Chair, by flattering Speeches, Orations, and fustian bombast letters, he went to work another way, and tried what might be done, by making great and valuable Presents to the Club, Introducing certain Seals, Medals, Canopies of State, Shields or Scutcheons, caps of State, Conundrums, and the like tinsel trumpery, which, we shall find in the Sequel raised great disturbance in the Club, set his honor the president, his State officers, and longstanding members together by the ears, and, this politic officer, at last compassed his ends, in a great measure, by picking up and securing to himself, whatever he could snatch, in these General hubbubs and Club hurly-burlys.

At Sederunt 100 March 4th 1748/9, Jealous Spyplot Junr Esqr being high Steward, and Huffman Snap Esqr, by commission, deputy president, the Secretary || offered to make the Club a present of a Seal, cut in Silver, [421] expressing the proper design and motto of the Club, to be used by the honorable the president, in the Sealing of Commissions &ct: which the Club accepted of, and the Secretary undertook and promised accordingly, to have this Seal done and finished at London, as soon as could be, com-

mitting the Care of the same to Capt: Comely Coppernose, (this evening
entertained as a Stranger by the Club, according to ancient Custom) who in
a little time Intended to go for England.

Jonathan Grog Esqr, was ordered by his honor the deputy and the
Club, to deliver the thanks of the Club to the Secretary, for this generous
proffer, which he did in the following form.

"Mr Secretary Sir,

Not only in obedience to the commands of the honorable the deputy
president and Club, but of my own frank and free Inclination, I return you
hearty thanks, in the name of the honorable the deputy and Club, for your
Generous offer to make us a present of a Silver Seal for the Club's use, and
in token that I do this Sincerely I drink your health" [then he took a hearty
pull of the bowl]

Then the Secretary moved the Club, that there should be badges of
Silver, prepared for each Regular member of the Club, weighing half an
ounce each, dowble gilt, with the proper Signatures and mottos of the Club
Imbossed, or raised thereupon, to be fixed upon ribbons, instead of the
[422] Card badges now used, and that the ‖ said badges, should be ordered to be
prepar'd and done at London, upon this motion of the Secretarie's, the yeas
and nays were put round, and it was unanimously agreed to; the Secretary
then received orders to commit the Care of this to Capt: Comely Coppernose, who undertook to have it done in the cheapest and the neatest manner, at the Common expence of the Regular members of the Club, The
Secretary moved next, that blank Commissions should be printed, for the
use of his honor the president, which was agreed to, and the Club, ordered
Jonathan Grog Esqr, to print the same.

At the time of making these motions by the Secretary, the Club did not
forsee the designs of this politic officer, in broaching them, but, the violent
heats and disputes, which the Seal, these Badges, and these Commissions
occasioned afterwards in Club, made them Sorely repent that ever they had
agreed to these motions.

On Sederunt 101, Quirpum Comic Esqr being high Steward, and Laconic Comus Esqr deputy president by Commission, the Club met again in
the School room, the ancient place of meeting of the Ugly Club, and the
Songs of, *Stand Around my brave boys,* and *Bumpers 'Squire Jones,*[1] were sung
by the deputy, at the express Injunction and Command of his honor the
President, who had made it a Condition at the bottom of his Commission,

1. Handel's "Stand Round My Brave Boys" was published in the *London Magazine* (November 1745), 560–561. "Bumpers Squire Jones" appears in *Calliope, or English Harmony* and was
also published in the *Gentleman's Magazine* (November 1744), 612.

to sing these Songs, besides which the deputy Complimented the Club with a Voluntaire Song, which as it was a favorite of his we shall here give a Copy of.

Club Song, sung by Laconic Comus Esqr D:P:[2]   [423]

She tells me, with Claret, she cannot agree,
And she thinks of a hogshead, whene'er she sees me,
For I smell like a beast, and therefore must I,
Resolve to forsake her, or Claret deny.

Must I Leave my dear bottle that was always my friend,
And I hope will Continue so, to my life's end,
Must I leave it for her, 'tis a very hard task,
Let her go to the Devil, bring 'tother full flask.

Had she found out my Chloris, up two pair of Stairs,
I had baulk'd her and gone to Saint James's to prayers,
Had she tax'd me with gaming, and bid me forbear,
Tis a thousand to one, I had lent her an ear.

Had she bid me read homilies, three times a day,
Perhaps she'd been humor'd, with little to say,
But at night to deny me, my dear flask of red,
Let her go to the Devil, there's no more to be said.

The honorable deputy sung this Song very pathetically, passion appearing in the twist of his features and glare of his eyes, especially, when he pronounced these words, *let her go to the Devil,* by which his hearers might easily know, that he was himself a dear lover of his bottle, and this was really the Case, for Mr Comus, tho he would talk but very little upon any Subject, yet, when the bowl or bottle came to be the Topic of discourse, he held forth very emphatically.

A letter from the high Steward, to his honor the presi- ‖ dent was   [424]
produced in Club as follows, vizt:

To the honorable Nasifer Jole Esqr,
President of the Tuesday Club, Annapolis.

Most Illustrious Sir,
    It is with the deepest concern, that being sat down to address your honor, agreeable to the practise of your honor's worthy members of this

2. This song appears as "The Jolly Toaper" in D'Urfey, *Wit and Mirth,* and in John Sadler, *The Muses Delight* (Liverpool, 1754), 165.

well Constituted Society, I find myself not only unable to equal the meanest
of their performances in this way, but even utterly unstock'd with a choice
of thoughts and diction, in any degree worthy of your honor's attention,
and therefore, not to detain your honor Longer, or occasion any further
loss of those precious moments, that are constantly employed by your
honor, in promoting the grandure and well being of this your honor's
Ancient Tuesday Club, I, an unworthy member thereof, humbly take the
Liberty to acquaint your honor, that this evening, being especially appointed, for the meeting of this most honorable Society, I propose to officiate in duty of high Steward at the free School, and am in hopes your honor
will favor the Club with your presence, I am your honor's

From my lodging in	Most obedient
Tabernacle Street	Most obliged
21, March 1748	Most devoted and
	Most humble Servt: & Subject
	Quirpum Comic.

We may observe from the tenor of this letter, what gradual Steps, the
members of this ancient and honorable Club took in raising up great titles
for their President, since he is here addressed by the title of *Most Illustrious
Sir,* a title never once thought of, or applied to him in Speeches or letters
before this time, (If we only except the Secretaries Stile in the Indict- ||
[425] ments against Sir John) these Imprudent steps in the members of this Club,
screwd up the pride of the Chair, to such an extravagant pitch, that it
became at last quite Intollerable, and a burden too heavy for them to
support, so that the Constitution of the Club, shook and Cracked under it.

The Secretary having wrote to his honor the President, Concerning
the proposals of last Sederunt, he had the following answer.

To Loquacious Scribble Esqr,
Secretary of the Tuesday Club, These.

Sir,

I approve of the proposals, and have sent you the Commission, which
please to deliver according to directions Immediatly after the Clubs meeting, you have also the high Stewards letter, and as it well deserves a place in
our book of records, desire it may be forthwith recorded, either by yourself
or Chief Clerk, I am Sir,

| March 21, 1748/9 | Your humble Servant |
| | *Nasifer Jole.* |

We find his honor the president as yet complaisant enough, to agree to what the Club had resolved in his absence, but we shall not always find it so, for by the machinations & practises of Sir John, and the plots of the Secretary, he became at last so Jealous and Suspicious, that he absolutely refused to give a Sanction, to the veriest triffles that were transacted in Club without him.

The Secretary reported to the Club, that he had this day delivered their Commissions concerning the badges and Seal to Captain Comely Coppernose, who is to have them done at London, and further, that he ordered them to be Cast with fine pinchbeck mettle, Instead of Silver according to the order of the Club, that mettle being fitter for gilding in Case the gilding should in time wear off, which orders of the Secretarie's the Club approved of.

Then the Secretary gave Jonathan Grog Esqr, thanks for his diligence,   [426] in printing 26 blank Commissions, for the use of his honor the president and Club, and Jonathan Grog Esqr, returned a very civil compliment, in answer to the Secretary.

This evening was produced, a curious distich, wrote upon the envelope of the Club's badge, sent to the high Steward by Jonathan Grog Esqr, to the following purpose.

To Mr ⌗

Inclos'd I've sent your Tuesday badge,
To night, you'll see, how well 'twill fadge.[3]

The Club approved so much of this distich, that they Immediatly Created Jonathan Grog Esqr *Poet Laureat of the Club,* and thus made a new officer, yet, by this addition the Club fund was by no means Impaired, that having been long agoe, Intirely swallowed up in the Philadelphian lottery, and, had there been any Club fund now In being, it would not have been affected by the Creation of this officer, for the Club wisely Judged, in not allowing him any Sallary, knowing he would Rhime the better, the poorer he was kept, like all his brethern bards, whose geniuses are only Clogged and Clouded, by too much pampering and Cramming, after his Creation, the Club ordered him to prepare an ode proper for the next anniversary Solemnity, to be sung by Mr Proto-musicus.

The turn, or Genius of Jonathan Grog Esqr, in his poetical performances, was so uncommon, that it might well be called an original Genius,

3. How well it will suit you, or agree with you.

no other being found to match it among all our ancient or moderen bards, in short, his Compositions had something in them peculiar to themselves and altogether Inimitable, they were pointed & edged, as one might say *I* [427] *dont know howish,* or as the ‖ french express it, they had a *Je ne sçai quoi* of a Salt or relish in them, which cannot well be expressed any other way, but by perusing Specimens of his performances, of which follows one, wrote in the epigrammatic Stile, upon a Subject so barren in itself, that one would be Surprized, how this keen wit could make any thing of it; it is upon a Gentleman's erecting a gate in an out o' the way place or Corner.

Epigram, by Jonathan Grog Esqr

Between these Sticks
This gate to fix
Was Esquire Bl——n's[4] fancy,
But why it was done
I'm Son of Gun,
If I at all can see.

The doggrell is here punctually observed and followed, and there is something of a delicate burlesque turn in the epigram, this Specimen alone will show how well qualified this Gentleman was for a Club poet.

At this Sederunt, there was an amendment made on Law 36th, vizt: after these words in the Law, *Excepting only the election of members,* the following words are to be added, *and matters of expence,* then the two following laws were passed in Club, vizt:

Law XXXVIII. Passed into a law, by the president and Club now met, this 21 of March 1748/9, that from henceforth, when the ballots are to be put round upon any Question, the Secretary is to give all the members present warning, before he destributes the Ballots, and propose the Question in [428] plain and Intelligible terms, and then ‖ destribute the ballots, and, after once going round, whatever the result be, they are to be put round no more upon the same question, during that Sederunt, and for three Succeeding Sederunts after that, and, that all the ballots, both yeas and nays, shall be taken in by two different persons, before those that the Secretary takes be examined.

This law was made, on a Suspicion the members had of some Juggling practises of the Secretary at Sederunt 100, when he procured by flattery and other artifices the consent of the Club, to his proposals concerning the

4. Hamilton's draft has Bladen, probably a reference to Thomas Bladen; see biographical sketch.

badges, for in that instance, the ballots at the first taking were not all unanimous, there being one Nay, but this Cunning officer, pretending there had been a mistake made, got the Club to ballot again, and the whole were Yeas, and it was even suspected, that at this Second balloting he by some Slight or Legerdemain had contrived to remove a nay from the hat, and put a yea in its place; the other law passed at this Sederunt was as follows.

Law XXXIX. Passed into a Law, by the President and Club now met, this 21 of March 1748/9, that no Law for the future shall be passed in Club, unless two thirds, at least, of the members be present.

After passing these Laws, Jonathan Grog Esqr proposed to prepare for the Club, Ballots made in such a manner, as that they might be thrown into the hat, without any person's discovering what was put in, a Nay or yea, which the Club accepted of.

At Sederunt 102, april 11th 1749, Prim Timorous Esqr, being high Steward, a magnificent Canopy appeared fixed upon the presidential Chair, in the Shape and model of a large Scallop Shell, and upon the forepart of it, was erected an oval Shi- ‖ eld, with the proper devices and mottos of the   [429]
Club, curiously delineated there-
upon, of which the figure in
minature is here in the margin
annexed; this too was a contrivance of that plodding officer, the
Secretary, and designed by him to
promote mischief in the Club, for
we shall soon find, this very device, triffling as it was, raise contentions, and hot disputes which
were not easily quell'd.

Sir John, after having taken
his Seat as usual, at the right hand
of the Chair, and deposited a na-
ked Sword upon the Club table *in terrorem*, casting a fierce eye upon this new Canopy, with a frown in his countenance, addressed the president, and spoke as follows.

"Mr President,

I cannot help taking notice of some Innovations here, which I pre-sume, have been contrived and Introduced, without advice or consent of the Club, pray Sir, may I presume to ask, by whose authority, advice and expence, this Sumptous and noble canopy, has been affixed to the Chair, for

[430] Sure ‖ I am, that I, tho a person of rank and consequence, in this here club, was neither consulted, advised with, nor Concerned, in preparing, ordering and erecting this seemingly Superflous ornament."

Before his honor could make any reply to this bold harangue of the knight's, the Secretary politicly moved, that the Club should proceed to business of more Importance, and the enquiry went no farther at this Juncture.

The Reverend Mr Smoothum Sly, late Master of the Ceremonies, and an old Standing member of this Club, having departed the City, the office of Master of Ceremonies by his leaving the Club, became vacant. These two Important offices, of Speaker, and Master of Ceremonies, being therefore, at this time vacant, the Club resolved at this Sederunt to elect new officers to fill their places, but when the Club was proceeding to this Election, a question was started, whether the title of Speaker, should be changed for that of orator, yea or nay, and, the ballots being put round, it was carried in the affirmative, eight yeas & three Nays.

Then Laconic Comus, Huffman Snap, and Jealous Spyplot Senr: Esqrs, were set up as Candidates for the office of orator, and the Election was carried in favor of Laconic Comus Esqr, who, accordingly, after Supper, took his place at the left hand of the Chair, as Orator and State officer of the Club, and privy Councellor to the Chair.

The Club then proceeded to the election of a master of the Ceremonies, and two questions were put, after the following Gentlemen were pro-
[431] posed, as Candidates ‖ for the office, vizt: Jealous Spyplot Junior, Jonathan Grog, and Quirpum Comic Esqrs, The first question proposed, was, whether Jonathan Grog Esqr, as already enjoying several offices and titles in the Club, vizt: Poet, punster, Printer, Punchmaker general and Purveyor, properly expressed by 5 Capital P's, after the manner of the old Romans, Thus, Jonathan Grog Esqr P.P.P.P.P. was to be burdened with any other offices in Club, or was a proper person to stand Candidate for another office, yea or nay, the ballots were put about, and, it passed in the negative, nine Nays, and two Yeas; upon which the Club by balloting, Chose Quirpum Comic Esqr, master of Ceremonies, who took his place accordingly, at the right hand of Sir John, after the Club had been long delay'd in their proceedings in this Election, by a dispute upon some nice distinctions, fomented by Mr Protomusicus Neverout, a gentleman remarkable for raising objections, where no body else could find any.

As Quirpum Comic Esqr, will at times make a Considerable figure in this Club History, both in the Quality of an officer and private Member,

Laconicus Comus Esq, Orator of the Tuesday Club.

[facing page 429]

it will be proper in this place, to give a short Sketch of his person and Character.

Quirpum Comic Esqr, is of a middle Stature, and wears on his Countenance a remarkable droll Cast or turn, altogether undescribable by words, there being as it were a Jest in the very turn of his features, posture of his [432] mouth, mold of his nose, and cast of his eye, || his disposition is comico-serious, or rather Serio-comical, having more of the Grave than Gelastic in his air, for he is seldom or never seen to laugh, tho' he has a Surprizing power, or faculty of setting every body else a laughing, which he does by his Superlative grave air, and *Judgematical countenance* that he puts on when talking of the most trivial or rather Clubical matters, and the queer Clubish gestures, which he uses while he speaks, which by the bye is but seldom, for he is not very fluent of tongue, he never speaks in Club, but it is much to the purpose, that is, his discourse is exactly adapted to the true turn and Nature of Clubical conversation, and always excites gelastic Commotions, in the muscles of every face but his own, for he never was but once observed to laugh in Club, and that was at the extravagant Speech and gestures of Mr Protomusicus Neverout, attempting to talk greek, in a Cause which he pled, in quality of Attorney General, to the Club, when the over exercised faculty of Risibility, had like to have made one half of the Longstanding members expire, to sum up the Character of this Club worthy, I shall give here, the four latin verses that were wrote under his picture, when the portraitures of the members were drawn.

> *Longostati corum Sociorum cerne Cremorem,*
> *Qui nos per noctes sepe delectat Jocis.*
> *Comici Ingenii Juvenis, tua verba per aures,*
> *Vadentia risum, Cachinnamque cient.*[5]

The Club at this Sederunt, having observed, that the book of Records, was too much bandied and tossed about, by certain overcurious and Inquisitive members, to the great hindrance of the Secretary in his office of reading the proceedings, and entering the minutes of the Club, and to the [433] stirring up || and encouraging needless disputes, and objections concerning the Laws; it was therefore resolved, that at next Sederunt, the Club should take some method to prevent this abuse for the future, that the book shall not be thus thumbed and looked Into, upon all occasions, by every member at his own pleasure, while the Club is sitting, without leave given by his

5. "Behold the cream of the longstanding members, / Who often delights us with jokes through the night. / Young man of comic genius, your words through our ears / Passing, stir up humor and laughter."

honor and the Club, and proper application made to the Secretary, who is the only person, with whom the book of Records ought to be trusted.

After Supper, Mr Orator Comus, repeated the same Question, which had been started by Sir John, before Supper, with regard to the Canopy of State affixed to the Chair, demanding by whose authority and orders it had been made? To which the Secretary made answer, that he had some considerable time agoe, received some money of his honor the president to be applied to the use of ornamenting the Chair, and that by means of this money, and a small addition of his own, he caused that canopy to be made and prepared, with which answer, Sir John, the orator, and the Club seemed satisfied. Thus we see this ambitious officer erecting his batteries on all hands, but a little while since, he attempted to corrupt the Club, by offering to make them a present of a Seal, and now is endeavoring to corrupt his honor, by covering his venerable head with a Canopy of State, we shall find this longstanding member barefacedly Walpolizing it in this here Club, that is promoting and establishing bribery and corruption.

Jonathan Grog Esqr, produced at this Sederunt, a Set of new ballots, done in the form of little oblong books, according to his promise last meeting, which the Club accepted of, and they were committed to the care and keeping of the Secretary.

The master of ceremonies moved in Club, that thanks should be returned to Jonathan Grog Esqr for providing || these ballots, for the use of [434] the Club, and, the said Master of Cerimonies being required to do the same, he spoke to the following purpose.

"Mr Jonathan Grog, Sir,

I am commanded by his honor and the Club to return you thanks, for presenting them with a neat Set of Ballots, and accordingly I comply with their commands, and, In the name of the honorable the President and Club, I thank you Sir, I thank you heartily and kindly for this favor."

To which Jonathan Grog Esqr Replied, that this was but a small token of his grateful Sense of the Clubs favors towards him.

Then the master of Ceremonies moved in Club, that there should be thanks returned to the honorable the President, and to the Secretary, for their procuring and causing to be made, a Stately canopy of State for the presidential Chair, upon which the Club appointed the said Master of Ceremonies, to return thanks to the honorable the president and Secretary, which he did as follows.

"Mr President Sir,

This here ancient and honorable Club, by means of me, your Honor's Master of ceremonies, return your honor thanks for your honors favor to them, in procuring or Causing to be made, this magnificent canopy, as an Ornament for your honor's Chair."

After which Speech his honor the president bowed to the master of ceremonies, but some of the Longstanding members, believed, and that with some reason, that this Speech verified the proverb, *Thank you for nothing says the Gallipot,*[6]—the master of Ceremonies then proceeded addressing himself to the Secretary.

"Mr Secretary Sir,

[435] I return you most hearty thanks, in the name of the most honorable the president and Club, for your honoring the || presidential Chair, with this most gorgeous and Splendid Canopy of State"—To which the Secretary replied

"Sir, The honor the Club does me, in returning thanks by the mouth of a person of your Consequence, & learning, is more than Sufficient recompense for any small trowble I may have taken in the way of my duty."

Then the Master of Ceremonies, after all this Ceremony taking his place, enquired of the Secretary, what were the duties of his office, "for Sir said he, I know not but in what I have Just now done, I have exceeded my Commission," to which the Secretary replied, and it stood as a rule for the future

1mo   That he is to Invest the president, as often as he ascends the Chair, with his proper badges of State, and affix the Canopy of State, as often as required so to do.

2do   That he is to present such Gentlemen Strangers as shall be entertained, according to ancient custom of the Club, To his honor the President, Sir John, the Orator, and the Longstanding members, recommending them to their favor.

3tio   That he is to Invest all new admitted members at their Inauguration, or confirmation, with the Club's badge, and deliver to them, the Master of Ceremonies form of confirmation, as recorded in the proceedings of Sederunt 99th—it is also expressed to be the mind of the Club that—

4to   He is to deliver the thanks, congratulations, or Compliments, of the honorable the president and Club, to any member or Gentleman, whom the Club shall think deserving of the same.

6. The phrase "thank you for nothing" appears in the works of several authors with whom Hamilton would have been familiar, but the only one that even remotely resembles the gallipot proverb appears in Thomas Shadwell's *The Sullen Lovers* (1668) as follows: "One . . . promised Jupiter a silver cup. Jupiter thanked him for nothing" (act 5, sc. 3). Hamilton has perhaps misremembered these lines and is confusing a gallipot (a small earthen cup) with the silver cup.

As to the duties of the orators office, they remain the same as those of the Speakers, as expressed below, only the Club think fit, that when Speeches are made in || Club, Mr President only, and no other officer or [436] member, shall be addressed, any Law passed, at Sederunt 46th to the contrary notwithstanding, so that now, it is resolved, to be no part of the orator's privileges, as formerly it was the Speakers, to be addressed to, when any motion is made in Club, but the Orators duties are as follow.

1mo   He is, as formerly the Speaker did, to sum up the whole of any argument or dispute, and report it to the Chair.

2do   He is to be a privy councellor to the honorable the Chair, in conjunction with Sir John, knight of the Club, and to demean and behave himself, like a State officer of the Club.

3tio   He is to moderate and regulate all disputes in Club, and call to order, when too much discord or noise arises in any dispute, and, in Case of disobedience, the Gelastic law is to be executed.

4to   He is to command the Master of Ceremonies to return thanks to any member or Gentleman, whom the Club shall think worthy of the same.

5to   He is to open the Solemnity of each Anniversary with a congratulatory Speech, to the president and Club, or in case he declines doing it himself, he shall have the power of commanding any other longstanding member properly qualified to do the same for him, giving him notice of the same, the Club or Committee, Imediatly preceeding the Anniversary.

6to   He shall have power to order the Clerk, to draw up Indictments, when gross trespasses are Committed in Club, that is, he is to exercise the office of prosecutor in the Club.

A member moved for the alteration of Law Second, and that two dishes of vittles should be allowed for Supper at || the Club Suppers, but his [437] motion was only faintly seconded and not complied with, this Satyrical motion was prompted by the Secretary, and done by way of Sneer on his honor and some of the members, particularly, Prim Timorous Esqr, who never paid any Regard to that frugal Law.

At Sederunt 103 April 25th 1749, Mr Orator Comus being high Steward, the worshipful Sir John produced in Club, a letter from the Reverend Mr Smoothum Sly, late an old Standing member and Master of Ceremonies of this Club, presenting his compliments to the honorable the president and the members, and declaring his Intention to come to the ensuing Anniversary, together with Signior Lardini, a worthy honorary member, provided the honorable the president should Celebrate that Solemnity himself, and he should be advertised of the time of its Celebration, upon which, the Secretary was ordered to write an answer to the Reverend Mr Sly, certifying him of the time of Solemnizing the Anniversary, and Returning the Club's compliments to him.

The Solemnity of the Anniversary was appointed to be held, upon Tuesday, the 16th Day of May next, at the house of the honorable Mr President Jole, and a Committee was appointed to meet at the house of Mr Secretary Scribble, upon the 9th of May next, being the Tuesday Immediatly preceeding the anniversary day, to consider of things preparatory for this great Solemnity, and this Committee was ordered, and instructed by the honorable the chair to consider of no other affairs, but such as were relative to the anniversary, The president by this Instruction showd his [438] Jealousy of encroachments on his prerogative and power, not || having yet forgot, the affair of the Sham Committee, of which Drawlum Quaint Esqr, had been Chairman, which proceeded without Instructions. The Gentlemen named by his honor for this Committee were Mess: Jonathan Grog, Prim Timorous, Jealous Spyplot Senr, Huffman Snap, Slyboots Pleasant, and Loquacious Scribble, or any three of them Exclusive of the Secretary, who was to act as Clerk to the Committee, and they were ordered to transmit a Copy of their proceedings to the honorable Mr President Jole, the next day after their sitting.

Chapter XI

Celebration of the fourth Anniversary, Speeches on that Occasion, by the Orator and Secretary, Anniversary Ode, foundation of the Eastren-shore Triumvirate.

This ancient and honorable Club, having now arrived at its greatest pitch of glory, grandure, and magnificence, very grand preparations began to be made for Solemnizing the ensuing anniversary, that every proceeding might be transacted with that dignity and State, becoming so noble a president, such noble State officers and noble Commoners and Longstanding members.

The Committee for the Anniversary, met upon the 9th of may 1749, at the Secretarie's house according to appointment, and having Elected Jonathan Grog Esqr Chairman, they dispatched the following message, to the [439] honorable the president, by Mr Protomusicus Never- || out and Slyboots Pleasant Esqr, two of their members, vizt:

To the honorable Nasifer Jole Esqr,
president of the Tuesday Club.

Honorable Sir,

Your Committee being now met, and having Elected Jonathan Grog Esqr, Chairman, we hope your honor will approve of our choice.

We only wait your honor's further orders, before we proceed to business, and, if your honor has any matters to recommend to our Consideration, besides what was appointed to be deliberated upon, last meeting of the Club, we request that your honor would let us know what it is, we are certainly Informed that there will be a great meeting of the members honorary and regular, at the Anniversary, vizt: upwards of twenty, and therefore, as Mr Quaint, late a worthy member of the Club, has made us a kind offer of a house where there are large rooms, we desire to know your honors mind, whether or not for the better conveniency of the Club, you will accept of that offer, and we shall appoint the meeting there accordingly.

Sig: per order,
Loquacious Scribble Clk: Com:

After dispatching this message, the Committee sent another to Mr Orator Comus, in the following words.

To Laconic Comus Esqr,
Orator of the Tuesday Club.

Sir,

The Committee desire to know, if you are to open ‖ the anniversary [440] solemnity with a speech, if so, you are to send no answer, but, if you appoint another person, you are to let the committee know who it is you appoint, you cannot appoint Mr Huffman Snap, he not being present at this committee, if you fix on any other, please to notify it, for the committee must know this night.

Sig: per order
Loquacious Scribble Clk: Com:

Upon the Return of the Gentlemen from the honorable the president, this answer was delivered, "That the Committee should proceed to the business appointed them to consider of at last Club, and also to appoint the place, where all the members are to meet, before they are to go in procession to attend the president, and as to the place for holding the anniversary, his honor acquaints the Committee that he Chuses his own house, preferable to any other place," and therefore the Committee, in obedience to his honors commands, acquiesce.

Mr Orator Comus, sent for answer to the Committees message, the following short billet.

Gentlemen,

As you apprehend that Mr Snap will not supply the office of orator, I desire Mr Secretary Scribble may officiate, and am yours &ct:

From my bed chamber   *Laconic Comus.*

In pursuance of these answers from the President and orator, the Committee Resolved as follows.

[441]   1mo   That the anniversary Solemnity shall be Celebrated at the house of the honorable Mr President Jole, upon Tuesday the 16th Day of may.

2do   That Mr Secretary Scribble open the Solemnity of the Anniversary with a Speech.

3tio   That the members shall convene at the secretarie's house upon Tuesday, the 16th Day of may, at half an hour after Six in the Evening precisely, bringing their badges with them.

4to   That the members after they are convened, shall send his honor the president notice of their coming to meet him a quarter of an hour before they proceed.

5to   That the members shall wear their badges at the grand anniversary procession, when they go forth to meet the president.

6to   That the Secretary shall give timely notice to all the members of the time and place of meeting.

After entering these Resolves, Jonathan Grog Esqr, Chairman, produced to the Committee, the ode, prepared to be sung at the Anniversary, according to an order passed at Sederunt 101, March 21, which Ode, tho' not yet quite finished, the Committee approved of, and ordered it to be set to music in two parts, ordered also, that the proceedings of this Committee be sent to his honor the president to morrow morning.

Signed,
Jonathan Grog, Chairman.

Pursuant to the order of the Committee, the Secretary sent a Copy of the proceedings to his honor the president at the time appointed.

[442]   The members convened at the Secretarie's house upon the 16th, according to the appointment of the Committee, and dispatched a message to the honorable Nasifer Jole Esqr, that they Intended to proceed to meet him

in a quarter of an hour, and they also resolved not to Invest themselves with their badges 'till they came to the President's gate.

At Seven o'Clock in the evening, the members proceeded accordingly, to meet his honor the president, and were Joined in the way by Prim Timorous Esqr; The honorable the president graciously advanced to meet them about ten paces from his own gate, and did each member the honor of a Salute by manuquassation. The members, before they entered the president's gate, Invested themselves with their badges, and walked in decent order to his honor's back yard, the way being strow'd with flowers, and the Club flag display'd, after sometime staying in the yard, they removed into his honor's great Saloon, and the honorable the president mounted the Chair.

Then Silence being commanded, by the Master of Ceremonies, Mr Orator Comus, was called upon to deliver a harangue to the Chair, upon this occasion, on which Mr Orator, rising up gravely, made a profound obeisance to the Chair, and pulling out a written paper, put on his Spectacles, and read as follows.

"Mr President, Sir,

Eight days agoe, there was a Committee of the Club held at the Secretaries house, which Committee sent a message to me, under the hand of Mr Secretary, ac- || quainting me, that they desired to know whether I Intended [443] to officiate upon the Anniversary, by delivering a Speech to the Chair, and, at the same time, Informing me, that Mr Huffman Snap, who I Intended should officiate for me, was not at the Club's committee, and declined serving me upon this occasion; I therefore sent an answer to the Committee, that I appointed Mr Secretary Scribble, to officiate for me on the anniversary day, by delivering a Speech to the Club, and, as I have not heard that Mr Secretary has refused, so I hope he will proceed, with your honor's and the Club's permission to perform that ceremony in my stead."

Mr Orator having thus delivered himself sat down, and after some debate, whether the Secretary should be permitted to deliver any Speech, it was concluded that he should, and he rising up, made a profound obeisance to the Chair, and delivered the following oration.

Anniversary Speech, delivered by the Secretary

Mr President, Sir,

I have the honor to be appointed by Mr Orator Comus, to perform the Ceremony of congratulating your honor, and the longstanding members of this here ancient and honorable Club, upon this agreeable occasion of the Anniversary.

Gentlemen,

It would be vanity and presumption in me, by arguments from personal weakness, and Inability, to disqualify myself from properly complimenting, the honorable the president and you, upon this Solemn occasion [444] of ‖ rejoicing, since that would be the same as calling Mr Orator's judgement in question.

I grant then I am fit gentlemen, and I hope without Imputation of vanity, since Mr Orator, and the worthy Committee have esteemed me fit, for the discharge of this grand task, their consenting that I should be called to this dignity silences me and leaves me without excuse, I must therefore acquiesce in their Commands, and shall acquit myself to the best of my ability.

Mr President Sir,

Not only myself, but all these here Longstanding members who now hear me, I shall be bold to speak for them and in their name, have a Singular pleasure and Satisfaction in seeing your honor possessed, of that there dignified Seat and office in this here Club, we have found by experience, Sir, that our Constitution has hitherto florished and prospered under your honor's benign management and oeconomy, for we all know, and must own that your honor's administration has more of the Sweet than the bitter in it, and has all along been carried on, with that even temper and Steadiness as to preserve an equal balance, between too rigid a Severity on the one hand, and a Supine mildness and Indifference on the other. Neither can we accuse your honor of partiality or respect of persons, for some of our first rate grandees, have found the resentment of the Chair, when Just cause was given, as effectually, as the most Inconsiderable of our commoners,— we have continued now Sir, for four years, a regular, harmonious and polite Society, under your honor's discreet conduct and direction, and, as we are all conscious that you are the fittest person among us to possess that there [445] Chair of State, and exercise the office of Supreme Governor ‖ of this here Club, so we wish you may long sit there, and Continue to bless us for many anniversaries to come with your wholesome and mild government.

Worshipful Sir John, knight of the order of the Tuesday Club,

Most Dignified and eloquent Mr Orator Comus,

I address you both in particular, as dignified State officers of this here Club, and the main props and Supporters of the honorable Chair.

It would be Impudence in me, to pretend to advise gentlemen of your rank and dignity, that Innate Generosity, that Inbred Spark of virtue and honor, which qualifies you for the high offices you hold in this here Club, together with the opinion you cannot but Justly entertain of the honorable the president's high merit and deserts, must prompt you to exert your powers and talents to the utmost for the Support, defence and honor of his chair and dignity.

Sir Clement Cotterell,

Mr Protomusicus[a] and

Mr Poet Laureat,

This occasion affords each of you an opportunity of putting your best foot foremost, the first in setting every thing in order, that might, without his care be misplaced, the next in warbling forth melodious and melliflous notes, to Charm our ears, and captivate our Senses, and our Sublime Son of the Muses may now pindarize it, in praise of the honble: the President & Club.

Gentlemen,   [446]

This present meeting Commences the fifth year of the Æra of our Society, and I hope, as it has hitherto florished and Increased, it will still continue so to do, not only for five years, but for fifty times five, that the name and being of so worthy and polite a Club, as this of ours, may not be lost to posterity, and unknown to future ages—In fine,

Mr President and Gentlemen,

This is not a time to speak much, but to act well and as becomes us upon this occasion, without many more words then, in order that our meeting here, may be as agreeable as the occasion Requires, permit me to make this motion, that our discourse and conversation be regular, orderly, free, humorous and Jocose, without reflection, without passion, without reserve, without Clamor, without noise, and also that this Speech and Motion of mine, may have your kind and Candid reception, as it proceeds from a heart full of good will and benevolence to the Society, and to conclude, let our Songs be in tune, our puns and repartees *a propos,* and not too poignant or Satyrical, our toasts loyal and Amorous, our Stomachs keen, to relish the elegant fare prepared for us by his honor the president, on this Joyful occasion, and our punch bowls always replete, with fragrant and nectarious liquor, for this Cordial Juice, taken with temperance and moderation [here the Secretary took the punch bowl in his hand,] lightens the Spirits, enlivens the wit, and will conduce not only to make me a more fluent orator, but you more Jolly and benevolent Long standing members [then the Secretary made ‖ some profound bows, first a grand bow to his honor the president, [447] then to all the members round, and drank a Stout pull of the punch to

(a) The compliments adapted to the musician, were not delivered by the Secretary, he not being in club, when this Speech was pronounced, tho' he came in afterwards.

moisten his desiccated pipes, Mr Ignotus Warble, an honorary member pledged him, drinking a new fangled toast, which he called the King and the Club.]

After the Secretary had delivered this Speech, it was moved, that thanks should be returned for the same, and the Master of Ceremonies was called upon to perform this office, but he declining it, Jealous Spyplot Senr Esqr, stood up, and in a handsom manner returned thanks to the Secretary, observing, that his Speech was devised in a very good method, first, being complimentary to the president and Club, and then monitory, or expressing some good advice, how they should behave themselves upon this occasion—To which thanks delivered by Mr Spyplot, the Secretary returned this compliment, saying That he took Mr Spyplot's Civility so much the more kindly, as that he had done it Spontaneously or undesired, whereas others whose proper business it was, and who had been appointed to compliment him, upon the occasion, had declined it, from a consciousness as he suppos'd of personal unfitness or dissability.

After Supper, which was served up in a very elegant manner and consisted of several curious dishes nicely prepared, there was a motion made, that thanks should be returned to his honor the president for his elegant entertainment, and the Secretary being desired to officiate stood up, and after setting his countenance in a proper order and trim, addressd his honor as follows.

[448]   "Mr President Sir,

I return thanks to your honor in the name of this here Club, for your most Sumptous and elegant entertainment, with which you have regaled them, upon this occasion of the Anniversary, the Club find Sir, that you not only exert yourself Strenuously to govern them well, by exhibiting and executing good and wholesome Laws, to keep them in decent order, but also, you study how to exalt and exhilirate their Spirits, by feeding them with rich and nourishing viands & cordial drinks, and therefore I may be allow'd on this occasion to quote a Certain witty and Celebrated poet,[1] *a propos* to the present case.

Who fed them for the public weal,
With marrow pudding many a meal,
And Cram'd them 'till their guts did ake
With Candle Custard and plum cake."

1. The author of these lines is Jonas Green, Tuesday Club poet laureate.

Then the Master of Ceremonies moved, that thanks should be returned for these thanks delivered by the Secretary, which was done in a Succinct manner by the Master of Ceremonies himself.

Then it was moved that thanks should be returned to Mr Orator Comus, for appointing so fit a person as the Secretary, to open the Anniversary Solemnity with a Speech, which was also done in a very Succinct manner, by the Master of ceremonies.

Then the Anniversary Ode, Composed by Jonathan Grog Esqr, Poet Laureat, was called for, and ordered ‖ to be read, and after some dispute, [449] whether the Secretary or the author should read it, 'twas determined that it should be read by the author, or poet Laureat of the Club, upon which Jonathan Grog Esqr, standing up, drank first a draught of punch, wiped his mouth, clear'd his pipes & read distinctly as follows.

An Anniversary Ode on the Tuesday Club

By Jonathan Grog Esqr Poet Laureat

> *Recitativo*
> The Tuesday Club, let the sweet music sound,
> Whose fame is spread from east to westren Clime,
> Honor'd in future Annals shall be found,
> And Jole's Great name endure to th'end of time.
> *Air*
> Her wholesome laws contriv'd and penn'd so well,
> Shall ages hence her Solid wisdom tell,
> To after Clubs a pattern she shall stand,
> With that most beauteous badge of hand in hand.
> *Chorus*
> Our President we honor and revere,
> Who most deserv'dly fills our Stately Chair.
> *Air*
>   He, oer the Judge and Advocate,
>   The Doctor, Gentleman beside,
>   With wisdom and with Judgment great
>   Does by one General choice preside.
> *Recitativo* [450]
> Had other Clubs so great and good a head
> As this, they need no dissolution dread.

Air

  Whene're we meet
  With bowl replete,
The Loyal healths go round,
  And in each toast
  We all can boast
We're honest, hearty Sound.

Recitativo

The Ladies too, with whom the President,
Their Constant friend and hero first begins,
In bumpers round the Spacious room are sent,
But no one yet his Sole affection wins.

Air

Long live the Tuesday Club, so wisely fram'd,
That 'mongst all those great Addison has nam'd,
Not one so great, Long may the members stand,
And still mantain their badge of hand in hand.

Chorus

Our president we honor and revere,
Who most deserv'dly fills our Stately Chair.

When the poet Laureat had read this ode, the Club approved of it, and the Chorus was only sung by Mr Protomusicus, who by the help of Mr [451] Ignotus Warble, an honorary member, set a tune to it, the performance ‖ of the rest of the ode being defferred, 'till the Club can procure their band of Instrumental music, and some asistance from that Ingenious composer Signior Lardini.

It was moved, that Jonathan Grog Esqr, poet Laureat should have the thanks of the Club, for composing this Elegant ode, and Mr Ignotus Warble, being ordered to deliver the thanks of the Club, spoke to the following purpose.

"Mr Poet Laureat, Sir,

I return you thanks, in the name of his honor the president and Club, for taking the pains to compose this elegant ode upon this occasion, in which the brightness of your poetical genius, and your great regard for the honorable the president and Club at the same time appear." To which Jonathan Grog Esqr, made answer,

"Mr Warble, Sir,

I thank you for your odd thanks for my ode"—In this Laconic Speech appears the poet Laureat's great propensity to punning.

Then the Reverend Mr Smoothum Sly, late a regular, and now an honorary member of the Club, standing up, spoke as follows.

"Mr President, Sir,

I am to Inform your honor, that there is a Club now a forming upon the Eastren Shore, of which I have the honor to be a member, this Club is yet in its Infancy and is not as yet perfectly modelled, but we hope ‖ that in [452] time we shall bring it to bear, and I am Commissioned from the Gentlemen of that Club, Sir, to pay their respects to your honor, and the Longstanding members of this here ancient and honorable Club, for, as you have acquired a great name far and near, by your wise and Just Conduct in that there Chair, as president of this here worthy Club, so, they having heard of your fame and Character, have a Just respect for you, and beg you would kindly receive their compliments, from my mouth, and Covet much your acquaintance and Correspondence, and to be regulated by your advice and direction."

To this the honorable the President made reply That he was mightily obliged to the Gentlemen for the honor they did him, and desired Mr Sly to Compliment them in his and the Club's name.

Then the Secretary standing up, remarked as follows.

"Mr President Sir,

I think the gentlemen pay this here Club, a piece of respect which they highly deserve, nor ought we to be remiss in returning their compliments, and we hope, as our Laws are allowed to be well framed and penned, and our constitution settled on a firm basis, that these Gentlemen, of that there other Club, will not think it beneath them, to consult our body of Laws, in order, the better to form a plan for theirs, as the Republic of Rome of old did that of Greece, when they sent for the tables of ‖ the grecian Laws, tho' [453] I would not have you Inferr from this, that either they are as great as were the ancient Romans, or we as wise as the ancient Greeks."

At the close of the Secretaries Speech, Sir John, frowned and said— "Sir!—Sir!—I make bold to affirm, that we of this here Club, are as great, and as wise as any body, not excepting either Greeks or Trojans."

This was the first foundation of the worshipful the Eastren Shore triumvirate, a Society, which we shall find in the Sequel, intirely dependant upon, and subjected to the honorable Mr President Jole, and his ancient and honorable Tuesday Club, and thus began the power Influence and Jurisdiction of this great and Illustrious President and Club, over the other presidents and Clubs in British America.

The Secretary then Informed the Club, that the Reverend Mr Roundhead Muddy, the new parson of the parish, desired to be admitted a long-

standing member, and the Club determined to proceed to his election at next Sederunt, then Jealous Spyplot Senr Esqr, made some motions with regard to regulating the Succession to the Chair, In case of the demise or removal of the honorable the president, which were dissagreeable to his honor & the Club, and therefore not seconded, the *Great Bell of Lincoln* was sung, the king and Ladies toasted after Supper, and every thing was trans-
[454] acted with ‖ that gaiety, vivacity, good humor and decorum, becoming the great and Solemn occasion, thus finished the fourth Anniversary, and thus I conclude the fifth book of our history.

A List of the members Regular and Honorary of the Ancient and honorable Tuesday Club, from the 9th of June 1747 to the 16th of May 1749.

Regular members	Honorary members
The Hon: Nasifer Jole Esqr Præs:	Mr Abraham Bumper
Sir John Knight & Champion	Doctor Polyhistor
Laconic Comus Esqr Orator	Mr Oldham Wisely
Solo Neverout Esqr,	Mr Joshua fluter
protomusicus	Mr Ignotus warble
Jonathan Grog Esqr P:P:P:P:P:	Signr: Lardini
Loquacious Scribble Esqr,	Revd Mr Broadface round
Secretry	Mr Merry Makefun
Drawlum Quaint Esqr Speaker	Mr Chantum Cheary
left the club novr 8, 1748	Coll: Courtly Phraze
Revd Mr Smoothum Sly	Mr Curious Courtly
Mr of Cer: left the club,	Mr Swillum Swagbelly
april 11, 1749	Mr Prim Laconic
Quirpum Comic Esqr, Mr of Cer:	Revd Mr Smoothum Sly
Jealous Spyplot Esqr Senr:	
Jealous Spyplot Esqr Junr	
Capt: Seemly Spruce	
Capt: Serious Social	
left the Club Octor: 13, 1747	
Slyboots Pleasant Esqr	
Huffman Snap Esqr	
Prim Timorous Esqr	

History of The Ancient and honorable Tuesday Club

Book VI

From the foundation of the eastren-Shore Triumvirate, to the Creation of the Chancellor, and Striking of the Club Medals at London.

Chapter I

Of the Witty Sayings, apothegms and Jests of Jonathan Grog Esqr, and other Ingenious men.

None of our Senses were given us but for good purposes, our faculties also were originally Intended to be exercised upon worthy objects and pursuits, by which we daily contribute to our own quiet and happiness, and to the benefit of the Society in which we have been plac'd—This is a doctrine, which has been preached up by Philosophers & Moralists, ever since the beginning of time, and I believe has never been either doubted or denied, 'till of late Certain upstart virtuosi, and Connoiseurs of Quality, who pretend to have made certain very useful discoveries for the ease of the looser part of mankind, and picque themselves in mantaining of, and dogmatizing upon ‖ certain new coined libertine principles and maxims, have [456] taken it into their heads to assert, That our chief happiness consists in giving a full Swing to Sensual pleasures, and Indulging every craving and Idle appetite in this life, seeing the wisdom of this age has lately discovered, that we have little or no hope, or probability (notwithstanding the fine Speeches of Divines and Philosophers) of enjoying any future being, therefore a short life and a merry is the best—If this be not the doctrine of some deep headed moderen Sceptics, what do they mean by treating the terms,

Honor, Justice, equity, Candor, temperance, Charity, piety and the like, in such a Slighting and Sarcastical manner, declaring them absolutely to be no other than Insignificant names, Invented by the more politic and Cunning Class of mankind, To keep the vulgar herd, or Ignorant mobile in awe, in so far as that is necessary to preserve decorum and Order in Society[1]—Tho' these wise Dons in my opinion here only beg the Question, while they grant the necessity of preserving order in Society, and yet sneer at the means of doing it, at least they act very Impoliticly, in publishing and mantaining these their new Coind philosophical Dogmas, for, should this many headed beast the vulgar or mobile, once give credit to these novell fine spun maxims, and be Convinced right or wrong, that they are true, the broachers must rack their Invention to discover some new devices, to keep them in order; since, if the abovenamed virtues (as they are called) are once strip'd

[457] of their value and Significancy, and || the prospect of all future rewards and punishments is struck off, it will not be halters, gibbets, Swords, axes, whips, racks, fire, faggot, and all the tormenting inventions of cruelty, that will keep this giddy multitude in awe, for they will Surely gratify their Lusts for the time present, at the Expence of the public, and every private Interest but their own, and to the ruin and Subversion of the whole civil oeconomy, and laugh at the most exquisite punishments, as if they were only flea bites.

But some may properly enough ask here, why this grave Moral dissertation in a Club History? does it become a Club Historian to turn a Lecturer in Ethics? I beseech you Gentlemen, to have a little patience, 'till you see the drift of my Introducing this book and Chapter with so grave a disquisition, and then I hope, you will neither wonder at nor condemn me.

Tho' it would seem by this preamble, that I Intended to discant, upon the use and abuse of the Senses and faculties, yet, I must here, before I go farther, let you know, my good discerning readers, that I purpose only to Insist alittle upon the use and abuse of the ear, or Sense of hearing, and the use and abuse of the tongue, or faculty of Speech, as these two members are chiefly concerned in Clubs, where various topics of conversation are carried on, and many things heard, as well as said, both consistent with, and repugnant to decency and good manners.

The Tongue and ear are two members pritty nighly related to each

1. Hamilton is alluding particularly to the libertine principles espoused by John Wilmot, earl of Rochester (1647–1680), and his circle of friends, and to the rather cynical social and moral views advanced by Mandeville in the early 18th century. For a good discussion of Epicurean philosophy in early-18th-century England, see Thomas Franklin Mayo, *Epicurus in England, 1650–1725* (Dallas, Tex., 1934), 165–216; see also James G. Turner, "The Properties of Libertinism," *Eighteenth-Century Life*, n.s., IX, no. 3 (1985), 75–87.

other, so as that they may properly be called cousin Germans, being in such a nigh ‖ Neighbourhood, that the anatomists tell us, the roots of the first [458] have a connexion or communication with the membranes and ligaments of the Latter, so that the first seldom wags, but the latter fixes itself into a listening posture, and often suffers Smartly for its Slips and trespasses, being not only liable on that Score, to many Dry drubs and boxes, but sometimes to the vindictive incision of the keen knife of Justice, by which one or both of these externall excrescencies, are shaved smack and smooth with the pericranium.

The first of these little members, has been reckoned by philosophers in all ages a very mischievous tool when not kept within a proper and decent compass, and so many books and treatises have been wrote upon the due Government of it, as might serve a man of leisure, who has a mind to collect them, to read and ponder upon all his life long, and therefore it will be needless for me to enlarge upon this trite Subject, since it is Impossible to say any thing upon it, which has not already been amply discussed by much better pens than mine, I shall therefore only say in General, that this little member, is very often apt to display the Ignorance, folly, Simplicity and wickedness of it's owner; for, as we are told somewhere in the Sacred Archives, *Out of the fullness of the heart the tongue speaketh,*[2] so when a fool, or Ignorant fellow, is stocked with a multitude of Silly, Idle, Impertinent, and pedantic Ideas, his tongue, if his natural Stupidity does not constrain it, (for his natural wisdom never can) will soon betray him ‖ for a rank cox- [459] comb, and altogether unfit for Solid or Sensible conversation, again, when an envious or Ill natured mortal, has not this Impertinent member under proper Governance, it becomes a mere conduit or Spout, of Scandal Invective and abuse, and the Innocent as well as guilty are smeared over with its poisonous ejections—If a busy meddling fellow, who minds other peoples affairs more than his own, cannot restrain this voluble member, the whole neighbourhood where he lives, are Sure to be set together by the ears, and quarrells will tread upon the heels of Quarrells, every triffling occurrence, and private piece of history or Lousy family transaction, supplying fresh fewell to feed the fire of discord, 'till every Individual in the Society, becomes an Inveterate enimy, either Conceal'd or open, one to another.

These foolish, Invidious and meddling people, who cannot keep this nimble member under a Strict guard, have by this means been the destruction of many an amicable Club, and dissolved that Strong band of Society and friendship, which, at it's first Institution was so firm that every one

2. See Luke 6:45.

would have thought it indissoluble, let all Clubs then beware how they admit or entertain such members, who have this depraved or Simple turn of mind, who cannot lay the least constraint upon that little member the tongue.

The ear again is a small organ, which in most people likes to be tickled, there is a Sort of Tentigo (as the Physicians call it) to which it is very subject [460] ‖ and nothing to which it is more open than Scandal, or the Secrets of others, this has been particularly remarked as a distemper peculiar to great men and rulers, a *tentigo auricularis,* or ear itch, whence it happens, that certain mean fellows, whose trade it is to pick up foolish Stories, and whisper them to such great men, their patrons, find mighty favor and countenance with them, and are promoted to places and honorable employments, for which neither their natural or acquired parts have by any means qualified them, and therefore, their only merit is this pitiful and depraved quality; those who have curious ears to draw in the worst and basest filth of conversation disgorged by these pitiful Scavengers, have also been of great hurt to Societies and Clubs of all kinds, and have often been very Instrumental in separating of those who have thought themselves happy, in being united in the Sacred bands of friendship.

Now, I question not, but I shall be told, that all this discourse is mighty good, and wonderfully grave and Satirical, and what we well knew before, but for what purpose, or to what end, such Sage, such pointed lectures? we are perswaded that mens ears and tongues, are very often ill Emploied, and what signifies our knowing all this unless we could find a certain remedy for it, useful and Instructing Subjects of discourse are now [461] become so stale, that people of all ‖ ranks begin to be tired of them. A man cannot always be philosophizing, moralizing, praying, singing of Psalms and Sacred hymns, hearing of Sermons, and leading a life of mortification, such as is prescribed by the reverend & pious Mr Law, in his rules for the life of a Christian.[3] These rules are now become altogether inconsistent with true politeness. To speak metaphorically, human nature cannot subsist with this Sort of Serious diet alone, the far greatest part of it must consist of Sauce compounded of triffles, to make the Serious relish the better; hence our moderen virtuosi, to keep men out of mischief, have Invented a Sort of Chip in porridge Conversation, which is in itself Indifferent, Importing neither good nor bad, is neither beneficial nor altogether useless, Such are these Sorts of pastimes and amusements, in which cards are con-

---

3. William Law (1686–1761) was a famous English spiritual leader and author of *A Practical Treatise upon Christian Perfection* (London, 1726) and *A Serious Call to a Devout and Holy Life* (London, 1729).

cerned, the Innocent tho' triffling amusements of those polite assemblies called Routs and Drums; There are also, the humorous games of Cross purposes, hunt the whistle, Break the friar's neck, and what is it like,[+] adapted to the humor and Capacity of the younger Class of persons of condition of both Sexes.

I grant you, that these conceits and Inventions are very well adapted for this purpose, where mixed assemblies of both Sexes are concerned, being to a tea suited to the humor and taste of our polite young Gentlemen and Ladies, who do not in the least understand Subjects of a more perplexed and abstruse nature, but, they will by no means answer the purpose of those assemblies Called || Clubs, which are of a more Solid and Philo- [462] sophical turn, and therefore, the remedy I would propose to prevent mischievous Conversation in these nocturnal meetings is this, Let them exercise themselves in merry Jests, Smart Sayings, pithy and Concise apothegms, quaint Repartees, Ingenious puns, and knotty conundrums, which has been the practice of many wise and politic Clubs, both in ancient and Moderen times, of which I Intend presently to give examples, but, I would by the bye put in this caution, that their Jests, Smart Sayings, apothegms, Repartees, puns and Conundrums, be not particularly pointed at any one in the Company, or his friend, or dipt in Gall or wormwood, else they will Surely give offence, and Instead of bearing the true Character and Spirit of Satyr, which always ought to be generally placed, and rather seem to laugh in a pleasant manner, than grin with a Sneer, they will deservedly come under the name and Imputation of Scandal or Invective and personal abuse. If they be generally placed, and the Chief Seasoning or Ingredient be of the Comic Sort, they will never fail to please, with such as have any humor at all, and afford a very agreeable and Sprightly conversation, well Seasoned with mirth and Laughter. This I take to be an effectual preservative against the abuse of the ear and tongue in Clubs; but here I may be told, that every member of a Club is not qualified for this Sort of Conversation, it requiring a lively Imagination, and quick turn of thought, I grant you this, but allow me || to affirm at the same time, that there are few Clubs that consist of ten [463] or a dozen members, where there are not at least one or two, that have a genius for this kind of Conversation, and this is Sufficient to enliven and furbish up all the rest and set them in motion, as a small quantity of yest does a huge barrell full of Small beer wort; and especially after five or Six

4. *Cross purposes* is a parlor game in which a ludicrous effect is produced by connecting questions and answers that have nothing to do with one another; in *hunt the whistle* the seeker is blindfolded and has a whistle fastened to him, which the other players blow at intervals; *what is it like* is perhaps Hamilton's phrase for charades.

rounds of the glass, which effectually brightens up our Clubical geniuses, that are naturally more slow and heavy, besides, there are the famous Collections of the Oxford, Cambridge, and London Jests, and the Curious Collection of Jests and Jokes, published by that Learned and Ingenious Gentleman Mr Joseph Miller, under the title of *Joe Miller's Jests,*[5] to which bright Constellation of Grubstreet, I must own it is matter of Surprize to me that the Royal Society have not shown some respect, in Dubbing him a brother or F.R.S. or at least bestowing upon him one of their annual medals, or that neither of our famous Universities have yet conferrd upon him the degree of Doctor, since it is notoriously known, that these learned bodies have heaped their favors and honors of Late, on geniuses far Inferior to his.—There is also the late Collections and publications of Conundrums, Composed for the entertainment of persons of quality,[6] which may all be purchased for the value of five Shillings (a small præmium for such an exhaustless fund of wit) and are abundantly Sufficient to stock any Gentleman, tho' naturally never so dull, with a never failing magazine, if he has

[464] only memory enough to con half a doz- || en Stories or conundrums every club night, and if he be one whose genius does not enable him to enter so far Into the Spirit of a Joke, as to tell it with a proper Emphasis and Grace, the Joke by this means is Improved upon, and becomes rather more Clubical, there being an additional Joke in the way of telling it.

I now proceed to give Instances both from ancient and moderen history of this kind of wit and humor, so Serviceable to, and so much fitted for the Genius of Clubs, and at the same time so effectual a Remedy against the epidemical distemper of Idle and mischievous conversation.

I shall begin with that Celebrated Ancient Droll Democritus of Abdera, who, tho' a profound Philosopher, was esteemed mad by his fellow Citizens, this notion they conceived of him, from his often breaking into violent fits of Laughter, when no body knew for what, little dreaming that he laughed at the Sempiternal Comedy, which he saw acted from day to day

5. *Oxford Jests, Refined and Enlarged,* 3d ed. (London, 1671), by Capt. William Hickes, was in its 14th edition by 1740. *Cambridge Jests; or, Witty Alarums for Melancholy Spirits* (London, 1674), by "a Lover of Ha, Ha, He," was reprinted in 1742. *London Jests; or, A Collection of the Choisest Joques and Repartees, Out of the Most Celebrated Authors, Ancient and Modern* (London, 1684) was in its 3d edition by 1740. *Joe Miller's Jests; or, The Wits Vade-Mecum* (London, 1739) was actually compiled by John Mottley under a pseudonym. Mottley (1692–1750) was the author of two dull tragedies, a few comedies, and lives of Peter the Great and Catherine I. Joseph Miller (1684–1738) was a Drury Lane actor and a reputed humorist.

6. Hamilton is referring to *The Witling: Being a Compleat Collection of the Most Celebrated Conundrums Now in Vogue among People of High Taste* (London, 1749) and *A Key to the Witling: Being Proper Answers to . . . the Conundrums* (London, 1750).

on this great earthly stage, by his fellow Mortals, this Philosopher used to teach, that the whole course of human life was only matter of Laughter, all men he said were a kind of two leg'd asses, monkies, or rather wild beasts of a more fierce nature, that Reasoned, Philosophized squabbled quarrelled and destroyed one another, about things that were In themselves triffles, and that there was no difference between men of a mature age and Children, excepting this trivial one, that the latter diverted themselves, with babies made up of rags and Remnants, and the first with Bawbles, composed of more costly Stuff, tho' alike perishable and vain.

There is a stale Story of Diogenes the Cynic, which I have sometimes seen curiously done on Japand tables and ‖ cupboards, he had no other [465] house than an old hogshead or wine cask, and no other cup but the hollow of his hand, and was one of your Sneering Solemn drolls, whom I esteem the most Gelastic and entertaining; of him it is said, that being one day asked by Alexander, the Macedonian Conqueror; what it was in his power to do for him? bidding him only declare and it should Immediatly be granted.—He replied with a Cynical grin, and a very gelastic contorsion of Countenance, tho' he did not Intend to make a laughing matter of it—Tis in your power said he to bestow upon me many triffles, on which, as I want them not, I set no value, but prithee take not that from me which thou canst not give, get you from between me and the Sun, for I dispise even your Shadow.

The same Diogenes, as he one day sat in his tub, scranching⁷ of turnips like a Hog, a certain Smart fellow passing by had a mind to be arch with the philosopher, and told him That if he would only learn the art of flattery, he might convert his tub into a palace, and his nasty roots into delicate viands,—And you vain Glorious Coxcomb (replied the Sage) if you could learn to be contented with this wholesome and homely fare, need never study and practice the fawning arts of a Spaniel.

Socrates, the famous Athenian Sage, tho' he was reckoned the wisest man of the age in which he lived, yet, when Aristophanes the Comedian introduced him upon the Stage, in a ridiculous Character, to promote the Jest, and at the same time, to disarm the Satyrist, mounted the public Theatre, and acted that very part himself, and when the same Socrates had taken abundance of pains to find out one wise man, conversing for that purpose with ‖ men of all degrees and professions, from the philosopher to [466] the Clown; he at length concluded that all were fools alike, and he himself

---

7. Crunching. The first story about Diogenes the Cynic appears in Diogenes Laertius 6.38. The second story is an adaptation of Diogenes Laertius 6.58.

as great a fool as any, since he publicly ownd and proclaimed it, that he was an Ignoramus, for he only knew one thing, and that was, *that he knew Nothing,* and, in this very opinion Tully long after agreed with him, expressly saying, *Stulte et Incaute omnia agi video.*[8]

> *Ille Sinistrorsum hic dextrorsum, unus utrique,*
> *Error, sed variis illudit partibus omnes.*

> One Reels to this, another to that wall,
> 'Tis the same error that deludes them all.[9]
>
> *Robertus Burton*

The Divine Plato, having defined a man to be *Animal bipes Implume facie Erecta,* or an unfledgd two legd animal,[10] a wag one day strip'd a cock of all his feathers and drove him into a School, where Philosophical Lectures were held, according to the Sect of the Platonists, and on being asked, what he meant by that conceit, he told them that he had sent them *Plato's man.*

When Demetrius took Megara he asked Stylphon a Philosopher, if he had lost any thing,—Not I Sir Indeed replied he, I carry nothing about me, which you can make prey of or take from me, that is of any value, This Philosopher esteeming nothing of such value, as to be reckoned wealth or riches or real possessions but the Moral virtues, upon the same conqueror's leaving the City, he told the same Philosopher, that he quitted the City to [467] him in an Intire State of freedom,—Very true Sir (replied || Stylphon) for once you and your dragoons are departed there will not be so much as one Slave left among us.[11]

One Agapestor, a cripple in his right leg, being at a merry making, the company in ridicule ordered that every man should stand on his right leg and drink off his Glass, when it came to his turn to Command he matched

---

8. "I see all things being done foolishly and without caution" (Cicero, *Epistulae ad Atticum* 7.10.10). Socrates appears as a caricature Sophist in Aristophanes' *Clouds;* in Plato's *Apology,* 19C, Socrates invites the court to compare the caricature with the reality. The allusion to his knowing nothing appears in Plato's *Apology* 21–23.

9. More literally, "That one to the left, this one to the right; either way, / One error deludes all in their various directions" (Horace, *Satirae* 2.3.50).

10. Literally, "unfeathered, biped animal, his face upright." The "wag" who plays the joke on Plato is Diogenes the Cynic (see Diogenes Laertius, 6.40).

11. Demetrius I (336–283 B.C.) of Macedonia established control over Greece but lacked wisdom as a ruler. Stilpon (ca. 380–300 B.C.) was a Megarian philosopher who strongly influenced Zeno the Stoic and maintained the monism characteristic of the Megarian school, denying the Platonic distinction between universals and individuals. This story appears in Plutarch's life of Demetrius.

them, for, getting a small pitcher, he put his withered right leg into it, and ordered that every man in the Company should do the same, while he tossed off his bumper, the whole company, like a parcel of fools, attempted to do it, but in vain, so Agapestor laugh'd in his turn and they drank kelty.[12]

Cato seeing two Ambassadors sent from Rome to a foreign State, one of whom had a very small head, like an owl, the other so lame, that he could not walk without Crutches, said very archly, and much like one of our moderen punsters, here's an Embassy that has neither head nor tail.[13]

The Philosopher Aristotle, being once teized with the Impertinence of a talkative fellow, who at every period would ask him, Is not this very Strange, Aristotle?—no Indeed says the Philosopher, but I think it very Strange that one who has Legs to run away, should stand to hear your Idle Stories; and the same Philosopher being asked once by a fellow, who had been several hours in telling him a tale of a tub, If he had not tired his patience—By my troth no, replied the Sage, for I have not heard one single word you said.

A Certain Indian Philosopher, Calanus by || name, an enimy to talk- [468] ing, showed Alexander the great, who consulted him about where he should fix the Seat of his Empire, a very Significant emblem of the nature of Civil Government, by throwing a dry raw hide on the ground and treading upon it all round the edges, by which the other Side still tilted up, but at last clapping his foot right in the middle of the hide, it lay flat and even.[14] One need be no conjurer to find out what Lesson the conqueror gathered by this example.

The Companions of Demosthenes, In his Embassy to Philip king of Macedon, commended that prince for his beauty, eloquence, and for his being a good toaper—These elogiums said the Orator, are more applicable to a woman, an advocate and a Spunge than to a king.

Zeno, a Certain Philosopher among the Sophists, once Lecturing in his School, argued thus against motion,—If a body moves at all, it must move either in it's place, or out of it's place; but in its place it cannot move, because the Idea of motion Implies a Constant Change of place, neither can it move out of its place, because a body must always possess some place or

12. Agamestor was an Academic philosopher, called Agapestor in Plutarch, *Quaestiones convivales* 1.4.3., the source of this anecdote.

13. The Cato story is loosely derived from Plutarch's life of Cato.

14. Calanus's (fl. 4th century B.C.) real name was Sphines, but he was wont to say *Cale*, the Indian form of salutation, so the Greeks called him Calanus. He acted as counselor to Alexander, who greatly mourned him after his death. The Calanus story appears in Plutarch's life of Alexander.

other, *Ergo,* there is no such thing as motion;[15] while this argument was going on, a certain Comical Crabbed fellow, stood in a corner of the School, at some distance from the Learned Lecturer. And when he had finished his argument, he advanced Gravely towards him, and gave him a Smart box on the ear, with his dowbled fist, and then returned to his [469] place,—The Sophister asked him || why he used him in such a rough manner?—It was not I Sir, replied he,—How says the other, did I not see you come from that corner where you are to this corner where I am and strike me?—That could never be Good Sir replied the Droll, since you and I are two bodies, and These corners two distant places, and, as no body can move either in its place, or out of it's place, I never could have moved from this corner to that to give you a box on the ear. This was a Solid and hard argument and a Sophism *ad hominem* as our Logicians call it.

But enough of ancient examples of this kind, I come now nigher our moderen times.

After the Gothic Barbarism had overclouded the face of Europe, the Intire abolition of Learning was followed by a still calm of Dullness, the Solemn and Subtile Doctors among the Schoolmen, groped thro' this Dusky Gloom, under the guidance of Aristotles Lanthorn, and consumed all their oil, and spent all their Labour, in refining and Commenting upon words and abstract notions, yawning over a vacuum, analysing of farts, unravelling of Cobwebs, distilling the moonshine, and the like useful and Curious operations, from whose Indefatigable brain work, it is thought, that curious moderen art of punning first took its rise, while this Laborious Scrutiny was going on, none had leisure to apply themselves to any other Study, and therefore, the progress of Quaint Stories, Sage apothegms, and Smart repartees, was at a stand till some early wits of the 15th Century, [470] about the time of the Sacking of Constantinople by the Turk, || of whom the famous french Philosopher Turlupin[16] was one, began to break out like the morning Star from a black horizontal Cloud, and threw some faint rays of wit and humor, over the Darkened face of Europe, then began the light of the Aristotelian Lanthorn to fade, & was at last lost in a certain fog, no body knows where or how, from which murky fog arose the celebrated Paracelsus and others, his followers, searchers after the Philosopher's Stone. But, as none durst in these bigotted times appear barefacedly in the Charac-

---

15. Born ca. 490 B.C., Zeno studied under Parmenides, employed his teacher's monistic principles to argue against motion, and according to Aristotle, invented the dialectic. Zeno's argument about the paradoxical laws of motion appears in Aristotle's *Physics* 239, B5.

16. On Turlupin, see p. 218n, above.

ter of drolls, being afraid of fire and faggot, the reward of heresy, for every
thing was damnable heresy, that differed in the least from the Jargon of the
Schools, and a parcel of aristotelian Lumber, They made the poor devil,
who with reason they esteemed fire proof, stand between them and all
harm, by cloathing him in a motely fool's coat, for men were at all times
very ready to roll the blame upon the Devil's back, and to clear their hands
of guilt, therefore this venerable old Don the Devil, was always brought
upon the Stage, whenever any piece of Drollery, mirth or Buffonery was to
be performed, and accordingly we find this ancient Sinner brought in like
an antic in several comic farces, where he diverts the audience, either by his
blunders or his Sufferings. Thus, in a representation of the Story of David
and Abigail where the Devil is made Lacquai to Nabal, the latter goes to
sheer his Sheep, and the Devil In Imitation of his master, falls tooth and
nail to the Sheering of a great overgrown hog, which makes a dreadful
vociferation and horrid Screaming, under Signior Satano's paws, and much
diverts the Spectators, hence the old proverb, *Great cry and little wool as* || *the*   [471]
devil said when he shore his Hogs.[17]

The Devil for a considerable Time held the honorable place of general
Droll, and master buffoon, being often brought on the Stage as a but or
Subject of Laughter, his task being often to dance in a circle of witches,
with a candle in his fundament, to ride long Journeys thro' the air on
broomsticks, to make long voyages in eggshells, to say prayers backwards in
a Short Cloak & high Crownd hat, while the candles burnt wonderfully
blue, and other such foolish amusements fit for his devilship, 'till at last,
having performed his parts with general approbation, he was advanced to
the honorable office of master of the revells, and appeared on the Stage in a
higher Character, as for instance, in the famous pantomime, of Harlequin
Doctor Faustus,[18] where he performs the majestic and dignified part, of
Soveraign monarch of hell, and struts in buskins, then the Ladies became so
familiar with his devilship, that they could look him in the face with the
same Indifference, as if he had been any mortal man of a course feature like

---

17. Hamilton appears to be the first author to associate this proverb with the devil (see
Apperson, *English Proverbs and Proverbial Phrases,* 432, where pre-19th-century uses typically
read "Much cry and little wool, as one said . . . " or "as a man said"). Since the devil is not
known for shearing hogs in the Bible, it seems evident that Hamilton has applied an old
proverb to a contemporary farce in which the devil does perform such shenanigans. What is
curious about the proverb as Hamilton has patched it together, however, is that it did become
popular as he uses it, in the 19th century.

18. *Harlequin Doctor Faustus* (1723), which established the tradition that Harlequin must play
someone other than himself, was written by John Thurmond, an 18th-century actor who
invented many profitable pantomimes for Drury Lane.

the Celebrated Mr Heydagger,[19] late regulator of the Masquerades and Ridottos.

When Signior Devil had thus served his apprintiship, and assumed a higher part, the office of Jesting was put into the hands of certain arch [472] fellows, who had more Cunning than their neigh- || bours, and were placed near the persons of great princes, under the title and Character of Fools, tho in fact they were nothing less, these fellows were very useful in their way, for they often gave advice, and wholesome Councel with Impunity, to the hot headed Tyrants their Masters, when none else, not even those of the greatest Sagacity and prudence among their Subjects durst open their mouths.

It is recorded of one of these fellows, belonging to the Tyrant Bajazet I king of the Turks,[20] that one day, his master being determined to put all his Kadilisquers or Judges to death, for accepting bribes in Causes that were brought before them, this fool dress'd himself up in the garb of an ambassador, and appeared with a very grave countenance before the Sultan his master, who asking what he meant by this device? replied that he came to solicit him to be sent Ambassador To the Emperor of Constantinople,— For what? said the Tyrant—To bring to court a posse of his grave monks and friars, replied the fool—and what then?—To supply the places of these venerable Judges, whom your majesty Intends to hang, said the fool—may not I supply their places from among my own Subjects said the Sultan—Ay, but these monks and friars will do very well replied the fool, on account of their grave and demure Countenances, since men of an adequate knowledge in the Laws, to these miserable Condemned Judges, are not to be found [473] among all your majestie's || Subjects. This made the Tyrant think alittle, and turning to one Alis Bassa of his privy Council, he told him that the fool was very right, and asked him what he had best do, the Bassa advised Bajazet to pardon and replace these Judges, and allow them Sufficient Sallaries, whereby they should be above Corruption, which the Tyrant accordingly did.

It is told of James I, that Royal Virtuoso, & reputed Solomon of the age in which he lived, that he kept nigh his person a fellow Called Archie,[21] to divert him with his Jests at times, this Archie, or rather Arch fellow, one day, while the king was at dinner, clapt his fools cap, bells and all, upon

19. John James Heidegger (1659?–1749) was the English theater manager of the Italian opera at Haymarket for the Royal Academy of Music from 1720 to 1728.

20. As ruler of the Ottomans (1389–1402), Bajazet I besieged Constantinople but was defeated and taken prisoner by Tamerlane.

21. Archie Armstrong (d. 1672) was a jester in the court of James I.

his majesties wise head, as some think, not Improperly, the master being thought by many more a fool by nature than the man,—How now Archie said the king, what's this for—For sending the prince your Son to Spain, replied the fool—what then, said the king, I hope he'll return safe—Then Nunkle, said Archie, I'll send mine nown Cap to the king of Spain, and he shall wear it.

A fool of this Sort, who belonged to one of the kings of France, having a small Spite at the master huntsman, was resolved to be revenged on him, and, one day, as he attempted to ford a river with his pack of hounds, being doubtful of the depth of the Channel, he asked this fool, if he might safely pass, who assured him he might, but the poor man and his horse were first mired, and then drowned in attempting it, while the fool stood by, Laughing all the ‖ while, a complaint of this being brought to the king, the fool [474] was asked why he had done this mischief, he replied That he was not at all to blame, for he had seen his majesties Geese pass the River at that very place, not ten minutes before, and Surely a man on horseback might wade where a parcel of geese did, on this the fool was excused, because he gave advice to the best of his knowledge, and the huntsman blamed, because he trusted too much to the advice of a fool.

A very recent example of this Sort, happened, in a question, put to his present Britannic majesty, by a certain Nobleman, who, tho' no fool by profession, yet in this Instance assumed the Character of a Jester or Buffoon, his majesty being much Incensed, with his Scots Subjects, on account of a rebellious Insurrection of the mob at Edinburgh, who had in an outragious manner hanged Capt: Porteous,[22] was asked by this Nobleman, at the time that the General Assembly of the kirk was about to meet there, who his majesty would please to nominate for his commissioner to represent him, in this assembly,—The Devil, replied the king in a huff,—The nobleman after some pause, asked his majesty how he would please to have the Devil addressed, if in the usual form, *To our Trusty and well beloved Cousin and Councellor.*

But the most remarkable quaint Saying, that I have yet met with, which was the more so, as it came from the mouth of a Natural fool, was the foll- ‖ owing. A dull parson, once holding forth in his pulpit, the whole [475] congregation, except this natural, fell fast asleep, upon which the preacher reproved them Smartly, and rousing them, with half a dozen Smart Cushion thumps, bid them take example by that fool, who did not sleep while

22. John Porteous (d. 1736), captain of the Edinburgh city guard, fired on a crowd gathered to rescue a popular smuggler and was later hanged by an armed group in disguise.

the word of God was a preaching,—Ah! Good Sir, said the Idiot, had I not been a fool, I should have been asleep too.

Many such Instances might be produced, of the Smart and witty Sayings of both fools and wise men, which shone forth by degrees, brighter and brighter, after the Revival of Learning in Europe, but I shall trowble you with no other examples of these times, but that of a certain Pope who was no fool. At the Installment of these holy fathers, there used to be a net laid upon a large table, instead of a Cloth, at which his holiness is to eat, as he represents Peter the poor fisherman, his predecessor, this Pope, after he found he had secured the Main Chance, or the papal Chair, coming into the Room, where this farcical net had been laid out, desired the waiters to Take away the Net, and lay a Cloth, for the fish was already caught.

About the beginning of the 16th Century, this kind of wit and Drollery, was much on the Increase, then was the Republic of letters blessed with a Rabelais, and a Verveille,[23] whose Instructive and witty writings have been of such General Service to Church and State, and have been carefully Com-
[476] mon placed ‖ by all our Succeeding Jesters, by the Celebrated Tom Brown, that comic Star of Grubstreet, by the Celebrated Mr Ward,[24] author of the *London Spy*, and even by the Incomparable Dean Swift, that delicate and modest writer, who has brought the art of Jesting and Buffonery, and writing huge essays upon nothing, to a greater perfection than any man ever did before or since.

In the wise and politic reign of King James I, This useful art was in great perfection at the English Court, and a good pun, Conundrum or Jest, would then recommend a man to a fat Bishoprick, or to any great office in Church or State.

There is a good Jest told of one Abbe Soray,[25] a poor poet, who, one day walking the Streets in a ragged habit, having a great hole or Chasm in the Crown of his hat, was taken in a Shower, and having no Money in his

23. François Béroalde de Verville (1558–1612) was a French mathematician, scientist, and author whose works include a poor imitation of *Utopia* called *Idée de la république* (1583), *Appréhensions spirituelles* (1583), *Le Cabinet de Minerve* (1601), and *Moyen de parvenir*, or *Salmigondes* (1610), a collection of licentious tales.

24. Thomas Brown (1663–1704) was an English satirist and author of the famous "I do not love thee, Dr. Fell" and *Amusements Serious and Comical* (London, 1700), humorous sketches of London life. Edward "Ned" Ward (1667–1731) was an English author of Hudibrastic doggerel verse and coarse, humorous prose, including *The London Spy* (London, 1698–1703), the observations of a country man in London, and *Hudibras Redivivus* (1705–1707).

25. Probably Nicholas Soret (fl. 17th century), a French priest and poet, whose works include *La Céciliade; ou, Martyre sanglant de Saincte-Cécile, patrone des musiciens* (1606), a five-act tragedy in verse.

pocket to hire a coach, went under a pent house to screen himself, a proud
Marquis Riding that way in his Chariot, happened to spy this Ragged
Bard, and having a mind to make himself merry at his expence, without the
least design to bestow a dinner upon him, sent his lacquai to ask him in
what battle he had received that terrible Gash or wound in his hat, the
Servant did as he was ordered, saying, that monsieur the marquis had sent
his compliments, and desired to know in what ‖ battle he had received that   [477]
dreadful wound in his hat, on which the Abbe elevated his cane, and letting
full drive at the fellows head made answer, at the Battle of *Cane-y* you
Rascal. The poor Lacquai went back with his bloody crown, and complain'd to his master, who, Jumping out of the Chariot, went boldly up to
the Ragged Son of Apollo, and asked him how he durst use the Servant of a
man of his quality in such a rude manner,—Because he was Saucy said the
Abbe,—Saucy says the marquis, pray Sir, do you know who I am—yes
replied the Bard—and who am I pray, said the marquis—you're a fool said
the poet, and so the Marquis mounted his Chariot again, hanging an Arse,
being afraid that if he should carry the conference any further, the poets
cane would know no difference between the master and valet,—Thus we see
how dangerous a thing it is to meddle with poets, or hungry sharp set wits,
but even poets will sometimes meet with their matches, as the following
instances will show.

Alexander Pope Esqr, our Celebrated English Poet, being lighted
home by a link boy, gave him a Sixpenny piece—bless your honor said the
boy, I have gone a great way with your honor, and hope your honor will
give me more,—God mend me boy, said Pope, his usual oath,—nay Sir,
said the boy Interrupting him, God had better make nine others than mend
such an odd figure as you. ‖ Mr Pope was so pleased with this smart   [478]
repartee that he gave the boy half a Crown.

It did not however turn out so well with the said Mr Pope on another
occasion, who being once in a Coffee house, surrounded by a Club of Town
wits, who were his most humble Servants and submitted to his Judgement
and decision in every thing, they were looking over a passage in Anacreon
the greek poet, which puzzled the whole Junto, none of them being able to
find out the meaning of it, a young Smart, Just fresh from the University,
dawbed over with lace, and decked with a Sword and Cockade, as having
Just entered into the army, beg'd leave to look at the book, Mr Pope handed
it to him, and leerd on him with great contempt, thinking it much out of
Character that such a foppish figure, should pretend to Learning of any
Sort, but the event soon Convinced him, that he trusted too much to a false

association of Ideas, as Mr Locke Calls it,[26] in making Ignorance an Insepa-
rable companion of foppery, for this young man explained the passage, and
convinced the whole Club of wits, that the difficulty arose only from an
error in the press, in the ommitting of a point of Interrogation.—Pray Sir,
says Mr Pope with a Sneer, Do you know what a point of Interrogation
[479]   is?—yes Sir.—what ‖ is it pray?—why 'tis a little crooked thing that asks
questions. This repartee effectually turned the laugh upon Mr Pope and
silenced him, for he was a man of a slender small body, and had a little
hump upon one of his Shoulders.

But now, since we talk of poets, we must not ommit our celebrated
Poet Laureat of the ancient & honorable Tuesday Club, vizt: Jonathan
Grog Esqr, who, I may safely say, is as well stocked with Jests, quaint
Stories, puns, conundrums, and other such conceits, as any wit, either
ancient or moderen, that ever was heard of, to recount all the Witticisms of
this bard, would be an endless Labor, and would require a huge ponderous
volume, therefore, a few specimens will serve to show the acute wit and
lively Imagination, of this moderen Club Bard.

His favorite Story was of a Stuttering boy, who was sent with a present
of a Roasting pig in a basket, to his master's friend, the basket was covered,
in which the pig was, which (to speak in the Stile of the Learned Doctor
Lister in his *Journey thro' Paris*)[27] was to prevent I suppose the pig's escap-
ing, the boy had occasion to step behind a hedge on his way, and deposited
the basket 'till he had dispatched a certain necessary business, a fellow
passing by in the mean time, stole the pig, and Clap'd a puppy in its place,
and Covered up the basket again, the boy not perceiving this, Carried it to
[480]   the Gentleman, for whom the present ‖ was Intended, and leisurly uncover-
ing the basket said Sis-Sis-Sis-Sis-Sir, m-m-my ma-ma-master has se-se-
sent you a ro-ro-roasting P-P-P-P-P-uppy by God!—and so out Jumped
the puppy.

Another Story, that this Ingenious Gentleman told, was of a poor
Scholar—A Gentleman, whose Charity was chiefly bestowed upon poor
Scholars, had a visit paid him one day by a fellow in a very ragged Condition, having opened his chamber door to him, he asked him who he was,—
a poor Scholar Sir, replied he,—'Tis well Sir, pray walk in said the Gentleman,—well, you say you are a poor Scholar, in what does your Scholar-craft

26. Locke discusses the dangers arising from a false association of ideas in *An Essay concerning Human Understanding* (1690), chap. 33, sec. 9.

27. Martin Lister (1638?–1712), English zoologist, physician, and fellow of the Royal Society,
published an account of his journey to Paris in 1698 with the earl of Portland, who was
ambassador there.

consist—In what your honor pleases good Sir—Nay, pray be particular Sir—as particular as your honor pleases Sir—do you understand any of the Learned Languages,—what Learned Languages Good Sir,—why, the greek, latin, hebrew, Chaldee or the oriental tongues,—Not a word of any of them Sir—are you a proficient in the Mathematics, algebra Arithmetic, or any of the arts or Sciences,—I never heard of such things 'till this minute, and like your honor—Can you read or write,—Never could in my life Good Sir—very well friend, heres half a Crown for you,—you are in every respect the poorest Scholar I ever yet met with.

If I mistake not, I have heard him tell a humorous Story, of the Great [481] and learned Bishop Hoadly,[28] who one day coming out of the parliament house, when it rained, looked round him, and asked, with an earnest voice, Where is my fellow?—I gad my Lord says a wag that stood near him, he is not to be found in all England.

One of the like nature, I think, was a favorite of this Club wit,—a fat peer one day in parliament time, meeting a lean commoner, who had a mind to pry into the Secrets of his house, asked his Lordship,—My Lord said he, what are you about now,—Just three yards if you measure the round of my belly answered his Lordship.

He used to give a curious, yet comical account of the foundation of the Ancient City of Edinburg in the kingdom of Scotland. Cain said he, after he had murdered his brother, went to the Land of Nod, which could be no other than Scotland (σκοτια) in the Greek Idiom signifying darkness, and a dark corner is The most likely to make one Nod, or go to sleep, and there he built a City, which could be no other than Edinburg corruptly, anciently Eden-burg; tho not named In Sacred writ, for Cain Called it Edenburg, in honor of the Garden of Eden, from which place his parents had been lately expelld.

But one arch Story in particular, I remember to have heard Mr Grog [482] often tell, It was of three companions riding the road together, and passing a place where were many unripe blackberries a growing, one said, Lord! how red these blackberries are—you fool, says another, who ever heard of red-blackberries; you're both fools alike said the third, for blackberries are always red, when they're green.

Another Jest he used often to tell of a Simple Country parson, nick-named Jockey Frizzle, who had a very Large parish, one asked him what he did with his flock, in the extreme parts of his parish—I e'en leave them

28. Benjamin Hoadly (1676–1761) was an English bishop famous as the initiator of the Bangorian Controversy, an attempt to reduce church authority.

to God Almighty, said the parson—The very best curate you could have pitched upon replied the other.

One Story more of this celebrated Club wit, and then I have done,—A woman once riding along the road, tumbled from her horse, and turning head over heels, discovered some Arcana, which the whole Sex are very Solicitous about concealing, when she got up, and had rectified her petticoats, she spied a fellow passing by, & could not forbear exclaiming, in Surprize and Confusion, Did you ever see the like!—yes by God, said the fellow, a hundred and a hundred times over, my wife has got Just such another.

With numberless such delectable and merry tales and Stories, this Celebrated Club Bard used to abound, and by his good natured and Comical way of relating them, was often very Serviceable, in keeping up a prop- ‖
[483] per Club conversation, and preventing the members, from entering upon mischievous topics of discourse.

I shall now mention some of the favorite maxims of this celebrated Club wit, and with them Conclude this long Introductory Chapter.

1   He used to say, that if one would gain a Ladie's affections, he ought to persevere, and stand stiffly to it without shrinking. This was a good Standing Joke, and fit for a Longstanding member, but not altogether consistent with Monsieur What d'ye call 'um's rules of decency in his reflections on ridicule.[29]

2   He would say sometimes, that if a man's Conscience lay heavy on his hands, he might put it out to Interest.

3   He declared often, that the Surest way to procure honor, and the General esteem of mankind, was to get rich any how, taking care, in your voyage, towards the Regions of Dis or Pluto, to keep but a very little, or Just touch and go, as they call it, to the windward of the Gallows, pillory and whiping post.

4   He often affirmed it to be his opinion, that a man must by all means acquire a mean Sneaking behavior, before he can step into the favor and good graces of the great, and also that eves-droppers and Tale bearers, or (when he had a mind to pun) Tail bearers, were very useful and necessary members of some political States, whether under Male-administration, or petticoat government.

[484]   5   He often said, that your petticoat pensioners were like the Miners in the west Indies, always digging and poaking in dark holes and Caverns, for little bits of gold and Silver, yet never lived to reach the bottom, being

---

29. Abbé Jean-Baptiste Morvan de Bellegarde (1648–1734) was the author of *Réflexions sur le ridicule, et sur les moyens de l'éviter* (Paris, 1696).

taken off by the Sulphurous Steams and Stinking mephites, of these Subter-
ranean dark Caverns.

6   Lies he often affirmed proved a very good home Staple, but seldom
or never yielded much at a foreign market, hence the small regard that is
usually paid, to the overgrown Lies of Travellers.

7   It was his custom to observe, that many devoured the favors of the
great, like Luscious dishes, which being well digested, produced fulsom
and Ill applied compliments, very much resembling the fætid Stools of an
epicure or glutton.

8   He affirmed that he knew many men, that lived as if they were
never to die, and died as if they had never lived.

9   It was a maxim of his that in case a man's father had been a thief,
and his mother a whore, their vices, (tho' he had nothing to do with them)
would be laid at his door, and thrown in his teeth from Generation to
generation everlastingly, unless he could have the good luck to get himself
created a peer.

10   He would affirm with a minc'd oath, for he seldom swore round
ones, that as Sure as two and two made four, so Sure a Lords bastard, was
base born, as much as the bastard of a Cobler.

11   He confidently asserted it for a truth, in Spite of the Sceptics of the   [485]
age, That all men were mortal, that black and white, day and night were
opposites and quite different things, that a Stool was a Stool, a table a table
and a gun a gun, and not an Idle notion or Idea, as some would persuade
us, and finally that there was no such thing as being a good man, or in other
words a good Christian, without morality.

12   He mantained that a man never was to be Cock Sure of having
Strict Justice done him, in any human court either of Law or equity, unless
he was furnished with a very ponderous purse.

13   He affirmed that the Pope of Rome had been poxed, above a
thousand years agoe by the whore of Babylon, as appeared by his Blue-
boars, which boars the Ignorant vulgar believed to be bulls, with blue
Leaden hoofs, like the bulls of Ireland, because the lying priests told them
so, this he spoke in the Spirit of a Presbyterian, for he was a true blue one.

14   He said that our Lawyers and divines differed very little from our
merchants, since they made trade and traffic of Justice and religion, and the
small difference was this, that they could not like the merchants suffer by
Shipwreck, since they never sent their wares over Seas.

15   He affirmed, that it was as absurd to stile Bishops my Lord, your
Grace, and Right Reverend father in God, as to call the Emperor of China
the Vicar of || Bray, this he spoke also in the Spirit of a Presbyterian.   [486]

16   He was firmly of opinion, that to return Injury for Injury, and affront for affront, was expressly contrary to the Spirit of Christianity, and the same as if you should spue in my porridge, because I had pissed in your drink.

17   If it should cost us as little to Drink as to laugh, said he pleasantly and Smilingly smacking his lips, we should have plenty of good grog for nothing.

18   Beware quoth he of too great familiarty with great men, if you sit too nigh a rousing Christenmass fire, you may chance to burn or blister your Shins.

19   He asserted that if a number of books upon Shelves, could make a man a Scholar, sleeping in a pew at Church would make him a very good Christian.

20   As good Cloths are always the worse for wearing, so, said he, good doctrines, are the worse for being put in practice, the reason why our prim Clergy, who are as careful of their doctrines, as they are of their beavers, bands, Gouns and Cassocks, dont care much to practise what they preach, this also he spoke as a presbyterian.

21   He was fond of Honoring the names of ancient worthies, by converting them into puns, for with him a pun was the quintessence of wit, for example, if you asked a Chaw of tobacco of him, he would hand you his
[487]   box, and say pleas- || antly "That's good old *Chaw-Sir*," meaning thereby to honor the name and memory of our ancient english bard.

22   Finally, he used to say of one Pandragoras, much addicted to lying when Sober, who one day in his cups said, with a Sigh, *All men are mortal,*—I know not how to believe you said his cousin Sobrio.

These Stories and apothegms, we reckon Sufficient to give a Specimen of the acute genius of our Club Bard.

Chapter II

Introduction of the Toast called the king and Club, Proposals for reviving the Box rejected, the orator lays down his office, abolition of that office in Club.

It is wonderful to observe, how old customs will be exploded, and new ones Introduced in their place; while no one can give better reasons for those odd Incidents, when they occurr in History, than that of blind caprice or fancy, and often the spirit of opposition, which has had force enough at times to 'stablish the most absurd customs that ever were Broached, for, once oppose or thwart, any particular fancy, or any particular maxim or opinion, and use endeavors to suppress them, they shall soon find number-less defenders and grow to a prodigious Size, however Inconsistent and absurd they may be in them- || selves, and however repugnant to the com-   [488] mon sense and reason of mankind; this we see abundantly exemplified in many Sects and maxims both religious and political.

We find here at this period, an instance of the thing in this our History, it had been established long agoe, by a Law of this Club, that the Ladies should be first toasted after Supper, but all of a Sudden, an odd and whim-sical Toast of the King and the Club, starts up, and takes the precedence, which toast was accidentaly Introduced by an honorary member, upon the Anniversary Night, vizt: Mr Ignotus Warble, who happening to toast the king and the Club, met with great opposition from the Long standing members, some affirming that this toast was not Clubical, and that it ought to be the *King of Clubs,* to make it more in Stile, others asserting that It should be the Club and the king, among whom was Sir John, who was for placing the Club before every thing, and the reason given for this was, the example of our high Church partizans, who in their toasts drink the Church and king, and not the king and Church, as the Phanatic whigs puritans and such low vermin do, a third party in the Club were of opinion, that the toast was too whiggish, and seemed to call in question the Loyalty of the Longstanding members, as if some among them were suspected of Jacobit-ism, and therefore declared against all such abominable test toasts. These disputes and Cavils, it is thought, Incenced his honor the president, to such a degree, who was not only || a high churchman, but a strenuous whig, (two   [489] extremes that seldom meet in one Character) that ever after, In opposition to these libertine principles, in the Longstanding members, he made the King and Club the first toast after Supper, but, as all earthly things are transitory, so this famous toast had it's time, and gave way at last, as we shall find to the High Stewards health.

At Sederunt 105 May 31, 1749, Mr Secretary Scribble being high Stew-ard, an accusation was exhibited against the high Steward, by some of the members, for Irregularly adjourning the Club to an unusual Day (being wednesday) on account of a public ball, but the prosecution of this affair was postpon'd, till other business was dispatched.

The Reverend Mr Roundhead Muddy, attended the Club, at this Sede-runt, in order for his admission, and Mr Secretary moved the thing to the Club, after some dispute, whether Mr Muddy could be duely elected a member of the Tuesday Club, upon wednesday, In which Argument Mr Orator Comus held out very stiffly, it was resolved, that the ballots should be put about, after Mr Muddys consent was asked.

Upon putting about the ballots, the Election was unanimous, and Mr Muddy was Saluted by his honor the president and the Club, as a Long-standing Member, and then addressing himself to the honorable the Chair, and to the Club, he spoke as follows with a Strong and loud voice.

[490]   "Most honorable Mr President, most worshipful Sir John, Most Noble Mr Orator, and you Gentlemen, the other worthy Longstanding members of this here ancient and Honorable Club, I return you thanks for the honor you have done me."—Then Mr Roundhead sat down and as a member of the Club, took his place accordingly, his confirmation, on account of the absence of the master of Ceremonies, being defferred till another time.

Mr Orator Comus, Lately created by his office a State member, we shall find now begin to truckle to the Chair, and become Intirely a creature to his honor the president, In such a manner, as to presume to Introduce again a Club box, for, at this Sederunt, It was moved by this State officer, that that pestilent fomenter of mischief in the Club, the Box, should again be set on foot, this he plainly did to curry favor with the Chair, the motion occasioned pritty warm disputes in Club, at last his honor the president appointed the Reverend Mr Roundhead Muddy, Jealous Spyplot Senior and Jonathan Grog Esqrs, a Committee to draw up proposals for establishing a box, to be reported to the Club at next Sederunt.

Then, his honor being Jealous of some Slippery tricks from the Secretary, gave orders from the Chair, that all the minutes of the Club proceedings, should be henceforth roughly drawn upon a waste piece of paper, and laid before the Club, before they were entered in the book, to prevent [491] errors, Interpolations || erazures and Interlineations, that might otherwise be practised, and, that after the Club had examined and ammended this rough draught, it should thus ammended be entered verbatim in the book of records, without adding or deminishing one title, and not afterwards altered upon any pretence whatsoever.

Accordingly at Sederunt 106 June 13th, 1749, Slyboots pleasant Esqr, being high Steward, the proceedings were produced upon a piece of waste paper, and being read, were corrected by the club, and Entered in the Record book.

Jealous Spyplot Esqr, Chairman of the Committee for drawing up proposals for establishing a Club box, which sat upon the 9th Instant, presented to his honor the president, the report of the said Committee, together with a Scheme for setting on foot a Club box, drawn up by Jonathan Grog Esqr, a member of the said Committee, and his honor delivered them to the Secretary, who read them to the Club.

A Letter under the hand of the Revd Mr Smoothum Sly, was presented in Club by Sir John, containing the Compliments of the Eastren-shore triumvirate to his honor and the Club, Then Quirpum Comic Esqr, the Master of Ceremonies, confirmed the Revd Mr Roundhead Muddy, a Longstanding member of the commoners of the ancient & honorable Tuesday Club, according to the usual form.

Then the Reverend Mr Muddy, addressed with a Loud voice his Honor and the Club as follows.

"Most honorable Mr President, most magnanimous Sir John, most [492] musical Mr Protomusicus, most polite Master of the Ceremonies, most Sublime Poet Laureat, most worthy Mr Secretary, and all ye Gentlemen Longstanding members of this here ancient and honorable Club, I thank you for the favor you have done me."—Then Mr Muddy sat down, and by this concise Speech we may understand, that Mr Orator Comus, was not in Club this night, as Indeed he was not, for an Embassy was dispatched to him by two officers of the Club, vizt: the Secretary and master of ceremonies, to require his attendance, but this Cunning State officer, excused himself to the Club, not caring, as is thought, to appear openly in the affair of the box, tho he operated in a conceald manner, to promote that mischievous Scheme.

The Secretary, in place of Mr Orator Comus, by appointment of the Committee, delivered a Speech to the Chair, concerning the box, now proposed to be set on foot, in which he set forth both the advantages and disadvantages, that might arise from having a Club box, and shut up his argument, by declaring his opinion, that this box should be admitted or rejected by the Club, as the one or the other prevailed.

Then the Club entered into the Consideration of the box, and, the first question proposed was, whether ‖ it should pass by a majority or unanimity, [493] it was Carried by Six against five, that it should pass by a majority, then the first report of the Committee was again read, vizt: That "your Committee are humbly of opinion, that It should be proposed to his honor the president and the Club, that there should be a Club box, set on foot." The Question was put, a box or no box, upon putting round the Ballots, it Carried in the negative, Seven nays against four yeas, thus was this pestilent Scheme knocked on the head for ever.

On the next Sederunt, which was the 107th, Mr Protomusicus Never-

out being high Steward, his honor the president produced a Letter, which
was read in Club, and ordered to be recorded as follows.

To the Honorable Nasifer Jole Esqr,
President of The Tuesday Club.

Sir,

    I confess that I had like to have forgot, that I have the honor to serve
as high Steward, to your ancient and worthy Club, and therefore Intreat the
favor of your most august company.

    But, if Sir, I am to be deprived of that happiness, please to let me
know, whom you Intend the honor of representing you, and you'll much
oblige Sir,

June 27th 1749   Your most humble Servt:
                                 Solo Neverout H:S: of the
                                 Tuesday Club.

[494]   This epistle is wrote in the true careless stile and jantee taste, much like that
of the Card billets of these our polite times, which shows that Mr Protomusicus was well versed in the Modish Phrazeology.

    At the following Sederunt July 11th, the Reverend Mr Roundhead
Muddy being high Steward, his honor produced in Club, a Letter from the
high Steward as follows.

To The right Honorable Nasifer Jole Esqr,
President of the Tuesday Club.

Sir,

    I expect your *precedential* highness, will honor me with your company,
this evening, and tho' I cannot subscribe myself your Honor's high Steward, yet will take it as a favor, if you will accept of such a Chair, as my
Lodgings affords, I am, with the most profound respect, your honors

Tuesday evening July the 11th 1749,   Most dutiful &
given at my Lodgings   Most obliged humble Servt:
                                 Roundhead Muddy.

    What a high Strain do we now see the Long Standing members run-
ning into, in their compliments to his honor the president, they now address him with the pompous titles of *Right Honorable,* and *highness,* one
would think they would stop here, but we shall find it otherwise.

[495]   At this Sederunt Mr Orator Comus, for what ‖ reasons remains a

secret, tho' it is conjectured by some, who reckon themselves well skilled in the designs and Secrets of politicians, that it was on account of his bad Success in the attempt made by him to re-establish the Club box; Pray'd his honor the president and Club, that he might lay down his office of Orator, after some dispute, whether he should be Indulged in this Strange request, his honor demanded the Reasons why he should give up his place, but Mr Orator declined giving any reasons, alledging that he was not obliged to do so.

This proposal much pleased the Secretary, whose ambition could stop no where, but at the degree of a State officer, to which dignified Station, he had now for a Long time been endeavoring to climb, and no sooner had he gaind two or three rounds of the Ladder, than he met with a repulse, in spite of all his artifice and Cunning, we shall see how his expectations were here again frustrated, for, tho' this place was given up by Mr Comus, the Secretary was baulkd in his expectations of succeeding him, the Club at last granted Mr Comus's request, and the Orator's Chair being thus vacant, it was next to be considered, who was to succeed in that office, but before the Club could proceed to determin this, Jealous Spyplot Esqr Senr: made the following proposition, That Mr Comus should be Indulged so far, as to have his office as a Sinecure, and be excused from officiating as orator ‖ in [496] consideration, that he was naturally a man of very few words, and of but an Indifferent action and delivery, but, that still retaining the dignity honors and profits, (if any should accrue) he should have leave given him to ap-point Deputies to Officiate for him, which proposal Mr Comus Declined, and Insisted upon giving up, place, titles, honors, profits, and every thing belonging to it, which request was most graciously granted him by his honor the President, and Consented to by the Club.

Then the Question was put, vizt: whether there should be any such officer as a Club Orator or not? it was Caried in the Negative, 7 nays against 4 yeas, this show'd a spirit of Liberty in the Longstanding members, who found that the Chair grew too Strong and powerful with two State officers, and at the same time, their determination in this point, did not displease his honor the president, for he was too Jealous of the other members, to trust them with such an office, particularly the Secretary.

Another Question was then proposed, whether or not there should be any such officer in the Club as a Speaker, the ballots were put round, and it Carried in the negative, Six nays against five yeas, and thus this great office and title in Club, droped, and was extinct, and tho' sometime after this, the title was revived, and the Secretary procured at last by his devices the office of Club orator, yet that officer was ever after only Classed among the officers of the Commons.

[497] ## Chapter III

Commotions in Club, the Records In danger of being burnt, Confirmation of a deputy Secretary.

Turbulent and ambitious Spirits, when they cannot by open practices and mere compulsion obtain their ends, often employ cunning and artifice, and place their whole Confidence in that Cursed Machiavelian maxim, *Divide et Impera;* Thus, some wicked politicians, who pretend to act for the good of the public, keeping still a Steddy eye, upon one little pitiful, diminutive point, vizt: their own private Interest and advancement, will clear their way, thro all difficulties and rubs, by exciting the fury of party and faction, among those whom they Intend to make their fools or gulls, and like the dog in the fable, pick up the bone, while their fellow Curs are a fighting,[1] or like a Turkish Janisar Aga, mount the breach of preferment, upon heaps of the Carcases of his own Asapi, or base Soldiery, thrown down by thousands for that purpose alone.

Thus, the Secretary, that ambitious, restless, and turbulent Club officer, still aiming at the Dignity of a State member, which he seemed resolved to procure at any rate Cost what it would, after having by his cunning practices, and fustian orations against the box, undermined and overset Mr Orator Comus, and in a manner wheedled him, into the Surrendry of his [498] honorable ‖ office, made long strides to get into that dignified place himself, and because his cunning and artifice failed him at that Juncture, as we shall see in the relation of what follows, he endeavored all he could to set his honor the president and the Club together by the Ears, in order to try if he could not succeed by that means.

At Sederunt 108, after Mr Orator Comus had made a Surrendry of his office, the Secretary moved to the Club, when he found that his ambitious expectations were quite frustrated, by the Club's proceeding, in abolishing the offices of Orator and Speaker, into one of which he expected to be promoted, That he should have an asistant in his office allowed him, for he

1. Hamilton is recalling Swift's "Republick of Dogs," in *The Battle of the Books* (*Prose Works of Swift,* ed. Davis, I, 141–142).

alledged That his was, of all offices in the Club the most trowblesome, especially, since he had been obliged, by an order of the honorable Chair, to make dowble entries, that he had served the Club now almost four years, in quality of Secretary, and that since by all his care and pains, he could not become *Emeritus,* yet he hoped, his honor and the Club would Indulge him at least as much as they had done Mr Orator Comus, whose office and place, was not attended with nigh so much trowble & pains, neither had he served the Club, in any office so long. Upon this, the Secretary delivered the book of Records to his honor the President, declaring That he would not receive it again, till his request was granted.

In making this motion, the Secretary had two ends in view, first to put the Club Into an uproar and confusion, and then to force them, as it were || by this Surrendry of his place to chuse another Secretary, and by some means to get the orators office revived in Club, so, that having removed the objection of his Enjoying a multiplicity of offices, he might the more easily step himself into that honorable place, but the Club made a timely discovery of his policy in this affair, and would by no means Listen to his proposals, however, the motion that he made, so far answered his purpose, as to excite a very hot dispute in Club, some taking one part, and some another, a terrible noise, Clamor, and vociferation arose among the Long standing members, all spoke at once, and all stood up at once, The Reverend Mr Muddy, who was gifted with a mighty Stentorian voice, was heard above all the rest, and his honor the president was not heard at all, it being only known that he spoke by the quick motion of his lips, his turning his face first to the right then to the left of the Chair, and his waving the book of records up and down, which he grasped in both hands, it was for sometime a Confused medley of broken Sentences and words, like those heard in Groenland upon the coming of a General thaw, as Pray Sir—nay Sir—I say Sir—by your leave Sir—what!—must I Con- —no by G—therefore—pox on it—patience alittle—here Club—Judgematic—holla!—damn the book —burn the—hey, hey!—and such like unintelligible Jargon, while the Secretary like a Sly bitch, sat silent all the time Laughing in his Sleeve, and expecting || what the Issue of this general confusion would be, in short, it seemed, as if the Longstanding members would go from words to blows, while the Loud laugh of Mr Protomusicus Neverout, Joined with the hoarse and Stentorian bass of the Revd Mr Roundhead Muddy, and the mingled Clamor of the other members, made the most horrid discord that ever was heard, a thing very unbecoming this musical Gentleman, whose business it was to promote and Improve concord and harmony In Sounds at least, if not in actions and behaviour.

[499]

[500]

Club Hubbub, concerning the Records.

[facing page 500]

During this hurly burly, and general Club hubbub and Scuffle, Capt: Nathaniel Sylvius, a plain honest and Simple Gentleman, Invited that night to the Club as a Stranger, according to ancient Custom, endeavored to stand mediator, between his honor & the members, and starting up from his Seat, in the middle of this Club altercation, cried out with great earnestness, expanding his arms, and separating the long Standing members one from another, as one passing thro' a marshe or Swamp, does the reeds or Sedges, "Pray Gentlemen,—good Gentlemen—good Sir President—Sweet Sir President,—pray be quiet—for Gods Sake be easy—Pray good Sir—I beseech you Sir President—gi' me leave Dear Sir—Psha forbear!—avast ho!—Stand aloof,—Let them alone pray—luff luff—port, port—Let them alone, theyll come too presently, the Storm ‖ will blow over." Thus did this [501] good man, with these short and pithy ejaculations, endeavor to make peace between his honor and the Longstanding members, and the Storm was laid by degrees.

When the general clamor was hushed, some proposed that his honor should appoint a Committee, to burn the book, and not only destroy all the Records of the Club hitherto made, but keep no more for the future, this procedure some were of opinion, would tend to the final dissolution of the Club, and therefore it was warmly opposed, and his honor the President, foreseeing, that by this one rash resolve, if he should unadvisedly give in to it, at the Instance of his privy Councellor and right hand man Sir John, who was warm for this motion's taking place, he should lose all the Security he had for his prerogative and authority, notwithstanding that his resentment would have prompted him to do any thing to thwart the Secretary, declared himself openly against this proceeding, and, by his honor's prudence and moderation, the precious book of records, was thus snatched from the devouring flames, and the memorable transactions of this ancient and honorable Club, from eternal oblivion, which, had they been lost, would have been an Irretrievable Dammage to posterity, and have occasioned a Lamentable Chasm or blank, in the Journal De Sçavants, or Republic of Letters.

At Last Quirpum Comic Esqr, Master of the Ceremonies stood up [502] with a grave Staid and Serio-Gelastic countenance, and adjusting his wig, and stroaking down his face and Chin, addressed his honor as follows.

"Mr President, Sir,—hem—

Tho I have heretofore, at the risque of my ears—hum—hum—served your honor's turbulent and ungrateful Secretary, in quality of his deputy without commission or order from your honor or this here Club, and had like to have been drawn by his means Into a premunire, at Sederunt 98, on

account of an Interpolation, added to your honor's Commission of deputation to Slyboots Pleasant Esqr, had not your honor graciously Interposed
and overlooked the trespass, which made me again lay down, this unthank-
ful office, yet to show your honor, and these here longstanding members,
that I bear no Spite or animosity, to this here turbulent officer, and that I
have a Sincere regard, for the peace and wellfare of this here ancient and
honorable Club, I freely, and of my own accord offer my Service to act as
[503] his deputy with your honor's and the Club's permission, which— ‖ hum—
hum—It is my duty to pay a regard to, and thus put a Stop to all his noise
and Complaints for the future—hum—hum."

When Mr Comic had thus addressed himself, he sat down, and his
honor the President was pleased to confirm him in the office of Deputy
Secretary according to his request, then the Secretary desired the President
to return him the Record book, which his honor refused first to do, 'till he
should make some Submission, and own to the Club, that he had been in
the wrong, which, he obstinately refusing to do, by the advice of the Club,
to prevent another uproar, which was Just ready to break out, the record
book was Solemnly delivered into his hands, by the honorable the president, without any other condition of Reaccceptance, but that of his being
allowed an asistant in his office.

Then the Club ordered for the greater ease of the Secretary, that
Dowble Entries and letters, are henceforth not to be permitted in recording, except the Latter, by a particular order from the President and Club.

Chapter IV

Sublime Club Letters, Eulogium on a Longstanding member deceased,
Letter of Cats, danger of a dissolution of the Club, The Master of
Ceremonies leaves the Club.

Tho Jesting and Joaking, is often a very pritty Innocent and entertain-
[504] ing amusement, when Introduced ‖ with proper prudence and discretion,
as we have somewhere else observed, being like a game at Shuttle Cock,
where the volatile and feathered witicism is bandied about from hand to
hand, with great Glee, vivacity and agility, which alighting upon any of
the bye standers or players, by reason of its light Substance, being Compounded only of Cork and feathers, neither hurts nor bruises, yet have I
often known that a Joke or Jest, tho' volatile and light enough in it's own

nature, would occasion abundance of Enmity and ill blood, and even out-ragious quarrells and blows both wet and dry, where the Shuttle Cock, (to Carry on our metaphor,) lighted upon a tender Skin or an Inflammed or excoriated part, or in a word galled an old Sore.

This makes it necessary, that in passing Joke or Jest, the quality of the Jester and the quality and temper of the Jested, or to speake in the manner of our Learned Lawyers, the *Jestor* and *Jestee*, must always be maturely weighed and Considered, In order to evade an ensuing mischief; The Dis-position of the But must be known, whether he be a person, that under-stands raillery, and also the nature and texture of the Jest it self,—Should the Jestor, for Instance, be a man of a Low degree, and the Jestee a Gran-dee, should the Jestor be a young Smart, and the Jestee an old Coxcomb or Choleric Don, should the Jestor ‖ be a poor fellow, and the Jestee rich, [505] should the Jestor be a reputed wit, and the Jestee an arrant dunce, it is by no means safe for the Jestor to exercise his talents upon these occasions, and in these cases, again, should the Jest touch some favorite or acquired vice, or natural failing, or expose some folly, or bodily deformity in the Jested, should it strike at any of the favorite maxims of politics or religion, of any party or person, should it affect the beauty, virtue or reputation of any woman, tho ugly as Hecate and leud as Messalene, it is in itself extremely dangerous, and by all means for peaces Sake to be avoided, for history abounds with Instances of the woeful and tragical effects, of such Jests, such as families ruined, Cities burnt and Razed, provinces laid waste, multitudes of men, women and Innocent babes put to the Sword, virgins and modest matrons Ravished &ct: &ct: &ct:

Hence I conclude, that it is a very rash, and Inconsiderate thing, to pass Jests upon Emperors, kings, popes, Lords, proud prelates, powerful fools, noble pimps, wealthy blockheads, Whores and presidents of Clubs. The mischievous and almost fatal effects of an unlucky Jest, to this here ancient and honorable Club, the occasion of this preamble, shall be related in its proper place in this very Chapter.

At Sederund 109, July 25th 1749, Jealous Spyplot Esqr, being high Steward, the following Laws were passed.

Law XL. Resolved and passed into a Law, by the president and Club [506] now met, this 25th of July 1749, that no member shall speak above once in a dispute, and that not above Six minutes, the person who first made the motion may reply, not exceeding the said limited time, and, in case two or three or more members rise up to speak at once, they are to be Called to order, and deliver their opinions one after another as nominated by his honor the president.

This Law was passed on occasion of the general Clamor and hurly burly, at last Sederunt. Against it Sir John Entered his protest, declaring that he was for an unlimited liberty of Speech in Club, and for his part would always use that Liberty—none durst contradict him.

Law XLI. Resolved *Nem: Con:* and passed into a Law by the President and Club now met, that for the future no honorary member shall be allowed to vote in any dispute whatsoever.

His Honor the President produced a letter from the high Steward, which was read and recorded as follows.

To Nasifer Jole Esqr,
President of the Tuesday Club.

Sir,

This night being the Tuesday Club, whereon it comes to my turn to serve, as Steward, *Custome* has made it necessary, not only so, but Instituted
[507] it Into a Law, for every Steward in his turn to serve ‖ to acquaint the President therewith, it therefore becomes a duty in me, so to do; I hope you'll favor me with your presence this evening at the Club, at my house, which shall esteem as a great honor Conferrd upon me, by a person of your exalted merit, I have the honor of being with great respect Sir,

July 25th 1749   Your most obedient
                                       Most obsequious and
                                       Most humble Servant
                                       Jealous Spyplot Senr:

This Letter is wrote in a plain honest and manly Stile, and, (except a little florish at the Conclusion) exactly in Character, for this Longstanding member was none of those that dealt in high sounding titles, such as, *your honor, your highness* and such like, tho' we shall find the force of bad example in this Club to be such, as to Corrupt the plain Simplicity and bluntness of even this very Gentleman, who grossly deviates from his usual manner in a Letter which he wrote sometime after this to his honor the president, tho' some suspect that letter to be none of his own Inditing, but his setting his hand to such fustian throws a Cloud over his wonted Sincerity.

It was moved this night, that the *Great bell of Lincoln* should be sung, in honor of the Admission of the Reverend Mr Roundhead Muddy, but, upon account of its having been too late, when the motion was made, his honor the president deferred that ceremony till another night, upon which
[508] Mr Muddy, with too ‖ much precipitation and warmth declared That he was no more a member of this here Club, and desired The Secretary to

eraze his name from the list. This astonished some of the Longstanding members very much, and they did not know which most to admire at, the caprice of his honor the president, in refusing such a legal and reasonable demand, or the thin Skin of Mr Muddy in resenting such a triffle, tho many believed that Mr Muddy was not in earnest, and that his resentment of this, was nothing but a Clubical resentment.

At Sederunt 110 augst: 8, 1749, The worshipful Sir John being high Steward, The Club took into their Serious consideration, the Revᵈ Mr Muddy's request to the Secretary as it stood upon the Record of last Sederunt, vizt: whether It should be complied with or not, but before they had proceeded far in the argument, the Revd Mr Muddy, came and took his Seat in Club, which determined, or put an end to the dispute.

His Honor the president produced a letter from the High Steward, which was read and recorded as follows.

To the Honorable Nasifer Jole Esqr,
President of the Honorable Tuesday Club.

Sir,

I am to have the pleasure of Entertaining The most worthy Tuesday Club, this night at my ‖ house, *whare* I hope you will give me the honor of [509] your good company, which is, not only to night, but at all times acceptable to, *grate* Sir, your Honor's

From my Castle	Most humble &
August the 8th, 1749	Most obedient Servant to Command
	Sir John, knight of the Most honble:
	Tuesday Club.

His honor the president sung the Catch called the *Great bell of Lincoln*, this night, on account of the admission of the Reverend Mr Muddy into the Club, we find in the records of this Sederunt the following entry.

"This night The honorable Mr President Jole, appeared in a mourning badge Ribbon, on account of the Death of Capt: Seemly Spruce, late a worthy regular member of this Club, and one of the oldest members, having been of the Club, since the time of it's first Institution, a Gentleman, whose humane and benevolent Character, whose friendly and Sociable disposition, procured him so much the esteem and affection of every one that knew him, in his life time, that his Death is most Justly and most Sincerely Lamented, and in a particular manner, by the members of this Club, who, out of regard and affection for his memory, have ordered their Secretary to enter this short, tho' Just eulogium in their Book of records."

At Sederunt III, augst 22d, Jonathan Grog Esqr being high Steward,
[510] his Honor the president pro- ‖ duced a Letter from the high Steward,
which was read and recorded, the Tenor of which follows.

To Nasifer Jole Esqr,
President of the Tuesday Club,
at his Mansion house in North East Street, Annapolis.

Honorable Sir,
    This short Epistle is a Messenger to acquaint you, that the Tuesday
Club, of which you are most deservedly the head, is to meet at my house in
Charles Street this evening, being the twenty Second of the month, where I
hope you will honor me with your *august* presence, as without that the
entertainment will be tastless and Insipid to the members, but especially
Great Sir to

                            Your much devoted
                            Very humble Servant & H:S:
                            Jonathan Grog.

    I come now to relate a transaction, seemingly triffling in itself, which
notwithstanding, occasioned such a difference between his honor the president and the Club, as that it had well nigh ended in a final dissolution of
this ancient and honorable Society, it was a Letter wrote to his honor the
President by the high Steward Mr Quirpum Comic, at Sederunt 112, September 5th 1749, which was Intended for a Jest, but not being properly
[511] Seasoned with discretion, or applied to a proper person, proved ‖ a mischievous Jest, Mr Comic being a Single man, and no house keeper, intended to hold his Club in the School Room, the ancient place of meeting
of the ugly Club as has been mentioned elsewhere, in this history, his honor
had an objection to this, alledging that a place where School boys met, was
not at all proper for such wise men as the Longstanding members of the
Tuesday Club to assemble in; besides, he objected to the place, on account
of its Nastiness, and professed publicly and openly, that if the Club was held
there, he would neither come himself, nor appoint a deputy, what his hon-
or's reason could be, for objecting to this place of meeting, at this particular
Juncture, (when it appears, he made no manner of objection to it at Sederunt 87, when the Club met there and his honor was there present himself at
the drawing up the articles for the Delivery of the Club box; and also at
Sederunt 101, when the said Mr Comic was high Steward and kept His Club
in that place, when his honor tho not present show'd his approbation by
appointing Laconic Comus Esqr his Deputy,) we can by no means conjec-

ture, I should be loath to say, that it was mere caprice, or out of some picque he had conceived at the high Steward, but be that as it will, Quirpum Comic Esqr, the high Steward, In order to please his honor *If possible,* had the room Cleaned, well sweeped and scrubbed, with mops, brushes, dusting Cloths brooms and Rubbers, and all in decent order for the Reception of the Club, which it had not been, for 50 years before, at least not in the memory of any body then Living, This Possibly might have brought his ‖ honor in some measure to comply, had the high Steward [512] gone no farther, but he being in some degree nettled by his honor's unreasonable and uncivil behavior, could not restrain his rash and unadvised hand, but wrote his honor a Satyrical letter, which I cannot call by a more proper name than the *letter of Cats,* this letter was not suffered to be recorded, but the passage in it that gave offence, was nearly to this purpose, "That he [the high Steward] Intended to hold his Club in the School room, and, that his honor might have no objection to it, on account of the nastiness of the room, he had swept it clean, and taken care to whip out all *Cats* and dogs, Cats especially, as being a vermin mighty apt to breed fleas, and to piss about, and excite a very disagreeable perfume." This was the pinch, not only talking in such a Slighting manner of Cats, his honors favorites, but besides, there was a Sting in the tail of this observation, which was contained in the Implication, that his honors rooms were nasty, and perfumed with a disagreeable Odor, as he kept always a great number of these domestic animals about him, and also, that his honor's taste in this particular was ridiculous and weak, in making such mighty favorites of those brutes, this raised his honors Spleen and resentment to such a height, that he was heard to swear in his wrath, that he never would come nigh the Club again, or be any way concerned in it, and had his honor kept to this rash vow, here would have been an end and final Dissolution of this ancient and honorable Club, The frame and Consti- ‖ tution of which, was now so [513] Interwoven with his honor's presence and countenance, that it could no ways subsist or exist without him, but the destinies had decreed otherwise, and his honor, as we shall see, was soon reconciled, tho the high Steward thought it his best prudence and policy to leave the Club, to evade the furious blow that threatened him from his honor's Just resentment, tho' like all great men, when they give up their offices and places, he pretended that his departure from the Club was voluntary, as we shall presently see.

At the same Sederunt, a few of the Longstanding members met (not at the School room as was Intended but) at the house of Prim Timerous Esqr; The high Steward having given up his purpose of meeting in the School room, in order, *if possible,* to be reconciled to his honor, and Induce him, either to come himself to Club, or send a deputation, but it was too late, for his honor, being Implacable at that time would do neither, Therefore, the members understanding the Cause of offence, was that Ill Contrived letter of Cats, as above related, they advised the high Steward to write a Submissive Letter to his honor, requesting him to come to Club, which advice he followed, and the Letter was sent to his honor, by a Special messenger, from the Club, but still to no purpose, his honor remained Inflexible, then a dispute arose among the members present, whether this meeting was a Club or not, as there was no Deputy appointed, and if it was not a Club, whether or not his honor the president, had not voluntarily and of his own

[514]   ‖ free will and accord, abdicated the Chair, in this dispute some doubts were started, whether the word *abdicated* was proper, as were in a very wise and august assembly at Westminster, in the year —88, but this appearing to be a dangerous argument to Insist upon, no determination was made thereon.

This was the first time, that his honor the president refused to send a deputation in his own absence, which obliged the Club afterwards for the Security of the Constitution, to pass a Law, whereby they took to themselves the power of electing a deputy, in case of his honor's refusing himself to appoint one, but his honor, to this day with some Show of Reason, (at least reason founded upon Law, which I think does not always come up to the Sterling Stamp, for tho we are told by Certain Grave Dons, that the Law is founded upon reason, yet Philosophers will not agree, that reason derived from Law is every where Current) Questions their power to make any such Law, as it plainly encroaches upon, and is contradictory to the presidential prerogative, which he is obliged Strictly to mantain against all attempts, for his own Sake, and that of his Successors in the Chair, thus, we see, how this ancient and honorable Club, by rashly giving too much to his honor the president, have entangled themselves in an Everlasting Labyrinth of Cavils, and disputes about prerogative and privilege, like some other Sagacious and politic Societies and States, who, bewitched by the Jargon of a Set of Quibbling Gownmen, Chuse rather to be Governed by rules and orders of their own Invention, than submit themselves to the direction and dictates of common Sense and reason.

[515]   After Supper, Mr Secretary Scribble came into the Club & reported to the members, from the honorable the president, (with whom he had been for some hours in private Conference) his high displeasure at the high Stewards Letter, for which the members expressed their concern and Sorrow, and resolved to consider on ways and means, against next Sederunt, to

accommodate matters to the Satisfaction of his honor the president, which the high Steward wisely foresaw was Impossible to be done without making a Sacrifice of him, for the good of the Common weal, and therefore like a wise and politic Statesman, he stood up with great gravity in his countenance, mixed with a small degree of Gelasticity, and declared His Intention to leave the Club, on account of the Great Inconvenience and trowble it was to him, to serve in his turn as H:S: he being a Single man, possessed of no house of his own, in which with Decency, to entertain his honor and the Club, and begged the members to Indulge him so far, as to take this his proposal in Good part; The members willingly & chearfully agreed to it, professing, That by their Constitution they were a free Society, and every man was at liberty to go and come at pleasure. Thus by this Impolitic Step, the Club lost a deputy Secretary & Master of Ceremonies at one blow.

Chapter V

More Sublime Club Letters, Petition to his honor the President from the Single females, several Club Speeches.

The resentments of Great men, must at all events be gratified, and suffered at first eruption to have their full Spring, for, should the Inferiour powers, || That is, the *profanum vulgus*,[1] endeavor to confine it, like a Spark [516] among gun powder pent up and rammd down, it produces a violent explosion, which tears and rends and drives every thing before it, with an Inexpressible and Irresistable fury, whereas, if it has free air, and is left to its Self, it will either Spontaneously die away, or go off with a puff, this politic maxim, the Longstanding members of this ancient and honorable Club seemed not to be Ignorant of, when to save their constitution, now In danger of a Lapse, they at Sederunt 113 Septr 26th, 1749, Jealous Spyplot Junr Esqr, being high Steward, gave way to the earnest desire of his honor the president, to have the Letters of the Late high Steward, which had given such offence, read, and Condemned to perpetual oblivion, a Just fate to all fomenters of mischief.

A letter from the High Steward, to his honor the President was read and entered as follows.

1. "Vulgar mob" (see, e.g., Horace, *Carmina* 3.1.1).

To the Honorable Nasifer Jole Esqr,
President of the Tuesday Club.

Honorable Sir,   Septr 26th 1749
    The Club, according to the appointment of the last meeting, is to be at
my Father's house this night, where I have the honor of serving as high
Steward, therefore Sir, according to the usual and Just manner, of the wise
[517] and worthy members, of our ancient || and well constituted Society, I (by
this) desire the honor and favor of your auspicious presence, the want of
which seemed to *boad,* a dissolution of our happiness and unanimity.
    I hope, by this nights Chearfulness, every thing that is past and un-
pleasant will be erased and forgot, I am, Honored Sir,

Your obedient & humble Servt:
Jealous Spyplot Junr:

    What the penman of this Letter (which seems to be wrote in a concise
and elegant Stile of Language) means by every thing that was passed being
erazed and forgot, must be left for future Criticks to find out, for, it exceeds
my ability to explain the passage, unless you will admit, (which I am very
loath to do) that this gentleman bore a Spite and animosity to all the Club
Records, and therefore wished, that every thing that was passed should be
erazed; As for his wishing that things unpleasant should be forgot &
erazed, I think that no Strange wish in any good natured man.
    Then the Secretary produced in Club, a letter from the Reverend Mr
Smoothum Sly, in the name of the Eastren Shore triumvirate, In answer to
one, which he had been ordered to write by the club, on Sederunt 110th, the
Transcript of which Letter follows.

To Loquacious Scribble Esqr, at Annapolis, These.

Sir,
[518]   Next to my acknowledging the receit of your Second || (tho the first to
me), I cannot forbear remarking, that the preamble or prologue of it, differs from most other modern prologues in this, vizt: whereas these have
little or no connexion with the pieces they stand before, yours on the
contrary is a very pertinent Introduction to the Letter it is prefixed to, and
the whole production is a manifest proof to me, how well you are qualified
for sustaining the office of Orator in the ancient Tuesday Club, in which,
however, I am sorry to understand, you were lately disappointed.
    The arduous Task of returning to Messrs Makefun and Lardini, the
compliments of the honorable the President and worthy members of the
ancient Tuesday Club, in a manner suited to the Dignity and excellence of

that Society, would have Indeed been too heavy for me to support, had not a reflection, upon the uncommon Candor of your August Club, on the one hand, and the Remarkable good nature of the Gentlemen on the other, come Seasonably in to my relief, but, to convince you, that I urge not this as a plea, for Indolence or Laziness, I assure you Sir, that after having Invocked Genius, eloquence and Learning to asist me, and being Inspired with some of Bacchus's richest Gifts in the hospitable house of the Generous Mr Makefun, I attempted to execute the Commands of the honorable the president, and the worthy members of the ancient Tuesday Club, in the handsomest and most polite manner, in the kindest and most expressive terms, I was able, the Message was received by the Gentlemen with the profoundest respect, and the most grateful acknowledgements, especially to the President, the *Grand Original*, of honor and Ex- || cellence, that adds a [519] dignity to, and spreads a Lusture over your society; a president, of whose body and mind, we are far from being able to describe the *Quantums* and the *Quales*, and indeed, in our opinion, the Sublimest panegyric, and the finest picture, must come far short of the *Original*, the Solemnity of his countenance prognosticates his wisdom, and his air of Insinuating address, a deep penetration, his good breeding is enough to polish a province, and his humor and facetious disposition to Charm the most Intelligent Club, his conversation is universally acknowledged to be the Standard of Sheer wit, and his picquant reflections to be big with the Sharpest and Justest Satir,—The humble and quiet member, might ever find a safe retreat, under the Shadow of his Eyebrows, and be covered with the wings of his authority, in a word, we may, without the Imputation of flattery, pronounce him a mantainer of the Dignity of the Chair, a friend to prerogative, and an enimy to false patriotism and faction. What a delightful figure must such a president make, at the head of a Club, Composed of members, in whose generous bosoms dwell the noble and disinterested friendship, the melting love, the humane benevolent Sentiment, the ardent Gratitude, the soft compassion, and the Candid opinion, (a) notwithstanding some little blemishes, *Quas humana parum Cavit Natura* (b), *macti este virtuti*, go on and

(a) Vide Fielding's *History of Tom Jones*. [2]
(b) Horace quoted by Fielding, *History of Tom Jones*. [3]

2. This passage is typical of the many panegyrical speeches in *Tom Jones*, such as the one Tom delivers on Nightingale's wife in bk. 14, chap. 7.
3. "Which human nature has failed to avoid, be honored for virtue" (Horace, *Ars poetica*, line 353; *Satirae* 1.2.31). The first passage appears twice in *Tom Jones*, at the end of bk. 10, chap. 1, and in bk. 11, chap. 1.

prosper, may your Society be lasting, and it's happiness equal to your wishes.

Certain it is, tho I know not how it happens, that the mind is more Sprightly and active in company, than alone, the Images crowd in faster, [520] and humor flows in a freer vein, ‖ perhaps it may be owing to the Sight of our friends, and I doubt not, the toasting of the Ladies, gives a brisk and agreeable motion to the Spirits, and by that means enlivens conversation and calls forth every humorous Sentiment, this made Mr Makefun Signior Lardini and myself, resolve to erect a Club in our neighborhood, tho' we are sorry to tell you, that we have not as yet been able to accomplish our design, if we had, we were determined fully, to copy after your original as near as possible.

Mr Musician Neverout's rude behavior upon many occasions, to the honorable the president, besides, the flemmish account he has made of the English beer, Sufficiently recommends him to Mr Makefun, but above all his Impudently disputing the prize with the honorable president, in Sing-ing, provokes our resentment, and raises our Indignation, in a word, we look upon the one to be a natural, the other to be a mere Nincompoop in vocal music, that is to say, the honorable the President is by nature fur-nished with these gifts, that are requisite to form a good Singer, whereas the other is nothing but an Artifice, artifice all, we have frequently heard Mr Musicians made tunes and unnatural Notes, to the great disquiet of our ears, and the no less danger of a headake, on the other hand, the proper tunes, thrilling notes and captivating Sounds of the honorable president, have frequently stilld our passions, commanded our Souls, and forced us to laugh, when we had a mind to appear grave, in short, when we hold up the musician to the light of the honorable the president, he is Intirely eclipsed, and we can only compare him to a Cat, that can pur alittle In time and tune, so that he seems to us to be as Imperfect in the vocal, as he has been deem'd short in the Instrument—al ways.

[521]   Tis with the utmost concern Sir, that we differ in any thing with your worthy Society, but their rejecting your offer as orator, is a piece of con-duct, that we cannot altogether reconcile ourselves to, especially, as you generously set yourself up as a candidate for that office, which motion, we understand, was not so much as seconded—This we take to be a procedure, by no means equal to the Judgement of the ancient Tuesday Club, or the merit of their faithful Secretary, for, from a passage in your letter, it appears to us, that your abilities as an orator, are far from being Inconsiderable. The passage is as follows, *"Sir, Please to tell Mr Makefun, in particular, that in case*

he should ever make another present of English beer to the Club, to be Sure to Commit it to more trusty hands than Mr Musician Neverout's"—what a rare collection of the most beautiful flowers of Rhetoric, and how wonderful a group of the finest Images is here, such as *Please!—another present!—English beer!—The Club!—Trusty hands!*—we think we might fairly challenge any orator, either ancient or modern, to muster up such a delightful knot of Rhetorical florishes, within so small a compass, besides, what a delicate hint is here given, to Mr Makefun, to make another present of English beer to the Club, In fine Sir, the beauties of this passage, could be owing to nothing less than the Inspiration of English beer, which Butler says has Inspired many,+ and, as we doubt not you excell as much in the declamatory, as in the petitory way, so, we think you exceedingly well ‖ qualified for the office of [522] an orator, this we thought proper for your Sake to remark *en passant*, as it may serve for a hint to the worthy Society, to consider better of your merit, and prefer you to the office you are so ambitious of, be that as it will, we have, upon this admirable Specimen of your abilities, constituted you honorary Orator of our Triumvirate, vizt: Mr Makefun, Signior Lardini & myself.

We have the honor to send our dutiful Compliments to the Illustrious and Serene President, and our best respects to the worthy Society, as well State as Common officers, not forgetting our honorary Orator, this, in the Name of the above Triumvirate, be pleased to represent from Sir,

Talbot County   Your most humble Servant
August 31st 1749   *Smoothum Sly.*

P:S: We Sincerely condole the Death of Capt: Seemly Spruce, and doubt not, but the Eulogium Mr Jonathan Grog [a] made upon him, was Intended both to do Justice to his memory, and to pay a Compliment to the Club, tho' some that pretend to see, as far into a Stone as a *free Mason*⁵ are of opinion that it was owing to his being a Gentleman born & bred in New England—*S:S:*

(a) Vide *Maryland Gazette* No 223.

4. In *Hudibras* Samuel Butler invokes the nameless muse who ". . . with Ale, or viler Liquors, / Didst inspire *Withers, Pryn,* and *Vickars,* / And force them, though it were in spight / Of nature and their stars, to write" (*Hudibras*, ed. John Wilders [Oxford, 1967], 1.1.639–642).

5. Again, Hamilton seems to have applied an old proverb in a new way. To "see as far into a stone as any other man" is the typical use of this proverb (see, e.g., Dryden's "I am a fool, . . . but yet I can see as far into a Mill-stone as the best of you" [*Amphitryon* V.i.]). Hamilton has adapted the proverb to the Freemasons, who were known for their secrecy, or in this case, for their ability to penetrate mysteries.

     To this Letter the Secretary was ordered to prepare an answer, and lay it before the Club, next Sederunt.

[523]   After Supper a petition was presented, to the honorable the president, from the Single Ladies of Annapolis, which was read, and ordered to be entered, the tenor of which follows.

To The Honorable Nasifer Jole Esqr, President of the worshipful and ancient Tuesday Club, the petition and remonstrance, of sundry of the Single females of Annapolis.

Showeth,

     That whereas it has been observed by sundry persons as well as your petitioners, that a Singular and Surprizing Success, has all along attended such happy females, as your honor has been pleased to pitch upon, as the toasts of the honorable Chair, every one of whom in a short time, after having been thus adopted by your honor, has Successfully and happily been provided, with a much more Eligible State, than that of a Single Life,

     Your petitioners therefore, earnestly pray, that your honor, instead of conferring your favors in so partial a manner, would, in Commiseration of our desperate Situation, Include us all in the circle of your favor, that the benign Influence of your honor's maritiferous notice, may henceforth equally shine upon us all, which benevolent Condescention of your honor, will have a tendency to multiply the Inhabitants of this City, as well as to better our present forlorn Situation.

                            And your petitioners shall ever
                            pray &ct:

     The honorable the president was pleased to declare that he would grant this petition as far as lay in his power.

[524]   I must not here omitt an arch Joke of Jonathan Grog Esqr, passed upon Jealous Spyplot Senr, the Latter was making a bowl of Rumbo, and wanted some nutmeg to grate upon it, when the facetious poet, put into his hand a pig nut, as hard as a pebble Stone, exactly of the Shape and colour of a nutmeg, at which he might have rubbed and scrubbed till dooms day, even upon a file, and not have procured a Democritic atom from it, so that the worthy Mr Spyplot was for one quarter of an hour at least *occupatus nihil agendo*,[6] and furnishing matter of laughter for the Club. The Ingenious Laureat, had several Jokes of this kind by which he used to make

---

    6. "Occupied doing nothing"; above, Hamilton is alluding to the atomic theory of Democritus (born ca. 460–457 B.C.), the famous "laughing philosopher" and the greatest of the Greek physical philosophers.

people stare and laugh, he had a curious punch bowl, Japaned exactly like China, which was not frangible, which he would often let drop out of his hand, as he gave it to his fellow, which excited both Surprize and fear in the Standers by, but he always took Special Care that almost all the Grog or Rumbo was evacuated before he put this Joke in practise, that there might be as little loss as possible, he had a small piece of Glass Cylender, which looked like Sealing wax, with which he duped many, by making them hold it to the candle, to melt it till they burnt their fingers, he had in his Chaw box, a small piece of the tail of a pig, which he gave to several persons who asked a Chaw of him, but they might have tugged, till they pulld out their teeth, but could not bite it, or make it separate. With these merry Jokes, this bard used often to divert himself.

Mr Protomusicus Neverout, having been absent, ever since the 27th of June Last when he was high Steward, It was disputed whether or not he had forfeited his Seat as a member, by the tenor of Law 13th, but it was made appear, that he had sent an excuse, upon the 22d of ‖ august, when [525] Jonathan Grog Esqr served as high Steward, which the Secretary had ommitted to enter.

The place of Master of Ceremonies being now vacant, it was disputed, who should next fill that office, and was at last determined, that it should be a privilege of the Chair, to nominate or appoint, a master of Ceremonies for the night, when necessity should require, thus, the longstanding members not considering the consequences, still keept heaping of new privileges on the Chair.

It was also thought expedient, that Laconic Comus Esqr, should formally resign his office of orator every Club night, Some may think this a very absurd resolution of the Club, but not so fast, there can be a very good precedent given for it, dont we all know, that his holiness the pope, who is Infallible, as we are told, for an old Grudge, formally excommunicates his Catholic majesty of Spain, sometime about Easter, once a year, and his catholic majesty, in order to get clear of that heavy Sentence, presents his holiness, with a fine milk white mare of the best breed, as our Ingenious English Lyric poet has observed.[7]

As once a twelvemonth, to the priest,
Holy at Rome, here anti-christ,
The Spanish king presents a Gennet,
To show his love, that's all that's in it,

7. Hamilton has accurately quoted the opening lines of Matthew Prior's lengthy "Epistle to Fleetwood Shephard, Esq."

For, if his holiness would thump
His reverend bum 'gainst horses rump,
He might b'equipp'd from his own Stable
With one as white and eke more able.

Some may alledge Indeed, that his holyness the pope has a very good lucrative reason for keeping up this form, whereas, we do not find, that his honor the president, or indeed any body else, made any gain ‖ or profit by Mr Comus's resuming or resigning his office every Club night, but, to silence all objections and Cavils of this Sort, does not the Doge of Venice yearly sail out in a Gondola, and formally wed the Adriatic Sea, by throwing into it a gold ring, that very Significant Symbol of matrimony.[8] If then this powerful high priest, and that magnificent Duke or Doge, observe these Superfluous ceremonies, why may not Laconic Comus Esqr do the same.

[526]

The Reverend Mr Roundhead Muddy after Supper, stood up, and addressed himself to his honor the president and Club as follows.

"Right Honorable Mr President,

And you most worthy Longstanding members, of this august and ancient Tuesday Club,

After I have in a grateful manner, acknowledged the many great favors, I have received from your honor, and this right worthy Society, I am to tell you with regret, that I am now obliged to leave it, the nature of my affairs so requiring it, that I must remove to a distant place, I should have thought myself happy always to have enjoyed the pleasure of your good company, and conversation, and to have continued a Constant and assiduous member of this here ancient and honorable Tuesday Club, but as this cannot be, I must now take my leave of your honor and these here Longstanding members, I only ask this favor, which I hope your honor and these worthy gentlemen will readily grant, ‖ that I may still be continued a regular member of this here Society, and as often as I am in the place when the Club meets, I shall always do myself the pleasure of waiting upon your honor and these worthy members, this Satisfaction I have however, upon my leaving the place, that I have left in my Room a worthy Gentleman, of established good Character, so that the people, not only of this parish, but, the Long Standing members of this here Club, (as I suppose the Gentleman will soon become one of our Society) have made a very advantageous exchange."

[527]

8. In 1177 Pope Alexander III gave the Doge, or chief magistrate of Venice, a gold ring in honor of the Venetian victory at Istria over Frederick Barbarossa; in annual commemoration of this event, the Doge threw a similar ring into the Adriatic, saying, "We wed thee, O sea, in token of perpetual domination."

Mr Muddy having thus spoke, sat down, and the Reverend Mr Philo Dogmaticus (entertained this night as a Stranger by the Club, according to their ancient custom of Civility to Strangers) for whom this Compliment was Intended, made a Low bow to the Speaker, and observed to the Club, that it was pity this Gentleman was going to leave the Club, for that he would make an excellent Club orator.

The Secretary then rising up spoke as follows, directing his discourse to Mr Muddy.

"Sir,

Our honorable president, and the Longstanding members of this here Club, are very Sensible of their loss, in being deprived of so worthy a member, as you, and nothing could so well compensate, or make a mends for this Incident, as their being assured that it is for your advantage, in many respects, || that you leave this parish to take the charge of a better, tho' [528] you will scarce find, that you leave this here Club to become a member of a better, as a better than this is no where to be found, this, together with the expectation that we shall not utterly be deprived of your Company, and, that when you are called to this place, you will visit us *en passant,* contributes to alleviate our Concern, for being deprived of so agreeable a member."

It was then Decreed, that the Reverend Mr Roundhead Muddy, should still continue a regular member of this Club, tho a non-resident.

Chapter VI

Proposal for writing the History of the Club rejected, Hieroglyphical Characters Introduced into the Club Letters, Jonathan Grog Esqr, created Master of Ceremonies.

As Slips will often overgrow the Stocks on which they are grafted, so, some Societies, that rise out of the bowels of others, will overgrow their parent Society, and some religions will outstrip in number of professors their parent Religion, this is evident in three particular Cases which I shall name, vizt: two Religious and one Civil Case, 1st Mahometanism, was Grafted upon Judaism and Christianity, and now has far out grown them Both, having overspread almost all Asia, and a great part of Europe and Afric, whereas the others are only scattered in very small || parcells here and [529] there, in Europe and America, and some other bye corners of the world; 2d The popish Religion, which is called the Catholic Church, was Engrafted upon Paganism & Xtianity, and tho' the Slip has overgrown the Stock so as quite to kill the Christian Scyon, yet the pagan Stock and the Graft are now so Incorporated, that you cannot distinguish the one from the other, and they have both become as it were one religion, only changing the names of the objects of worship, vizt: those of the ancient heathen Deities for those of Saints, for a Confirmation of which Consult Doctor Conyers Middletons *Letter from Rome*,[1] 3d, the Eastren Shore Triumvirate, at first a small Society, founded upon the policy, and springing from the bowels of the ancient and honorable Tuesday Club, consisting at first only of three members called Triumvirs, has now, as it were become a centumvirate, spreading itself all over the Spacious Territory of Talbot county, and part of Queen Annes, on the Eastren main, whereas, its parent, the Tuesday Club, is Confined to the narrow Limits of the City of Annapolis, and a Scattering of a few honorary members, in the Counties of both Shores.

This Triumvirate was now become so great and numerous, that they began to assume to themselves pompous names and titles, and like the free masons, stile their Society the *Worshipful* and *right Worshipful,* and had [530] wrote, (as we have seen) by || their Secretary, a Long letter to the ancient and honorable Tuesday Club, which was there read.

At Sederunt 114 October 10th 1749, Huffman Snap Esqr, being high Steward, the Secretary produced an answer to the triumvirates Letter, drawn up by him, according to the order of Last Sederunt, but before he read it to the Club, he made the following motion, at the Instance, (as he said) of the Worshipful Triumvirate.

"That an exact and accurate History of the ancient and honorable Tuesday Club, should be undertaken and penned, from its first foundation, to this present time, and, that an able Historiographer, should be appointed to compose and Collect the same."

To which motion the Honorable the President and the Club, gave a Categorical answer in the negative and would by no means Consent, that any such History should be compiled, this repulse very much chagrined the Secretary, as he expected to be employed, in this great work, being the only proper person for it, as keeper of the Records, for he promised himself not only great Profits, as the Club's Historiographer, but also flattered his vanity, that he should make a very great figure in the Republic of Letters, In quality of an Historian.

The answer to the Triumvirates Letter was read as follows.

1. Hamilton is referring especially to chapter 4, "Worship of Images," in which Middleton argues that the Catholic Church has simply replaced the gods of the Pantheon with idols of its own.

To The Revd: Mr Smoothum Sly, Talbot County.

Sir,

Your Letter in the name of the worshipful Eastren ‖ Shore triumvirate [531] was read in Club, upon Tuesday the 26th *ultimo;* I had the honor to read it, and did it with a *bon grace,* and a Stentorian voice, it was received with Infinite Satisfaction and respect by the whole Society, and in a particular manner by the most honorable the president, who wore upon his countenance, during the whole time of the lecture, a most gracious and Serene Smile, which added a peculiar Grace and Comliness to the Corrigations of his countenance, among the rest of the members, (I mean the Commoners) the effect was of a rougher, or more unpolished Cast, for my voice, loud as it was, several times was drowned with *Grandes eclats de rire,*[2] notwithstanding our Laughter Master general, Mr Musician Neverout happened not to be in Club, and it was more the pity that he missed the opportunity of hearing himself Justly enough pictured out, tho' not to any great advantage.

The honorable president and Club, were all very well pleased with your opinion of the musician, & think it exactly Just, but some of our Stricter politicians took somewhat in bad part your opinion of the Club, concerning their Conduct In my unhappy affair of the Orator, as for my own part, modesty forbids me to say so much of the matter, Tis like, the honorable president & Club, who are competent Judges in affairs of this Nature, might see some Ineptitude in me, for that dignified office, which the worshipful Triumvirate, from the abundance of their good nature and humanity might overlook, or not readily perceive, but one motive, I am Sure Influenced our honorable pre- ‖ sident and Club, which was this, that I was [532] already Secretary and Chief Clerk of the Club, and therefore they were unwilling to Load me with another Charge, lest I should be negligent in my office, as Secretary, which office they esteemed more essential and necessary in the Club than that of orator.

I am mightily obliged to the worshipful Triumvirate for the honor they have done me, in appointing me their honorary Orator, a dignified place, in which, I am afraid my slender abilities, will not enable me Conspicuously to shine, however, I shall to the utmost of my power endeavor to deserve it, by a most bombast and Sonorous Oration, to be delivered, the first time I am so happy as to visit your parts.

As for your high Compliments upon the Rhetorical touches in my Letter, it is not for me to take much notice of them, or to Insist much on the affair, one way or other, lest I should unwarily betray some vanity,

---

2. "Great bursts of laughter."

however, if there appears any excellence in the Phraze, or Stile, I must not take all the glory to myself, but frankly ascribe the largest half to the honorable president's accurate pen, for his honor was pleased to Revise the Letter, before it was sent away, he refined and interlined it, and added some touches of Inexpressible elegance, and that particular passage, which you Quote, vizt: *Please tell Mr Makefun in Particular, if ever he makes another present of English beer to the Club &ct:* was Inserted by his express Com-

[533] mand, || which, I agree with you comprehends so much wit and archness in a few words, that the author of that short sentence, whoever he be, might well pass in the eyes of the world for an original.

Gratitude obliges us here to take notice of the elegancies of your Letter, since you did us the honor, to touch somewhat largely on what you are pleased to call most beautiful flowers of Rhetoric, and a wonderful Group of fine Images in ours. Your whole Letter is such a fluent and finished piece of the true Sublime, that the honorable president and Club cannot Sufficiently recompense the author, for giving them an opportunity to adorn and decorate their archives, with such a masterpiece of wit and eloquence, where, among the many Elegant touches, that shine in the body of the work, the divine art of punning stands in the most conspicous view, what a beautiful and Striking pun is couched under these words, *Short in the Instrument—al way,* what a master Stroke is there in *Some who pretend to see as far into a Stone as a free Mason,* what an elegant and Succinct Definition of a *Nincompoop,* have we got in these words, *Artifice, Artifice all,* what a droll but Just Contrast Is Introduced betwixt the said *Nincompoop* and a *Natural,* what an apt Simile is that of a *Cat's purring alittle in time and tune,* and in fine, what a Consistent group of fine tropes and touches, is there in the honorable President's *Thrilling notes, Commanding our Souls, stilling our*

[534] *passions, and at the same time forceing us to laugh* || *when we had a great mind to appear grave,* there are besides these Inimitable beauties, the *Quantums* & *Quales,* the *quas humana parum Cavit natura,* the *macti este virtuti,* elegant, and I may safely say, Classical ejaculations, which shine in the body of your elaborate epistle like Splendid and precious Sapphires set in Gold, and which, as they are wrote in Large text Characters in our book of Records, will recommend us all to posterity as very Learned men, and most profound Scholars; Oh! how can we recompense or retalliate such a profusion of Learned bounty and benevolence? when shall the ancient Tuesday Club have a Secretary of such erudition, as to make equal returns or answers to such elaborate and Superlative Sketches of Learning and wit? and can we ever put too great a value upon such a learned friend and Correspondent?

Ah! can the worshipful Triumvirate, ever Sufficiently caress, so valuable and so accomplished a penman? and *Proh dolor!*[3] can the ancient Tuesday Club ever enough bewail, the being deprived of so facetious and Erudite a member.

> *Quis desiderio sit pudor, aut modus*
> *Tam Cari Capitis?*[4]

I am commissioned to return to your worshipful Triumvirate, the Compliments of the honorable the President, and the members of our ancient Tuesday Club, and upon all occasions, we shall never fail to express that true and sincere regard, which with so much Justice we profess for the worthy gentlemen || of the triumvirate, all of whom, the honorable presi- [535] dent esteems as his own Children, and the members of the ancient Tuesday Club, look upon them as their bretheren, they being all members of that ancient and worthy Society, as for the abstract of the Clubs history, which you mentioned to me in another Letter, the thing has not as yet been laid before the honorable the president with proper form and ceremony, so that his Consent is yet wanting, and his Superlative prudence will not permit him to give his consent to any proposition suddenly, let it appear ever so Simple or plain, but there must be mature Consideration upon the matter, before the Determining *fiat* be pronounced from the Chair, there is also as yet wanting, a proper and able Historiographer, to connect and form into an uniform Rhapsody affairs and facts of such Singular Importance, but so soon as these weighty points are discussed, I shall give you further notice, in the mean time, permit me, in the name of the honorable the president and members of our ancient Tuesday Club, to subscribe myself Sir,

Octor: 10th 1749   Your most Devoted and obedient
             Humble Servant
             Loquacious Scribble Secr:

P:S: Some observed, during the reading of your letter, tho I will not vouch it for a truth, because my eyes were fixed another way, that the worshipful Sir John, knight of the Tuesday Club, wore an austere frown upon his countenance, but whether || it was that he thought himself slighted in not [536] being mentioned respectfully or so much as taken notice of in your Letter, or, because he often delights to act a Counterpart to his honor the presi-

---

3. "For sorrow!"
4. "What shame or restraint should there be for the mourning of so dear a head?" (Horace, *Carmina* 1.24.1).

dent, who smiled all the time, I shall leave to nicer physiognomists than I to determin; as for Jonathan Grog Esqr, he heard with great composure and Sedateness, and a taciturnity becoming a free Mason, the Conjecture made Concerning him in your postscript, and, when I had Just finished reading your Letter, he took it in his hand, gravely perused the postscript to himself, returned it to me, with a half Smile, rolled his chaw over his tongue, to the other corner of his mouth, and Clasping his two hands together over his belly, sat in a Settled posture, appearing no more moved, than if he had been the corner Stone of a great Cathedral. *L:S:*

The Secretary was ordered to dispatch the above letter to the Reverend Mr Sly, by the first opportunity, delivering a copy of the same to the honorable the president.

After Supper, two Letters from the high Steward, to the honorable the president, and to the worshipful Sir John, were presented, and read in Club, vizt:

To the Honorable Nasifer Jole Esqr,
President of the Tuesday Club.

Most worthy President,
Having the honor of serving as high Steward to the ancient Tuesday Club this Evening at my house, I trowble you with this Scrowl by way of notice, and humbly request the gracious favor of your presence, I am, most worthy Sir,

10th octor, 1749   Your honors most obedient &
                                          Most humble Servt:
                                          Huffman Snap.

[537]   To the most magnanimous Sir John.

Sir John,
As have the honor of serving as high Steward to the Ancient and worthy Tuesday Club this evening, it becomes my duty, as well as Inclination, to request your presence amongst us at my house; I am, Sir John,

10th octor 1749   Your worships most obedient
                                          Humble Servant
                                          Huffman Snap.

These Laconic letters show how much this Gentleman's conversation with the club, had Improved him since his admission into it, having striped

him much of that verbosity and prolixity of Stile, peculiar to those gentlemen, his bretheren by profession, who study that voluminous and perplexed Science called the *Common Law of England*.

After reading and recording the above Letters, the Club passed the
following Law.

Law XLII. Resolved by the president and Club, that no person whatsoever, that does not reside in the place, and attend the Club regularly at its
meetings, or serve in his turn as high Steward, shall be a regular member of
this Club, therefore, the entry of last Sederunt, concerning the Reverend
Mr Roundhead Muddy, is hereby annulled, as also all other such entries, if
such there be, granting the like privilege to any other person, and he and
they, are henceforth to be deemed only honorary members of this Club.

This law was procured, at the Instance and desire of his honor the
president, who being Jealous and tenacious of the prerogative of the Chair,
was afraid of its being Infringed or Impaired, by the Increase of the number
of extraneous regular ‖ members, who all had a title to vote in Club, and [538]
who being non residents were not so Immediatly under his eye, as those
regular members who remained on the Spot, and therefore he got them
Reduced to the Station and degree of honorary members, who, by a preceeding law, had no vote in Club.

At Sederunt 115 octor: 24, 1749, Prim Timorous Esqr being high Steward, the Secretary reported in Club, that he had dispatched the Answer to
the Triumvirate's Letter, and delivered a copy of the same to his honor the
president.

Then the Club took it under their Serious consideration, that the
badge Card of the honorable the President was so gone to decay, and out of
Repair, that the Letters were scarce legible, and the ornaments were become
dim, and their Lusture faded, it was therefore resolved, that there should be
a new Badge Card prepared for his honor, that the grandure and dignity of
the Chair in this Club, may duely be kept up, and the Secretary was ordered
to prepare the same, and produce it at next Sederunt.

A Letter from the high Steward to his honor the president was produced in Club, the tenor of which Follows.

To The honorable Nasifer Jole Esqr,
President of the Tuesday Club in Annapolis.

Sir,

This being my time to serve as high Steward of the Tuesday Club,
think it my duty to acquaint your honor therewith, and, as I am convinced,

there cannot be any thing more conduceive, to the Satisfaction of the ||
[539] whole Club, than to see you placed in the great Chair, hope we shall not be
dissappointed, I remain your honor's

(a)   Most obedient humble Servant
                                                 Prim Timerous.

For an explication of the Cypher or hieroglyphic at the end of this
Letter, we must refer, to his honor the president's original Copy, tho' some
presume to say, upon what grounds, I cannot tell, that these mystical Characters contain a Club Secret of State, between the high steward and his
honor, not fit for all the members to be let into, but, the explication given
in the note below, if genuine, seems to point at no such Secret, and as it
speaks in the third person, seems not to have been penned by the high
Steward himself, at least, If penned by him, he talks, as well as writes in
mysteries after the manner of the Celebrated Bishop Atterbury,[5] and his
political Correspondents, but this is only the first Introduction of hieroglyphical Characters Into the Club writings and Letters, we shall find one
more Instance of it in the Sequel of this History, which has not as yet, nor I
believe ever will be explained, unless Mr Protomusicus Neverout, the Ingenious author and Inventor of that particular way of Cyphering, gives us a
key to it.

At Sederunt 116, Novr 7th 1749, Laconic Comus Esqr being high Steward, the Secretary, according to an order of Last Sederunt, presented to
[540] his honor the President || and the club, the presidential badge, properly
adorned and lettered, with a variation from the former Inscription, tho the
form of the Card was still retained, viz: *Nasifer Jole Armiger, Societatis Annapolitanæ,* THE TUESDAY CLUB *dicta Præses.* The Secretary, when he presented this addressed himself to his Honor the President, and the Club, in a
Speech proper upon the occasion, but so loaded with hard, obselete and
new Coined words, That some present, who did not comprehend his meaning, particularly the Reverend Mr Roundhead Muddy, thought it was a
rebellious Jacobitish harangue.

(a) The meaning of this is conjectured, by the most Skillful decypherers, to be— Signior
——— would not Let me write this Letter, he Intends to leave you this night, God bless the
president, so says the Parson.

5. Francis Atterbury (1662–1732), bishop of Rochester, frequently engaged in the political
and theological disputes of the day and was imprisoned in 1720 for allegedly plotting to restore
the Stuarts to power; he was a strong supporter of the Church of England and the author of
numerous political pieces.

The honorable The President appointed Jonathan Grog Esqr Master of Ceremonies for the night, who in a decent and proper manner, Invested his honor with his new badge, then Jonathan Grog Esqr, was ordered by his honor to return thanks to the Secretary, for his diligence in preparing the presidential badge, which he did in an Elegant and Succinct manner.

The Honorable The President this night expressed some concern, that the high Steward had not wrote him a Letter, according to the usual Custom, by which the Records for this Sederunt would appear Imperfect, but he declared to the Club, that the H:S: had made him amends for that neglect, by waiting upon him in person, upon which the Club was satisfied, there seemed at this Sederunt, to be a more than Common Intimacy and Cordiality, between his honor the president and Sir John, they sitting by the fire || face to face, and foot to foot, smiling upon each other for a consider-   [541] able time, but the conversation of these two great men, consisted more in political nods, winks and Shrugs than in a flow of words, which made the Club suspect, that some grand design was *in petto.*

It was moved by the Secretary, that the ancient Custom of this Club, relating to a Side board, and a gammon of bacon, or any other one dish of dressed vittles, should be revived, and Strictly adhered to, or, that at least, if there was to be a table in form, and a Cloth laid, no person, except his honor the President, who is privileged, should exceed one dish of roast or boiled, for the Club Supper, and that under high penalty, but this Salutary motion was set aside, under pretence that there was not a full Club, mark here the Clubs disregard to a Law, that was not as yet repealed.

Jonathan Grog Esqr, applied to his honor the president and Club, to be permitted to lay down four of his five P offices, retaining only that of the Poet Laureat, which request was granted, then he applied to be created Master of Ceremonies, and the honble: the President and Club, finding him a person Sufficiently qualified, and the potent objection of the five Ps removed, he was accordingly created Mr of Ceremonies, *Quam diu bene se gesserit,*[6] the honorable the president taking him by the hand in token of approbation, at the same time always reserving to himself, the privilege granted at Sederunt 113, thus were the five Ps, of || Jonathan Grog Esqr,   [542] converted into P.L.M.C. That is to say, *Poeta Laureatus, Magister Ceremoniarum.*

After Supper, Mr Roundhead Muddy spoke against the Law passed at Sederunt 114 and showed by his councel, Mr Secretary Scribble, that that Law was not balloted according to form, and therefore was of no force, and

6. "So long as he behaves himself well."

could by no means annull the entry of Sederunt 113, after some dispute on the point, the Subject was waved till a more full meeting.

Upon the Honorable The President's giving the Signal, the gelastic Law was put in execution against the Reverend Mr Muddy, who talked alittle more upon this ungrateful Subject, than came to his Share, but the Gentleman bore this Severe Club punishment, with great patience and Resignation, and was utterly silent upon the argument, not pretending to say one word more to the point, either by himself, or his learned Councel.

Chapter VII

Eulogium of the poet Laureat on his honor the President's Entertainment, arrival of the Great Seal, more Sublime Club Letters.

It was well observed by a certain Peripatetic Philosopher, that Praise is a tribute due to the great, whether they Justly deserve it or not,[1] where- ||
[543] fore we find, that all Inferiors think themselves obliged to pay a deference or respect to their Superiors, and this respect they express both by words and gestures, and for once that they apply their praise and panegyric Justly, they ten times strain it too high, and carry it to a pitch beyond all reason and truth, thus have I seen many a Sage and grave Philosopher, uncover his Sagacious head to an arrant blockhead, whom capricious fortune has in the eye of the world raised above him, with regard to birth titles and posses-sions; I have seen also a grey headed venerable and worthy elder, bow to the grownd, when he came in the presence of a foolish princely greenheaded puppy; but as this is, and has constantly been, the way of the world, and providence, for the good order of human Society, has wisely ordained Sub-ordinations among men, we must submit to it, however absurd it may appear at first view to wise men.

Some may perhaps Incline to apply this observation to the Eastren Shore Triumvirate, and To Jonathan Grog Esqr, poet Laureat, when they examin into the Conduct of both, and may condemn the first for writing in such a flattering strain to the Club, and the latter for smoothing up his honor the president, in a Set of fustian verses, which we shall presently

1. Hamilton is playfully referring to Aristotle, who says exactly the opposite in the *Nicomachean Ethics* 1.12.2 ("we praise just men and brave men . . . because of their actions and the results they produce").

exhibit, upon the Supper given by him to the Club, but, when they Consider, that the Eastren Shore Triumvirate, owed it's rise, Increase and Glory, to the ancient and hon- ‖ orable Tuesday Club, even granting that the   [544] members of that Triumvirate were as good, by family birth and titles, and as wise men as the members of the ancient and honorable Tuesday Club; when they Consider also that Jonathan Grog Esqr, was lately promoted, by his honor's grace and favor, to the high office of Master of the Ceremonies, tho' the said Jonathan Grog Esqr, might be a man of a more ancient family, a readier wit, quicker genius, and a greater poet, than his honor the president or any other of his Longstanding members, they will Surely agree with me, that those praises and panegyrics, were properly and Justly enough applied to both the President and the Club, by that there Triumvirate, and this here poet Laureat, and were not altogether so ill placed and premature as the fulsome praises and flattery of some Impudent, Indefatigable and persevering Sycophants, who extoll their foolish or wicked patrons, at the expence of truth, candor and Sincerity, e'er they have received either promises or favors, but continue in the uncertain and hungry State of expecters and hangers on.

At Sederunt 117, Novr 21 1749, The honorable Mr President Jole being high Steward, a Letter from Capt: Comely Coppernose to the Secretary was produced after Supper, read, and ordered to be recorded, the tenor of which follows.

To Doctor Loquacious Scribble, Annapolis.   [545]

Dear Sir,   London June 24th 1749
    I have your kind favor, the 11th of april via Ireland, I am extremely obliged to you and all my good friends for your kind wishes, I believe they had a good effect, for we had a charming passage.
    The honorable the president, the principal officers, and worthy members of the Club, do me a very great honor in Laying their further Commands on me, I shall execute them to the best of my power, but I am afraid to tell you what they will cost, I consulted most of the workmen in what manner such a thing must be done, I had but two Choices, to have a dye cut, and so have them struck, or to have them engraved, the Latter would look very plain and ordinary, and come very near the price of the first method, vizt: struck, and this will look bold and Handsom, and be a beautiful medal, I have agreed to have the Dye cut for Six Guineas and a half, the other expences will come to about two and Sixpence a piece, besides the Gilding, what that will Cost, I cannot tell, suppose about 2/ or 2/6, They

will weigh each very near one onz ½ of Silver, and it must be quite pure, for
[546] fear of hurting the Dye, so, that ‖ had you dowble the number, they would
still be Cheaper, I shall have them in my possession, so that any number
may be supplied on proper notice, I would send them to you, but they
would not be Serviceable, as you have no engine to strike them with, the
Engraver would not engrave them for Less than ten Shillings a piece. The
great Seal comes by the bearer, and, I hope you'll think it well done, and not
dear, the medals will be done in about 6 weeks, and come by another
opportunity that will then offer.

If I please the worthy Gentlemen of the Club, in this commission, I
hope to be favored with a patent under the great Seal, as agent for the Club
in London, you'll do me the favor of presenting my duty to the honorable
the President, and my humble Service to all the gentlemen of the Club and
believe me, Dear Sir,

Your most humble Servant
Comely Coppernose.

This Letter was well received by his honor and the Club, and the
Secretary was ordered to prepare a proper answer to it, and dispatch it with
the first opportunity.

His honor at this Sederunt, having as it was usual with him, given the
Club a very elegant entertainment, Jonathan Grog Esqr, Master of Ceremo-
nies and Poet Laureat, after Supper, when his honor had resumed the
Chair, stood up & delivered himself as follows.

[547]   The President our Lofty chair has grac'd,
The Brimming bowls in decent order plac'd,
We all have tasted rich delicious Cheer,
Sure nothing but good humor can be here.
Come, fellow members, let the bowl go round,(a)
Let this grand hall with Songs and Jokes resound,
Sure, from Joves board, Ambrosial Cates we share,
And heavenly nectar flows to sooth our Care,
Such Cates as these, Celestial feasts may grace,
And this rich punch of nectar take the place,
To you, Great Sir, our humble Thanks we pay,
Who spare no pains or cost to make us gay,
We, in our turn, our wits shall exercise,
To tell the world, you're Noble Generous, wise,

(a) Here the poet Laureat took the bowl in his hand.

And for fine feasting and the Sparkling bowl,
First thank the Gods, and then Illustrious Jole.

This Sublime poetical Speech met with great applause from all the Longstanding members, and the poet Laureat having delivered it, took a hearty pull at the bowl & sat down.

His honor having drank the king and the Club after Supper, some of the members murmured at his giving the preference to that foolish Toast as they Called it, upon which, his honor, after his usual peremptory way declared That none of the Longstanding members had any right to dictate to him, in these matters, or pretend to direct him in his choice of a toast, and therefore his honor expressly ordered from the Chair, that this toast of the king and the Club, should henceforth be the || first toast proposed after [548] Supper, The longstanding members on this were silent, and said no more, perceiving that his honor had assumed his peremptory face, and could not brook Contradiction.

At Sederunt 118 December 5th 1749, Mr Secretary Scribble being high Steward, his honor produced in Club the following Letter from the high Steward.

To The Honorable Nasifer Jole Esqr
President of the Tuesday Club, These.

Honorable Sir,
The title with which I address your honor, is undoubtedly your Due upon many accounts too prolix here to ennumerate, but plainly Conspicuous to every member of our ancient Club, who observes with what Impartial Justice, with what mild and Gentle moderation, with what modesty and tender humanity, with what regard to merit and Just abhorrence of Iniquity you moderate and regulate all affairs, relating to your humble Subjects, the members of the Ancient Tuesday Club, how like an exuberant Cornu-copia, you plentifully and magnificently entertain and regale them, how like a kind father, you administer to all their wants, and wink at and pass over all their Infirmities, and, how like a humane and mild ruler, you comply with all their proposals and demands, tho sometimes bordering upon extravagance.

These great qualities and Enduements, In my humble opinion, give a Juster Claim to the titles of *your honor* and *honorable Sir,* than all the foppery of Stars and gar- || ters, golden fleeces, Georges, St Andrews crosses, This- [549] tles, and such like farcical trash and Trumpery, nay even than the Royal patents, where these good qualities are wanting, for, it is certain, that many peers of noble blood and ancient extract, and also, many new upstarts who

have been dizened out, with the Tinsel badges of Titulary Honor, have
appeared in this age, in that age, and In every age, mere fools, knaves,
Scoundrells and Coxcombs, whilst men, who are placed in a lower rank, as
the world esteems it, such as the honest Presidents of ancient and worthy
Clubs, like this here Club of ours, have in effect been men of more Intrinsic
honor, and more noble principles.

I have the pleasure here to observe, that, as I had the honor to be
Steward (not high Steward) of that auspicious Club, in which your honor
was created president, and ascended our stately Chair, vizt: the memorable
26th of November, 1745, so, by some propitious fate and good fortune, it
has so fallen out, that I always have been honored with your honor's presence, for these eight successive times, which I have since served, sometimes
Steward, and sometimes as high Steward, this time is now the 9th, in which
I solicit and apply for the same favor, Some augurs have observed, that nine
is an unlucky number, I pray it may not prove so in this Instance, so as to
deprive me of your honor's company this night (tho' if it should, I have less
reason to complain, than any other Longstanding member of our ancient
Club) If it happens otherwise, I shall have a meaner opinion than ever I yet
[550] had of these idle and Super- || stitious maxims, and it will more and more
oblige, Honorable Sir,

Decr: 5th 1749   Your honor's obsequious Servant
                                      and faithful H:S: and Secretary
                                      Loquacious Scribble.

In this Letter, we find the Secretary very much upon the flattering and
cajoling Strain, and it must be observed here, that this officer, after he
found that he could not obtain his darling preferment, by violent methods
and by exciting tumults and hubbubs in the Club, had recourse to this
Smoothing method with his honor and Sir John, but his machinery still
proved insufficient, for these two great politic and wise men, easily saw
thro' his designs, and would by no means make themselves Gudgeons, to be
Entraped in his Subtile Snares, however, the Secretary did not turn flatterer
on the same grounds as the Eastren Shore Triumvirate and Jonathan Grog
Esqr did, for he was still a dependant and hanger on, so, that he might
properly be classed among those Sempiternal Sycophants, mentioned in the
beginning of this Chapter.

Another Letter was presented in Club, by the worshipful Sir John, writ
to him by the same High Steward.

To The worshipful Sir John,
knight of the Noble order of the Tuesday Club, These.

Most undaunted and magnanimous knight,

It would be Impertinent and Idle to tell a man of your understanding, and knowledge in Chronology, how ancient the order of knighthood is, and for ‖ what purpose instituted, the worthy knights of old were defenders and [551] champions of virtue, and friends to the fair Sex, and mighty princes have not thought it beneath them, to gird the Sword of Justice upon their manly thighs, to protect the Innocent and relieve the oppressed, but alas, this Noble order is now degenerated, into I dont know what kind of a farce, and our moderen pigmy knights, Instead of Swords, helmets, and coats of mail, the ponderous and manly badges of heroes, wear delicate soft silks, velvets, Ribbons, garters, Stars, Jewels, Golden fleeces, crosses and other gewgaws, Just enough emblems of their Softness, effeminacy and cowardice, and, instead of the noble feats of arms in the fields of Mars, and defending the oppressed and mantaining the Cause of the fair, they storm bawdy houses, kick poor whores, bilk hackney Coach men, break windows, knock down the watch, Cudgel drunken Constables, smoke Coblers, dance, fiddle, sing, shuffle Cards, rattle dice, make fantastical legs and foppish grimaces at the Ladies, and make a figure no where but at bagnios, masquerades, Ridottos, Italian operas, Drums, routs, taverens, gaming Tables, cock pits, horse races and Broughtons Amphitheatre.[2] This would almost tempt one to think that the long expected *Annus mirabilis,* was nigh at hand, when the women shall put on breeches and armor, and the men step into Smokes and petticoats.

Observing this degeneracy, in the ancient and noble order of knighthood, I should long ago have given up all for lost, and Imagined, that true Valor ‖ and courage was banished out of the world, did I not find that there [552] is yet extant, one valiant and tremendous knight, of courage right Stéel'd and tried bravery, even Sir John, (heretofore Oldcastle) the renownd and Invincible Champion of the Ancient Tuesday Club, under whose puisant arm, the longstanding members sit in Safety, and, by whose brave presence and Influence, The honorable president is stuck fast and Immoveable in his Chair, and hugs himself, secure from all violent assaults, both from within doors, and from without, your worship being therefore so necessary a person, upon whom we depend for Safety, and in whom we place our Confidence, the only remaining type of the true and ancient chivalry, I must

2. The British prizefighter John Broughton established a theater for boxing in 1743 (John Ford, *Prizefighting: The Age of Regency Boximania* [New York, 1972]).

request the honor of your magnanimous presence this night, in the name of the Ancient Tuesday Club, to which is high Steward, under favor of the honorable the president, most magnanimous Sir John,

Decr 5th 1749					Your worships most humble
						Servt: and faithful Squire
						Loquacious Scribble.

The other great and Important transactions of this most memorable Sederunt, are reserved as the Subject of the following Chapter, to which we refer the reader if he desires to know them.

---

[553]		## Chapter VIII

Admission of Philo Dogmaticus Esqr, Speeches in prose and verse at the Delivery of the Great Seal, Creation of the Chancellor, and an account of the Club Medals being struck at London.

Hope is a passion by which all mankind are buoy'd up, be their Circumstance what it will, prosperous, or adverse, this Strange Phantom still haunts and attends them, thro all the windings and turnings of this foolish life as the Philosophers call it; if they enjoy good fortune Hope still promises a better, if they Labor under distresses and difficulties, Hope whispers them, that they shall sometime or other be relieved; In fine this flattering power is still in view, unless when despair takes place, for this latter, being her mortal and sworn Enimy, she always takes flight at the Sight of his horrid front, as a beautiful modest and Coy virgin would fly at the Sight of a Rude rake or ravisher, and yet some people have as little ground or reason for Entertaining this flattering Phantome, as those who hope for the Millennium, have a chance to live to see those halcyon days, or those who fear the Sky will fall and smother the Larks, run a risk to be smothered and Crushed in their Company.

But tho this vain propensity, may often present us golden Scenes at a distance, and promise us relief in our greatest distresses and difficulties, ‖
[554]	yet such is the caprice of Lady fortune In human affairs, or, to speak more Intelligibly, such is the Indiscretion and Imprudence of the bulk of mankind, that ten to one, those that hope for, and desire most, enjoy the Least of the good things of life, and many, who scarce ever hoped or expected a better fortune, than that they are at present possesed of, or ever longed after

places and titles of honor, have them, I know not how, pop suddenly into their mouths to the great Surprize and astonishment of every one, who cannot comprehend how they came to have such good Luck, these are such as have been born with a Silver Spoon in their mouths, or a Cawl on their heads, as the proverb goes; a remarkable Instance of this, we shall find in the case of the Reverend Mr Philo Dogmaticus, who, at one and the same Instant, as it were, was made a Long Standing member of this Club, Chancellor, State officer and privy Councellor to the Honorable The Chair, as also, keeper of his honors political Conscience, which transaction shall presently be related.

On the aforesaid Sederunt 118 the Secretary presented to the Honorable the president and Club, a petition from the Reverend Mr Philo Dogmaticus, who being desired to withdraw into an adjoining Chamber, it was read as follows.

To the honorable Nasifer Jole Esqr President, ‖ The honored Sir   [555]
John knight, and the other worshipful officers, and worthy members
of the ancient and honorable Tuesday Club.

Gentlemen,

As without Society, man would be the most wretched Creature upon earth, so to this he owes, tho' not his rational powers and faculties, yet the use and Improvement of them, arts Sciences, and all the advantages and pleasures of life flow from this fountain, which alone renders it more secure, and Comfortable, than the Condition of the Irrational tribes, for without this, even reason it self would avail us very little, our nobler powers would Languish and perhaps be employed in mutual destruction, but Society, founded upon principles of right reason, directed by Just Laws, Impartially executed, under the administration of wise and virtuous Rulers, what a glorious Idea is it! what heart can conceive a greater blessing upon Earth! it is the very prelude, or rather type of heaven, where nothing is to be found but order, peace, love and all happy enjoyments worthy of the rational nature.

Wherever such well Constituted Societies are ‖ to be met with upon   [556]
Earth, be they more public or more private, formed for more General advantage or the Comforts of a more private life, what wonder is it that men should wish and endeavour, to be members of such Societies, who, being prompted by a natural and reasonable Self love, wish themselves happy.

Moved by this principle, and the fame of this ancient, honorable and worthy Society of the Tuesday Club, the pleasures and benefits of which, I have also shared in, thro' that generosity, which has once and again Invited and admitted me, a Stranger among you, to the honor and pleasure of being a witness and partaker of your most ravishing Conversation, I humbly beg and petition, the honorable the president, the honored Sir John, knight, and the other worshipful officers, and all the Respectful worthy members of the ancient Tuesday Club, to perfect the honor they have already done me, by admitting me a member of it, and, however unworthy I may be at present, your noble examples, and Improving Conversation, will I hope, render me by degrees more worthy of such an honor, and lay under an Infinite obligation,

Your most Loving, Devoted and
Obedient humble Servant
Philo Dogmaticus.

This petition being read, the ballots of yeas & nays were put round, [557] and, the Reverend Mr Philo dog- ‖ maticus being unanimously elected a member of the Tuesday Club, Jonathan Grog Esqr, Master of Ceremonies and the Secretary, waited upon him in the next Room, acquainting him that he was elected a member, upon which they conducted him into the Club Room, where the honorable the president met him at the Door, and Saluted him with a hearty manuquassation, an honor, which was never done to any longstanding member, either before or since, and a happy Presage, or pompous prelude, to the great honors, that were soon to be heaped upon him.

Then Jonathan Grog Esqr, Master of Ceremonies, placeing him nigh the presidential Chair, confirmed him in the following manner.

"Sir,

I as master of Ceremonies to our ancient and honorable Tuesday Club, with all the Ceremony I am master of, which mastery in Ceremonies, I acknowledge to be conveyd to me, by the authority of our honorable President, do Inaugurate, constitute and confirm you, Philo Dogmaticus Esqr, a good firm and Longstanding member of the Commoners, of this our ancient and honorable Tuesday Club, in token of which, I Invest you, with this the Club's badge, and here Solemnly present you, to the honorable the president, recommending it to you, to make your acknowledgements to the honorable the president and Club, in the handsomest and best Speech you can devise, upon this Important, and honorable occasion."

Then Mr Dogmaticus, standing in a proper posture and attitude, addressed the honorable the president and Club as follows.

"Honorable Mr President,   [558]
Honored Knight,
and all ye other worshipful officers, and,
Worthy members of the ancient & honorable Tuesday Club,
      I Joyfully acknowledge the honor you have done me by my admission
into your most noble Society, for which I return you my most grateful
thanks, from a heart that shall always be devoted to the promoting of the
honor and benefit of this Club in opposition to all Envious Rivals, and
malicious Enimies, who can distinguish themselves only by reviling or de-
tracting from that worth, which they must for ever despair of equalling.
      May the ancient and honorable Tuesday Club, subsist and florish,
while the Sun and moon Endures, and you my honored Superiors, and
other worthy fellow members of it *Macti virtuti, omnique Genere foelicitatis
estote,*[1] *Amen* and *Amen.*"
      Mr Dogmaticus, having thus finished his gratulatory Speech, was Sa-
luted by all round as a member, and took his Seat in Club accordingly.
      Then the Secretary rising up, Informed the Club, that he had received
the Great Seal, sent by Captain Comely Copper Nose, and that he had
further Intelligence from the said Gentleman, that the Club medals were
already struck at London, and would very soon be sent over, then putting
his Countenance in a proper order, he delivered the following Speech.
      "Mr President Sir,
      It is a Certain truth, which will be granted by every man of plain Sense
and understanding, as well as your professed Sage or Philosopher, that the
noblest and most eminent ‖ marks or Signatures, which can dignify or   [559]
decorate men or distinguish human Societies, are Virtue, honor and Integrity, since these more effectually recommend men to the regard of their
Contemporaries, to the esteem of posterity, and form a more eloquent
Eulogium in the mouth of fame, than all the blazoning of the Herald's
office, or the utmost Skill of the Sculptor or engraver, tho exercised upon
the most durable Substances of Stone and metal, hence it is, that many
Societies have made these mechanic arts, only Subservient, to the abovenamed excellent virtues, but using them to fabricate Certain material monuments, and Significant designs, by which either the effigies of great and
virtuous men, or particular virtues and qualities peculiar to themselves,
were preserved and signified to posterity, and remained legible in these

      1. "Be honored with virtue and every kind of happiness" (first phrase echoes Horace, *Satirae*
1.2.31).

Characters, whatever they were. To give an Instance from Antiquity, we find an old Classic Author, saying of the famous Mythologist Æsop.

Æsopo Ingentem Statuam, posuere Attici,
Servumqʒ collocarunt Æterno in basi,
Patere honoris, scirent ut cumque viam,
Nec Generi Tribui, sed virtuti Gloriam.

Athens of old, admiring virtuous fame,
A Statue reard, to Æsop's honor'd name,
Him tho a Slave, in Lasting brass they plac'd,
His Image, tho deformd, their City grac'd,
Thus Deemd they birth and Sounding titles nought,
Since virtue only lasting Glory brought.[2]

[560] Now Sir, as I flatter myself, that this worthy Society the ‖ ancient Tuesday Club, is not in a mean degree possessed of some great virtues and excellencies in which true Intrinsic worth and merit essentially consist, so, I hope this worthy Club, may assume to themselves that privilege, which other associations and Corporations have taken before them, that is to devise and invent for themselves, Certain Significant Characters or Hieroglyphics, which being engraved or Cut upon Stone, Metal, or such like durable Substances, may be expressive or significant of certain virtues, peculiar to that ancient, honorable and worthy Society, such as, amity, concord, benevolence, Generosity, Good fellowship, and the like, and thus not only Inform the present generation, and their contemporaries, how well disposed the members of this worthy Club are, but also, leave a lasting and permanent Character behind them by which posterity may be put in mind, that such a worthy Society once florished, and by this means the Succeeding generations may be prompted to follow so fair an example.

Gentlemen,

We may go farther back, than the History or records of the Heralds office, an Institution at best but modern and Gothic, we may take an earlier date than even the oldest order of knighthood, now extant in Christendome, In searching for Authorities from antiquity, when particular Societies of men, first Invented for themselves Certain marks and Signatures, by which they were distinguished and known from other Societies, were I to

[561] Instance ‖ The many Signatures and hieroglyphics used by ancient Ægypt,

2. More literally, "The men of Attica erected a great statue to Aesop; / They placed this slave on an eternal pedestal / That they might know the road of honor was always open, / And that glory was given to virtue, not family" (Phaedrus, *Fabulae*, II, epilogue).

the Symbols wore by the magistrates and priests, which notified or Implied some peculiar virtue or excellency, were I to ennumerate the things of this Sort, used even by the Jewish priesthood, such as the Urim and Thummum, the Seraphs and Cherubs, the Ephods and Candlesticks and lavers &ct: by which, I might like some learned historians derive this mode even from divine Institution, I doubt I should become not only too refined, but abundantly too tedious and prolix, and keep your honor, and these here Gentlemen, the Longstanding members, if you had a mind to hear me out, sitting here till Christenmass, which is now pritty nigh at hand.

Therefore, since it appears, to have been a prevailing custom in all ages, for certain men, and Societies of men, to adopt particular marks and Signatures, by which they desire to be known, and distinguished, which often, if not always, are expressive of some virtues or excellencies, peculiar to the Society to which they belong, it seems highly Just and reasonable, that this worthy Society, the ancient and honorable Tuesday Club, whose honorable President and Longstanding members, have now, for some years distinguished themselves in this present age, and, in this City wherein they live, by exhibiting an example of good fellowship, and a friendly and Sociable disposition, should in conformity with so many || worthy patterns of [562] antiquity, who have florished in former ages, and lived in greater Cities, Invent and Design for themselves, some Laudable and Ingenious device expressive of that amity and Sociable Spirit, which prevails among them, this Indeed has been done, in an elegant and well contrived, tho Simple device, of two hands Joined over a heart, with the Mottos of CONCORDIA RES PARVÆ CRESCUNT, and LIBERTAS ET NATALE SOLUM. This device then Mr President and Gentlemen, formerly delineated upon a fragile Card of no duration or permanency, I, out of the great Regard I have for this worthy Society, and out of Gratitude for the trust they have reposed in me, in honoring me with the office of their Secretary, have caused to be here curiously engraved on Silver, in the form of a Seal, which Seal, I humbly present to the worthy Society for their use, to be affixed to all Commissions Summons, writings, or Instruments of whatsoever kind, which shall henceforth be Issued in the name of the honorable

president and Club, to which writings, I humbly request, that this Seal,
[563] may be for the time to come ‖ a Sanction and Corroboration, and, that
some trusty person, from among the members of this worthy Society, not
already dignified with an office, may be chosen *Chancellor*, or keeper of this
great Seal, to affix it to such writings, as the honorable the president and
Club shall Command, and, if this my present is chearfully accepted by the
honorable the president and worthy members, and it is put upon Record,
that this was the gift of their faithful Secretary, I shall esteem myself,
dowbly and Trebly rewarded, for any little Expence or trowble it may have
cost me."

The Secretary having thus spoke, presented the Seal and Impression,
to the honorable the president & Club, who were pleased to give their
approbation.

Then Jonathan Grog Esqr, Master of Ceremonies, being Commanded
by his honor the President, to return thanks to the Secretary for his present,
stood up and addressed himself to this purpose.

Whilst the Club's thanks my task is to rehearse,
I leave Dull prose for my beloved verse,
For great must be the wit that can Compose,
Fine florid Speeches in Phlegmatic prose,
My Rhiming Genius, therefore fixes here,
Plain thoughts in Rhime will better please your ear.
    While your Indulgent Smiles great Sir, [a] Inspire,
I slight Apollo, and his virgin Choir,
[564] While propd by thy bold Courage O Sir John,
I need no Pegasus to ride upon,
While this rare punch, is on the table brought,
The Streams of Helicon to me are nought,
Cheer'd by your Smiles, [a] by this rich liquor warmd,
'Gainst Critics and the Bathos I am armd,
Th'obsequious bard, your orders then obeys,
And thus proclaims our Secretaries praise.
    For this rich present, Generous Sir, to you [b]
The thanks I pay, which Justly are your due,
Illustrious Jole Commands, and I obey,
He and the Club, assent to what I say,

(a) To the president.
(a) To the members of the Club.
(b) To the Secretary, with the Seal and Impression in hand.

They speak by me, my Words their Sense express,
My Lays are pregnant with their Thankfulness,
Accept our grateful thanks, this Seal you give,
Will make our Club to distant ages live,
The Sculptors art, displays to future times
The worth of virtue and the Guilt of Crimes,
This art, or praise or Satyr speaks as Strong
As painters Coloring, or the poet's Song,
These types (c) the virtue of our Club declare,
Here hand Joins hand, while but one heart we share.
Posterity shall see, and shall admire,
How pure amongst us Glows the Social fire.
A Social Club our Sons shall have in view,   [565]
And all the bright example shall pursue.
   If this bright Seal, our Club shall Eternize,
No mean one, bounteous Sir, shall be your prize,
Your Generous name shall live, our grateful page
Shall sound your name to every distant age,
And if these humble lays a place may Claim
In Records Sage, 'twill swell the poet's fame,
And you, and I, and every Social Soul
Immortal praise shall share with Noble Jole.

This poetical Speech had the applause of the whole Club, and Jonathan Grog Esqr, making a reverend bow to the honorable president and Club, sat down.

Then the Club proceeded to chuse a Chancellor, and keeper of the great Seal, and the Revd: Mr Philo dogmaticus, by a great majority was elected for that Important office, and the great Seal being Solemnly delivered to him by Jonathan Grog Esqr, master of Ceremonies, he in a handsom manner gave Thanks for the great and Important trust Committed to him, of Chancellor and keeper of the honorable the Presidents Clubical Conscience, solemnly promising a faithful execution of it, and then took his place appointed by the Club, on the left hand of his honor's Chair of State, in quality of a State officer, and privy Councellor to the Chair, the wonted place of the Orator and Speaker, before these offices were taken away and quite discontinued in Club.

Thus we find, in a most Surprizing and astonishing ‖ manner, this   [566]
gentleman promoted to a great and new office of trust in the Club, on the

(c) Showing the Impression in wax.

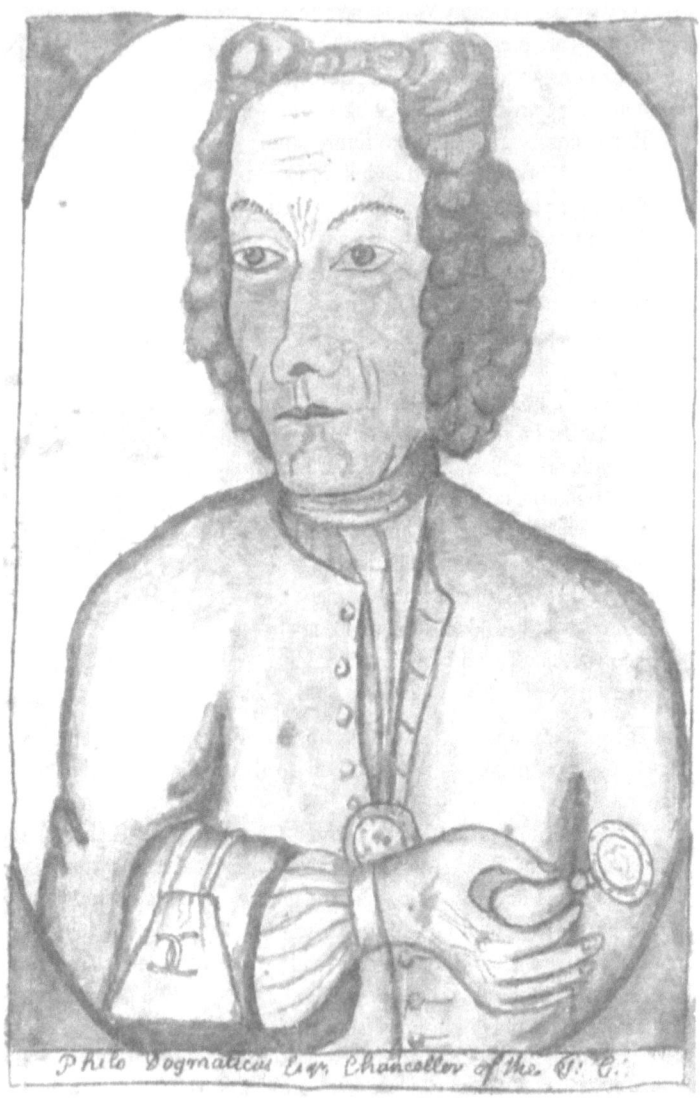

Philo Dogmaticus Esqr. Chancellor of the &c. &c.

[facing page 563]

very night, in which he was admitted a Longstanding member, without so much as applying or making Interest for it, which is a sign of either the great personal merit and Capacity of this gentleman, or at least, of the great opinion, his honor the president and Club had of his abilities and parts, but be that as it will, his honor never was so much mistaken in his man as now, ever since he was a president, for he thought he had now got a firm friend to the prerogative and power of the Chair, but in a little time found himself most woefully baulked, for Mr Dogmaticus turned out to be a Zealous Republican, and a Stiff advocate for, and mantainer of Clubical liberty, and, we shall find this State officer, in the Sequel of our History, giving many a bold check to the petulence of the Chair, and occasioning many heartburns, broils, dissentions and Contentions, between his honor & the Longstanding members, and the principal author, exciter and fomenter of a great, dangerous & bloody rebellion, which broke out in the Club, as in due time shall be related.

The Secretary, by this remarkable occurrence, was now for ever deprived of all his hopes of becoming a State member of the Club, which he still expected some time or other to be, by his stepping into the orator's Chair, for tho he sometime after Indeed, procured that office and title, yet he did not become thereby a State officer, || the Chancellor taking the [567] precedence of him in that quality, neither did he by his office of orator enjoy the degree of Chief officer of the Commons long, for a new officer was created, under the name of his honor's Attorney General, who took place of all the other Commoners.

The Club ordered at the same Sederunt, that Commissions should be made out for the worshipful Sir John, and the other officers, under the Great Seal, and that a patent should be granted under the said Seal, to Capt: Comely Coppernose, to be agent for the Club at London, and also, that the said Capt: Comely Coppernose, should be entered and enrolled among the honorary members of this Club.

Ordered also, that a Letter of thanks be drawn up to Capt: Comely Coppernose, with the patent and Commissions, by Huffman Snap Esqr, and the Secretary, a Committee of two for that purpose, and laid before the Club at next Sederunt.

Thus, we find this ancient Club now taking great State upon itself, and the prophesy of Jealous Spyplot Senr Esqr, in a great measure accomplished, with regard to the Club's becoming a state Club, for now indeed it was a State Club with a witness, tho' not thro' the operation or Means of Mr Protomusicus Neverout, who was for the most part absent from the

Club during these grand transactions, but this is nothing at all, to the State, pomp, pageantry and lofty titles, which this here Club and it's president took upon themselves, a short while after, which shall be minutely and circumstantially related in the following Books.

End of the 6th Book & of Volume I.

A List of the members Regular and Honorary of the Ancient and honorable Tuesday Club, from the 16th of may 1749 to the 5th of December, the same year. [568]

Regular members	Honorary members
The Hon: Nasifer Jole Esqr, præs:	Mr Abraham Bumper
	Doctor Polyhistor
Sir John, knight and Champn	Mr Oldham wisely
Philo dogmaticus Esqr Cancell:	Mr Joshua fluter
Laconic Comus Esqr, Orator	Mr Ignotus warble
Jonathan Grog Esqr, P:L:M:C:	Signior Lardini
Solo Neverout Esqr Proto-mus:	Mr Broadface round
Loquacious Scribble Esqr Secrty	Mr Merry Makefun
Quirpum Comic Esqr dep: Secr:	Mr Chantum Cheary
Slyboots pleasant (Esqrs)	Coll: Courtly Phraze
Capt: Seemly Spruce (Esqrs)	Mr Curious Courtly
Jealous Spyplot Senr (Esqrs)	Mr Swillum Swagbelly
Jealous Spyplot Junr: (Esqrs)	Mr Prim Laconic
Huffman Snap (Esqrs)	Revd Mr Smoothum Sly
Prim Timorous (Esqrs)	Revd Mr Roundhead Muddy
Roundhead Muddy (Esqrs)	Capt: Comely Coppernose

Index of the
Contents of this Volume

www.ingramcontent.com/pod-product-compliance
Lightning Source LLC
Chambersburg PA
CBHW020644110726
47901CB00001B/47